THE KEY TO REBECCA

"Brilliant . . . breathless high adventure . . . by the most romantic of all the top thriller writers!"

—*Time*

"From the opening sentence to the gripping climax . . . Ken Follett delivers the surefire suspense readers have come to expect from the author of *Triple* and *Eye of the Needle*!"

—*Los Angeles Times*

" . . . steaming intrigue spiced with a gorgeous belly dancer, a stoic British hero, the courageous Jewish girl he recruits and a master Nazi spy."

—*Cosmopolitan*

"It can keep you up all night—grabbed, gripped, and thrilled!"
—*Chicago Sun-Times*

"Ken Follett does it again."

—*Newsweek*

"Thrills unlimited . . . the most exciting novel in years!"
—*Cincinnati Enquirer*

"A top-flight adventure thriller . . . violence, intrigue, and exotic passions . . . a vivid page-turner!"
—*Washington Post*

THE MAN FROM ST. PETERSBURG

"Ken Follett has done it once more . . . [*The Man from St. Petersburg*] goes down with the ease and impact of a well-prepared martini."
—*The New York Times Book Review*

"A grabber with a pace that never flags!"
—*Cosmopolitan*

"Follett is a master!"
—*Washington Post Book World*

"A truly thrilling story by a master . . . builds with such high intensity that your heart races with pounding anticipation and sticks in your throat as the climactic moments near."
—*Chattanooga News-Free Press*

"The perfect entertainment!"
—*Chicago Tribune*

"The plot is eerily plausable . . . the denouement one of Follett's finest!"
—*Time*

"Both a superb thriller and a fine novel. . . . Can Follett write! . . . He out classes his competitors!"
—*Newsday*

" . . . Can keep you up at night!"
—*The Wall Street Journal*

"Right from the start the pulse-beat rises . . . and you have a thriller that keeps you on tenterhooks to the last page."
—*John Barkham Reviews*

KEN FOLLETT
Two Complete Novels

THE KEY TO REBECCA

THE MAN FROM ST. PETERSBURG

SEAFARER • NEW YORK

SEAFARER BOOKS
a Division of Penguin Books USA Inc.
375 Hudson Street, New York, New York 10014

Published by Seafarer Books, a division of Penguin Books USA Inc.
The Key to Rebecca and *The Man from St. Petersburg* were previously
published in individual volumes by Signet, an imprint of Dutton/Signet,
a division of Penguin Books USA Inc.

First Seafarer Printing, September 1994

The Key to Rebecca and *The Man from St. Petersburg* were both originally
published in hardcover editions by William Morrow and Company, Inc.

In *The Man from St. Petersburg,* the quotation on page 57 is taken from
The London Times of June 14, 1914. The quotation on pp. 226-227 is taken
from *The London Times* of June 29, 1914. "After the Ball" on p. 206 was
written by Charles K. Harris and published in Great Britain by Francis
Day & Hunter.

ISBN 0-8289-0874-5
Printed in the USA
10 9 8 7 6 5 4 3 2 1

THE KEY
TO REBECCA

TO ROBIN McGIBBON

"Our spy in Cairo is the greatest hero of them all."
—ERWIN ROMMEL, September 1942

(Quoted by Anthony Cave Brown in *Bodyguard of Lies*)

PART ONE

———

TOBRUK

1

The last camel collapsed at noon.

It was the five-year-old white bull he had bought in Gialo, the youngest and strongest of the three beasts, and the least ill-tempered: he liked the animal as much as a man could like a camel, which is to say that he hated it only a little.

They climbed the leeward side of a small hill, man and camel planting big clumsy feet in the inconstant sand, and at the top they stopped. They looked ahead, seeing nothing but another hillock to climb, and after that a thousand more, and it was as if the camel despaired at the thought. Its forelegs folded, then its rear went down, and it couched on top of the hill like a monument, staring across the empty desert with the indifference of the dying.

The man hauled on its nose rope. Its head came forward and its neck stretched out, but it would not get up. The man went behind and kicked its hindquarters as hard as he could, three or four times. Finally he took out a razor-sharp curved Bedouin knife with a narrow point and stabbed the camel's rump. Blood flowed from the wound but the camel did not even look around.

The man understood what was happening. The very tissues

of the animal's body, starved of nourishment, had simply stopped working, like a machine that has run out of fuel. He had seen camels collapse like this on the outskirts of an oasis, surrounded by life-giving foliage which they ignored, lacking the energy to eat.

There were two more tricks he might have tried. One was to pour water into its nostrils until it began to drown; the other to light a fire under its hindquarters. He could not spare the water for one nor the firewood for the other, and besides neither method had a great chance of success.

It was time to stop, anyway. The sun was high and fierce. The long Saharan summer was beginning, and the midday temperature would reach 110 degrees in the shade.

Without unloading the camel, the man opened one of his bags and took out his tent. He looked around again, automatically: there was no shade or shelter in sight—one place was as bad as another. He pitched his tent beside the dying camel, there on top of the hillock.

He sat cross-legged in the open end of the tent to make his tea. He scraped level a small square of sand, arranged a few precious dry twigs in a pyramid and lit the fire. When the kettle boiled he made tea in the nomad fashion, pouring it from the pot into the cup, adding sugar, then returning it to the pot to infuse again, several times over. The resulting brew, very strong and rather treacly, was the most revivifying drink in the world.

He gnawed at some dates and watched the camel die while he waited for the sun to pass overhead. His tranquillity was practiced. He had come a long way in this desert, more than a thousand miles. Two months earlier he had left El Agela, on the Mediterranean coast of Libya, and traveled due south for five hundred miles, via Gialo and Kufra, into the empty heart of the Sahara. There he had turned east and crossed the border into Egypt unobserved by man or beast. He had traversed the rocky wasteland of the Western Desert and turned north near Kharga; and now he was not far from his destination. He knew the desert, but he was afraid of it—all intelligent men were, even the nomads who lived all their lives here. But he never allowed that fear to take hold of him, to panic him, to use up his nervous energy. There were always catastrophes: mistakes in navigation that made you miss a well by a couple of miles; water bottles that leaked or burst; apparently healthy camels that got sick a couple of days out. The only response was to say *Inshallah*: It is the will of God.

Eventually the sun began to dip toward the west. He looked at the camel's load, wondering how much of it he could carry. There were three small European suitcases, two heavy and one light, all important. There was a little bag of clothes, a sextant, the maps, the food and the water bottle. It was already too much: he would have to abandon the tent, the tea set, the cooking pot, the almanac and the saddle.

He made the three cases into a bundle and tied the clothes, the food and the sextant on top, strapping the lot together with a length of cloth. He could put his arms through the cloth straps and carry the load like a rucksack on his back. He slung the goatskin water bag around his neck and let it dangle in front.

It was a heavy load.

Three months earlier he would have been able to carry it all day then play tennis in the evening, for he was a strong man; but the desert had weakened him. His bowels were water, his skin was a mass of sores, and he had lost twenty or thirty pounds. Without the camel he could not go far.

Holding his compass in his hand, he started walking.

He followed the compass wherever it led, resisting the temptation to divert around the hills, for he was navigating by dead reckoning over the final miles, and a fractional error could take him a fatal few hundred yards astray. He settled into a slow, long-strided walk. His mind emptied of hopes and fears and he concentrated on the compass and the sand. He managed to forget the pain of his ravaged body and put one foot in front of the other automatically, without thought and therefore without effort.

The day cooled into evening. The water bottle became lighter around his neck as he consumed its contents. He refused to think about how much water was left: he was drinking six pints a day, he had calculated, and he knew there was not enough for another day. A flock of birds flew over his head, whistling noisily. He looked up, shading his eyes with his hand, and recognized them as Lichtenstein's sandgrouse, desert birds like brown pigeons that flocked to water every morning and evening. They were heading the same way as he was, which meant he was on the right track, but he knew they could fly fifty miles to water, so he could take little encouragement from them.

Clouds gathered on the horizon as the desert cooled. Behind him, the sun sank lower and turned into a big yellow balloon. A little later a white moon appeared in a purple sky.

He thought about stopping. Nobody could walk all night. But he had no tent, no blanket, no rice and no tea. And he was sure he was close to the well: by his reckoning he should have been there.

He walked on. His calm was deserting him now. He had set his strength and his expertise against the ruthless desert, and it began to look as if the desert would win. He thought again of the camel he had left behind, and how it had sat on the hillock, with the tranquillity of exhaustion, waiting for death. He would not wait for death, he thought: when it became inevitable he would rush to meet it. Not for him the hours of agony and encroaching madness—that would be undignified. He had his knife.

The thought made him feel desperate, and now he could no longer repress the fear. The moon went down, but the landscape was bright with starlight. He saw his mother in the distance, and she said: "Don't say I never warned you!" He heard a railway train that chugged along with his heartbeat, slowly. Small rocks moved in his path like scampering rats. He smelled roast lamb. He breasted a rise and saw, close by, the red glow of the fire over which the meat had been roasted, and a small boy beside it gnawing the bones. There were the tents around the fire, the hobbled camels grazing the scattered thorns, and the wellhead beyond. He walked into the hallucination. The people in the dream looked up at him, startled. A tall man stood up and spoke. The traveler pulled at his howli, partially unwinding the cloth to reveal his face.

The tall man stepped forward, shocked, and said. "My cousin!"

The traveler understood that this was not, after all, an illusion; and he smiled faintly and collapsed.

∽

When he awoke he thought for a moment that he was a boy again, and that his adult life had been a dream.

Someone was touching his shoulder and saying "Wake up, Achmed," in the tongue of the desert. Nobody had called him Achmed for years. He realized he was wrapped in a coarse blanket and lying on the cold sand, his head swathed in a howli. He opened his eyes to see the gorgeous sunrise like a straight rainbow against the flat black horizon. The icy morning wind blew into his face. In that instant he experienced again all the confusion and anxiety of his fifteenth year.

He had felt utterly lost, that first time he woke up in the desert. He had thought *My father is dead*, and then *I have a new father*. Snatches from the Surahs of the Koran had run through his head, mixed with bits of the Creed which his mother still taught him secretly, in German. He remembered the recent sharp pain of his adolescent circumcision, followed by the cheers and rifle shots of the men as they congratulated him on at last becoming one of them, a true man. Then there had been the long train journey, wondering what his desert cousins would be like, and whether they would despise his pale body and his city ways. He had walked briskly out of the railway station and seen the two Arabs, sitting beside their camels in the dust of the station yard, wrapped in traditional robes which covered them from head to foot except for the slit in the howli which revealed only their dark, unreadable eyes. They had taken him to the well. It had been terrifying: nobody had spoken to him, except in gestures. In the evening he had realized that these people had *no toilets*, and he became desperately embarrassed. In the end he had been forced to ask. There was a moment of silence, then they all burst out laughing. It transpired that they had thought he could not speak their language, which was why everyone had tried to communicate with him in signs; and that he had used a baby word in asking about toilet arrangements, which made it funnier. Someone had explained to him about walking a little way beyond the circle of tents and squatting in the sand, and after that he had not been so frightened, for although these were hard men they were not unkind.

All these thoughts had run through his mind as he looked at his first desert sunrise, and they came back again twenty years later, as fresh and as painful as yesterday's bad memories, with the words "Wake up, Achmed."

He sat up abruptly, the old thoughts clearing rapidly like the morning clouds. He had crossed the desert on a vitally important mission. He had found the well, and it had not been a hallucination: his cousins were here, as they always were at this time of the year. He had collapsed with exhaustion, and they had wrapped him in blankets and let him sleep by the fire. He suffered a sudden sharp panic as he thought of his precious baggage—had he still been carrying it when he arrived?—then he saw it, piled neatly at his feet.

Ishmael was squatting beside him. It had always been like this: throughout the year the two boys had spent together in the desert, Ishmael had never failed to wake first in the morning. Now he said: "Heavy worries, cousin."

Achmed nodded. "There is a war."

Ishmael proffered a tiny jeweled bowl containing water. Achmed dipped his fingers in the water and washed his eyes. Ishmael went away. Achmed stood up.

One of the women, silent and subservient, gave him tea. He took it without thanking her and drank it quickly. He ate some cold boiled rice while the unhurried work of the encampment went on around him. It seemed that this branch of the family was still wealthy: there were several servants, many children and more than twenty camels. The sheep nearby were only a part of the flock—the rest would be grazing a few miles away. There would be more camels, too. They wandered at night in search of foliage to eat, and although they were hobbled they sometimes went out of sight. The young boys would be rounding them up now, as he and Ishmael had done. The beasts had no names, but Ishmael knew each one individually, and its history. He would say: "This is the bull my father gave to his brother Abdel in the year many women died, and the bull became lame so my father gave Abdel another and took this one back, and it still limps, see?" Achmed had come to know camels well, but he had never quite adopted the nomad attitude to them: he had not, he remembered, lit a fire underneath his dying white yesterday. Ishmael would have.

Achmed finished his breakfast and went back to his baggage. The cases were not locked. He opened the top one, a small leather suitcase; and when he looked at the switches and dials of the compact radio neatly fitted into the rectangular case he had a sudden vivid memory like a movie: the bustling frantic city of Berlin; a tree-lined street called the Tirpitzufer; a four-story sandstone building; a maze of hallways and staircases; an outer office with two secretaries; an inner office, sparsely furnished with desk, sofa, filing cabinet, small bed and on the wall a Japanese painting of a grinning demon and a signed photograph of Franco; and beyond the office, on a balcony overlooking the Landwehr Canal, a pair of dachshunds and a prematurely white-haired admiral who said: "Rommel wants me to put an agent into Cairo."

The case also contained a book, a novel in English. Idly, Achmed read the first line: "Last night I dreamt I went to Manderley again." A folded sheet of paper fell out from between the leaves of the book. Carefully, Achmed picked it up and put it back. He closed the book, replaced it in the case, and closed the case.

Ishmael was standing at his shoulder. He said: "Was it a long journey?"

Achmed nodded. "I came from El Agela, in Libya." The names meant nothing to his cousin. "I came from the sea."

"From the sea!"

"Yes."

"*Alone?*"

"I had some camels when I started."

Ishmael was awestruck: even the nomads did not make such

long journeys, and he had never seen the sea. He said: "But why?"

"It is to do with this war."

"One gang of Europeans fighting with another over who shall sit in Cairo—what does this matter to the sons of the desert?"

"My mother's people are in the war," Achmed said.

"A man should follow his father."

"And if he has two fathers?"

Ishmael shrugged. He understood dilemmas.

Achmed lifted the closed suitcase. "Will you keep this for me?"

"Yes." Ishmael took it. "Who is winning the war?"

"My mother's people. They are like the nomads—they are proud, and cruel, and strong. They are going to rule the world."

Ishmael smiled. "Achmed, you always did believe in the desert lion."

Achmed remembered: he had learned, in school, that there had once been lions in the desert, and that it was possible a few of them remained, hiding in the mountains, living off deer and fennec fox and wild sheep. Ishmael had refused to believe him. The argument had seemed terribly important then, and they had almost quarreled over it. Achmed grinned. "I still believe in the desert lion," he said.

The two cousins looked at one another. It was five years since the last time they had met. The world had changed. Achmed thought of the things he could tell: the crucial meeting in Beirut in 1938, his trip to Berlin, his great coup in Istanbul . . . None of it would mean anything to his cousin —and Ishmael was probably thinking the same about the events of *his* last five years. Since they had gone together as boys on the pilgrimage to Mecca they had loved each other fiercely, but they never had anything to talk about.

After a moment Ishmael turned away, and took the case to his tent. Achmed fetched a little water in a bowl. He opened another bag, and took out a small piece of soap, a brush, a mirror and a razor. He stuck the mirror in the sand, adjusted it, and began to unwind the howli from around his head.

The sight of his own face in the mirror shocked him.

His strong, normally clear forehead was covered with sores. His eyes were hooded with pain and lined in the corners. The dark beard grew matted and unkempt on his fine-boned cheeks, and the skin of his large hooked nose was red and split. He parted his blistered lips and saw that his fine, even teeth were filthy and stained.

He brushed the soap on and began to shave.

Gradually his old face emerged. It was strong rather than handsome, and normally wore a look which he recognized, in his more detached moments, to be faintly dissolute; but now it was simply ravaged. He had brought a small phial of scented lotion across hundreds of miles of desert for this moment, but now he did not put it on because he knew it would sting unbearably. He gave it to a girl-child who had been watching him, and she ran away, delighted with her prize.

He carried his bag into Ishmael's tent and shooed out the women. He took off his desert robes and donned a white English shirt, a striped tie, gray socks and a brown checked suit. When he tried to put on the shoes he discovered that his feet had swollen: it was agonizing to attempt to force them into the hard new leather. However, he could not wear his European suit with the improvised rubber-tire sandals of the desert. In the end he slit the shoes with his curved knife and wore them loose.

He wanted more: a hot bath, a haircut, cool soothing cream for his sores, a silk shirt, a gold bracelet, a cold bottle of champagne and a warm soft woman. For those he would have to wait.

When he emerged from the tent the nomads looked at him as if he were a stranger. He picked up his hat and hefted the two remaining cases—one heavy, one light. Ishmael came to him carrying a goatskin water bottle. The two cousins embraced.

Achmed took a wallet from the pocket of his jacket to check his papers. Looking at the identity card, he realized that once again he was Alexander Wolff, age thirty-four, of Villa les

Oliviers, Garden City, Cairo, a businessman, race—European.

He put on his hat, picked up his cases and set off in the cool of the dawn to walk across the last few miles of desert to the town.

❧

The great and ancient caravan route, which Wolff had followed from oasis to oasis across the vast empty desert, led through a pass in the mountain range and at last merged with an ordinary modern road. The road was like a line drawn on the map by God, for on one side were the yellow, dusty, barren hills, and on the other were lush fields of cotton squared off with irrigation ditches. The peasants, bent over their crops, wore galabiyas, simple shifts of striped cotton, instead of the cumbersome protective robes of the nomads. Walking north on the road, smelling the cool damp breeze off the nearby Nile, observing the increasing signs of urban civilization, Wolff began to feel human again. The peasants dotted about the fields came to seem less like a crowd. Finally he heard the engine of a car, and he knew he was safe.

The vehicle was approaching him from the direction of Assyut, the town. It came around a bend and into sight, and he recognized it as a military jeep. As it came closer he saw the British Army uniforms of the men in it, and he realized he had left behind one danger only to face another.

Deliberately he made himself calm. I have every right to be here, he thought. I was born in Alexandria. I am Egyptian by nationality. I own a house in Cairo. My papers are all genuine. I am a wealthy man, a European and a German spy behind enemy lines—

The jeep screeched to a halt in a cloud of dust. One of the men jumped out. He had three cloth pips on each shoulder of his uniform shirt: a captain. He looked terribly young, and walked with a limp.

The captain said: "Where the devil have you come from?"

Wolff put down his cases and jerked a thumb back over his shoulder. "My car broke down on the desert road."

The captain nodded, accepting the explanation instantly: it

would never have occurred to him, or to anyone else, that a European might have walked here from Libya. He said: "I'd better see your papers, please."

Wolff handed them over. The captain examined them, then looked up. Wolff thought: There has been a leak from Berlin, and every officer in Egypt is looking for me; or they have changed the papers since last time I was here, and mine are out of date; or—

"You look about all in, Mr. Wolff," the captain said. "How long have you been walking?"

Wolff realized that his ravaged appearance might get some useful sympathy from another European. "Since yesterday afternoon," he said with a weariness that was not entirely faked. "I got a bit lost."

"You've been out here all *night?*" The captain looked more closely at Wolff's face. "Good Lord, I believe you have. You'd better have a lift with us." He turned to the jeep. "Corporal, take the gentleman's cases."

Wolff opened his mouth to protest, then shut it again abruptly. A man who had been walking all night would be only too glad to have someone take his luggage. To object would not only discredit his story, it would draw attention to the bags. As the corporal hefted them into the back of the jeep, Wolff realized with a sinking feeling that he had not even bothered to lock them. How could I be so stupid? he thought. He knew the answer. He was still in tune with the desert, where you were lucky to see other people once a week, and the last thing they wanted to steal was a radio transmitter that had to be plugged in to a power outlet. His senses were alert to all the wrong things: he was watching the movement of the sun, smelling the air for water, measuring the distances he was traveling, and scanning the horizon as if searching for a lone tree in whose shade he could rest during the heat of the day. He had to forget all that now, and think instead of policemen and papers and locks and lies.

He resolved to take more care, and climbed into the jeep.

The captain got in beside him and said to the driver: "Back into town."

Wolff decided to bolster his story. As the jeep turned in the dusty road he said: "Have you got any water?"

"Of course." The captain reached beneath his seat and pulled up a tin bottle covered in felt, like a large whiskey flask. He unscrewed the cap and handed it to Wolff.

Wolff drank deeply, swallowing at least a pint. "Thanks," he said, and handed it back.

"Quite a thirst you had. Not surprising. Oh, by the way— I'm Captain Newman." He stuck out his hand.

Wolff shook it and looked more closely at the man. He *was* young—early twenties, at a guess—and fresh-faced, with a boyish forelock and a ready smile; but there was in his demeanor that weary maturity that comes early to fighting men. Wolff asked him: "Seen any action?"

"Some." Captain Newman touched his own knee. "Did the leg at Cyrenaica, that's why they sent me to this one-horse town." He grinned. "I can't honestly say I'm panting to get back into the desert, but I'd like to be doing something a bit more positive than this, minding the shop hundreds of miles from the war. The only fighting we ever see is between the Christians and the Moslems in the town. Where does your accent come from?"

The sudden question, unconnected with what had gone before, took Wolff by surprise. It had surely been intended to, he thought: Captain Newman was a sharp-witted young man. Fortunately Wolff had a prepared answer. "My parents were Boers who came from South Africa to Egypt. I grew up speaking Afrikaans and Arabic." He hesitated, nervous of overplaying his hand by seeming too eager to explain. "The name Wolff is Dutch, originally; and I was christened Alex after the town where I was born."

Newman seemed politely interested. "What brings you here?"

Wolff had prepared for that one, too. "I have business interests in several towns in Upper Egypt." He smiled. "I like to pay them surprise visits."

They were entering Assyut. By Egyptian standards it was a large town, with factories, hospitals, a Muslim university, a famous convent and some sixty thousand inhabitants. Wolff was about to ask to be dropped at the railway station when Newman saved him from that error. "You need a garage," the captain said. "We'll take you to Nasif's: he has a tow truck."

Wolff forced himself to say: "Thank you." He swallowed drily. He was still not thinking hard enough or fast enough. I wish I could pull myself together, he thought; it's the damn desert, it's slowed me down. He looked at his watch. He had time to go through a charade at the garage and still catch the daily train to Cairo. He considered what he would do. He would have to go into the place, for Newman would watch. Then the soldiers would drive away. Wolff would have to make some inquiries about car parts or something, then take his leave and walk to the station.

With luck, Nasif and Newman might never compare notes on the subject of Alex Wolff.

The jeep drove through the busy, narrow streets. The familiar sights of an Egyptian town pleased Wolff: the gay cotton clothes, the women carrying bundles on their heads, the officious policemen, the sharp characters in sunglasses, the tiny shops spilling out into the rutted streets, the stalls, the battered cars and the overloaded asses. They stopped in front of a row of low mud-brick buildings. The road was half blocked by an ancient truck and the remains of a cannibalized Fiat. A small boy was working on a cylinder block with a wrench, sitting on the ground outside the entrance.

Newman said: "I'll have to leave you here, I'm afraid; duty calls."

Wolff shook his hand. "You've been very kind."

"I don't like to dump you this way," Newman continued. "You've had a bad time." He frowned, then his face cleared. "Tell you what—I'll leave Corporal Cox to look after you."

Wolff said: "It's kind, but really—"

Newman was not listening. "Get the man's bags, Cox, and look sharp. I want you to take care of him—and don't you leave anything to the wogs, understand?"

"Yes, sir!" said Cox.

Wolff groaned inwardly. Now there would be more delay

while he got rid of the corporal. Captain Newman's kindness was becoming a nuisance—could that possibly be intentional?

Wolff and Cox got out, and the jeep pulled away. Wolff walked into Nasif's workshop, and Cox followed, carrying the cases.

Nasif was a smiling young man in a filthy galabiya, working on a car battery by the light of an oil lamp. He spoke to them in English. "You want to rent a beautiful automobile? My brother have Bentley—"

Wolff interrupted him in rapid Egyptian Arabic. "My car has broken down. They say you have a tow truck."

"Yes. We can leave right away. Where is the car?"

"On the desert road, forty or fifty miles out. It's a Ford. But we're not coming with you." He took out his wallet and gave Nasif an English pound note. "You'll find me at the Grand Hotel by the railway station when you return."

Nasif took the money with alacrity. "Very good! I leave immediately!"

Wolff nodded curtly and turned around. Walking out of the workshop with Cox in tow, he considered the implications of his short conversation with Nasif. The mechanic would go out into the desert with his tow truck and search the road for the car. Eventually he would return to the Grand Hotel to confess failure. He would learn that Wolff had left. He would consider he had been reasonably paid for his wasted day, but that would not stop him telling all and sundry the story of the disappearing Ford and its disappearing driver. The likelihood was that all this would get back to Captain Newman sooner or later. Newman might not know quite what to make of it all, but he would certainly feel that here was a mystery to be investigated.

Wolff's mood darkened as he realized that his plan of slipping unobserved into Egypt might have failed.

He would just have to make the best of it. He looked at his watch. He still had time to catch the train. He would be able to get rid of Cox in the lobby of the hotel, then get something to eat and drink while he was waiting, if he was quick.

Cox was a short, dark man with some kind of British regional accent which Wolff could not identify. He looked about Wolff's age, and as he was still a corporal he was probably not too bright. Following Wolff across the Midan el-Mahatta, he said: "You know this town, sir?"

"I've been here before," Wolff replied.

They entered the Grand. With twenty-six rooms it was the larger of the town's two hotels. Wolff turned to Cox. "Thank you, Corporal. I think you could get back to work now."

"No hurry, sir," Cox said cheerfully. "I'll carry your bags upstairs."

"I'm sure they have porters here—"

"Wouldn't trust 'em, sir, if I were you."

The situation was becoming more and more like a nightmare or a farce, in which well-intentioned people pushed him into increasingly senseless behavior in consequence of one small lie. He wondered again whether this was entirely accidental, and it crossed his mind with terrifying absurdity that perhaps they knew everything and were simply toying with him.

He pushed the thought aside and spoke to Cox with as much grace as he could muster. "Well, thank you."

He turned to the desk and asked for a room. He looked at his watch: he had fifteen minutes left. He filled in the form quickly, giving an invented address in Cairo—there was a chance Captain Newman would forget the true address on the identity papers, and Wolff did not want to leave a reminder.

A Nubian porter led them upstairs to the room. Wolff tipped him off at the door. Cox put the cases down on the bed.

Wolff took out his wallet: perhaps Cox expected a tip too. "Well, Corporal," he began, "you've been very helpful—"

"Let me unpack for you, sir," Cox said. "Captain said not to leave anything to the wogs."

"No, thank you," Wolff said firmly. "I want to lie down right now."

"You go ahead and lie down," Cox persisted generously. "It won't take me—"

"Don't open that!"

Cox was lifting the lid of the case. Wolff reached inside his jacket, thinking *Damn the man* and *Now I'm blown* and *I should have locked it* and *Can I do this quietly?* The little corporal stared at the neat stacks of new English pound notes which filled the small case. He said: "Jesus Christ, you're loaded!" It crossed Wolff's mind, even as he stepped forward, that Cox had never seen so much money in his life. Cox began to turn, saying: "What do you want with all that—" Wolff pulled the wicked curved Bedouin knife, and it glinted in his hand as his eyes met Cox's, and Cox flinched and opened his mouth to shout; and then the razor-sharp blade sliced deep into the soft flesh of his throat, and his shout of fear came as a bloody gurgle and he died; and Wolff felt nothing, only disappointment.

2

It was May, and the khamsin was blowing, a hot dusty wind from the south. Standing under the shower, William Vandam had the depressing thought that this would be the only time he would feel cool all day. He turned off the water and dried himself rapidly. His body was full of small aches. He had played cricket the day before, for the first time in years. General Staff Intelligence had got up a team to play the doctors from the field hospital—spies versus quacks, they had called it—and Vandam, fielding on the boundary, had been run ragged as the medics hit the Intelligence Department's bowling all over the park. Now he had to admit he was not in good condition. Gin had sapped his strength and cigarettes had shortened his wind, and he had too many worries to give the game the fierce concentration it merited.

He lit a cigarette, coughed and started to shave. He always smoked while he was shaving—it was the only way he knew to relieve the boredom of the inevitable daily task. Fifteen years ago he had sworn he would grow a beard as soon as he got out of the Army, but he was still in the Army.

He dressed in the everyday uniform: heavy sandals, socks,

31

bush shirt and the khaki shorts with the flaps that could be let down and buttoned below the knee for protection against mosquitoes. Nobody ever used the flaps, and the younger officers usually cut them off, they looked so ridiculous.

There was an empty gin bottle on the floor beside the bed. Vandam looked at it, feeling disgusted with himself: it was the first time he had taken the damn bottle to bed with him. He picked it up, replaced the cap and threw the bottle into the wastebasket. Then he went downstairs.

Gaafar was in the kitchen, making tea. Vandam's servant was an elderly Copt with a bald head and a shuffling walk, and pretensions to be an English butler. That he would never be, but he had a little dignity and he was honest, and Vandam had not found those qualities to be common among Egyptian house servants.

Vandam said: "Is Billy up?"

"Yes, sir, he's coming down directly."

Vandam nodded. A small pan of water was bubbling on the stove. Vandam put an egg in to boil and set the timer. He cut two slices from an English-type loaf and made toast. He buttered the toast and cut it into fingers, then he took the egg out of the water and decapitated it.

Billy came into the kitchen and said: "Good morning, Dad."

Vandam smiled at his ten-year-old son. "Morning. Breakfast is ready."

The boy began to eat. Vandam sat opposite him with a cup of tea, watching. Billy often looked tired in the mornings recently. Once upon a time he had been infallibly daisy-fresh at breakfast. Was he sleeping badly? Or was his metabolism simply becoming more like an adult's? Perhaps it was just that he was staying awake late, reading detective stories under the sheet by the light of a flashlight.

People said Billy was like his father, but Vandam could not see the resemblance. However, he could see traces of Billy's mother: the gray eyes, the delicate skin and the faintly supercilious expression which came over his face when someone crossed him.

Vandam always prepared his son's breakfast. The servant was perfectly capable of looking after the boy, of course, and most of the time he did; but Vandam liked to keep this little ritual for himself. Often it was the only time he was with Billy all day. They did not talk much—Billy ate and Vandam smoked—but that did not matter: the important thing was that they were together for a while at the start of each day.

After breakfast Billy brushed his teeth while Gaafar got out Vandam's motorcycle. Billy came back wearing his school cap, and Vandam put on his uniform cap. As they did every day, they saluted each other. Billy said: "Right, sir—let's go and win the war."

Then they went out.

⌒

Major Vandam's office was at Gray Pillars, one of a group of buildings surrounded by barbed-wire fencing which made up GHQ Middle East. There was an incident report on his desk when he arrived. He sat down, lit a cigarette and began to read.

The report came from Assyut, three hundred miles south, and at first Vandam could not see why it had been marked for Intelligence. A patrol had picked up a hitchhiking European who had subsequently murdered a corporal with a knife. The body had been discovered last night, almost as soon as the corporal's absence was noted, but several hours after the death. A man answering the hitchhiker's description had bought a ticket to Cairo at the railway station, but by the time the body was found the train had arrived in Cairo and the killer had melted into the city.

There was no indication of motive.

The Egyptian police force and the British Military Police would be investigating already in Assyut, and their colleagues in Cairo would, like Vandam, be learning the details this morning. What reason was there for Intelligence to get involved?

Vandam frowned and thought again. A European is picked up in the desert. He says his car has broken down. He checks into a hotel. He leaves a few minutes later and catches a train. His car is not found. The body of a soldier is discovered that night in the hotel room.

Why?

Vandam got on the phone and called Assyut. It took the army camp switchboard a while to locate Captain Newman, but eventually they found him in the arsenal and got him to a phone.

Vandam said: "This knife murder almost looks like a blown cover."

"That occurred to me, sir," said Newman. He sounded a young man. "That's why I marked the report for Intelligence."

"Good thinking. Tell me, what was your impression of the man?"

"He was a big chap—"

"I've got your description here—six foot, twelve stone, dark hair and eyes—but that doesn't tell me what he was *like*."

"I understand," Newman said. "Well, to be candid, at first I wasn't in the least suspicious of him. He looked all in, which fitted with his story of having broken down on the desert road, but apart from that he seemed an upright citizen: a white man, decently dressed, quite well spoken with an accent he said was Dutch, or rather Afrikaans. His papers were perfect—I'm still quite sure they were genuine."

"But . . . ?"

"He told me he was checking on his business interests in Upper Egypt."

"Plausible enough."

"Yes, but he didn't strike me as the kind of man to spend his life investing in a few shops and small factories and cotton farms. He was much more the assured cosmopolitan type: if he had money to invest it would probably be with a London stockbroker or a Swiss bank. He just wasn't a small-timer . . . It's very vague, sir, but do you see what I mean?"

"Indeed." Newman sounded a bright chap, Vandam thought. What was he doing stuck out in Assyut?

Newman went on: "And then it occurred to me that he had, as it were, just appeared in the desert, and I didn't really

know where he might have come from . . . so I told poor old
Cox to stay with him, on the pretense of helping him, to make
sure he didn't do a bunk before we had a chance to check
his story. I should have arrested the man, of course, but quite
honestly, sir, at the time I had only the most slender suspicion—"

"I don't think anyone's blaming you, Captain," said Vandam. "You did well to remember the name and address from
the papers. Alex Wolff, Villa les Oliviers, Garden City, right?"

"Yes, sir."

"All right, keep me in touch with any developments at your
end, will you?"

"Yes, sir."

Vandam hung up. Newman's suspicions chimed with his own
instincts about the killing. He decided to speak to his immediate superior. He left his office, carrying the incident report.

General Staff Intelligence was run by a brigadier with the
title of Director of Military Intelligence. The DMI had two
deputies: DDMI(O)—for Operational—and DDMI(I)—for Intelligence. The deputies were colonels. Vandam's boss, Lieutenant Colonel Bogge, came under the DDMI(I). Bogge was
responsible for personnel security, and most of his time was
spent administering the censorship apparatus. Vandam's concern was security leaks by means other than letters. He and
his men had several hundred agents in Cairo and Alexandria;
in most clubs and bars there was a waiter who was on his pay-
roll, he had an informant among the domestic staffs of the
more important Arab politicians, King Farouk's valet worked
for Vandam, and so did Cairo's wealthiest thief. He was interested in who was talking too much, and who was listening;
and among the listeners, Arab nationalists were his main target.
However, it seemed possible that the mystery man from Assyut
might be a different kind of threat.

Vandam's wartime career had so far been distinguished by
one spectacular success and one great failure. The failure took
place in Turkey. Rashid Ali had escaped there from Iraq.
The Germans wanted to get him out and use him for propaganda; the British wanted him kept out of the limelight; and

the Turks, jealous of their neutrality, wanted to offend nobody. Vandam's job had been to make sure Ali stayed in Istanbul, but Ali had switched clothes with a German agent and slipped out of the country under Vandam's nose. A few days later he was making propaganda speeches to the Middle East on Nazi radio. Vandam had somewhat redeemed himself in Cairo. London had told him they had reason to believe there was a major security leak there, and after three months of painstaking investigation Vandam had discovered that a senior American diplomat was reporting to Washington in an insecure code. The code had been changed, the leak had been stopped up and Vandam had been promoted to major.

Had he been a civilian, or even a peacetime soldier, he would have been proud of his triumph and reconciled to his defeat, and he would have said: "You win some, you lose some." But in war an officer's mistakes killed people. In the aftermath of the Rashid Ali affair an agent had been murdered, a woman, and Vandam was not able to forgive himself for that.

He knocked on Lieutenant Colonel Bogge's door and walked in. Reggie Bogge was a short, square man in his fifties, with an immaculate uniform and brilliantined black hair. He had a nervous, throat-clearing cough which he used when he did not know quite what to say, which was often. He sat behind a huge curved desk—bigger than the DMI's—going through his in tray. Always willing to talk rather than work, he motioned Vandam to a chair. He picked up a bright-red cricket ball and began to toss it from hand to hand. "You played a good game yesterday," he said.

"You didn't do badly yourself," Vandam said. It was true: Bogge had been the only decent bowler on the Intelligence team, and his slow googlies had taken four wickets for forty-two runs. "But are we winning the war?"

"More bloody bad news, I'm afraid." The morning briefing had not yet taken place, but Bogge always heard the news by word of mouth beforehand. "We expected Rommel to attack the Gazala Line head on. Should have known better—fellow never fights fair and square. He went around our southern flank, took the Seventh Armored's headquarters, and captured General Messervy."

It was a depressingly familiar story, and Vandam suddenly felt weary. "What a shambles," he said.

"Fortunately he failed to get through to the coast, so the divisions on the Gazala Line didn't get isolated. Still . . ."

"Still, when are we going to *stop* him?"

"He won't get much farther." It was an idiotic remark: Bogge simply did not want to get involved in criticism of generals. "What have you got there?"

Vandam gave him the incident report. "I propose to follow this one through myself."

Bogge read the report and looked up, his face blank. "I don't see the point."

"It looks like a blown cover."

"Uh?"

"There's no motive for the murder, so we have to speculate," Vandam explained. "Here's one possibility: the hitchhiker was not what he said he was, and the corporal discovered that fact, and so the hitchhiker killed the corporal."

"Not what he said he was—you mean he was a spy?" Bogge laughed. "How d'you suppose he got to Assyut—by parachute? Or did he walk?"

That was the trouble with explaining things to Bogge, thought Vandam: he had to ridicule the idea, as an excuse for not thinking of it himself. "It's not impossible for a small plane to sneak through. It's not impossible to cross the desert, either."

Bogge sailed the report through the air across the vast expanse of his desk. "Not very likely, in my view," he said. "Don't waste any time on that one."

"Very good, sir." Vandam picked up the report from the floor, suppressing the familiar frustrated anger. Conversations with Bogge always turned into points-scoring contests, and the smart thing to do was not to play. "I'll ask the police to keep us informed of their progress—copies of memos, and so on, just for the file."

"Yes." Bogge never objected to making people send him

copies for the file: it enabled him to poke his finger into things without taking any responsibility. "Listen, how about arranging some cricket practice? I noticed they had nets and a catching boat there yesterday. I'd like to lick our team into shape and get some more matches going."

"Good idea."

"See if you can organize something, will you?"

"Yes, sir." Vandam went out.

On the way back to his own office, he wondered what was so wrong with the administration of the British Army that it could promote to lieutenant colonel a man as empty-headed as Reggie Bogge. Vandam's father, who had been a corporal in the first war, had been fond of saying that British soldiers were "lions led by donkeys." Sometimes Vandam thought it was still true. But Bogge was not merely dull. Sometimes he made bad decisions because he was not clever enough to make good decisions; but mostly, it seemed to Vandam, Bogge made bad decisions because he was playing some other game, making himself look good or trying to be superior or something, Vandam did not know what.

A woman in a white hospital coat saluted him and he returned the salute absent-mindedly. The woman said: "Major Vandam, isn't it?"

He stopped and looked at her. She had been a spectator at the cricket match, and now he remembered her name. "Dr. Abuthnot," he said. "Good morning." She was a tall, cool woman of about his age. He recalled that she was a surgeon—highly unusual for a woman, even in wartime—and that she held the rank of captain.

She said: "You worked hard yesterday."

Vandam smiled. "And I'm suffering for it today. I enjoyed myself, though."

"So did I." She had a low, precise voice and a great deal of confidence. "Shall we see you on Friday?"

"Where?"

"The reception at the Union."

"Ah." The Anglo-Egyptian Union, a club for bored Europeans, made occasional attempts to justify its name by holding a reception for Egyptian guests. "I'd like that. What time?"

"Five o'clock, for tea."

Vandam was professionally interested: it was an occasion at which Egyptians might pick up service gossip, and service gossip sometimes included information useful to the enemy. "I'll come," he said.

"Splendid. I'll see you there." She turned away.

"I look forward to it," Vandam said to her back. He watched her walk away, wondering what she wore under the hospital coat. She was trim, elegant and self-possessed: she reminded him of his wife.

He entered his office. He had no intention of organizing a cricket practice, and he had no intention of forgetting about the Assyut murder. Bogge could go to hell. Vandam would go to work.

First he spoke again to Captain Newman, and told him to make sure the description of Alex Wolff got the widest possible circulation.

He called the Egyptian police and confirmed that they would be checking the hotels and flophouses of Cairo today.

He contacted Field Security, a unit of the prewar Canal Defense Force, and asked them to step up their spot checks on identity papers for a few days.

He told the British paymaster general to keep a special watch for forged currency.

He advised the wireless listening service to be alert for a new, local transmitter; and thought briefly how useful it would be if the boffins ever cracked the problem of locating a radio by monitoring its broadcasts.

Finally he detailed a sergeant on his staff to visit every radio shop in Lower Egypt—there were not many—and ask them to report any sales of parts and equipment which might be used to make or repair a transmitter.

Then he went to the Villa les Oliviers.

～

The house got its name from a small public garden across the street where a grove of olive trees was now in bloom, shedding white petals like dust on to the dry, brown grass.

The house had a high wall broken by a heavy, carved wooden gate. Using the ornamentation for footholds, Vandam climbed over the gate and dropped on the other side to find himself in a large courtyard. Around him the whitewashed walls were smeared and grubby, their windows blinded by closed, peeling shutters. He walked to the center of the courtyard and looked at the stone fountain. A bright-green lizard darted across the dry bowl.

The place had not been lived in for at least a year.

Vandam opened a shutter, broke a pane of glass, reached through to unfasten the window, and climbed over the sill into the house.

It did not look like the home of a European, he thought as he walked through the dark cool rooms. There were no hunting prints on the walls, no neat rows of bright-jacketed novels by Agatha Christie and Dennis Wheatley, no three-piece suite imported from Maples or Harrods. Instead the place was furnished with large cushions and low tables, handwoven rugs and hanging tapestries.

Upstairs he found a locked door. It took him three or four minutes to kick it open. Behind it there was a study.

The room was clean and tidy, with a few pieces of rather luxurious furniture: a wide, low divan covered in velvet, a hand-carved coffee table, three matching antique lamps, a bear-skin rug, a beautifully inlaid desk and a leather chair.

On the desk were a telephone, a clean white blotter, an ivory-handled pen and a dry inkwell. In the desk drawer Vandam found company reports from Switzerland, Germany and the United States. A delicate beaten-copper coffee service gathered dust on the little table. On a shelf behind the desk were books in several languages: nineteenth-century French novels, the Shorter Oxford Dictionary, a volume of what appeared to Vandam to be Arabic poetry, with erotic illustrations, and the Bible in German.

There were no personal documents.

There were no letters.

There was not a single photograph in the house.

Vandam sat in the soft leather chair behind the desk and looked around the room. It was a masculine room, the home of a cosmopolitan intellectual, a man who was on the one hand careful, precise and tidy and on the other hand sensitive and sensual.

Vandam was intrigued.

A European name, a totally Arabic house. A pamphlet about investing in business machines, a book of Arab verse. An antique coffee jug and a modern telephone. A wealth of information about a character, but not a single clue which might help find the man.

The room had been carefully cleaned out.

There should have been bank statements, bills from tradesmen, a birth certificate and a will, letters from a lover and photographs of parents or children. The man had collected all those things and taken them away, leaving no trace of his identity, as if he knew that one day someone would come looking for him.

Vandam said aloud: "Alex Wolff, who are you?"

He got up from the chair and left the study. He walked through the house and across the hot, dusty courtyard. He climbed back over the gate and dropped into the street. Across the road an Arab in a green-striped galabiya sat cross-legged on the ground in the shade of the olive trees, watching Vandam incuriously. Vandam felt no impulse to explain that he had broken into the house on official business: the uniform of a British officer was authority enough for just about anything in this town. He thought of the other sources from which he could seek information about the owner of this house: municipal records, such as they were; local tradesmen who might have delivered there when the place was occupied; even the neighbors. He would put two of his men on to it, and tell Bogge some story to cover up. He climbed onto his motorcycle and kicked it into life. The engine roared enthusiastically, and Vandam drove away.

3

Full of anger and despair Wolff sat outside his home and watched the British officer drive away.

He remembered the house as it had been when he was a boy, loud with talk and laughter and life. There by the great carved gate there had always been a guard, a black-skinned giant from the south, sitting on the ground, impervious to the heat. Each morning a holy man, old and almost blind, would recite a chapter from the Koran in the courtyard. In the cool of the arcade on three sides the men of the family would sit on low divans and smoke their hubble-bubbles while servant boys brought coffee in long-necked jugs. Another black guard stood at the door to the harem, behind which the women grew bored and fat. The days were long and warm, the family was rich and the children were indulged.

The British officer, with his shorts and his motorcycle, his arrogant face and his prying eyes hidden in the shadow of the peaked uniform cap, had broken in and violated Wolff's childhood. Wolff wished he could have seen the man's face, for he would like to kill him one day.

He had thought of this place all through his journey. In Berlin and Tripoli and El Agela, in the pain and exhaustion of the desert crossing, in the fear and haste of his flight from Assyut, the villa had represented a safe haven, a place to rest and get clean and whole again at the end of the voyage. He had looked forward to lying in the bath and sipping coffee in the courtyard and bringing women home to the great bed.

Now he would have to go away and stay away.

He had remained outside all morning, alternately walking the street and sitting under the olive trees, just in case Captain Newman should have remembered the address and sent somebody to search the house; and he had bought a galabiya in the souk beforehand, knowing that if someone did come they would be looking for a European, not an Arab.

It had been a mistake to show genuine papers. He could see that with hindsight. The trouble was, he mistrusted Abwehr forgeries. Meeting and working with other spies he had heard horror stories about crass and obvious errors in the documents made by German Intelligence: botched printing, inferior-quality paper, even misspellings of common English words. In the spy school where he had been sent for his wireless cipher course the current rumor had been that every policeman in England knew that a certain series of numbers on a ration card identified the holder as a German spy.

Wolff had weighed the alternatives and picked what seemed the least risky. He had been wrong, and now he had no place to go.

He stood, picked up his cases and began to walk.

He thought of his family. His mother and his stepfather were dead, but he had three stepbrothers and a stepsister in Cairo. It would be hard for them to hide him. They would be questioned as soon as the British realized the identity of the owner of the villa, which might be today; and while they might tell lies for his sake, their servants would surely talk. Furthermore, he could not really trust them, for when his stepfather had died, Alex as the eldest son had got the house as well as a share of the inheritance, although he was European and an adopted, rather than natural, son. There had been some bitterness, and meetings with lawyers; Alex had stood firm and the others had never really forgiven him.

He considered checking in to Shepheard's Hotel. Unfortunately the police were sure to think of that, too: Shepheard's would by now have the description of the Assyut murderer. The other major hotels would have it soon. That left the pensions. Whether they were warned depended on how thorough the police wanted to be. Since the British were involved, the police might feel obliged to be meticulous. Still, the managers of small guest houses were often too busy to pay a lot of attention to nosy policemen.

He left the Garden City and headed downtown. The streets were even more busy and noisy than when he had left Cairo. There were countless uniforms—not just British but Australian, New Zealand, Polish, Yugoslav, Palestinian, Indian and Greek. The slim, pert Egyptian girls in their cotton frocks and heavy jewelry competed successfully with their red-faced, dispirited European counterparts. Among the older women it seemed to Wolff that fewer wore the traditional black robe and veil. The men still greeted one another in the same exuberant fashion, swinging their right arms outward before bringing their hands together with a loud clap, shaking hands for at least a minute or two while grasping the shoulder of the other with the left hand and talking excitedly. The beggars and peddlers were out in force, taking advantage of the influx of naïve Europeans. In his galabiya Wolff was immune, but the foreigners were besieged by cripples, women with fly-encrusted babies, shoeshine boys and men selling everything from secondhand razor blades to giant fountain pens guaranteed to hold six months' supply of ink.

The traffic was worse. The slow, verminous trams were more crowded than ever, with passengers clinging precariously to the outside from a perch on the running board, crammed into the cab with the driver and sitting cross-legged on the roof. The buses and taxis were no better: there seemed to be a shortage of vehicle parts, for so many of the cars had broken windows, flat tires and ailing engines, and were lacking headlights or windshield wipers. Wolff saw two taxis—an elderly Morris and an even older Packard—which had finally stopped running and were now being drawn by donkeys. The only decent cars were the monstrous American limousines of the wealthy pashas and the occasional prewar English Austin. Mixing with the motor vehicles in deadly competition were the horse-drawn gharries, the mule carts of the peasants, and the livestock— camels, sheep and goats—which were banned from the city center by the most unenforceable law on the Egyptian statute book.

And the noise—Wolff had forgotten the noise.

The trams rang their bells continuously. In traffic jams all the cars hooted all the time, and when there was nothing to hoot at they hooted on general principles. Not to be outdone, the drivers of carts and camels yelled at the tops of their voices. Many shops and all cafés blared Arab music from cheap radios turned to full volume. Street vendors called continually and pedestrians told them to go away. Dogs barked and circling kites screamed overhead. From time to time it would all be swamped by the roar of an airplane.

This is my town, Wolff thought; they can't catch me here.

There were a dozen or so well-known pensions catering for tourists of different nationalities: Swiss, Austrian, German, Danish and French. He thought of them and rejected them as too obvious. Finally he remembered a cheap lodging house run by nuns at Bulaq, the port district. It catered mainly for the sailors who came down the Nile in steam tugs and feluccas laden with cotton, coal, paper and stone. Wolff could be sure he would not get robbed, infected or murdered, and nobody would think to look for him there.

As he headed out of the hotel district the streets became a little less crowded, but not much. He could not see the river itself, but occasionally he glimpsed, through the huddled buildings, the high triangular sail of a felucca.

The hostel was a large, decaying building which had once been the villa of some pasha. There was now a bronze crucifix over the arch of the entrance. A black-robed nun was watering a tiny bed of flowers in front of the building. Through the arch Wolff saw a cool quiet hall. He had walked several miles today, with his heavy cases: he looked forward to a rest.

Two Egyptian policemen came out of the hostel.

Wolff took in the wide leather belts, the inevitable sunglasses and the military haircuts in a swift glance, and his heart sank. He turned his back on the men and spoke in French to the nun in the garden. "Good day, Sister."

She unbent from her watering and smiled at him. "Good day." She was shockingly young. "Do you want lodgings?"

"No lodgings. Just your blessing."

The two policemen approached, and Wolff tensed, preparing his answers in case they should question him, considering which direction he should take if he had to run away; then they went past, arguing about a horse race.

"God bless you," said the nun.

Wolff thanked her and walked on. It was worse than he had imagined. The police must be checking *everywhere*. Wolff's feet were sore now, and his arms ached from carrying the luggage. He was disappointed, and also a little indignant, for everything in this town was notoriously haphazard, yet it seemed they were mounting an efficient operation just for him. He doubled back, heading for the city center again. He was beginning to feel as he had in the desert, as if he had been walking forever without getting anywhere.

In the distance he saw a familiar tall figure: Hussein Fahmy, an old school friend. Wolff was momentarily paralyzed. Hussein would surely take him in, and perhaps he could be trusted; but he had a wife, and three children, and how would one explain to them that Uncle Achmed was coming to stay, but it was a secret, they must not mention his name to their friends . . . How, indeed, would Wolff explain it all to Hussein himself? Hussein looked in Wolff's direction, and Wolff turned quickly and crossed the road, darting behind a tram. Once on the opposite pavement he went quickly down an alley without looking back. No, he could not seek shelter with old school friends.

He emerged from the alley into another street, and realized he was close to the German School. He wondered if it were still open: a lot of German nationals in Cairo had been interned. He walked toward it, then saw, outside the building, a

Field Security patrol checking papers. He turned about quickly and headed back the way he had come.

He had to get off the streets.

He felt like a rat in a maze—every way he turned he was blocked. He saw a taxi, a big old Ford with steam hissing out from under its hood. He hailed it and jumped in. He gave the driver an address and the car jerked away in third gear, apparently the only gear that worked. On the way they stopped twice to top up the boiling radiator, and Wolff skulked in the back seat, trying to hide his face.

The taxi took him to Coptic Cairo, the ancient Christian ghetto.

He paid the driver and went down the steps to the entrance. He gave a few piasters to the old woman who held the great wooden key, and she let him in.

It was an island of darkness and quiet in the stormy sea of Cairo. Wolff walked its narrow passages, hearing faintly the low chanting from the ancient churches. He passed the school and the synagogue and the cellar where Mary was supposed to have brought the baby Jesus. Finally he went into the smallest of the five churches.

The service was about to begin. Wolff put down his precious cases beside a pew. He bowed to the pictures of saints on the wall, then approached the altar, knelt and kissed the hand of the priest. He returned to the pew and sat down.

The choir began to chant a passage of scripture in Arabic. Wolff settled into his seat. He would be safe here until darkness fell. Then he would try his last shot.

∾

The Cha-Cha was a large open-air nightclub in a garden beside the river. It was packed, as usual. Wolff waited in the queue of British officers and their girls while the safragis set up extra tables on trestles in every spare inch of space. On the stage a comic was saying: "Wait till Rommel gets to Shepheard's—that will hold him up."

Wolff finally got a table and a bottle of champagne. The evening was warm and the stage lights made it worse. The audience was rowdy—they were thirsty, and only champagne was served, so they quickly got drunk. They began to shout for the star of the show, Sonja el-Aram.

First they had to listen to an overweight Greek woman sing "I'll See You in My Dreams" and "I Ain't Got Nobody" (which made them laugh). Then Sonja was announced. However, she did not appear for a while. The audience became noisier and more impatient as the minutes ticked by. At last, when they seemed to be on the verge of rioting, there was a roll of drums, the stage lights went off and silence descended.

When the spotlight came on Sonja stood still in the center of the stage with her arms stretched skyward. She wore diaphanous trousers and a sequined halter, and her body was powdered white. The music began—drums and a pipe—and she started to move.

Wolff sipped champagne and watched, smiling. She was still the best.

She jerked her hips slowly, stamping one foot and then the other. Her arms began to tremble, then her shoulders moved and her breasts shook; and then her famous belly rolled hypnotically. The rhythm quickened. She closed her eyes. Each part of her body seemed to move independently of the rest. Wolff felt, as he always did, as every man in the audience did, that he was alone with her, that her display was just for him, and that this was not an act, not a piece of show-business wizardry, but that her sensual writhings were compulsive, she did it because she had to, she was driven to a sexual frenzy by her own voluptuous body. The audience was tense, silent, perspiring, mesmerized. She went faster and faster, seeming to be transported. The music climaxed with a bang. In the instant of silence that followed Sonja uttered a short, sharp cry; then she fell backward, her legs folded beneath her, her knees apart, until her head touched the boards of the stage. She held the position for a moment, then the lights went out. The audience rose to their feet with a roar of applause.

The lights came up, and she was gone.

Sonja never took encores.

Wolff got out of his seat. He gave a waiter a pound—three

months' wages for most Egyptians—to lead him backstage. The waiter showed him the door to Sonja's dressing room, then went away.

Wolff knocked on the door.

"Who is it?"

Wolff walked in.

She was sitting on a stool, wearing a silk robe, taking off her makeup. She saw him in the mirror and spun around to face him.

Wolff said: "Hello, Sonja."

She stared at him. After a long moment she said: "You bastard."

∽

She had not changed.

She was a handsome woman. She had glossy black hair, long and thick; large, slightly protruding brown eyes with lush eyelashes; high cheekbones which saved her face from roundness and gave it shape; an arched nose, gracefully arrogant; and a full mouth with even white teeth. Her body was all smooth curves, but because she was a couple of inches taller than average she did not look plump.

Her eyes flashed with anger. "What are you doing here? Where did you go? What happened to your face?"

Wolff put down his cases and sat on the divan. He looked up at her. She stood with her hands on her hips, her chin thrust forward, her breasts outlined in green silk. "You're beautiful," he said.

"Get out of here."

He studied her carefully. He knew her too well to like or dislike her: she was part of his past, like an old friend who remains a friend, despite his faults, just because he has always been there. Wolff wondered what had happened to Sonja in the years since he had left Cairo. Had she got married, bought a house, fallen in love, changed her manager, had a baby? He had given a lot of thought, that afternoon in the cool, dim church, to how he should approach her; but he had reached no conclusions, for he was not sure how she would be with him. He was still not sure. She appeared angry and scornful, but did she mean it? Should he be charming and full of fun, or aggressive and bullying, or helpless and pleading?

"I need help," he said levelly.

Her face did not change.

"The British are after me," he went on. "They're watching my house, and all the hotels have my description. I've nowhere to sleep. I want to move in with you."

"Go to hell," she said.

"Let me tell you why I walked out on you."

"After two years no excuse is good enough."

"Give me a minute to explain. For the sake of . . . all that."

"I owe you nothing." She glared at him a moment longer, then she opened the door. He thought she was going to throw him out. He watched her face as she looked back at him, holding the door. Then she put her head outside and yelled: "Somebody get me a drink!"

Wolff relaxed a little.

Sonja came back inside and closed the door. "A minute," she said to him.

"Are you going to stand over me like a prison guard? I'm not dangerous." He smiled.

"Oh yes you are," she said, but she went back to her stool and resumed working on her face.

He hesitated. The other problem he had mulled over during that long afternoon in the Coptic church had been how to explain why he had left her without saying good-bye and never contacted her since. Nothing less than the truth sounded convincing. Reluctant as he was to share his secret, he had to tell her, for he was desperate and she was his only hope.

He said: "Do you remember I went to Beirut in nineteen thirty-eight?"

"No."

"I brought back a jade bracelet for you."

Her eyes met his in the mirror. "I don't have it anymore."

He knew she was lying. He went on: "I went there to see a German army officer called Heinz. He asked me to work for Germany in the coming war. I agreed."

She turned from her mirror and faced him, and now he saw in her eyes something like hope.

"They told me to come back to Cairo and wait until I heard from them. Two years ago I heard. They wanted me to go to Berlin. I went. I did a training course, then I worked in the Balkans and the Levant. I went back to Berlin in February for briefing on a new assignment. They sent me here—"

"What are you telling me?" she said incredulously. "You're a *spy?*"

"Yes."

"I don't believe you."

"Look." He picked up a suitcase and opened it. "This is a radio, for sending messages to Rommel." He closed it again and opened the other. "This is my financing."

She stared at the neat stacks of notes. "My God!" she said. "It's a *fortune.*"

There was a knock at the door. Wolff closed the case. A waiter came in with a bottle of champagne in a bucket of ice. Seeing Wolff, he said: "Shall I bring another glass?"

"No," Sonja said impatiently. "Go away."

The waiter left. Wolff opened the wine, filled the glass, gave it to Sonja, then took a long drink from the bottle.

"Listen," he said. "Our army is winning in the desert. We can help them. They need to know about the British strength—numbers of men, which divisions, names of commanders, quality of weapons and equipment and—if possible—battle plans. We're here, in Cairo; we can find these things out. Then, when the Germans take over, we will be heroes."

"We?"

"You can help me. And the first thing you can do is give me a place to live. You hate the British, don't you? You want to see them thrown out?"

"I would do it for anyone but you." She finished her champagne and refilled her glass.

Wolff took the glass from her hand and drank. "Sonja. If I had sent you a postcard from Berlin the British would have thrown you in jail. You must not be angry, now that you know the reasons why." He lowered his voice. "We can bring those old times back. We'll have good food and the best champagne, new clothes and beautiful parties and an American car. We'll go to Berlin, you've always wanted to dance in Berlin, you'll be a star there. Germany is a new *kind* of nation—we're going to rule the world, and you can be a princess. We—" He paused. None of this was getting through to her. It was time to play his last card. "How is Fawzi?"

Sonja lowered her eyes. "She left, the bitch."

Wolff set down the glass, then he put both hands to Sonja's neck. She looked up at him, unmoving. With his thumbs under her chin he forced her to stand. "I'll find another Fawzi for us," he said softly. He saw that her eyes were suddenly moist. His hands moved over the silk robe, descending her body, stroking her flanks. "I'm the only one who understands what you need." He lowered his mouth to hers, took her lip between his teeth, and bit until he tasted blood.

Sonja closed her eyes. "I hate you," she moaned.

∾

In the cool of the evening Wolff walked along the towpath beside the Nile toward the houseboat. The sores had gone from his face and his bowels were back to normal. He wore a new white suit, and he carried two bags full of his favorite groceries.

The island suburb of Zamalek was quiet and peaceful. The raucous noise of central Cairo could be heard only faintly across a wide stretch of water. The calm, muddy river lapped gently against the houseboats lined along the bank. The boats, all shapes and sizes, gaily painted and luxuriously fitted out, looked pretty in the late sunshine.

Sonja's was smaller and more richly furnished than most. A plank led from the path to the top deck, which was open to the breeze but shaded from the sun by a green-and-white striped canopy. Wolff boarded the boat and went down the ladder to the interior. It was crowded with furniture: chairs and divans and tables and cabinets full of knickknacks. There was a tiny kitchen in the prow. Floor-to-ceiling curtains of maroon velvet divided the space in two, closing off the bedroom. Beyond the bedroom, in the stern, was a bathroom.

Sonja was sitting on a cushion painting her toenails. It was extraordinary how slovenly she could look, Wolff thought. She wore a grubby cotton dress, her face looked drawn and her hair was uncombed. In half an hour, when she left for the Cha-Cha Club, she would look like a dream.

Wolff put his bags on a table and began to take things out. "French champagne . . . English marmalade . . . German sausage . . . quail's eggs . . . Scotch salmon . . ."

Sonja looked up, astonished. "Nobody can find things like that—there's a war on."

Wolff smiled. "There's a little Greek grocer in Qulali who remembers a good customer."

"Is he safe?"

"He doesn't know where I'm living—and besides, his shop is the only place in North Africa where you can get caviar."

She came across and dipped into a bag. "Caviar!" She took the lid off the jar and began to eat with her fingers. "I haven't had caviar since—"

"Since I went away," Wolff finished. He put a bottle of champagne in the icebox. "If you wait a few minutes you can have cold champagne with it."

"I can't wait."

"You never can." He took an English-language newspaper out of one of the bags and began to look through it. It was a rotten paper, full of press releases, its war news censored more heavily than the BBC broadcasts which everyone listened to, its local reporting even worse—it was illegal to print speeches by the official Egyptian opposition politicians. "Still nothing about me in here," Wolff said. He had told Sonja of the events in Assyut.

"They're always late with the news," she said through a mouthful of caviar.

"It's not that. If they report the murder they need to say what the motive was—or, if they don't, people will guess. The British don't want people to suspect that the Germans have spies in Egypt. It looks bad."

She went into the bedroom to change. She called through the curtain: "Does that mean they've stopped looking for you?"

"No. I saw Abdullah in the souk. He says the Egyptian police aren't really interested, but there's a Major Vandam who's keeping the pressure on." Wolff put down the newspaper, frowning. He would have liked to know whether Vandam was the officer who had broken into the Villa les Oliviers. He wished he had been able to look more closely at that man, but from across the street the officer's face, shaded by the peaked cap, had been a dark blank.

Sonja said: "How does Abdullah know?"

"I don't know." Wolff shrugged. "He's a thief, he hears things." He went to the icebox and took out the bottle. It was not really cold enough, but he was thirsty. He poured two glasses. Sonja came out, dressed: as he had anticipated, she was transformed, her hair perfect, her face lightly but cleverly made up, wearing a sheer cherry-red dress and matching shoes.

A couple of minutes later there were footsteps on the gangplank and a knock at the hatch. Sonja's taxi had arrived. She drained her glass and left. They did not say hello and good-bye to one another.

Wolff went to the cupboard where he kept the radio. He took out the English novel and the sheet of paper bearing the key to the code. He studied the key. Today was May 28. He had to add 42—the year—to 28 to arrive at the page number in the novel which he must use to encode his message. May was the fifth month, so every fifth letter on the page would be discounted.

He decided to send HAVE ARRIVED. CHECKING IN. ACKNOWLEDGE. Beginning at the top of page 70 of the book, he looked along the line of print for the letter H. It was the tenth character, discounting every fifth letter. In his code it would therefore be represented by the tenth letter of the alphabet, J. Next he needed an A. In the book, the third letter after the H was an A. The A of HAVE would therefore be represented by the third letter of the alphabet, C. There were special ways of dealing with rare letters, like X.

This type of code was a variation on the one-time pad, the only kind of code which was unbreakable in theory and in practice. To decode the message a listener had to have both the book and the key.

When he had encoded his message he looked at his watch. He was to transmit at midnight. He had a couple of hours before he needed to warm up the radio. He poured another glass of champagne and decided to finish the caviar. He found a spoon and picked up the pot. It was empty. Sonja had eaten it all.

∽

The runway was a strip of desert hastily cleared of camel thorn and large rocks. Rommel looked down as the ground came up to meet him. The Storch, a light aircraft used by German commanders for short trips around the battlefield, came down like a fly, its wheels on the ends of long, spindly front legs. The plane stopped and Rommel jumped out.

The heat hit him first, then the dust. It had been relatively cool, up in the sky; now he felt as if he had stepped into a furnace. He began to perspire immediately. As soon as he breathed in, a thin layer of sand coated his lips and the end of his tongue. A fly settled on his big nose, and he brushed it away.

Von Mellenthin, Rommel's Ic—intelligence officer—ran toward him across the sand, his high boots kicking up dusty clouds. He looked agitated. "Kesselring's here," he said.

"*Auch, das noch,*" said Rommel. "That's all I need."

Kesselring, the smiling field marshal, represented everything Rommel disliked in the German armed forces. He was a General Staff officer, and Rommel hated the General Staff; he was a founder of the Luftwaffe, which had let Rommel down so often in the desert war; and he was—worst of all—a snob. One of his acid comments had gotten back to Rommel. Complaining that Rommel was rude to his subordinate officers, Kesselring had said: "It might be worth speaking to him about it, were it not that he's a Wuerttemberger." Wuerttemberg was the provincial state where Rommel was born, and the remark epitomized the prejudice Rommel had been fighting all his career.

He stumped across the sand toward the command vehicle, with von Mellenthin in tow. "General Cruewell has been captured," von Mellenthin said. "I had to ask Kesselring to take over. He's spent the afternoon trying to find out where you were."

"Worse and worse," Rommel said sourly.

They entered the back of the command vehicle, a huge truck. The shade was welcome. Kesselring was bent over a map, brushing away flies with his left hand while tracing a line with his right. He looked up and smiled. "My dear Rommel, thank heaven you're back," he said silkily.

Rommel took off his cap. "I've been fighting a battle," he grunted.

"So I gather. What happened?"

Rommel pointed to the map. "This is the Gazala Line." It was a string of fortified "boxes" linked by minefields which ran from the coast at Gazala due south into the desert for fifty miles. "'We made a dogleg around the southern end of the line and hit them from behind."

"Good idea. What went wrong?"

"We ran out of gasoline and ammunition." Rommel sat down heavily, suddenly feeling very tired. "Again," he added. Kesselring, as commander in chief (South), was responsible for Rommel's supplies, but the field marshal seemed not to notice the implied criticism.

An orderly came in with mugs of tea on a tray. Rommel sipped his. There was sand in it.

Kesselring spoke in a conversational tone. "I've had the unusual experience, this afternoon, of taking the role of one of your subordinate commanders."

Rommel grunted. There was some piece of sarcasm coming, he could tell. He did not want to fence with Kesselring now, he wanted to think about the battle.

Kesselring went on: "I found it enormously difficult, with

my hands tied by subordination to a headquarters that issued no orders and could not be reached."

"I was at the heart of the battle, giving my orders on the spot."

"Still, you might have stayed in touch."

"That's the way the British fight," Rommel snapped. "The generals are miles behind the lines, staying in touch. But I'm winning. If I'd had my supplies, I'd be in Cairo now."

"You're not going to Cairo," Kesselring said sharply. "You're going to Tobruk. There you'll stay until I've taken Malta. Such are the Fuehrer's orders."

"Of course." Rommel was not going to reopen that argument; not yet. Tobruk was the immediate objective. Once that fortified port was taken, the convoys from Europe—inadequate though they were—could come directly to the front line, cutting out the long journey across the desert which used so much gasoline. "And to reach Tobruk we have to break the Gazala Line."

"What's your next step?"

"I'm going to fall back and regroup." Rommel saw Kesselring raise his eyebrows: the field marshal knew how Rommel hated to retreat.

"And what will the enemy do?" Kesselring directed the question to von Mellenthin, who as Ic was responsible for detailed assessment of the enemy position.

"They will chase us, but not immediately," said von Mellenthin. "They are always slow to press an advantage, fortunately. But sooner or later they will try a breakout."

Rommel said: "The question is, when and where?"

"Indeed," von Mellenthin agreed. He seemed to hesitate, then said. "There is a little item in today's summaries which will interest you. The spy checked in."

"The spy?" Rommel frowned. "Oh, him!" Now he remembered. He had flown to the Oasis of Gialo, deep in the Libyan desert, to brief the man finally before the spy began a long marathon walk. Wolff, that was his name. Rommel had been impressed by his courage, but pessimistic about his chances. "Where was he calling from?"

"Cairo."

"So he got there. If he's capable of that, he's capable of anything. Perhaps he can foretell the breakout."

Kesselring broke in: "My God, you're not relying on spies now, are you?"

"I'm not relying on anyone!" Rommel said. "I'm the one upon whom everyone else relies."

"Good." Kesselring was unruffled, as always. "Intelligence is never much use, as you know; and intelligence from spies is the worst kind."

"I agree," Rommel said more calmly. "But I have a feeling this one could be different."

"I doubt it," said Kesselring.

4

Elene Fontana looked at her face in the mirror and thought: I'm twenty-three, I must be losing my looks.

She leaned closer to the glass and examined herself carefully, searching for signs of deterioration. Her complexion was perfect. Her round brown eyes were as clear as a mountain pool. There were no wrinkles. It was a childish face, delicately modeled, with a look of waiflike innocence. She was like an art collector checking on his finest piece: she thought of the face as *hers*, not as *her*. She smiled, and the face in the mirror smiled back at her. It was a small, intimate smile, with a hint of mischief about it: she knew it could make a man break out into a cold sweat.

She picked up the note and read it again.

Thursday

My dear Elene,

I'm afraid it is all over. My wife has found out. We have patched things up, but I've had to promise never to see you again. Of course you can stay in the flat, but I can't pay the rent anymore. I'm so sorry it happened this way

—but I suppose we both knew it could not last forever. Good luck—

Your,

Claud.

Just like that, she thought.

She tore up the note and its cheap sentiments. Claud was a fat, half-French and half-Greek businessman who owned three restaurants in Cairo and one in Alexandria. He was cultured and jolly and kind, but when it came to the crunch he cared nothing for Elene.

He was the third in six years.

It had started with Charles, the stockbroker. She had been seventeen years old, penniless, unemployed and frightened to go home. Charles had set her up in the flat and visited her every Tuesday night. She had thrown him out after he offered her to his brother as if she were a dish of sweetmeats. Then there had been Johnnie, the nicest of the three, who wanted to divorce his wife and marry Elene: she had refused. Now Claud, too, had gone.

She had known from the start there was no future in it.

It was her fault as much as theirs that the affairs broke up. The ostensible reasons—Charles's brother, Johnnie's proposal, Claud's wife—were just excuses, or maybe catalysts. The real cause was always the same: Elene was unhappy.

She contemplated the prospect of another affair. She knew how it would be. For a while she would live on the little nest egg she had in Barclays Bank in the Shari Kasr-el-Nil—she always managed to save, when she had a man. Then she would see the balance slowly going down, and she would take a job in a dance troupe, kicking up her legs and wiggling her bottom in some club for a few days. Then . . . She looked into the mirror and through it, her eyes unfocusing as she visualized her fourth lover. Perhaps he would be an Italian, with flashing eyes and glossy hair and perfectly manicured hands. She might meet him in the bar of the Metropolitan Hotel, where the reporters drank. He would speak to her, then offer her a drink. She would smile at him, and he would be lost. They would make a date for dinner the next day. She would look stunning as she walked into the restaurant on his arm. All heads would turn, and he would feel proud. They would have more dates. He would give her presents. He would make a pass at her, then another: his third would be successful. She would enjoy making love with him—the intimacy, the touching, the endearments—and she would make him feel like a king. He would leave her at dawn, but he would be back that evening. They would stop going to restaurants together—"too risky," he would say—but he would spend more and more time at the flat, and he would begin to pay the rent and the bills. Elene would then have everything she wanted: a home, money and affection. She would begin to wonder why she was so miserable. She would throw a tantrum if he arrived half an hour late. She would go into a black sulk if he so much as mentioned his wife. She would complain that he no longer gave her presents, but accept them nonchalantly when he did. The man would be irritated but he would be unable to leave her, for by this time he would be eager for her grudging kisses, greedy for her perfect body; and she would still make him feel like a king in bed. She would find his conversation boring; she would demand from him more passion than he was able to give; there would be rows. Finally the crisis would come. His wife would get suspicious, or a child would fall ill, or he would have to take a six-month business trip, or he would run short of money. And Elene would be back where she was now: drifting, alone, disreputable—and a year older.

Her eyes focused, and she saw again her face in the mirror. Her face was the cause of all this. It was because of her face that she led this pointless life. Had she been ugly, she would always have yearned to live like this, and never discovered its hollowness. You led me astray, she thought; you deceived me, you pretended I was somebody else. You're not my face, you're a mask. You should stop trying to run my life.

I'm not a beautiful Cairo socialite, I'm a slum girl from Alexandria.

I'm not a woman of independent means, I'm the next thing to a whore.

I'm not Egyptian, I'm Jewish.

My name is not Elene Fontana. It's Abigail Asnani.

And I want to go home.

∽

The young man behind the desk at the Jewish Agency in Cairo wore a yarmulke. Apart from a wisp of beard, his cheeks were smooth. He asked for her name and address. Forgetting her resolution, she called herself Elene Fontana.

The young man seemed confused. She was used to this: most men got a little flustered when she smiled at them. He said: "Would you— I mean, do you mind if I ask you why you want to go to Palestine?"

"I'm Jewish," she said abruptly. She could not explain her life to this boy. "All my family are dead. I'm wasting my life." The first part was not true, but the second part was.

"What work would you do in Palestine?"

She had not thought of that. "Anything."

"It's mostly agricultural labor."

"That's fine."

He smiled gently. He was recovering his composure. "I mean no offense, but you don't look like a farmhand."

"If I didn't want to change my life, I wouldn't want to go to Palestine."

"Yes." He fiddled with his pen. "What work do you do now?"

"I sing, and when I can't get singing I dance, and when I can't get dancing I wait on tables." It was more or less true. She had done all three at one time or another, although dancing was the only one she did successfully, and she was not brilliant at that. "I told you, I'm wasting my life. Why all the questions? Is Palestine accepting only college graduates now?"

"Nothing like that," he said. "But it's very tough to get in. The British have imposed a quota, and all the places are taken by refugees from the Nazis."

"Why didn't you tell me that before?" she said angrily.

"Two reasons. One is that we can get people in illegally.

The other . . . the other takes a little longer to explain. Would you wait a minute? I must telephone someone."

She was still angry with him for questioning her before he told her there were no places. "I'm not sure there's any point in my waiting."

"There is, I promise you. It's quite important. Just a minute or two."

"Very well."

He went into a back room to phone. Elene waited impatiently. The day was warming up, and the room was poorly ventilated. She felt a little foolish. She had come here impulsively, without thinking through the idea of emigration. Too many of her decisions were made like that. She might have guessed they would ask her questions; she could have prepared her answers. She could have come dressed in something a little less glamorous.

The young man came back. "It's so warm," he said. "Shall we go across the street for a cold drink?"

So that was the game, she thought. She decided to put him down. She gave him an appraising look, then said: "No. You're much too young for me."

He was terribly embarrassed. "Oh, please don't misunderstand me. There's someone I want you to meet, that's all."

She wondered whether to believe him. She had nothing to lose, and she was thirsty. "All right."

He held the door for her. They crossed the street, dodging the rickety carts and broken-down taxis, feeling the sudden blazing heat of the sun. They ducked under a striped awning and stepped into the cool of a café. The young man ordered lemon juice; Elene had gin and tonic.

She said: "You can get people in illegally."

"Sometimes." He took half his drink in one gulp. "One reason we do it is if the person is being persecuted. That's why I asked you some questions."

"I'm not being persecuted."

"The other reason is if people have done a lot for the cause, some way."

"You mean I have to earn the right to go to Palestine?"

"Look, maybe one day all Jews will have the right to go there to live. But while there are quotas there have to be criteria."

She was tempted to ask: Who do I have to sleep with? But she had misjudged him that way once already. All the same, she thought he wanted to use her somehow. She said: "What do I have to do?"

He shook his head. "I can't make a bargain with you. Egyptian Jews can't get into Palestine, except for special cases, and you're not a special case. That's all there is to it."

"What are you trying to tell me, then?"

"You can't go to Palestine, but you can still fight for the cause."

"What, exactly, did you have in mind?"

"The first thing we have to do is defeat the Nazis."

She laughed. "Well, I'll do my best!"

He ignored that. "We don't like the British much, but any enemy of Germany's is a friend of ours, so at the moment— strictly on a temporary basis—we're working with British Intelligence. I think you could help them."

"For God's sake! How?"

A shadow fell across the table, and the young man looked up. "Ah!" he said. He looked back at Elene. "I want you to meet my friend Major William Vandam."

∾

He was a tall man, and broad: with those wide shoulders and mighty legs he might once have been an athlete, although now, Elene guessed, he was close to forty and just beginning to go a little soft. He had a round, open face topped by wiry brown hair which looked as if it might curl if it were allowed to grow a little beyond the regulation length. He shook her hand, sat down, crossed his legs, lit a cigarette and ordered gin. He wore a stern expression, as if he thought life was a very serious business and he did not want anybody to start fooling around.

Elene thought he was a typical frigid Englishman.

The young man from the Jewish Agency asked him: "What's the news?"

"The Gazala Line is holding, but it's getting very fierce out there."

Vandam's voice was a surprise. English officers usually spoke with the upper-class drawl which had come to symbolize arrogance for ordinary Egyptians. Vandam spoke precisely but softly, with rounded vowels and a slight burr on the r: Elene had a feeling this was the trace of a country accent, although she could not remember how she knew.

She decided to ask him. "Where do you come from, Major?"

"Dorset. Why do you ask?"

"I was wondering about your accent."

"Southwest of England. You're observant. I thought I had no accent."

"Just a trace."

He lit another cigarette. She watched his hands. They were long and slender, rather at odds with the rest of his body; the nails were well manicured and the skin was white except for the deep amber stains where he held his cigarette.

The young man took his leave. "I'll let Major Vandam explain everything to you. I hope you will work with him; I believe it's very important."

Vandam shook his hand and thanked him, and the young man went out.

Vandam said to Elene: "Tell me about yourself."

"No," she said. "You tell me about yourself."

He raised an eyebrow at her, faintly startled, a little amused and suddenly not at all frigid. "All right," he said after a moment. "Cairo is full of officers and men who know secrets. They know our strengths, our weaknesses and our plans. The enemy wants to know those secrets. We can be sure that at any time the Germans have people in Cairo trying to get information. It's my job to stop them."

"That simple."

He considered. "It's simple, but it's not easy."

He took everything she said seriously, she noticed. She thought it was because he was humorless, but all the same she rather liked it: men generally treated her conversation like background music in a cocktail bar, a pleasant enough but largely meaningless noise.

He was waiting. "It's your turn," he said.

Suddenly she wanted to tell him the truth. "I'm a lousy singer and a mediocre dancer, but sometimes I find a rich man to pay my bills."

He said nothing, but he looked taken aback.

Elene said: "Shocked?"

"Shouldn't I be?"

She looked away. She knew what he was thinking. Until now he had treated her politely, as if she were a respectable woman, one of his own class. Now he realized he had been mistaken. His reaction was completely predictable, but all the same she felt bitter. She said: "Isn't that what most women do, when they get married—find a man to pay the bills?"

"Yes," he said gravely.

She looked at him. The imp of mischief seized her. "I just turn them around a little faster than the average housewife."

Vandam burst out laughing. Suddenly he looked a different man. He threw back his head, his arms and legs spread sideways, and all the tension went out of his body. When the laugh subsided he was relaxed, just briefly. They grinned at one another. The moment passed, and he crossed his legs again. There was a silence. Elene felt like a schoolgirl who has been giggling in class.

Vandam was serious again. "My problem is information," he said. "Nobody tells an Englishman anything. That's where you come in. Because you're Egyptian, you hear the kind of gossip and street talk that never comes my way. And because you're Jewish, you'll pass it to me. I hope."

"What kind of gossip?"

"I'm interested in anyone who's curious about the British Army." He paused. He seemed to be wondering how much to tell her. "In particular . . . At the moment I'm looking for a man called Alex Wolff. He used to live in Cairo and he has recently returned. He may be hunting for a place to live, and he probably has a lot of money. He is certainly making inquiries about British forces."

Elene shrugged. "After all that buildup I was expecting to be asked to do something much more dramatic."

"Such as?"

"I don't know. Waltz with Rommel and pick his pockets."

Vandam laughed again. Elene thought: I could get fond of that laugh.

He said: "Well, mundane though it is, will you do it?"

"I don't know." But I do know, she thought; I'm just trying to prolong the interview, because I'm enjoying myself.

Vandam leaned forward. "I need people like you, Miss Fontana." Her name sounded silly when he said it so politely. "You're observant, you have a perfect cover and you're obviously intelligent; please excuse me for being so direct—"

"Don't apologize, I love it," she said. "Keep talking."

"Most of my people are not very reliable. They do it for the money, whereas you have a better motive—"

"Wait a minute," she interrupted. "I want money, too. What does the job pay?"

"That depends on the information you bring in."

"What's the minimum?"

"Nothing."

"That's a little less than what I was hoping for."

"How much do you want?"

"You might be a gentleman and pay the rent of my flat." She bit her lip: it sounded so tarty, put like that.

"How much?"

"Seventy-five a month."

Vandam's eyebrows rose. "What have you got, a palace?"

"Prices have gone up. Haven't you heard? It's all these English officers desperate for accommodation."

"Touché." He frowned. "You'd have to be awfully useful to justify seventy-five a month."

Elene shrugged. "Why don't we give it a try?"

"You're a good negotiator." He smiled. "All right, a month's trial."

Elene tried not to look triumphant. "How do I contact you?"

"Send me a message." He took a pencil and a scrap of paper from his shirt pocket and began to write. "I'll give you my address and phone number, at GHQ and at home. As soon as I hear from you I'll come to your place."

"All right." She wrote down her address, wondering what the major would think of her flat. "What if you're seen?"

"Will it matter?"

"I might be asked who you are."

"Well, you'd better not tell the truth."

She grinned. "I'll say you're my lover."

He looked away. "Very well."

"But you'd better act the part." She kept a straight face. "You must bring armfuls of flowers and boxes of chocolates."

"I don't know—"

"Don't Englishmen give their mistresses flowers and chocolates?"

He looked at her unblinkingly. She noticed that he had gray eyes. "I don't know," he said levelly. "I've never had a mistress."

Elene thought: I stand corrected. She said: "Then you've got a lot to learn."

"I'm sure. Would you like another drink?"

And now I'm dismissed, she thought. You're a little too much, Major Vandam: there's a certain self-righteousness about you, and you rather like to be in charge of things; you're so masterful. I may take you in hand, puncture your vanity, do you a little damage.

"No, thanks," she said. "I must go."

He stood up. "I'll look forward to hearing from you."

She shook his hand and walked away. Somehow she had the feeling that he was not watching her go.

∽

Vandam changed into a civilian suit for the reception at the Anglo-Egyptian Union. He would never have gone to the Union while his wife was alive: she said it was "plebby." He told her to say "plebeian" so that she would not sound like a county snob. She said she was a county snob, and would he kindly stop showing off his classical education.

Vandam had loved her then and he did now.

Her father was a fairly wealthy man who became a diplomat because he had nothing better to do. He had not been pleased at the prospect of his daughter marrying a postman's son. He was not much mollified when he was told that Vandam had gone to a minor public school (on a scholarship) and London University, and was considered one of the most promising of his generation of junior army officers. But the daughter was adamant in this as in all things, and in the end the father had accepted the match with good grace. Oddly enough, on the one occasion when the fathers met they got on rather well. Sadly, the mothers hated each other and there were no more family gatherings.

None of it mattered much to Vandam; nor did the fact that his wife had a short temper, an imperious manner and an ungenerous heart. Angela was graceful, dignified and beautiful. For him she was the epitome of womanhood, and he thought himself a lucky man.

The contrast with Elene Fontana could not have been more striking.

He drove to the Union on his motorcycle. The bike, a BSA 350, was very practical in Cairo. He could use it all the year round, for the weather was almost always good enough; and he could snake through the traffic jams that kept cars and taxis waiting. But it was a rather quick machine, and it gave him a secret thrill, a throwback to his adolescence, when he had coveted such bikes but had not been able to buy one. Angela had loathed it—like the Union, it was plebby—but for once Vandam had resolutely defied her.

The day was cooling when he parked at the Union. Passing the clubhouse, he looked through a window and saw a snooker game in full swing. He resisted the temptation and walked on to the lawn.

He accepted a glass of Cyprus sherry and moved into the

crowd, nodding and smiling, exchanging pleasantries with people he knew. There was tea for the teetotal Muslim guests, but not many had turned up. Vandam tasted the sherry and wondered whether the barman could be taught to make a martini.

He looked across the grass to the neighboring Egyptian Officers' Club, and wished he could eavesdrop on conversations there. Someone spoke his name, and he turned to see the woman doctor. Once again he had to think before he could remember her name. "Dr. Abuthnot."

"We might be informal here," she said. "My name is Joan."

"William. Is you husband here?"

"I'm not married."

"Pardon me." Now he saw her in a new light. She was single and he was a widower, and they had been seen talking together in public three times in a week: by now the English colony in Cairo would have them practically engaged. "You're a surgeon?" he said.

She smiled. "All I do these days is sew people up and patch them—but yes, before the war I was a surgeon."

"How did you manage that? It's not easy for a woman."

"I fought tooth and nail." She was still smiling, but Vandam detected an undertone of remembered resentment. "You're a little unconventional yourself, I'm told."

Vandam thought himself to be utterly conventional. "How so?" he said with surprise.

"Bringing up your child yourself."

"No choice. If I had wanted to send him back to England, I wouldn't have been able to: you can't get a passage unless you're disabled or a general."

"But you didn't want to."

"No."

"That's what I mean."

"He's my son," Vandam said. "I don't want anyone else to bring him up—nor does he."

"I understand. It's just that some fathers would think it . . . unmanly."

He raised his eyebrows at her, and to his surprise she blushed.

He said: "You're right, I suppose. I'd never thought of it that way."

"I'm ashamed of myself, I've been prying. Would you like another drink?"

Vandam looked into his glass. "I think I shall have to go inside in search of a real drink."

"I wish you luck." She smiled and turned away.

Vandam walked across the lawn to the clubhouse. She was an attractive woman, courageous and intelligent, and she had made it clear she wanted to know him better. He thought: Why the devil do I feel so indifferent to her? All these people are thinking how well matched we are—and they're right.

He went inside and spoke to the bartender. "Gin. Ice. One olive. And *a few drops* of very dry vermouth."

The martini when it came was quite good, and he had two more. He thought again of the woman Elene. There were a thousand like her in Cairo—Greek, Jewish, Syrian and Palestinian as well as Egyptian. They were dancers for just as long as it took to catch the eye of some wealthy roué. Most of them probably entertained fantasies of getting married and being taken back to a large house in Alexandria or Paris or Surrey, and they would be disappointed.

They all had delicate brown faces and feline bodies with slender legs and pert breasts, but Vandam was tempted to think that Elene stood out from the crowd. Her smile was devastating. The idea of her going to Palestine to work on a farm was, at first sight, ridiculous; but she had tried, and when that failed she had agreed to work for Vandam. On the other hand, retailing street gossip was easy money, like being a kept woman. She was probably the same as all the other dancers: Vandam was not interested in that kind of woman, either.

The martinis were beginning to take effect, and he was afraid he might not be as polite as he should to the ladies when they came in, so he paid his bill and went out.

He drove to GHQ to get the latest news. It seemed the day had ended in a standoff after heavy casualties on both sides—rather more on the British side. It was just bloody demoralizing, Vandam thought: we had a secure base, good supplies,

superior weapons and greater numbers; we planned thoughtfully and we fought carefully, and we never damn well won
anything. He went home.

Gaafar had prepared lamb and rice. Vandam had another
drink with his dinner. Billy talked to him while he ate. Today's
geography lesson had been about wheat farming in Canada.
Vandam would have liked the school to teach the boy something about the country in which he lived.

After Billy went to bed Vandam sat alone in the drawing
room, smoking, thinking about Joan Abuthnot and Alex Wolff
and Erwin Rommel. In their different ways they all threatened
him. As night fell outside, the room came to seem claustrophobic. Vandam filled his cigarette case and went out.

The city was as much alive now as at any time during the
day. There were a lot of soldiers on the streets, some of them
very drunk. These were hard men who had seen action in the
desert, had suffered the sand and the heat and the bombing
and the shelling, and they often found the wogs less grateful
than they should be. When a shopkeeper gave short change or
a restaurant owner overcharged or a barman refused to serve
drunks, the soldiers would remember seeing their friends
blown up in the defense of Egypt, and they would start fighting
and break windows and smash the place up. Vandam understood why the Egyptians were ungrateful—they did not much
care whether it was the British or the Germans who oppressed
them—but still he had little sympathy for the Cairo shopkeepers, who were making a fortune out of the war.

He walked slowly, cigarette in hand, enjoying the cool night
air, looking into the tiny open-fronted shops, refusing to buy
a cotton shirt made-to-measure-while-you-wait, a leather handbag for the lady or a secondhand copy of a magazine called
Saucy Snips. He was amused by a street vendor who had filthy
pictures in the left-hand side of his jacket and crucifixes in the
right. He saw a bunch of soldiers collapse with laughter at the
sight of two Egyptian policemen patrolling the street hand in
hand.

He went into a bar. Outside of the British clubs it was wise
to avoid the gin, so he ordered zibib, the aniseed drink which

turned cloudy with water. At ten o'clock the bar closed, by mutual consent of the Muslim Wafd government and the kill-joy provost marshal. Vandam's vision was a little blurred when he left.

He headed for the Old City. Passing a sign saying OUT OF BOUNDS TO TROOPS he entered the Birka. In the narrow streets and alleys the women sat on steps and leaned from windows, smoking and waiting for customers, chatting to the military police. Some of them spoke to Vandam, offering their bodies in English, French and Italian. He turned into a little lane, crossed a deserted courtyard and entered an unmarked open doorway.

He climbed the staircase and knocked at a door on the first floor. A middle-aged Egyptian woman opened it. He paid her five pounds and went in.

In a large, dimly lit inner room furnished with faded luxury, he sat on a cushion and unbuttoned his shirt collar. A young woman in baggy trousers passed him the nargileh. He took several deep lungfuls of hashish smoke. Soon a pleasant feeling of lethargy came over him. He leaned back on his elbows and looked around. In the shadows of the room there were four other men. Two were pashas—wealthy Arab landowners—sitting together on a divan and talking in low, desultory tones. A third, who seemed almost to have been sent to sleep by the hashish, looked English and was probably an officer like Vandam. The fourth sat in the corner talking to one of the girls. Vandam heard snatches of conversation and gathered that the man wanted to take the girl home, and they were discussing a price. The man was vaguely familiar, but Vandam, drunk and now doped too, could not get his memory in gear to recall who he was.

One of the girls came over and took Vandam's hand. She led him into an alcove and drew the curtain. She took off her halter. She had small brown breasts. Vandam stroked her cheek. In the candlelight her face changed constantly, seeming old, then very young, then predatory, then loving. At one point she looked like Joan Abuthnot. But finally, as he entered her, she looked like Elene.

5

Alex Wolff wore a galabiya and a fez and stood thirty yards from the gate of GHQ—British headquarters—selling paper fans which broke after two minutes of use.

The hue and cry had died down. He had not seen the British conducting a spot check on identity papers for a week. This Vandam character could not keep up the pressure indefinitely.

Wolff had gone to GHQ as soon as he felt reasonably safe. Getting into Cairo had been a triumph; but it was useless unless he could exploit the position to get the information Rommel wanted—and quickly. He recalled his brief interview with Rommel in Gialo. The Desert Fox did not look foxy at all. He was a small, tireless man with the face of an aggressive peasant: a big nose, a downturned mouth, a cleft chin, a jagged scar on his left cheek, his hair cut so short that none showed beneath the rim of his cap. He had said: "Numbers of troops, names of divisions, in the field and in reserve, state of training. Numbers of tanks, in the field and in reserve, state of repair. Supplies of ammunition, food and gasoline. Personalities and attitudes of commanding officers. Strategic and tactical intentions. They say you're good, Wolff. They had better be right."

It was easier said than done.

There was a certain amount of information Wolff could get just by walking around the city. He could observe the uniforms of the soldiers on leave and listen to their talk, and that told him which troops had been where and when they were going back. Sometimes a sergeant would mention statistics of dead and wounded, or the devastating effect of the 88-millimeter guns—designed as antiaircraft weapons—which the Germans had fitted to their tanks. He had heard an army mechanic complain that thirty-nine of the fifty new tanks which arrived yesterday needed major repairs before going into service. All this was useful information which could be sent to Berlin, where Intelligence analysts would put it together with other snippets in order to form a big picture. But it was not what Rommel wanted.

Somewhere inside GHQ there were pieces of paper which said things like: "After resting and refitting, Division A, with 100 tanks and full supplies, will leave Cairo tomorrow and join forces with Division B at the C Oasis in preparation for the counterattack west of D next Saturday at dawn."

It was those pieces of paper Wolff wanted.

That was why he was selling fans outside GHQ.

For their headquarters the British had taken over a number of the large houses—most of them owned by pashas—in the Garden City suburb. (Wolff was grateful that the Villa les Oliviers had escaped the net.) The commandeered homes were surrounded by a barbed-wire fence. People in uniform were passed quickly through the gate, but civilians were stopped and questioned at length while the sentries made phone calls to verify credentials.

There were other headquarters in other buildings around the city—the Semiramis Hotel housed something called British Troops in Egypt, for example—but this was GHQ Middle East, the powerhouse. Wolff had spent a lot of time, back in the Abwehr spy school, learning to recognize uniforms, regimental identification marks and the faces of literally hundreds of senior British officers. Here, several mornings running, he had observed the large staff cars arriving and had peeked through the windows to see colonels, generals, admirals, squadron leaders and the commander in chief, Sir Claude Auchinleck, himself. They all looked a little odd, and he was puzzled until he realized that the pictures of them which he had burned into his brain were in black and white, and now he was seeing them for the first time in color.

The General Staff traveled by car, but their aides walked. Each morning the captains and majors arrived on foot, carrying their little briefcases. Toward noon—after the regular morning conference, Wolff presumed—some of them left, still carrying their briefcases.

Each day Wolff followed one of the aides.

Most of the aides worked at GHQ, and their secret papers would be locked up in the office at the end of the day. But these few were men who had to be at GHQ for the morning conference, but had their own offices in other parts of the city; and they had to carry their briefing papers with them in between one office and another. One of them went to the Semiramis. Two went to the barracks in the Kasr-el-Nil. A fourth went to an unmarked building in the Shari Suleiman Pasha.

Wolff wanted to get into those briefcases.

Today he would do a dry run.

Waiting under the blazing sun for the aides to come out, he thought about the night before, and a smile curled the corners of his mouth below the newly-grown mustache. He had promised Sonja that he would find her another Fawzi. Last night he had gone to the Birka and picked out a girl at Madame Fahmy's establishment. She was not a Fawzi—*that* girl had been a real enthusiast—but she was a good temporary substitute. They had enjoyed her in turn, then together; then they had played Sonja's weird, exciting games . . . It had been a long night.

When the aides came out, Wolff followed the pair that went to the barracks.

A minute later Abdullah emerged from a café and fell into step beside him.

"Those two?" Abdullah said.

"Those two."

Abdullah was a fat man with a steel tooth. He was one of the richest men in Cairo, but unlike most rich Arabs he did not ape the Europeans. He wore sandals, a dirty robe and a fez. His greasy hair curled around his ears and his fingernails were black. His wealth came not from land, like the pashas', nor from trade, like the Greeks'. It came from crime.

Abdullah was a thief.

Wolff liked him. He was sly, deceitful, cruel, generous, and always laughing: for Wolff he embodied the age-old vices and virtues of the Middle East. His army of children, grandchildren, nephews, nieces and second cousins had been burgling houses and picking pockets in Cairo for thirty years. He had tentacles everywhere: he was a hashish wholesaler, he had influence with politicians, and he owned half the houses in the Birka, including Madame Fahmy's. He lived in a large crumbling house in the Old City with his four wives.

They followed the two officers into the modern city center. Abdullah said: "Do you want one briefcase, or both?"

Wolff considered. One was a casual theft; two looked organized. "One," he said.

"Which?"

"It doesn't matter."

Wolff had considered going to Abdullah for help after the discovery that the Villa les Oliviers was no longer safe. He had decided not to. Abdullah could certainly have hidden Wolff away somewhere—probably in a brothel—more or less indefinitely. But as soon as he had Wolff concealed, he would have opened negotiations to sell him to the British. Abdullah divided the world in two: his family and the rest. He was utterly loyal to his family and trusted them completely; he would cheat everyone else and expected them to try to cheat him. All business was done on the basis of mutual suspicion. Wolff found this worked surprisingly well.

They came to a busy corner. The two officers crossed the road, dodging the traffic. Wolff was about to follow when Abdullah put a hand on his arm to stop him.

"We'll do it here," Abdullah said.

Wolff looked around, observing the buildings, the pavement,

the road junction and the street vendors. He smiled slowly, and nodded. "It's perfect," he said.

✧

They did it the next day.

Abdullah had indeed chosen the perfect spot for the snatch. It was where a busy side street joined a main road. On the corner was a café with tables outside, reducing the pavement to half its width. Outside the café, on the side of the main road, was a bus stop. The idea of queueing for the bus had never really caught on in Cairo despite sixty years of British domination, so those waiting simply milled about on the already crowded pavement. On the side street it was a little clearer, for although the café had tables out here too, there was no bus stop. Abdullah had observed this little shortcoming, and had put it right by detailing two acrobats to perform on the street there.

Wolff sat at the corner table, from where he could see along both the main road and the side street, and worried about the things that might go wrong.

The officers might not go back to the barracks today.

They might go a different way.

They might not be carrying their briefcases.

The police might arrive too early and arrest everyone on the scene.

The boy might be grabbed by the officers and questioned.

Wolff might be grabbed by the officers and questioned.

Abdullah might decide he could earn his money with less trouble simply by contacting Major Vandam and telling him he could arrest Alex Wolff at the Café Nasif at twelve noon today.

Wolff was afraid of going to prison. He was more than afraid, he was terrified. The thought of it brought him out in a cold sweat under the noonday sun. He could live without good food and wine and girls, if he had the vast wild emptiness of the desert to console him; and he could forego the freedom of the desert to live in a crowded city if he had the urban luxuries to console him; but he could not lose both. He had never told anyone of this: it was his secret nightmare. The idea of living in a tiny, colorless cell, among the scum of the earth (and all of them men), eating bad food, never seeing the blue sky or the endless Nile or the open plains . . . panic touched him glancingly even while he contemplated it. He pushed it out of his mind. It was not going to happen.

At eleven forty-five the large, grubby form of Abdullah waddled past the café. His expression was vacant but his small black eyes looked around sharply, checking his arrangements. He crossed the road and disappeared from view.

At five past twelve Wolff spotted two military caps among the massed heads in the distance.

He sat on the edge of his chair.

The officers came nearer. They were carrying their briefcases.

Across the street a parked car revved its idling engine.

A bus drew up to the stop, and Wolff thought: Abdullah can't possibly have arranged *that*: it's a piece of luck, a bonus.

The officers were five yards from Wolff.

The car across the street pulled out suddenly. It was a big black Packard with a powerful engine and soft American springing. It came across the road like a charging elephant, motor screaming in low gear, regardless of the main road traffic, heading for the side street, its horn blowing continuously. On the corner, a few feet from where Wolff sat, it plowed into the front of an old Fiat taxi.

The two officers stood beside Wolff's table and stared at the crash.

The taxi driver, a young Arab in a Western shirt and a fez, leaped out of his car.

A young Greek in a mohair suit jumped out of the Packard.

The Arab said the Greek was the son of a pig.

The Greek said the Arab was the back end of a diseased camel.

The Arab slapped the Greek's face and the Greek punched the Arab on the nose.

The people getting off the bus, and those who had been intending to get on it, came closer.

Around the corner, the acrobat who was standing on his colleague's head turned to look at the fight, seemed to lose his balance, and fell into his audience.

A small boy darted past Wolff's table. Wolff stood up, pointed at the boy and shouted at the top of his voice: "Stop, thief!"

The boy dashed off. Wolff went after him, and four people sitting near Wolff jumped up and tried to grab the boy. The child ran between the two officers, who were staring at the fight in the road. Wolff and the people who had jumped up to help him cannoned into the officers, knocking both of them to the ground. Several people began to shout "Stop, thief!" although most of them had no idea who the alleged thief was. Some of the newcomers thought it must be one of the fighting drivers. The crowd from the bus stop, the acrobats' audience, and most of the people in the café surged forward and began to attack one or other of the drivers—Arabs assuming the Greek was the culprit and everyone else assuming it was the Arab. Several men with sticks—most people carried sticks— began to push into the crowd, beating on heads at random in an attempt to break up the fighting which was entirely counterproductive. Someone picked up a chair from the café and hurled it into the crowd. Fortunately it overshot and went through the windshield of the Packard. However the waiters, the kitchen staff and the proprietor of the café now rushed out and began to attack everyone who swayed, stumbled or sat on their furniture. Everyone yelled at everyone else in five languages. Passing cars halted to watch the melee, the traffic backed up in three directions, and every stopped car sounded its horn. A dog struggled free of its leash and started biting people's legs in a frenzy of excitement. Everyone got off the bus. The brawling crowd became bigger by the second. Drivers who had stopped to watch the fun regretted it, for when the fight engulfed their cars they were unable to move away (because everyone else had stopped too) and they had to lock their doors and roll up their windows while men, women and children, Arabs and Greeks and Syrians and Jews and Australians and Scotsmen, jumped on their roofs and fought on their hoods and fell on their running boards and bled all over their paintwork. Somebody fell through the window of the tailor's shop next to the café, and a frightened goat ran into the souvenir shop which flanked the café on the other side and began to knock down all the tables laden with china and pottery and glass. A baboon came from somewhere—it had probably been riding the goat, in a common form of street entertainment— and ran across the heads in the crowd, nimble-footed, to disappear in the direction of Alexandria. A horse broke free of its harness and bolted along the street between the lines of cars. From a window above the café a woman emptied a bucket of dirty water into the melee. Nobody noticed.

At last the police arrived.

When people heard the whistles, suddenly the shoves and pushes and insults which had started their own individual fights seemed a lot less important. There was a scramble to get away before the arrests began. The crowd diminished rapidly. Wolff, who had fallen over early in the proceedings, picked himself up and strolled across the road to watch the dénouement. By the time six people had been handcuffed it was all over, and there was no one left fighting except for an old woman in black and a one-legged beggar feebly shoving each other in the gutter. The café proprietor, the tailor and the owner of the souvenir shop were wringing their hands and berating the police for not coming sooner while they mentally doubled and trebled the damage for insurance purposes.

The bus driver had broken his arm, but all the other injuries were cuts and bruises.

There was only one death: the goat had been bitten by the dog and consequently had to be destroyed.

When the police tried to move the two crashed cars, they discovered that during the fight the street urchins had jacked up the rear ends of both vehicles and stolen the tires.

Every single light bulb in the bus had also disappeared.

And so had one British Army briefcase.

⌇

Alex Wolff was feeling pleased with himself as he walked

briskly through the alleys of Old Cairo. A week ago the task of prizing secrets out of GHQ had seemed close to impossible. Now it looked as if he had pulled it off. The idea of getting Abdullah to orchestrate a street fight had been brilliant.

He wondered what would be in the briefcase.

Abdullah's house looked like all the other huddled slums. Its cracked and peeling façade was irregularly dotted with small misshapen windows. The entrance was a low doorless arch with a dark passage beyond. Wolff ducked under the arch, went along the passage and climbed a stone spiral staircase. At the top he pushed through a curtain and entered Abdullah's living room.

The room was like its owner—dirty, comfortable and rich. Three small children and a puppy chased each other around the expensive sofas and inlaid tables. In an alcove by a window an old woman worked on a tapestry. Another woman was drifting out of the room as Wolff walked in: there was no strict Muslim separation of the sexes here, as there had been in Wolff's boyhood home. In the middle of the floor Abdullah sat cross-legged on an embroidered cushion with a baby in his lap. He looked up at Wolff and smiled broadly. "My friend, what a success we have had!"

Wolff sat on the floor opposite him. "It was wonderful," he said. "You're a magician."

"Such a riot! And the bus arriving at just the right moment —and the baboon running away . . ."

Wolff looked more closely at what Abdullah was doing. On the floor beside him was a pile of wallets, handbags, purses and watches. As he spoke he picked up a handsome tooled leather wallet. He took from it a wad of Egyptian banknotes, some postage stamps and a tiny gold pencil, and put them somewhere under his robe. Then he put down the wallet, picked up a handbag and began to rifle through that.

Wolff realized where they had come from. "You old rogue," he said. "You had your boys in the crowd picking pockets."

Abdullah grinned, showing his steel tooth. "To go to all that trouble and then steal only one briefcase . . ."

"But you have got the briefcase."

"Of course."

Wolff relaxed. Abdullah made no move to produce the case. Wolff said: "Why don't you give it to me?"

"Immediately," Abdullah said. Still he did nothing. After a moment he said: "You were to pay me another fifty pounds on delivery."

Wolff counted out the notes and they disappeared beneath the grubby robe. Abdullah leaned forward, holding the baby to his chest with one arm, and with the other reached under the cushion he was sitting on and pulled out the briefcase.

Wolff took it from him and examined it. The lock was broken. He felt cross: surely there should be a limit to duplicity. He made himself speak calmly. "You've opened it already."

Abdullah shrugged. He said: *"Maaleesh."* It was a conveniently ambiguous word which meant both "Sorry" and "So what?"

Wolff sighed. He had been in Europe too long; he had forgotten how things were done at home.

He lifted the lid of the case. Inside was a sheaf of ten or twelve sheets of paper closely typewritten in English. As he began to read someone put a tiny coffee cup beside him. He glanced up to see a beautiful young girl. He said to Abdullah "Your daughter?"

Abdullah laughed. "My wife."

Wolff took another look at the girl. She seemed about fourteen years old. He turned his attention back to the papers.

He read the first, then with growing incredulity leafed through the rest.

He put them down. "Dear God," he said softly. He started to laugh.

He had stolen a complete set of barracks canteen menus for the month of June.

❧

Vandam said to Colonel Bogge: "I've issued a notice reminding officers that General Staff papers are not to be carried about the town other than in exceptional circumstances."

Bogge was sitting behind his big curved desk, polishing the red cricket ball with his handkerchief. "Good idea," he said. "Keep chaps on their toes."

Vandam went on: "One of my informants, the new girl I told you about—"

"The tart."

"Yes." Vandam resisted the impulse to tell Bogge that "tart" was not the right word for Elene. "She heard a rumor that the riot had been organized by Abdullah—"

"Who's he?"

"He's a kind of Egyptian Fagin, and he also happens to be an informant, although selling me information is the least of his many enterprises."

"For what purpose was the riot organized, according to this rumor?"

"Theft."

"I see." Bogge looked dubious.

"A lot of stuff was stolen, but we have to consider the possibility that the main object of the exercise was the briefcase."

"A conspiracy!" Bogge said with a look of amused skepticism. "But what would this Abdullah want with our canteen menus, eh?" He laughed.

"He wasn't to know what the briefcase contained. He may simply have assumed that they were secret papers."

"I repeat the question," Bogge said with the air of a father patiently coaching a child. "What would he want with secret papers?"

"He may have been put up to it."

"By whom?"

"Alex Wolff."

"Who?"

"The Assyut knife man."

"Oh, now really, Major, I thought we had finished with all that."

Bogge's phone rang, and he picked it up. Vandam took the opportunity to cool off a little. The truth about Bogge, Vandam reflected, was probably that he had no faith in himself, no trust in his own judgment; and, lacking the confidence to make real decisions, he played one-upmanship, scoring points off people in a smart-alec fashion to give himself the illusion that he *was* clever after all. Of course Bogge had no idea whether the briefcase theft was significant or not. He might have listened to what Vandam had to say and then made up his own mind; but he was frightened of that. He could not engage in a fruitful discussion with a subordinate, because he spent all his intellectual energy looking for ways to trap you in a contradiction or catch you in an error or pour scorn on your ideas; and by the time he had finished making himself feel superior that way the decision had been taken, for better or worse and more or less by accident, in the heat of the exchange.

Bogge was saying: "Of course, sir, I'll get on it right away." Vandam wondered how he coped with superiors. The colonel hung up. He said: "Now, then, where were we?"

"The Assyut murderer is still at large," Vandam said. "It may be significant that soon after his arrival in Cairo a General Staff officer is robbed of his briefcase."

"Containing canteen menus."

Here we go again, Vandam thought. With as much grace as he could muster he said: "In Intelligence, we don't believe in coincidence, do we?"

"Don't lecture me, laddie. Even if you were right—and I'm sure you're not—what could we do about it, other than issue the notice you've sent out?"

"Well. I've talked to Abdullah. He denies all knowledge of Alex Wolff, and I think he's lying."

"If he's a thief, why don't you tip off the Egyptian police about him?"

And what would be the point of that? thought Vandam. He said: "They know all about him. They can't arrest him because too many senior officers are making too much money from his bribes. But we could pull him in and interrogate him, sweat him a little. He's a man without loyalty, he'll change sides at the drop of a hat—"

"General Staff Intelligence does not pull people in and sweat them, Major—"

"Field Security can, or even the military police "

Bogge smiled. "If I went to Field Security with this story of an Arab Fagin stealing canteen menus I'd be laughed out of the office."

"But—"

"We've discussed this long enough, Major—too long, in fact."

"For Christ's sake—"

Bogge raised his voice. "I don't believe the riot was organized, I don't believe Abdullah intended to steal the briefcase, and I don't believe Wolff is a Nazi spy. Is that clear?"

"Look, all I want—"

"Is that *clear?*"

"Yes, sir."

"Good. Dismissed."

Vandam went out.

6

I am a small boy. My father told me how old I am, but I forgot. I will ask him again next time he comes home. My father is a soldier. The place he goes to is called a Sudan. A Sudan is a long way away.

I go to school. I learn the Koran. The Koran is a holy book I also learn to read and write. Reading is easy, but it is difficult to write without making a mess. Sometimes I pick cotton or take the beasts to drink.

My mother and my grandmother look after me. My grandmother is a famous person. Practically everyone in the whole world comes to see her when they are sick. She gives them medicines made of herbs.

She gives me treacle. I like it mixed with curdled milk. I lie on top of the oven in my kitchen and she tells me stories. My favorite story is the ballad of Zahran, the hero of Denshway. When she tells it, she always says that Denshway is nearby. She must be getting old and forgetful, because Denshway is a long way away. I walked there once with Abdel and it took us all morning.

Denshway is where the British were shooting pigeons when

one of their bullets set fire to a barn. All the men of the village come running to find out who had started the fire. One of the soldiers was frightened by the sight of all the strong men of the village running toward him, so he fired at them. There was a fight between the soldiers and the villagers. Nobody won the fight, but the soldier who had fired on the barn was killed. Soon more soldiers came and arrested all the men in the village.

The soldiers made a thing out of wood called a scaffold. I don't know what a scaffold is but it is used to hang people. I don't know what happens to people when they are hanged. Some of the villagers were hanged and the others were flogged. I know about flogging. It is the worst thing in the world, even worse than hanging, I should think.

Zahran was the first to be hanged, for he had fought the hardest against the soldiers. He walked to the scaffold with his head high, proud that he had killed the man who set fire to the barn.

I wish I were Zahran.

I have never seen a British soldier, but I know that I hate them.

My name is Anwar el-Sadat, and I am going to be a hero.

∽

Sadat fingered his mustache. He was rather pleased with it. He was only twenty-two years old, and in his captain's uniform he looked a bit like a boy soldier: the mustache made him seem older. He needed all the authority he could get, for what he was about to propose was—as usual—faintly ludicrous. At these little meetings he was at pains to talk and act as if the handful of hotheads in the room really were going to throw the British out of Egypt any day now.

He deliberately made his voice a little deeper as he began to speak. "We have all been hoping that Rommel would defeat the British in the desert and so liberate our country." He looked around the room: a good trick, that, in large or small meetings, for it made each one think Sadat was talking to him personally. "Now we have some very bad news. Hitler has agreed to give Egypt to the Italians."

Sadat was exaggerating: this was not news, it was a rumor. Furthermore most of the audience knew it to be a rumor. However, melodrama was the order of the day, and they responded with angry murmurs.

Sadat continued: "I propose that the Free Officers Movement should negotiate a treaty with Germany, under which we would organize an uprising against the British in Cairo, and they would guarantee the independence and sovereignty of Egypt after the defeat of the British." As he spoke the risibility of the situation struck him afresh: here he was, a peasant boy just off the farm, talking to half a dozen discontented subalterns about negotiations with the German Reich. And yet, who else would represent the Egyptian people? The British were conquerors, the Parliament was a puppet and the King was a foreigner.

There was another reason for the proposal, one which would not be discussed here, one which Sadat would not admit to himself except in the middle of the night: Abdel Nasser had been posted to the Sudan with his unit, and his absence gave Sadat a chance to win for himself the position of leader of the rebel movement.

He pushed the thought out of his mind, for it was ignoble. He had to get the others to agree to the proposal, then to agree to the means of carrying it out.

It was Kemel who spoke first. "But will the Germans take us seriously?" he asked. Sadat nodded, as if he too thought that was an important consideration. In fact he and Kemel had agreed beforehand that Kemel should ask this question, for it was a red herring. The real question was whether the Germans could be trusted to keep to any agreement they made with a group of unofficial rebels: Sadat did *not* want the meeting to discuss that. It was unlikely that the Germans would stick to their part of the bargain; but if the Egyptians did rise up against the British, and if they were then betrayed by the Germans, they would see that nothing but independence was good enough—and perhaps, too, they would turn for leadership to the man who had organized the uprising. Such hard political realities were not for meetings such as this: they were too sophisticated, too calculating. Kemel was the only person with whom Sadat could discuss tactics. Kemel was a policeman, a detective with the Cairo force, a shrewd, careful man: perhaps police work had made him cynical.

The others began to talk about whether it would work. Sadat made no contribution to the discussion. Let them talk, he thought; it's what they really like to do. When it came to action they usually let him down.

As they argued, Sadat recalled the failed revolution of the previous summer. It had started with the sheik of al-Azhar, who had preached: "We have nothing to do with the war." Then the Egyptian Parliament, in a rare display of independence, had adopted the policy: "Save Egypt from the scourge of war." Until then the Egyptian Army had been fighting side by side with the British Army in the desert, but now the British ordered the Egyptians to lay down their arms and withdraw. The Egyptians were happy to withdraw but did not want to be disarmed. Sadat saw a heaven-sent opportunity to foment strife. He and many other young officers refused to hand in their guns and planned to march on Cairo. To Sadat's great disappointment, the British immediately yielded and let them keep their weapons. Sadat continued to try to fan the spark of rebellion into the flame of revolution, but the British had outmaneuvered him by giving way. The march on Cairo was a fiasco: Sadat's unit arrived at the assembly point but nobody else came. They washed their vehicles, sat down, waited awhile, then went on to their camp.

Six months later Sadat had suffered another failure. This time it centered on Egypt's fat, licentious, Turkish King. The British gave an ultimatum to King Farouk: either he was to instruct his Premier to form a new, pro-British government, or he was to abdicate. Under pressure the King summoned Mustafa el-Nahas Pasha and ordered him to form a new government. Sadat was no royalist, but he was an opportunist: he announced that this was a violation of Egyptian sovereignty, and the young officers marched to the palace to salute the King in protest. Once again Sadat tried to push the rebellion further. His plan was to surround the palace in token defense of the

King. Once again, he was the only one who turned up.

He had been bitterly disappointed on both occasions. He had felt like abandoning the whole rebel cause: let the Egyptians go to hell their own way, he had thought in the moments of blackest despair. Yet those moments passed, for he knew the cause was right and he knew he was smart enough to serve it well.

"But we haven't any means of contacting the Germans." It was Imam speaking, one of the pilots. Sadat was pleased that they were already discussing *how to* do it rather than *whether to.*

Kemel had the answer to the question. "We might send the message by plane."

"Yes!" Imam was young and fiery. "One of us could go up on a routine patrol and then divert from the course and land behind German lines."

One of the older pilots said: "On his return he would have to account for his diversion—"

"He could not come back at all," Imam said, his expression turning forlorn as swiftly as it had become animated.

Sadat said quietly: "He could come back with Rommel."

Imam's eyes lit up again, and Sadat knew that the young pilot was seeing himself and Rommel marching into Cairo at the head of an army of liberation. Sadat decided that Imam should be the one to take the message.

"Let us agree on the text of the message," Sadat said democratically. Nobody noticed that such a clear decision had not been required on the question of whether a message should be sent at all. "I think we should make four points. One: We are honest Egyptians who have an organization within the Army. Two: Like you, we are fighting the British. Three: We are able to recruit a rebel army to fight on your side. Four: We will organize an uprising against the British in Cairo, if you will in return guarantee the independence and sovereignty of Egypt after the defeat of the British." He paused. With a frown, he added: "I think perhaps we should offer them some token of our good faith."

There was a silence. Kemel had the answer to this question,

too, but it would look better coming from one of the others.

Imam rose to the occasion. "We could send some useful military information along with the message."

Kemel now pretended to oppose the idea. "What sort of information could *we* get? I can't imagine—"

"Aerial photographs of British positions."

"How is that possible?"

"We can do it on a routine patrol, with an ordinary camera."

Kemel looked dubious. "What about developing the film?"

"Not necessary," Imam said excitedly. "We can just send the film."

"Just one film?"

"As many as we like."

Sadat said: "I think Imam is right." Once again they were discussing the practicalities of an idea instead of its risks. There was only one more hurdle to jump. Sadat knew from bitter experience that these rebels were terribly brave until the moment came when they really had to stick their necks out. He said: "That leaves only the question of which of us will fly the plane." As he spoke he looked around the room, letting his eyes rest finally on Imam.

After a moment's hesitation, Imam stood up.

Sadat's eyes blazed with triumph.

～

Two days later Kemel walked the three miles from central Cairo to the suburb where Sadat lived. As a detective inspector, Kemel had the use of an official car whenever he wanted it, but he rarely used one to go to rebel meetings, for security reasons. In all probability his police colleagues would be sympathetic to the Free Officers Movement; still, he was not in a hurry to put them to the test.

Kemel was fifteen years older than Sadat, yet his attitude to the younger man was one almost of hero worship. Kemel shared Sadat's cynicism, his realistic understanding of the levers of political power; but Sadat had something more, and that was a burning idealism which gave him unlimited energy and boundless hope.

Kemel wondered how to tell him the news.

The message to Rommel had been typed out, signed by Sadat and all the leading Free Officers except the absent Nasser and sealed in a big brown envelope. The aerial photographs of British positions had been taken. Imam had taken off in his Gladiator, with Baghdadi following in a second plane. They had touched down in the desert to pick up Kemel, who had given the brown envelope to Imam and climbed into Baghdadi's plane. Imam's face had been shining with youthful idealism.

Kemel thought: How will I break it to Sadat?

It was the first time Kemel had flown. The desert, so featureless from ground level, had been an endless mosaic of shapes and patterns: the patches of gravel, the dots of vegetation and the carved volcanic hills. Baghdadi said: "You're going to be cold," and Kemel thought he was joking—the desert was like a furnace—but as the little plane climbed the temperature dropped steadily, and soon he was shivering in his thin cotton shirt.

After a while both planes had turned due east, and Baghdadi spoke into his radio, telling base that Imam had veered off course and was not replying to radio calls. As expected, base told Baghdadi to follow Imam. This little pantomime was necessary so that Baghdadi, who was to return, should not fall under suspicion.

They flew over an army encampment. Kemel saw tanks, trucks, field guns and jeeps. A bunch of soldiers waved: they must be British, Kemel thought. Both planes climbed. Directly ahead they saw signs of battle: great clouds of dust, explosions and gunfire. They turned to pass to the south of the battlefield.

Kemel had thought: We flew over a British base, then a battlefield—next we should come to a German base.

Ahead, Imam's plane lost height. Instead of following, Baghdadi climbed a little more—Kemel had the feeling that the Gladiator was near its ceiling—and peeled off to the south.

Looking out of the plane to the right, Kemel saw what the pilots had seen: a small camp with a cleared strip marked as a runway.

Approaching Sadat's house, Kemel recalled how elated he had felt, up there in the sky above the desert, when he realized they were behind German lines, and the treaty was almost in Rommel's hands.

He knocked on the door. He still did not know what to tell Sadat.

It was an ordinary family house, rather poorer than Kemel's home. In a moment Sadat came to the door, wearing a galabiya and smoking a pipe. He looked at Kemel's face, and said immediately: "It went wrong."

"Yes." Kemel stepped inside. They went into the little room Sadat used as a study. There were a desk, a shelf of books and some cushions on the bare floor. On the desk an army pistol lay on top of a pile of papers.

They sat down. Kemel said: "We found a German camp with a runway. Imam descended. Then the Germans started to fire on his plane. It was an English plane, you see—we never considered that."

Sadat said: "But surely, they could see he was not hostile—he did not fire, did not drop bombs—"

"He just kept on going down," Kemel went on. "He waggled his wings, and I suppose he tried to raise them on the radio; anyway they kept firing. The tail of the plane took a hit."

"Oh, God."

"He seemed to be going down very fast. The Germans stopped firing. Somehow he managed to land on his wheels. The plane seemed to bounce. I don't think Imam could control it any longer. Certainly he could not slow down. He went off the hard surface and into a patch of sand; the port wing hit the ground and snapped; the nose dipped and plowed into the sand; then the fuselage fell on the broken wing."

Sadat was staring at Kemel, blank-faced and quite still, his pipe going cold in his hand. In his mind Kemel saw the plane lying broken on the sand, with a German fire truck and ambulance speeding along the runway toward it, followed by ten or fifteen soldiers. He would never forget how, like a blossom opening its petals, the belly of the plane had burst skyward in a riot of red and yellow flame.

"It blew up," he told Sadat.

"And Imam?"

"He could not possibly live through such a fire."

"We must try again," Sadat said. "We must find another way to get a message through."

Kemel stared at him, and realized that his brisk tone of voice was phony. Sadat tried to light his pipe, but the hand holding the match was shaking too much. Kemel looked closely, and saw that Sadat had tears in his eyes.

"The poor boy," Sadat whispered.

7

Wolff was back at square one: he knew where the secrets were, but he could not get at them.

He might have stolen another briefcase the way he had taken the first, but that would begin to look, to the British, like a conspiracy. He might have thought of another way to steal a briefcase, but even that might lead to a security clampdown. Besides, one briefcase on one day was not enough for his needs: he had to have regular, unimpeded access to secret papers.

That was why he was shaving Sonja's pubic hair.

Her hair was black and coarse, and it grew very quickly. Because she shaved it regularly she was able to wear her translucent trousers without the usual heavy, sequined G-string on top. The extra measure of physical freedom—and the persistent and accurate rumor that she had nothing on under the trousers —had helped to make her the leading belly dancer of the day.

Wolff dipped the brush into the bowl and began to lather her.

She lay on the bed, her back propped up by a pile of pillows, watching him suspiciously. She was not keen on this, his latest perversion. She thought she was not going to like it.

Wolff knew better.

He knew how her mind worked, and he knew her body better than she did, and he wanted something from her.

He stroked her with the soft shaving brush and said: "I've thought of another way to get into those briefcases."

"What?"

He did not answer her immediately. He put down the brush and picked up the razor. He tested its sharp edge with his thumb, then looked at her. She was watching him with horrid fascination. He leaned closer, spread her legs a little more, put the razor to her skin, and drew it upward with a light, careful stroke.

He said: "I'm going to befriend a British officer."

She did not answer: she was only half listening to him. He wiped the razor on a towel. With one finger of his left hand he touched the shaved patch, pulling down to stretch the skin, then he brought the razor close.

"Then I'll bring the officer here," he said.

Sonja said: "Oh, no."

He touched her with the edge of the razor and gently scraped upward.

She began to breathe harder.

He wiped the razor and stroked again once, twice, three times.

"Somehow I'll get the officer to bring his briefcase."

He put his finger on her most sensitive spot and shaved around it. She closed her eyes.

He poured hot water from a kettle into a bowl on the floor beside him. He dipped a flannel into the water and wrung it out.

"Then I'll go through the briefcase while the officer is in bed with you."

He pressed the hot flannel against her shaved skin.

She gave a sharp cry like a cornered animal: "Ahh, God!"

Wolff slipped out of his bathrobe and stood naked. He picked up a bottle of soothing skin oil, poured some into the palm of his right hand, and knelt on the bed beside Sonja; then he anointed her pubis.

"I won't," she said as she began to writhe.

He added more oil, massaging it into all the folds and crevices. With his left hand he held her by the throat, pinning her down. "You will."

His knowing fingers delved and squeezed, becoming less gentle.

She said: "No."

He said: "Yes."

She shook her head from side to side. Her body wriggled, helpless in the grip of intense pleasure. She began to shudder, and finally she said: "Oh. Oh. Oh. Oh. Oh. Oh!" Then she relaxed.

Wolff would not let her stop. He continued to stroke her smooth, hairless skin while with his left hand he pinched her brown nipples. Unable to resist him, she began to move again.

She opened her eyes and saw that he, too, was aroused. She said: "You bastard, stick it in me."

He grinned. The sense of power was like a drug. He lay over her and hesitated, poised.

She said: "Quickly!"

"Will you do it?"

"Quickly!"

He let his body touch hers, then paused again. "Will you do it?"

"Yes! Please!"

"Aaah," Wolff breathed, and lowered himself to her.

∽

She tried to go back on it afterward, of course.

"That kind of promise doesn't count," she said.

Wolff came out of the bathroom wrapped in a big towel. He looked at her. She was lying on the bed, still naked, eating chocolates from a box. There were moments when he was almost fond of her.

He said: "A promise is a promise."

"You promised to find us another Fawzi." She was sulking. She always did after sex.

"I brought that girl from Madame Fahmy's," Wolff said.

"She wasn't another Fawzi. Fawzi didn't ask for ten pounds every time, and she didn't go home in the morning."

"All right. I'm still looking."

"You didn't promise to *look,* you promised to *find.*"

Wolff went into the other room and got a bottle of champagne out of the icebox. He picked up two glasses and took them back into the bedroom. "Do you want some?"

"No," she said. "Yes."

He poured and handed her a glass. She drank some and took another chocolate. Wolff said: "To the unknown British officer who is about to get the nicest surprise of his life."

"I won't go to bed with an Englishman," Sonja said. "They smell bad and they have skin like slugs and I hate them."

"That's why you'll do it—because you hate them. Just imagine it: while he's screwing you and thinking how lucky he is, I'll be reading his secret papers."

Wolff began to dress. He put on a shirt which had been made for him in one of the tiny tailor shops in the Old City—a British uniform shirt with captain's pips on the shoulders.

Sonja said: "What are you wearing?"

"British officer's uniform. They don't talk to foreigners, you know."

"You're going to pretend to be British?"

"South African, I think."

"But what if you slip up?"

He looked at her. "I'll probably be shot as a spy."

She looked away.

Wolff said: "If I find a likely one, I'll take him to the Cha-Cha." He reached into his shirt and drew his knife from its underarm sheath. He went close to her and touched her naked shoulder with its point. "If you let me down, I'll cut your lips off."

She looked into his face. She did not speak, but there was fear in her eyes.

Wolff went out.

∽

Shepheard's was crowded. It always was.

Wolff paid off his taxi, pushed through the pack of hawkers and dragomans outside, mounted the steps and went into the foyer. It was packed with people: Levantine merchants holding noisy business meetings, Europeans using the post office and the banks, Egyptian girls in their cheap gowns and British officers—the hotel was out of bounds to Other Ranks. Wolff passed between two larger-than-life bronze ladies holding lamps and entered the lounge. A small band played nondescript music while more crowds, mostly European now, called constantly for waiters. Negotiating the divans and marble-topped tables Wolff made his way through to the long bar at the far end.

Here it was a little quieter. Women were banned, and serious drinking was the order of the day. It was here that a lonely officer would come.

Wolff sat at the bar. He was about to order champagne, then he remembered his disguise and asked for whiskey and water.

He had given careful thought to his clothes. The brown shoes were officer pattern and highly polished; the khaki socks were turned down at exactly the right place; the baggy brown shorts had a sharp crease; the bush shirt with captain's pips was worn outside the shorts, not tucked in; the flat cap was just slightly raked.

He was a little worried about his accent. He had his story ready to explain it—the line he had given Captain Newman, in Assyut, about having been brought up in Dutch-speaking South Africa—but what if the officer he picked up was a South African? Wolff could not distinguish English accents well enough to recognize a South African.

He was more worried about his knowledge of the Army. He was looking for an officer from GHQ, so he would say that he himself was with BTE—British Troops in Egypt—which was a separate and independent outfit. Unfortunately he knew little else about it. He was uncertain what BTE did and how it was organized, and he could not quote the name of a single one of its officers. He imagined a conversation:

"How's old Buffy Jenkins?"

"Old Buffy? Don't see much of him in my department."

"Don't see much of him? He runs the show! Are we talking about the same BTE?"

Then again:

"What about Simon Frobisher?"

"Oh, Simon's the same, you know."

"Wait a minute—someone said he'd gone back home. Yes, I'm sure he has—how come you didn't know?"

Then the accusations, and the calling of the military police, and the fight, and finally the jail.

Jail was the only thing that really frightened Wolff. He pushed the thought out of his mind and ordered another whiskey.

A perspiring colonel came in and stood at the bar next to Wolff's stool. He called to the barman: "*Ezma!*" It meant "Listen," but all the British thought it meant "Waiter." The colonel looked at Wolff.

Wolff nodded politely and said: "Sir."

"Cap off in the bar, Captain," said the colonel. "What are you thinking of?"

Wolff took off his cap, cursing himself silently for the error. The colonel ordered beer. Wolff looked away.

There were fifteen or twenty officers in the bar, but he recognized none of them. He was looking for any one of the eight aides who left GHQ each midday with their briefcases. He had memorized the face of each one, and would recognize them instantly. He had already been to the Metropolitan Hotel and the Turf Club without success, and after half an hour in Shepheard's he would try the Officers' Club, the Gezira Sporting Club and even the Anglo-Egyptian Union. If he failed tonight he would try again tomorrow: sooner or later he was sure to bump into at least one of them.

Then everything would depend on his skill.

His scheme had a lot going for it. The uniform made him one of them, trustworthy and a comrade. Like most soldiers they were probably lonely and sex-starved in a foreign country. Sonja was undeniably a very desirable woman—to look at, anyway—and the average English officer was not well armored against the wiles of an Oriental seductress.

And anyway, if he was unlucky enough to pick an aide smart enough to resist temptation, he would have to drop the man and look for another.

He hoped it would not take that long.

In fact it took him five more minutes.

The major who walked in was a small man, very thin, and about ten years older than Wolff. His cheeks had the broken veins of a hard drinker. He had bulbous blue eyes, and his thin sandy hair was plastered to his head.

Every day he left GHQ at midday and walked to an unmarked building in the Shari Suleiman Pasha—carrying his briefcase.

Wolff's heart missed a beat.

The major came up to the bar, took off his cap, and said: "*Ezma!* Scotch. No ice. Make it snappy." He turned to Wolff. "Bloody weather," he said conversationally.

"Isn't it always, sir?" Wolff said.

"Bloody right. I'm Smith, GHQ."

"How do you do, sir," Wolff said. He knew that, since Smith went from GHQ to another building every day, the major could not really be at GHQ; and he wondered briefly why the man should lie about it. He put the thought aside for the moment and said: "I'm Slavenburg, BTE."

"Jolly good. Get you another?"

It was proving even easier than he had expected to get into conversation with an officer. "Very kind of you, sir," Wolff said.

"Ease up on the sirs. No bull in the bar, what?"

"Of course." Another error.

"What'll it be?"

"Whiskey and water, please."

"Shouldn't take water with it if I were you. Comes straight out of the Nile, they say."

Wolff smiled. "I must be used to it."

"No gippy tummy? You must be the only white man in Egypt who hasn't got it."

"Born in Africa, been in Cairo ten years." Wolff was slipping into Smith's abbreviated style of speech. I should have been an actor, he thought.

Smith said: "Africa, eh? I thought you had a bit of an accent."

"Dutch father, English mother. We've got a ranch in South Africa."

Smith looked solicitous. "It's rough for your father, with Jerry all over Holland."

Wolff had not thought of that. "He died when I was a boy," he said.

"Bad show." Smith emptied his glass.

"Same again?" Wolff offered.

"Thanks."

Wolff ordered more drinks. Smith offered him a cigarette: Wolff refused.

Smith complained about the poor food, the way bars kept running out of drinks, the rent of his flat and the rudeness of Arab waiters. Wolff itched to explain that the food was poor because Smith insisted on English rather than Egyptian dishes, that drinks were scarce because of the European war, that rents were sky-high because of the thousands of foreigners like Smith who had invaded the city, and that the waiters were rude to him because he was too lazy or arrogant to learn a few phrases of courtesy in their language. Instead of explaining he bit his tongue and nodded as if he sympathized.

In the middle of this catalogue of discontent Wolff looked past Smith's shoulder and saw six military policemen enter the bar.

Smith noticed his change of expression and said: "What's the matter—seen a ghost?"

There were an army MP, a navy MP in white leggings, an Australian, a New Zealander, a South African and a turbaned Gurkha. Wolff had a crazy urge to run for it. What would they ask him? What would he say?

Smith looked around, saw the MPs and said: "The usual nightly picket—looking for drunken officers and German spies. This is an officers' bar, they won't disturb us. What's the matter —you breaking bounds or something?"

"No, no." Wolff improvised hastily: "The navy man looks just like a chap I knew who got killed at Halfaya." He continued to stare at the picket. They appeared very businesslike with their steel hats and holstered pistols. Would they ask to see papers?

Smith had forgotten them. He was saying: "And as for the servants . . . Bloody people. I'm bloody sure my man's been watering the gin. I'll find him out though. I've filled an empty gin bottle with zibib—you know, that stuff that turns cloudy when you add water? Wait till he tries to dilute that. He'll have to buy a whole new bottle and pretend nothing happened. Haha! Serve him right."

The officer in charge of the picket walked over to the colonel who had told Wolff to take off his hat. "Everything in order, sir?" the MP said.

"Nothing untoward," the colonel replied.

"What's the matter with you?" Smith said to Wolff. "I say, you are entitled to those pips, aren't you?"

"Of course," Wolff said. A drop of perspiration ran into his eye, and he wiped it away with a too-rapid gesture.

"No offense intended," Smith said. "But, you know, Shepheard's being off limits to Other Ranks, it's not unknown for subalterns to sew a few pips on their shirts just to get in here."

Wolff pulled himself together. "Look here, sir, if you'd care to check—"

"No, no, no," Smith said hastily.

"The resemblance was rather a shock."

"Of course, I understand. Let's have another drink. *Ezma!*"

The MP who had spoken to the colonel was taking a long look around the room. His armband identified him as the assistant provost marshal. He looked at Wolff. Wolff wondered whether the man remembered the description of the Assyut knife murderer. Surely not. Anyway, they would not be looking for a British officer answering the description. And Wolff had grown a mustache to confuse the issue. He forced himself to meet the MP's eyes, then let his gaze drift casually away. He picked up his drink, sure the man was still staring at him.

Then there was a clatter of boots and the picket went out.

By an effort Wolff prevented himself from shaking with relief. He raised his glass in a determinedly steady hand and said: "Cheers."

They drank. Smith said: "You know this place. What's a chap to do in the evening, other than drink in Shepheard's bar?"

Wolff pretended to consider the question. "Have you seen any belly dancing?"

Smith gave a disgusted snort. "Once. Some fat wog wiggling her hips."

"Ah. Then you ought to see the real thing."

"Should I?"

"Real belly dancing is the most erotic thing you've ever seen."

There was an odd light in Smith's eyes. "Is that so?"

Wolff thought: Major Smith, you are just what I need. He said: "Sonja is the best. You must try to see her act."

Smith nodded. "Perhaps I shall."

"Matter of fact, I was toying with the idea of going on to the Cha-Cha Club myself. Care to join me?"

"Let's have another drink first," said Smith.

Watching Smith put away the liquor Wolff reflected that the major was, at least on the surface, a highly corruptible man. He seemed bored, weak-willed and alcoholic. Provided he was normally heterosexual, Sonja would be able to seduce him easily. (Damn, he thought, she had better do her stuff.) Then they would have to find out whether he had in his briefcase anything more useful than menus. Finally they would have to find a way to get the secrets out of him. There were too many maybes and too little time.

He could only go step by step, and the first step was to get Smith in his power.

They finished their drinks and set out for the Cha-Cha. They could not find a taxi, so they took a gharry, a horse-drawn open carriage. The driver mercilessly whipped his elderly horse.

Smith said: "Chap's a bit rough on the beast."

"Isn't he," Wolff said, thinking: You should see what we do to camels.

The club was crowded and hot, again. Wolff had to bribe a waiter to get a table.

Sonja's act began moments after they sat down. Smith

watched Sonja while Wolff watched Smith. In minutes the major was drooling.

Wolff said: "Good, isn't she?"

"Fantastic," Smith replied without looking around.

"Matter of fact, I know her slightly," Wolff said. "Shall I ask her to join us afterwards?"

This time Smith did look around. "Good Lord!" he said. "Would you?"

∽

The rhythm quickened. Sonja looked out across the crowded floor of the club. Hundreds of men feasted their eyes greedily on her magnificent body. She closed her eyes.

The movements came automatically: the sensations took over. In her imagination she still saw the sea of rapacious faces staring at her. She felt her breasts shake and her belly roll and her hips jerk, and it was as if someone else was doing it to her, as if all the hungry men in the audience were manipulating her body. She went faster and faster. There was no artifice in her dancing, not any more; she was doing it for herself. She did not even follow the music—it followed her. Waves of excitement swept her. She rode the excitement, dancing, until she knew she was on the edge of ecstasy, knew she only had to jump and she would be flying. She hesitated on the brink. She spread her arms. The music climaxed with a bang. She uttered a cry of frustration and fell backward, her legs folded beneath her, her thighs open to the audience, until her head hit the stage. Then the lights went out.

It was always like that.

In the storm of applause she got up and crossed the darkened stage to the wings. She walked quickly to her dressing room, head down, looking at no one. She did not want their words or their smiles. They did not understand. Nobody knew how it was for her, nobody knew what she went through every night when she danced.

She took off her shoes, her filmy pantaloons and her sequined halter, and put on a silk robe. She sat in front of the mirror to remove her makeup. She always did this immediately, for the makeup was bad for the skin. She had to look after her body. Her face and throat were getting that fleshy look again, she observed. She would have to stop eating chocolates. She was already well past the age at which women began to get fat. Her age was another secret the audience must never discover. She was almost as old as her father had been when he died. Father . . .

He had been a big, arrogant man whose achievements never lived up to his hopes. Sonja and her parents had slept together in a narrow hard bed in a Cairo tenement. She had never felt so safe and warm since those days. She would curl up against her father's broad back. She could remember the close familiar smell of him. Then, when she should have been asleep, there had been another smell, something that excited her unaccountably. Mother and father would begin to move in the darkness, lying side by side; and Sonja would move with them. A few times her mother realized what was happening. Then her father would beat her. After the third time they made her sleep on the floor. Then she could hear them but could not share the pleasure: it seemed so cruel. She blamed her mother. Her father was willing to share, she was sure; he had known all along what she had been doing. Lying on the floor, cold, excluded, listening, she had tried to enjoy it at a distance, but it had not worked. Nothing had worked since then, until the arrival of Alex Wolff . . .

She had never spoken to Wolff about that narrow bed in the tenement, but somehow he understood. He had an instinct for the deep needs that people never acknowledged. He and the girl Fawzi had re-created the childhood scene for Sonja, and it had worked.

He did not do it out of kindness, she knew. He did these things so that he could use people. Now he wanted to use her to spy on the British. She would do almost anything to spite the British—anything but go to bed with them . . .

There was a knock on the door of her dressing room. She called: "Come in."

One of the waiters entered with a note. She nodded dismissal at the boy and unfolded the sheet of paper. The message said simply: "Table 41. Alex."

She crumpled the paper and dropped it on the floor. So he had found one. That was quick. His instinct for weakness was working again.

She understood him because she was like him. She, too, used people—although less cleverly than he did. She even used him. He had style, taste, high-class friends and money; and one day he would take her to Berlin. It was one thing to be a star in Egypt, and quite another in Europe. She wanted to dance for the aristocratic old generals and the handsome young Storm Troopers; she wanted to seduce powerful men and beautiful white girls; she wanted to be queen of the cabaret in the most decadent city in the world. Wolff would be her passport. Yes, she was using him.

It must be unusual, she thought, for two people to be so close and yet to love each other so little.

He *would* cut her lips off.

She shuddered, stopped thinking about it and began to dress. She put on a white gown with wide sleeves and a low neck. The neckline showed off her breasts while the skirt slimmed her hips. She stepped into white high-heeled sandals. She fastened a heavy gold bracelet around each wrist, and around her neck she hung a gold chain with a teardrop pendant which lay snugly in her cleavage. The Englishman would like that. They had the most coarse taste.

She took a last look at herself in the mirror and went out into the club.

A zone of silence went with her across the floor. People fell quiet as she approached and then began to talk about her when she had passed. She felt as if she were inviting mass rape. Onstage it was different: she was separated from them by an invisible wall. Down here they could touch her, and they all wanted to. They never did, but the danger thrilled her.

She reached table 41 and both men stood up.

Wolff said: "Sonja, my dear, you were magnificent, as always."

She acknowledged the compliment with a nod.

"Allow me to introduce Major Smith."

Sonja shook his hand. He was a thin, chinless man with a fair mustache and ugly, bony hands. He looked at her as if she were an extravagant dessert which had just been placed before him.

Smith said: "Enchanted, absolutely."

They sat down. Wolff poured champagne. Smith said: "Your dancing was splendid, mademoiselle, just splendid. Very . . . artistic."

"Thank you."

He reached across the table and patted her hand. "You're very lovely."

And you're a fool, she thought. She caught a warning look from Wolff: he knew what was in her mind. "You're very kind, Major," she said.

Wolff was nervous, she could tell. He was not sure whether she would do what he wanted. In truth she had not yet decided.

Wolff said to Smith: "I knew Sonja's late father."

It was a lie, and Sonja knew why he had said it. He wanted to remind her.

Her father had been a part-time thief. When there was work he worked, and when there was none he stole. One day he had tried to snatch the handbag of a European woman in the Shari el-Koubri. The woman's escort had made a grab for Sonja's father, and in the scuffle the woman had been knocked down, spraining her wrist. She was an important woman, and Sonja's father had been flogged for the offense. He had died during the flogging.

Of course, it was not supposed to kill him. He must have had a weak heart, or something. The British who administered the law did not care. The man had committed the crime, he had been given the due punishment and the punishment had killed him: one wog less. Sonja, twelve years old, had been heartbroken. Since then she had hated the British with all her being.

Hitler had the right idea but the wrong target, she believed. It was not the Jews whose racial weakness infected the world—

it was the British. The Jews in Egypt were more or less like everyone else: some rich, some poor, some good, some bad. But the British were uniformly. arrogant, greedy and vicious. She laughed bitterly at the high-minded way in which the British tried to defend Poland from German oppression while they themselves continued to oppress Egypt.

Still, for whatever reasons, the Germans were fighting the British, and that was enough to make Sonja pro-German.

She wanted Hitler to defeat, humiliate and ruin Britain.

She would do anything she could to help.

She would even seduce an Englishman.

She leaned forward. "Major Smith," she said, "you're a *very* attractive man."

Wolff relaxed visibly.

Smith was startled. His eyes seemed about to pop out of his head. "Good Lord!" he said. "Do you think so?"

"Yes, I do, Major."

"I say, I wish you'd call me Sandy."

Wolff stood up. "I'm afraid I've got to leave you. Sonja, may I escort you home?"

Smith said: "I think you can leave that to me, Captain."

"Yes, sir."

"That is, if Sonja . . ."

Sonja batted her eyelids. "Of course, Sandy."

Wolff said: "I hate to break up the party, but I've got an early start."

"Quite all right," Smith told him. "You just run along."

As Wolff left a waiter brought dinner. It was a European meal—steak and potatoes—and Sonja picked at it while Smith talked to her. He told her about his successes in the school cricket team. He seemed to have done nothing spectacular since then. He was very boring.

Sonja kept remembering the flogging.

He drank steadily through dinner. When they left he was weaving slightly. She gave him her arm, more for his benefit than for hers. They walked to the houseboat in the cool night air. Smith looked up at the sky and said: "Those stars . . . beautiful." His speech was a little thick.

They stopped at the houseboat. "Looks pretty," Smith said.

"It's very nice," Sonja said. "Would you like to see inside?"

"Rather."

She led him over the gangplank, across the deck, and down the stairs.

He looked around, wide-eyed. "I must say, it's very luxurious."

"Would you like a drink?"

"Very much."

Sonja hated the way he said "very" all the time. He slurred the *r* and pronounced it "vey." She said: "Champagne, or something stronger?"

"A drop of whiskey would be very nice."

"Do sit down."

She gave him his drink and sat close to him. He touched her shoulder, kissed her cheek, and roughly grabbed her breast. She shuddered. He took that as a sign of passion, and squeezed harder.

She pulled him down on top of her. He was very clumsy: his elbows and knees kept digging into her. He fumbled beneath the skirt of her dress.

She said: "Oh, Sandy, you're so strong."

She looked over his shoulder and saw Wolff's face. He was on deck, kneeling down and watching through the hatch, laughing soundlessly.

8

William Vandam was beginning to despair of ever finding Alex Wolff. The Assyut murder was almost three weeks in the past, and Vandam was no closer to his quarry. As time went by the trail got colder. He almost wished there would be another briefcase snatch, so that at least he would know what Wolff was up to.

He knew he was becoming a little obsessed with the man. He would wake up in the night, around 3 A.M. when the booze had worn off, and worry until daybreak. What bothered him was something to do with Wolff's *style*: the sideways manner in which he had slipped into Egypt, the suddenness of the murder of Corporal Cox, the ease with which Wolff had melted into the city. Vandam went over these things, again and again, all the time wondering why he found the case so fascinating.

He had made no real progress, but he had gathered some information, and the information had fed his obsession—fed it not as food feeds a man, making him satisfied, but as fuel feeds a fire, making it burn hotter.

The Villa les Oliviers was owned by someone called Achmed Rahmha. The Rahmhas were a wealthy Cairo family. Achmed had inherited the house from his father, Gamal Rahmha, a lawyer. One of Vandam's lieutenants had dug up the record of a marriage between Gamal Rahmha and one Eva Wolff, widow of Hans Wolff, both German nationals; and then adoption papers making Hans and Eva's son Alex the legal child of Gamal Rahmha . . .

Which made Achmed Rahmha a German, and explained how he got legitimate Egyptian papers in the name of Alex Wolff.

Also in the records was a will which gave Achmed, or Alex, a share of Gamal's fortune, plus the house.

Interviews with all surviving Rahmhas had produced nothing. Achmed had disappeared two years ago and had not been heard from since. The interviewer had come back with the impression that the adopted son of the family was not much missed.

Vandam was convinced that when Achmed disappeared he had gone to Germany.

There was another branch of the Rahmha family, but they were nomads, and no one knew where they could be found. No doubt, Vandam thought, they had helped Wolff somehow with his reentry into Egypt.

Vandam understood that now. Wolff could not have come into the country through Alexandria. Security was tight at the port: his entry would have been noted, he would have been investigated, and sooner or later the investigation would have revealed his German antecedents, whereupon he would have been interned. By coming from the south he had hoped to get in unobserved and resume his former status as a born-and-bred Egyptian. It had been a piece of luck for the British that Wolff had run into trouble in Assyut.

It seemed to Vandam that that was the last piece of luck they had had.

He sat in his office, smoking one cigarette after another, worrying about Wolff.

The man was no low-grade collector of gossip and rumor. He was not content, as other agents were, to send in reports based on the number of soldiers he saw in the street and the shortage of motor spares. The briefcase theft proved he was after top-level stuff, and he was capable of devising ingenious ways of getting it. If he stayed at large long enough he would succeed sooner or later.

Vandam paced the room—from the coat stand to the desk, around the desk for a look out of the window, around the other side of the desk, and back to the coat stand.

The spy had his problems, too. He had to explain himself to inquisitive neighbors, conceal his radio somewhere, move about the city and find informants. He could run out of money, his radio could break down, his informants could betray him or someone could quite accidentally discover his secret. One way or another, traces of the spy had to appear.

The cleverer he was, the longer it would take.

Vandam was convinced that Abdullah, the thief, was involved with Wolff. After Bogge refused to have Abdullah arrested, Vandam had offered a large sum of money for Wolff's whereabouts. Abdullah still claimed to know nothing of anyone called Wolff, but the light of greed had flickered in his eyes.

Abdullah might not know where Wolff could be found—Wolff was surely careful enough to take that precaution with a notoriously dishonest man—but perhaps Abdullah could find out. Vandam had made it clear that the money was still on offer. Then again, once Abdullah had the information he might simply go to Wolff, tell him of Vandam's offer and invite him to bid higher.

Vandam paced the room.

Something to do with *style*. Sneaking in; murder with a knife; melting away; and . . . Something else went with all that. Something Vandam knew about, something he had read in a report or been told in a briefing. Wolff might almost have been a man Vandam had known, long ago, but could no longer bring to mind. Style.

The phone rang.

He picked it up. "Major Vandam."

"Oh, hello, this is Major Calder in the paymaster's office."

Vandam tensed. "Yes?"

"You sent us a note, a couple of weeks ago, to look out for forged sterling. Well, we've found some."

That was it—that was the trace. "Good!" Vandam said.

"Rather a lot, actually," the voice continued.

Vandam said: "I need to see it as soon as possible."

"It's on its way. I'm sending a chap round—he should be there soon."

"Do you know who paid it in?"

"There's been more than one lot, actually, but we've got some names for you."

"Marvelous. I'll ring you back when I've seen the notes. Did you say Calder?"

"Yes." The man gave his phone number. "We'll speak later, then."

Vandam hung up. Forged sterling—it fitted: this could be the breakthrough. Sterling was no longer legal tender in Egypt. Officially Egypt was supposed to be a sovereign country. However, sterling could always be exchanged for Egyptian money at the office of the British paymaster general. Consequently people who did a lot of business with foreigners usually accepted pound notes in payment.

Vandam opened his door and shouted along the hall. "Jakes!"

"Sir!" Jakes shouted back equally loudly.

"Bring me the file on forged banknotes."

"Yes, sir!"

Vandam stepped to the next office and spoke to his secretary. "I'm expecting a package from the paymaster. Bring it in as soon as it comes, would you?"

"Yes, sir."

Vandam went back into his office. Jakes appeared a moment later with a file. The most senior of Vandam's team, Jakes was an eager, reliable young man who would follow orders to the letter, as far as they went, then use his initiative. He was even taller than Vandam, thin and black-haired, with a somewhat lugubrious look. He and Vandam were on terms of easy formality: Jakes was very scrupulous about his salutes and sirs, yet they discussed their work as equals, and Jakes used bad language with great fluency. Jakes was very well connected, and would almost certainly go further in the Army than Vandam would.

Vandam switched on his desk light and said: "Right, show me a picture of Nazi-style funny money."

Jakes put down the file and flicked through it. He extracted a sheaf of glossy photographs and spread them on the desk. Each print showed the front and the back of a banknote, somewhat larger than actual size.

Jakes sorted them out. "Pound notes, fivers, tenners and twenties."

Black arrows on the photographs indicated the errors by which the forgeries might be identified.

The source of the information was counterfeit money taken from German spies captured in England. Jakes said: "You'd think they'd know better than to give their spies funny money."

Vandam replied without looking up from the pictures. "Espionage is an expensive business, and most of the money is wasted. Why should they buy English currency in Switzerland when they can make it themselves? A spy has forged papers, he might as well have forged money. Also, it has a slightly damaging effect on the British economy if it gets into circulation. It's inflationary, like the government printing money to pay its debts."

"Still, you'd think they would have cottoned on by now to the fact that we're catching the buggers."

"Ah—but when we catch 'em, we make sure the Germans don't *know* we've caught 'em."

"All the same, I hope our spies aren't using counterfeit Reichmarks."

"I shouldn't think so. We take Intelligence rather more seriously than they do, you know. I wish I could say the same about tank tactics."

Vandam's secretary knocked and came in. He was a bespectacled twenty-year-old corporal. "Package from the paymaster, sir."

"Good show!" Vandam said.

"If you'd sign the slip, sir."

Vandam signed the receipt and tore open the envelope. It contained several hundred pound notes.

Jakes said: "Bugger me!"

"They told me there were a lot," Vandam said. "Get a magnifying glass, Corporal, on the double."

"Yes, sir."

Vandam put a pound note from the envelope next to one of the photographs and looked for the identifying error.

He did not need the magnifying glass.

"Look, Jakes."

Jakes looked.

The note bore the same error as the one in the photograph.

"That's it, sir," said Jakes.

"Nazi money, made in Germany," said Vandam. "*Now* we're on his trail."

～

Lieutenant Colonel Reggie Bogge knew that Major Vandam was a smart lad, with the kind of low cunning one sometimes finds among the working class; but the major was no match for the likes of Bogge.

That night Bogge played snooker with Brigadier Povey, the Director of Military Intelligence, at the Gezira Sporting Club. The brigadier was shrewd, and he did not like Bogge all that much, but Bogge thought he could handle him.

They played for a shilling a point, and the brigadier broke.

While they played, Bogge said: "Hope you don't mind talking shop in the club, sir."

"Not at all," said the brigadier.

"It's just that I don't seem to get a chance to leave m'desk in the day."

"What's on your mind?" The brigadier chalked his cue.

Bogge potted a red ball and lined up the pink. "I'm pretty sure there's a fairly serious spy at work in Cairo." He missed the pink.

The brigadier bent over the table. "Go on."

Bogge regarded the brigadier's broad back. A little delicacy was called for here. Of course the head of a department was responsible for that department's successes, for it was only well-run departments which had successes, as everyone knew; nevertheless it was necessary to be subtle about how one took the credit. He began: "You remember a corporal was stabbed in Assyut a few weeks ago?"

"Vaguely."

"I had a hunch about that, and I've been following it up ever since. Last week a General Staff aide had his briefcase pinched during a street brawl. Nothing very remarkable about that, of course, but I put two and two together."

The brigadier potted the white. "Damn," he said. "Your shot."

"I asked the paymaster general to look out for counterfeit English money. Lo and behold, he found some. I had my boys examine it. Turns out to have been made in Germany."

"Aha!"

Bogge potted a red, the blue and another red, then he missed the pink again.

"I think you've left me rather well off," said the brigadier, scrutinizing the table through narrowed eyes. "Any chance of tracing the chap through the money?"

"It's a possibility. We're working on that already."

"Pass me that bridge, will you?"

"Certainly."

The brigadier laid the bridge on the baize and lined up his shot.

Bogge said: "It's been suggested that we might instruct the paymaster to continue to accept the forgeries, in case he can bring in any new leads." The suggestion had been Vandam's, and Bogge had turned it down. Vandam had argued—something that was becoming wearyingly familiar—and Bogge had had to slap him down. But it was an imponderable, and if things turned out badly Bogge wanted to be able to say he had consulted his superiors.

The brigadier unbent from the table and considered. "Rather depends how much money is involved, doesn't it?"

"Several hundred pounds so far."

"It's a lot."

"I feel it's not really necessary to continue to accept the counterfeits, sir."

"Jolly good." The brigadier pocketed the last of the red balls and started on the colors.

Bogge marked the score. The brigadier was ahead, but Bogge had got what he came for.

"Who've you got working on this spy thing?" the brigadier asked.

"Well, I'm handling it myself basically—"

"Yes, but which of your majors are you using?"

"Vandam, actually."

"Ah, Vandam. Not a bad chap."

Bogge did not like the turn the conversation was taking. The brigadier did not really understand how careful you had to be with the likes of Vandam: give them an inch and they would take the Empire. The Army *would* promote these people above their station. Bogge's nightmare was to find himself taking orders from a postman's son with a Dorset accent. He said: "Vandam's got a bit of a soft spot for the wog, unfortunately; but as you say, he's good enough in a plodding sort of fashion."

"Yes." The brigadier was enjoying a long break, potting the colors one after another. "He went to the same school as I. Twenty years later, of course."

Bogge smiled. "He was a scholarship boy, though, wasn't he, sir?"

"Yes," said the brigadier. "So was I." He pocketed the black.

"You seem to have won, sir," said Bogge.

∾

The manager of the Cha-Cha Club said that more than half his customers settled their bills in sterling, he could not possibly identify who payed in which currency, and even if he could he did not know the names of more than a few regulars.

The chief cashier of Shepheard's Hotel said something similar.

So did two taxi drivers, the proprietor of a soldiers' bar and the brothel keeper Madame Fahmy.

Vandam was expecting much the same story from the next location on his list, a shop owned by one Mikis Aristopoulos.

Aristopolous had changed a large amount of sterling, most of it forged, and Vandam imagined his shop would be a business of considerable size, but it was not so. Aristopoulos had a small grocery store. It smelled of spices and coffee but there was not much on the shelves. Aristopoulos himself was a short Greek of about twenty-five years with a wide, white-toothed smile. He wore a striped apron over his cotton trousers and white shirt.

He said: "Good morning, sir. How can I help you?"

"You don't seem to have much to sell," Vandam said.

Aristopoulos smiled. "If you're looking for something particular, I may have it in the stock room. Have you shopped here before, sir?"

So that was the system: scarce delicacies in the back room for regular customers only. It meant he might know his clientele. Also, the amount of counterfeit money he had exchanged probably represented a large order, which he would remember.

Vandam said: "I'm not here to buy. Two days ago you took one hundred and forty-seven pounds in English money to the British paymaster general and exchanged it for Egyptian currency."

Aristopoulos frowned and looked troubled. "Yes . . ."

"One hundred and twenty-seven pounds of that was counterfeit—forged—no good."

Aristopoulos smiled and spread his arms in a huge shrug. "I am sorry for the paymaster. I take the money from English, I give it back to English . . . What can I do?"

"You can go to jail for passing counterfeit notes."

Aristopoulos stopped smiling. "Please. This is not justice. How could I know?"

"Was all that money paid to you by one person?"

"I don't know—"

"Think!" Vandam said sharply. "Did anyone pay you one hundred and twenty-seven pounds?"

"Ah . . . yes! Yes!" Suddenly Aristopoulos looked hurt. "A very respectable customer. One hundred twenty-six pounds ten shillings."

"His name?" Vandam held his breath.

"Mr. Wolff—"

"Ahhh."

"I am so shocked. Mr. Wolff has been a good customer for many years, and no trouble with paying, never."

"Listen," Vandam said, "did you deliver the groceries?"

"No."

"*Damn.*"

"We offered to deliver, as usual, but this time Mr. Wolff—"

"You usually deliver to Mr. Wolff's home?"

"Yes, but this time—"

"What's the address?"

"Let me see. Villa les Oliviers, Garden City."

Vandam banged his fist on the counter in frustration. Aristopoulos looked a little frightened. Vandam said: "You haven't delivered there recently, though."

"Not since Mr. Wolff came back. Sir, I am very sorry that this bad money has passed through my innocent hands. Perhaps something can be arranged . . . ?"

"Perhaps," Vandam said thoughtfully.

"Let us drink coffee together."

Vandam nodded. Aristopoulos led him into the back room. The shelves here were well laden with bottles and tins, most of them imported. Vandam noticed Russian caviar, American canned ham and English jam. Aristopoulos poured thick strong coffee into tiny cups. He was smiling again.

Aristopoulos said: "These little problems can always be worked out between friends."

They drank coffee.

Aristopoulos said: "Perhaps, as a gesture of friendship, I could offer you something from my store. I have a little stock of French wine—"

"No, no—"

"I can usually find some Scotch whiskey when everyone else in Cairo has run out—"

"I'm not interested in *that* kind of arrangement," Vandam said impatiently.

"Oh!" said Aristopoulos. He had become quite convinced that Vandam was seeking a bribe.

"I want to find Wolff," Vandam continued. "I need to know where he is living now. You said he was a regular customer?"

"Yes."

"What sort of stuff does he buy?"

"Much champagne. Also some caviar. Coffee, quite a lot. Foreign liquor. Pickled walnuts, garlic sausage, brandied apricots . . ."

"Hm." Vandam drank in this incidental information greedily. What kind of a spy spent his funds on imported delicacies? Answer: one who was not very serious. But Wolff *was* serious. It was a question of style. Vandam said: "I was wondering how soon he is likely to come back."

"As soon as he runs out of champagne."

"All right. When he does, I must find out where he lives."

"But, sir, if he again refuses to allow me to deliver . . . ?"

"That's what I've been thinking about. I'm going to give you an assistant."

Aristopoulos did not like that idea. "I want to help you, sir, but my business is private—"

"You've got no choice," Vandam said. "It's help me, or go to jail."

"But to have an English officer working here in my shop—"

"Oh, it won't be an English officer." He would stick out like a sore thumb, Vandam thought, and probably scare Wolff away as well. Vandam smiled. "I think I know the ideal person for the job."

⌒

That evening after dinner Vandam went to Elene's apartment, carrying a huge bunch of flowers, feeling foolish.

She lived in a graceful, spacious old apartment house near

the Place de l'Opéra. A Nubian concierge directed Vandam to the third floor. He climbed the curving marble staircase which occupied the center of the building and knocked on the door of 3A.

She was not expecting him, and it occurred to him suddenly that she might be entertaining a man friend.

He waited impatiently in the corridor, wondering what she would be like in her own home. This was the first time he had been here. Perhaps she was out. Surely she had plenty to do in the evenings—

The door opened.

She was wearing a yellow cotton dress with a full skirt, rather simple but almost thin enough to see through. The color looked very pretty against her light-brown skin. She gazed at him blankly for a moment, then recognized him and gave her impish smile.

She said: "Well, hello!"

"Good evening."

She stepped forward and kissed his cheek. "Come in."

He went inside and she closed the door.

"I wasn't expecting the kiss," he said.

"All part of the act. Let me relieve you of your disguise."

He gave her the flowers. He had the feeling he was being teased.

"Go in there while I put these in water," she said.

He followed her pointing finger into the living room and looked around. The room was comfortable to the point of sensuality. It was decorated in pink and gold and furnished with deep soft seats and a table of pale oak. It was a corner room with windows on two sides, and now the evening sun shone in and made everything glow slightly. There was a thick rug of brown fur on the floor that looked like bearskin. Vandam bent down and touched it: it was genuine. He had a sudden, vivid picture of Elene lying on the rug, naked and writhing. He blinked and looked elsewhere. On the seat beside him was a book which she had, presumably, been reading when he knocked. He picked up the book and sat on the seat. It was warm from her body. The book was called *Stamboul*

Train. It looked like cloak-and-dagger stuff. On the wall opposite him was a rather modern-looking painting of a society ball: all the ladies were in gorgeous formal gowns and all the men were naked. Vandam went and sat on the couch beneath the painting so that he would not have to look at it. He thought it peculiar.

She came in with the flowers in a vase, and the smell of wistaria filled the room. "Would you like a drink?"

"Can you make martinis?"

"Yes. Smoke if you want to."

"Thank you." She knew how to be hospitable, Vandam thought. He supposed she had to, given the way she earned her living. He took out his cigarettes. "I was afraid you'd be out."

"Not this evening." There was an odd note in her voice when she said that, but Vandam could not figure it out. He watched her with the cocktail shaker. He had intended to conduct the meeting on a businesslike level, but he was not able to, for it was she who was conducting it. He felt like a clandestine lover.

"Do you like this stuff?" He indicated the book.

"I've been reading thrillers lately."

"Why?"

"To find out how a spy is supposed to behave."

"I shouldn't think you—" He saw her smiling, and realized he was being teased again. "I never know whether you're serious."

"Very rarely." She handed him a drink and sat down at the opposite end of the couch. She looked at him over the rim of her glass. "To espionage."

He sipped his martini. It was perfect. So was she. The mellow sunshine burnished her skin. Her arms and legs looked smooth and soft. He thought she would be the same in bed as she was out of it: relaxed, amusing and game for anything. Damn. She had had this effect on him last time, and he had gone on one of his rare binges and ended up in a wretched brothel.

"What are you thinking about?" she said.

"Espionage."

She laughed: it seemed that somehow she knew he was lying. "You must love it," she said.

Vandam thought: How does she do this to me? She kept him always off balance, with her teasing and her insight, her innocent face and her long brown limbs. He said: "Catching spies can be very satisfying work, but I don't love it."

"What happens to them when you've caught them?"

"They hang, usually."

"Oh."

He had managed to throw her off balance for a change. She shivered. He said: "Losers generally die in wartime."

"Is that why you don't love it—because they hang?"

"No. I don't love it because I don't always catch them."

"Are you proud of being so hardhearted?"

"I don't think I'm hardhearted. We're trying to kill more of them than they can kill of us." He thought: How did I come to be defending myself?

She got up to pour him another drink. He watched her walk across the room. She moved gracefully—like a cat, he thought; no, like a kitten. He looked at her back as she stooped to pick up the cocktail shaker, and he wondered what she was wearing beneath the yellow dress. He noticed her hands as she poured the drink: they were slender and strong. She did not give herself another martini.

He wondered what background she came from. He said: "Are your parents alive?"

"No," she said abruptly.

"I'm sorry," he said. He knew she was lying.

"Why did you ask me that?"

"Idle curiosity. Please forgive me."

She leaned over and touched his arm lightly, brushing his skin with her fingertips, a caress as gentle as a breeze. "You apologize too much." She looked away from him, as if hesitating; and then, seeming to yield to an impulse, she began to tell him of her background.

She had been the eldest of five children in a desperately poor family. Her parents were cultured and loving people—"My father taught me English and my mother taught me to wear clean clothes," she said—but the father, a tailor, was ultra-orthodox and had estranged himself from the rest of the Jewish community in Alexandria after a doctrinal dispute with the ritual slaughterer. When Elene was fifteen years old her father began to go blind. He could no longer work as a tailor—but he would neither ask nor accept help from the "back-sliding" Alexandrian Jews. Elene went as a live-in maid to a British home and sent her wages to her family. From that point on, her story was one which had been repeated, Vandam knew, time and again over the last hundred years in the homes of the British ruling class: she fell in love with the son of the house, and he seduced her. She had been fortunate in that they had been found out before she became pregnant. The son was sent away to university and Elene was paid off. She was terrified to return home to tell her father she had been fired for fornication—and with a gentile. She lived on her payoff, continuing to send home the same amount of cash each week, until the money ran out. Then a lecherous business-man whom she had met at the house had set her up in a flat, and she was embarked upon her life's work. Soon afterward her father had been told how she was living, and he made the family sit shiva for her.

"What is shiva?" Vandam asked.

"Mourning."

Since then she had not heard from them, except for a message from a friend to tell her that her mother had died.

Vandam said: "Do you hate your father?"

She shrugged. "I think it turned out rather well." She spread her arms to indicate the apartment.

"But are you happy?"

She looked at him. Twice she seemed about to speak and then said nothing. Finally she looked away. Vandam felt she was regretting the impulse that had made her tell him her life story. She changed the subject. "What brings you here tonight, Major?"

Vandam collected his thoughts. He had been so interested in her—watching her hands and her eyes as she spoke of her past—that he had forgotten for a while his purpose. "I'm still looking for Alex Wolff," he began. "I haven't found him, but I've found his grocer."

"How did you do that?"

He decided not to tell her. Better that nobody outside Intelligence should know that German spies were betrayed by their forged money. "That's a long story," he said. "The important thing is, I want to put someone inside the shop in case he comes back."

"Me."

"That's what I had in mind."

"Then, when he comes in, I hit him over the head with a bag of sugar and guard the unconscious body until you come along."

Vandam laughed. "I believe you would," he said. "I can just see you leaping over the counter." He realized how much he was relaxing, and resolved to pull himself together before he made a fool of himself.

"Seriously, what do I have to do?" she said.

"Seriously, you have to discover where he lives."

"How?"

"I'm not sure." Vandam hesitated. "I thought perhaps you might befriend him. You're a very attractive woman—I imagine it would be easy for you."

"What do you mean by 'befriend'?"

"That's up to you. Just as long as you get his address."

"I see." Suddenly her mood had changed, and there was bitterness in her voice. The switch astonished Vandam: she was too quick for him to follow her. Surely a woman like Elene would not be offended by this suggestion? She said: "Why don't you just have one of your soldiers follow him home?"

"I may have to do that, if you fail to win his confidence. The trouble is, he might realize he was being followed and shake off the tail—then he would never go back to the grocer's, and we would have lost our advantage. But if you can persuade him, say, to invite you to his house for dinner, then we'll get the information we need without tipping our hand. Of course, it might not work. Both alternatives are risky. But I prefer the subtle approach."

"I understand that."

Of course she understood, Vandam thought; the whole thing was as plain as day. What the devil was the matter with her? She was a strange woman: at one moment he was quite enchanted by her, and at the next he was infuriated. For the first time it crossed his mind that she might refuse to do what he was asking. Nervously he said: "Will you help me?"

She got up and filled his glass again, and this time she took another drink herself. She was very tense, but it was clear she was not willing to tell him why. He always felt very annoyed with women in moods like this. It would be a damn nuisance if she refused to cooperate now.

At last she said: "I suppose it's no worse than what I've been doing all my life."

"That's what I thought," said Vandam with relief.

She gave him a very black look.

"You start tomorrow," he said. He gave her a piece of paper with the address of the shop written on it. She took it without looking at it. "The shop belongs to Mikis Aristopoulos," he added.

"How long do you think this will take?" she said.

"I don't know." He stood up. "I'll get in touch with you every few days, to make sure everything's all right—but you'll contact me as soon as he makes an appearance, won't you?"

"Yes."

Vandam remembered something. "By the way, the shopkeeper thinks we're after Wolff for forgery. Don't talk to him about espionage."

"I won't."

The change in her mood was permanent. They were no longer enjoying each other's company. Vandam said: "I'll leave you to your thriller."

She stood up. "I'll see you out."

They went to the door. As Vandam stepped out, the tenant of the neighboring flat approached along the corridor. Vandam had been thinking of this moment, in the back of his mind, all evening, and now he did what he had been determined not to do. He took Elene's arm, bent his head and kissed her mouth.

Her lips moved briefly in response. He pulled away. The neighbor passed by. Vandam looked at Elene. The neighbor unlocked his door, entered his flat and closed the door behind him. Vandam released Elene's arm.

She said: "You're a good actor."

"Yes," he said. "Good-bye." He turned away and strolled briskly down the corridor. He should have felt pleased with his evening's work, but instead he felt as if he had done something a little shameful. He heard the door of her apartment bang shut behind him.

～

Elene leaned back against the closed door and cursed William Vandam.

He had come into her life, full of English courtesy, asking her to do a new kind of work and help win the war; and then he had told her she must go whoring again.

She had really believed he was going to change her life. No more rich businessmen, no more furtive affairs, no more dancing or waiting on tables. She had a worthwhile job, something she believed in, something that mattered. Now it turned out to be the same old game.

For seven years she had been living off her face and her body, and now she wanted to stop.

She went into the living room to get a drink. His glass was there on the table, half empty. She put it to her lips. The drink was warm and bitter.

At first she had not liked Vandam: he had seemed a stiff, solemn, dull man. Then she had changed her mind about him. When had she first thought there might be another, different man beneath the rigid exterior? She remembered: it had been when he laughed. That laugh intrigued her. He had done it again tonight, when she said she would hit Wolff over the head with a bag of sugar. There was a rich vein of fun deep, deep inside him, and when it was tapped the laughter bubbled up and took over his whole personality for a moment. She suspected that he was a man with a big appetite for life—an appetite which he had firmly under control, too firmly. It made Elene want to get under his skin, to make him be himself. That was why she teased him, and tried to make him laugh again.

That was why she had kissed him, too.

She had been curiously happy to have him in her home, sitting on her couch, smoking and talking. She had even thought how nice it would be to take this strong, innocent man to bed and show him things he never dreamed of. Why did she like him? Perhaps it was that he treated her as a person, not as a girlie. She knew he would never pat her bottom and say: "Don't you worry your pretty little head . . ."

And he had spoiled it all. Why was she so bothered by this thing with Wolff? One more insincere act of seduction would do her no harm. Vandam had more or less said that. And in saying so, he had revealed that he regarded her as a whore. That was what had made her so mad. She wanted his esteem, and when he asked her to "befriend" Wolff, she knew she was never going to get it, not really. Anyway the whole thing was foolish: the relationship between a woman such as she and an English officer was doomed to turn out like all Elene's relationships— manipulation on one side, dependence on the other and respect nowhere. Vandam would always see her as a whore. For a while she had thought he might be different from all the rest, but she had been wrong.

And she thought: But why do I mind so much?

∽

Vandam was sitting in darkness at his bedroom window in the middle of the night, smoking cigarettes and looking out at the moonlit Nile, when a memory from his childhood sprang, fully formed, into his mind.

He is eleven years old, sexually innocent, physically still a child. He is in the terraced gray brick house where he has always lived. The house has a bathroom, with water heated by the coal fire in the kitchen below: he has been told that this makes his family very fortunate, and he must not boast about it; indeed, when he goes to the new school, the posh school in Bournemouth, he must pretend that he thinks it is perfectly normal to have a bathroom and hot water coming out of the taps. The bathroom has a water closet too. He is going there now to pee. His mother is in there, bathing his sister, who is seven years old, but they won't mind him going in to pee, he has done it before, and the other toilet is a long cold walk down the garden. What he has forgotten is that his cousin is also being bathed. She is eight years old. He walks into the bathroom. His sister is sitting in the bath. His cousin is standing, about to come out. His mother holds a towel. He looks at his cousin.

She is naked, of course. It is the first time he has seen any girl other than his sister naked. His cousin's body is slightly plump, and her skin is flushed with the heat of the water. She is quite the loveliest sight he has ever seen. He stands inside the bathroom doorway looking at her with undisguised interest and admiration.

He does not see the slap coming. His mother's large hand seems to come from nowhere. It hits his cheek with a loud clap. She is a good hitter, his mother, and this is one of her best efforts. It hurts like hell, but the shock is even worse than the pain. Worst of all is that the warm sentiment which had engulfed him has been shattered like a glass window.

"Get out!" his mother screams, and he leaves, hurt and humiliated.

Vandam remembered this as he sat alone watching the Egyptian night, and he thought, as he had thought at the time it happened: Now why did she do that?

9

In the early morning the tiled floor of the mosque was cold to Alex Wolff's bare feet. The handful of dawn worshipers was lost in the vastness of the pillared hall. There was a silence, a sense of peace, and a bleak gray light. A shaft of sunlight pierced one of the high narrow slits in the wall, and at that moment the muezzin began to cry:

"*Allahu akbar! Allahu akbar! Allahu akbar! Allahu akbar!*"

Wolff turned to face Mecca.

He was wearing a long robe and a turban, and the shoes in his hand were simple Arab sandals. He was never quite sure why he did this. He was a True Believer only in theory. He had been circumcised according to Islamic doctrine, and he had completed the pilgrimage to Mecca; but he drank alcohol and ate pork, he never paid the zakat tax, he never observed the fast of Ramadan and he did not pray every day, let alone five times a day. But every so often he felt the need to immerse himself, just for a few minutes, in the familiar, mechanical ritual of his stepfather's religion. Then, as he had done today, he would get up while it was still dark, and dress in traditional clothes, and walk through the cold quiet streets of the city to the mosque his father had attended, and perform the ceremonial ablutions in the forecourt, and enter in time for the first prayers of the new day.

He touched his ears with his hands, then clasped his hands in front of him, the left within the right. He bowed, then knelt down. Touching his forehead to the floor at appropriate moments, he recited the el-fatha:

"In the name of God the merciful and compassionate. Praise be to God, the lord of the worlds, the merciful and compassionate, the Prince of the day of judgment; Thee we serve, and to Thee we pray for help; lead us in the right way, the way of those to whom Thou hast shown mercy, upon whom no wrath resteth, and who go not astray."

He looked over his right shoulder, then his left, to greet the two recording angels who wrote down his good and bad acts.

When he looked over his left shoulder, he saw Abdullah.

Without interrupting his prayer the thief smiled broadly, showing his steel tooth.

Wolff got up and went out. He stopped outside to put on his sandals, and Abdullah came waddling after him. They shook hands.

"You are a devout man, like myself," Abdullah said. "I knew you would come, sooner or later, to your father's mosque."

"You've been looking for me?"

"Many people are looking for you."

Together they walked away from the mosque. Abdullah said: "Knowing you to be a True Believer, I could not betray you to the British, even for so large a sum of money; so I told Major Vandam that I knew nobody by the name of Alex Wolff, or Achmed Rahmha."

Wolff stopped abruptly. So they were still hunting him. He had started to feel safe—too soon. He took Abdullah by the arm and steered him into an Arab café. They sat down

Wolff said: "He knows my Arab name."

"He knows all about you—except where to find you."

Wolff felt worried, and at the same time intensely curious. "What is this major like?" he asked.

Abdullah shrugged. "An Englishman. No subtlety. No manners. Khaki shorts and a face the color of a tomato."

"You can do better than that."

Abdullah nodded. "This man is patient and determined. If I were you, I should be afraid of him."

Suddenly Wolff *was* afraid.

He said: "What has he been doing?"

"He has found out all about your family. He has talked to all your brothers. They said they knew nothing of you."

The café proprietor brought each of them a dish of mashed fava beans and a flat loaf of coarse bread. Wolff broke his bread and dipped it into the beans. Flies began to gather around the bowls. Both men ignored them.

Abdullah spoke through a mouthful of food. "Vandam is offering one hundred pounds for your address. Ha! As if we would betray one of our own for money."

Wolff swallowed. "Even if you knew my address."

Abdullah shrugged. "It would be a small thing to find out."

"I know," Wolff said. "So I am going to tell you, as a sign of my faith in your friendship. I am living at Shepheard's Hotel."

Abdullah looked hurt. "My friend, I know this is not true. It is the first place the British would look—"

"You misunderstand me." Wolff smiled. "I am not a guest there. I work in the kitchens, cleaning pots, and at the end of the day I lie down on the floor with a dozen or so others and sleep there."

"So cunning!" Abdullah grinned: he was pleased with the idea and delighted to have the information. "You hide under their very noses!"

"I know you will keep this secret," Wolff said. "And, as a sign of my gratitude for your friendship, I hope you will accept from me a gift of one hundred pounds."

"But this is not necessary—"

"I insist."

Abdullah sighed and gave in reluctantly. "Very well."

"I will have the money sent to your house."

Abdullah wiped his empty bowl with the last of his bread.

"I must leave you now," he said. "Allow me to pay for your breakfast."

"Thank you."

"Ah! But I have come with no money. A thousand pardons—"

"It's nothing," Wolff said. "*Alallah*—in God's care."

Abdullah replied conventionally: "*Allah yisallimak*—may God protect thee." He went out.

Wolff called for coffee and thought about Abdullah. The thief would betray Wolff for a lot less than a hundred pounds, of course. What had stopped him so far was that he did not know Wolff's address. He was actively trying to discover it—that was why he come to the mosque. Now he would attempt to check on the story about living in the kitchens of Shepheard's. This might not be easy, for of course no one would admit that staff slept on the kitchen floor—indeed Wolff was not at all sure it was true—but he had to reckon on Abdullah discovering the lie sooner or later. The story was no more than a delaying tactic; so was the bribe. However, when at last Abdullah found out that Wolff was living on Sonja's houseboat, he would probably come to Wolff for more money instead of going to Vandam.

The situation was under control—for the moment.

Wolff left a few millièmes on the table and went out.

The city had come to life. The streets were already jammed with traffic, the pavements crowded with vendors and beggars, the air full of good and bad smells. Vandam made his way to the central post office to use a telephone. He called GHQ and asked for Major Smith.

"We have seventeen of them," the operator told him. "Have you got a first name?"

"Sandy."

"That will be Major Alexander Smith. He's not here at the moment. May I take a message?"

Wolff had known the major would not be at GHQ—it was too early. "The message is: Twelve noon today at Zamalek. Would you sign it: S. Have you got that?"

"Yes, but if I may have your full—"

Wolff hung up. He left the post office and headed for Zamalek.

Since Sonja had seduced Smith, the major had sent her a dozen roses, a box of chocolates, a love letter and two hand-delivered messages asking for another date. Wolff had for-bidden her to reply. By now Smith was wondering whether he would ever see her again. Wolff was quite sure that Sonja was the first beautiful woman Smith had ever slept with. After a couple of days of suspense Smith would be desperate to see her again, and would jump at any chance.

On the way home Wolff bought a newspaper, but it was full of the usual rubbish. When he got to the houseboat Sonja was still asleep. He threw the rolled-up newspaper at her to wake her. She groaned and turned over.

Wolff left her and went through the curtains back into the living room. At the far end, in the prow of the boat, was a tiny open kitchen. It had one quite large cupboard for brooms and cleaning materials. Wolff opened the cupboard door. He could just about get inside if he bent his knees and ducked his head. The catch of the door could be worked only from the outside. He searched through the kitchen drawers and found a knife with a pliable blade. He thought he could probably work the catch from inside the cupboard by sticking the knife through the crack of the door and easing it against the spring-loaded bolt. He got into the cupboard, closed the door and tried it. It worked

However, he could not see through the doorjamb.

He took a nail and a flatiron and banged the nail through the thin wood of the door at eye level. He used a kitchen fork to enlarge the hole. He got inside the cupboard again and closed the door. He put his eye to the hole.

He saw the curtains part, and Sonja came into the living room. She looked around, surprised that he was not there. She shrugged, then lifted her nightdress and scratched her belly. Wolff suppressed a laugh. She came across to the kitchen, picked up the kettle and turned on the tap.

Wolff slipped the knife into the crack of the door and

worked the catch. He opened the door, stepped out and said: "Good morning."

Sonja screamed.

Wolff laughed.

She threw the kettle at him, and he dodged. He said: "It's a good hiding place, isn't it?"

"You terrified me, you bastard," she said.

He picked up the kettle and handed it to her. "Make the coffee," he told her. He put the knife in the cupboard, closed the door and went to sit down.

Sonja said: "What do you need a hiding place for?"

"To watch you and Major Smith. It's very funny—he looks like a passionate turtle."

"When is he coming?"

"Twelve noon today."

"Oh, no. Why so early in the morning?"

"Listen. If he's got anything worthwhile in that briefcase, then he certainly isn't allowed to go wandering around the city with it in his hand. He should take it straight to his office and lock it in the safe. We mustn't give him time to do that—the whole thing is useless unless he brings his case here. What we want is for him to come rushing here straight from GHQ. In fact, if he gets here late and without his briefcase, we're going to lock up and pretend you're out—then next time he'll know he has to get here fast."

"You've got it all worked out, haven't you?"

Wolff laughed. "You'd better start getting ready. I want you to look irresistible."

"I'm always irresistible." She went through to the bedroom.

He called after her: "Wash your hair." There was no reply.

He looked at his watch. Time was running out. He went around the houseboat hiding traces of his own occupation, putting away his shoes, his razor, his toothbrush and his fez. Sonja went up on deck in a robe to dry her hair in the sun. Wolff made the coffee and took her a cup. He drank his own, then washed his cup and put it away. He took out a bottle of champagne, put it in a bucket of ice and placed it beside the bed with two glasses. He thought of changing the sheets, then decided to do it after Smith's visit, not before. Sonja came down from the deck. She dabbed perfume on her thighs and between her breasts. Wolff took a last look around. All was ready. He sat on a divan by a porthole to watch the towpath.

It was a few minutes after noon when Major Smith appeared. He was hurrying, as if afraid to be late. He wore his uniform shirt, khaki shorts, socks and sandals, but he had taken off his officer's cap. He was sweating in the midday sun.

He was carrying his briefcase.

Wolff grinned with satisfaction.

"Here he comes," Wolff called. "Are you ready?"

"No."

She was trying to rattle him. She would be ready. He got into the cupboard, closed the door, and put his eye to the peephole.

He heard Smith's footsteps on the gangplank and then on the deck. The major called: "Hello?"

Sonja did not reply.

Looking through the peephole, Wolff saw Smith come down the stairs into the interior of the boat.

"Is anybody there?"

Smith looked at the curtains which divided off the bedroom. His voice was full of the expectation of disappointment. "Sonja?"

The curtains parted. Sonja stood there, her arms lifted to hold the curtains apart. She had put her hair up in a complex pyramid as she did for her act. She wore the baggy trousers of filmy gauze, but at this distance her body was visible through the material. From the waist up she was naked except for a jeweled collar around her neck. Her brown breasts were full and round. She had put lipstick on her nipples.

Wolff thought: Good girl!

Major Smith stared at her. He was quite bowled over. He said: "Oh, dear. Oh, good Lord. Oh, my soul."

Wolff tried not to laugh.

Smith dropped his briefcase and went to her. As he embraced her, she stepped back and closed the curtains behind his back.

Wolff opened the cupboard door and stepped out.

The briefcase lay on the floor just this side of the curtains. Wolff knelt down, hitching up his galabiya, and turned the case over. He tried the catches. The case was locked.

Wolff whispered: *"Lieber Gott."*

He looked around. He needed a pin, a paper clip, a sewing needle, something with which to pick the locks. Moving quietly, he went to the kitchen area and carefully pulled open a drawer. Meat skewer, too thick; bristle from a wire brush, too thin; vegetable knife, too broad . . . In a little dish beside the sink he found one of Sonja's hair clips.

He went back to the case and poked the end of the clip into the keyhole of one of the locks. He twisted and turned it experimentally, encountered a kind of springy resistance, and pressed harder

The clip broke.

Again Wolff cursed under his breath.

He glanced reflexively at his wristwatch. Last time Smith had screwed Sonja in about five minutes. I should have told her to make it last, Wolff thought.

He picked up the flexible knife he had been using to open the cupboard door from the inside. Gently, he slid it into one of the catches on the briefcase. When he pressed, the knife bent.

He could have broken the locks in a few seconds, but he did not want to, for then Smith would know that his case had been opened. Wolff was not afraid of Smith, but he wanted the major to remain oblivious to the real reason for the seduction: if there was valuable material in the case, Wolff wanted to open it regularly.

But if he could not open the case, Smith would always be useless.

What would happen if he broke the locks? Smith would finish with Sonja, put on his pants, pick up his case and realize it had been opened. He would accuse Sonja. The houseboat would be blown unless Wolff killed Smith. What would be the consequences of killing Smith? Another British soldier murdered, this time in Cairo. There would be a terrific manhunt. Would they be able to connect the killing with Wolff? Had Smith told anyone about Sonja? Who had seen them together in the Cha-Cha Club? Would inquiries lead the British to the houseboat?

It would be risky—but the worst of it would be that Wolff would be without a source of information, back at square one.

Meanwhile his people were fighting a war out there in the desert, and they needed information.

Wolff stood silent in the middle of the living room, racking his brains. He had thought of something, back there, which gave him his answer, and now it had slipped his mind. On the other side of the curtain, Smith was muttering and groaning. Wolff wondered if he had his pants off yet—

His pants off, that was it.

He would have the key to his briefcase in his pocket.

Wolff peeped between the curtains. Smith and Sonja lay on the bed. She was on her back, eyes closed. He lay beside her, propped up on one elbow, touching her. She was arching her back as if she were enjoying it. As Wolff watched, Smith rolled over, half lying on her, and put his face to her breasts.

Smith still had his shorts on.

Wolff put his head through the curtains and waved an arm, trying to attract Sonja's attention. He thought: Look at me, woman! Smith moved his head from one breast to the other. Sonja opened her eyes, glanced at the top of Smith's head, stroked his brilliantined hair, and caught Wolff's eye.

He mouthed: Take off his pants.

She frowned, not understanding.

Wolff stepped through the curtains and mimed removing pants.

Sonja's face cleared as enlightenment dawned.

Wolff stepped back through the curtains and closed them silently, leaving only a tiny gap to look through.

He saw Sonja's hands go to Smith's shorts and begin to

struggle with the buttons of the fly. Smith groaned. Sonja rolled her eyes upward, contemptuous of his credulous passion. Wolff thought: I hope she has the sense to throw the shorts this way.

After a minute Smith grew impatient with her fumbling, rolled over, sat up and took them off himself. He dropped them over the end of the bed and turned back to Sonja.

The end of the bed was about five feet away from the curtain.

Wolff got down on the floor and lay flat on his belly. He parted the curtains with his hands and inched his way through, Indian fashion.

He heard Smith say: "Oh, God, you're so beautiful."

Wolff reached the shorts. With one hand he carefully turned the material over until he saw a pocket. He put his hand in the pocket and felt for a key.

The pocket was empty.

There was the sound of movement from the bed. Smith grunted. Sonja said: "No, lie still."

Wolff thought: Good *girl*.

He turned the shorts over until he found the other pocket. He felt in it. That, too, was empty.

There might be more pockets. Wolff grew reckless. He felt the garment, searching for hard lumps that might be metal. There were none. He picked up the shorts—

A bunch of keys lay beneath them.

Wolff breathed a silent sigh of relief.

The keys must have slipped out of the pocket when Smith dropped the shorts on the floor.

Wolff picked up the keys and the shorts and began to inch backward through the curtains.

Then he heard footsteps on deck.

Smith said: "Good God, what's that!" in a high-pitched voice.

"Hush!" Sonja said. "Only the postman. Tell me if you like this . . ."

"Oh, yes."

Wolff made it through the curtains and looked up. The postman was placing a letter on the top step of the stairs, by the hatch. To Wolff's horror the postman saw him and called out: "*Sabah el-kheir*—good morning!"

Wolff put a finger to his lips for silence, then lay his cheek against his hand to mime sleep, then pointed to the bedroom.

"Your pardon!" the postman whispered.

Wolff waved him away.

There was no sound from the bedroom.

Had the postman's greeting made Smith suspicious? Probably not, Wolff decided: a postman might well call good morning even if he could see no one, for the fact that the hatch was open indicated that someone was at home.

The lovemaking noises in the next room resumed, and Wolff breathed more easily.

He sorted through the keys, found the smallest, and tried it in the locks of the case.

It worked.

He opened the other catch and lifted the lid. Inside was a sheaf of papers in a stiff cardboard folder. Wolff thought: No more menus, please. He opened the folder and looked at the top sheet.

He read:

OPERATION ABERDEEN

1. Allied forces will mount a major counterattack at dawn on 5 June.

2. The attack will be two-pronged . .

Wolff looked up from the papers. "My God," he whispered. "This is it!"

He listened. The noises from the bedroom were louder now. He could hear the springs of the bed, and he thought the boat itself was beginning to rock slightly. There was not much time.

The report in Smith's possession was detailed. Wolff was not sure exactly how the British chain of command worked, but presumably the battles were planned in detail by General Ritchie at desert headquarters then sent to GHQ in Cairo for approval by Auchinleck. Plans for more important battles would be discussed at the morning conferences, which Smith obviously attended in some capacity. Wolff wondered again which department it was that was housed in the unmarked building in the Shari Suleiman Pasha to which Smith returned each afternoon; then he pushed the thought aside. He needed to make notes.

He hunted around for pencil and paper, thinking: I should have done this beforehand. He found a writing pad and a red pencil in a drawer. He sat down by the briefcase and read on.

The main Allied forces were besieged in an area they called the Cauldron. The June 5 counterattack was intended to be a breakout. It would begin at 0250 with the bombardment, by four regiments of artillery, of the Aslagh Ridge, on Rommel's eastern flank. The artillery was to soften up the opposition in readiness for the spearhead attack by the infantry of the 10th Indian Brigade. When the Indians had breached the line at Aslagh Ridge, the tanks of the 22nd Armored Brigade would rush through the gap and capture Sidi Muftah while the 9th Indian Brigade followed through and consolidated.

Meanwhile the 32nd Army Tank Brigade, with infantry support, would attack Rommel's northern flank at Sidra Ridge.

When he came to the end of the report Wolff realized he had been so absorbed that he had heard, but had not taken notice of, the sound of Major Smith reaching his climax. Now the bed creaked and a pair of feet hit the floor.

Wolff tensed.

Sonja said: "Darling, pour some champagne."

"Just a minute—"

"I want it now."

"I feel a bit silly with me pants off, m'dear."

Wolff thought: Christ, he wants his pants.

Sonja said: "I like you undressed. Drink a glass with me before you put your clothes on."

"Your wish is my command."

Wolff relaxed. She may bitch about it, he thought, but she does what I want!

He looked quickly through the rest of the papers, determined that he would not be caught now: Smith was a wonderful find, and it would be a tragedy to kill the goose the first time it laid a golden egg. He noted that the attack would employ four hundred tanks, three hundred and thirty of them with the eastern prong and only seventy with the northern; that Generals Messervy and Briggs were to establish a combined headquarters; and that Auchinleck was demanding—a little peevishly, it seemed—thorough reconnaissance and close cooperation between infantry and tanks.

A cork popped loudly as he was writing. He licked his lips, thinking: I could use some of that. He wondered how quickly Smith could drink a glass of champagne. He decided to take no chances.

He put the papers back in the folder and the folder back in the case. He closed the lid and keyed the locks. He put the bunch of keys in a pocket of the shorts. He stood up and peeped through the curtain.

Smith was sitting up in bed in his army-issue underwear with a glass in one hand and a cigarette in the other, looking pleased with himself. The cigarettes must have been in his shirt pocket: it would have been awkward if they had been in his shorts.

At the moment Wolff was within Smith's field of view. He took his face away from the tiny gap between the curtains, and waited. He heard Sonja say: "Pour me some more, please." He looked through again. Smith took her glass and turned away to the bottle. His back was now to Wolff. Wolff pushed the shorts through the curtains and put them on the floor. Sonja saw him and raised her eyebrows in alarm. Wolff withdrew his arm. Smith handed Sonja the glass.

Wolff got into the cupboard, closed the door and eased himself to the floor. He wondered how long he would have to wait before Smith left. He did not care: he was jubilant. He had struck gold.

It was half an hour before he saw, through the peephole, Smith come into the living room, wearing his clothes again. By this time Wolff was feeling very cramped. Sonja followed Smith, saying: "Must you go so soon?"

"I'm afraid so," he said. "It's a very awkward time for me, you see." He hesitated. "To be perfectly frank, I'm not actually supposed to carry this briefcase around with me. I had the very devil of a job to come here at noon. You see, I have to go from GHQ straight to my office. Well, I didn't do that today—I was desperately afraid I might miss you if I came late. I told my office I was lunching at GHQ, and told the chaps at GHQ I was lunching at my office. However, next time I'll go to my office, dump the briefcase, and come on here—if that's all right with you, my little poppet."

Wolff thought: For God's sake, Sonja, say something!

She said: "Oh, but, Sandy, my housekeeper comes every afternoon to clean—we wouldn't be alone."

Smith frowned. "Damn. Well, we'll just have to meet in the evenings."

"But I have to work—and after my act, I have to stay in the club and talk to the customers. And I couldn't sit at your table every night: people would gossip."

The cupboard was very hot and stuffy. Wolff was perspiring heavily.

Smith said: "Can't you tell your cleaner not to come?"

"But darling, I couldn't clean the place myself—I wouldn't know how."

Wolff saw her smile, then she took Smith's hand and placed it between her legs. "Oh, Sandy, say you'll come at noon."

It was much more than Smith could withstand. "Of course I will, my darling," he said.

They kissed, and at last Smith left. Wolff listened to the footsteps crossing the deck and descending the gangplank, then he got out of the cupboard.

Sonja watched with malicious glee as he stretched his aching limbs. "Sore?" she said with mock sympathy.

"It was worth it," Wolff said. "You were wonderful."

"Did you get what you wanted?"

"Better than I could have dreamed."

Wolff cut up bread and sausage for lunch while Sonja took a bath. After lunch he found the English novel and the key to the code, and drafted his signal to Rommel. Sonja went to the racetrack with a crowd of Egyptian friends: Wolff gave her fifty pounds to bet with.

In the evening she went to the Cha-Cha Club and Wolff sat at home drinking whiskey and reading Arab poetry. As midnight approached, he set up the radio.

At exactly 2400 hours, he tapped out his call sign, Sphinx. A few seconds later Rommel's desert listening post, or Horch Company, answered. Wolff sent a series of V's to enable them to tune in exactly, then asked them what his signal strength was. In the middle of the sentence he made a mistake, and sent a series of E's—for Error—before beginning again. They told him his signal was maximum strength and made GA for Go Ahead. He made KA to indicate the beginning of his message; then, in code, he began: "Operation Aberdeen. . . ."

At the end he added AR for Message Finished and K for Over. They replied with a series of R's, which meant: "Your message has been received and understood."

Wolff packed away the radio, the code book and the key, then he poured himself another drink.

All in all, he thought he had done incredibly well.

10

The signal from the spy was only one of twenty or thirty reports on the desk of von Mellenthin, Rommel's Ic—intelligence officer—at seven o'clock on the morning of June 4. There were several other reports from listening units: infantry had been heard talking to tanks *au clair*; field headquarters had issued instructions in low-grade codes which had been deciphered overnight; and there was other enemy radio traffic which, although indecipherable, nevertheless yielded hints about enemy intentions simply because of its location and frequency. As well as radio reconnaissance there were the reports from the Ics in the field, who got information from captured weapons, the uniforms of enemy dead, interrogation of prisoners and simply looking across the desert and *seeing* the people they were fighting. Then there was aerial reconnaissance, a situation report from an order-of-battle expert and a summary—just about useless—of Berlin's current assessment of Allied intentions and strength.

Like all field intelligence officers, von Mellenthin despised spy reports. Based on diplomatic gossip, newspaper stories and sheer guesswork, they were wrong at least as often as they were right, which made them effectively useless.

He had to admit that this one *looked* different.

The run-of-the-mill secret agent might report: "9th Indian Brigade have been told they will be involved in a major battle in the near future," or: "Allies planning a breakout from the Cauldron in early June," or: "Rumors that Auchinleck will be replaced as commander in chief." But there was nothing indefinite about this report.

The spy, whose call sign was Sphinx, began his message: "Operation Aberdeen." He gave the date of the attack, the brigades involved and their specific roles, the places they would pounce, and the tactical thinking of the planners.

Von Mellenthin was not convinced, but he was interested.

As the thermometer in his tent passed the 100-degree mark he began his routine round of morning discussions. In person, by field telephone and—rarely—by radio, he talked to the divisional Ics, the Luftwaffe liaison officer for aerial reconnaissance, the Horch Company liaison man and a few of the better brigade Ics. To all of these men he mentioned the 9th and 10th Indian Brigades, the 22nd Armored Brigade, and the 32nd Army Tank Brigade. He told them to look out for these brigades. He also told them to watch for battle preparations in the areas from which, according to the spy, the counterthrust would come. They would also observe the enemy's observers: if the spy were right, there would be increased aerial reconnaissance by the Allies of the positions they planned to attack, namely Aslagh Ridge, Sidra Ridge and Sidi Muftah. There might be increased bombing of those positions, for the purpose of softening up, although this was such a giveaway that most commanders would resist the temptation. There might be *de*creased bombing, as a bluff, and this too could be a sign.

These conversations also enabled the field Ics to update their overnight reports. When they were finished von Mellenthin wrote *his* report for Rommel, and took it to the command vehicle. He discussed it with the chief of staff, who then presented it to Rommel.

The morning discussion was brief, for Rommel had made his major decisions and given his orders for the day during the previous evening. Besides, Rommel was not in a reflective mood in the mornings: he wanted action. He tore around the desert, going from one front-line position to another in his staff car or his Storch aircraft, giving new orders, joking with the men and taking charge of skirmishes—and yet, although he constantly exposed himself to enemy fire, he had not been wounded since 1914. Von Mellenthin went with him today, taking the opportunity to get his own picture of the front-line situation, and making his personal assessment of the Ics who were sending in his raw material: some were overcautious, omitting all unconfirmed data, and others exaggerated in order to get extra supplies and reinforcements for their units.

In the early evening, when at last the thermometer showed a fall, there were more reports and conversations. Von Mellenthin sifted the mass of detail for information relating to the counterattack predicted by Sphinx.

The Ariete Armored—the Italian division occupying the Aslagh Ridge—reported increased enemy air activity. Von Mellenthin asked them whether this was bombing or reconnaissance, and they said reconnaissance: bombing had actually ceased.

The Luftwaffe reported activity in no-man's-land which might, or might not, have been an advance party marking out an assembly point.

There was a garbled radio intercept in a low-grade cipher in which the something Indian Brigade requested urgent clarification of the morning's something (orders?) with particular reference to the timing of something artillery bombardment. In British tactics, von Mellenthin knew, artillery bombardment generally preceded an attack.

The evidence was building.

Von Mellenthin checked his card index for the 32nd Army Tank Brigade and discovered that they had recently been sighted at Rigel Ridge—a logical position from which to attack Sidra Ridge.

The task of an Ic was an impossible one: to forecast the enemy's moves on the basis of inadequate information. He looked at the signs, he used his intuition and he gambled.

Von Mellenthin decided to gamble on Sphinx.

At 1830 hours he took his report to the command vehicle.

Rommel was there with his chief of staff Colonel Bayerlein and Kesselring. They stood around a large camp table looking at the operations map. A lieutenant sat to one side ready to take notes.

Rommel had taken his cap off, and his large, balding head appeared too big for his small body. He looked tired and thin. He suffered recurring stomach trouble, von Mellenthin knew, and was often unable to eat for days. His normally pudgy face had lost flesh, and his ears seemed to stick out more than usual. But his slitted dark eyes were bright with enthusiasm and the hope of victory.

Von Mellenthin clicked his heels and formally handed over the report, then he explained his conclusions on the map. When he had done Kesselring said: "And all this is based on the report of a spy, you say?"

"No, Field Marshal," von Mellenthin said firmly. "There are confirming indications."

"You can find confirming indications for anything," Kesselring said.

Out of the corner of his eye von Mellenthin could see that Rommel was getting cross.

Kesselring said: "We really can't plan battles on the basis of information from some grubby little secret agent in Cairo."

Rommel said: "I am inclined to believe this report."

Von Mellenthin watched the two men. They were curiously balanced in terms of power—curiously, that was, for the Army, where hierarchies were normally so well defined. Kesselring was C in C South, and outranked Rommel, but Rommel did not take orders from him, by some whim of Hitler's. Both men had patrons in Berlin—Kesselring, the Luftwaffe man, was Goering's favorite, and Rommel produced such good publicity that Goebbels could be relied upon to support him. Kesselring was popular with the Italians, whereas Rommel always insulted them. Ultimately Kesselring was more powerful, for as a field marshal he had direct access to Hitler, while Rommel had to go through Jodl; but this was a card Kesselring could not afford to play too often. So the two men quarreled; and although Rommel had the last word here in the desert, back in Europe

—von Mellenthin knew—Kesselring was maneuvering to get rid of him.

Rommel turned to the map. "Let us be ready, then, for a two-pronged attack. Consider first the weaker, northern prong. Sidra Ridge is held by the Twenty-first Panzer Division with antitank guns. Here, in the path of the British advance, is a minefield. The panzers will lure the British into the minefield and destroy them with antitank fire. If the spy is right, and the British throw only seventy tanks into this assault, the Twenty-first Panzers should deal with them quickly and be free for other action later in the day."

He drew a thick forefinger down across the map. "Now consider the second prong, the main assault, on our eastern flank. This is held by the Italian Army. The attack is to be led by an Indian brigade. Knowing those Indians, and knowing our Italians, I assume the attack will succeed. I therefore order a vigorous riposte.

"One: The Italians will counterattack from the west. Two: The Panzers, having repelled the other prong of the attack at Sidra Ridge, will turn about and attack the Indians from the north. Three: Tonight our engineers will clear a gap in the minefield at Bir el-Harmat, so that the Fifteenth Panzers can make a swing to the south, emerge through the gap, and attack the British forces from the rear."

Von Mellenthin, listening and watching, nodded appreciation. It was a typical Rommel plan, involving rapid switching of forces to maximize their effect, an encircling movement, and the surprise appearance of a powerful division where it was least expected, in the enemy's rear. If it all worked, the attacking Allied brigades would be surrounded, cut off and wiped out.

If it all worked.

If the spy was right.

Kesselring said to Rommel: "I think you could be making a big mistake."

"That's your privilege," Rommel said calmly.

Von Mellenthin did not feel calm. If it worked out badly, Berlin would soon hear about Rommel's unjustified faith in poor intelligence; and von Mellenthin would be blamed for supplying that intelligence. Rommel's attitude to subordinates who let him down was savage.

Rommel looked at the note-taking lieutenant. "Those, then, are my orders for tomorrow." He glared defiantly at Kesselring.

Von Mellenthin put his hands in his pockets and crossed his fingers.

❦

Von Mellenthin remembered that moment when, sixteen days later, he and Rommel watched the sun rise over Tobruk.

They stood together on the escarpment northeast of El Adem, waiting for the start of the battle. Rommel was wearing the goggles he had taken from the captured General O'Connor, the goggles which had become a kind of trademark of his. He was in top form: bright-eyed, lively and confident. You could almost hear his brain tick as he scanned the landscape and computed how the battle might go.

Von Mellenthin said: "The spy was right."

Rommel smiled. "That's exactly what I was thinking."

The Allied counterattack of June 5 had come precisely as forecast, and Rommel's defense had worked so well that it had turned into a counter-counterattack. Three of the four Allied brigades involved had been wiped out, and four regiments of artillery had been captured. Rommel had pressed his advantage remorselessly. On June 14 the Gazala Line had been broken and today, June 20, they were to besiege the vital coastal garrison of Tobruk.

Von Mellenthin shivered. It was astonishing how cold the desert could be at five o'clock in the morning.

He watched the sky.

At twenty minutes past five the attack began.

A sound like distant thunder swelled to a deafening roar as the Stukas approached. The first formation flew over, dived toward the British positions, and dropped their bombs. A great cloud of dust and smoke arose, and with that Rommel's entire artillery forces opened fire with a simultaneous ear-splitting crash. Another wave of Stukas came over, then another: there were hundreds of bombers.

Von Mellenthin said: "Fantastic. Kesselring really did it."

It was the wrong thing to say. Rommel snapped: "No credit to Kesselring: today we are directing the planes ourselves."

The Luftwaffe was putting on a good show, even so, von Mellenthin thought; but he did not say it.

Tobruk was a concentric fortress. The garrison itself was within a town, and the town was at the heart of a larger British-held area surrounded by a thirty-five-mile perimeter wire dotted with strongpoints. The Germans had to cross the wire, then penetrate the town, then take the garrison.

A cloud of orange smoke arose in the middle of the battlefield. Von Mellenthin said: "That's a signal from the assault engineers, telling the artillery to lengthen their range."

Rommel nodded. "Good. We're making progress."

Suddenly von Mellenthin was seized by optimism. There was booty in Tobruk: petrol, and dynamite, and tents, and trucks—already more than half Rommel's motorized transport consisted of captured British vehicles—and food. Von Mellenthin smiled and said: "Fresh fish for dinner?"

Rommel understood his train of thought. "Liver," he said. "Fried potatoes. Fresh bread."

"A real bed, with a feather pillow."

"In a house with stone walls to keep out the heat and the bugs."

A runner arrived with a signal. Von Mellenthin took it and read it. He tried to keep the excitement out of his voice as he said: "They've cut the wire at Strongpoint Sixty-nine. Group Menny is attacking with the infantry of the Afrika Korps."

"That's it," said Rommel. "We've opened a breach. Let's go."

⌒

It was ten-thirty in the morning when Lieutenant Colonel Reggie Bogge poked his head around the door of Vandam's office and said: "Tobruk is under siege."

It seemed pointless to work then. Vandam went on mechanically, reading reports from informants, considering the case of a lazy lieutenant who was due for promotion but did not deserve it, trying to think of a fresh approach to the Alex Wolff case; but everything seemed hopelessly trivial. The news became more depressing as the day wore on. The Germans breached the perimeter wire; they bridged the antitank ditch; they crossed the inner minefield; they reached the strategic road junction known as King's Cross.

Vandam went home at seven to have supper with Billy. He could not tell the boy about Tobruk: the news was not to be released at present. As they ate their lamb chops, Billy said that his English teacher, a young man with a lung condition who could not get into the Army, never stopped talking about how he would love to get out into the desert and have a bash at the Hun. "I don't believe him, though," Billy said. "Do you?"

"I expect he means it," Vandam said. "He just feels guilty."

Billy was at an argumentative age. "Guilty? He can't feel *guilty*—it's not his fault."

"Unconsciously he can."

"What's the difference?"

I walked into that one, Vandam thought. He considered for a moment, then said: "When you've done something wrong, and you know it's wrong, and you feel bad about it, and you know why you feel bad, that's conscious guilt. Mr. Simkisson has done nothing wrong, but he *still* feels bad about it, and he doesn't know why he feels bad. That's unconscious guilt. It makes him feel better to talk about how much he wants to fight."

"Oh," said Billy.

Vandam did not know whether the boy had understood or not.

Billy went to bed with a new book. He said it was a "tec," by which he meant a detective story. It was called *Death on the Nile.*

Vandam went back to GHQ. The news was still bad. The 21st Panzers had entered the town of Tobruk and fired from the quay on to several British ships which were trying, belatedly, to escape to the open sea. A number of vessels had been sunk. Vandam thought of the men who made a ship, and the tons of precious steel that went into it, and the training of the sailors, and the welding of the crew into a team; and now the men were dead, the ship sunk, the effort wasted.

He spent the night in the officers' mess, waiting for news. He drank steadily and smoked so much that he gave himself a headache. Bulletins came down periodically from the Operations Room. During the night Ritchie, as commander of the Eighth Army, decided to abandon the frontier and retreat to Mersa Matruh. It was said that when Auchinleck, the commander in chief, heard this news he stalked out of the room with a face as black as thunder.

Toward dawn Vandam found himself thinking about his parents. Some of the ports on the south coast of England had suffered as much as London from the bombing, but his parents were a little way inland, in a village in the Dorset countryside. His father was postmaster at a small sorting office. Vandam looked at his watch: it would be four in the morning in England now, the old man would be putting on his cycle clips, climbing on his bike and riding to work in the dark. At sixty years of age he had the constitution of a teen-age farmboy. Vandam's chapelgoing mother forbade smoking, drinking and all kinds of dissolute behavior, a term she used to encompass everything from darts matches to listening to the wireless. The regime seemed to suit her husband, but she herself was always ailing.

Eventually booze, fatigue and tedium sent Vandam into a doze. He dreamed he was in the garrison at Tobruk with Billy and Elene and his mother. He was running around closing all the windows. Outside, the Germans—who had turned into firemen—were leaning ladders against the wall and climbing up. Suddenly Vandam's mother stopped counting her forged banknotes and opened a window, pointing at Elene and screaming: "The Scarlet Woman!" Rommel came through the window in a fireman's helmet and turned a hose on Billy. The force of the jet pushed the boy over a parapet and he fell into the sea. Vandam knew he was to blame, but he could not figure out what he had done wrong. He began to weep bitterly. He woke up.

He was relieved to discover that he had not really been crying. The dream left him with an overwhelming sense of despair. He lit a cigarette. It tasted foul.

The sun rose. Vandam went around the mess turning out the lights, just for something to do. A breakfast cook came in with a pot of coffee. As Vandam was drinking his, a captain came down with another bulletin. He stood in the middle of the mess, waiting for silence.

He said: "General Klopper surrendered the garrison of Tobruk to Rommel at dawn today."

Vandam left the mess and walked through the streets of the city toward his house by the Nile. He felt impotent and useless, sitting in Cairo catching spies while out there in the desert his country was losing the war. It crossed his mind that Alex Wolff might have had something to do with Rommel's latest series of victories; but he dismissed the thought as somewhat farfetched. He felt so depressed that he wondered whether things could possibly get any worse, and he realized that, of course, they could.

When he got home he went to bed.

PART TWO

MERSA MATRUH

11

The Greek was a feeler.

Elene did not like feelers. She did not mind straightforward lust; in fact, she was rather partial to it. What she objected to was furtive, guilty, unsolicited groping.

After two hours in the shop she had disliked Mikis Aristo-poulos. After two weeks she was ready to strangle him.

The shop itself was fine. She liked the spicy smells and the rows of gaily colored boxes and cans on the shelves in the back room. The work was easy and repetitive, but the time passed quickly enough. She amazed the customers by adding up their bills in her head very rapidly. From time to time she would buy some strange imported delicacy and take it home to try: a jar of liver paste, a Hershey bar, a bottle of Bovril, a can of baked beans. And for her it was novel to do an ordinary, dull, eight-hours-a-day job.

But the boss was a pain. Every chance he got he would touch her arm, her shoulder or her hip; each time he passed her, behind the counter or in the back room, he would brush against her breasts or her bottom. At first she had thought it was accidental, because he did not look the type: he was in his twenties, quite good-looking, with a big smile that showed his white teeth. He must have taken her silence for acquiescence. She would have to tread on him a little.

She did not need this. Her emotions were too confused already. She both liked and loathed William Vandam, who talked to her as an equal, then treated her like a whore; she was supposed to seduce Alex Wolff, whom she had never met; and she was being groped by Mikis Aristopoulos, for whom she felt nothing but scorn.

They all use me, she thought; it's the story of my life.

She wondered what Wolff would be like. It was easy for Vandam to tell her to befriend him, as if there were a button she could press which made her instantly irresistible. In reality a lot depended on the man. Some men liked her immediately. With others it was hard work. Sometimes it was impossible. Half of her hoped it would be impossible with Wolff. The other half remembered that he was a spy for the Germans, and Rommel was coming closer every day, and if the Nazis ever got to Cairo . . .

Aristopoulos brought a box of pasta out from the back room. Elene looked at her watch: it was almost time to go home. Aristopoulos dropped the box and opened it. On his way back, as he squeezed past her, he put his hands under her arms and touched her breasts. She moved away. She heard someone come into the shop. She thought: I'll teach the Greek a lesson. As he went into the back room, she called after him loudly, in Arabic: "If you touch me again I'll cut your cock off!"

There was a burst of laughter from the customer. She turned and looked at him. He was a European, but he must understand Arabic, she thought. She said: "Good afternoon."

He looked toward the back room and called out: "What have you been doing, Aristopoulos, you young goat?"

Aristopoulos poked his head around the door. "Good day, sir. This is my niece, Elene." His face showed embarrassment and something else which Elene could not read. He ducked back into the storeroom.

"Niece!" said the customer, looking at Elene. "A likely tale."

He was a big man in his thirties with dark hair, dark skin and dark eyes. He had a large hooked nose which might have been typically Arab or typically European-aristocratic. His mouth was thin-lipped, and when he smiled he showed small even teeth—like a cat's, Elene thought. She knew the signs of wealth and she saw them here: a silk shirt, a gold wristwatch, tailored cotton trousers with a crocodile belt, handmade shoes and a faint masculine cologne.

Elene said: "How can I help you?"

He looked at her as if he were contemplating several possible answers, then he said: "Let's start with some English marmalade."

"Yes." The marmalade was in the back room. She went there to get a jar.

"It's him!" Aristopoulos hissed.

"What are you talking about?" she asked in a normal voice. She was still mad at him.

"The bad-money man—Mr. Wolff—that's him!"

"Oh, God!" For a moment she had forgotten why she was here. Aristopoulos' panic infected her, and her mind went blank. "What shall I say to him? What should I do?"

"I don't know—give him the marmalade—I don't know—"

"Yes, the marmalade, right . . ." She took a jar of Cooper's Oxford from a shelf and returned to the shop. She forced herself to smile brightly at Wolff as she put the jar down on the counter. "What else?"

"Two pounds of the dark coffee, ground fine."

He was watching her while she weighed the coffee and put it through the grinder. Suddenly she was afraid of him. He was not like Charles, Johnnie and Claud, the men who had kept her. They had been soft, easygoing, guilty and pliable. Wolff seemed poised and confident: it would be hard to deceive him and impossible to thwart him, she guessed.

"Something else?"

"A tin of ham."

She moved around the shop, finding what he wanted and putting the goods on the counter. His eyes followed her everywhere. She thought: I must talk to him, I can't keep saying

"Something else?" I'm supposed to befriend him. "Something else?" she said.

"A half case of champagne."

The cardboard box containing six full bottles was heavy. She dragged it out of the back room. "I expect you'd like us to deliver this order," she said. She tried to make it sound casual. She was slightly breathless with the effort of bending to drag the case, and she hoped this would cover her nervousness.

He seemed to look through her with his dark eyes. "Deliver?" he said. "No, thank you."

She looked at the heavy box. "I hope you live nearby."

"Close enough."

"You must be very strong."

"Strong enough."

"We have a thoroughly reliable delivery man—"

"No delivery," he said firmly.

She nodded. "As you wish." She had not really expected it to work, but she was disappointed all the same. "Something else?"

"I think that's all."

She began to add up the bill. Wolff said: "Aristopoulos must be doing well, to employ an assistant."

Elene said: "Five pounds twelve and six, you wouldn't say that if you knew what he pays me, five pounds thirteen and six, six pounds—"

"Don't you like the job?"

She gave him a direct look. "I'd do *anything* to get out of here."

"What did you have in mind?" He was very quick.

She shrugged, and went back to her addition. Eventually she said: "Thirteen pounds ten shillings and fourpence."

"How did you know I'd pay in sterling?"

He was *quick*. She was afraid she had given herself away. She felt herself begin to blush. She had an inspiration, and said: "You're a British officer, aren't you?"

He laughed loudly at that. He took out a roll of pound notes and gave her fourteen. She gave him his change in Egyptian coins. She was thinking: What else can I do? What else can I say? She began to pack his purchases into a brown-paper shopping bag.

She said: "Are you having a party? I love parties."

"What makes you ask?"

"The champagne."

"Ah. Well, life is one long party."

She thought: I've failed. He will go away now, and perhaps he won't come back for weeks, perhaps never; I've had him in my sights, I've talked to him, and now I have to let him walk away and disappear into the city.

She should have felt relieved, but instead she felt a sense of abject failure.

He lifted the case of champagne on to his left shoulder, and picked up the shopping bag with his right hand. "Good-bye," he said.

"Good-bye."

He turned around at the door. "Meet me at the Oasis Restaurant on Wednesday night at seven-thirty."

"All right!" she said jubilantly. But he was gone.

∽

It took them most of the morning to get to the Hill of Jesus. Jakes sat in the front next to the driver; Vandam and Bogge sat in the back. Vandam was exultant. An Australian company had taken the hill in the night, and they had captured—almost intact—a German wireless listening post. It was the first good news Vandam had heard for months.

Jakes turned around and shouted over the noise of the engine. "Apparently the Aussies charged in their socks, to surprise 'em," he said. "Most of the Italians were taken prisoner in their pajamas."

Vandam had heard the same story. "The Germans weren't sleeping, though," he said. "It was quite a rough show."

They took the main road to Alexandria, then the coast road to El Alamein, where they turned on to a barrel track—a route through the desert marked with barrels. Nearly all the traffic was going in the opposite direction, retreating. Nobody knew what was happening. They stopped at a supply dump to fill up with petrol, and Bogge had to pull rank on the officer in charge to get a chitty.

Their driver asked for directions to the hill. "Bottle track," the officer said brusquely. The tracks, created by and for the Army, were named Bottle, Boot, Moon and Star, the symbols for which were cut into the empty barrels and petrol cans along the routes. At night little lights were placed in the barrels to illuminate the symbols.

Bogge asked the officer: "What's happening out here? Everything seems to be heading back east."

"Nobody tells me anything," said the officer.

They got a cup of tea and a bully-beef sandwich from the NAAFI truck. When they moved on they went through a recent battlefield, littered with wrecked and burned-out tanks, where a graveyard detail was desultorily collecting corpses. The barrels disappeared, but the driver picked them up again on the far side of the gravel plain.

They found the hill at midday. There was a battle going on not far away: they could hear the guns and see clouds of dust rising to the west. Vandam realized he had not been this near the fighting before. The overall impression was one of dirt, panic and confusion. They reported to the command vehicle and were directed to the captured German radio trucks.

Field intelligence men were already at work. Prisoners were being interrogated in a small tent, one at a time, while the others waited in the blazing sun. Enemy ordnance experts were examining weapons and vehicles, noting manufacturers' serial numbers. The Y Service was there looking for wavelengths and codes. It was the task of Bogge's little squad to investigate how much the Germans had been learning in advance about Allied movements.

They took a truck each. Like most people in Intelligence, Vandam had a smattering of German. He knew a couple of hundred words, most of them military terms, so that while he could not have told the difference between a love letter and a laundry list, he could read army orders and reports.

There was a lot of material to be examined: the captured post was a great prize for Intelligence. Most of the stuff would have to be boxed, transported to Cairo and perused at length by a large team. Today's job was a preliminary overview.

Vandam's truck was a mess. The Germans had begun to destroy their papers when they realized the battle was lost. Boxes had been emptied and a small fire started, but the damage had been arrested quickly. There was blood on a cardboard folder: someone had died defending his secrets.

Vandam went to work. They would have tried to destroy the important papers first, so he began with the half-burned pile. There were many Allied radio signals, intercepted and in some cases decoded. Most of it was routine—most of everything was routine—but as he worked Vandam began to realize that German Intelligence's wireless interception was picking up an awful lot of useful information. They were better than Vandam had imagined—and Allied wireless security was very bad.

At the bottom of the half-burned pile was a book, a novel in English. Vandam frowned. He opened the book and read the first line: "Last night I dreamt I went to Manderley again." The book was called *Rebecca*, and it was by Daphne du Maurier. The title was vaguely familiar. Vandam thought his wife might have read it. It seemed to be about a young woman living in an English country house.

Vandam scratched his head. It was, to say the least, peculiar reading for the Afrika Korps.

And why was it in English?

It might have been taken from a captured English soldier, but Vandam thought that unlikely: in his experience soldiers read pornography, hard-boiled private eye stories and the Bible. Somehow he could not imagine the Desert Rats getting interested in the problems of the mistress of Manderley.

No, the book was here for a purpose. What purpose? Vandam could think of only one possibility: it was the basis of a code.

A book code was a variation on the one-time pad. A one-time pad had letters and numbers randomly printed in five-character groups. Only two copies of each pad were made: one for the sender and one for the recipient of the signals. Each sheet of the pad was used for one message, then torn off and destroyed. Because each sheet was used only once the code could not be broken. A book code used the pages of a printed book in the same way, except that the sheets were not necessarily destroyed after use.

There was one big advantage which a book had over a pad. A pad was unmistakably for the purpose of encipherment, but a book looked quite innocent. In the battlefield this did not matter; but it did matter to an agent behind enemy lines.

This might also explain why the book was in English. German soldiers signaling to one another would use a book in German, if they used a book at all, but a spy in British territory would need to carry a book in English.

Vandam examined the book more closely. The price had been written in pencil on the endpaper, then rubbed out with an eraser. That might mean the book had been bought secondhand. Vandam held it up to the light, trying to read the impression the pencil had made in the paper. He made out the number 50, followed by some letters. Was it *eic*? It might be *erc*, or *esc*. It was *esc*, he realized—fifty escudos. The book had been bought in Portugal. Portugal was neutral territory, with both German and British embassies, and it was a hive of low-level espionage.

As soon as he got back to Cairo he would send a message to the Secret Intelligence Service station in Lisbon. They could check the English-language bookshops in Portugal—there could not be very many—and try to find out where the book had been bought, and if possible by whom.

At least two copies would have been bought, and a bookseller might remember such a sale. The interesting question was, where was the other copy? Vandam was pretty sure it was in Cairo, and he thought he knew who was using it.

He decided he had better show his find to Lieutenant Colonel Bogge. He picked up the book and stepped out of the truck.

Bogge was coming to find him.

Vandam stared at him. He was white-faced, and angry to the point of hysteria. He came stomping across the dusty sand, a sheet of paper in his hand.

Vandam thought: What the devil has got into him?

Bogge shouted: "What do you do all day, anyway?"

Vandam said nothing. Bogge handed him the sheet of paper. Vandam looked at it.

It was a coded radio signal, with the decrypt written between the lines of code. It was timed at midnight on June 3. The sender used the call sign Sphinx. The message, after the usual preliminaries about signal strength, bore the heading OPERATION ABERDEEN.

Vandam was thunderstruck. Operation Aberdeen had taken place on June 5, and the Germans had received a signal about it on June 3.

Vandam said: "Jesus Christ Almighty, this is a disaster."

"Of course it's a bloody disaster!" Bogge yelled. "It means Rommel is getting full details of our attacks before they bloody begin!"

Vandam read the rest of the signal. "Full details" was right. The message named the brigades involved, the timing of various stages of the attack, and the overall strategy.

"No wonder Rommel's winning," Vandam muttered.

"Don't make bloody jokes!" Bogge screamed.

Jakes appeared at Vandam's side, accompanied by a full colonel from the Australian brigade that had taken the hill, and said to Vandam: "Excuse me, sir—"

Vandam said abruptly: "Not now, Jakes."

"Stay here, Jakes," Bogge countermanded. "This concerns you, too."

Vandam handed the sheet of paper to Jakes. Vandam felt as if someone had struck him a physical blow. The information was so good that it had to have originated in GHQ.

Jakes said softly: "Bloody hell."

Bogge said: "They must be getting this stuff from an English officer, you realize that, do you?"

"Yes," Vandam said.

"What do you mean, yes? Your job is personnel security—this is your bloody responsibility!"

"I realize that, sir."

"Do you also realize that a leak of this magnitude will have to be reported to the commander in chief?"

The Australian colonel, who did not appreciate the scale of the catastrophe, was embarrassed to see an officer getting a public dressing down. He said: "Let's save the recriminations for later, Bogge. I doubt the thing is the fault of any one individual. Your first job is to discover the extent of the damage and make a preliminary report to your superiors."

It was clear that Bogge was not through ranting yet; but he was outranked. He suppressed his wrath with a visible effort, and said: "Right, get on with it, Vandam." He stumped off, and the colonel went away in the other direction.

Vandam sat down on the step of the truck. He lit a cigarette with a shaking hand. The news seemed worse as it sunk in. Not only had Alex Wolff penetrated Cairo and evaded Vandam's net, he had gained access to high-level secrets.

Vandam thought: Who is this man?

In just a few days he had selected his target, laid his groundwork, and then bribed, blackmailed or corrupted the target into treachery.

Who was the target; who was giving Wolff the information? Literally hundreds of people had the information: the generals, their aides, the secretaries who typed written messages, the men who encoded radio messages, the officers who carried verbal messages, all Intelligence staff, all interservice liaison people . . .

Somehow, Vandam assumed, Wolff had found one among those hundreds of people who was prepared to betray his country for money, or out of political conviction, or under pressure of blackmail. Of course it was possible that Wolff had nothing to do with it—but Vandam thought that unlikely, for a traitor needed a channel of communication with the enemy, and Wolff had such a channel, and it was hard to believe there might be two like Wolff in Cairo.

Jakes was standing beside Vandam, looking dazed. Vandam said: "Not only is this information getting through, but Rommel is using it. If you recall the fighting on five June—"

"Yes, I do," Jakes said. "It was a massacre."

And it was my fault, Vandam thought. Bogge had been right

about that: Vandam's job was to stop secrets getting out, and when secrets got out it was Vandam's responsibility.

One man could not win the war, but one man could lose it. Vandam did not want to be that man.

He stood up. "All right, Jakes, you heard what Bogge said. Let's get on with it."

Jakes snapped his fingers. "I forgot what I came to tell you: you're wanted on the field telephone. It's GHQ. Apparently there's an Egyptian woman in your office, asking for you, refusing to leave. She says she has an urgent message and she won't take no for an answer."

Vandam thought: Elene!

Maybe she had made contact with Wolff. She must have—why else would she be desperate to speak to Vandam? Vandam ran to the command vehicle, with Jakes hard on his heels.

The major in charge of communications handed him the phone. "Make it snappy, Vandam, we're using that thing."

Vandam had swallowed enough abuse for one day. He snatched the phone, thrust his face into the major's face, and said loudly: "I'll use it as long as I need it." He turned his back on the major and spoke into the phone. "Yes?"

"William?"

"Elene!" He wanted to tell her how good it was to hear her voice, but instead he said: "What happened?"

"He came into the shop."

"You saw him! Did you get his address?"

"No—but I've got a date with him."

"Well done!" Vandam was full of savage delight—he would catch the bastard now. "Where and when?"

"Tomorrow night, seven-thirty, at the Oasis Restaurant."

Vandam picked up a pencil and a scrap of paper. "Oasis Restaurant, seven-thirty," he repeated. "I'll be there."

"Good."

"Elene . . ."

"Yes?"

"I can't tell you how grateful I am. Thank you."

"Until tomorrow."

"Good-bye." Vandam put down the phone.

Bogge was standing behind him, with the major in charge of communications. Bogge said: "What the devil do you mean by using the field telephone to make dates with your bloody girl friends?"

Vandam gave him a sunny smile. "That wasn't a girl friend, it was an informant," he said. "She's made contact with the spy. I expect to arrest him tomorrow night."

12

Wolff watched Sonja eat. The liver was underdone, pink and soft, just as she liked it. She ate with relish, as usual. He thought how alike the two of them were. In their work they were competent, professional and highly successful. They both lived in the shadows of childhood shocks: her father's death, his mother's remarriage into an Arab family. Neither of them had ever come close to marrying, for they were too fond of themselves to love another person. What brought them together was not love, not even affection, but shared lusts. The most important thing in life, for both of them, was the indulgence of their appetites. They both knew that Wolff was taking a small but unnecessary risk by eating in a restaurant, and they both felt the risk was worth it, for life would hardly be worth living without good food.

She finished her liver and the waiter brought an ice-cream dessert. She was always very hungry after performing at the Cha-Cha Club. It was not surprising: she used a great deal of energy in her act. But when, finally, she quit dancing, she would grow fat. Wolff imagined her in twenty years' time: she would have three chins and a vast bosom, her hair would be brittle and graying, she would walk flat-footed and be breathless after climbing the stairs.

"What are you smiling at?" Sonja said.

"I was picturing you as an old woman, wearing a shapeless black dress and a veil."

"I won't be like that. I shall be very rich, and live in a palace surrounded by naked young men and women eager to gratify my slightest whim. What about you?"

Wolff smiled. "I think I shall be Hitler's ambassador to Egypt, and wear an SS uniform to the mosque."

"You'd have to take off your jackboots."

"Shall I visit you in your palace?"

"Yes, please—wearing your uniform."

"Would I have to take off my jackboots in your presence?"

"No. Everything else, but not the boots."

Wolff laughed. Sonja was in a rare gay mood. He called the waiter and asked for coffee, brandy and the bill. He said to Sonja: "There's some good news. I've been saving it. I think I've found another Fawzi."

She was suddenly very still, looking at him intently. "Who is she?" she said quietly.

"I went to the grocer's yesterday. Aristopoulos has his niece working with him."

"A shopgirl!"

"She's a real beauty. She has a lovely, innocent face and a slightly wicked smile."

"How old?"

"Hard to say. Around twenty, I think. She has such a girlish body."

Sonja licked her lips. "And you think she will . . . ?"

"I think so. She's dying to get away from Aristopoulos, and she practically threw herself at me."

"When?"

"I'm taking her to dinner tomorrow night."

"Will you bring her home?"

"Maybe. I have to feel her out. She's so perfect, I don't want to spoil everything by rushing her."

"You mean you want to have her first."

"If necessary."

"Do you think she's a virgin?"

"It's possible."

"If she is . . ."

"Then I'll save her for you. You were so good with Major Smith, you deserve a treat." Wolff sat back, studying Sonja. Her face was a mask of sexual greed as she anticipated the corruption of someone beautiful and innocent. Wolff sipped his brandy. A warm glow spread in his stomach. He felt good: full of food and wine, his mission going remarkably well and a new sexual adventure in view.

The bill came, and he paid it with English pound notes.

∽

It was a small restaurant, but a successful one. Ibrahim managed it and his brother did the cooking. They had learned the trade in a French hotel in Tunisia, their home; and when their father died they had sold the sheep and come to Cairo to seek their fortune. Ibrahim's philosophy was simple: they knew only French-Arab cuisine, so that was all they offered. They might, perhaps, have attracted more customers if the menu in the window had offered spaghetti bolognaise or roast beef and Yorkshire pudding; but those customers would not have returned, and anyhow Ibrahim had his pride.

The formula worked. They were making a good living, more money than their father had ever seen. The war had brought even more business. But wealth had not made Ibrahim careless.

Two days earlier he had taken coffee with a friend who was a cashier at the Metropolitan Hotel. The friend had told him how the British paymaster general had refused to exchange four of the English pound notes which had been passed in the hotel bar. The notes were counterfeit, according to the British. What was so unfair was that they had confiscated the money.

This was not going to happen to Ibrahim.

About half his customers were British, and many of them paid in sterling. Since he heard the news he had been checking carefully every pound note before putting it into the till. His friend from the Metropolitan had told him how to spot the forgeries.

It was typical of the British. They did not make a public announcement to help the businessmen of Cairo to avoid being cheated. They simply sat back and confiscated the dud notes. The businessmen of Cairo were used to this kind of treatment, and they stuck together. The grapevine worked well.

When Ibrahim received the counterfeit notes from the tall European who was dining with the famous belly dancer, he was not sure what to do next. The notes were all crisp and new, and bore the identical fault. Ibrahim double-checked them against one of the good notes in his till: there was no doubt. Should he, perhaps, explain the matter quietly to the customer? The man might take offense, or at least pretend to; and he would probably leave without paying. His bill was a heavy one—he had taken the most expensive dishes, plus imported wine—and Ibrahim did not want to risk such a loss.

He would call the police, he decided. They would prevent the customer running off, and might help persuade him to pay by check, or at least leave an IOU.

But which police? The Egyptian police would probably argue that it was not their responsibility, take an hour to get here, and then require a bribe. The customer was presumably an Englishman—why else would he have sterling?—and was probably an officer, and it was British money that had been counterfeited. Ibrahim decided he would call the military.

He went over to their table, carrying the brandy bottle. He gave them a smile. "Monsieur, madame, I hope you have enjoyed your meal."

"It was excellent," said the man. He talked like a British officer.

Ibrahim turned to the woman. "It is an honor to serve the greatest dancer in the world."

She gave a regal nod.

Ibrahim said: "I hope you will accept a glass of brandy, with the compliments of the house."

"Very kind," said the man.

Ibrahim poured them more brandy and bowed away. That should keep them sitting still for a while longer, he thought. He left by the back door and went to the house of a neighbor who had a telephone.

～

If I had a restaurant, Wolff thought, I would do things like that. The two glasses of brandy cost the proprietor very little, in relation to Wolff's total bill, but the gesture was very effective in making the customer feel wanted. Wolff had often toyed with the idea of opening a restaurant, but it was a pipe dream: he knew there was too much hard work involved.

Sonja also enjoyed the special attention. She was positively glowing under the combined influences of flattery and liquor. Tonight in bed she would snore like a pig.

The proprietor had disappeared for a few minutes, then returned. Out of the corner of his eye, Wolff saw the man whispering to a waiter. He guessed they were talking about Sonja. Wolff felt a pang of jealousy. There were places in Cairo where, because of his good custom and lavish tips, he was known by name and welcomed like royalty; but he had thought it wise not to go to places where he would be recognized, not while the British were hunting him. Now he wondered whether he could afford to relax his vigilance a little more.

Sonja yawned. It was time to put her to bed. Wolff waved to a waiter and said: "Please fetch Madame's wrap." The man went off, paused to mutter something to the proprietor, then continued on toward the cloakroom.

An alarm bell sounded, fain and distant, somewhere in the back of Wolff's mind.

He toyed with a spoon as he waited for Sonja's wrap. Sonja ate another petit four. The proprietor walked the length of the restaurant, went out of the front door, and came back in again. He approached their table and said: "May I get you a taxi?"

Wolff looked at Sonja. She said: "I don't mind."

Wolff said: "I'd like a breath of air. Let's walk a little way, then hail one."

"Okay."

Wolff looked at the proprietor. "No taxi."

"Very good, sir."

The waiter brought Sonja's wrap. The proprietor kept looking at the door. Wolff heard another alarm bell, this one louder. He said to the proprietor: "Is something the matter?"

The man looked very worried. "I must mention an extremely delicate problem, sir."

Wolff began to get irritated. "Well, what is it, man? We want to go home."

There was the sound of a vehicle noisily drawing up outside the restaurant.

Wolff took hold of the proprietor's lapels. "What is going on here?"

"The money with which you paid your bill, sir, is not good."

"You don't accept sterling? Then why didn't—"

"It's not that, sir. The money is counterfeit."

The restaurant door burst open and three military policemen marched in.

Wolff stared at them openmouthed. It was all happening so quickly, he couldn't catch his breath . . . Military police. Counterfeit money. He was suddenly afraid. He might go to jail. Those imbeciles in Berlin had given him forged notes, it was so *stupid,* he wanted to take Canaris by the throat and *squeeze*—

He shook his head. There was no time to be angry now. He had to keep calm and try to slide out of this mess—

The MPs marched up to the table. Two were British and the third was Australian. They wore heavy boots and steel helmets, and each of them had a small gun in a belt holster. One of the British said: "Is this the man?"

"Just a moment," Wolff said, and was astonished at how cool and suave his voice sounded. "The proprietor has, this very minute, told me that my money is no good. I don't believe this, but I'm prepared to humor him, and I'm sure we can make some arrangement which will satisfy him." He gave the proprietor a reproachful look. "It really wasn't necessary to call the police."

The senior MP said: "It's an offense to pass forged money."

"Knowingly," Wolff said. "It is an offense *knowingly* to pass forged money." As he listened to his own voice, quiet and persuasive, his confidence grew. "Now, then, what I propose is this. I have here my checkbook and some Egyptian money. I will write a check to cover my bill, and use the Egyptian money for the tip. Tomorrow I will take the allegedly counterfeit notes to the British paymaster general for examination, and if they really are forgeries I will surrender them." He smiled at the group surrounding him. "I imagine that should satisfy everyone."

The proprietor said: "I would prefer if you could pay entirely in cash, sir."

Wolff wanted to hit him in the face.

Sonja said: "I may have enough Egyptian money."

Wolff thought: Thank God.

Sonja opened her bag.

The senior MP said: "All the same, sir, I'm going to ask you to come with me."

Wolff's heart sank again. "Why?"

"We'll need to ask you some questions."

"Fine. Why don't you call on me tomorrow morning. I live—"

"You'll have to come with me. Those are my orders."

"From whom?"

"The assistant provost marshal."

"Very well, then," said Wolff. He stood up. He could feel the fear pumping desperate strength into his arms. "But either you or the provost will be in very deep trouble in the morning." Then he picked up the table and threw it at the MP.

He had planned and calculated the move in a couple of seconds. It was a small circular table of solid wood. Its edge struck the MP on the bridge of the nose, and as he fell back the table landed on top of him.

Table and MP were on Wolff's left. On his right was the proprietor. Sonja was opposite him, still sitting, and the other two MPs were on either side of her and slightly behind her.

Wolff grabbed the proprietor and pushed him at one of the MPs. Then he jumped at the other MP, the Australian, and punched his face. He hoped to get past the two of them and run away. It did not work. The MPs were chosen for their size, belligerence and brutality, and they were used to dealing with soldiers desert-hardened and fighting drunk. The Australian took the punch and staggered back a pace, but he did not fall over. Wolff kicked him in the knee and punched his face again; then the other MP, the second Englishman, pushed the proprietor out of the way and kicked Wolff's feet from under him.

Wolff landed heavily. His chest and his cheek hit the tiled floor. His face stung, he was momentarily winded and he saw stars. He was kicked again, in the side; the pain made him jerk convulsively and roll away from the blow. The MP jumped on him, beating him about the head. He struggled to push the man off. Someone else sat on Wolff's feet. Then Wolff saw, above him and behind the English MP on his chest, Sonja's face, twisted with rage. The thought flashed through his mind that she was remembering another beating that had been administered by British soldiers. Then he saw that she was raising high in the air the chair she had been sitting on. The MP on Wolff's chest glimpsed her, turned around, looked up, and raised his arms to ward off the blow. She brought the heavy chair down with all her might. A corner of the seat struck the MP's mouth, and he gave a shout of pain and anger as blood spurted from his lips.

The Australian got off Wolff's feet and grabbed Sonja from behind, pinning her arms. Wolff flexed his body and threw off the wounded Englishman, then scrambled to his feet.

He reached inside his shirt and whipped out his knife.

The Australian threw Sonja aside, took a pace forward, saw the knife and stopped. He and Wolff stared into each other's eyes for an instant. Wolff saw the other man's eyes flicker to one side, then the other, seeing his two partners lying on the floor. The Australian's hand went to his holster.

Wolff turned and dashed for the door. One of his eyes was closing: he could not see well. The door was closed. He grabbed for the handle and missed. He felt like screaming. He found the handle and flung the door open wide. It hit the wall with a crash. A shot rang out.

ᴖ

Vandam drove the motorcycle through the streets at a dangerous speed. He had ripped the blackout mask off the headlight—nobody in Cairo took the blackout seriously anyway—and he drove with his thumb on the horn. The streets were still busy, with taxis, gharries, army trucks, donkeys and camels. The pavements were crowded and the shops were bright with electric lights, oil lamps and candles. Vandam weaved recklessly through the traffic, ignoring the outraged hooting of the cars, the raised fists of the gharry drivers, and the blown whistle of an Egyptian policeman.

The assistant provost marshal had called him at home. "Ah, Vandam, wasn't it you who sent up the balloon about this funny money? Because we've just had a call from a restaurant where a European is trying to pass—"

"*Where?*"

The APM gave him the address, and Vandam ran out of the house.

He skidded around a corner, dragging a heel in the dusty road for traction. It had occurred to him that, with so much counterfeit money in circulation, some of it must have got into the hands of other Europeans, and the man in the restaurant might well be an innocent victim. He hoped not. He wanted desperately to get his hands on Alex Wolff. Wolff had outwitted and humiliated him and now, with his access to secrets and his direct line to Rommel, he threatened to bring about the fall of Egypt; but it was not just that. Vandam was consumed with curiosity about Wolff. He wanted to see the man and touch him, to find out how he would move and speak. Was he clever, or just lucky? Courageous, or foolhardy? Determined, or stubborn? Did he have a handsome face and a warm smile, or beady eyes and an oily grin? Would he fight or come quietly? Vandam wanted to know. And, most of all, Vandam wanted to take him by the throat and drag him off to jail, chain him to the wall and lock the door and throw away the key.

He swerved to avoid a pothole, then opened the throttle and roared down a quiet street. The address was a little out of the city center, toward the Old Town: Vandam was acquainted with the street but not with the restaurant. He turned two more corners, and almost hit an old man riding an ass with his wife walking along behind. He found the street he was looking for.

It was narrow and dark, with high buildings on either side. At ground level there were some shop fronts and some house entrances. Vandam pulled up beside two small boys playing in the gutter and said the name of the restaurant. They pointed vaguely along the street.

Vandam cruised along, pausing to look wherever he noticed a lit window. He was half way down the street when he heard the *crack!* of a small firearm, slightly muffled, and the sound of glass shattering. His head jerked around toward the source of the noise. Light from a broken window glinted off shards of falling glass, and as he looked a tall man ran out of a door into the street.

It had to be Wolff.

He ran in the opposite direction.

Vandam felt a surge of savagery. He twisted the throttle of the motorcycle and roared after the running man. As he passed the restaurant an MP ran out and fired three shots. The fugitive's pace did not falter.

Vandam caught him in the beam of the headlight. He was running strongly, steadily, his arms and legs pumping rhythmically. When the light hit him he glanced back over his shoulder without breaking his stride, and Vandam glimpsed a hawk nose and a strong chin, and a mustache above a mouth open and panting.

Vandam could have shot him, but officers at GHQ did not carry guns.

The motorcycle gained fast. When they were almost level Wolff suddenly turned a corner. Vandam braked and went into a back-wheel skid, leaning the bike against the direction of the skid to keep his balance. He came to a stop, jerked upright and shot forward again.

He saw the back of Wolff disappear into a narrow alleyway. Without slowing down, Vandam turned the corner and drove into the alley. The bike shot out into empty space. Vandam's stomach turned over. The white cone of his headlight illuminated nothing. He thought he was falling into a pit. He gave an involuntary shout of fear. The back wheel hit something. The front wheel went down, down, then hit. The headlight showed a flight of steps. The bike bounced, and landed again. Vandam fought desperately to keep the front wheel straight. The bike descended the steps in a series of spine-jarring bumps, and with each bump Vandam was sure he would lose control and crash. He saw Wolff at the bottom of the stairs, still running.

Vandam reached the foot of the staircase and felt incredibly lucky. He saw Wolff turn another corner, and followed. They were in a maze of alleys. Wolff ran up a short flight of steps.

Vandam thought: Jesus, no.

He had no choice. He accelerated and headed squarely for the steps. A moment before hitting the bottom step he jerked the handlebars with all his might. The front wheel lifted. The bike hit the steps, bucked like a wild thing and tried to throw him. He hung on grimly. The bike bumped crazily up. Vandam fought it. He reached the top.

He found himself in a long passage with high, blank walls on either side. Wolff was still in front of him, still running. Vandam thought he could catch him before Wolff reached the end of the passage. He shot forward.

Wolff looked back over his shoulder, ran on, and looked again. His pace was flagging, Vandam could see. His stride was no longer steady and rhythmic: his arms flew out to either side and he ran raggedly. Glimpsing Wolff's face, Vandam saw that it was taut with strain.

Wolff put on a burst of speed, but it was not enough. Vandam drew level, eased ahead, then braked sharply and twisted the handlebars. The back wheel skidded and the front wheel hit the wall. Vandam leaped off as the bike fell to the ground. Vandam landed on his feet, facing Wolff. The smashed headlight threw a shaft of light into the darkness of the passage.

There was no point in Wolff's turning and running the other way, for Vandam was fresh and could easily catch him. Without pausing in his stride Wolff jumped over the bike, his body passing through the pillar of light from the headlight like a knife slicing a flame, and crashed into Vandam. Vandam, still unsteady, stumbled backward and fell. Wolff staggered and took another step forward. Vandam reached out blindly in the dark, found Wolff's ankle, gripped and yanked. Wolff crashed to the ground.

The broken headlight gave a little light to the rest of the alley. The engine of the bike had cut out, and in the silence Vandam could hear Wolff's breathing, ragged and hoarse. He could smell him, too: a smell of booze and perspiration and fear. But he could not see his face.

There was a split second when the two of them lay on the ground, one exhausted and the other momentarily stunned. Then they both scrambled to their feet. Vandam jumped at Wolff, and they grappled.

Wolff was strong. Vandam tried to pin his arms, but he could not hold on to him. Suddenly he let go and threw a punch. It landed somewhere soft, and Wolff said: "Ooff." Vandam punched again, this time aiming for the face; but Wolff dodged, and the fist hit empty space. Suddenly something in Wolff's hand glinted in the dim light.

Vandam thought: A knife!

The blade flashed toward his throat. He jerked back reflexively. There was a searing pain all across his cheek. His hand flew to his face. He felt a gush of hot blood. Suddenly the pain was unbearable. He pressed on the wound and his fingers touched something hard. He realized he was feeling his own teeth, and that the knife had sliced right through the flesh of his cheek; and then he felt himself falling, and he heard Wolff running away, and everything turned black.

13

Wolff took a handkerchief from his trousers pocket and wiped the blood from the blade of the knife. He examined the blade in the dim light, then wiped it again. He walked along, polishing the thin steel vigorously. He stopped, and thought: What am I doing? It's clean already. He threw away the handkerchief and replaced the knife in the sheath under his arm. He emerged from the alley into a street, got his bearings, and headed for the Old City.

He imagined a prison cell. It was six feet long by four feet wide, and half of it was taken up by a bed. Beneath the bed was a chamber pot. The walls were of smooth gray stone. A small light bulb hung from the ceiling by a cord. In one end of the cell was a door. In the other end was a small square window, set just above eye level: through it he could see the bright blue sky. He imagined that he woke up in the morning and saw all this, and remembered that he had been here for a year, and he would be here for another nine years. He used the chamberpot, then washed his hands in the tin bowl in the corner. There was no soap. A dish of cold porridge was pushed through the hatch in the door. He picked up the spoon and took a mouthful, but he was unable to swallow, for he was weeping.

He shook his head to clear it of nightmare visions. He thought: I got away, didn't I? *I got away.* He realized that some of the people on the street were staring at him as they passed. He saw a mirror in a shop window, and examined himself in it. His hair was awry, one side of his face was bruised and swollen, his sleeve was ripped and there was blood on his collar. He was still panting from the exertion of running and fighting. He thought: I look dangerous. He walked on, and turned at the next corner to take an indirect route which would avoid the main streets.

Those imbeciles in Berlin had given him counterfeit money! No wonder they were so generous with it—they were printing it themselves. It was so foolish that Wolff wondered if it might be more than foolishness. The Abwehr was run by the military, not by the Nazi Party; its chief, Canaris, was not the staunchest of Hitler's supporters.

When I get back to Berlin there will be such a purge . . .

How had it caught up with him, here in Cairo? He had been spending money fast. The forgeries had got into circulation. The banks had spotted the dud notes—no, not the banks, the paymaster general. Anyway, someone had begun to refuse the money, and word had got around Cairo. The proprietor of the restaurant had noticed that Wolff's money was fake and had called the military. Wolff grinned ruefully to himself when he recalled how flattered he had been by the proprietor's complimentary brandy—it had been no more than a ruse to keep him there until the MPs arrived.

He thought about the man on the motorcycle. He must be a determined bastard, to ride the bike around those alleys and up and down the steps. He had no gun, Wolff guessed: if he had, he would surely have used it. Nor had he a tin hat, so presumably he was not an MP. Someone from Intelligence, perhaps? Major Vandam, even?

Wolff hoped so.

I cut the man, he thought. Quite badly, probably. I wonder where? The face?

I hope it was Vandam.

He turned his mind to his immediate problem. They had Sonja. She would tell them she hardly knew Wolff—she would make up some story about a quick pickup in the Cha-Cha Club. They would not be able to hold her for long, because she was famous, a star, a kind of hero among the Egyptians, and to imprison her would cause a great deal of trouble. So they would let her go quite soon. However, she would have to give them her address; which meant that Wolff could not go back to the houseboat, not yet. But he was exhausted, bruised and disheveled: he had to clean himself up and get a few hours' rest, somewhere.

He thought: I've been here before—wandering the city, tired and hunted, with nowhere to go.

This time he would have to fall back on Abdullah.

He had been heading for the Old City, knowing all along, in the back of his mind, that Abdullah was all he had left; and now he found himself a few steps from the old thief's house. He ducked under an arch, went along a short dark passage and climbed a stone spiral staircase to Abdullah's home.

Abdullah was sitting on the floor with another man. A nargileh stood between them, and the air was full of the herbal smell of hashish. Abdullah looked up at Wolff and gave a slow, sleepy smile. He spoke in Arabic. "Here is my friend Achmed, also called Alex. Welcome, Achmed-Alex."

Wolff sat on the floor with them and greeted them in Arabic.

Abdullah said: "My brother Yasef here would like to ask you a riddle, something that has been puzzling him and me for some hours now, ever since we started the hubble-bubble, speaking of which . . ." He passed the pipe across, and Wolff took a lungful.

Yasef said: "Achmed-Alex, friend of my brother, welcome. Tell me this: Why do the British call us wogs?"

Yasef and Abdullah collapsed into giggles. Wolff realized they were heavily under the influence of hashish: they must have been smoking all evening. He drew on the pipe again, and pushed it over to Yasef. It was strong stuff. Abdullah always had the best. Wolff said: "As it happens, I know the answer.

Egyptian men working on the Suez Canal were issued with special shirts, to show that they had the right to be on British property. They were Working On Government Service, so on the backs of their shirts were printed the letters W.O.G.S."

Yasef and Abdullah giggled all over again. Abdullah said: "My friend Achmed-Alex is clever. He is as clever as an Arab, almost, because he is almost an Arab. He is the only European who has ever got the better of me, Abdullah."

"I believe this to be untrue," Wolff said, slipping into their stoned style of speech. "I would never try to outwit my friend Abdullah, for who can cheat the devil?"

Yasef smiled and nodded his appreciation of this witticism.

Abdullah said: "Listen, my brother, and I will tell you." He frowned, collecting his doped thoughts. "Achmed-Alex asked me to steal something for him. That way I would take the risk and he would get the reward. Of course, he did not outwit me so simply. I stole the thing—it was a case—and of course my intention was to take its contents for myself, since the thief is entitled to the proceeds of his crime, according to the laws of God. Therefore I should have outwitted him, should I not?"

"Indeed," said Yasef, "although I do not recall the passage of Holy Scripture which says that a thief is entitled to the proceeds of his crime. However . . ."

"Perhaps not," said Abdullah. "Of what was I speaking?"

Wolff, who was still more or less compos mentis, told him: "You should have outwitted me, because you opened the case yourself."

"Indeed! But wait. There was nothing of value in the case, so Achmed-Alex had outwitted me. But wait! I made him pay me for rendering this service; therefore I got one hundred pounds and he got nothing."

Yasef frowned. "You, then, got the better of him."

"No." Abdullah shook his head sadly. "He paid me in forged banknotes."

Yasef stared at Abdullah. Abdullah stared back. They both burst out laughing. They slapped each other's shoulders, stamped their feet on the floor and rolled around on the cushions, laughing until the tears came to their eyes.

Wolff forced a smile. It was just the kind of funny story that appealed to Arab businessmen, with its chain of double crosses. Abdullah would be telling it for years. But it sent a chill through Wolff. So Abdullah, too, knew about the counterfeit notes. How many others did? Wolff felt as if the hunting pack had formed a circle around him, so that every way he ran he came up against one of them, and the circle drew tighter every day.

Abdullah seemed to notice Wolff's appearance for the first time. He immediately became very concerned. "What has happened to you? Have you been robbed?" He picked up a tiny silver bell and rang it. Almost immediately, a sleepy woman came in from the next room. "Get some hot water," Abdullah told her. "Bathe my friend's wounds. Give him my European shirt. Bring a comb. Bring coffee. Quickly!"

In a European house Wolff would have protested at the women being roused, after midnight, to attend to him; but here such a protest would have been very discourteous. The women existed to serve the men, and they would be neither surprised nor annoyed by Abdullah's peremptory demands.

Wolff explained: "The British tried to arrest me, and I was obliged to fight with them before I could get away. Sadly, I think they may now know where I have been living, and this is a problem."

"Ah." Abdullah drew on the nargileh, and passed it around again. Wolff began to feel the effects of the hashish: he was relaxed, slow-thinking, a little sleepy. Time slowed down. Two of Abdullah's wives fussed over him, bathing his face and combing his hair. He found their ministrations very pleasant indeed.

Abdullah seemed to doze for a while, then he opened his eyes and said: "You must stay here. My house is yours. I will hide you from the British."

"You are a true friend," Wolff said. It was odd, he thought. He had planned to offer Abdullah money to hide him. Then Abdullah had revealed that he knew the money was no good, and Wolff had been wondering what else he could do. Now Abdullah was going to hide him for nothing. A true friend.

What was odd was that Abdullah was not a true friend. There were no friends in Abdullah's world: there was the family, for whom he would do anything, and the rest, for whom he would do nothing. How have I earned this special treatment? Wolff thought sleepily.

His alarm bell was sounding again. He forced himself to think: it was not easy after the hashish. Take it one step at a time, he told himself. Abdullah asks me to stay here. Why? Because I am in trouble. Because I am his friend. Because I have outwitted him.

Because I have outwitted him. That story was not finished. Abdullah would want to add another double cross to the chain. How? By betraying Wolff to the British. That was it. As soon as Wolff fell asleep, Abdullah would send a message to Major Vandam. Wolff would be picked up. The British would pay Abdullah for the information, and the story could be told to Abdullah's credit at last.

Damn.

A wife brought a white European shirt. Wolff stood up and took off his torn and bloody shirt. The wife averted her eyes from his bare chest.

Abdullah said: "He doesn't need it yet. Give it to him in the morning."

Wolff took the shirt from the woman and put it on.

Abdullah said: "Perhaps it would be undignified for you to sleep in the house of an Arab, my friend Achmed?"

Wolff said: "The British have a proverb: He who sups with the devil must use a long spoon."

Abdullah grinned, showing his steel tooth. He knew that Wolff had guessed his plan. "Almost an Arab," he said.

"Good-bye, my friends," said Wolff.

"Until the next time," Abdullah replied.

Wolff went out into the cold night, wondering where he could go now.

～

In the hospital a nurse froze half of Vandam's face with a local anesthetic, then Dr. Abuthnot stitched up his cheek with her long, sensitive, clinical hands. She put on a protective dressing and secured it by a long strip of bandage tied around his head.

"I must look like a toothache cartoon," he said.

She looked grave. She did not have a big sense of humor. She said: "You won't be so chirpy when the anesthetic wears off. Your face is going to hurt badly. I'm going to give you a pain-killer."

"No, thanks," said Vandam.

"Don't be a tough guy, Major," she said. "You'll regret it."

He looked at her, in her white hospital coat and her sensible flat-heeled shoes, and wondered how he had ever found her even faintly desirable. She was pleasant enough, even pretty, but she was also cold, superior and antiseptic. Not like—

Not like Elene.

"A pain-killer will send me to sleep," he told her.

"And a jolly good thing, too," she said. "If you sleep we can be sure the stitches will be undisturbed for a few hours."

"I'd love to, but I have some important work that won't wait."

"You can't *work*. You shouldn't really walk around. You should talk as little as possible. You're weak from loss of blood, and a wound like this is mentally as well as physically traumatic—in a few hours you'll feel the backlash, and you'll be dizzy, nauseous, exhausted and confused."

"I'll be worse if the Germans take Cairo," he said. He stood up.

Dr. Abuthnot looked cross. Vandam thought how well it suited her to be in a position to tell people what to do. She was not sure how to handle outright disobedience. "You're a silly boy," she said.

"No doubt. Can I eat?"

"No. Take glucose dissolved in warm water."

I might try it in warm gin, he thought. He shook her hand. It was cold and dry.

Jakes was waiting outside the hospital with a car. "I knew they wouldn't be able to keep you long, sir," he said. "Shall I drive you home?"

"No." Vandam's watch had stopped. "What's the time?"

"Five past two."

"I presume Wolff wasn't dining alone."

"No, sir. His companion is under arrest at GHQ."

"Drive me there."

"If you're sure . . ."

"Yes."

The car pulled away. Vandam said: "Have you notified the hierarchy?"

"About this evening's events? No, sir."

"Good. Tomorrow will be soon enough." Vandam did not say what they both knew: that the department, already under a cloud for letting Wolff gather intelligence, would be in utter disgrace for letting him slip through their fingers.

Vandam said: "I presume Wolff's dinner date was a woman."

"Very much so, if I may say so, sir. A real dish. Name of Sonja."

"The dancer?"

"No less."

They drove on in silence. Wolff was a cool customer, Vandam thought, to go out with the most famous belly dancer in Egypt in between stealing British military secrets. Well, he would not be so cool now. That was unfortunate in a way: having been warned by this incident that the British were on to him, he would be more careful from now on. Never scare them, just catch them.

They arrived at GHQ and got out of the car. Vandam said: "What's been done with her since she arrived?"

"The no-treatment treatment," Jakes said. "A bare cell, no food, no drink, no questions."

"Good." It was a pity, all the same, that she had been given time to collect her thoughts. Vandam knew from prisoner-of-war interrogations that the best results were achieved immediately after the capture, when the prisoner was still frightened of being killed. Later on, when he had been herded here and there and given food and drink, he began to think of himself as a prisoner rather than as a soldier, and remembered that he had new rights and duties; and then he was better able to keep his mouth shut. Vandam should have interviewed Sonja immediately after the fight in the restaurant. As that was not possible, the next best thing was for her to be kept in isolation and given no information until he arrived.

Jakes led the way along a corridor to the interview room. Vandam looked in through the judas. It was a square room, without windows but bright with electric light. There were a table, two upright chairs and an ashtray. To one side was a doorless cubicle with a toilet.

Sonja sat on one of the chairs facing the door. Jakes was right, Vandam thought; she's a dish. However she was by no means *pretty*. She was something of an Amazon, with her ripe, voluptuous body and strong, well-proportioned features. The young women in Egypt generally had a slender, leggy grace, like downy young deer: Sonja was more like . . . Vandam frowned, then thought: a tigress. She wore a long gown of bright yellow which was garish to Vandam but would be quite *à la mode* in the Cha-Cha Club. He watched her for a minute or two. She was sitting quite still, not fidgeting, not darting nervous glances around the bare cell, not smoking or biting her nails. He thought: She will be a tough nut to crack. Then the expression on her handsome face changed, and she stood up and began pacing up and down, and Vandam thought: Not so tough.

He opened the door and went in.

He sat down at the table without speaking. This left her standing, which was a psychological disadvantage for a woman: Score the first point to me, he thought. He heard Jakes come in behind him and close the door. He looked up at Sonja. "Sit down."

She stood gazing at him, and a slow smile spread across her face. She pointed at his bandages. "Did he do that to you?" she said.

Score the second point to her.

"Sit down."

"Thank you." She sat.

"Who is 'he'?"

"Alex Wolff, the man you *tried* to beat up tonight."

"And who is Alex Wolff?"

"A wealthy patron of the Cha-Cha Club."

"How long have you known him?"

She looked at her watch. "Five hours."

"What is your relationship with him?"

She shrugged. "He was a date."

"How did you meet?"

"The usual way. After my act, a waiter brought a message inviting me to sit at Mr. Wolff's table."

'Which one?"

"Which table?"

"Which *waiter*."

"I don't remember."

"Go on."

"Mr. Wolff gave me a glass of champagne and asked me to have dinner with him. I accepted, we went to the restaurant, and you know the rest."

"Do you usually sit with members of the audience after your act?"

"Yes, it's a custom."

"Do you usually go to dinner with them?"

"Occasionally."

"Why did you accept this time?"

"Mr. Wolff seemed like an unusual sort of man." She looked at Vandam's bandage again, and grinned. "He was an unusual sort of man."

"What is your full name?"

"Sonja el-Aram."

"Address?"

"*Jihan*, Zamalek. It's a houseboat."

"Age?"

"How discourteous."

"Age?"

"I refuse to answer."

"You're on dangerous ground—"

"No, *you* are on dangerous ground." Suddenly she startled Vandam by letting her feelings show, and he realized that all this time she had been suppressing a fury. She wagged a finger in his face. "At least ten people saw your uniformed bullies arrest me in the restaurant. By midday tomorrow half of Cairo will know that the British have put Sonja in jail. If I don't appear at the Cha-Cha tomorrow night there will be a riot. My people will burn the city. You'll have to bring troops back from the desert to deal with it. And if I leave here with a single bruise or scratch, I'll show it to the world onstage tomorrow night, and the result will be the same. No, mister, it isn't me who's on dangerous ground."

Vandam looked at her blankly throughout the tirade, then spoke as if she had said nothing extraordinary. He had to ignore what she said, because she was right, and he could not deny it. "Let's go over this again," he said mildly. "You say you met Wolff at the Cha-Cha—"

"No," she interrupted. "I won't go over it again. I'll cooperate with you, and I'll answer questions, but I will not be interrogated." She stood up, turned her chair around, and sat down with her back to Vandam.

Vandam stared at the back of her head for a moment. She had well and truly outmaneuvered him. He was angry with himself for letting it happen, but his anger was mixed with a sneaking admiration for her for the way she had done it. Abruptly, he got up and left the room. Jakes followed.

Out in the corridor Jakes said: "What do you think?"

"We'll have to let her go."

Jakes went to give instructions. While he waited, Vandam thought about Sonja. He wondered from what source she had been drawing the strength to defy him. Whether her story was true or false, she should have been frightened, confused, intimidated and ultimately compliant. It was true that her fame gave her some protection; but, in threatening him with her fame, she ought to have been blustering, unsure and a little desperate, for an isolation cell normally frightened anyone—especially celebrities, because the sudden excommunication from the familiar glittering world made them wonder even more than usually whether that familiar glittering world could possibly be real.

What gave her strength? He ran over the conversation in his mind. The question she had balked at had been the one about her age. Clearly her talent had enabled her to keep going past the age at which run-of-the-mill dancers retired, so perhaps she was living in fear of the passing years. No clues there. Otherwise she had been calm, expressionless and blank, except when she had smiled at his wound. Then, at the end, she had allowed herself to explode, but even then she had used her fury, she had not been controlled by it. He called to mind her face as she had raged at him. What had he seen there? Not just anger. Not fear.

Then he had it. It had been hatred.

She hated him. But he was nothing to her, nothing but a British officer. Therefore she hated the British. And her hatred had given her strength.

Suddenly Vandam was tired. He sat down heavily on a bench in the corridor. From where was *he* to draw strength? It was easy to be strong if you were insane, and in Sonja's hatred there had been a hint of something a little crazy. He had no such refuge. Calmly, rationally, he considered what was at stake. He imagined the Nazis marching into Cairo; the Gestapo in the streets; the Egyptian Jews herded into concentration camps; the Fascist propaganda on the wireless . . .

People like Sonja looked at Egypt under British rule and felt that the Nazis had already arrived. It was not true, but if one tried for a moment to see the British through Sonja's eyes it had a certain plausibility: the Nazis said that Jews were sub-human, and the British said that blacks were like children; there was no freedom of the press in Germany, but there was none in Egypt either; and the British, like the Germans, had their political police. Before the war Vandam had sometimes heard Hitler's politics warmly endorsed in the officers' mess: they disliked him, not because he was a Fascist, but because he had been a corporal in the Army and a house painter in civilian life. There were brutes everywhere, and sometimes they got into power, and then you had to fight them.

It was a more rational philosophy than Sonja's, but it just was not inspirational.

The anesthetic in his face was wearing off. He could feel a sharp, clear line of pain across his cheek, like a new burn. He realized he also had a headache. He hoped Jakes would be a long time arranging Sonja's release, so that he could sit on the bench a little while longer.

He thought of Billy. He did not want the boy to miss him at breakfast. Perhaps I'll stay awake until morning, then take him to school, then go home and sleep, he thought. What would Billy's life be like under the Nazis? They would teach him to despise the Arabs. His present teachers were no great admirers of African culture, but at least Vandam could do a little to make his son realize that people who were different were not necessarily stupid. What would happen in the Nazi classroom when he put up his hand and said: "Please, sir, my dad says a dumb Englishman is no smarter than a dumb Arab"?

He thought of Elene. Now she was a kept woman, but at least she could choose her lovers, and if she didn't like what they wanted to do in bed she could kick them out. In the brothel of a concentration camp she would have no such choice . . . He shuddered.

Yes. We're not very admirable, especially in our colonies, but the Nazis are worse, whether the Egyptians know it or not. It is worth fighting. In England decency is making slow progress; in Germany it's taking a big step backward. Think about the people you love, and the issues become clearer.

Draw strength from that. Stay awake a little longer. Stand up.

He stood up.

Jakes came back.

Vandam said: "She's an Anglophobe."

"I beg your pardon, sir?"

"Sonja. She hates the British. I don't believe Wolff was a casual pickup. Let's go."

They walked out of the building together. Outside it was still dark. Jakes said: "Sir, you're very tired—"

"Yes. I'm very tired. But I'm still thinking straight, Jakes. Take me to the main police station."

"Sir."

They pulled away. Vandam handed his cigarette case and lighter to Jakes, who drove one-handed while he lit Vandam's cigarette. Vandam had trouble sucking: he could hold the cigarette between his lips and breathe the smoke, but he could not draw on it hard enough to light it. Jakes handed him the lit cigarette. Vandam thought: I'd like a martini to go with it.

Jakes stopped the car outside police headquarters. Vandam said: "We want the chief of detectives, whatever they call him."

"I shouldn't think he'll be there at this hour—"

"No. Get his address. We'll wake him up."

Jakes went into the building. Vandam stared ahead through the windshield. Dawn was on its way. The stars had winked out, and now the sky was gray rather than black. There were a few people about. He saw a man leading two donkeys loaded with vegetables, presumably going to market. The muezzins had not yet called the first prayer of the day.

Jakes came back. "Gezira," he said as he put the car in gear and let in the clutch.

Vandam thought about Jakes. Someone had told Vandam that Jakes had a terrific sense of humor. Vandam had always found him pleasant and cheerful, but he had never seen any evidence of actual humor. Am I such a tyrant, Vandam thought, that my staff are terrified of cracking a joke in my presence? Nobody makes me laugh, he thought.

Except Elene.

"You never tell *me* jokes, Jakes."

"Sir?"

"They say you have a terrific sense of humor, but you never tell me jokes."

"No, sir."

"Would you care to be candid for a moment and tell me why?"

There was a pause, then Jakes said: "You don't invite familiarity, sir."

Vandam nodded. How would they know how much he liked to throw back his head and roar with laughter? He said: "Very tactfully put, Jakes. The subject is closed."

The Wolff business is getting to me, he thought. I wonder whether perhaps I've never really been any good at my job, and then I wonder if I'm any good for anything at all. And my face hurts.

They crossed the bridge to the island. The sky turned from slate-gray to pearl. Jakes said: "I'd like to say, sir, that, if you'll pardon me, you're far and away the best superior officer I've ever had."

"Oh." Vandam was quite taken aback. "Good Lord. Well, thank you, Jakes. Thank you."

"Not at all, sir. We're there."

He stopped the car outside a small, pretty single-story house with a well-watered garden. Vandam guessed that the chief of detectives was doing well enough out of his bribes, but not too well. A cautious man, perhaps: it was a good sign.

They walked up the path and hammered on the door. After a couple of minutes a head looked out of a window and spoke in Arabic.

Jakes put on his sergeant major's voice. "Military Intelligence—open up the bloody door!"

A minute later a small, handsome Arab opened up, still belting his trousers. He said in English: "What's going on?"

Vandam took charge. "An emergency. Let us in, will you?"

"Of course." The detective stood aside and they entered. He led them into a small living room. "What has happened?" He seemed frightened, and Vandam thought: Who wouldn't be? The knock on the door in the middle of the night . . .

Vandam said: "There's nothing to panic about, but we want you to set up a surveillance, and we need it right away."

"Of course. Please sit down." The detective found a notebook and pencil. "Who is the subject?"

"Sonja el-Aram."

"The dancer?"

"Yes. I want you to put a twenty-four-hour watch on her home, which is a houseboat called *Jihan* in Zamalek."

As the detective wrote down the details, Vandam wished he did not have to use the Egyptian police for this work. However, he had no choice: it was impossible, in an African country, to use conspicuous, white-skinned, English-speaking people for surveillance.

The detective said: "And what is the nature of the crime?"

I'm not telling *you*, Vandam thought. He said: "We think

she may be an associate of whoever is passing counterfeit sterling in Cairo."

"So you want to know who comes and goes, whether they carry anything, whether meetings are held aboard the boat . . ."

"Yes. And there is a particular man that we're interested in. He is Alex Wolff, the man suspected of the Assyut knife murder; you should have his description already."

"Of course. Daily reports?"

"Yes, except that if Wolff is seen I want to know immediately. You can reach Captain Jakes or me at GHQ during the day. Give him our home phone numbers, Jakes."

"I know these houseboats," the detective said. "The towpath is a popular evening walk, I think, especially for sweethearts."

Jakes said: "That's right."

Vandam raised an eyebrow at Jakes.

The detective went on: "A good place, perhaps, for a beggar to sit. Nobody ever sees a beggar. At night . . . well, there are bushes. Also popular with sweethearts."

Vandam said: "Is that right, Jakes?"

"I wouldn't know, sir." He realized he was being ribbed, and he smiled. He gave the detective a piece of paper with the phone numbers written on it.

A little boy in pajamas walked into the room, rubbing his eyes. He was about five or six years old. He looked around the room sleepily, then went to the detective.

"My son," the detective said proudly.

"I think we can leave you now," Vandam said. "Unless you want us to drop you in the city?"

"No, thank you, I have a car, and I should like to put on my jacket and tie and comb my hair."

"Very well, but make it fast." Vandam stood up. Suddenly he could not see straight. It was as if his eyelids were closing involuntarily, yet he knew he had his eyes wide open. He felt himself losing his balance. Then Jakes was beside him, holding his arm.

"All right, sir?"

His vision returned slowly. "All right now," he said.

"You've had a nasty injury," the detective said sympathetically.

They went to the door. The detective said: "Gentlemen, be assured that I will handle this surveillance personally. They won't get a mouse aboard that houseboat without your knowing it." He was still holding the little boy, and now he shifted him on to his left hip and held out his right hand.

"Good-bye," Vandam said. He shook hands. "By the way, I'm Major Vandam."

The detective gave a little bow. "Superintendent Kemel, at your service, sir."

14

Sonja brooded. She had half expected Wolff to be at the house-boat when she returned toward dawn, but she had found the place cold and empty. She was not sure how she felt about that. At first, when they had arrested her, she had felt nothing but rage toward Wolff for running away and leaving her at the mercy of the British thugs. Being alone, being a woman and being an accomplice of sorts in Wolff's spying, she was terrified of what they might do to her. She thought Wolff should have stayed to look after her. Then she had realized that that would not have been smart. By abandoning her he had diverted suspicion away from her. It was hard to take, but it was for the best. Sitting alone in the bare little room at GHQ, she had turned her anger away from Wolff and toward the British.

She had defied them, and they had backed down.

At the time she had not been sure that the man who interrogated her had been Major Vandam, but later, when she was being released, the clerk had let the name slip. The confirmation had delighted her. She smiled again when she thought of the grotesque bandage on Vandam's face. Wolff must have cut him with the knife. He should have killed him. But all the same, what a night, what a glorious night!

She wondered where Wolff was now. He would have gone to ground somewhere in the city. He would emerge when he thought the coast was clear. There was nothing she could do. She would have liked him here, though, to share the triumph.

She put on her nightdress. She knew she ought to go to bed, but she did not feel sleepy. Perhaps a drink would help. She found a bottle of scotch whiskey, poured some into a glass, and added water. As she was tasting it she heard footsteps on the gangplank. Without thinking she called: "Achmed . . . ?" Then she realized the step was not his, it was too light and quick. She stood at the foot of the ladder in her nightdress, with the drink in her hand. The hatch was lifted and an Arab face looked in.

"Sonja?"

"Yes—"

"You were expecting someone else, I think." The man climbed down the ladder. Sonja watched him, thinking: What now? He stepped off the ladder and stood in front of her. He was a small man with a handsome face and quick, neat movements. He wore European clothes: dark trousers, polished black shoes and a short-sleeved white shirt. "I am Detective Superintendent Kemel, and I am honored to meet you." He held out his hand.

Sonja turned away, walked across to the divan and sat down. She thought she had dealt with the police. Now the Egyptians wanted to get in on the act. It would probably come down to a bribe in the end, she reassured herself. She sipped her drink, staring at Kemel. Finally she said: "What do you want?"

Kemel sat down uninvited. "I am interested in your friend, Alex Wolff."

"He's not my friend."

Kemel ignored that. "The British have told me two things about Mr. Wolff: one, that he knifed a soldier in Assyut; two, that he tried to pass counterfeit English banknotes in a restaurant in Cairo. Already the story is a little curious. Why was he in Assyut? Why did he kill the soldier? And where did he get the forged money?"

"I don't know anything about the man," said Sonja, hoping he would not come home right now.

"I do, though," said Kemel. "I have other information that the British may or may not possess. I know who Alex Wolff is. His stepfather was a lawyer, here in Cairo. His mother was German. I know, too, that Wolff is a nationalist. I know that he used to be your lover. And I know that you are a nationalist."

Sonja had gone cold. She sat still, her drink untouched, watching the sly detective unreel the evidence against her. She said nothing.

Kemel went on: "Where did he get the forged money? Not in Egypt. I don't think there is a printer in Egypt capable of doing the work; and if there were, I think he would make Egyptian currency. Therefore the money came from Europe. Now Wolff, also known as Achmed Rahmha, quietly disappeared a couple of years ago. Where did he go? Europe? He came back—via Assyut. Why? Did he want to sneak into the country unnoticed? Perhaps he teamed up with an English counterfeiting gang, and has now returned with his share of the profits; but I don't think so, for he is not a poor man, nor is he a criminal. So, there is a mystery."

He knows, Sonja thought. Dear God, he knows.

"Now the British have asked me to put a watch on this houseboat, and tell them of everyone who comes and goes here. Wolff will come here, they hope; and then they will arrest him; and then they will have the answers. Unless I solve the puzzle first."

A watch on the boat! He could never come back. But—but why, she thought, is Kemel telling me?

"The key, I think, lies in Wolff's nature: he is both a German and an Egyptian." Kemel stood up, and crossed the floor to sit beside Sonja and look into her face. "I think he is fighting in this war. I think he is fighting for Germany and for Egypt. I think the forged money comes from the Germans. I think Wolff is a spy."

Sonja thought: But you don't know where to find him. That's why you're here. Kemel was staring at her. She looked away, afraid that he might read her thoughts in her face.

Kemel said: "If he is a spy, I can catch him. Or I can save him."

Sonja jerked her head around to look at him. "What does that mean?"

"I want to meet him. Secretly."

"But why?"

Kemel smiled his sly, knowing smile. "Sonja, you are not the only one who wants Egypt to be free. There are many of us. We want to see the British defeated, and we are not fastidious about who does the defeating. We want to work with the Germans. We want to contact them. We want to talk to Rommel."

"And you think Achmed can help you?"

"If he is a spy, he must have a way of getting messages to the Germans."

Sonja's mind was in a turmoil. From being her accuser, Kemel had turned into a co-conspirator—unless this was a trap. She did not know whether to trust him or not. She did not have enough time to think about it. She did not know what to say, so she said nothing.

Kemel persisted gently. "Can you arrange a meeting?"

She could not possibly make such a decision on the spur of the moment. "No," she said.

"Remember the watch on the houseboat," he said. "The surveillance reports will come to me before being passed on to Major Vandam. If there is a chance, just a chance, that you might be able to arrange a meeting, I in turn can make sure that the reports which go to Vandam are carefully edited so as to contain nothing . . . embarrassing."

Sonja had forgotten the surveillance. When Wolff came back—and he would, sooner or later—the watchers would report it, and Vandam would know, unless Kemel fixed it. This changed everything. She had no choice. "I'll arrange a meeting," she said.

"Good." He stood up. "Call the main police station and

leave a message saying that Sirhan wants to see me. When I get that message I'll contact you to arrange date and time."

"Very well."

He went to the ladder, then came back. "By the way." He took a wallet from his trousers pocket and extracted a small photograph. He handed it to Sonja. It was a picture of her. "Would you sign this for my wife? She's a great fan of yours." He handed her a pen. "Her name is Hesther."

Sonja wrote: "To Hesther, with all good wishes, Sonja." She gave him the photograph, thinking: This is incredible.

"Thank you so much. She will be overjoyed."

Incredible.

Sonja said: "I'll get in touch just as soon as I can."

"Thank you." He held out his hand. This time she shook it. He went up the ladder and out, closing the hatch behind him.

Sonja relaxed. Somehow she had handled it right. She was still not completely convinced of Kemel's sincerity; but if there was a trap she could not see it.

She felt tired. She finished the whiskey in the glass, then went through the curtains into the bedroom. She still had her nightdress on, and she was quite cold. She went to the bed and pulled back the covers. She heard a tapping sound. Her heart missed a beat. She whirled around to look at the porthole on the far side of the boat, the side that faced across the river. There was a head behind the glass.

She screamed.

The face disappeared.

She realized it had been Wolff.

She ran up the ladder and out on to the deck. Looking over the side, she saw him in the water. He appeared to be naked. He clambered up the side of the little boat, using the portholes for handholds. She reached for his arm and pulled him on to the deck. He knelt there on all fours for a moment, glancing up and down the river bank like an alert water rat; then he scampered down the hatch. She followed him.

He stood on the carpet, dripping and shivering. He *was* naked. She said: "What happened?"

"Run me a bath," he said.

She went through the bedroom into the bathroom. There was a small tub with an electric water heater. She turned the taps on and threw a handful of scented crystals into the water. Wolff got in and let the water rise around him.

"What happened?" Sonja repeated.

He controlled his shivering. "I didn't want to risk coming down the towpath, so I took off my clothes on the opposite bank and swam across. I looked in, and saw that man with you—I suppose he was another policeman."

"Yes."

"So I had to wait in the water until he went away."

She laughed. "You poor thing."

"It's not funny. My God, I'm cold. The fucking Abwehr gave me dud money. Somebody will be strangled for that, next time I'm in Germany."

"Why did they do it?"

"I don't know whether it's incompetence or disloyalty. Canaris has always been lukewarm on Hitler. Turn off the water, will you?" He began to wash the river mud off his legs.

"You'll have to use your own money," she said.

"I can't get at it. You can be sure the bank has instructions to call the police the moment I show my face. I could pay the occasional bill by check, but even that might help them get a line on me. I could sell some of my stocks and shares, or even the villa, but there again the money has to come through a bank . . ."

So you will have to use my money, Sonja thought. You won't ask, though: you'll just take it. She filed the thought for further consideration. "That detective is putting a watch on the boat—on Vandam's instructions."

Wolff grinned. "So it was Vandam."

"Did you cut him?"

"Yes, but I wasn't sure where. It was dark."

"The face. He had a huge bandage."

Wolff laughed aloud. "I wish I could see him." He became sober, and asked: "Did he question you?"

"Yes."

"What did you tell him?"

"That I hardly knew you."

"Good girl." He looked at her appraisingly, and she knew that he was pleased, and a little surprised, that she had kept her head. He said: "Did he believe you?"

"Presumably not, since he ordered this surveillance."

Wolff frowned. "That's going to be awkward. I can't swim the river every time I want to come home . . ."

"Don't worry," Sonja said. "I've fixed it."

"*You* fixed it?"

It was not quite so, Sonja knew, but it sounded good. "The detective is one of us," she explained.

"A nationalist?"

"Yes. He wants to use your radio."

"How does he know I've got one?" There was a threatening note in Wolff's voice.

"He doesn't," Sonja said calmly. "From what the British have told him he deduces that you're a spy; and he presumes a spy has a means of communicating with the Germans. The nationalists want to send a message to Rommel."

Wolff shook his head. "I'd rather not get involved."

She would not have him go back on a bargain she had made. "You've got to get involved," she said sharply.

"I suppose I do," he said wearily.

She felt an odd sense of power. It was as if she were taking control. She found it exhilarating.

Wolff said: "They're closing in. I don't want any more surprises like last night. I'd like to leave this boat, but I don't know where to go. Abdullah knows my money's no good—he'd like to turn me over to the British. Damn."

"You'll be safe here, while you string the detective along."

"I haven't any choice."

She sat on the edge of the bathtub, looking at his naked body. He seemed . . . not defeated, but at least cornered. His face was lined with tension, and there was in his voice a faint note of panic. She guessed that for the first time he was wondering whether he could hold out until Rommel arrived. And, also for the first time, he was dependent on her. He needed her money, he needed her home. Last night he had depended on her silence under interrogation, and—he now believed—he had been saved by her deal with the nationalist detective. He was slipping into her power. The thought intrigued her. She felt a little horny.

Wolff said: "I wonder if I should keep my date with that girl, Elene, tonight."

"Why not? She's nothing to do with the British. You picked her up in a shop!"

"Maybe. I just feel it might be safer to lie low. I don't know."

"No," said Sonja firmly. "I want her."

He looked up at her through narrowed eyes. She wondered whether he was considering the issue or thinking about her newfound strength of will. "All right," he said finally. "I'll just have to take precautions."

He had given in. She had tested her strength against his, and she had won. It gave her a kind of thrill. She shivered.

"I'm still cold," Wolff said. "Put some more hot water in."

"No." Without removing her nightdress, Sonja got into the bath. She knelt astride him, facing him, her knees jammed against the sides of the narrow tub. She lifted the wet hem of the nightdress to the level of her waist. She said: "Eat me."

He did.

∾

Vandam was in high spirits as he sat in the Oasis Restaurant, sipping a cold martini, with Jakes beside him. He had slept all day and had woken up feeling battered but ready to fight back. He had gone to the hospital, where Dr. Abuthnot had told him he was a fool to be up and about, but a lucky fool, for his wound was mending. She had changed his dressing for a smaller, neater one that did not have to be secured by a yard of bandage around his head. Now it was a quarter past seven, and in a few minutes he would catch Alex Wolff.

Vandam and Jakes were at the back of the restaurant, in a position from which they could see the whole place. The table nearest to the entrance was occupied by two hefty sergeants eating fried chicken paid for by Intelligence. Outside, in an unmarked car parked across the road, were two MPs in civilian clothes with their handguns in their jacket pockets. The trap was set: all that was missing was the bait. Elene would arrive at any minute.

Billy had been shocked by the bandage at breakfast that morning. Vandam had sworn the boy to secrecy, then told him the truth. "I had a fight with a German spy. He had a knife. He got away, but I think I may catch him tonight." It was a breach of security, but what the hell, the boy needed to know why his father was wounded. After hearing the story Billy had not been worried anymore, but thrilled. Gaafar had been awestruck, and inclined to move around softly and talk in whispers, as if there had been a death in the family.

With Jakes, he found that last night's impulsive intimacy had left no overt trace. Their formal relationship had returned: Jakes took orders, called him sir, and did not offer opinions without being asked. It was just as well, Vandam thought: they were a good team as things were, so why make changes?

He looked at his wristwatch. It was seven-thirty. He lit another cigarette. At any moment now Alex Wolff would walk through the door. Vandam felt sure he would recognize Wolff —a tall, hawk-nosed European with brown hair and brown eyes, a strong, fit man—but he would make no move until Elene came in and sat by Wolff. Then Vandam and Jakes would move in. If Wolff fled the two sergeants would block the door, and in the unlikely event that he got past them, the MPs outside would shoot at him.

Seven thirty-five. Vandam was looking forward to interrogating Wolff. What a battle of wills that would be. But Vandam would win it, for he would have all the advantages. He would feel Wolff out, find the weak points, and then apply pressure until the prisoner cracked.

Seven thirty-nine. Wolff was late. Of course it was possible that he would not come at all. God forbid. Vandam shuddered when he recalled how superciliously he had said to Bogge: "I expect to arrest him tomorrow night." Vandam's section was in very bad odor at the moment, and only the prompt arrest of Wolff would enable them to come up smelling of roses. But suppose that, after last night's scare, Wolff had decided to lie low for a while, wherever it was that he was lying? Somehow Vandam felt that lying low was not Wolff's style. He hoped not.

At seven-forty the restaurant door opened and Elene walked in. Vandam heard Jakes whistle under his breath. She looked stunning. She wore a silk dress the color of clotted cream. Its simple lines drew attention to her slender figure, and its color and texture flattered her smooth tan skin: Vandam felt a sudden urge to stroke her.

She looked around the restaurant, obviously searching for Wolff and not finding him. Her eyes met Vandam's and moved on without hesitating. The headwaiter approached, and she spoke to him. He seated her at a table for two close to the door.

Vandam caught the eye of one of the sergeants and inclined his head in Elene's direction. The sergeant gave a little nod of acknowledgment and checked his watch.

Where was Wolff?

Vandam lit a cigarette and began to worry. He had assumed that Wolff, being a gentleman, would arrive a little early; and Elene would arrive a little late. According to that scenario the arrest would have taken place the moment she sat down. It's going wrong, he thought, it's going bloody wrong.

A waiter brought Elene a drink. It was seven forty-five. She looked in Vandam's direction and gave a small, dainty shrug of her slight shoulders.

The door of the restaurant opened. Vandam froze with a cigarette half way to his lips, then relaxed again, disappointed: it was only a small boy. The boy handed a piece of paper to a waiter then went out again.

Vandam decided to order another drink.

He saw the waiter go to Elene's table and hand her the piece of paper.

Vandam frowned. What was this? An apology from Wolff, saying he could not keep the date? Elene's face took on an expression of faint puzzlement. She looked at Vandam and gave that little shrug again.

Vandam considered whether to go over and ask her what was going on—but that would have spoiled the ambush, for what if Wolff should walk in while Elene was talking to Vandam? Wolff could turn around at the door and run, and he would have only the MPs to get past, two people instead of six.

Vandam murmured to Jakes: "Wait."

Elene picked up her clutch bag from the chair beside her and stood up. She looked at Vandam again, then turned around. Vandam thought she was going to the ladies' room. Instead she went to the door and opened it.

Vandam and Jakes got to their feet together. One of the sergeants half rose, looking at Vandam, and Vandam waved him down: no point in arresting Elene. Vandam and Jakes hurried across the restaurant to the door.

As they passed the sergeants Vandam said: "Follow me."

They went through the door into the street. Vandam looked around. There was a blind beggar sitting against the wall, holding out a cracked dish with a few piasters in it. Three soldiers in uniform staggered along the pavement, already drunk, arms around each other's shoulders, singing a vulgar song. A group of Egyptians had met just outside the restaurant and were vigorously shaking hands. A street vendor offered Vandam cheap razor blades. A few yards away Elene was getting into a taxi.

Vandam broke into a run.

The door of the taxi slammed and it pulled away.

Across the street, the MPs' car roared, shot forward and collided with a bus.

Vandam caught up with the taxi and leaped on to the running board. The car swerved suddenly. Vandam lost his grip, hit the road running and fell down.

He got to his feet. His face blazed with pain: his wound was bleeding again, and he could feel the sticky warmth under the dressing. Jakes and the two sergeants gathered around him. Across the road the MPs were arguing with the bus driver.

The taxi had disappeared.

15

Elene was terrified. It had all gone wrong. Wolff was supposed to have been arrested in the restaurant, and now he was here, in a taxi with her, smiling a feral smile. She sat still, her mind a blank.

"Who was he?" Wolff said, still smiling.

Elene could not think. She looked at Wolff, looked away again, and said: "What?"

"That man who ran after us. He jumped on the running board. I couldn't see him properly, but I thought he was a European. Who was he?"

Elene fought down her fear. *He's William Vandam, and he was supposed to arrest you.* She had to make up a story. Why would someone follow her out of a restaurant and try to get into her taxi? "He . . . I don't know him. He was in the restaurant." Suddenly she was inspired. "He was bothering me. I was alone. It's your fault, you were late."

"I'm so sorry," he said quickly.

Elene had an access of confidence after he swallowed her story so readily. "And why are we in a taxi?" she demanded. "What's it all about? Why aren't we having dinner?" She heard a whining note in her voice, and hated it.

"I had a wonderful idea." He smiled again, and Elene suppressed a shudder. "We're going to have a picnic. There's a basket in the trunk."

She did not know whether to believe him. Why had he pulled that stunt at the restaurant, sending a boy in with the message "Come outside.—A.W." unless he suspected a trap? What would he do now, take her into the desert and knife her? She had a sudden urge to leap out of the speeding car. She closed her eyes and forced herself to think calmly. If he suspected a trap, why did he come at all? No, it had to be more complex than that. He seemed to have believed her about the man on the running board—but she could not be sure what was going on behind his smile.

She said: "Where are we going?"

"A few miles out of town, to a little spot on the riverbank where we can watch the sun go down. It's going to be a lovely evening."

"I don't want to go."

"What's the matter?"

"I hardly know you."

"Don't be silly. The driver will be with us all the time—and I'm a gentleman."

"I should get out of the car."

"Please don't." He touched her arm lightly. "I have some smoked salmon, and a cold chicken, and a bottle of champagne. I get so bored with restaurants."

Elene considered. She could leave him now, and she would be safe—she would never see him again. That was what she wanted, to get away from the man forever. She thought: But I'm Vandam's only hope. What do I care for Vandam? I'd be happy never to see him again, and go back to the old peaceful life—

The old life.

She did care for Vandam, she realized; at least enough for her to hate the thought of letting him down. She had to stay with Wolff, cultivate him, angle for another date, try to find out where he lived.

Impulsively she said: "Let's go to your place."

He raised his eyebrows. "That's a sudden change of heart."

She realized she had made a mistake. "I'm confused," she said. "You sprung a surprise on me. Why didn't you ask me first?"

"I only thought of the idea an hour ago. It didn't occur to me that it might scare you."

Elene realized that she was, unintentionally, fufilling her role as a dizzy girl. She decided not to overplay her hand. "All right," she said. She tried to relax.

Wolff was studying her. He said: "You're not quite as vulnerable as you seem, are you?"

"I don't know."

"I remember what you said to Aristopoulos, that first day I saw you in the shop."

Elene remembered: she had threatened to cut off Mikis' cock if he touched her again. She should have blushed, but she could not do so voluntarily. "I was so angry," she said.

Wolff chuckled. "You sounded it," he said. "Try to bear in mind that I am not Aristopoulos."

She gave him a weak smile. "Okay."

He turned his attention to the driver. They were out of the city, and Wolff began to give directions. Elene wondered where he had found this taxi: by Egyptian standards it was luxurious. It was some kind of American car, with big soft seats and lots of room, and it seemed only a few years old.

They passed through a series of villages, then turned on to an unmade road. The car followed the winding track up a small hill and emerged on a little plateau atop a bluff. The river was immediately below them, and on its far side Elene could see the neat patchwork of cultivated fields stretching into the distance until they met the sharp tan-colored line of the edge of the desert.

Wolff said: "Isn't this a lovely spot?"

Elene had to agree. A flight of swifts rising from the far bank of the river drew her eye upward, and she saw that the evening clouds were already edged in pink. A young girl was walking away from the river with a huge water jug on her head. A lone felucca sailed upstream, propelled by a light breeze.

The driver got out of the car and walked fifty yards away. He sat down, pointedly turning his back on them, lit a cigarette and unfolded a newspaper.

Wolff got a picnic hamper out of the trunk and set it on the floor of the car between them. As he began to unpack the food, Elene asked him: "How did you discover this place?"

"My mother brought me here when I was a boy." He handed her a glass of wine. "After my father died, my mother married an Egyptian. From time to time she would find the Muslim household oppressive, so she would bring me here in a gharry and tell me about . . . Europe, and so on."

"Did you enjoy it?"

He hesitated. "My mother had a way of spoiling things like that. She was always interrupting the fun. She used to say: 'You're so selfish, just like your father.' At that age I preferred my Arab family. My stepbrothers were wicked, and nobody tried to control them. We used to steal oranges from other people's gardens, throw stones at horses to make them bolt, puncture bicycle tires . . . Only my mother minded, and all she could do was warn us that we'd get punished eventually. She was always saying that—'They'll catch you one day, Alex!' "

The mother was right, Elene thought: they would catch Alex one day.

She was relaxing. She wondered whether Wolff was carrying the knife he had used in Assyut, and that made her tense again. The situation was so normal—a charming man taking a girl on a picnic beside the river—that for a moment she had forgotten she wanted something from him.

She said: "Where do you live now?"

"My house has been . . . commandeered by the British. I'm living with friends." He handed her a slice of smoked salmon on a china plate, then sliced a lemon in half with a kitchen knife. Elene watched his deft hands. She wondered what *he* wanted from *her*, that he should work so hard to please her.

∽

Vandam felt very low. His face hurt, and so did his pride. The great arrest had been a fiasco. He had failed professionally, he had been outwitted by Alex Wolff and he had sent Elene into danger.

He sat at home, his cheek newly bandaged, drinking gin to ease the pain. Wolff had evaded him so damn *easily*. Vandam was sure the spy had not really known about the ambush— otherwise he would not have turned up at all. No, he had just been taking precautions; and the precautions had worked beautifully.

They had a good description of the taxi. It had been a distinctive car, quite new, and Jakes had read the number plate. Every policeman and MP in the city was looking out for it, and had orders to stop it on sight and arrest all the occupants. They would find it, sooner or later, and Vandam felt sure it would be too late. Nevertheless he was sitting by the phone.

What was Elene doing now? Perhaps she was in a candlelit restaurant, drinking wine and laughing at Wolff's jokes. Vandam pictured her, in the cream-colored dress, holding a glass, smiling her special, impish smile, the one that promised you anything you wanted. Vandam checked his watch. Perhaps they had finished dinner by now. What would they do then? It was traditional to go and look at the pyramids by moonlight: the black sky, the stars, the endless flat desert and the clean triangular planes of the pharaohs' tombs. The area would be deserted, except perhaps for another pair of lovers. They might climb a few levels, he springing up ahead and then reaching down to lift her; but soon she would be exhausted, her hair and her dress a little awry, and she would say that these shoes were not designed for mountaineering; so they would sit on the great stones, still warm from the sun, and breathe the mild night air while they watched the stars. Walking back to the taxi, she would shiver in her sleeveless evening gown, and he might put an arm around her shoulders to keep her warm. Would he kiss her in the taxi? No, he was too old for that. When he made his pass, it would be in some sophisticated manner. Would he suggest going back to his place, or hers? Vandam did not know which to hope for. If they went to his place, Elene would report in the morning, and Vandam would be able to arrest Wolff at home, with his radio, his code book and perhaps even his back traffic. Professionally, that would be better—but it would also mean that Elene would spend a night with Wolff, and that thought made Vandam more angry than it should have done. Alternatively, if they went to her place, where Jakes was waiting with ten men and three cars, Wolff would be grabbed before he got a chance to—

Vandam got up and paced the room. Idly, he picked up the book *Rebecca*, the one he thought Wolff was using as the basis of his code. He read the first line: "Last night I dreamt I went to Manderley again." He put the book down, then opened it again and read on. The story of the vulnerable, bullied girl was a welcome distraction from his own worries. When he realized that the girl would marry the glamorous, older widower, and that the marriage would be blighted by the ghostly presence of the man's first wife, he closed the book and put it down again. What was the age difference between himself and Elene? How long would he be haunted by Angela? She, too, had been coldly perfect; Elene, too, was young, impulsive and in need of rescue from the life she was living. These thoughts irritated him, for he was not going to marry Elene. He lit a cigarette. Why did the time pass so slowly? Why did the phone not ring? How could he have let Wolff slip through his fingers twice in two days? Where was Elene?

Where was Elene?

He had sent a woman into danger once before. It had happened after his other great fiasco, when Rashid Ali had slipped out of Turkey under Vandam's nose. Vandam had sent a woman agent to pick up the German agent, the man who had changed clothes with Ali and enabled him to escape. He had hoped to salvage something from the shambles by finding out all about the man. But next day the woman had been found dead in a hotel bed. It was a chilling parallel.

There was no point in staying in the house. He could not possibly sleep, and there was nothing else he could do there. He would go and join Jakes and the others, despite Dr. Abuthnot's orders. He put on a coat and his uniform cap, went outside, and wheeled his motorcycle out of the garage.

❧

Elene and Wolff stood together, close to the edge of the bluff, looking at the distant lights of Cairo and the nearer, flickering glimmers of peasant fires in dark villages. Elene was thinking of an imaginary peasant—hardworking, poverty-stricken, superstitious—laying a straw mattress on the earth floor, pulling a rough blanket around him, and finding consolation in the arms of his wife. Elene had left poverty behind, she hoped forever, but sometimes it seemed to her that she had left something else behind with it, something she could not do without. In Alexandria when she was a child people would put blue palm prints on the red mud walls, hand shapes to ward off evil. Elene did not believe in the efficacy of the palm prints; but despite the rats, despite the nightly screams as the moneylender beat both of his wives, despite the ticks that infested everyone, despite the early death of many babies, she believed there had been *something* there that warded off evil. She had been looking for that something when she took men home, took them into her bed, accepted their gifts and their caresses and their money; but she had never found it.

She did not want to do that anymore. She had spent too much of her life looking for love in the wrong places. In particular, she did not want to do it with Alex Wolff. Several times she had said to herself: "Why not do it just once more?" That was Vandam's coldly reasonable point of view. But, each time she contemplated making love with Wolff, she saw again the daydream that had plagued her for the last few weeks, the daydream of seducing William Vandam. She knew *just* how Vandam would be: he would look at her with innocent wonder, and touch her with wide-eyed delight; thinking of it, she felt momentarily helpless with desire. She knew how Wolff would be, too. He would be knowing, selfish, skillful and unshockable.

Without speaking she turned from the view and walked back toward the car. It was time for him to make his pass. They had finished the meal, emptied the champagne bottle and the flask of coffee, picked clean the chicken and the bunch of grapes. Now he would expect his just reward. From the back seat of the car she watched him. He stayed a moment longer on the edge of the bluff, then walked toward her, calling to the driver. He had the confident grace that height often seemed to give to men. He was an attractive man, much more glamorous than any of Elene's lovers had been, but she was afraid of him, and her fear came not just from what she knew about him, his history and his secrets and his knife, but from an intuitive understanding of his nature: somehow she knew that his charm was not spontaneous but manipulative, and that if he was kind it was because he wanted to use her.

She had been used enough.

Wolff got in beside her. "Did you enjoy the picnic?"

She made an effort to be bright. "Yes, it was lovely. Thank you."

The car pulled away. Either he would invite her to his place or he would take her to her flat and ask for a nightcap. She would have to find an encouraging way to refuse him. This struck her as ridiculous: she was behaving like a frightened virgin. She thought: What am I doing—saving myself for Mr. Right?

She had been silent for too long. She was supposed to be witty and engaging. She should talk to him. "Have you heard the war news?" she asked, and realized at once it was not the most lighthearted of topics.

"The Germans are still winning," he said. "Of course."

"Why 'of course'?"

He smiled condescendingly at her. "The world is divided into masters and slaves, Elene." He spoke as if he were explaining simple facts to a schoolboy. "The British have been masters too long. They've gone soft, and now it will be someone else's turn."

"And the Egyptians—are they masters, or slaves?" She knew she should shut up, she was walking on thin ice, but his complacency infuriated her.

"The Bedouin are masters," he said. "But the average Egyptian is a born slave."

She thought: He means every word of it. She shuddered.

They reached the outskirts of the city. It was after midnight, and the suburbs were quiet, although downtown would still be buzzing. Wolff said: "Where do you live?"

She told him. So it was to be her place.

Wolff said: "We must do this again."

"I'd like that."

They reached the Sharia Abbas, and he told the driver to stop. Elene wondered what was going to happen now. Wolff turned to her and said: "Thank you for a lovely evening. I'll see you soon." He got out of the car.

She stared in astonishment. He bent down by the driver's window, gave the man some money and told him Elene's address. The driver nodded. Wolff banged on the roof of the car, and the driver pulled away. Elene looked back and saw Wolff waving. As the car began to turn a corner, Wolff started walking toward the river.

She thought: What do you make of that?

No pass, no invitation to his place, no nightcap, not even a good-night kiss—what game was he playing, hard-to-get?

She puzzled over the whole thing as the taxi took her home. Perhaps it was Wolff's technique to try to intrigue a woman. Perhaps he was just eccentric. Whatever the reason, she was very grateful. She sat back and relaxed. She was not obliged to choose between fighting him off and going to bed with him. Thank God.

The taxi drew up outside her building. Suddenly, from nowhere, three cars roared up. One stopped right in front of the taxi, one close behind, and one alongside. Men materialized out of the shadows. All four doors of the taxi were flung open, and four guns pointed in. Elene screamed.

Then a head was poked into the car, and Elene recognized Vandam.

"Gone?" Vandam said.

Elene realized what was happening. "I thought you were going to shoot me," she said.

"Where did you leave him?"

"Sharia Abbas."

"How long ago?"

"Five or ten minutes. May I get out of the car?"

He gave her a hand, and she stepped on to the pavement. He said: "I'm sorry we scared you."

"This is called slamming the stable door after the horse has bolted."

"Quite." He looked utterly defeated.

She felt a surge of affection for him. She touched his arm. "You've no idea how happy I am to see your face," she said.

He gave her an odd look, as if he was not sure whether to believe her.

She said: "Why don't you send your men home and come and talk inside?"

He hesitated. "All right." He turned to one of his men, a captain. "Jakes, I want you to interrogate the taxi driver, see what you can get out of him. Let the men go. I'll see you at GHQ in an hour or so."

"Very good, sir."

Elene led the way inside. It was so good to enter her own apartment, slump on the sofa, and kick off her shoes. The trial was over, Wolff had gone, and Vandam was here. She said: "Help yourself to a drink."

"No, thanks."

"What went wrong, anyway?"

Vandam sat down opposite her and took out his cigarettes. "We expected him to walk into the trap all unawares—but he was suspicious, or at least cautious, and we missed him. What happened then?"

She rested her head against the back of the sofa, closed her eyes, and told him in a few words about the picnic. She left out her thoughts about going to bed with Wolff, and she did not tell Vandam that Wolff had hardly touched her all evening. She spoke abruptly: she wanted to forget, not remember. When she had told him the story she said: "Make me a drink, even if you won't have one."

He went to the cupboard. Elene could see that he was angry. She looked at the bandage on his face. She had seen it in the restaurant, and again a few minutes ago when she arrived, but now she had time to wonder what it was. She said: "What happened to your face?"

"We almost caught Wolff last night."

"Oh, no." So he had failed twice in twenty-four hours: no wonder he looked defeated. She wanted to console him, to put her arms around him, to lay his head in her lap and stroke his hair; the longing was like an ache. She decided—impulsively, the way she always decided things—that she would take him to her bed tonight.

He gave her a drink. He had made one for himself after all. As he stooped to hand her the glass she reached up, touched his chin with her fingertips and turned his head so that she could look at his cheek. He let her look, just for a second, then moved his head away.

She had not seen him as tense as this before. He crossed the room and sat opposite her, holding himself upright on the edge of the chair. He was full of a suppressed emotion, something like rage, but when she looked into his eyes she saw not anger but pain.

He said: "How did Wolff strike you?"

She was not sure what he was getting at. "Charming. Intelligent. Dangerous."

"His appearance?"

"Clean hands, a silk shirt, a mustache that doesn't suit him. What are you fishing for?"

He shook his head irritably. "Nothing. Everything." He lit another cigarette.

She could not reach him in this mood. She wanted him to come and sit beside her, and tell her she was beautiful and brave and she had done well; but she knew it was no use asking.

All the same she said: "How did I do?"

"I don't know," he said. "*What* did you do?"

"You know what I did."

"Yes. I'm most grateful."

He smiled, and she knew the smile was insincere. What was the matter with him? There was something familiar in his anger, something she would understand as soon as she put her finger on it. It was not just that he felt he had failed. It was his attitude to her, the way he spoke to her, the way he sat across from her and especially the way he looked at her. His expression was one of . . . it was almost one of disgust.

"He said he would see you again?" Vandam asked.

"Yes."

"I hope he does." He put his chin in his hands. His face was strained with tension. Wisps of smoke rose from his cigarette. "Christ, I hope he does."

"He also said: 'We must do this again,' or something like that," Elene told him.

"I see. 'We must do this again,' eh?"

"Something like that."

"What do you think he had in mind, exactly?"

She shrugged. "Another picnic, another date—damn it, William, what has got into you?"

"I'm just curious," he said. His face wore a twisted grin, one she had never seen on him before. "I'd like to know what the two of you did, other than eat and drink, in the back of that big taxi, and on the riverbank; you know, all that time together, in the dark, a man and a woman—"

"Shut up." She closed her eyes. Now she understood; now she knew. Without opening her eyes she said: "I'm going to bed. You can see yourself out."

A few seconds later the front door slammed.

She went to the window and looked down to the street. She saw him leave the building, and get on his motorcycle. He kicked the engine into life and roared off down the road at a breakneck speed and took the corner at the end as if he were in a race. Elene was very tired, and a little sad that she would be spending the night alone after all, but she was not unhappy, for she had understood his anger, she knew the cause of it, and that gave her hope. As he disappeared from sight she smiled faintly and said softly: "William Vandam, I do believe you're jealous."

16

By the time Major Smith made his third lunchtime visit to
the houseboat, Wolff and Sonja had gotten into a slick routine.
Wolff hid in the cupboard when the major approached. Sonja
met him in the living room with a drink in her hand ready
for him. She made him sit down there, ensuring that his
briefcase was put down before they went into the bedroom.
After a minute or two she began kissing him. By this time
she could do what she liked with him, for he was paralyzed by
lust. She contrived to get his shorts off, then soon afterward
took him into the bedroom.

It was clear to Wolff that nothing like this had ever happened
to the major before: he was Sonja's slave as long as she allowed
him to make love to her. Wolff was grateful: things would not
have been quite so easy with a more strong-minded man.

As soon as Wolff heard the bed creak he came out of the
cupboard. He took the key out of the shorts pocket and opened
the case. His notebook and pencil were beside him, ready.

Smith's second visit had been disappointing, leading Wolff
to wonder whether perhaps it was only occasionally that Smith
saw battle plans. However, this time he struck gold again.

General Sir Claude Auchinleck, the C in C Middle East, had taken over direct control of the Eighth Army from General Neil Ritchie. As a sign of Allied panic, that alone would be welcome news to Rommel. It might also help Wolff, for it meant that battles were now being planned in Cairo rather than in the desert, in which case Smith was more likely to get copies.

The Allies had retreated to a new defense line at Mersa Matruh, and the most important paper in Smith's briefcase was a summary of the new dispositions.

The new line began at the coastal village of Matruh and stretched south into the desert as far as an escarpment called Sidi Hamza. Tenth Corps was at Matruh; then there was a heavy minefield fifteen miles long; then a lighter minefield for ten miles; then the escarpment; then, south of the escarpment, the 13th Corps.

With half an ear on the noises from the bedroom, Wolff considered the position. The picture was fairly clear: the Allied line was strong at either end and weak in the middle.

Rommel's likeliest move, according to Allied thinking, was a dash around the southern end of the line, a classic Rommel outflanking maneuver, made more feasible by his capture of an estimated 500 tons of fuel at Tobruk. Such an advance would be repelled by the 13th Corps, which consisted of the strong 1st Armored Division and the 2nd New Zealand Division, the latter—the summary noted helpfully—freshly arrived from Syria.

However, armed with Wolff's information, Rommel could instead hit the soft center of the line and pour his forces through the gap like a stream bursting a dam at its weakest point.

Wolff smiled to himself. He felt he was playing a major role in the struggle for German domination of North Africa: he found it enormously satisfying.

In the bedroom, a cork popped.

Smith always surprised Wolff by the rapidity of his love-making. The cork popping was the sign that it was all over, and Wolff had a few minutes in which to tidy up before Smith came in search of his shorts.

He put the papers back in the case, locked it and put the key back in the shorts pocket. He no longer got back into the cupboard afterward—once had been enough. He put his shoes in his trousers pockets and tiptoed, soundlessly in his socks, up the ladder, across the deck, and down the gangplank to the towpath. Then he put his shoes on and went to lunch.

∾

Kemel shook hands politely and said: "I hope your injury is healing rapidly, Major."

"Sit down," Vandam said. "The bandage is more damn nuisance than the wound. What have you got?"

Kemel sat down and crossed his legs, adjusting the crease of his black cotton trousers. "I thought I would bring the surveillance report myself, although I'm afraid there's nothing of interest in it."

Vandam took the proffered envelope and opened it. It contained a single typewritten sheet. He began to read.

Sonja had come home—presumably from the Cha-Cha Club—at eleven o'clock the previous night. She had been alone. She had surfaced at around ten the following morning, and had been seen on deck in a robe. The postman had come at one. Sonja had gone out at four and returned at six carrying a bag bearing the name of one of the more expensive dress shops in Cairo. At that hour the watcher had been relieved by the night man.

Yesterday Vandam had received by messenger a similar report from Kemel covering the first twelve hours of the surveillance. For two days, therefore, Sonja's behavior had been routine and wholly innocent, and neither Wolff nor anyone else had visited her on the houseboat.

Vandam was bitterly disappointed.

Kemel said: "The men I am using are completely reliable, and they are reporting directly to me."

Vandam grunted, then roused himself to be courteous.

"Yes, I'm sure," he said. "Thank you for coming in."

Kemel stood up. "No trouble," he said. "Good-bye." He went out.

Vandam sat brooding. He read Kemel's report again, as if there might have been clues between the lines. If Sonja was connected with Wolff—and Vandam still believed she was, somehow—clearly the association was not a close one. If she was meeting anyone, the meetings must be taking place away from the houseboat.

Vandam went to the door and called: "Jakes!"

"Sir!"

Vandam sat down again and Jakes came in. Vandam said: "From now on I want you to spend your evenings at the Cha-Cha Club. Watch Sonja, and observe whom she sits with after the show. Also, bribe a waiter to tell you whether anyone goes to her dressing room."

"Very good, sir."

Vandam nodded dismissal, and added with a smile: "Permission to enjoy yourself is granted."

The smile was a mistake: it hurt. At least he was no longer trying to live on glucose dissolved in warm water: Gaafar was giving him mashed potatoes and gravy, which he could eat from a spoon and swallow without chewing. He was existing on that and gin. Dr. Abuthnot had also told him he drank too much and smoked too much, and he had promised to cut down—after the war. Privately he thought: After I've caught Wolff.

If Sonja was not going to lead him to Wolff, only Elene could. Vandam was ashamed of his outburst at Elene's apartment. He had been angry at his own failure, and the thought of her with Wolff had maddened him. His behavior could be described only as a fit of bad temper. Elene was a lovely girl who was risking her neck to help him, and courtesy was the least he owed her.

Wolff had said he would see Elene again. Vandam hoped he would contact her soon. He still felt irrationally angry at the thought of the two of them together; but now that the houseboat angle had turned out to be a dead end, Elene was his only hope. He sat at his desk, waiting for the phone to ring, dreading the very thing he wanted most.

∽

Elene went shopping in the late afternoon. Her apartment had come to seem claustrophobic after she had spent most of the day pacing around, unable to concentrate on anything, alternately miserable and happy; so she put on a cheerful striped dress and went out into the sunshine.

She liked the fruit-and-vegetable market. It was a lively place, especially at this end of the day when the tradesmen were trying to get rid of the last of their produce. She stopped to buy tomatoes. The man who served her picked up one with a slight bruise, and threw it away dramatically before filling a paper bag with undamaged specimens. Elene laughed, for she knew that the bruised tomato would be retrieved, as soon as she was out of sight, and put back on the display so that the whole pantomime could be performed again for the next customer. She haggled briefly over the price, but the vendor could tell that her heart was not in it, and she ended up paying almost what he had asked originally.

She bought eggs, too, having decided to make an omelet for supper. It was good, to be carrying a basket of food, more food than she could eat at one meal: it made her feel safe. She could remember days when there had been no supper.

She left the market and went window shopping for dresses. She bought most of her clothes on impulse: she had firm ideas about what she liked, and if she planned a trip to buy something specific, she could never find it. She wanted one day to have her own dressmaker.

She thought: I wonder if William Vandam could afford that for his wife?

When she thought of Vandam she was happy, until she thought of Wolff.

She knew she could escape, if she wished, simply by refusing to see Wolff, refusing to make a date with him, refusing to answer his message. She was under no obligation to act as the bait in a trap for a knife murderer. She kept returning to this idea, worrying at it like a loose tooth: I don't have to.

She suddenly lost interest in dresses, and headed for home. She wished she could make omelet for two, but omelet for one was something to be thankful for. There was a certain unforgettable pain in the stomach which came when, having gone to bed with no supper, you woke up in the morning to no breakfast. The ten-year-old Elene had wondered, secretly, how long people took to starve to death. She was sure Vandam's childhood had not suffered such worries.

When she turned into the entrance to her apartment block, a voice said: "Abigail."

She froze with shock. It was the voice of a ghost. She did not dare to look. The voice came again.

"Abigail."

She made herself turn around. A figure came out of the shadows: an old Jew, shabbily dressed, with a matted beard, veined feet in rubber-tire sandals . . .

Elene said: "Father."

He stood in front of her, as if afraid to touch her, just looking. He said: "So beautiful still, and not poor . . ."

Impulsively, she stepped forward, kissed his cheek, then stepped back again. She did not know what to say.

He said: "Your grandfather, my father, has died."

She took his arm and led him up the stairs. It was all unreal, irrational, like a dream.

Inside the apartment she said: "You should eat," and took him into the kitchen. She put a pan on to heat and began to beat the eggs. With her back to her father she said: "How did you find me?"

"I've always known where you were," he said. "Your friend Esme writes to her father, who sometimes I see."

Esme was an acquaintance, rather than a friend, but Elene ran into her every two or three months. She had never let on that she was writing home. Elene said: "I didn't want you to ask me to come back."

"And what would I have said to you? 'Come home, it is your duty to starve with your family.' No. But I knew where you were."

She sliced tomatoes into the omelet. "You would have said it was better to starve than to live immorally."

"Yes, I would have said that. And would I have been wrong?"

She turned to look at him. The glaucoma which had taken the sight of his left eye years ago was now spreading to the right. He was fifty-five, she calculated: he looked seventy. "Yes, you would have been wrong," she said. "It is always better to live."

"Perhaps it is."

Her surprise must have shown on her face, for he explained: "I'm not as certain of these things as I used to be. I'm getting old."

Elene halved the omelet and slid it on to two plates. She put bread on the table. Her father washed his hands, then blessed the bread. "Blessed art thou O Lord our God, King of the Universe . . ." Elene was surprised that the prayer did not drive her into a fury. In the blackest moments of her lonely life she had cursed and raged at her father and his religion for what it had driven her to. She had tried to cultivate an attitude of indifference, perhaps mild contempt; but she had not quite succeeded. Now, watching him pray, she thought: And what do I do, when this man whom I hate turns up on the doorstep? I kiss his cheek, and I bring him inside, and I give him supper.

They began to eat. Her father had been very hungry, and wolfed his food. Elene wondered why he had come. Was it just to tell her of the death of her grandfather? No. That was part of it, perhaps, but there would be more.

She asked about her sisters. After the death of their mother all four of them, in their different ways, had broken with their father. Two had gone to America, one had married the son of her father's greatest enemy, and the youngest, Naomi, had chosen the surest escape, and died. It dawned on Elene that her father was destroyed.

He asked her what she was doing. She decided to tell him the truth. "The British are trying to catch a man, a German, they think is a spy. It's my job to befriend him . . . I'm the

bait in a snare. But . . I think I may not help them anymore."

He had stopped eating. "Are you afraid?"

She nodded. "He's very dangerous. He killed a soldier with
a knife. Last night . . . I was to meet him in a restaurant
and the British were to arrest him there, but something went
wrong and I spent the whole evening with him, I was so
frightened, and when it was over, the Englishman . . ." She
stopped, and took a deep breath. "Anyway, I may not help
them anymore."

Her father went on eating. "Do you love this Englishman?"

"He isn't Jewish," she said defiantly.

"I've given up judging everyone," he said.

Elene could not take it all in. Was there *nothing* of the old
man left?

They finished their meal, and Elene got up to make him a
glass of tea. He said: "The Germans are coming. It will be
very bad for Jews. I'm getting out."

She frowned. "Where will you go?"

"Jerusalem."

"How will you get there? The trains are full, there's a
quota for Jews—"

"I am going to walk."

She stared at him, not believing he could be serious, not
believing he would joke about such a thing. "Walk?"

He smiled. "It's been done before."

She saw that he meant it, and she was angry with him. "As
I recall, Moses never made it."

"Perhaps I will be able to hitch a ride."

"It's crazy!"

"Haven't I always been a little crazy?"

"Yes!" she shouted. Suddenly her anger collapsed. "Yes,
you've always been a little crazy, and I should know better than
to try to change your mind."

"I will pray to God to preserve you. You will have a chance
here—you're young and beautiful, and maybe they won't know
you're Jewish. But me, a useless old man muttering Hebrew
prayers . . . me they would send to a camp where I would

surely die. It is always better to live. You said that."

She tried to persuade him to stay with her, for one night at least, but he would not. She gave him a sweater, and a scarf, and all the cash she had in the house, and told him that if he waited a day she could get more money from the bank, and buy him a good coat; but he was in a hurry. She cried, and dried her eyes, and cried again. When he left she looked out of her window and saw him walking along the street, an old man going up out of Egypt and into the wilderness, following in the footsteps of the Children of Israel. There *was* something of the old man left: his orthodoxy had mellowed, but he still had a will of iron. He disappeared into the crowd, and she left the window. When she thought of his courage, she knew she could not run out on Vandam.

∾

"She's an intriguing girl," Wolff said. "I can't quite figure her out." He was sitting on the bed, watching Sonja get dressed. "She's a little jumpy. When I told her we were going on a picnic she acted quite scared, said she hardly knew me, as if she needed a chaperone."

"With you, she did," Sonja said.

"And yet she can be very earthy and direct."

"Just bring her home to me. I'll figure her out."

"It bothers me." Wolff frowned. He was thinking aloud. "Somebody tried to jump into the taxi with us."

"A beggar."

"No, he was a European."

"A European beggar." Sonja stopped brushing her hair to look at Wolff in the mirror. "This town is full of crazy people, you know that. Listen, if you have second thoughts, just picture her writhing on that bed with you and me on either side of her."

Wolff grinned. It was an appealing picture, but not an irresistible one: it was Sonja's fantasy, not his. His instinct told him to lay low now, and not to make dates with anyone. But Sonja was going to insist—and he still needed her.

Sonja said: "And when am I going to contact Kemel? He must know by now that you're living here."

Wolff sighed. Another date; another claim on him; another danger; also, another person whose protection he needed. "Call him tonight from the club. I'm not in a rush for this meeting, but we've got to keep him sweet."

"Okay." She was ready, and her taxi was waiting. "Make a date with Elene." She went out.

She was not in his power the way she had once been, Wolff realized. The walls you build to protect you also close you in. Could he afford to defy her? If there had been a clear and immediate danger, yes. But all he had was a vague nervousness, an intuitive inclination to keep his head down. And Sonja might be crazy enough to betray him if she really got angry. He was obliged to choose the lesser danger.

He got up from the bed, found paper and a pen and sat down to write a note to Elene.

17

The message came the day after Elene's father left for Jerusalem. A small boy came to the door with an envelope. Elene tipped him and read the letter. It was short. "My dear Elene, let us meet at the Oasis Restaurant at eight o'clock next Thursday. I eagerly look forward to it. Fondly, Alex Wolff." Unlike his speech, his writing had a stiffness which seemed German—but perhaps it was her imagination. Thursday—that was the day after tomorrow. She did not know whether to be elated or scared. Her first thought was to telephone Vandam; then she hesitated.

She had become intensely curious about Vandam. She knew so little about him. What did he do when he was not catching spies? Did he listen to music, collect stamps, shoot duck? Was he interested in poetry or architecture or antique rugs? What was his home like? With whom did he live? What color were his pajamas?

She wanted to patch up their quarrel, and she wanted to see where he lived. She had an excuse to contact him now, but instead of telephoning she would go to his home.

She decided to change her dress, then she decided to take a

bath first, then she decided to wash her hair as well. Sitting in the bath she thought about which dress to wear. She recalled the occasions she had seen Vandam, and tried to remember which clothes she had worn. He had never seen the pale pink one with puffed shoulders and buttons all down the front: that was very pretty.

She put on a little perfume, then the silk underwear Johnnie had given her, which always made her feel so feminine. Her short hair was dry already, and she sat in front of the mirror to comb it. The dark, fine locks gleamed after washing. I look ravishing, she thought, and she smiled at herself seductively.

She left the apartment, taking Wolff's note with her. Vandam would be interested to see his handwriting. He was interested in every little detail where Wolff was concerned, perhaps because they had never met face to face, except in the dark or at a distance. The handwriting was very neat, easily legible, almost like an artist's lettering: Vandam would draw some conclusion from that.

She headed for Garden City. It was seven o'clock, and Vandam worked until late, so she had time to spare. The sun was still strong, and she enjoyed the heat on her arms and legs as she walked. A bunch of soldiers whistled at her, and in her sunny mood she smiled at them, so they followed her for a few blocks before they got diverted into a bar.

She felt gay and reckless. What a good idea it was to go to his house—so much better than sitting alone at home. She had been alone too much. For her men, she had existed only when they had time to visit her; and she had made their attitudes her own, so that when they were not there she felt she had nothing to do, no role to play, no one to be. Now she had broken with all that. By doing this, by going to see him uninvited, she felt she was being herself instead of a person in someone else's dream. It made her almost giddy.

She found the house easily. It was a small French-colonial villa, all pillars and high windows, its white stone reflecting the evening sun with painful brilliance. She walked up the short drive, rang the bell and waited in the shadow of the portico.

An elderly, bald Egyptian came to the door. "Good evening, Madam," he said, speaking like an English butler.

Elene said: "I'd like to see Major Vandam. My name is Elene Fontana."

"The major has not yet returned home, Madam." The servant hesitated.

"Perhaps I could wait," Elene said.

"Of course, Madam." He stepped aside to admit her.

She crossed the threshold. She looked around with nervous eagerness. She was in a cool tiled hall with a high ceiling. Before she could take it all in the servant said: "This way, Madam." He led her into a drawing room. "My name is Gaafar. Please call me if there is anything you require."

"Thank you, Gaafar."

The servant went out. Elene was thrilled to be in Vandam's house and left alone to look around. The drawing room had a large marble fireplace and a lot of very English furniture: somehow she thought he had not furnished it himself. Everything was clean and tidy and not very lived-in. What did this say about his character? Perhaps nothing.

The door opened and a young boy walked in. He was very good-looking, with curly brown hair and smooth, preadolescent skin. He seemed about ten years old. He looked vaguely familiar.

He said: "Hello, I'm Billy Vandam."

Elene stared at him in horror. A son—Vandam had a son! She knew now why he seemed familiar: he resembled his father. Why had it never occurred to her that Vandam might be married? A man like that—charming, kind, handsome, clever —was unlikely to have reached his late thirties without getting hooked. What a fool she had been to think that she might have been the first to desire him! She felt so stupid that she blushed.

She shook Billy's hand. "How do you do," she said. "I'm Elene Fontana."

"We never know what time Dad's coming home," Billy said. "I hope you won't have to wait too long."

She had not yet recovered her composure. "Don't worry, I don't mind, it doesn't matter a bit . . ."

"Would you like a drink, or anything?"

He was very polite, like his father, with a formality that was somehow disarming. Elene said: "No, thank you."

"Well, I've got to have my supper. Sorry to leave you alone."

"No, no . . ."

"If you need anything, just call Gaafar."

"Thank you."

The boy went out, and Elene sat down heavily. She was disoriented, as if in her own home she had found a door to a room she had not known was there. She noticed a photograph on the marble mantelpiece, and got up to look at it. It was a picture of a beautiful woman in her early twenties, a cool, aristocratic-looking woman with a faintly supercilious smile. Elene admired the dress she was wearing, something silky and flowing, hanging in elegant folds from her slender figure. The woman's hair and makeup were perfect. The eyes were startlingly familiar, clear and perceptive and light in color: Elene realized that Billy had eyes like that. This, then, was Billy's mother—Vandam's wife. She was, of course, exactly the kind of woman who would be his wife, a classic English beauty with a superior air.

Elene felt she had been a fool. Women like that were queuing up to marry men like Vandam. As if he would have bypassed all of them only to fall for an Egyptian courtesan! She rehearsed the things that divided her from him: he was respectable and she was disreputable; he was British and she was Egyptian; he was Christian—presumably—and she was Jewish; he was well bred and she came out of the slums of Alexandria; he was almost forty and she was twenty-three . . . The list was long.

Tucked into the back of the photograph frame was a page torn from a magazine. The paper was old and yellowing. The page bore the same photograph. Elene saw that it had come from a magazine called *The Tatler*. She had heard of it: it was much read by the wives of colonels in Cairo, for it reported all the trivial events of London society—parties, balls, charity lunches, gallery openings and the activities of English royalty. The picture of Mrs. Vandam took up most of this page, and a paragraph of type beneath the picture reported that Angela, daughter of Sir Peter and Lady Beresford, was engaged to be married to Lieutenant William Vandam, son of Mr. and Mrs. John Vandam of Gately, Dorset. Elene refolded the cutting and put it back.

The family picture was complete. Attractive British officer, cool, self-assured English wife, intelligent charming son, beautiful home, money, class and happiness. Everything else was a dream.

She wandered around the room, wondering if it held any more shocks in store. The room had been furnished by Mrs. Vandam, of course, in perfect, bloodless taste. The decorous print of the curtains toned with the restrained hue of the upholstery and the elegant striped wallpaper. Elene wondered what their bedroom would be like. It too would be coolly tasteful, she guessed. Perhaps the main color would be blue-green, the shade they called eau de Nil although it was not a bit like the muddy water of the Nile. Would they have twin beds? She hoped so. She would never know.

Against one wall was a small upright piano. She wondered who played. Perhaps Mrs. Vandam sat here sometimes, in the evenings, filling the air with Chopin while Vandam sat in the armchair, over there, watching her fondly. Perhaps Vandam accompanied himself as he sang romantic ballads to her in a strong tenor. Perhaps Billy had a tutor, and fingered hesitant scales every afternoon when he came home from school. She looked through the pile of sheet music in the seat of the piano stool. She had been right about the Chopin: they had all the waltzes here in a book.

She picked up a novel from the top of the piano and opened it. She read the first line: "Last night I dreamt I went to Manderley again." The opening sentences intrigued her, and she wondered whether Vandam was reading the book. Perhaps she could borrow it: it would be good to have something of his. On the other hand, she had the feeling he was not a great reader of fiction. She did not want to borrow it from his wife.

Billy came in. Elene put the book down suddenly, feeling

irrationally guilty, as if she had been prying. Billy saw the gesture. "That one's no good," he said. "It's about some silly girl who's afraid of her husband's housekeeper. There's no action."

Elene sat down, and Billy sat opposite her. Obviously he was going to entertain her. He was a miniature of his father, except for those clear gray eyes. She said: "You've read it, then?"

"*Rebecca?* Yes. But I didn't like it much. I always finish them, though."

"What *do* you like to read?"

"I like tecs best."

"Tecs?"

"Detectives. I've read all of Agatha Christie's and Dorothy Sayers'. But I like the American ones most of all—S. S. Van Dine and Raymond Chandler."

"Really?" Elene smiled. "I like detective stories too—I read them all the time."

"Oh! Who's your favorite tec?"

Elene considered. "Maigret."

"I've never heard of him. What's the author's name?"

"Georges Simenon. He writes in French, but now some of the books have been translated into English. They're set in Paris, mostly. They're very . . . complex."

"Would you lend me one? It's so hard to get new books, I've read all the ones in this house, and in the school library. And I swap with my friends but they like, you know, stories about children having adventures in the school holidays."

"All right," Elene said. "Let's swap. What have you got to lend me? I don't think I've read any American ones."

"I'll lend you a Chandler. The American ones are much more true to life, you know. I've gone off those stories about English country houses and people who probably couldn't murder a fly."

It was odd, Elene thought, that a boy for whom the English country house might be part of everyday life should find stories about American private eyes more "true to life." She hesitated, then asked: "Does your mother read detective stories?"

Billy said briskly: "My mother died last year in Crete."

"Oh!" Elene put her hand to her mouth; she felt the blood drain from her face. So Vandam was *not* married!

A moment later she felt ashamed that that had been her first thought, and sympathy for the child her second. She said: "Billy, how awful for you. I'm so sorry." Real death had suddenly intruded into their lighthearted talk of murder stories, and she felt embarrassed.

"It's all right," Billy said. "It's the war, you see."

And now he was like his father again. For a while, talking about books, he had been full of boyish enthusiasm, but now the mask was on, and it was a smaller version of the mask used by his father: courtesy, formality, the attitude of the considerate host. *It's the war, you see*: he had heard someone else say that, and had adopted it as his own defense. She wondered whether his preference for "true-to-life" murders, as opposed to implausible country-house killings, dated from the death of his mother. Now he was looking around him, searching for something, inspiration perhaps. In a moment he would offer her cigarettes, whiskey, tea. It was hard enough to know what to say to a bereaved adult: with Billy she felt helpless. She decided to talk of something else.

She said awkwardly: "I suppose, with your father working at GHQ, you get more news of the war than the rest of us."

"I suppose I do, but usually I don't really understand it. When he comes home in a bad mood I know we've lost another battle." He started to bite a fingernail, then stuffed his hands into his shorts pockets. "I wish I was *older*."

"You want to fight?"

He looked at her fiercely, as if he thought she was mocking him. "I'm not one of those kids who thinks it's all jolly good fun, like the cowboy films."

She murmured: "I'm sure you're not."

"It's just that I'm afraid the Germans will *win*."

Elene thought: Oh, Billy, if you were ten years older I'd fall in love with you, too. "It might not be so bad," she said. "They're not monsters."

He gave her a skeptical look: she should have known better

than to soft-soap him. He said: "They'd only do to us what we've been doing to the Egyptians for fifty years."

It was another of his father's lines, she was sure.

Billy said: "But then it would all have been for nothing." He bit his nail again, and this time he did not stop himself. Elene wondered *what* would have been for nothing: the death of his mother? His own personal struggle to be brave? The two-year seesaw of the desert war? European civilization?

"Well, it hasn't happened yet," she said feebly.

Billy looked at the clock on the mantelpiece. "I'm supposed to go to bed at nine." Suddenly he was a child again.

"I suppose you'd better go, then."

"Yes." He stood up.

"May I come and say good night to you, in a few minutes?"

"If you like." He went out.

What kind of life did they lead in this house? Elene wondered. The man, the boy and the old servant lived here together, each with his own concerns. Was there laughter, and kindness, and affection? Did they have time to play games and sing songs and go on picnics? By comparison with her own childhood Billy's was enormously privileged; nevertheless she feared this might be a terribly adult household for a boy to grow up in. His young-old wisdom was charming, but he seemed like a child who did not have much fun. She experienced a rush of compassion for him, a motherless child in an alien country besieged by foreign armies.

She left the drawing room and went upstairs. There seemed to be three or four bedrooms on the second floor, with a narrow staircase leading up to a third floor where, presumably, Gaafar slept. One of the bedroom doors was open, and she went in.

It did not look much like a small boy's bedroom. Elene did not know a lot about small boys—she had had four sisters— but she was expecting to see model airplanes, jigsaw puzzles, a train set, sports gear and perhaps an old, neglected teddy bear. She would not have been surprised to see clothes on the floor, a construction set on the bed and a pair of dirty football boots

on the polished surface of a desk. But the place might almost
have been the bedroom of an adult. The clothes were folded
neatly on a chair, the top of the chest of drawers was clear,
schoolbooks were stacked tidily on the desk and the only toy
in evidence was a cardboard model of a tank. Billy was in
bed, his striped pajama top buttoned to the neck, a book on
the blanket beside him.

"I like your room," Elene said deceitfully.

Billy said: "It's fine."

"What are you reading?"

"*The Greek Coffin Mystery.*"

She sat on the edge of the bed. "Well, don't stay awake too
late."

"I've to put out the light at nine-thirty."

She leaned forward suddenly and kissed his cheek.

At that moment the door opened and Vandam walked in.

∽

It was the familiarity of the scene that was so shocking: the
boy in bed with his book, the light from the bedside lamp
falling just so, the woman leaning forward to kiss the boy
good night. Vandam stood and stared, feeling like one who
knows he is in a dream but still cannot wake up.

Elene stood up and said: "Hello, William."

"Hello, Elene."

"Good night, Billy."

"Good night, Miss Fontana."

She went past Vandam and left the room. Vandam sat on the
edge of the bed, in the dip in the covers which she had vacated.
He said: "Been entertaining our guest?"

"Yes."

"Good man."

"I like her—she reads detective stories. We're going to swap
books."

"That's grand. Have you done your prep?"

"Yes—French vocab."

"Want me to test you?"

"It's all right, Gaafar tested me. I say, she's ever so pretty, isn't she."

"Yes. She's working on something for me—it's a bit hush-hush, so . . ."

"My lips are sealed."

Vandam smiled. "That's the stuff."

Billy lowered his voice. "Is she, you know, a secret agent?"

Vandam put a finger to his lips. "Walls have ears."

The boy looked suspicious. "You're having me on."

Vandam shook his head silently.

Billy said: "Gosh!"

Vandam stood up. "Lights out at nine-thirty."

"Right-ho. Good night."

"Good night, Billy." Vandam went out. As he closed the door it occurred to him that Elene's good-night kiss had probably done Billy a lot more good than his father's man-to-man chat.

He found Elene in the drawing room, shaking martinis. He felt he should have resented more than he did the way she had made herself at home in his house, but he was too tired to strike attitudes. He sank gratefully into a chair and accepted a drink.

Elene said: "Busy day?"

Vandam's whole section had been working on the new wireless security procedures that were being introduced following the capture of the German listening unit at the Hill of Jesus, but Vandam was not going to tell Elene that. Also, he felt she was playacting the role of housewife, and she had no right to do that. He said: "What made you come here?"

"I've got a date with Wolff."

"Wonderful!" Vandam immediately forgot all lesser concerns. "When?"

"Thursday." She handed him a sheet of paper.

He studied the message. It was a peremptory summons written in a clear, stylish script. "How did this come?"

"A boy brought it to my door."

"Did you question the boy? Where he was given the message and by whom, and so on?"

She was crestfallen. "I never thought to do that."

"Never mind." Wolff would have taken precautions, anyway; the boy would have known nothing of value.

"What will we do?" Elene asked.

"The same as last time, only better." Vandam tried to sound more confident than he felt. It should have been simple. The man makes a date with a girl, so you go to the meeting place and arrest the man when he turns up. But Wolff was unpredictable. He would not get away with the taxi trick again: Vandam would have the restaurant surrounded, twenty or thirty men and several cars, roadblocks in readiness and so on. But he might try a different trick. Vandam could not imagine what—and that was the problem.

As if she were reading his mind Elene said: "I don't want to spend another evening with him."

"Why?"

"He frightens me."

Vandam felt guilty—*remember Istanbul*—and suppressed his sympathy. "But last time he did you no harm."

"He didn't try to seduce me, so I didn't have to say no. But he will, and I'm afraid he won't take no for an answer."

"We've learned our lesson," Vandam said with false assurance. "There'll be no mistakes this time." Secretly he was surprised by her simple determination not to go to bed with Wolff. He had assumed that such things did not matter much, one way or the other, to her. He had misjudged her, then. Seeing her in this new light somehow made him very cheerful. He decided he must be honest with her. "I should rephrase that," he said. "I'll do everything in my power to make sure that there are no mistakes this time."

Gaafar came in and said: "Dinner is served, sir." Vandam smiled: Gaafar was doing his English-butler act in honor of the feminine company.

Vandam said to Elene: "Have you eaten?"

"No."

"What have we got, Gaafar?"

"For you, sir, clear soup, scrambled eggs and yoghurt. But I took the liberty of grilling a chop for Miss Fontana."

Elene said to Vandam: "Do you always eat like that?"

"No, it's because of my cheek, I can't chew." He stood up.

As they went into the dining room Elene said: "Does it still hurt?"

"Only when I laugh. It's true—I can't stretch the muscles on that side. I've got into the habit of smiling with one side of my face."

They sat down, and Gaafar served the soup.

Elene said: "I like your son very much."

"So do I," Vandam said.

"He's old beyond his years."

"Do you think that's a bad thing?"

She shrugged. "Who knows?"

"He's been through a couple of things that ought to be reserved for adults."

"Yes." Elene hesitated. "When did your wife die?"

"May the twenty-eighth, nineteen-forty-one, in the evening."

"Billy told me it happened in Crete."

"Yes. She worked on cryptanalysis for the Air Force. She was on a temporary posting to Crete at the time the Germans invaded the island. May twenty-eighth was the day the British realized they had lost the battle and decided to get out. Apparently she was hit by a stray shell and killed instantly. Of course, we were trying to get live people away then, not bodies, so . . . There's no grave, you see. No memorial. Nothing left."

Elene said quietly: "Do you still love her?"

"I think I'll always be in love with her. I believe it's like that with people you really love. If they go away, or die, it makes no difference. If ever I were to marry again, I would still love Angela."

"Were you very happy?"

"We . . ." He hesitated, unwilling to answer, then he realized that the hesitation was an answer in itself. "Ours wasn't an idyllic marriage. It was I who was *devoted* . . . Angela was fond of me."

"Do you think you will marry again?"

"Well. The English in Cairo keep thrusting replicas of Angela at me." He shrugged. He did not know the answer to the question. Elene seemed to understand, for she fell silent and began to eat her dessert.

Afterward Gaafar brought them coffee in the drawing room. It was at this time of day that Vandam usually began to hit the bottle seriously, but tonight he did not want to drink. He sent Gaafar to bed, and they drank their coffee. Vandam smoked a cigarette.

He felt the desire for music. He had loved music, at one time, although lately it had gone out of his life. Now, with the mild night air coming in through the open windows and the smoke curling up from his cigarette, he wanted to hear clear, delightful notes, and sweet harmonies, and subtle rhythms. He went to the piano and looked at the music. Elene watched him in silence. He began to play "Für Elise." The first few notes sounded, with Beethoven's characteristic, devastating simplicity; then the hesitation; then the rolling tune. The ability to play came back to him instantly, almost as if he had never stopped. His hands knew what to do in a way he always felt was miraculous.

When the song was over he went back to Elene, sat next to her, and kissed her cheek. Her face was wet with tears. She said: "William, I love you with all my heart."

∽

They whisper.

She says, "I like your ears."

He says, "Nobody has ever licked them before."

She giggles. "Do you like it?"

"Yes, yes." He sighs. "Can I . . . ?"

"Undo the buttons—here—that's right—aah."

"I'll put out the light."

"No, I want to see you—"

"There's a moon." *Click.* "There, see? The moonlight is enough."

"Come back here quickly—"

"I'm here."

"Kiss me again, William."

They do not speak for a while. Then:

"Can I take this thing off?" he says.

"Let me help . . . there."

"Oh! Oh, they're so *pretty*."

"I'm so glad you like them . . . would you do that harder . . . suck a little . . . aah, God—"

And a little later she says:

"Let me feel *your* chest. Damn buttons—I've ripped your shirt—"

"The hell with that."

"Ah, I knew it would be like this . . . Look."

"What?"

"Our skins in the moonlight—you're so pale and I'm nearly black, look—"

"Yes."

"Touch me. Stroke me. Squeeze, and pinch, and explore, I want to feel your hands all over me—"

"Yes—"

"—everywhere, your hands, there, yes, especially there, oh, you *know*, you know *exactly* where, oh!"

"You're so soft inside."

"This is a dream."

"No, it's real."

"I never want to wake up."

"So soft . . ."

"And you're so hard . . . Can I kiss it?"

"Yes, please . . . Ah . . . Jesus it feels good—*Jesus*—"

"William?"

"Yes?"

"Now, William?"

"Oh, yes."

". . . Take them off."

"Silk."

"Yes. Be quick."

"Yes."

"I've wanted this for so long—"

She gasps, and he makes a sound like a sob, and then there is only their breathing for many minutes, until finally he begins to shout aloud, and she smothers his cries with her kisses and then she, too, feels it, and she turns her face into the cushion and opens her mouth and screams into the cushion, and he not being used to this thinks something is wrong and says:

"It's all right, it's all right, it's all right—"

—and finally she goes limp, and lies with her eyes closed for a while, perspiring, until her breathing returns to normal, then she looks up at him and says:

"So *that's* how it's supposed to be!"

And he laughs, and she looks quizzically at him, so he explains:

"That's exactly what I was thinking."

Then they both laugh, and he says:

"I've done a lot of things after . . . you know, afterwards . . . but I don't think I've ever laughed."

"I'm so glad," she says. "Oh, William, I'm so glad."

18

Rommel could smell the sea. At Tobruk the heat and the dust and the flies were as bad as they had been in the desert, but it was all made bearable by that occasional whiff of salty dampness in the faint breeze.

Von Mellenthin came into the command vehicle with his intelligence report. "Good evening, Field Marshal."

Rommel smiled. He had been promoted after the victory at Tobruk, and he had not yet gotten used to the new title. "Anything new?"

"A signal from the spy in Cairo. He says the Mersa Matruh Line is weak in the middle."

Rommel took the report and began to glance over it. He smiled when he read that the Allies anticipated he would try a dash around the southern end of the line: it seemed they were beginning to understand his thinking. He said: "So the minefield gets thinner at this point . . . but there the line is defended by two columns. What is a column?"

"It's a new term they're using. According to one of our prisoners of war, a column is a brigade group that has been twice overrun by Panzers."

"A weak force, then."

"Yes."

Rommel tapped the report with his forefinger. "If this is correct, we can burst through the Mersa Matruh Line as soon as we get there."

"I'll be doing my best to check the spy's report over the next day or two, of course," said von Mellenthin. "But he was right last time."

The door to the vehicle flew open and Kesselring came in.

Rommel was startled. "Field Marshall" he said. "I thought you were in Sicily."

"I was," Kesselring said. He stamped the dust off his hand-made boots. "I've just flown here to see you. Damn it, Rommel, this has got to stop. Your orders are quite clear: you were to advance to Tobruk and no farther."

Rommel sat back in his canvas chair. He had hoped to keep Kesselring out of this argument. "The circumstances have changed," he said.

"But your original orders have been confirmed by the Italian Supreme Command," said Kesselring. "And what was your re-action? You declined the 'advice' and invited Bastico to lunch with you in Cairo!"

Nothing infuriated Rommel more than orders from Italians. "The Italians have done *nothing* in this war," he said angrily.

"That is irrelevant. Your air and sea support is now needed for the attack on Malta. After we have taken Malta your com-munications will be secure for the advance to Egypt."

"You people have learned nothing!" Rommel said. He made an effort to lower his voice. "While we are digging in the enemy, too, will be digging in. I did not get this far by playing the old game of advance, consolidate, then advance again. When they attack, I dodge; when they defend a position I go around that position; and when they retreat I chase them. They are running now, and now is the time to take Egypt."

Kesselring remained calm. "I have a copy of your cable to Mussolini." He took a piece of paper from his pocket and read: "The state and morale of the troops, the present supply posi-tion owing to captured dumps and the present weakness of the enemy permit our pursuing him into the depths of the Egyptian area." He folded the sheet of paper and turned to von Mellenthin. "How many German tanks and men do we have?"

Rommel suppressed the urge to tell von Mellenthin not to answer: he knew this was a weak point.

"Sixty tanks, Field Marshal, and two thousand five hundred men."

"And the Italians?"

"Six thousand men and fourteen tanks."

Kesselring turned back to Rommel. "And you're going to take Egypt with a total of seventy-four tanks? Von Mellenthin, what is our estimate of the enemy's strength?"

"The Allied forces are approximately three times as numerous as ours, but—"

"There you are."

Von Mellenthin went on: "—but we are very well supplied with food, clothing, trucks and armored cars, and fuel; and the men are in tremendous spirits."

Rommel said: "Von Mellenthin, go to the communications truck and see what has arrived."

Von Mellenthin frowned, but Rommel did not explain, so he went out.

Rommel said: "The Allies are regrouping at Mersa Matruh. They expect us to move around the southern end of their line. Instead we will hit the middle, where they are weakest—"

"How do you know all this?" Kesselring interrupted.

"Our intelligence assessment—"

"On what is the assessment based?"

"Primarily on a spy report—"

"My God!" For the first time Kesselring raised his voice. "You've no tanks, but you have your spy!"

"He was right last time."

Von Mellenthin came back in.

Kesselring said: "All this makes no difference. I am here to confirm the Fuehrer's orders: you are to advance no farther."

Rommel smiled. "I have sent a personal envoy to the Fuehrer."

"You . . . ?"

"I am a Field Marshal now, I have direct access to Hitler."

"Of course."

"I think von Mellenthin may have the Fuehrer's reply."

"Yes," said von Mellenthin. He read from a sheet of paper. "It is only once in a lifetime that the Goddess of Victory smiles. Onward to Cairo. Adolf Hitler."

There was a silence.

Kesselring walked out.

19

When Vandam got to his office he learned that, the previous evening, Rommel had advanced to within sixty miles of Alexandria.

Rommel seemed unstoppable. The Mersa Matruh Line had broken in half like a matchstick. In the south, the 13th Corps had retreated in a panic, and in the north the fortress of Mersa Matruh had capitulated. The Allies had fallen back once again —but this would be the last time. The new line of defense stretched across a thirty-mile gap between the sea and the impassable Qattara Depression, and if that line fell there would be no more defenses, Egypt would be Rommel's.

The news was not enough to dampen Vandam's elation. It was more than twenty-four hours since he had awakened at dawn, on the sofa in his drawing room, with Elene in his arms. Since then he had been suffused with a kind of adolescent glee. He kept remembering little details: how small and brown her nipples were, the taste of her skin, her sharp fingernails digging into his thighs. In the office he had been behaving a little out of character, he knew. He had given back a letter to his typist, saying: "There are seven errors in this, you'd better do it again," and smiled at her sunnily. She had nearly fallen off her chair. He thought of Elene, and he thought: "Why not? Why the hell not?" and there was no reply.

He was visited early by an officer from the Special Liaison Unit. Anybody with his ear to the ground in GHQ now knew that the SLUs had a very special, ultra-secret source of intelligence. Opinions differed as to how good the intelligence was, and evaluation was always difficult because they would never tell you the source. Brown, who held the rank of captain but was quite plainly not a military man, leaned on the edge of the table and spoke around the stem of his pipe. "Are you being evacuated, Vandam?"

These chaps lived in a world of their own, and there was no point in telling them that a captain had to call a major "sir." Vandam said: "What? Evacuated? Why?"

"Our lot's off to Jerusalem. So's everyone who knows too much. Keep people out of enemy hands, you know."

"The brass is getting nervous, then." It was logical, really: Rommel could cover sixty miles in a day.

"There'll be riots at the station, you'll see—half Cairo's trying to get out and the other half is preening itself ready for the liberation. Ha!"

"You won't tell too many people that you're going . . ."

"No, no, no. Now, then, I've got a little snippet for you. We all know Rommel's got a spy in Cairo."

"How did you know?" Vandam said.

"Stuff comes through from London, old boy. Anyhow, the chap has been identified as, and I quote, 'the hero of the Rashid Ali affair.' Mean anything to you?"

Vandam was thunderstruck. "It does!" he said.

"Well, that's it." Brown got off the table.

"Just a minute," Vandam said. "Is that *all*?"

"I'm afraid so."

"What is this, a decrypt or an agent report?"

"Suffice it to say that the source is reliable."

"You always say that."

"Yes. Well, I may not see you for a while. Good luck."

"Thanks," Vandam muttered distractedly.

"Toodle-oo!" Brown went out, puffing smoke.

The hero of the Rashid Ali affair. It was incredible that Wolff should have been the man who outwitted Vandam in Istanbul. Yet it made sense: Vandam recalled the odd feeling he had had about Wolff's *style,* as if it were familiar. The girl whom Vandam had sent to pick up the mystery man had had her throat cut.

And now Vandam was sending Elene in against the same man.

A corporal came in with an order. Vandam read it with mounting disbelief. All departments were to extract from their files those papers which might be dangerous in enemy hands, and burn them. Just about anything in the files of an intelligence section might be dangerous in enemy hands. We might as well burn the whole damn lot, Vandam thought. And how would departments operate afterward? Clearly the brass thought the departments would not be operating at all for very much longer. Of course it was a precaution, but it was a very drastic one: they would not destroy the accumulated results of years of work unless they thought there was a very strong chance indeed of the Germans taking Egypt.

It's going to pieces, he thought; it's falling apart.

It was unthinkable. Vandam had given three years of his life to the defense of Egypt. Thousands of men had died in the desert. After all that, was it possible that we could lose? Actually give up, and turn and run away? It did not bear contemplating.

He called Jakes in and watched him read the order. Jakes just nodded, as if he had been expecting it. Vandam said: "Bit drastic, isn't it?"

"It's rather like what's been happening in the desert, sir," Jakes replied. "We establish huge supply dumps at enormous cost, then as we retreat we blow them up to keep them out of enemy hands."

Vandam nodded. "All right, you'd better get on with it. Try and play it down a bit, for the sake of morale—you know, brass getting the wind up unnecessarily, that sort of thing."

"Yes, sir. We'll have the bonfire in the yard at the back, shall we?"

"Yes. Find an old dustbin and poke holes in its bottom. Make sure the stuff burns up properly."

"What about your own files?"

"I'll go through them now."

"Very good, sir." Jakes went out.

Vandam opened his file drawer and began to sort through his papers. Countless times over the last three years he had thought: I don't need to remember that, I can always look it up. There were names and addresses, security reports on individuals, details of codes, systems of communication of orders, case notes and a little file of jottings about Alex Wolff. Jakes brought in a big cardboard box with "Lipton's Tea" printed on its side, and Vandam began to dump papers into it, thinking: This is what it is like to be the losers.

The box was half full when Vandam's corporal opened the door and said: "Major Smith to see you, sir."

"Send him in." Vandam did not know a Major Smith.

The major was a small, thin man in his forties with bulbous blue eyes and an air of being rather pleased with himself. He shook hands and said: "Sandy Smith, S.I.S."

Vandam said: "What can I do for the Secret Intelligence Service?"

"I'm sort of the liaison man between S.I.S. and the General Staff," Smith explained. "You made an inquiry about a book called *Rebecca* . . ."

"Yes."

"The answer got routed through us." Smith produced a piece of paper with a flourish.

Vandam read the message. The S.I.S. Head of Station in Portugal had followed up the query about *Rebecca* by sending one of his men to visit all the English-language bookshops in the country. In the holiday area of Estoril he had found a bookseller who recalled selling his entire stock—six copies—of *Rebecca* to one woman. On further investigation the woman had turned out to be the wife of the German military attaché in Lisbon.

Vandam said: "This confirms something I suspected. Thank you for taking the trouble to bring it over."

"No trouble," Smith said. "I'm over here every morning anyway. Glad to be able to help." He went out.

Vandam reflected on the news while he went on with his work. There was only one plausible explanation of the fact that the book had found its way from Estoril to the Sahara. Undoubtedly it was the basis of a code—and, unless there were two successful German spies in Cairo, it was Alex Wolff who was using that code.

The information would be useful, sooner or later. It was a pity the key to the code had not been captured along with the book and the decrypt. That thought reminded him of the importance of burning his secret papers, and he determined to be more ruthless about what he destroyed.

At the end he considered his files on pay and promotion of subordinates, and decided to burn those too since they might help enemy interrogation teams fix their priorities. The cardboard box was full. He hefted it on to his shoulder and went outside.

Jakes had the fire going in a rusty steel water tank propped up on bricks. A corporal was feeding papers to the flames. Vandam dumped his box and watched the blaze for a while. It reminded him of Guy Fawkes Night in England, fireworks and baked potatoes and the burning effigy of a seventeenth-century traitor. Charred scraps of paper floated up on a pillar of hot air. Vandam turned away.

He wanted to think, so he decided to walk. He left GHQ and headed downtown. His cheek was hurting. He thought he should welcome the pain, for it was supposed to be a sign of healing. He was growing a beard to cover the wound so that he would look a little less unsightly when the dressing came off. Every day he enjoyed not having to shave in the morning.

He thought of Elene, and remembered her with her back arched and perspiration glistening on her naked breasts. He had been shocked by what had happened after he had kissed her—shocked, but thrilled. It had been a night of firsts for him: first time he had made love anywhere other than on a bed, first time he had seen a woman have a climax like a man's, first time sex had been a mutual indulgence rather than the imposition of his will on a more or less reluctant woman. It was, of course, a disaster that he and Elene had fallen so joyfully in love. His parents, his friends and the Army would be aghast at the idea of his marrying a wog. His mother would also feel bound to explain why the Jews were wrong to reject Jesus. Vandam decided not to worry over all that. He and Elene might be dead within a few days. We'll bask in the sunshine while it lasts, he thought, and to hell with the future.

His thoughts kept returning to the girl whose throat had been cut, apparently by Wolff, in Istanbul. He was terrified that something might go wrong on Thursday and Elene might find herself alone with Wolff again.

Looking around him, he realized that there was a festive feeling in the air. He passed a hairdresser's salon and noticed that it was packed out, with women standing waiting. The dress shops seemed to be doing good business. A woman came out of a grocer's with a basket full of canned food, and Vandam saw that there was a queue stretching out of the shop and along the pavement. A sign in the window of the next shop said, in hasty scribble: "Sorry, no maekup." Vandam realized that the Egyptians were preparing to be liberated, and looking forward to it.

He could not escape a sense of impending doom. Even the sky seemed dark. He looked up: the sky *was* dark. There seemed to be a gray swirling mist, dotted with particles, over the city. He realized that it was smoke mixed with charred paper. All across Cairo the British were burning their files, and the sooty smoke had blotted out the sun.

Vandam was suddenly furious with himself and the rest of the Allied armies for preparing so equably for defeat. Where was the spirit of the Battle of Britain? What had happened to that famous mixture of obstinacy, ingenuity and courage which was supposed to characterize the nation? What, Vandam asked himself, are *you* planning to do about it?

He turned around and walked back toward Garden City, where GHQ was billeted in commandeered villas. He visualized the map of the El Alamein Line, where the Allies would make their last stand. This was one line Rommel could not circumvent, for at its southern end was the vast impassable Qattara Depression. So Rommel would have to break the line.

Where would he try to break through? If he came through the northern end, he would then have to choose between dashing straight for Alexandria and wheeling around and attacking the Allied forces from behind. If he came through the southern end he must either dash for Cairo or, again, wheel around and destroy the remains of the Allied forces.

Immediately behind the line was the Alam Halfa ridge, which Vandam knew was heavily fortified. Clearly it would be better for the Allies if Rommel wheeled around after breaking through the line, for then he might well spend his strength attacking Alam Halfa.

There was one more factor. The southern approach to Alam Halfa was through treacherous soft sand. It was unlikely that Rommel knew about the quicksand, for he had never penetrated this far east before, and only the Allies had good maps of the desert.

So, Vandam thought, my duty is to prevent Alex Wolff telling Rommel that Alam Halfa is well defended and cannot be attacked from the south.

It was a depressingly negative plan.

Vandam had come, without consciously intending it, to the Villa les Oliviers, Wolff's house. He sat in the little park opposite it, under the olive trees, and stared at the building as if it might tell him where Wolff was. He thought idly: If only Wolff would make a mistake, and encourage Rommel to attack Alam Halfa from the south.

Then it hit him.

Suppose I do capture Wolff. Suppose I also get his radio. Suppose I even find the key to his code.

Then I could impersonate Wolff, get on the radio to Rommel, and tell him to attack Alam Halfa from the south.

The idea blossomed rapidly in his mind, and he began to feel elated. By now Rommel was convinced, quite rightly, that Wolff's information was good. Suppose he got a message from Wolff saying the El Alamein Line was weak at the southern end, that the southern approach to Alam Halfa was hard going, and that Alam Halfa itself was weakly defended.

The temptation would be too much for Rommel to resist.

He would break through the line at the southern end and then swing northward, expecting to take Alam Halfa without much trouble. Then he would hit the quicksand. While he was struggling through it, our artillery would decimate his forces. When he reached Alam Halfa he would find it heavily defended. At that point we would bring in more forces from the front line and squeeze the enemy like a nutcracker.

If the ambush worked well, it might not only save Egypt but annihilate the Afrika Korps.

He thought: I've got to put this idea up to the brass.

It would not be easy. His standing was not very high just now—in fact his professional reputation was in ruins on account of Alex Wolff. But surely they would see the merit of the idea.

He got up from the bench and headed for his office. Suddenly the future looked different. Perhaps the jackboot would not ring out on the tiled floors of the mosques. Perhaps the treasures of the Egyptian Museum would not be shipped to Berlin. Perhaps Billy would not have to join the Hitler Youth. Perhaps Elene would not be sent to Dachau.

We could all be saved, he thought.

If I catch Wolff.

PART THREE

ALAM HALFA

20

One of these days, Vandam thought, I'm going to punch Bogge on the nose.

Today Lieutenant Colonel Bogge was at his worst: indecisive, sarcastic and touchy. He had a nervous cough which he used when he was afraid to speak, and he was coughing a lot now. He was also fidgeting: tidying piles of papers on his desk, crossing and uncrossing his legs and polishing his wretched cricket ball.

Vandam sat still and quiet, waiting for him to tie himself up in knots.

"Now look here, Vandam, strategy is for Auchinleck. Your job is personnel security—and you're not doing very well."

"Nor is Auchinleck," Vandam said.

Bogge pretended not to hear. He picked up Vandam's memo. Vandam had written out his deception plan and formally submitted it to Bogge, with a copy to the brigadier. "For one thing, this is full of holes," Bogge said.

Vandam said nothing.

"Full of holes." Bogge coughed. "For one thing, it involves letting old Rommel through the line, doesn't it?"

Vandam said: "Perhaps the plan could be made contingent on his getting through."

"Yes. Now, you see? This is the kind of thing I mean. If you put up a plan that's full of holes like that, given that your reputation is at a pretty damn low point around here at the moment, well, you'll be laughed out of Cairo. Now." He coughed. "You want to encourage Rommel to attack the line at its weakest point—giving him a better chance of getting through! You see?"

"Yes. Some parts of the line are weaker than others, and since Rommel has air reconnaissance there's a chance he'll know which parts."

"And you want to turn a chance into a certainty."

"For the sake of the subsequent ambush, yes."

"Now, it seems to me that we want old Rommel to attack the *strongest* part of the line, so that he won't get through at all."

"But if we repel him, he'll just regroup and hit us again. Whereas if we trap him we could finish him off finally."

"No, no, no. Risky. Risky. This is our last line of defense, laddie." Bogge laughed. "After this, there's nothing but one little canal between him and Cairo. You don't seem to realize—"

"I realize very well, sir. Let me put it this way. One: if Rommel gets through the line he must be diverted to Alam Halfa by the false prospect of an easy victory. Two: it is preferable that he attack Alam Halfa from the south, because of the quicksand. Three: either we must wait and see which end of the line he attacks, and take the risk that he will go north; or we must encourage him to go south, and take the risk that we will thereby increase his chances of breaking through the line in the first place."

"Well," said Bogge, "now that we've rephrased it, the plan is beginning to make a bit more sense. Now look here: you're going to have to leave it with me for a while. When I've got a moment I'll go through the thing with a fine-toothed comb, and see if I can knock it into shape. Then perhaps we'll put it up to the brass."

I see, Vandam thought: the object of the exercise is to make it Bogge's plan. Well, what the hell? If Bogge can be bothered to play politics at this stage, good luck to him. It's winning that matters, not getting the credit.

Vandam said: "Very good, sir. If I might just emphasize the time factor . . . If the plan is to be put into operation, it must be done quickly."

"I think I'm the best judge of its urgency, Major, don't you?"

"Yes, sir."

"And, after all, everything depends on catching the damn spy, something at which you have not so far been entirely successful, am I right?"

"Yes, sir."

"I'll be taking charge of tonight's operation myself, to ensure that there are no further foul-ups. Let me have your proposals this afternoon, and we'll go over them together—"

There was a knock at the door and the brigadier walked in. Vandam and Bogge stood up.

Bogge said: "Good morning, sir."

"At ease, gentlemen," the brigadier said. "I've been looking for you, Vandam."

Bogge said: "We were just working on an idea we had for a deception plan—"

"Yes, I saw the memo."

"Ah, Vandam sent you a copy," Bogge said. Vandam did not look at Bogge, but he knew the lieutenant colonel was furious with him.

"Yes, indeed," said the brigadier. He turned to Vandam. "You're supposed to be catching spies, Major, not advising generals on strategy. Perhaps if you spent less time telling us how to win the war you might be a better security officer."

Vandam's heart sank.

Bogge said: "I was just saying—"

The brigadier interrupted him. "However, since you have done this, and since it's such a splendid plan, I want you to come with me and sell it to Auchinleck. You can spare him, Bogge, can't you?"

"Of course, sir," Bogge said through clenched teeth.

"All right, Vandam. The conference will be starting any minute. Let's go."

Vandam followed the brigadier out and shut the door very softly on Bogge.

◇

On the day that Wolff was to see Elene again, Major Smith came to the houseboat at lunchtime.

The information he brought with him was the most valuable yet.

Wolff and Sonja went through their now-familiar routine. Wolff felt like an actor in a French farce, who has to hide in the same stage wardrobe night after night. Sonja and Smith, following the script, began on the couch and moved into the bedroom. When Wolff emerged from the cupboard the curtains were closed, and there on the floor were Smith's briefcase, his shoes and his shorts with the key ring poking out of the pocket.

Wolff opened the briefcase and began to read.

Once again Smith had come to the houseboat straight from the morning conference at GHQ, at which Auchinleck and his staff discussed Allied strategy and decided what to do.

After a few minutes' reading Wolff realized that what he held in his hand was a complete rundown of the Allies' last-ditch defense on the El Alamein Line.

The line consisted of artillery on the ridges, tanks on the level ground and minefields all along. The Alam Halfa ridge, five miles behind the center of the line, was also heavily fortified. Wolff noted that the southern end of the line was weaker, both in troops and mines.

Smith's briefcase also contained an enemy-position paper. Allied Intelligence thought Rommel would probably try to break through the line at the southern end, but noted that the northern end was possible.

Beneath this, written in pencil in what was presumably Smith's handwriting, was a note which Wolff found more exciting than all the rest of the stuff put together. It read: "Major Vandam proposes deception plan. Encourage Rommel to break through at southern end, lure him toward Alam Halfa, catch him in quicksand, then nutcracker. Plan accepted by Auk."

"Auk" was Auchinleck, no doubt. What a discovery this was! Not only did Wolff hold in his hand the details of the Allied defense line—he also knew what they expected Rommel to do, *and* he knew their deception plan.

And the deception plan was Vandam's!

This would be remembered as the greatest espionage coup of the century. Wolff himself would be responsible for assuring Rommel's victory in North Africa.

They should make me King of Egypt for this, he thought, and he smiled.

He looked up and saw Smith standing between the curtains, staring down at him.

Smith roared: "Who the devil are you?"

Wolff realized angrily that he had not been paying attention to the noises from the bedroom. Something had gone wrong, the script had not been followed, there had been no champagne-cork warning. He had been totally absorbed in the strategic appreciation. The endless names of divisions and brigades, the numbers of men and tanks, the quantities of fuel and supplies, the ridges and depressions and quicksands had monopolized his attention to the exclusion of local sounds. He was suddenly terribly afraid that he might be thwarted in his moment of triumph.

Smith said: "That's my bloody briefcase!"

He took a step forward.

Wolff reached out, caught Smith's foot, and heaved sideways. The major toppled over and hit the floor with a heavy thud.

Sonja screamed.

Wolff and Smith both scrambled to their feet.

Smith was a small, thin man, ten years older than Wolff and in poor shape. He stepped backward, fear showing in his face. He bumped into a shelf, glanced sideways, saw a cut-glass fruit bowl on the shelf, picked it up and hurled it at Wolff.

It missed, fell into the kitchen sink, and shattered loudly.

The noise, Wolff thought: if he makes any more noise people will come to investigate. He moved toward Smith.

Smith, with his back to the wall, yelled: "Help!"

Wolff hit him once, on the point of the jaw, and he collapsed, sliding down the wall to sit, unconscious, on the floor.

Sonja came out and stared at him.

Wolff rubbed his knuckles. "It's the first time I've ever done that," he said.

"What?"

"Hit somebody on the chin and knocked him out. I thought only boxers could do that."

"Never mind that, what are we going to do about him?"

"I don't know." Wolff considered the possibilities. To kill Smith would be dangerous, for the death of an officer—and the disappearance of his briefcase—would now cause a terrific rumpus throughout the city. There would be the problem of what to do with the body. And Smith would bring home no more secrets.

Smith groaned and stirred.

Wolff wondered whether it might be possible to let him go. After all, if Smith were to reveal what had been going on in the houseboat he would implicate himself. Not only would it ruin his career, he would probably be thrown in jail. He did not look like the kind of man to sacrifice himself for a higher cause.

Let him go free? No, the chance was too much to take. To know that there was a British officer in the city who possessed all of Wolff's secrets . . . Impossible.

Smith had his eyes open. "You . . ." he said. "You're Slavenburg . . ." He looked at Sonja, then back at Wolff. "It was you who introduced . . . in the Cha-Cha . . . this was all planned . . ."

"Shut up," Wolff said mildly. Kill him or let him go: what other options were there? Only one: to keep him here, bound and gagged, until Rommel reached Cairo.

"You're damned spies," Smith said. His face was white.

Sonja said nastily: "And you thought I was crazy for your miserable body."

"Yes." Smith was recovering. "I should have known better than to trust a wog bitch."

Sonja stepped forward and kicked his face with her bare foot.

"Stop it!" Wolff said. "We've got to think what to do with him. Have we got any rope to tie him with?"

Sonja thought for a moment. "Up on deck, in that locker at the forward end."

Wolff took from the kitchen drawer the heavy steel he used for sharpening the carving knife. He gave the steel to Sonja. "If he moves, hit him with that," he said. He did not think Smith would move.

He was about to go up the ladder to the deck when he heard footsteps on the gangplank.

Sonja said: "Postman!"

Wolff knelt in front of Smith and drew his knife. "Open your mouth."

Smith began to say something, and Wolff slid the knife between Smith's teeth.

Wolff said: "Now, if you move or speak, I'll cut out your tongue."

Smith sat dead still, staring at Wolff with a horrified look.

Wolff realized that Sonja was stark naked. "Put something on, quickly!"

She pulled a sheet off the bed and wrapped it around her as she went to the foot of the ladder. The hatch was opening. Wolff knew that he and Smith could be seen from the hatch. Sonja let the sheet slide down a little as she reached up to take the letter from the postman's outstretched hand.

"Good morning!" the postman said. His eyes were riveted on Sonja's half-exposed breasts.

She went farther up the ladder toward him, so that he had to back away, and let the sheet slip even more. "Thank you," she simpered. She reached for the hatch and pulled it shut.

Wolff breathed again.

The postman's footsteps crossed the deck and descended the gangplank.

Wolff said to Sonja: "Give me that sheet."

She unwrapped herself and stood naked again.

Wolff withdrew the knife from Smith's mouth and used it

to cut off a foot or two of the sheet. He crumpled the cotton into a ball and stuffed it into Smith's mouth. Smith did not resist. Wolff slid the knife into its underarm sheath. He stood up. Smith closed his eyes. He seemed limp, defeated.

Sonja picked up the sharpening steel and stood ready to hit Smith while Wolff went up the ladder and on to the deck. The locker Sonja had mentioned was in the riser of a step in the prow. Wolff opened it. Inside was a coil of slender rope. It had perhaps been used to tie up the vessel in the days before she became a houseboat. Wolff took the rope out. It was strong, but not too thick: ideal for tying someone's hands and feet.

He heard Sonja's voice, from below, raised in a shout. There was a clatter of feet on the ladder.

Wolff dropped the rope and whirled around.

Smith, wearing only his underpants, came up through the hatch at a run.

He had not been as defeated as he looked—and Sonja must have missed him with the steel.

Wolff dashed across the deck to the gangplank to head him off.

Smith turned, ran to the other side of the boat, and jumped into the water.

Wolff said: "Shit!"

He looked all around quickly. There was no one on the decks of the other houseboats—it was the hour of the siesta. The towpath was deserted except for the "beggar"—Kemel would have to deal with him—and one man in the distance walking away. On the river there were a couple of feluccas, at least a quarter of a mile away, and a slow-moving steam barge beyond them.

Wolff ran to the edge. Smith surfaced, gasping for air. He wiped his eyes and looked around to get his bearings. He was clumsy in the water, splashing a lot. He began to swim, in-expertly, away from the houseboat.

Wolff stepped back several paces and took a running jump into the river.

He landed, feet first, on Smith's head.

For several seconds all was confusion. Wolff went underwater in a tangle of arms and legs—his and Smith's—and struggled to reach the surface and push Smith down at the same time. When he could hold his breath no longer he wriggled away from Smith and came up.

He sucked air and wiped his eyes. Smith's head bobbed up in front of him, coughing and spluttering. Wolff reached forward with both hands, grabbed Smith's head, and pulled it toward himself and down. Smith wriggled like a fish. Wolff got him around the neck and pushed down. Wolff himself went under the water, then came up again a moment later. Smith was still under, still struggling.

Wolff thought: How long does it take a man to drown?

Smith gave a convulsive jerk and freed himself. His head came up and he heaved a great lungful of air. Wolff tried to punch him. The blow landed, but it had no force. Smith was coughing and retching between shuddering gasps. Wolff himself had taken in water. Wolff reached for Smith again. This time he got behind the major and crooked one arm around the man's throat while he used the other to push down on the top of his head.

He thought: Christ, I hope no one is watching.

Smith went under. He was facedown in the water now, with Wolff's knees in his back, and his head held in a firm grip. He continued to thrash around under water, turning, jerking, flailing his arms, kicking his legs and trying to twist his body. Wolff tightened his grip and held him under.

Drown, you bastard, drown!

He felt Smith's jaws open and knew the man was at last breathing water. The convulsions grew more frantic. Wolff felt he was going to have to let go. Smith's struggle pulled Wolff under. Wolff squeezed his eyes shut and held his breath. It seemed Smith was weakening. By now his lungs must be half full of water, Wolff thought. After a few seconds Wolff himself began to need air.

Smith's movements became feeble. Holding the major less tightly, Wolff kicked himself upward and found air. For a minute he just breathed. Smith became a dead weight. Wolff used his legs to swim toward the houseboat, pulling Smith with him. Smith's head came up out of the water, but there was no sign of life.

Wolff reached the side of the boat. Sonja was up on deck, wearing a robe, staring over the side.

Wolff said: "Did anybody see?"

"I don't think so. Is he dead?"

"Yes."

Wolff thought: What the hell do I do now?

He held Smith against the side of the boat. If I let him go, he'll just float, he thought. The body will be found near here and there will be a house-to-house search. But I can't carry a body half across Cairo to get rid of it.

Suddenly Smith jerked and spewed water.

"Jesus Christ, he's alive!" Wolff said.

He pushed Smith under again. This was no good, it took too long. He let Smith go, pulled out his knife, and lunged. Smith was underwater, moving feebly. Wolff could not direct the knife. He slashed wildly. The water hampered him. Smith thrashed about. The foaming water turned pink. At last Wolff was able to grab Smith by the hair and hold his head still while he cut his throat.

Now he was dead.

Wolff let Smith go while he sheathed the knife again. The river water turned muddy red all around him. I'm swimming in blood, he thought, and he was suddenly filled with disgust.

The body was drifting away. Wolff pulled it back. He realized, too late, that a drowned major might simply have fallen in the river, but a major with his throat cut had unquestionably been murdered. Now he *had* to hide the body.

He looked up. "Sonja!"

"I feel ill."

"Never mind that. We have to make the body sink to the bottom."

"Oh, God, the water's all bloody."

"Listen to me!" He wanted to yell at her, to make her snap

out of it, but he had to keep his voice low. "Get . . . get that rope. Go on!"

She disappeared from view for a moment, and returned with the rope. She was helpless, Wolff decided: he would have to tell her exactly what to do.

"Now—get Smith's briefcase and put something heavy in it."

"Something heavy . . . but what?"

"Jesus Christ . . . What have we got that's heavy? What's heavy? Um . . . books, books are heavy, no, that might not be enough . . . I know, bottles. Full bottles—champagne bottles. Fill his briefcase with full bottles of champagne."

"Why?"

"My God, stop dithering, do what I tell you!"

She went away again. Through the porthole he could see her coming down the ladder and into the living room. She was moving very slowly, like a sleepwalker.

Hurry, you fat bitch, hurry!

She looked around her dazedly. Still moving in slow motion, she picked up the briefcase from the floor. She took it to the kitchen area and opened the icebox. She looked in, as if she were deciding what to have for dinner.

Come *on.*

She took out a champagne bottle. She stood with the bottle in one hand and the briefcase in the other, and she frowned, as if she could not remember what she was supposed to be doing with them. At last her expression cleared and she put the bottle in the case, laying it flat. She took another bottle out.

Wolff thought: Lay them head to toe, idiot, so you get more in.

She put the second bottle in, looked at it, then took it out and turned it the other way.

Brilliant, Wolff thought.

She managed to get four bottles in. She closed the icebox and looked around for something else to add to the weight. She picked up the sharpening steel and a glass paperweight. She put those into the briefcase and fastened it. Then she came up on deck.

"What now?" she said.

"Tie the end of the rope around the handle of the briefcase."

She was coming out of her daze. Her fingers moved more quickly.

"Tie it very tight," Wolff said.

"Okay."

"Is there anyone around?"

She glanced to left and right. "No."

"Hurry."

She finished the knot.

"Throw me the rope," Wolff said.

She threw down the other end of the rope and he caught it. He was tiring with the effort of keeping himself afloat and holding on to the corpse at the same time. He had to let Smith go for a moment because he needed both hands for the rope, which meant he had to tread water furiously to stay up. He threaded the rope under the dead man's armpits and pulled it through. He wound it around the torso twice, then tied a knot. Several times during the operation he found himself sinking, and once he took a revolting mouthful of bloody water.

At last the job was done.

"Test your knot," he told Sonja.

"It's tight."

"Throw the briefcase into the water—throw it as far out as you can."

She heaved the briefcase over the side. It splashed a couple of yards away from the houseboat—it had been too heavy for her to throw far—and went down. Slowly the rope followed the case. The length of rope between Smith and the case became taut, then the body went under. Wolff watched the surface. The knots were holding. He kicked his legs, underwater where the body had gone down: they did not contact anything. The body had sunk deep.

Wolff muttered: "*Liebe Gott,* what a shambles."

He climbed on deck. Looking back down, he saw that the pink tinge was rapidly disappearing from the water.

A voice said: "Good morning!"

Wolff and Sonja whirled around to face the towpath.

"Good morning!" Sonja replied. She muttered to Wolff in an undertone: "A neighbor."

The neighbor was a half-caste woman of middle age, carrying a shopping basket. She said: "I heard a lot of splashing—is there anything wrong?"

"Um . . . no," Sonja said. "My little dog fell in the water, and Mr. Robinson here had to rescue him."

"How gallant!" the woman said. "I didn't know you had a dog."

"He's a puppy, a gift."

"What kind?"

Wolff wanted to scream: Go away, you stupid old woman!

"A poodle," Sonja replied.

"I'd love to see him."

"Tomorrow, perhaps—he's been locked up as a punishment now."

"Poor thing."

Wolff said: "I'd better change my wet clothes."

Sonja said to the neighbor: "Until tomorrow."

"Lovely to meet you, Mr. Robinson," the neighbor said.

Wolff and Sonja went below.

Sonja slumped on the couch and closed her eyes. Wolff stripped off his wet clothes.

Sonja said: "It's the worst thing that's ever happened to me."

"You'll survive," Wolff said.

"At least it was an Englishman."

"Yes. You should be jumping for joy."

"I will when my stomach settles."

Wolff went into the bathroom and turned on the taps of the tub. When he came back Sonja said: "Was it worth it?"

"Yes." Wolff pointed to the military papers which were still on the floor, where he had dropped them when Smith surprised him. "That stuff is red-hot—the best he's ever brought us. With that, Rommel can win the war."

"When will you send it?"

"Tonight, at midnight."

"Tonight you're going to bring Elene here."

He stared at her. "How can you think of that when we've just killed a man and sunk his body?"

She stared at him defiantly. "I don't know, I just know it makes me feel very sexy."

"My God."

"You *will* bring her home tonight. You owe it to me."

Wolff hesitated. "I'd have to make the broadcast while she's here."

"I'll keep her busy while you're on the radio."

"I don't know—"

"Damn it, Alex, you *owe* me!"

"All right."

"Thank you."

Wolff went into the bathroom. Sonja was unbelievable, he thought. She took depravity to new heights of sophistication. He got into the hot water.

She called from the bedroom: "But now Smith won't be bringing you any more secrets."

"I don't think we'll need them, after the next battle," Wolff replied. "He's served his purpose."

He picked up the soap and began to wash off the blood.

21

Vandam knocked at the door of Elene's flat an hour before she was due to meet Alex Wolff.

She came to the door wearing a black cocktail dress and high-heeled black shoes with silk stockings. Around her neck was a slender gold chain. Her face was made up, and her hair gleamed. She had been expecting Vandam.

He smiled at her, seeing someone familiar yet at the same time astonishingly beautiful. "Hello."

"Come in." She led him into the living room. "Sit down."

He had wanted to kiss her, but she had not given him the chance. He sat on the couch. "I wanted to tell you the details for tonight."

"Okay." She sat on a chair opposite him. "Do you want a drink?"

"Sure."

"Help yourself."

He stared at her. "Is something wrong?"

"Nothing. Give yourself a drink, then brief me."

Vandam frowned. "What is this?"

"Nothing. We've got work to do, so let's do it."

He stood up, went across to her, and knelt in front of her chair. "Elene. What are you doing?"

She glared at him. She seemed close to tears. She said loudly: "Where have you been for the last two days?"

He looked away from her, thinking. "I've been at work."

"And where do you think I've been?"

"Here, I suppose."

"Exactly!"

He did not understand what that meant. It crossed his mind that he had fallen in love with a woman he hardly knew. He said: "I've been working, and you've been here, and so you're mad at me?"

She shouted: "Yes!"

Vandam said: "Calm down. I don't understand why you're so cross, and I want you to explain it to me."

"No!"

"Then I don't know what to say." Vandam sat on the floor with his back to her and lit a cigarette. He truly did not know what had upset her, but there was an element of willfulness in his attitude: he was ready to be humble, to apologize for whatever he had done, and to make amends—but he was not willing to play guessing games.

They sat in silence for a minute, not looking at one another. Elene sniffed. Vandam could not see her, but he knew the kind of sniff that came from weeping. She said: "You could have sent me a note, or even a bunch of bloody flowers!"

"A note? What for? You knew we were to meet tonight."

"Oh, my God."

"Flowers? What do you want with flowers? We don't need to play that game anymore."

"Oh, really?"

"What do you want me to say?"

"Listen. We made love the night before last, in case you've forgotten—"

"Don't be silly—"

"You brought me home and kissed me good-bye. Then—nothing."

He drew on his cigarette. "In case *you* have forgotten, a certain Erwin Rommel is knocking at the gates with a bunch of Nazis in tow, and I'm one of the people who's trying to keep him out."

"Five minutes, that's all it would have taken to send me a note."

"What *for?*"

"Well, exactly, what for? I'm a loose woman, am I not? I give myself to a man the way I take a drink of water. An hour later I've forgotten—is that what you think? Because that's how it seems to me! Damn you, William Vandam, you make me feel cheap!"

It made no more sense than it had at the start, but now he could hear the pain in her voice. He turned to face her. "You're the most wonderful thing that's happened to me for a long time, perhaps ever. Please forgive me for being a fool." He took her hand in his own.

She looked toward the window, biting her lip, fighting back tears. "Yes, you are," she said. She looked down at him and touched his hair. "You bloody, bloody fool," she whispered, stroking his head. Her eyes spilled tears.

"I've such a lot to learn about you," he said.

"And I about you."

He looked away, thinking aloud. "People resent my equanimity—always have. Those who work for me don't, they like it. They know that when they feel like panicking, when they feel they can't cope, they can come to me and tell me about the dilemma; and if I can't see a way through it, I'll tell them what is the best thing to do, the lesser evil; and because I say it in a calm voice, because I see that it's a dilemma and I don't panic, they go away reassured and do what they have to do. All I do is clarify the problem and refuse to be frightened by it; but that's just what they need. However . . . exactly the same attitude often infuriates other people—my superiors, my friends, Angela, you . . . I've never understood why."

"Because sometimes you *should* panic, fool," she said softly. "Sometimes you should show that you are frightened, or obsessed, or crazy for something. It's human, and it's a sign that you care. When you're so calm all the time we think it's because you don't give a damn."

Vandam said: "Well, people should know better. Lovers should know better, and so should friends, and bosses if they're any good." He said this honestly, but in the back of his mind he realized that there was indeed an element of ruthlessness, of cold-heartedness, in his famous equanimity.

"And if they don't know better . . . ?" She had stopped crying now.

"I should be different? No." He wanted to be honest with her now. He could have told her a lie to make her happy: Yes, you're right, I'll try to be different. But what was the point? If he could not be *himself* with her, it was all worthless, he would be manipulating her the way all men had manipulated her, the way he manipulated people he did not love. So he told her the truth. "You see, this is the way I win. I mean, win everything . . . the game of life—so to speak." He gave a wry grin. "I *am* detached. I look at everything from a distance. I *do* care, but I refuse to do pointless things, symbolic gestures, empty fits of rage. Either we love each other or we don't, and all the flowers in the world won't make any difference. But the work I did today could affect whether we live or die. I *did* think of you, all day; but each time I thought of you, I turned my mind to more urgent things. I work efficiently, I set priorities and I don't worry about you when I know you're okay. Can you imagine yourself getting used to that?"

She gave him a watery smile. "I'll try."

And all the time, in the back of his mind, he was thinking: For how long? Do I want this woman forever? What if I don't?

He pushed the thought down. Right now it was low priority. "What I want to say, after all that, is: Forget about tonight, don't go, we'll manage without you. But I can't. We need you, and it's terribly important."

"That's okay, I understand."

"But first of all, may I kiss you hello?"

"Yes, please."

Kneeling beside the arm of her chair, he took her face in

his big hand, and kissed her lips. Her mouth was soft and yielding, and slightly moist. He savored the feel and the taste of her. Never had he felt like this, as though he could go on kissing, just so, all night and never get tired.

Eventually she drew back, took a deep breath, and said: "My, my, I do believe you mean it."

"You may be sure of that."

She laughed. "When you said that, you were the old Major Vandam for a moment—the one I used to know before I knew you."

"And your 'My, my,' in that provocative voice was the old Elene."

"Brief me, Major."

"I'll have to get out of kissing distance."

"Sit over there and cross your legs. Anyway, what *were* you doing today?"

Vandam crossed the room to the drinks cupboard and found the gin. "A major in Intelligence has disappeared—along with a briefcase full of secrets."

"Wolff?"

"Could be. It turns out that this major has been disappearing at lunchtime, a couple of times a week, and nobody knows where he's been going. I've a hunch that he might have been meeting Wolff."

"So why would he disappear?"

Vandam shrugged. "Something went wrong."

"What was in his briefcase today?"

Vandam wondered how much to tell her. "A rundown of our defenses which was so complete that we think it could alter the result of the next battle." Smith had also been in possession of Vandam's proposed deception plan, but Vandam did not tell Elene this: he trusted her all the way, but he also had security instincts. He finished: "So, we'd better catch Wolff tonight."

"But it might be too late already!"

"No. We found the decrypt of one of Wolff's signals, a while back. It was timed at midnight. Spies have a set time for reporting, generally the same time every day. At other times their masters won't be listening—at least, not on the right wavelength—so even if they do signal nobody picks it up. Therefore, I think Wolff will send this information tonight at midnight—unless I catch him first." He hesitated, then changed his mind about security and decided she ought to know the full importance of what she was doing. "There's something else. He's using a code based on a novel called *Rebecca*. I've got a copy of the novel. If I can get the key to the code—"

"What's that?"

"Just a piece of paper telling him how to use the book to encode signals."

"Go on."

"If I can get the key to the *Rebecca* code, I can impersonate Wolff over the radio and send false information to Rommel. It could turn the tables completely—it could save Egypt. But I must have the key."

"All right. What's tonight's plan?"

"It's the same as before, only more so. I'll be in the restaurant with Jakes, and we'll both have pistols."

Her eyes widened. "You've got a gun?"

"I haven't got it now. Jakes is bringing it to the restaurant. Anyway, there will be two other men in the restaurant, and six more outside on the pavement, trying to look inconspicuous. There will also be civilian cars ready to block all exits from the street at the sound of a whistle. No matter what Wolff does tonight, if he wants to see you he's going to be caught."

There was a knock at the apartment door.

Vandam said: "What's that?"

"The door—"

"Yes, I know, are you expecting someone? Or something?"

"No, of course not, it's almost time for me to leave."

Vandam frowned. Alarm bells were sounding. "I don't like this. Don't answer."

"All right," Elene said. Then she changed her mind. "I have to answer. It might be my father. Or news of him."

"Okay, answer it."

Elene went out of the living room. Vandam sat listening.

The knock came again, then she opened the door.

Vandam heard her say: "Alex!"

Vandam whispered: "Christ!"

He heard Wolff's voice. "You're all ready. How delightful." It was a deep, confident voice, the drawled English spoken with only the faintest trace of an unidentifiable accent.

Elene said: "But we were to meet in the restaurant—"

"I know. May I come in?"

Vandam leaped over the back of the sofa and lay on the floor behind it.

Elene said: "Of course . . ."

Wolff's voice came closer. "My dear, you look exquisite tonight."

Vandam thought: Smooth bastard.

The front door slammed shut.

Wolff said: "This way?"

"Um . . . yes . . ."

Vandam heard the two of them enter the room. Wolff said: "What a lovely apartment. Mikis Aristopoulos must pay you well."

"Oh, I don't work there regularly. He's a distant relation, it's family, I help out."

"Uncle. He must be your uncle."

"Oh . . . great-uncle, second cousin, something. He calls me his niece for simplicity."

"Well. These are for you."

"Oh, flowers. Thank you."

Vandam thought: Fuck that.

Wolff said: "May I sit down?"

"Of course."

Vandam felt the sofa shift as Wolff lowered his weight onto it. Wolff was a big man. Vandam remembered grappling with him in the alley. He also remembered the knife, and his hand went to the wound on his cheek. He thought: What can I do?

He could jump Wolff now. The spy was here, practically in his hands! They were about the same weight, and evenly matched—except for the knife. Wolff had had the knife that night when he had been dining with Sonja, so presumably he took it everywhere with him, and had it now.

If they fought, and Wolff had the advantage of the knife, Wolff would win. It had happened before, in the alley. Vandam touched his cheek again.

He thought: Why didn't I bring the gun here?

If they fought, and Wolff won, what would happen then? Seeing Vandam in Elene's apartment, Wolff would know she had been trying to trap him. What would he do to her? In Istanbul, in a similar situation, he had slit the girl's throat.

Vandam blinked to shut out the awful image.

Wolff said: "I see you were having a drink before I arrived. May I join you?"

"Of course," Elene said again. "What would you like?"

"What's that?" Wolff sniffed. "Oh, a little gin would be very nice."

Vandam thought: That was my drink. Thank God Elene didn't have a drink as well—two glasses would have given the game away. He heard ice clink.

"Cheers!" Wolff said.

"Cheers."

"You don't seem to like it."

"The ice has melted."

Vandam knew why she had made a face when she sipped his drink: it had been straight gin. She was coping so well with the situation, he thought. What did she think he, Vandam, was planning to do? She must have guessed by now where he was hiding. She would be trying desperately not to look in this direction. Poor Elene! Once again she had got more than she bargained for.

Vandam hoped she would be passive, take the line of least resistance and trust him.

Did Wolff still plan to go to the Oasis Restaurant? Perhaps he did. If only I could be sure of that, Vandam thought, I could leave it all to Jakes.

Wolff said: "You seem nervous, Elene. Did I confuse your plans by coming here? If you want to go and finish getting ready, or something—not that you look a whit less than perfect right now—just leave me here with the gin bottle."

"No, no . . . Well, we did say we'd meet at the restaurant . . ."

"And here I am, altering everything at the last minute again. To be truthful, I'm bored with restaurants, and yet they are, so to speak, the conventional meeting place; so I arrange to have dinner with people, then when the time comes I can't face it, and I think of something else to do."

So they're not going to the Oasis, Vandam thought. Damn.

Elene said: "What do you want to do?"

"May I surprise you again?"

Vandam thought: Make him tell you!

Elene said: "All right."

Vandam groaned inwardly. If Wolff would reveal where they were going, Vandam could contact Jakes and have the whole ambush moved to the new venue. Elene was not thinking the right way. It was understandable: she sounded terrified.

Wolff said: "Shall we go?"

"All right."

The sofa creaked as Wolff got up. Vandam thought: I could go for him now!

Too risky.

He heard them leave the room. He stayed where he was for a moment. He heard Wolff, in the hallway, say: "After you." Then the front door was slammed shut.

Vandam stood up. He would have to follow them, and take the first available opportunity of calling GHQ and contacting Jakes. Elene did not have a telephone, not many people did in Cairo. Even if she had there was no time now. He went to the front door and listened. He heard nothing. He opened it a fraction: they had gone. He went out, closed the door and hurried along the corridor and down the stairs.

As he stepped out of the building he saw them on the other side of the road. Wolff was holding open a car door for Elene to get in. It was not a taxi: Wolff must have rented, borrowed or stolen a car for the evening. Wolff closed the door on Elene and walked around to the driver's side. Elene looked out of the window and caught Vandam's eye. She stared at him. He looked away from her, afraid to make any kind of gesture in case Wolff should see it.

Vandam walked to his motorcycle, climbed on and started the engine.

Wolff's car pulled away, and Vandam followed.

The city traffic was still heavy. Vandam was able to keep five or six cars between himself and Wolff without risking losing Wolff. It was dusk, but few cars had their lights on.

Vandam wondered where Wolff was going. They were sure to stop somewhere, unless the man intended to drive around all night. If only they would stop someplace where there was a telephone . . .

They headed out of the city, toward Giza. Darkness fell and Wolff illuminated the lights of the car. Vandam left his motorcycle lights off, so that Wolff would not be able to see that he was being followed.

It was a nightmare ride. Even in daylight, in the city, riding a motorcycle was a little hair-raising: the roads were strewn with bumps, potholes and treacherous patches of oil, and Vandam found he had to watch the surface as much as the traffic. The desert road was worse, and yet he now had to drive without lights and keep an eye on the car ahead. Three or four times he almost came off the bike.

He was cold. Not anticipating this ride, he had worn only a short-sleeved uniform shirt, and at speed the wind cut through it. How far was Wolff planning to go?

The pyramids loomed ahead.

Vandam thought: No phone there.

Wolff's car slowed down. They were going to picnic by the pyramids. Vandam cut the motorcycle engine and coasted to a halt. Before Wolff had a chance to get out of the car, Vandam wheeled his bike off the road on to the sand. The desert was not level, except when seen from a distance, and he found a rocky hump behind which to lay down the motorcycle. He lay in the sand beside the hump and watched the car.

Nothing happened.

The car stayed still, its engine off, its interior dark. What were they doing in there? Vandam was seized by jealousy. He told himself not to be stupid—they were eating, that was all. Elene had told him about the last picnic: the smoked salmon, the cold chicken, the champagne. You could not kiss a girl with a mouthful of fish. Still, their fingers would touch as he handed her the wine . . .

Shut up.

He decided to risk a cigarette. He moved behind the hump to light it, then cupped it in his hand, army fashion, to hide the glow as he returned to his vantage point.

Five cigarettes later the car doors opened.

The cloud had cleared and the moon was out. The whole landscape was dark blue and silver, the complex shadow work of the pyramids rising out of shining sand. Two dark figures got out of the car and walked toward the nearest of the ancient tombs. Vandam could see that Elene walked with her arms folded across her chest, as if she were cold, or perhaps because she did not want to hold Wolff's hand. Wolff put an arm lightly across her shoulders, and she made no move to resist him.

They stopped at the base of the monument and talked. Wolff pointed upward, and Elene seemed to shake her head: Vandam guessed she did not want to climb. They walked around the base and disappeared behind the pyramid.

Vandam waited for them to emerge on the other side. They seemed to take a very long time. What were they doing behind there? The urge to go and see was almost irresistible.

He could get to the car now. He toyed with the idea of sabotaging it, rushing back to the city, and returning with his team. But Wolff would not be here when Vandam got back; it would be impossible to search the desert at night; by the morning Wolff might be miles away.

It was almost unbearable to watch and wait and do nothing, but Vandam knew it was the best course.

At last Wolff and Elene came back into view. He still had his arm around her. They returned to the car, and stood beside the door. Wolff put his hands on Elene's shoulders, said something, and leaned forward to kiss her.

Vandam stood up.

Elene gave Wolff her cheek, then turned away, slipping out of his grasp, and got into the car.

Vandam lay down on the sand again.

The desert silence was broken by the roar of Wolff's car. Vandam watched it turn in a wide circle and take the road. The headlights came on, and Vandam ducked his head involuntarily, although he was well concealed. The car passed him, heading toward Cairo.

Vandam jumped up, wheeled his cycle on to the road and kicked the starter. The engine would not turn over. Vandam cursed: he was terrified he might have gotten sand in the carburetor. He tried again, and this time it fired. He got on and followed the car.

The moonlight made it easier for him to spot the holes and bumps in the road surface, but it also made him more visible. He stayed well behind Wolff's car, knowing there was nowhere to go but Cairo. He wondered what Wolff planned next. Would he take Elene home? If so, where would he go afterward? He might lead Vandam to his base.

Vandam thought: I wish I had that gun.

Would Wolff take Elene to *his* home? The man had to be staying somewhere, had to have a bed in a room in a building in the city. Vandam was sure Wolff was planning to seduce Elene. Wolff had been rather patient and gentlemanly with her, but Vandam knew that in reality he was a man who liked to get his way quickly. Seduction might be the least of the dangers Elene faced. Vandam thought: What wouldn't I give for a phone!

They reached the outskirts of the city, and Vandam was obliged to pull up closer to the car, but fortunately there was plenty of traffic about. He contemplated stopping and giving a message to a policeman, or an officer, but Wolff was driving fast, and anyway, what would the message say? Vandam still did not know where Wolff was going.

He began to suspect the answer when they crossed the bridge to Zamalek. This was where the dancer, Sonja, had her houseboat. It was surely not possible that Wolff was living there,

Vandam thought, for the place had been under surveillance for days. But perhaps he was reluctant to take Elene to his real home, and so was borrowing the houseboat.

Wolff parked in a street and got out. Vandam stood his motorcycle against a wall and hurriedly chained the wheel to prevent theft—he might need the bike again tonight.

He followed Wolff and Elene from the street to the towpath. From behind a bush he watched as they walked a short distance along the path. He wondered what Elene was thinking. Had she expected to be rescued before this? Would she trust that Vandam was still watching her? Would she now lose hope?

They stopped beside one of the boats—Vandam noted carefully which one—and Wolff helped Elene on to the gangplank. Vandam thought: Has it not occurred to Wolff that the houseboat might be under surveillance? Obviously not. Wolff followed Elene on to the deck, then opened a hatch. The two of them disappeared below.

Vandam thought: What now? This was surely his best chance to fetch help. Wolff must be intending to spend some time on the boat. But supposing that did not happen? Suppose, while Vandam was dashing to a phone, something went wrong—Elene insisted on being taken home, Wolff changed his plans, or they decided to go to a nightclub?

I could still lose the bastard, Vandam thought.

There must be a policeman around here somewhere.

"Hey!" he said in a stage whisper. "Is anybody there? Police? This is Major Vandam. Hey, where are—"

A dark figure materialized from behind a tree. An Arab voice said: "Yes?"

"Hello. I'm Major Vandam. Are you the police officer watching the houseboat?"

"Yes, sir."

"Okay, listen. The man we're chasing is on the boat now. Do you have a gun?"

"No, sir."

"Damn." Vandam considered whether he and the Arab could raid the boat on their own, and decided they could not: the Arab could not be trusted to fight enthusiastically, and in that confined space Wolff's knife could wreak havoc. "Right, I want you to go to the nearest telephone, ring GHQ, and get a message through to Captain Jakes or Colonel Bogge, absolutely top priority: they are to come here in force and raid the houseboat immediately. Is that clear?"

"Captain Jakes or Colonel Bogge, GHQ, they are to raid the houseboat immediately. Yes, sir."

"All right. Be quick!"

The Arab left at a trot.

Vandam found a position in which he was concealed from view but could still watch the houseboat and the towpath. A few minutes later the figure of a woman came along the path. Vandam thought she looked familiar. She boarded the houseboat, and Vandam realized she was Sonja.

He was relieved: at least Wolff could not molest Elene while there was another woman on the boat.

He settled down to wait.

22

The Arab was worried. "Go to the nearest telephone," the Englishman had said. Well, there were telephones in some of the nearby houses. But houses with phones were occupied by Europeans, who would not take kindly to an Egyptian—even a police officer—banging on their doors at eleven o'clock at night and demanding to use the phone. They would almost certainly refuse, with oaths and curses: it would be a humiliating experience. He was not in uniform, not even wearing his usual plainclothes outfit of white shirt and black trousers, but was dressed like a fellah. They would not even believe he was a policeman.

There were no public phones on Zamalek that he knew of. That left him only one option: to phone from the station house. He headed that way, still trotting.

He was also worried about calling GHQ. It was an unwritten rule for Egyptian officials in Cairo that no one ever voluntarily contacted the British. It always meant trouble. The switchboard at GHQ would refuse to put through the call, or they would leave the message until morning—then deny they had ever received it—or they would tell him to call back later. And if anything went wrong there would be hell to pay. How, anyway, did he know that the man on the towpath had been genuine? He did not know Major Vandam from Adam, and anyone could put on the uniform shirt of a major. Suppose it was a hoax? There was a certain type of young English officer who just loved to play practical jokes on well-meaning Egyptians.

He had a standard response to situations like this: pass the buck. Anyway, he had been instructed to report to his superior officer and no one else on this case. He would go to the station house and from there, he decided, he would call Superintendent Kemel at home.

Kemel would know what to do.

∽

Elene stepped off the ladder and looked nervously around the interior of the houseboat. She had expected the decor to be sparse and nautical. In fact it was luxurious, if a little overripe. There were thick rugs, low divans, a couple of elegant occasional tables, and rich velvet floor-to-ceiling curtains which divided this area from the other half of the boat, which was presumably the bedroom. Opposite the curtains, where the boat narrowed to what had been its stern, was a tiny kitchen with small but modern fittings.

"Is this yours?" she asked Wolff.

"It belongs to a friend," he said. "Do sit down."

Elene felt trapped. Where the hell was William Vandam? Several times during the evening she had thought there was a motorcycle behind the car, but she had been unable to look carefully for fear of alerting Wolff. Every second, she had been expecting soldiers to surround the car, arrest Wolff and set her free; and as the seconds turned into hours she had begun to wonder if it was all a dream, if William Vandam existed at all.

Now Wolff was going to the icebox, taking out a bottle of champagne, finding two glasses, unwrapping the silver foil from the top of the bottle, unwinding the wire fastening, pulling the cork with a loud pop and pouring the champagne into the glasses and *where the hell was William?*

She was terrified of Wolff. She had had many liaisons with

men, some of them casual, but she had always trusted the man, always known he would be kind, or if not kind, at least considerate. It was her body she was frightened for: if she let Wolff play with her body, what kind of games would he invent? Her skin was sensitive, she was soft inside, so easy to hurt, so vulnerable lying on her back with her legs apart . . . To be like that with someone who loved her, someone who would be as gentle with her body as she herself, would be a joy—but with Wolff, who wanted only to *use* her body . . . she shuddered.

"Are you cold?" Wolff said as he handed her a glass.

"No, I wasn't shivering . . ."

He raised his glass. "Your health."

Her mouth was dry. She sipped the cold wine, then took a gulp. It made her feel a little better.

He sat beside her on the couch and twisted around to look at her. "What a super evening," he said. "I enjoy your company so much. You're an enchantress."

Here it comes, she thought.

He put his hand on her knee.

She froze.

"You're enigmatic," he said. "Desirable, rather aloof, very beautiful, sometimes naïve and sometimes so knowing . . . will you tell me something?"

"I expect so." She did not look at him.

With his fingertip he traced the silhouette of her face: forehead, nose, lips, chin. He said: "Why do you go out with me?"

What did he mean? Was it possible he suspected what she was really doing? Or was this just the next move in the game?

She looked at him and said: "You're a very attractive man."

"I'm glad you think so." He put his hand on her knee again, and leaned forward to kiss her. She offered him her cheek, as she had done once before this evening. His lips brushed her skin, then he whispered: "Why are you frightened of me?"

There was a noise up on deck—quick, light footsteps—and then the hatch opened.

Elene thought: William!

A high-heeled shoe and a woman's foot appeared. The woman came down, closing the hatch above her, and stepped off the ladder. Elene saw her face and recognized her as Sonja, the belly dancer.

She thought: What on earth is going on?

⌒

"All right, Sergeant," Kemel said into the telephone. "You did exactly the right thing in contacting me. I'll deal with everything myself. In fact, you may go off duty now."

"Thank you, sir," said the sergeant. "Good night."

"Good night." Kemel hung up. This was a catastrophe. The British had followed Alex Wolff to the houseboat, and Vandam was trying to organize a raid. The consequences would be two-fold. First, the prospect of the Free Officers using the German's radio would vanish, and then there would be no possibility of negotiations with the Reich before Rommel conquered Egypt. Second, once the British discovered that the houseboat was a nest of spies, they would quickly figure out that Kemel had been concealing the facts and protecting the agents. Kemel regretted that he had not pushed Sonja harder, forced her to arrange a meeting within hours instead of days; but it was too late for regrets. What was he going to do now?

He went back into the bedroom and dressed quickly. From the bed his wife said softly: "What is it?"

"Work," he whispered.

"Oh, no." She turned over.

He took his pistol from the locked drawer in the desk and put it in his jacket pocket, then he kissed his wife and left the house quietly. He got into his car and started the engine. He sat thinking for a minute. He had to consult Sadat about this, but that would take time. In the meanwhile Vandam might grow impatient, waiting at the houseboat, and do something precipitate. Vandam would have to be dealt with first, quickly; then he could go to Sadat's house.

Kemel pulled away, heading for Zamalek. He wanted time to think, slowly and clearly, but time was what he lacked. Should he kill Vandam? He had never killed a man and did not know whether he would be capable of it. It was years since he had so much as hit anyone. And how would he cover up his involvement in all this? It might be days yet before the Germans reached Cairo—indeed it was possible, even at this stage, that they might be repulsed. Then there would be an investigation into what had happened on the towpath tonight, and sooner or later the blame would be laid at Kemel's door. He would probably be shot.

"Courage," he said aloud, remembering the way Imam's stolen plane had burst into flames as it crash-landed in the desert.

He parked near the towpath. From the trunk of the car he took a length of rope. He stuffed the rope into the pocket of his jacket, and carried the gun in his right hand.

He held the gun reversed, for clubbing. How long since he had used it? Six years, he thought, not counting occasional target practice.

He reached the riverbank. He looked at the silver Nile, the black shapes of the houseboats, the dim line of the towpath and the darkness of the bushes. Vandam would be in the bushes somewhere. Kemel stepped forward, walking softly.

➣

Vandam looked at his wristwatch in the glow of his cigarette. It was eleven-thirty. Clearly something had gone wrong. Either the Arab policeman had given the wrong message, or GHQ had been unable to locate Jakes, or Bogge had somehow fouled everything up. Vandam could not take the chance of letting Wolff get on the radio with the information he had now. There was nothing for it but to go aboard the houseboat himself, and risk everything.

He put out his cigarette, then he heard a footstep somewhere in the bushes. "Who is it?" he hissed. "Jakes?"

A dark figure emerged and whispered: "It's me."

Vandam could not recognize the whispered voice, nor could he see the face. "Who?"

The figure stepped nearer and raised an arm. Vandam said: "Who—" then he realized that the arm was sweeping down in a blow. He jerked sideways, and something hit the side of his head and bounced on his shoulder. Vandam shouted with pain, and his right arm went numb. The arm was lifted again. Vandam stepped forward, reaching clumsily for his assailant with his left hand. The figure stepped back and struck again, and this time the blow landed squarely on top of Vandam's head. There was a moment of intense pain, then Vandam lost consciousness.

❧

Kemel pocketed the gun and knelt beside Vandam's prone figure. First he touched Vandam's chest, and was relieved to feel a strong heartbeat. Working quickly, he took off Vandam's sandals, removed the socks, rolled them into a ball and stuffed them into the unconscious man's mouth. That should stop him from calling out. Next he rolled Vandam over, crossed his wrists behind his back, and tied them together with the rope. With the other end of the rope he bound Vandam's ankles. Finally he tied the rope to a tree.

Vandam would come round in a few minutes, but he would find it impossible to move. Nor could he cry out. He would remain there until somebody stumbled on him. How soon was that likely to happen? Normally there might have been people in these bushes, young men with their sweethearts and soldiers with their girls, but tonight there had surely been enough comings and goings here to frighten them away. There was a chance that a latecoming couple would see Vandam, or perhaps hear him groaning . . . Kemel would have to take that chance, there was no point standing around and worrying.

He decided to take a quick look at the houseboat. He walked light-footedly along the towpath to the *Jihan*. There were lights on inside, but little curtains were drawn across the portholes. He was tempted to go aboard, but he wanted to consult with Sadat first, for he was not sure what should be done.

He turned around and headed back toward his car.

❧

Sonja said: "Alex has told me all about you, Elene." She smiled.

Elene smiled back. Was this the friend of Wolff's who owned

the houseboat? Was Wolff living with her? Had he not expected her back so early? Why was neither of them angry, or puzzled, or embarrassed? Just for something to say, Elene asked her: "Have you just come from the Cha-Cha Club?"

"Yes."

"How was it?"

"As always—exhausting, thrilling, successful."

Sonja was not a humble woman, clearly.

Wolff handed Sonja a glass of champagne. She took it without looking at him, and said to Elene: "So you work in Mikis' shop?"

"No, I don't," Elene said, thinking: Are you really interested in this? "I helped him for a few days, that's all. We're related."

"So you're Greek?"

"That's right." The small talk was giving Elene confidence. Her fear receded. Whatever happened, Wolff was not likely to rape her at knifepoint in front of one of the most famous women in Egypt. Sonja gave her a breathing space, at least. William was determined to capture Wolff before midnight—

Midnight!

She had almost forgotten. At midnight Wolff was to contact the enemy by wireless, and hand over the details of the defense line. But where was the radio? Was it here, on the boat? If it was somewhere else, Wolff would have to leave soon. If it was here, would he send his message in front of Elene and Sonja? What was in his mind?

He sat down beside Elene. She felt vaguely threatened, with the two of them on either side of her. Wolff said: "What a lucky man I am, to be sitting here with the two most beautiful women in Cairo."

Elene looked straight ahead, not knowing what to say.

Wolff said: "Isn't she beautiful, Sonja?"

"Oh, yes." Sonja touched Elene's face, then took her chin and turned her head. "Do you think I'm beautiful, Elene?"

"Of course." Elene frowned. This was getting weird. It was almost as if—

"I'm so glad," Sonja said, and she put her hand on Elene's knee.

And then Elene understood.

Everything fell into place: Wolff's patience, his phony court-
liness, the houseboat, the unexpected appearance of Sonja . .
Elene realized she was not safe at all. Her fear of Wolff came
back, stronger than before. The pair of them wanted to use
her, and she would have no choice, she would have to lie there,
mute and unresisting, while they did whatever they wanted,
Wolff with the knife in one hand—

Stop it.

I won't be afraid. I can stand being mauled about by a pair
of depraved old fools. There's more at stake here. Forget about
your precious little body, think about the radio, and how to
stop Wolff using it.

This threesome might be turned to advantage.

She looked furtively at her wristwatch. It was a quarter to
midnight. Too late, now, to rely on William. She, Elene, was
the only one who could stop Wolff.

And she thought she knew how.

A look passed between Sonja and Wolff like a signal. Each
with a hand on one of Elene's thighs, they leaned across her
and kissed each other in front of her eyes.

She looked at them. It was a long, lascivious kiss. She
thought: What do they expect me to do?

They drew apart.

Wolff kissed Elene the same way. Elene was unresistant.
Then she felt Sonja's hand on her chin. Sonja turned Elene's
face toward her and kissed her lips.

Elene closed her eyes, thinking: It won't hurt me, it won't
hurt.

It did not hurt, but it was *strange*, to be kissed so tenderly
by a woman's mouth.

Elene thought: Somehow I have to get control of this scene.

Sonja pulled open her own blouse. She had big brown
breasts. Wolff bent his head and took a nipple into his mouth.
Elene felt Sonja pushing her head down. She realized she was
supposed to follow Wolff's example. She did so. Sonja moaned.

All this was for Sonja's benefit: it was clearly her fantasy,
her kink; she was the one who was panting and groaning now,

not Wolff. Elene was afraid that any minute now Wolff might break away and go to his radio. As she went mechanically through the motions of making love to Sonja, she cast about in her mind for ways to drive Wolff out of his mind with lust.

But the whole scene was so silly, so farcical, that everything she thought of doing seemed merely comical.

I've got to keep Wolff from that radio.

What's the *key* to all this? What do they *really* want?

She moved her face away from Sonja and kissed Wolff. He turned his mouth to hers. She found his hand, and pressed it between her thighs. He breathed deeply, and Elene thought: At least he's interested.

Sonja tried to push them apart.

Wolff looked at Sonja, then slapped her face, hard.

Elene gasped with surprise. Was this the key? It must be a game they play, it must be.

Wolff turned his attention back to Elene. Sonja tried to get between them again.

This time Elene slapped her.

Sonja moaned deep in her throat.

Elene thought: I've done it, I've guessed the game, I'm in *control*.

She saw Wolff look at his wristwatch.

Suddenly she stood up. They both stared at her. She lifted her arms then, slowly, she pulled her dress up over her head, threw it to one side, and stood there in her black underwear and stockings. She touched herself, lightly, running her hands between her thighs and across her breasts. She saw Wolff's face change: his look of composure vanished, and he gazed at her, wide-eyed with desire. He was tense, mesmerized. He licked his lips. Elene raised her left foot, planted a high-heeled shoe between Sonja's breasts and pushed Sonja backward. Then she grasped Wolff's head and drew it to her belly.

Sonja started kissing Elene's foot.

Wolff made a sound between a groan and a sigh, and buried his face between Elene's thighs.

Elene looked at her watch.

It was midnight.

23

Elene lay on her back in the bed, naked. She was quite still, rigid, her muscles tense, staring straight up at the blank ceiling. On her right was Sonja, facedown, arms and legs spread all ways over the sheets, fast asleep, snoring. Sonja's right hand rested limply on Elene's hip. Wolff was on Elene's left. He lay on his side, facing her, sleepily stroking her body.

Elene was thinking: Well, it didn't kill me.

The game had been all about rejecting and accepting Sonja. The more Elene and Wolff rejected her and abused her, the more passionate she became, until in the dénouement Wolff rejected Elene and made love to Sonja. It was a script that Wolff and Sonja obviously knew well: they had played it before.

It had given Elene very little pleasure, but she was not sickened or humiliated or disgusted. What she felt was that she had been betrayed, and betrayed by herself. It was like pawning a jewel given by a lover, or having your long hair cut off to sell for money, or sending a small child to work in a mill. She had abused herself. Worst of all, what she had done was the logical culmination of the life she had been living: in the eight years since she had left home she had been on the slippery slope that ended in prostitution, and now she felt she had arrived there.

The stroking stopped, and she glanced sideways at Wolff's face. His eyes were closed. He was falling asleep.

She wondered what had happened to Vandam.

Something had gone wrong. Perhaps Vandam had lost sight of Wolff's car in Cairo. Maybe he had had an accident in the traffic. Whatever the reason, Vandam was no longer watching over her. She was on her own.

She had succeeded in making Wolff forget his midnight transmission to Rommel—but what now was to stop him sending the message another night? Elene would have to get to GHQ and tell Jakes where Wolff was to be found. She would have to slip away, right now, find Jakes, get him to pull his team out of bed . . .

It would take too long. Wolff might wake, find she was gone, and vanish again.

Was his radio here, on the houseboat, or somewhere else? That might make all the difference.

She remembered something Vandam had said last evening—was it really only a few hours ago? "If I can get the key to the *Rebecca* code, I can impersonate him over the radio . . . it could turn the tables completely . . ."

Elene thought: Perhaps I can find the key.

He had said it was a sheet of paper explaining how to use the book to encode messages.

Elene realized that she now had a chance to locate the radio and the key to the code.

She had to search the houseboat.

She did not move. She was frightened again. If Wolff should discover her searching . . . She remembered his theory of human nature: the world is divided into masters and slaves. A slave's life was worth nothing.

No, she thought; I'll leave here in the morning, quite normally, and then I'll tell the British where Wolff is to be found, and they'll raid the houseboat, and—

And what if Wolff had gone by then? What if the radio was not here?

Then it would all have been for nothing.

Wolff's breathing was now slow and even: he was fast asleep. Elene reached down, gently picked up Sonja's limp hand, and moved it from her thigh on to the sheet. Sonja did not stir.

Now neither of them was touching Elene. It was a great relief.

Slowly, she sat upright.

The shift of weight on the mattress disturbed both of the other two. Sonja grunted, lifted her head, turned it the other way, and fell to snoring again. Wolff rolled over on his back without opening his eyes.

Moving slowly, wincing with every movement of the mattress, Elene turned around so that she was on her hands and knees, facing the head of the bed. She began painfully to crawl backward: right knee, left hand, left knee, right hand. She watched the two sleeping faces. The foot of the bed seemed miles away. The silence rang in her ears like thunder. The houseboat itself rocked from side to side on the wash of a passing barge, and Elene backed off the bed quickly under cover of the disturbance. She stood there, rooted to the spot, watching the other two, until the boat stopped moving. They stayed asleep.

Where should the search start? Elene decided to be methodical, and begin at the front and work backward. In the prow of the boat was the bathroom. Suddenly she realized she had to go there anyway. She tiptoed across the bedroom and went into the tiny bathroom.

Sitting on the toilet, she looked around. Where might a radio be hidden? She did not really know how big it would be: the size of a suitcase? A briefcase? A handbag? Here there were a basin, a small tub and a cupboard on the wall. She stood up and opened the cupboard. It contained shaving gear, pills and a small roll of bandage.

The radio was not in the bathroom.

She did not have the courage to search the bedroom while they slept, not yet. She crossed it and passed through the curtains into the living room. She looked quickly all around. She felt the need to hurry, and forced herself to be calm and careful. She began on the starboard side. Here there was a divan couch. She tapped its base gently: it seemed hollow. The radio might be underneath. She tried to lift it, and could not. Looking around its edge, she saw that it was screwed to the floor. The screws were tight. The radio would not be there. Next there was a tall cupboard. She opened it gently. It squeaked a little, and she froze. She heard a grunt from the bedroom. She waited for Wolff to come bounding through the curtains and catch her red-handed. Nothing happened.

She looked in the cupboard. There was a broom, and some dusters, and cleaning materials, and a flashlight. No radio. She closed the door. It squeaked again.

She moved into the kitchen area. She had to open six smaller cupboards. They contained crockery, tinned food, saucepans, glasses, supplies of coffee and rice and tea, and towels. Under the sink there was a bucket for kitchen waste. Elene looked in the icebox. It contained one bottle of champagne. There were several drawers. Would the radio be small enough to fit in a drawer? She opened one. The rattle of cutlery shredded her nerves. No radio. Another: a massive selection of bottled spices and flavorings, from vanilla essence to curry powder—somebody liked to cook. Another drawer: kitchen knives.

Next to the kitchen was a small escritoire with a fold-down desk top. Beneath it was a small suitcase. Elene picked up the suitcase. It was heavy. She opened it. There was the radio.

Her heart skipped.

It was an ordinary, plain suitcase, with two catches, a leather handle and reinforced corners. The radio fitted inside exactly, as if it had been designed that way. The recessed lid left a little room on top of the radio, and here there was a book. Its board covers had been torn off to make it fit into the space in the lid. Elene picked up the book and looked inside. She read: "Last night I dreamt I went to Manderley again." It was *Rebecca*.

She flicked the pages of the book. In the middle there was something between the pages. She let the book fall open and a sheet of paper dropped to the floor. She bent down and picked it up. It was a list of numbers and dates, with some words in German. This was surely the key to the code.

She held in her hand what Vandam needed to turn the tide of the war.

Suddenly the responsibility weighed her down.

Without this, she thought, Wolff cannot send messages to Rommel—or if he sends messages in plain language the Germans will suspect their authenticity and also worry that the Allies have overheard them . . . Without this, Wolff is useless. With this, Vandam can win the war.

She had to run away, now, taking the key with her.

She remembered that she was stark naked.

She broke out of her trance. Her dress was on the couch, crumpled and wrinkled. She crossed the boat, put down the book and the key to the code, picked up her dress and slipped it over her head.

The bed creaked.

From behind the curtains came the unmistakable sound of someone getting up, someone heavy, it had to be him. Elene stood still, paralyzed. She heard Wolff walk toward the curtains, then away again. She heard the bathroom door.

There was no time to put her panties on. She picked up her bag, her shoes, and the book with the key inside. She heard Wolff come out of the bathroom. She went to the ladder and ran up it, wincing as her bare feet cut into the edges of the narrow wooden steps. Glancing down, she saw Wolff appear between the curtains and glance up at her in astonishment. His eyes went to the suitcase opened on the floor. Elene looked away from him to the hatch. It was secured on the inside with two bolts. She slid them both back. From the corner of her eye she saw Wolff dash to the ladder. She pushed up the hatch and scrambled out. As she stood upright on the deck she saw Wolff scrambling up the ladder. She bent swiftly and lifted the heavy wooden hatch. As Wolff's right hand grasped the rim of the opening, Elene slammed the hatch down on his fingers with all her might. There was a roar of pain. Elene ran across the deck and down the gangplank.

It was just that: a plank, leading from the deck to the riverbank. She stooped, picked up the end of the plank, and threw it into the river.

Wolff came up through the hatch, his face a mask of pain and fury.

Elene panicked as she saw him come across the deck at a run. She thought: he's naked, he can't chase me! He took a flying jump over the rail of the boat.

He can't make it!

He landed on the very edge of the riverbank, his arms windmilling for balance. With a sudden access of courage Elene ran at him and, while he was still off balance, pushed him backward into the water.

She turned and ran along the towpath.

When she reached the lower end of the pathway that led to the street, she stopped and looked back. Already her heart was pounding and she was breathing in long, shuddering gasps. She felt elated when she saw Wolff, dripping wet and naked, climbing out of the water up the muddy riverbank. It was getting light: he could not chase her far in that state. She spun around toward the street, broke into a run and crashed into someone.

Strong arms caught her in a tight grip. She struggled desperately, got free and was seized again. She slumped in defeat: after all that, she thought; after all that.

She was turned around, grasped by the arms and marched toward the houseboat. She saw Wolff walking toward her. She struggled again, and the man holding her got an arm around her throat. She opened her mouth to scream for help, but before she could make a sound the man had thrust his fingers down her throat, making her retch.

Wolff came up and said: "Who are you?"

"I'm Kemel. You must be Wolff."

"Thank God you were there."

"You're in trouble, Wolff," said the man called Kemel.

"You'd better come aboard—oh, shit, she threw away the fucking plank." Wolff looked down at the river and saw the plank floating beside the houseboat. "I can't get any wetter," he said. He slid down the bank and into the water, grabbed the plank, shoved it up on to the bank and climbed up after it. He picked it up again and laid it across the gap between the houseboat and the bank.

"This way," he said.

Kemel marched Elene across the plank, over the deck and down the ladder.

"Put her over there," Wolff said, pointing to the couch.

Kemel pushed Elene over to the couch, not ungently, and made her sit down.

Wolff went through the curtains and came back a moment later with a big towel. He proceeded to rub himself dry with it. He seemed quite unembarrassed by his nakedness.

Elene was surprised to see that Kemel was quite a small man. From the way he had grabbed her, she had imagined he was Wolff's build. He was a handsome, dark-skinned Arab. He was looking away from Wolff uneasily.

Wolff wrapped the towel around his waist and sat down. He examined his hand. "She nearly broke my fingers," he said. He looked at Elene with a mixture of anger and amusement.

Kemel said: "Where's Sonja?"

"In bed," Wolff said, jerking his head toward the curtains. "She sleeps through earthquakes, especially after a night of lust."

Kemel was uncomfortable with such talk, Elene observed, and perhaps also impatient with Wolff's levity. "You're in trouble," he said again.

"I know," Wolff said. "I suppose she's working for Vandam."

"I don't know about that. I got a call in the middle of the night from my man on the towpath. Vandam had come along and sent my man to fetch help."

Wolff was shocked. "We came close!" he said. He looked worried. "Where's Vandam now?"

"Out there still. I knocked him on the head and tied him up."

Elene's heart sank. Vandam was out there in the bushes, hurt and incapacitated—and nobody else knew where she was. It had all been for nothing, after all.

Wolff nodded. "Vandam followed her here. That's two people who know about this place. If I stay here I'll have to kill them both."

Elene shuddered: he talked of killing people so lightly. Masters and slaves, she remembered.

"Not good enough," Kemel said. "If you kill Vandam the murder will eventually be blamed on me. You can go away, but I have to live in this town." He paused, watching Wolff with narrowed eyes. "And if you were to kill me, that would still leave the man who called me last night."

"So . . ." Wolff frowned and made an angry noise. "There's no choice. I have to go. Damn."

Kemel nodded. "If you disappear, I think I can cover up. But I want something from you. Remember the reason we've been helping you."

"You want to talk to Rommel."

"Yes."

"I'll be sending a message tomorrow night—tonight, I mean, damn, I've hardly slept. Tell me what you want to say, and I'll—"

"Not good enough," Kemel interrupted. "We want to do it ourselves. We want your radio."

Wolff frowned. Elene realized that Kemel was a nationalist rebel, cooperating or trying to cooperate with the Germans.

Kemel added: "We could send your message for you . . ."

"Not necessary," Wolff said. He seemed to have reached a decision. "I have another radio."

"It's agreed, then."

"There's the radio." Wolff pointed to the open case, still on the floor where Elene had left it. "It's already tuned to the correct wavelength. All you have to do is broadcast at midnight, any night."

Kemel went over to the radio and examined it. Elene wondered why Wolff had said nothing about the *Rebecca* code. Wolff did not care whether Kemel got through to Rommel or not, she decided; and to give him the code would be to risk that he might give it to someone else. Wolff was playing safe again.

Wolff said: "Where does Vandam live?"

Kemel told him the address.

Elene thought: *Now* what is he after?

Wolff said: "He's married, I suppose."

"No."

"A bachelor. Damn."

"Not a bachelor," Kemel said, still looking at the wireless transmitter. "A widower. His wife was killed in Crete last year."

"Any children?"

"Yes," Kemel said. "A small boy called Billy, so I'm told. Why?"

Wolff shrugged. "I'm interested, a little obsessed, with the man who's come so close to catching me."

Elene was sure he was lying.

Kemel closed the suitcase, apparently satisfied. Wolff said to him: "Keep an eye on her for a minute, would you?"

"Of course."

Wolff turned away, then turned back. He had noticed that Elene still had *Rebecca* in her hand. He reached down and took it from her. He disappeared through the curtains.

Elene thought: If I tell Kemel about the code, then maybe Kemel will make Wolff give it to him, and maybe then Vandam will get it from Wolff--but what will happen to me?

Kemel said to her: "What—" He stopped abruptly as Wolff came back, carrying his clothes, and began to dress.

Kemel said to him: "Do you have a call sign?"

"Sphinx," Wolff said shortly.

"A code?"

"No code."

"What was in that book?"

Wolff looked angry. "A code," he said. "But you can't have it."

"We need it."

"I can't give it to you," Wolff said. "You'll have to take your chance, and broadcast in clear."

Kemel nodded.

Suddenly Wolff's knife was in his hand. "Don't argue," he

said. "I know you've got a gun in your pocket. Remember, if you shoot, you'll have to explain the bullet to the British. You'd better go now."

Kemel turned, without speaking, and went up the ladder and through the hatch. Elene heard his footsteps above. Wolff went to the porthole and watched him walk away along the towpath.

Wolff put his knife away and buttoned his shirt over the sheath. He put on his shoes and laced them tightly. He got the book from the next room, extracted from it the sheet of paper bearing the key to the code, crumpled the paper, dropped it into a large glass ashtray, took a box of matches from a kitchen drawer and set fire to the paper.

He must have another key with the other radio, Elene thought.

Wolff watched the flames to make sure the paper was entirely burned. He looked at the book, as if contemplating burning that too, then he opened a porthole and dropped it into the river.

He took a small suitcase from a cupboard and began to pack a few things into it.

"Where are you going?" Elene said.

"You'll find out—you're coming."

"Oh, no." What would he do with her? He had caught her deceiving him—had he dreamed up some appropriate punishment? She felt very weary and afraid. Nothing she had done had turned out well. At one time she had been afraid merely that she would have to have sex with him. How much more there was to fear now. She thought of trying again to run away—she had almost made it last time—but she no longer had the spirit.

Wolff continued packing his case. Elene saw some of her own clothes on the floor, and remembered that she had not dressed properly. There were her panties, her stockings and her brassiere. She decided to put them on. She stood up and pulled her dress over her head. She bent down to pick up her underwear. As she stood up Wolff embraced her. He pressed a rough kiss against her lips, not seeming to care that she was completely unresponsive. He reached between her legs and thrust a finger inside her. He withdrew his finger from her vagina and shoved it into her anus. She tensed. He pushed his finger in farther, and she gasped with pain.

He looked into her eyes. "Do you know, I think I'd take you with me even if I didn't have a use for you."

She closed her eyes, humiliated. He turned from her abruptly and returned to his packing.

She put on her clothes.

When he was ready, he took a last look around and said: "Let's go."

Elene followed him up on to the deck, wondering what he planned to do about Sonja.

As if he knew what she was thinking, he said: "I hate to disturb Sonja's beauty sleep." He grinned. "Get moving."

They walked along the towpath. Why was he leaving Sonja behind? Elene wondered. She could not figure it out, but she knew it was callous. Wolff was a completely unscrupulous man, she decided; and the thought made her shudder, for she was in his power.

She wondered whether she could kill him

He carried his case in his left hand and gripped her arm with his right. They turned on to the footpath, walked to the street, and went to his car. He unlocked the door on the driver's side and made her climb in over the gear stick to the passenger side. He got in beside her and started the car.

It was a miracle the car was still in one piece after being left on the road all night: normally anything detachable would have been stolen, including wheels. He gets all the luck there is, Elene thought.

They drove away. Elene wondered where they were going. Wherever it was, Wolff's second radio was there, along with another copy of *Rebecca* and another key to the code. When we get there, I'll have to try again, she thought wearily. It was all up to her now. Wolff had left the houseboat, so there was nothing Vandam could do even after somebody untied him. Elene, on her own, had to try to stop Wolff from contacting Rommel, and if possible steal the key to the code.

The idea was ridiculous, shooting for the moon. All she really wanted was to get away from this evil, dangerous man, to go home, to forget about spies and codes and war, to feel safe again.

She thought of her father, walking to Jerusalem, and she knew she had to try.

Wolff stopped the car. Elene realized where they were She said: "This is Vandam's house!"

"Yes."

She gazed at Wolff, trying to read the expression on his face. She said: "But Vandam isn't there."

"No." Wolff smiled bleakly. "But Billy is."

24

Anwar el-Sadat was delighted with the radio.

"It's a Hallicrafter/Skychallenger," he told Kemel. "American." He plugged it in to test it, and pronounced it very powerful.

Kemel explained that he had to broadcast at midnight on the preset wavelength, and that the call sign was Sphinx. He said that Wolff had refused to give him the code, and that they would have to take the risk of broadcasting in clear.

They hid the radio in the oven in the kitchen of the little house.

Kemel left Sadat's home and drove from Kubri al-Qubbah back to Zamalek. On the way he considered how he was to cover up his role in the events of the night.

His story would have to tally with that of the sergeant whom Vandam had sent for help, so he would have to admit that he had received the phone call. Perhaps he would say that, before alerting the British, he had gone to the houseboat himself to investigate, in case "Major Vandam" was an impostor. What then? He had searched the towpath and the bushes for Vandam, and then he, too, had been knocked on the head. The snag was that he would not have stayed unconscious all these hours. So he would have to say that he had been tied up. Yes, he would say he had been tied up and had just managed to free himself. Then he and Vandam would board the houseboat—and find it empty.

It would serve.

He parked his car and went cautiously down to the towpath. Looking into the shrubbery, he figured out roughly where he had left Vandam. He went into the bushes thirty or forty yards away from that spot. He lay down on the ground and rolled over, to make his clothes dirty, then he rubbed some of the sandy soil on his face and ran his fingers through his hair. Then, rubbing his wrists to make them look sore, he went in search of Vandam.

He found him exactly where he had left him. The bonds were still tight and the gag still in place. Vandam looked at Kemel with wide, staring eyes.

Kemel said: "My God, they got you, too!"

He bent down, removed the gag, and began to untie Vandam. "The sergeant contacted me," he explained. "I came down here looking for you, and the next thing I knew, I woke up bound and gagged with a headache. That was hours ago. I just got free."

Vandam said nothing.

Kemel threw the rope aside. Vandam stood up stiffly. Kemel said: "How do you feel?"

"I'm all right."

"Let's board the houseboat and see what we can find," Kemel said. He turned around.

～

As soon as Kemel turned his back, Vandam stepped forward and hit him as hard as he possibly could with an edge-of-the-hand blow to the back of the neck. It might have killed Kemel, but Vandam did not care. Vandam had been bound and gagged, and he had been unable to see the towpath; but he had been able to hear: "I'm Kemel. You must be Wolff." That was how he knew that Kemel had betrayed him. Kemel had not thought of that possibility, obviously. Since overhearing those words, Vandam had been seething, and all his pent-up anger had gone into the blow.

Kemel lay on the ground, stunned. Vandam rolled him over, searched him and found the gun. He used the rope that had bound his own hands to tie Kemel's hands behind his back. Then he slapped Kemel's face until he came around.

"Get up," Vandam said.

Kemel looked blank, then fear came into his eyes. "What are you doing?"

Vandam kicked him. "Kicking you," he said. "Get up."

Kemel struggled to his feet.

"Turn around."

Kemel turned around. Vandam took hold of Kemel's collar with his left hand, keeping the gun in his right.

"Move."

They walked to the houseboat. Vandam pushed Kemel ahead, up the gangplank and across the deck.

"Open the hatch."

Kemel put the toe of his shoe into the handle of the hatch and lifted it open.

"Go down."

Awkwardly, with his hands tied, Kemel descended the ladder. Vandam bent down to look inside. There was nobody there. He went quickly down the ladder. Pushing Kemel to one side, he pulled back the curtain, covering the space behind with the gun.

He saw Sonja in bed, sleeping.

"Get in there," he told Kemel.

Kemel went through and stood beside the head of the bed.

"Wake her."

Kemel touched Sonja with his foot. She turned over, rolling away from him, without opening her eyes. Vandam realized vaguely that she was naked. He reached over and tweaked her nose. She opened her eyes and sat up immediately, looking cross. She recognized Kemel, then she saw Vandam with the gun.

She said: "What's going on?"

Then she and Vandam said simultaneously: "Where's Wolff?"

Vandam was quite sure she was not dissembling. It was clear now that Kemel had warned Wolff, and Wolff had fled without waking Sonja. Presumably he had taken Elene with him—although Vandam could not imagine why.

Vandam put the gun to Sonja's chest, just below her left breast. He spoke to Kemel. "I'm going to ask you a question. If you give the wrong answer, she dies. Understand?"

Kemel nodded tensely.

Vandam said: "Did Wolff send a radio message at midnight last night?"

"No!" Sonja screamed. "No, he didn't, he didn't!"

"What *did* happen here?" Vandam asked, dreading the answer.

"We went to bed."

"Who did?"

"Wolff, Elene and me."

"Together?"

"Yes."

So that was it. And Vandam had thought she was safe, because there was another woman around! That explained Wolff's continuing interest in Elene: they had wanted her for their threesome. Vandam was sick with disgust, not because of what they had done, but because he had caused Elene to be forced to be part of it.

He put the thought out of his mind. Was Sonja telling the truth—had Wolff failed to radio Rommel last night? Vandam could not think of a way to check. He could only hope it was true.

"Get dressed," he told Sonja.

She got off the bed and hurriedly put on a dress. Keeping both of them covered with the gun, Vandam went to the prow of the boat and looked through the little doorway. He saw a tiny bathroom with two small portholes.

"Get in there, both of you."

Kemel and Sonja went into the bathroom. Vandam closed the door on them and began to search the houseboat. He opened all the cupboards and drawers, throwing their contents on the floor. He stripped the bed. With a sharp knife from the kitchen he slashed the mattress and the upholstery of the couch. He went through all the papers in the escritoire. He found a large glass ashtray full of charred paper and poked through it, but all of the paper was completely burned up. He emptied the icebox. He went up on deck and cleaned out the lockers. He checked all around the outside of the hull, looking for a rope dangling into the water.

After half an hour he was sure that the houseboat contained no radio, no copy of *Rebecca* and no code key.

He got the two prisoners out of the bathroom. In one of the deck lockers he had found a length of rope. He tied Sonja's hands, then roped Sonja and Kemel together.

He marched them off the boat, along the towpath and up to the street. They walked to the bridge, where he hailed a taxi. He put Sonja and Kemel in the back then, keeping the gun pointed at them, he got in the front beside the wide-eyed, frightened Arab driver.

"GHQ," he told the driver.

The two prisoners would have to be interrogated, but really there were only two questions to be asked:

Where was Wolff?

And where was Elene?

ᔕ

Sitting in the car, Wolff took hold of Elene's wrist. She tried to pull away but his grip was too strong. He drew out his knife and ran its blade lightly across the back of her hand. The knife was very sharp. Elene stared at her hand in horror. At first there was just a line like a pencil mark. Then blood welled up in the cut, and there was a sharp pain. She gasped.

Wolff said: "You're to stay very close to me and say nothing."

Suddenly Elene hated him. She looked into his eyes. "Otherwise you'll cut me?" she said with all the scorn she could muster.

"No," he said. "Otherwise I'll cut Billy."

He released her wrist and got out of the car. Elene sat still, feeling helpless. What could she do against this strong, ruthless man? She took a little handkerchief from her bag and wrapped it around her bleeding hand.

Impatiently, Wolff came around to her side of the car and pulled open the door. He took hold of her upper arm and made her get out of the car. Then, still holding her, he crossed the road to Vandam's house.

They walked up the short drive and rang the bell. Elene remembered the last time she had stood in this portico waiting for the door to open. It seemed years ago, but it was only days. Since then she had learned that Vandam had been married, and that his wife had died; and she had made love to Vandam; and he had failed to send her flowers—how could she have made such a fuss about that?—and they had found Wolff; and—

The door opened. Elene recognized Gaafar. The servant remembered her, too, and said: "Good morning, Miss Fontana."

"Hello, Gaafar."

Wolff said: "Good morning, Gaafar. I'm Captain Alexander. The major asked me to come round. Let us in, would you?"

"Of course, sir." Gaafar stood aside. Wolff, still gripping Elene's arm, stepped into the house. Gaafar closed the door. Elene remembered this tiled hall. Gaafar said: "I hope the major is all right . . ."

"Yes, he's fine," Wolff said. "But he can't get home this morning, so he asked me to come round, tell you that he's well, and drive Billy to school."

Elene was aghast. It was awful—Wolff was going to kidnap Billy. She should have guessed that as soon as Wolff mentioned the boy's name—but it was unthinkable, she must not let it happen! What could she do? She wanted to shout No, Gaafar, he's lying, take Billy and get away, run, run! But Wolff had the knife, and Gaafar was old, and Wolff would get Billy anyway.

Gaafar seemed to hesitate. Wolff said: "All right, Gaafar, snap it up. We haven't got all day."

"Yes, sir," Gaafar said, reacting with the reflex of an Egyptian servant addressed in an authoritative manner by a European. "Billy is just finishing his breakfast. Would you wait in here for a moment?" He opened the drawing-room door.

Wolff propelled Elene into the room and at last let go of

her arm. Elene looked at the upholstery, the wallpaper, the marble fireplace and the *Tatler* photograph of Angela Vandam: these things had the eerie look of familiar objects seen in a nightmare. Angela would have known what to do, Elene thought miserably. "Don't be ridiculous!" she would have said; then, raising an imperious arm, she would have told Wolff to get out of her house. Elene shook her head to dispel the fantasy: Angela would have been as helpless as she.

Wolff sat down at the desk. He opened a drawer, took out a pad and a pencil, and began to write.

Elene wondered what Gaafar might do. Was it possible he might call GHQ to check with Billy's father? Egyptians were very reluctant to make phone calls to GHQ, Elene knew: Gaafar would have trouble getting past the switchboard operators and secretaries. She looked around, and saw that anyway the phone was here in this room, so that if Gaafar tried, Wolff would know and stop him.

"Why did you bring me here?" she cried. Frustration and fear made her voice shrill.

Wolff looked up from his writing. "To keep the boy quiet. We've got a long way to go."

"Leave Billy here," she pleaded. "He's a child."

"Vandam's child," Wolff said with a smile.

"You don't need him."

"Vandam may be able to guess where I'm going," Wolff said. "I want to make sure he doesn't come after me."

"Do you really think he'll sit at home while you have his son?"

Wolff appeared to consider the point. "I hope so," he said finally. "Anyway, what have I got to lose? If I don't take the boy he'll definitely come after me."

Elene fought back tears. "Haven't you got any *pity*?"

"Pity is a decadent emotion," Wolff said with a gleam in his eye. "Scepticism regarding morality is what is decisive. The end of the moral interpretation of the world, which no longer has any sanction . . ." He seemed to be quoting.

Elene said: "I don't think you're doing this to make Vandam

stay home. I think you're doing it out of spite. You're thinking about the anguish you'll cause him, and you love it. You're a crude, twisted, loathsome man."

"Perhaps you're right."

"You're sick."

"That's enough!" Wolff reddened slightly. He appeared to calm himself with an effort. "Shut up while I'm writing."

Elene forced herself to concentrate. They were going on a long journey. He was afraid Vandam would follow them. He had told Kemel he had another wireless set. Vandam might be able to guess where they were going. At the end of the journey, surely, there was the spare radio, with a copy of *Rebecca* and a copy of the key to the code. Somehow she had to help Vandam follow them, so that he could rescue them and capture the key. If Vandam could guess the destination, Elene thought, then so could I. Where would Wolff have kept a spare radio? It was a long journey away. He might have hidden one somewhere before he reached Cairo. It might be somewhere in the desert, or somewhere between here and Assyut. Maybe—

Billy came in. "Hello," he said to Elene. "Did you bring me that book?"

She did not know what he was talking about. "Book?" She stared at him, thinking that he was still very much a child, despite his grown-up ways. He wore gray flannel shorts and a white shirt, and there was no hair on the smooth skin of his bare forearm. He was carrying a school satchel and wearing a school tie.

"You forgot," he said, and looked betrayed. "You were going to lend me a detective story by Simenon."

"I did forget. I'm sorry."

"Will you bring it next time you come?"

"Of course."

Wolff had been staring at Billy all this time, like a miser looking into his treasure chest. Now he stood up. "Hello, Billy," he said with a smile. "I'm Captain Alexander."

Billy shook hands and said: "How do you do, sir."

"Your father asked me to tell you that he's very busy indeed."

"He always comes home for breakfast," Billy said.

"Not today. He's pretty busy coping with old Rommel, you know."

"Has he been in another fight?"

Wolff hesitated. "Matter of fact he has, but he's okay. He got a bump on the head."

Billy seemed more proud than worried, Elene observed.

Gaafar came in and spoke to Wolff. "You are sure, sir, that the major said you were to take the boy to school?"

He *is* suspicious, Elene thought.

"Of course," Wolff said. "Is something wrong?"

"No, but I am responsible for Billy, and we don't actually know you . . ."

"But you know Miss Fontana," Wolff said. "She was with me when Major Vandam spoke to me, weren't you, Elene?" Wolff stared at her and touched himself under the left arm, where the knife was sheathed.

"Yes," Elene said miserably.

Wolff said: "However, you're quite right to be cautious, Gaafar. Perhaps you should call GHQ and speak to the major yourself." He indicated the phone.

Elene thought: No, don't Gaafar, he'll kill you before you finish dialing.

Gaafar hesitated, then said: "I'm sure that won't be necessary, sir. As you say, we know Miss Fontana."

Elene thought: It's all my fault.

Gaafar went out.

Wolff spoke to Elene in rapid Arabic. "Keep the boy quiet for a minute." He continued writing.

Elene looked at Billy's satchel, and had the glimmer of an idea. "Show me your schoolbooks," she said.

Billy looked at her as if she were crazy.

"Come on," she said. The satchel was open, and an atlas stuck out. She reached for it. "What are you doing in geography?"

"The Norwegian fjords."

Elene saw Wolff finish writing and put the sheet of paper in an envelope He licked the flap, sealed the envelope, and put it in his pocket.

· "Let's find Norway," Elene said. She flipped the pages of the atlas.

Wolff picked up the telephone and dialed. He looked at Elene, then looked away, out of the window.

Elene found the map of Egypt.

Billy said: "But that's—"

Quickly, Elene touched his lips with her finger. He stopped speaking and frowned at her.

She thought: Please, little boy, be quiet and leave this to me.

She said: "Scandinavia, yes, but Norway is in Scandinavia, look." She unwrapped the handkerchief from around her hand. Billy stared at the cut. With her fingernail Elene opened the cut and made it bleed again. Billy turned white. He seemed about to speak, so Elene touched his lips and shook her head with a pleading look.

Elene was sure Wolff was going to Assyut. It was a likely guess, and Wolff had said he was afraid Vandam would correctly guess their destination. As she thought this, she heard Wolff say into the phone: "Hello? Give me the time of the train to Assyut."

I was right! she thought. She dipped her finger in the blood from her hand. With three strokes, she drew an arrow in blood on the map of Egypt, with the point of the arrow on the town of Assyut, three hundred miles south of Cairo. She closed the atlas. She used her handkerchief to smear blood on the cover of the book, then pushed the book behind her.

Wolff said: "Yes—and what time does it arrive?"

Elene said: "But why are there fjords in Norway and not in Egypt?"

Billy seemed dumbstruck. He was staring at her hand. She had to make him snap out of it before he gave her away. She said: "Listen, did you ever read an Agatha Christie story called *The Clue of the Bloodstained Atlas?*"

"No, there's no such—"

"It's very clever, the way the detective is able to figure everything out on the basis of *that one clue.*"

He frowned at her, but instead of the frown of the utterly amazed, it was the frown of one who is working something out.

Wolff put down the phone and stood up. "Let's go," he said. "You don't want to be late for school, Billy." He went to the door and opened it.

Billy picked up his satchel and went out. Elene stood up, dreading that Wolff would spot the atlas.

"Come on," he said impatiently.

She went through the door and he followed her. Billy was on the porch already. There was a little pile of letters on a kidney-shaped table in the hall. Elene saw Wolff drop his envelope on top of the pile.

They went out through the front door.

Wolff asked Elene: "Can you drive?"

"Yes," she answered, then cursed herself for thinking slowly —she should have said no.

"You two get in the front," Wolff instructed. He got in the back.

As she pulled away, Elene saw Wolff lean forward. He said: "See this?"

She looked down. He was showing the knife to Billy.

"Yes," Billy said in an unsteady voice.

Wolff said: "If you make trouble, I'll cut your head off."

Billy began to cry.

25

"Stand to attention!" Jakes barked in his sergeant major's voice.

Kemel stood to attention.

The interrogation room was bare but for a table. Vandam followed Jakes in, carrying a chair in one hand and a cup of tea in the other. He sat down.

Vandam said: "Where is Alex Wolff?"

"I don't know," said Kemel, relaxing slightly.

"Attention!" Jakes yelled. "Stand straight, boy!"

Kemel came to attention again.

Vandam sipped his tea. It was part of the act, a way of saying that he had all the time in the world and was not very concerned about anything, whereas the prisoner was in real trouble. It was the reverse of the truth.

He said: "Last night you received a call from the officer on surveillance at houseboat *Jihan*."

Jakes shouted: "Answer the major!"

"Yes," Kemel said.

"What did he say to you?"

"He said that Major Vandam had come to the towpath and sent him to summon assistance."

"Sir!" said Jakes. "To summon assistance, sir!"

"To summon assistance, sir."

Vandam said: "And what did you do?"

"I went personally to the towpath to investigate, sir."

"And then?"

"I was struck on the head and knocked unconscious. When I recovered I was bound hand and foot. It took me several hours to free myself. Then I freed Major Vandam, whereupon he attacked me."

Jakes went close to Kemel. "You're a bloody lying little bloody wog!" Kemel took a pace back. "Stand forward!" Jakes shouted. "You're a lying little wog, what are you?" Kemel said nothing.

Vandam said: "Listen, Kemel. As things stand you're going to be shot for spying. If you tell us all you know, you could get off with a prison sentence. Be sensible. Now, you came to the towpath and knocked me out, didn't you?"

"No, sir."

Vandam sighed. Kemel had his story and he was sticking to it. Even if he knew, or could guess, where Wolff had gone, he would not reveal it while he was pretending innocence.

Vandam said: "What is your wife's involvement in all this?"

Kemel said nothing, but he looked scared.

Vandam said: "If you won't answer my questions, I'll have to ask her."

Kemel's lips were pressed together in a hard line.

Vandam stood up. "All right, Jakes," he said. "Bring in the wife on suspicion of spying."

Kemel said: "Typical British justice."

Vandam looked at him. "Where is Wolff?"

"I don't know."

Vandam went out. He waited outside the door for Jakes. When the captain came out, Vandam said: "He's a policeman, he knows the techniques. He'll break, but not today." And Vandam had to find Wolff today.

Jakes asked: "Do you want me to arrest the wife?"

"Not yet. Maybe later." And where was Elene?

They walked a few yards to another cell. Vandam said: "Is everything ready here?"

"Yes."

"Okay." He opened the door and went in. This room was not so bare. Sonja sat on a hard chair, wearing a coarse gray prison dress. Beside her stood a woman army officer who would have scared Vandam, had he been her prisoner. She was short and stout, with a hard masculine face and short gray hair. There was a cot in one corner of the cell and a cold-water basin in the other.

As Vandam walked in the woman officer said: "Stand up!"

Vandam and Jakes sat down. Vandam said: "Sit down, Sonja."

The woman officer pushed Sonja into the chair.

Vandam studied Sonja for a minute. He had interrogated her once before, and she had been stronger than he. It would be different this time: Elene's safety was in the balance, and Vandam had few scruples left.

He said: "Where is Alex Wolff?"

"I don't know."

"Where is Elene Fontana?"

"I don't know."

"Wolff is a German spy, and you have been helping him."

"Ridiculous."

"You're in trouble."

She said nothing. Vandam watched her face. She was proud, confident, unafraid. Vandam wondered what, exactly, had happened on the houseboat this morning. Surely, Wolff had gone off without warning Sonja. Did she not feel betrayed?

"Wolff betrayed you," Vandam said. "Kemel, the policeman, warned Wolff of the danger; but Wolff left you sleeping and went off with another woman. Are you going to protect him after that?"

She said nothing.

"Wolff kept his radio on your boat. He sent messages to Rommel at midnight. You knew this, so you were an accessory to espionage. You're going to be shot for spying."

"All Cairo will riot! You wouldn't dare!"

"You think so? What do we care if Cairo riots now? The Germans are at the gates—let them put down the rebellion."

"You dare not touch me."

"Where has Wolff gone?"

"I don't know."

"Can you guess?"

"No."

"You're not being helpful, Sonja. It will make things worse for you."

"You can't touch me."

"I think I'd better prove to you that I can." Vandam nodded to the woman officer.

The woman held Sonja still while Jakes tied her to the chair. She struggled for a moment, but it was hopeless. She looked at Vandam, and for the first time there was a hint of fear in her eyes. She said: "What are you doing, you bastards?"

The woman officer took a large pair of scissors from her bag. She lifted a hank of Sonja's long, thick hair and cut it off.

"You can't do this!" Sonja shrieked.

Swiftly, the woman cut Sonja's hair. As the heavy locks fell away the woman dropped them in Sonja's lap. Sonja screamed, cursing Vandam and Jakes and the British in language which Vandam had never heard from a woman.

The woman officer took a smaller pair of scissors and cropped Sonja's hair close to the scalp.

Sonja's screams subsided into tears. When he could be heard Vandam said: "You see, we don't care much about legality and justice anymore, nor do we care about Egyptian public opinion. We've got our backs to the wall. We may all be killed soon. We're desperate."

The woman took soap and a shaving brush and lathered Sonja's head, then began to shave her scalp.

Vandam said: "Wolff was getting information from someone at GHQ. Who?"

"You're evil," said Sonja.

Finally the woman officer took a mirror from her bag and held it in front of Sonja's face. At first Sonja would not look in the glass, but after a moment she gave in. She gasped when she saw the reflection of her totally bald head. "No," she said. "It's not me." She burst into tears.

All the hatred was gone, now; she was completely demoralized. Vandam said softly: "Where was Wolff getting his information?"

"From Major Smith," Sonja replied.

Vandam heaved a sigh of relief. She had broken: thank God. "First name?" he asked.

"Sandy Smith."

Vandam glanced at Jakes. That was the name of the major from MI6 who had disappeared—it was as they had feared.

"How did he get the information?"

"Sandy came to the houseboat in his lunch break to visit me. While we were in bed Alex went through his briefcase."

As simple as that, Vandam thought. Jesus, I feel tired. Smith was liaison man between the Secret Intelligence Service—also known as MI6—and GHQ, and in that role he had been privy to all strategic planning, for MI6 needed to know what the Army was doing so that it could tell its spies what information to look for. Smith had been going straight from the morning conferences at GHQ to the houseboat, with a briefcase full of secrets. Vandam had already learned that Smith had been telling people at GHQ he was lunching at the MI6 office, and telling his superiors at MI6 he was lunching at GHQ, so that nobody would know he was screwing a dancer. Vandam had previously assumed Wolff was bribing or blackmailing someone: it had never occurred to him that Wolff might be getting information from someone without that someone's knowledge.

Vandam said: "Where is Smith now?"

"He caught Alex going through his briefcase. Alex killed him."

"Where's the body?"

"In the river by the houseboat."

Vandam nodded to Jakes, and Jakes went out.

Vandam said to Sonja: "Tell me about Kemel."

She was in full flood now, eager to tell all she knew, her resistance quite crushed; she would do anything to make people be nice to her. "He came and told me you had asked him to have the houseboat watched. He said he would censor his surveillance reports if I would arrange a meeting between Alex and Sadat."

"Alex and whom?"

"Anwar el-Sadat. He's a captain in the Army."

"Why did he want to meet Wolff?"

"So the Free Officers could send a message to Rommel."

Vandam thought: there are elements to this that I never thought of. He said: "Where does Sadat live?"

"Kubri al-Qubbah."

"The address?"

"I don't know."

Vandam said to the woman officer: "Go and find out the exact address of Captain Anwar el-Sadat."

"Yes, sir." The woman's face broke into a smile that was astonishingly pretty. She went out.

Vandam said: "Wolff kept his radio on your houseboat."

"Yes."

"He used a code for his messages."

"Yes, he had an English novel which he used to use to make up the code words."

"*Rebecca.*"

"Yes."

"And he had a key to the code."

"A key?"

"A piece of paper telling him which pages of the book to use."

She nodded slowly. "Yes, I think he did."

"The radio, the book and the key have gone. Do you know where?"

"No," she said. She got scared. "Honestly, no, I don't know, I'm telling the truth—"

"It's all right, I believe you. Do you know where Wolff might have gone?"

"He has a house . . . Villa les Oliviers."

"Good idea. Any other suggestions?"

"Abdullah. He might have gone to Abdullah."

"Yes. Any more?"

"His cousins, in the desert."

"And where would they be found?"

"No one knows. They're nomads."

"Might Wolff know their movements?"

"I suppose he might."

Vandam sat looking at her for a little while longer. She was
no actress: she could not have faked this. She was totally broken
down, not only willing but eager to betray her friends and tell
all her secrets. She was telling the truth.

"I'll see you again," Vandam said, and went out.

The woman officer handed him a slip of paper with Sadat's
address on it, then went into the cell. Vandam hurried to the
muster room. Jakes was waiting. "The Navy is lending us a
couple of divers," Jakes said. "They'll be here in a few minutes."

"Good." Vandam lit a cigarette. "I want you to raid Abdullah's place. I'm going to arrest this Sadat fellow. Send a small
team to the Villa les Oliviers, just in case—I don't suppose
they'll find anything. Has everyone been briefed?"

Jakes nodded. "They know we're looking for a wireless transmitter, a copy of *Rebecca,* and a set of coding instructions."

Vandam looked around, and noticed for the first time that
there were Egyptian policemen in the room. "Why have we
got bloody Arabs on the team?" he said angrily.

"Protocol, sir," Jakes replied formally. "Colonel Bogge's
idea."

Vandam bit back a retort. "After you've done Abdullah,
meet me at the houseboat."

"Yes, sir."

Vandam stubbed his cigarette. "Let's go."

They went out into the morning sunshine. A dozen or more
jeeps were lined up, their engines idling. Jakes gave instructions to the sergeants in the raiding parties, then nodded to
Vandam. The men boarded the jeeps, and the teams pulled
out.

Sadat lived in a suburb three miles out of Cairo in the direction of Heliopolis. His home was an ordinary family house
in a small garden. Four jeeps roared up outside, and the soldiers immediately surrounded the house and began to search

the garden. Vandam rapped on the front door. A dog began to bark loudly. Vandam knocked again. The door was opened.

"Captain Anwar el-Sadat?"

"Yes."

Sadat was a thin, serious young man of medium height. His curly brown hair was already receding. He wore his captain's uniform and fez, as if he was about to go out.

"You're under arrest," Vandam said, and pushed past him into the house. Another young man appeared in a doorway. "Who is he?" Vandam demanded.

"My brother, Tal'at," said Sadat.

Vandam looked at Sadat. The Arab was calm and dignified, but he was hiding some tension. He's afraid, Vandam thought; but he's not afraid of me, and he's not afraid of going to prison; he's afraid of something else.

What kind of deal had Kemel done with Wolff this morning? The rebels needed Wolff to help them get in touch with Rommel. Were they hiding Wolff somewhere?

Vandam said: "Which is your room, Captain?"

Sadat pointed. Vandam went into the room. It was a simple bedroom, with a mattress on the floor and a galabiya hanging from a hook. Vandam pointed to two British soldiers and an Egyptian policeman, and said: "All right, go ahead." They began to search the room.

"What is the meaning of this?" Sadat said quietly.

"You know Alex Wolff," Vandam said.

"No."

"He also calls himself Achmed Rahmha, but he's a European."

"I've never heard of him."

Clearly Sadat was a fairly tough personality, not the kind to break down and confess everything just because a few burly soldiers started messing up his house. Vandam pointed across the hall. "What's that room?"

"My study—"

Vandam went to the door.

Sadat said: "But the women of the family are in there, you must let me warn them—"

"They know we're here. Open the door."

Vandam let Sadat enter the room first. There were no women inside, but a back door was open as if someone had just stepped out. That was okay: the garden was full of soldiers, no one would escape. Vandam saw an army pistol on the desk holding down some sheets of paper covered with Arabic script. He went to the bookshelf and examined the books: *Rebecca* was not there.

A shout came from another part of the house: "Major Vandam!"

Vandam followed the sound into the kitchen. A sergeant MP was standing beside the oven, with the house dog yapping at his booted feet. The oven door stood open, and the sergeant lifted out a suitcase-radio.

Vandam looked at Sadat, who had followed him into the kitchen. The Arab's face was twisted with bitterness and disappointment. So this was the deal they had done: they warned Wolff, and in exchange they got his radio. Did that mean he had another? Or had Wolff arranged to come here, to Sadat's house, to broadcast?

Vandam spoke to his sergeant. "Well done. Take Captain Sadat to GHQ."

"I protest," Sadat said. "The law states that officers in the Egyptian Army may be detained only in the officers' mess and must be guarded by a fellow officer."

The senior Egyptian policeman was standing nearby. "This is correct," he said.

Once again Vandam cursed Bogge for bringing the Egyptians into this. "The law also states that spies are to be shot," he told Sadat. He turned to the sergeant. "Send out my driver. Finish searching the house. Then have Sadat charged with espionage."

He looked again at Sadat. The bitterness and disappointment had gone from his face, to be replaced by a calculating look. He's figuring out how to make the most of all this, Vandam thought; he's preparing to play martyr. He's very adaptable— he should be a politician.

Vandam left the house and went out to the jeep. A few moments later his driver came running out and jumped into the seat beside him. Vandam said: "To Zamalek."

"Yes, sir." The driver started the jeep and pulled away.

When Vandam reached the houseboat the divers had done their work and were standing on the towpath getting out of their gear. Two soldiers were hauling something extremely grisly out of the Nile. The divers had attached ropes to the body they had found on the bottom and then washed their hands of the affair.

Jakes came over to Vandam. "Look at this, sir." He handed him a waterlogged book. The board covers had been torn off. Vandam examined the book: it was *Rebecca*.

The radio went to Sadat; the code book went into the river. Vandam remembered the ashtray full of charred paper in the houseboat: had Wolff burned the key to the code?

Why had he gotten rid of the radio, the book and the key, when he had a vital message to send to Rommel? The conclusion was inescapable: he had *another* radio, book and key hidden away somewhere.

The soldiers got the body on to the bank and then stepped back as if they wanted nothing more to do with it. Vandam stood over it. The throat had been cut and the head was almost severed from the body. A briefcase was roped to the waist. Vandam bent down and gingerly opened the case. It was full of bottles of champagne.

Jakes said: "My God."

"Ugly, isn't it," Vandam said. "Throat cut, then dumped in the river with a case of champagne to weigh him down."

"Cool bastard."

"And damn quick with that knife." Vandam touched his cheek: the dressing had been taken off, now, and several days' growth of beard hid the wound. *But not Elene, not with the knife, please.* "I gather you haven't found him."

"I haven't found anything. I've had Abdullah brought in, just on general principles, but there was nothing at his house. And I called in at the Villa les Oliviers on the way back—same story."

"And at Captain Sadat's house." Suddenly Vandam felt utterly drained. It seemed that Wolff outwitted him at every turn. It occurred to him that he might simply not be smart enough to catch this sly, evasive spy. "Perhaps we've lost," he said. He rubbed his face. He had not slept in the last twenty-four hours. He wondered what he was doing here, standing over the hideous corpse of Major Sandy Smith. There was no more to be learned from it. "I think I'll go home and sleep for an hour," he said. Jakes looked surprised. Vandam added: "It might help me think more clearly. This afternoon we'll interrogate all the prisoners again."

"Very good, sir."

Vandam walked back to his vehicle. Driving across the bridge from Zamalek to the mainland, he recalled that Sonja had mentioned one other possibility: Wolff's nomad cousins. He looked at the boats on the wide, slow river. The current took them downstream and the wind blew them upstream—a coincidence of enormous importance to Egypt. The boatmen were still using the single triangular sail, a design which had been perfected . . . How long ago? Thousands of years, perhaps. So many things in this country were done the way they had been done for thousands of years. Vandam closed his eyes and saw Wolff, in a felucca, sailing upriver, manipulating the triangular sail with one hand while with the other he tapped out messages to Rommel on the transmitter. The car stopped suddenly and Vandam opened his eyes, realizing he had been daydreaming, or dozing. Why would Wolff go upriver? To find his nomad cousins. But who could tell where they would be? Wolff might be able to find them, if they followed some annual pattern in their wanderings.

The jeep had stopped outside Vandam's house. He got out. "I want you to wait for me," he told the driver. "You'd better come in." He led the way into the house, then directed the driver to the kitchen. "My servant, Gaafar, will give you something to eat, so long as you don't treat him like a wog."

"Thank you very much, sir," said the driver.

There was a small stack of mail on the hall table. The top envelope had no stamp, and was addressed to Vandam in a vaguely familiar hand. It had "Urgent" scribbled in the top left-hand corner. Vandam picked it up.

There was more he should do, he realized. Wolff could well be heading south now. Roadblocks should be set up at all major towns on the route. There should be someone at every stop on the railway line, looking for Wolff. And the river itself . . . There had to be some way of checking the river, in case Wolff really had gone by boat, as in the daydream. Vandam was finding it hard to concentrate. We could set up riverblocks on the same principle as roadblocks, he thought; why not? None of it would be any good if Wolff had simply gone to ground in Cairo. Suppose he were hiding in the cemeteries? Many Muslims buried their dead in tiny houses, and there were acres of such empty buildings in the city: Vandam would have needed a thousand men to search them all. Perhaps I should do it anyway, he thought. But Wolff might have gone north, toward Alexandria; or east or west into the desert . . .

He went into the drawing room, looking for a letter opener. Somehow the search had to be narrowed down Vandam did not have thousands of men at his disposal—they were all in the desert, fighting. He had to decide what was the best bet. He remembered where all this had started: Assyut. Perhaps he should contact Captain Newman in Assyut. That seemed to be where Wolff had come in from the desert, so maybe he would go out that way. Maybe his cousins were in that vicinity. Vandam looked indecisively at the telephone. Where was that damned letter opener? He went to the door and called: "Gaafar!" He came back into the room, and saw Billy's school atlas on a chair. It looked mucky. The boy had dropped it in a puddle, or something. He picked it up. It was sticky. Vandam realized there was blood on it. He felt as if he were in a nightmare. What was going on? No letter opener, blood on the atlas, nomads at Assyut . . .

Gaafar came in. Vandam said: "What's this mess?"

Gaafar looked. "I'm sorry, sir, I don't know. They were looking at it while Captain Alexander was here—"

"Who's they? Who's Captain Alexander?"

"The officer you sent to take Billy to school, sir. His name was—"

"Stop." A terrible fear cleared Vandam's brain in an instant.

"A British Army captain came here this morning and took Billy away?"

"Yes, sir, he took him to school. He said you sent him—"

"Gaafar, *I sent nobody*."

The servant's brown face turned gray.

Vandam said: "Didn't you check that he was genuine?"

"But, sir, Miss Fontana was with him, so it seemed all right "

"Oh, my God." Vandam looked at the envelope in his hand. Now he knew why the handwriting was familiar: it was the same as that on the note that Wolff had sent to Elene. He ripped open the envelope. Inside was a message in the same hand:

> *Dear Major Vandam,*
>
> Billy is with me. Elene is taking care of him. He will be quite all right as long as I am safe. I advise you to stay where you are and do nothing. We do not make war on children, and I have no wish to harm the boy. All the same, the life of one child is as nothing beside the future of my two nations, Egypt and Germany; so be assured that if it suits my purpose I will kill Billy.
>
> Yours truly,
> *Alex Wolff.*

It was a letter from a madman: the polite salutations, the correct English, the semicolon, the attempt to justify the kidnapping of an innocent child . . . Now Vandam knew that, somewhere deep down inside, Wolff was insane.

And he had Billy.

Vandam handed the note to Gaafar, who put on his spectacles with a shaky hand. Wolff had taken Elene with him when he left the houseboat. It would not have been difficult to coerce her into helping him: all he had to do was threaten Billy, and she would have been helpless. But what was the point of the kidnap, really? And where had they gone? And why the blood?

Gaafar was weeping openly. Vandam said: "Who was hurt? Who was bleeding?"

"There was no violence," Gaafar said. "I think Miss Fontana had cut her hand."

And she had smeared blood on Billy's atlas and left it on the chair. It was a sign, a message of some kind. Vandam held the book in his hands and let it fall open. Immediately he saw the map of Egypt with a blotted red arrow roughly drawn. It pointed to Assyut.

Vandam picked up the phone and dialed GHQ. When the switchboard answered he hung up. He thought: If I report this, what will happen? Bogge will order a squad of light infantry to arrest Wolff at Assyut. There will be a fight. Wolff will know he has lost, know he is to be shot for spying, not to mention kidnapping and murder—and what will he do then?

He is insane, Vandam thought; he will kill my son.

He felt paralyzed by fear. Of course that was what Wolff wanted, that was his aim in taking Billy, to paralyze Vandam. That was how kidnapping worked.

If Vandam brought the Army in, there would be a shootout. Wolff might kill Billy out of mad spite. So there was only one option.

Vandam had to go after them alone.

"Get me two bottles of water," he told Gaafar. The servant went off. Vandam went into the hall and put on his motorcycle goggles, then found a scarf and wound it around his mouth and neck. Gaafar came from the kitchen with the bottles of water. Vandam left the house and went to his motorcycle. He put the bottles in the pannier and climbed on the bike. He kicked it into life and revved the engine. The fuel tank was full. Gaafar stood beside him, still weeping. Vandam touched the old man's shoulder. "I'll bring them back," he said. He rocked the bike off its stand, drove into the street and turned south.

26

My God, the station was a shambles. I suppose everyone wants to get out of Cairo in case it gets bombed. No first-class seats on the trains to Palestine—not even standing room. The wives and children of the British are running like rats. Fortunately south-bound trains are less in demand. The booking office still claimed there were no seats, but they always say that; a few piasters here and a few more there always gets a seat, or three. I was afraid I might lose Elene and the boy on the platform, among all the hundreds of peasants, barefoot in their dirty galabiyas, carrying boxes tied with string, chickens in crates, sitting on the plat-form eating their breakfast, a fat mother in black handing out boiled eggs and pita bread and caked rice to her husband and sons, cousins and daughters and in-laws; smart idea of mine, to hold the boy's hand—if I keep him close by, Elene will follow; smart idea, I have smart ideas, Christ I'm smart, smarter than Vandam, eat your heart out, Major Vandam, I've got your son. Somebody had a goat on a lead. Fancy taking a goat on a train ride. I never had to travel economy with the peasants and their goats. What a job, to clean the economy coach at the end of the journey, I wonder who does it, some poor fellah, a different breed, a different race, born slaves, thank God we got first-class seats, I travel first class through life, I hate dirt, God that station was dirty. Vendors on the platform: cigarettes, newspapers, a man with a huge basket of bread on his head. I like the women when they carry baskets on their heads, looking so graceful and proud, makes you want to do it to them there and then, standing up, I like women when they like to do it, when they lose their minds with pleasure, when they scream, Gesundheit! Look at Elene, sitting there beside the boy, so frightened, so beautiful, I want to do it with her again soon, forget Sonja, I'd like to do it with Elene right now, here on the train, in front of all these people, humiliate her, with Vandam's son watching, terrified, ha! Look at the mud-brick suburbs, houses leaning against one another for support, cows and sheep in the narrow dusty streets, I always wondered what they ate, those city sheep with their fat tails, where do they graze? No plumbing in those dark little houses beside the railway line. Women in the doorways peeling vegetables, sitting cross-legged on the dusty ground. Cats. So graceful, the cats. European cats are different, slower and much fatter; no wonder cats are sacred here, they are so beautiful, a kitten brings luck. The English like dogs. Disgusting animals, dogs: unclean, undignified, slobbering, fawning, sniffing. A cat is superior, and knows it. It is so important to be superior. One is a master or a slave. I hold my head up, like a cat; I walk about, ignoring the hoi polloi, intent on my own mysterious tasks, using people the way a cat uses its owner, giving no thanks and accepting no affection, taking what they offer as a right, not a gift. I'm a master, a German Nazi, an Egyptian Bedouin, a born ruler. How many hours to Assyut, eight, ten? Must move fast. Find Ishmael. He should be at the well, or not far away. Pick up the radio. Broadcast at midnight tonight. Complete British defense, what a coup, they'll give me medals. Germans in charge in Cairo. Oh, boy, we'll get the place into shape. What a combination, Germans and Egyptians, efficiency by day and sensuality by night, Teutonic technology and Bedouin savagery, Beethoven and hashish. If I can survive, make it to Assyut, contact Rommel; then Rommel can cross the last bridge, destroy the last line of defense, dash to Cairo, anni-

hilate the British, what a victory that will be. If I can make it.
What a triumph! What a triumph! What a triumph!

∽

I *will* not be *sick*, I *will* not be *sick*, I *will* not be *sick*. The
train says it for me, rattling on the tracks. I'm too old to throw
up on trains now, I used to do that when I was eight. Dad
took me to Alexandria, bought me candy and oranges and
lemonade, I ate too much, don't think about it, it makes me
ill to think about it, Dad said it wasn't my fault it was his,
but I always used to feel sick even if I didn't eat, today Elene
bought chocolate but I said no, thanks, I'm pretty grown-up
to say no to chocolate, kids never say no to chocolate, look, I
can see the pyramids, one, two, and the little one makes
three, this must be Giza. Where are we going? He was supposed to take me to school. Then he got out the knife. It's
curved. He'll cut off my head, where's Dad? I should be in
school, we have geography in the first period today, a test on
the Norwegian fjords, I learned it all last night, I needn't
have bothered, I've missed the test. They've already finished
it by now, Mr. Johnstone collecting up the papers, *You call
that a map, Higgins? Looks more like a drawing of your ear,
boy!* Everybody laughs. *Smythe can't spell Moskenstraumen.
Write it fifty times, lad.* Everyone is glad he isn't Smythe. Old
Johnstone opens the textbook. *Next, the Arctic tundra.* I wish
I was in school. I wish Elene would put her arm round me. I
wish the man would stop looking at me, staring at me like
that, so pleased with himself, I think he's crazy, where's Dad?
If I don't think about the knife, it will be just as if it wasn't
there. I mustn't think about the knife. If I concentrate on
not thinking about the knife, that's the same as thinking about
the knife. It's impossible to deliberately not think about
something. How does anyone stop thinking of something?
Accidentally. Accidental thoughts. All thoughts are accidental.
There, I stopped thinking about the knife for a second. If I
see a policeman, I'll rush up to him and yell Save me, save
me! I'll be so quick that *he* won't be able to stop me. I can
run like the wind, I'm quick. I might see an officer. I might

see a general. I'll shout, Good morning, General! He'll look
at me, surprised, and say Well, young fellow-me-lad, you're a
fine boy! Pardon me, sir, I'll say, I'm Major Vandam's son,
and this man is taking me away, and my father doesn't know,
I'm sorry to trouble you, but I need help. What? says the
general. Look here, sir, you can't do this to the son of a
British officer! Not cricket, you know! Just clear off, d'you
hear? Who the devil d'you think you are? And you needn't
flash that little penknife at me, I've got a pistol! You're a
brave lad, Billy. I'm a brave lad. All day men get killed in the
desert. Bombs fall, Back Home. Ships in the Atlantic get sunk
by U-boats, men fall into the icy water and drown. RAF chaps
shot down over France. Everybody is brave. Chin up! Damn
this war. That's what they say: Damn this war. Then they
climb into the cockpit, hurry down the air-raid shelter, attack
the next dune, fire torpedoes at the U-boats, write letters
home. I used to think it was exciting. Now I know better. It
isn't exciting at all. It makes you feel sick.

ᔓ

Billy is so pale. He looks it. He's trying to be brave. He
shouldn't, he should act like a child, he should scream and
cry and throw a tantrum, Wolff couldn't cope with that; but
he won't, of course, for he has been taught to be tough, to
bite back the cry, to suppress the tears, to have self-control. He
knows how his father would be, what else does a boy do but
copy his father? Look at Egypt. A canal alongside the railway
line. A grove of date palms. A man crouching in a field, his
galabiya hitched up above his long white undershorts, doing
something to the crops; an ass grazing, so much healthier than
the miserable specimens you see pulling carts in the city; three
women sitting beside the canal, washing clothes, pounding
them on stones to get them clean; a man on horseback, gallop-
ing, must be the local effendi, only the richest peasants have
horses; in the distance, the lush green countryside ends abruptly
in a range of dusty tan hills. Egypt is only thirty miles wide,
really: the rest is desert. What am I going to do? That chill,
deep in my chest, every time I look at Wolff. The way he

stares at Billy. The gleam in his eye. His restlessness: the way
he looks out of the window, then around the carriage, then
at Billy, then at me, then at Billy again, always with that
gleam in his eye, the look of triumph. I should comfort Billy.
I wish I knew more about boys, I had four sisters. What a
poor stepmother I should be for Billy. I'd like to touch him,
put my arm around him, give him a quick squeeze, or even
a cuddle, but I'm not sure that's what he wants, it might
make him feel worse. Perhaps I could take his mind off things
by playing a game. What a ridiculous idea. Perhaps not so
ridiculous. Here is his school satchel. Here is an exercise book.
He looks at me curiously. What game? Noughts and crosses.
Four lines for the grid; my cross in the center. The way he
looks at me as he takes the pencil, I do believe he's going
along with this crazy idea in order to comfort me! His nought
in the corner. Wolff snatches the book, looks at it, shrugs,
and gives it back. My cross, Billy's nought; it will be a drawn
game. I should let him win next time. I can play this game
without thinking, more's the pity. Wolff has a spare radio at
Assyut. Perhaps I should stay with him, and try to prevent
him using the radio. Some hope! I have to get Billy away, then
contact Vandam and tell him where I am. I hope Vandam
saw the atlas. Perhaps the servant saw it, and called GHQ.
Perhaps it will lie on the chair all day, unnoticed. Perhaps
Vandam will not go home today. I have to get Billy away
from Wolff, away from that knife. Billy makes a cross in the
center of a new grid. I make a nought, then scribble hastily:
We must escape—be ready. Billy makes another cross, and:
OK. My nought. Billy's cross and *When?* My nought and
Next station. Billy's third cross makes a line. He scores through
the line of crosses, then smiles up at me jubilantly. He has
won. The train slows down.

ᔆ

Vandam knew the train was still ahead of him. He had
stopped at the station at Giza, close to the pyramids, to ask
how long ago the train had passed through; then he had
stopped and asked the same question at three subsequent

stations. Now, after traveling for an hour, he had no need to stop and ask, for the road and the railway line ran parallel, on either side of a canal, and he would see the train when he caught up with it.

Each time he stopped he had taken a drink of water. With his uniform cap, his goggles and the scarf around his mouth and neck, he was protected from the worst of the dust; but the sun was terribly hot and he was continually thirsty. Eventually he realized he was running a slight fever. He thought he must have caught cold, last night, lying on the ground beside the river for hours. His breath was hot in his throat, and the muscles of his back ached.

He had to concentrate on the road. It was the only road which ran the length of Egypt, from Cairo to Aswan, and consequently much of it was paved; and in recent months the Army had done some repair work: but he still had to watch for bumps and potholes. Fortunately the road ran straight as an arrow, so he could see, far ahead, the hazards of cattle, wagons, camel trains and flocks of sheep. He drove very fast, except through the villages and towns, where at any moment people might wander out into the road: he would not kill a child to save a child, not even to save his own child.

So far he had passed only two cars—a ponderous Rolls-Royce and a battered Ford. The Rolls had been driven by a uniformed chauffeur, with an elderly English couple in the back seat; and the old Ford had contained at least a dozen Arabs. By now Vandam was fairly sure Wolff was traveling by train.

Suddenly he heard a distant hoot. Looking ahead and to his left he saw, at least a mile away, a rising plume of white smoke which was unmistakably that of a steam engine. Billy! he thought. Elene! He went faster.

Paradoxically, the engine smoke made him think of England, of gentle slopes, endless green fields, a square church tower peeping over the tops of a cluster of oak trees, and a railway line through the valley with a puffing engine disappearing into the distance. For a moment he was in that English valley, tasting the damp air of morning; then the vision passed, and he saw again the steel-blue African sky, the paddy fields, the palm trees and the far brown cliffs.

The train was coming into a town. Vandam did not know the names of the places anymore: his geography was not that good, and he had rather lost track of the distance he had traveled. It was a small town. It would have three or four brick buildings and a market.

The train was going to get there before him. He had made his plans, he knew what he was going to do; but he needed time, it was impossible for him to rush into the station and jump on the train without making preparations. He reached the town and slowed right down. The street was blocked by a small flock of sheep. From a doorway an old man smoking a hookah watched Vandam: a European on a motorcycle would be a rare, but not unknown, sight. An ass tied to a tree snarled at the bike. A water buffalo drinking from a bucket did not even look up. Two filthy children in rags ran alongside, holding imaginary handlebars and saying "Brrrm, brrrm," in imitation. Vandam saw the station. From the square he could not see the platform, for that was obscured by a long, low station building; but he could observe the exit and see anyone who came out. He would wait outside until the train left, just in case Wolff got off; then he would go ahead, and reach the next stop in plenty of time. He brought the motorcycle to a halt and killed the engine.

ᵔ

The train rolled slowly over a level crossing. Elene saw the patient faces of the people behind the gate, waiting for the train to pass so that they could cross the line: a fat man on a donkey, a very small boy leading a camel, a horse-drawn cab, a group of silent old women. The camel couched, the boy began to beat it about the face with a stick and then the scene slid sideways out of view. In a moment the train would be in the station. Elene's courage deserted her. Not this time, she thought. I haven't had time to think of a plan. The next station, let me leave it until the next station. But she had told Billy they would try to get away at this station. If she did nothing he would not trust her any longer. It had to be this time.

She tried to devise a plan. What was her priority? To get Billy away from Wolff. That was the only thing that counted. Give Billy a chance to run, then try to prevent Wolff from giving chase. She had a sudden, vivid memory of a childhood fight in a filthy slum street in Alexandria: a big boy, a bully, hitting her, and another boy intervening and struggling with the bully, the smaller boy shouting to her "Run, run!" while she stood watching the fight, horrified but fascinated. She could not remember how it had ended.

She looked around. Think quickly! They were in an open carriage, with fifteen or twenty rows of seats. She and Billy sat side by side, facing forward. Wolff was opposite them. Beside him was an empty seat. Behind him was the exit door to the platform. The other passengers were a mixture of Europeans and wealthy Egyptians, all of them in Western clothing. Everyone was hot, weary and enervated. Several people were asleep. The trainmaster was serving tea in glasses to a group of Egyptian Army officers at the far end of the carriage.

Through the window she saw a small mosque, then a French courthouse, then the station. A few trees grew in the dusty soil beside the concrete platform. An old man sat cross-legged beneath a tree, smoking a cigarette. Six boyish-looking Arab soldiers were crowded on to one small bench. A pregnant woman carried a baby in her arms. The train stopped.

Not yet, Elene thought; not yet. The time to move would be when the train was about to pull out again—that would give Wolff less time to catch them. She sat feverishly still. There was a clock on the platform with roman numerals. It had stopped at five to five. A man came to the window offering fruit drinks, and Wolff waved him away.

A priest in Coptic robes boarded the train and took the seat next to Wolff, saying politely: *"Vous permettez, m'sieur?"*

Wolff smiled charmingly and replied: *"Je vous en prie."*

Elene murmured to Billy: "When the whistle blows, run

for the door and get off the train." Her heart beat faster: now she was committed.

Billy said nothing. Wolff said: "What was that?" Elene looked away. The whistle blew.

Billy looked at Elene, hesitating.

Wolff frowned.

Elene threw herself at Wolff, reaching for his face with her hands. She was suddenly possessed by rage and hatred toward him for the humiliation, anxiety and pain he had inflicted on her. He put up his arms protectively, but they did not stop her rush. Her strength astonished her. She raked his face with her fingernails, and saw blood spurt.

The priest gave a shout of surprise.

Over the back of Wolff's seat she saw Billy run to the door and struggle to open it.

She collapsed on Wolff, banging her face against his forehead. She lifted herself again and tried to scratch his eyes.

At last he found his voice, and roared with anger. He pushed himself out of his seat, driving Elene backward. She grabbed at him and caught hold of his shirt front with both hands. Then he hit her. His hand came up from below his waist, bunched into a fist, then struck the side of her jaw. She had not known a punch could hurt so much. For an instant she could not see. She lost her grip on Wolff's shirt, and fell back into her seat. Her vision returned and she saw him heading for the door. She stood up.

Billy had got the door open. She saw him fling it wide and jump on to the platform. Wolff leaped after him. Elene ran to the door.

Billy was racing along the platform, running like the wind. Wolff was charging after him. The few Egyptians standing around were looking on, mildly astonished, and doing nothing. Elene stepped down from the train and ran after Wolff. The train shuddered, about to move. Wolff put on a burst of speed. Elene yelled: "Run, Billy, run!" Billy looked over his shoulder. He was almost at the exit now. A ticket collector in a raincoat stood there, looking on openmouthed. Elene thought: They won't let him out, he has no ticket. It did not matter, she realized, for the train was now inching forward, and Wolff had to get back on it. Wolff looked at the train, but did not slow his pace. Elene saw that Wolff was not going to catch Billy, and she thought: We did it! Then Billy fell.

He had slipped on something, a patch of sand or a leaf. He lost his balance completely, and went flying through the air, carried by the momentum of his running, to hit the ground hard. Wolff was on him in a flash, bending to lift him. Elene caught up with them and jumped on Wolff's back. Wolff stumbled, losing his grip on Billy. Elene clung to Wolff. The train was moving slowly but steadily. Wolff grabbed Elene's arms, broke her grip, and shook his wide shoulders, throwing her to the ground.

For a moment she lay stunned. Looking up, she saw that Wolff had thrown Billy across his shoulder. The boy was yelling and hammering on Wolff's back, without effect. Wolff ran alongside the moving train for a few paces, then jumped in through an open door. Elene wanted to stay where she was, never to see Wolff again; but she could not leave Billy. She struggled to her feet.

She ran, stumbling, alongside the train. Someone reached out a hand to her. She took it, and jumped. She was aboard.

She had failed miserably. She was back where she started. She felt crushed.

She followed Wolff through the carriages back to their seats. She did not look at the faces of the people she passed. She saw Wolff give Billy one sharp smack on the bottom and dump him into his seat. The boy was crying silently.

Wolff turned to Elene. "You're a silly, crazy girl," he said loudly, for the benefit of the other passengers. He grabbed her arm and pulled her closer to him. He slapped her face with the palm of his hand, then with the back, then with the palm, again and again. It hurt, but Elene had no energy to resist. At last the priest stood up, touched Wolff's shoulder, and said something.

Wolff let her go and sat down. She looked around. They were all staring at her. None of them would help her, for she was not just an Egyptian, she was an Egyptian woman, and women, like camels, had to be beaten from time to time. As she met the eyes of the other passengers they looked away, embarrassed, and turned to their newspapers, their books and the view from the windows. No one spoke to her.

She fell into her seat. Useless, impotent rage boiled within her. Almost, they had almost escaped.

She put her arm around the child and pulled him close. She began to stroke his hair. After a while he fell asleep.

27

Vandam heard the train puff, pull and puff again. It gathered speed and moved out of the station. Vandam took another drink of water. The bottle was empty. He put it back in his pannier. He drew on his cigarette and threw away the butt. No one but a few peasants had gotten off the train. Vandam kicked his motorcycle into life and drove away.

In a few moments he was out of the little town and back on the straight, narrow road beside the canal. Soon he had left the train behind. It was noon: the sunshine was so hot it seemed tangible. Vandam imagined that if he stuck out his arm the heat would drag on it like a viscous liquid. The road ahead stretched into a shimmering infinity. Vandam thought: If I were to drive straight into the canal, how cool and refreshing it would be!

Somewhere along the road he had made a decision. He had set out from Cairo with no thought in his mind but to rescue Billy; but at some point he had realized that that was not his only duty. There was still the war.

Vandam was almost certain that Wolff had been too busy at midnight last night to use his radio. This morning he had given away the radio, thrown the book in the river and burned the key to the code. It was likely that he had another radio, another copy of *Rebecca* and another key to the code; and that the place they were all hidden was Assyut. If Vandam's deception plan were to be implemented, he had to have the radio and the key—and that meant he had to let Wolff get to Assyut and retrieve his spare set.

It ought to have been an agonizing decision, but somehow Vandam had taken it with equanimity. He had to rescue Billy and Elene, yes; but *after* Wolff had picked up his spare radio. It would be tough on the boy, savagely tough, but the worst of it—the kidnapping—was already in the past and irreversible, and living under Nazi rule, with his father in a concentration camp, would also be savagely tough.

Having made the decision, and hardened his heart, Vandam needed to be certain that Wolff really was on that train. And in figuring out how to check, he had thought of a way to make things a little easier for Billy and Elene at the same time.

When he reached the next town he reckoned he was at least fifteen minutes ahead of the train. It was the same kind of place as the last town: same animals, same dusty streets, same slow-moving people, same handful of brick buildings. The police station was in a central square, opposite the railway station, flanked by a large mosque and a small church. Vandam pulled up outside and gave a series of peremptory blasts on the horn of his bike.

Two Arab policemen came out of the building: a gray-haired man in a white uniform with a pistol at his belt, and a boy of eighteen or twenty years who was unarmed. The older man was buttoning his shirt. Vandam got off the bike and bawled: "Attention!" Both men stood straight and saluted. Vandam returned the salute, then shook the older man's hand. "I'm chasing a dangerous criminal, and I need your help," he said dramatically. The man's eyes glittered. "Let's go inside."

Vandam led the way. He felt he needed to keep the initiative firmly in his own hands. He was by no means sure of his own status here, and if the policemen were to choose to be uncooperative there would be little he could do about it. He entered the building. Through a doorway he saw a table with a telephone. He went into that room, and the policemen followed him.

Vandam said to the older man: "Call British headquarters in Cairo." He gave him the number, and the man picked up the phone. Vandam turned to the younger policeman. "Did you see the motorcycle?"

"Yes, yes." He nodded violently.

"Could you ride it?"

The boy was thrilled by the idea. "I ride it very well."

"Go out and try it."

The boy looked doubtfully at his superior, who was shouting into the telephone.

"Go on," Vandam said.

The boy went out.

The older man held the phone out to Vandam. "This is GHQ."

Vandam spoke into the phone. "Connect me with Captain Jakes, fast." He waited.

Jakes' voice came on the line after a minute or two. "Hello, yes?"

"This is Vandam. I'm in the south, following a hunch."

"There's a right panic on here since the brass heard what happened last night—the brigadier's having kittens and Bogge is running around like a fart in a colander—where in buggeration are you, sir?"

"Never mind where exactly, I won't be here much longer and I have to work alone at the moment. In order to assure the maximal support of the indigenous constabulary—" He spoke like this so that the policeman would not be able to understand—"I want you to do your Dutch uncle act. Ready?"

"Yes, sir."

Vandam gave the phone to the gray-haired policeman and stood back. He could guess what Jakes was saying. The policeman unconsciously stood straighter and squared his shoulders as Jakes instructed him, in no uncertain terms, to do everything Vandam wanted and do it fast. "Yes, sir!" the policeman said, several times. Finally he said: "Please be assured, sir and gentle-man, that we will do all in our power—" He stopped abruptly. Vandam guessed that Jakes had hung up. The policeman glanced at Vandam then said "Good-bye" to the empty wire.

Vandam went to the window and looked out. The young policeman was driving around and around the square on the motorcycle, hooting the horn and overrevving the engine. A small crowd had gathered to watch him, and a bunch of children were running behind the bike. The boy was grinning from ear to ear. He'll do, Vandam thought.

"Listen," he said. "I'm going to get on the Assyut train when it stops here in a few minutes. I'll get off at the next station. I want your boy to drive my bike to the next station and meet me there. Do you understand?"

"Yes, sir," said the man. "The train will stop here, then?"

"Doesn't it usually?"

"The Assyut train does not stop here usually."

"Then go to the station and tell them to stop it!"

"Yes, sir!" He went out at a run.

Vandam watched him cross the square. He could not hear the train yet. He had time for one more phone call. He picked up the receiver, waited for the operator, then asked for the army base in Assyut. It would be a miracle if the phone system worked properly twice in a row. It did. Assyut answered, and Vandam asked for Captain Newman. There was a long wait while they found him. At last he came on the line.

"This is Vandam. I think I'm on the trail of your knife man."

"Jolly good show, sir!" said Newman. "Anything I can do?"

"Well, now, listen. We have to go very softly. For all sorts of reasons which I'll explain to you later, I'm working entirely on my own, and to go after Wolff with a big squad of armed men would be worse than useless."

"Understood. What do you need from me?"

"I'll be arriving in Assyut in a couple of hours. I need a taxi, a large galabiya and a small boy. Will you meet me?"

"Of course, no problem. Are you coming by road?"

"I'll meet you at the city limits, how's that?"

"Fine." Vandam heard a distant chuff-chuff-chuff. "I have to go."

"I'll be waiting for you."

Vandam hung up. He put a five-pound note on the table beside the telephone: a little baksheesh never hurt. He went out into the square. Away to the north he could see the approaching smoke of the train. The younger policeman drove up to him on the bike. Vandam said: "I'm getting on the train. You drive the motorcycle to the next station and meet me there. Okay?"

"Okay, okay!" He was delighted.

Vandam took out a pound note and tore it in half. The young policeman's eyes widened. Vandam gave him half the note. "You get the other half when you meet me."

"Okay!"

The train was almost in the station. Vandam ran across the square. The older policeman met him. "The stationmaster is stopping the train."

Vandam shook his hand. "Thank you. What's your name?"

"Sergeant Nesbah."

"I'll tell them about you in Cairo. Goodbye." Vandam hurried into the station. He ran south along the platform, away from the train, so that he could board it at the front end without any of the passengers seeing him through the windows.

The train came in, billowing smoke. The stationmaster came along the platform to where Vandam was standing. When the train stopped the stationmaster spoke to the engine driver and the footplateman. Vandam gave all three of them baksheesh and boarded the train.

He found himself in an economy carriage. Wolff would surely travel first class. He began to walk along the train, picking his way over the people sitting on the floor with their boxes and crates and animals. He noticed that it was mainly women and children on the floor: the slatted wooden seats were occupied by the men with their bottles of beer and their cigarettes. The carriages were unbearably hot and smelly. Some of the women were cooking on makeshift stoves: surely that was dangerous! Vandam almost trod on a tiny baby crawling on the filthy floor. He had a feeling that if he had not avoided the child in the nick of time they would have lynched him.

He passed through three economy carriages, then he was at the door to a first-class coach. He found a guard just outside, sitting on a little wooden stool, drinking tea from a glass. The guard stood up. "Some tea, General?"

"No, thank you." Vandam had to shout to make himself heard over the noise of the wheels beneath them. "I have to check the papers of all first-class passengers."

"All in order, all very good," said the guard, trying to be helpful.

"How many first-class carriages are there?"

"All in order—"

Vandam bent to shout in the man's ear. "How many first-class coaches?"

The guard held up two fingers.

Vandam nodded and unbent. He looked at the door. Suddenly he was not sure that he had the nerve to go through with this. He thought that Wolff had never got a good look at him—they had fought in the dark, in the alley—but he could not be absolutely sure. The gash on his cheek might have given him away, but it was almost completely covered now by his beard; still he should try to keep that side of his face away from Wolff. Billy was the real problem. Vandam had to warn his son, somehow, to keep quiet and pretend not to recognize his father. There was no way to plan it, that was the trouble. He just had to go in there and think on his feet.

He took a deep breath and opened the door.

Stepping through, he glanced quickly and nervously at the first few seats and did not recognize anyone. He turned his back to the carriage as he closed the door, then turned around again. His gaze swept the rows of seats quickly: no Billy.

He spoke to the passengers nearest him. "Your papers, please, gentlemen."

"What's this, Major?" said an Egyptian Army officer, a colonel.

"Routine check, sir," Vandam replied.

He moved slowly along the aisle, checking people's papers. By the time he was halfway down the carriage he had studied the passengers well enough to be sure that Wolff, Elene and Billy were not here. He felt he had to finish the pantomime of checking papers before going on to the next coach. He began to wonder whether his guesswork might have gone wrong. Perhaps they weren't on the train at all; perhaps they weren't even heading for Assyut; perhaps the atlas clue had been a trick . . .

He reached the end of the carriage and passed through the door into the space between the coaches. If Wolff is on the train, I'll see him now, he thought. If Billy is here—if Billy is here—

He opened the door.

He saw Billy immediately. He felt a pang of distress like a wound. The boy was asleep in his seat, his feet only just reaching the floor, his body slumped sideways, his hair falling over his forehead. His mouth was open, and his jaws were moving slightly: Vandam knew, for he had seen this before, that Billy was grinding his teeth in his sleep.

The woman who had her arm around him, and on whose bosom his head rested, was Elene. Vandam had a disorienting sense of déjà vu: it reminded him of the night he had come upon Elene kissing Billy good night . . .

Elene looked up.

She caught Vandam's eye. He saw her face begin to change expression: her eyes widening, her mouth coming open for a cry of surprise; and, because he was prepared for something like this, he was very quick to raise a finger to his lips in a hushing sign. She understood immediately, and dropped her eyes; but Wolff had caught her look, and he was turning his head to find out what she had seen.

They were on Vandam's left, and it was his left cheek which had been cut by Wolff's knife. Vandam turned around so that his back was to the carriage, then he spoke to the people on the side of the aisle opposite Wolff's. "Your papers, please."

He had not reckoned on Billy being asleep.

He had been ready to give the boy a quick sign, as he had done with Elene, and he had hoped that Billy was alert enough to mask his surprise rapidly, as Elene had done. But this was a different situation. If Billy were to wake up and see his father standing there, he would probably give the game away before he had time to collect his thoughts.

Vandam turned to Wolff and said: "Papers, please."

It was the first time he had seen his enemy face to face. Wolff was a handsome bastard. His big face had strong features: a wide forehead, a hooked nose, even white teeth, a broad jaw. Only around the eyes and the corners of the mouth was there a hint of weakness, of self-indulgence, of depravity. He handed over his papers then looked out of the window, bored. The papers identified him as Alex Wolff, of Villa les Oliviers, Garden City. The man had remarkable nerve.

Vandam said: "Where are you going, sir?"

"Assyut."

"On business?"

"To visit relations." The voice was strong and deep, and Vandam would not have noticed the accent if he had not been listening for it.

Vandam said: "Are you people together?"

"That's my son and his nanny," Wolff said.

Vandam took Elene's papers and glanced at them. He wanted to take Wolff by the throat and shake him until his bones rattled. *That's my son and his nanny.* You bastard.

He gave Elene her papers. "No need to wake the child," he said. He looked at the priest sitting next to Wolff, and took the proffered wallet.

Wolff said: "What's this about, Major?"

Vandam looked at him again, and noticed that he had a fresh scratch on his chin, a long one: perhaps Elene had put up some resistance. "Security, sir," Vandam replied.

The priest said: "I'm going to Assyut, too."

"I see," said Vandam. "To the convent?"

"Indeed. You've heard of it, then."

"The place where the Holy Family stayed after their sojourn in the desert."

"Quite. Have you been there?"

"Not yet—perhaps I'll make it this time."

"I hope so," said the priest.

Vandam handed back the papers. "Thank you." He backed away, along the aisle to the next row of seats, and continued to examine papers. When he looked up he met Wolff's eyes. Wolff was watching him expressionlessly. Vandam wondered whether he had done anything suspicious. Next time he looked up, Wolff was staring out of the window again.

What was Elene thinking? She must be wondering what I'm up to, Vandam thought. Perhaps she can guess my intentions. It must be hard for her all the same, to sit still and see me walk by without a word. At least now she knows she's not alone.

What was Wolff thinking? Perhaps he was impatient, or gloating, or frightened, or eager . . . No, he was none of those, Vandam realized; he was bored.

He reached the end of the carriage and examined the last of the papers. He was handing them back, about to retrace his steps along the aisle, when he heard a cry that pierced his heart:

"THAT'S MY DAD!"

He looked up. Billy was running along the aisle toward him, stumbling, swaying from side to side, bumping against the seats, his arms outstretched.

Oh, God.

Beyond Billy, Vandam could see Wolff and Elene standing up, watching; Wolff with intensity, Elene with fear. Vandam opened the door behind him, pretending to take no notice of Billy, and backed through it. Billy came flying through. Vandam slammed the door. He took Billy in his arms.

"It's all right," Vandam said. "It's all right."

Wolff would be coming to investigate.

"They took me away!" Billy said. "I missed geography and I was really really scared!"

"It's all right now." Vandam felt he could not leave Billy now; he would have to keep the boy and kill Wolff, he would have to abandon his deception plan and the radio and the key to the code . . . No, it had to be done, it *had* to be done . . . He fought down his instincts. "Listen," he said. "I'm here, and I'm watching over you, but I have to catch that man, and I don't want him to know who I am. He's the German spy I'm after, do you understand?"

"Yes, yes . . ."

"Listen. Can you pretend you made a mistake? Can you pretend I'm not your father? Can you go back to him?"

Billy stared, openmouthed. He said nothing, but his whole expression said *No, no, no!*

Vandam said: "This is a real-life tec story, Billy, and we're in it, you and I. You have to go back to that man, and pretend you made a mistake; but remember, I'll be nearby, and together we'll catch the spy. Is that okay? Is it okay?"

Billy said nothing.

The door opened and Wolff came through.

"What's all this?" Wolff said.

Vandam made his face bland and forced a smile. "He seems to have woken up from a dream and mistaken me for his father. We're the same build, you and I . . . You did say you were his father, didn't you?"

Wolff looked at Billy. "What nonsense!" he said brusquely. "Come back to your seat at once."

Billy stood still.

Vandam put a hand on Billy's shoulder. "Come on, young man," he said. "Let's go and win the war."

The old catchphrase did the trick. Billy gave a brave grin. "I'm sorry, sir," he said. "I must have been dreaming."

Vandam felt as though his heart would break.

Billy turned away and went back inside the coach. Wolff went after him, and Vandam followed. As they walked along the aisle the train slowed down. Vandam realized they were already approaching the next station, where his motorcycle would be waiting. Billy reached his seat and sat down. Elene was staring at Vandam uncomprehendingly. Billy touched her arm and said: "It's okay, I made a mistake, I must have been dreaming." She looked at Billy, then at Vandam, and a strange light came into her eyes: she seemed on the point of tears.

Vandam did not want to walk past them. He wanted to sit down, to talk, to do anything to prolong the time he spent with them. Outside the train windows, another dusty little town appeared. Vandam yielded to temptation and paused at the carriage door. "Have a good trip," he said to Billy.

"Thank you, sir."

Vandam went out.

The train pulled into the station and stopped. Vandam got off and walked forward along the platform a little way. He stood in the shade of an awning and waited. Nobody else got off, but two or three people boarded the economy coaches. There was a whistle, and the train began to move. Vandam's eye was fixed on the window which he knew to be next to Billy's seat. As the window passed him, he saw Billy's face. Billy raised his hand in a little wave. Vandam waved back, and the face was gone.

Vandam realized he was trembling all over.

He watched the train recede into the hazy distance. When it was almost out of sight he left the station. There outside was his motorcycle, with the young policeman from the last town sitting astride it explaining its mysteries to a small crowd of admirers. Vandam gave him the other half of the pound note. The young man saluted.

Vandam climbed on the motorcycle and started it. He did not know how the policeman was going to get home, and he did not care. He drove out of town on the road south. The sun had passed its zenith, but the heat was still terrific.

Soon Vandam passed the train. He would reach Assyut thirty or forty minutes ahead of it, he calculated. Captain Newman would be there to meet him. Vandam knew in outline what he was going to do thereafter, but the details would have to be improvised as he went along.

He pulled ahead of the train which carried Billy and Elene, the only people he loved. He explained to himself again that he had done the right thing, the best thing for everyone, the best thing for Billy; but in the back of his mind a voice said: Cruel, cruel, cruel.

28

The train entered the station and stopped. Elene saw a sign which said, in Arabic and English, Assyut. She realized with a shock that they had arrived.

It had been an enormous relief to see Vandam's kind, worried face on the train. For a while she had been euphoric: surely, she had felt, it was all over. She had watched his pantomime with the papers, expecting him at any moment to pull a gun, reveal his identity, or attack Wolff. Gradually she had realized that it would not be that simple. She had been astonished, and rather horrified, at the icy nerve with which Vandam had sent his own son back to Wolff; and the courage of Billy himself had seemed incredible. Her spirits had plunged farther when she saw Vandam on the station platform, waving as the train pulled out. What game was he playing?

Of course, the *Rebecca* code was still on his mind. He must have some scheme to rescue her and Billy and also get the key to the code. She wished she knew how. Fortunately Billy did not seem to be troubled by such thoughts: his father had the situation under control, and apparently the boy did not even entertain the idea that his father's schemes could fail. He had perked up, taking an interest in the countryside through which the train was passing, and had even asked Wolff where he got his knife. Elene wished she had as much faith in William Vandam.

Wolff was also in good spirits. The incident with Billy had scared him, and he had looked at Vandam with hostility and anxiety; but he seemed reassured when Vandam got off the train. After that his mood had oscillated between boredom and nervous excitement, and now, arriving in Assyut, the excitement became dominant. Some kind of change had occurred in Wolff in the last twenty-four hours, she thought. When she first met him he had been a very poised, suave man. His face had rarely shown any spontaneous emotion other than a faint arrogance, his features had been generally rather still, his movements had been almost languid. Now all that had gone. He fidgeted, he looked about him restlessly, and every few seconds the corner of his mouth twitched almost imperceptibly, as if he were about to grin, or perhaps to grimace, at his thoughts. The poise which had once seemed to be part of his deepest nature now turned out to be a cracked façade. She guessed this was because his fight with Vandam had become vicious. What had begun as a deadly game had turned into a deadly battle. It was curious that Wolff, the ruthless one, was getting desperate while Vandam just got cooler.

Elene thought: Just so long as he doesn't get too damn cool.

Wolff stood up and took his case from the luggage rack. Elene and Billy followed him from the train and on to the platform. This town was bigger and busier than the others they had passed through, and the station was crowded. As they stepped down from the train they were jostled by people trying to get on. Wolff, a head higher than most of the people, looked around for the exit, spotted it, and began to carve a path through the throng. Suddenly a dirty boy in bare feet and green striped pajamas snatched Wolff's case, shouting: "I get taxi! I get taxi!" Wolff would not let go of the case, but neither would the boy. Wolff gave a good-humored shrug, touched with embarrassment, and let the boy pull him to the gate.

They showed their tickets and went out into the square. It

was late afternoon, but here in the south the sun was still very hot. The square was lined with quite tall buildings, one of them called the Grand Hotel. Outside the station was a row of horse-drawn cabs. Elene looked around, half expecting a detachment of soldiery ready to arrest Wolff. There was no sign of Vandam. Wolff told the Arab boy: "Motor taxi, I want a motor taxi." There was one such car, an old Morris parked a few yards behind the horse cabs. The boy led them to it.

"Get in the front," Wolff told Elene. He gave the boy a coin and got into the back of the car with Billy. The driver wore dark glasses and an Arab headdress to keep the sun off. "Go south, toward the convent," Wolff told the driver in Arabic.

"Okay," the driver said.

Elene's heart missed a beat. She knew that voice. She stared at the driver. It was Vandam.

∽

Vandam drove away from the station, thinking: So far, so good—except for the Arabic. It had not occurred to him that Wolff would speak to a taxi-driver in Arabic. Vandam's knowledge of the language was rudimentary, but he was able to give—and therefore to understand—directions. He could reply in monosyllables, or grunts, or even in English, for those Arabs who spoke a little English were always keen to use it, even when addressed by a European in Arabic. He would be all right as long as Wolff did not want to discuss the weather and the crops.

Captain Newman had come through with everything Vandam had asked for, including discretion. He had even loaned Vandam his revolver, a six-shot Enfield .380 which was now in the pocket of Vandam's trousers beneath his borrowed galabiya. While waiting for the train Vandam had studied Newman's map of Assyut and the surrounding area, so he had some idea of how to find the southbound road out of the city. He drove through the souk, honking his horn more or less continually in the Egyptian fashion, steering dangerously close to the great wooden wheels of the carts, nudging sheep out of the way with his fenders. From the buildings on either side shops, cafés and workshops spilled out into the street. The unpaved road was surfaced with dust, rubbish and dung. Glancing into his rearview mirror Vandam saw that four or five children were riding his back bumper.

Wolff said something, and this time Vandam did not understand. He pretended not to have heard. Wolff repeated it. Vandam caught the word for petrol. Wolff was pointing to a garage. Vandam tapped the gauge on the dashboard, which showed a full tank. "Kifaya," he said. "Enough." Wolff seemed to accept that.

Pretending to adjust his mirror, Vandam stole a glance at Billy, wondering if he had recognized his father. Billy was staring at the back of Vandam's head with an expression of delight. Vandam thought: Don't give the game away, for God's sake!

They left the town behind and headed south on a straight desert road. On their left were the irrigated fields and groves of trees; on their right, the wall of granite cliffs, colored beige by a layer of dusty sand. The atmosphere in the car was peculiar. Vandam could sense Elene's tension, Billy's euphoria and Wolff's impatience. He himself was very edgy. How much of all that was getting through to Wolff? The spy needed only to take one good look at the taxi driver to realize he was the man who had inspected papers on the train. Vandam hoped Wolff was preoccupied with thoughts of his radio.

Wolff said: *"Ruh alyaminak."*

Vandam knew this meant "Turn right." Up ahead he saw a turn-off which seemed to lead straight to the cliff. He slowed the car and took the turn, then saw that he was headed for a pass through the hills.

Vandam was surprised. Farther along the southbound road there were some villages and the famous convent, according to Newman's map; but beyond these hills there was nothing but the Western Desert. If Wolff had buried the radio in the sand he would never find it again. Surely he knew better? Vandam hoped so, for if Wolff's plans were to collapse, so would his.

The road began to climb, and the old car struggled to take the gradient. Vandam changed down once, then again. The car made the summit in second gear. Vandam looked out across an apparently endless desert. He wished he had a jeep. He wondered how far Wolff had to go. They had better get back to Assyut before nightfall. He could not ask Wolff questions for fear of revealing his ignorance of Arabic.

The road became a track. Vandam drove across the desert, going as fast as he dared, waiting for instructions from Wolff. Directly ahead, the sun rolled down the edge of the sky. After an hour they passed a small flock of sheep grazing on tufty, sparse camel thorn, guarded by a man and a boy. Wolff sat up in his seat and began to look about him. Soon afterward the road intersected a wadi. Cautiously Vandam let the car roll down the bank of the dried-up river.

Wolff said: "*Ruh ashshimalak.*"

Vandam turned left. The going was firm. He was astonished to see groups of people, tents and animals in the wadi. It was like a secret community. A mile farther on they saw the explanation: a wellhead.

The mouth of the well was marked by a low circular wall of mud brick. Four roughly dressed tree trunks leaned together over the hole, supporting a crude winding mechanism. Four or five men hauled water continuously, emptying the buckets into four radiating troughs around the wellhead. Camels and women crowded around the troughs.

Vandam drove close to the well. Wolff said: "*Andak.*" Vandam stopped the car. The desert people were incurious, although it must have been rare for them to see a motor vehicle: perhaps, Vandam thought, their hard lives left them no time to investigate oddities. Wolff was asking questions of one of the men in rapid Arabic. There was a short exchange. The man pointed ahead. Wolff said to Vandam: "*Dughri.*" Vandam drove on.

At last they came to a large encampment where Wolff made Vandam stop. There were several tents in a cluster, some penned sheep, several hobbled camels and a couple of cooking fires. With a sudden quick movement Wolff reached into the front of the car, switched off the engine and pulled out the key. Without a word he got out.

∽

Ishmael was sitting by the fire, making tea. He looked up and said: "Peace be with you," as casually as if Wolff had dropped in from the tent next door.

"And with you be health and God's mercy and blessing," Wolff replied formally.

"How is thy health?"

"God bless thee; I am well, thank God." Wolff squatted in the sand.

Ishmael handed him a cup. "Take it."

"God increase thy good fortune," Wolff said.

"And thy good fortune also."

Wolff drank the tea. It was hot, sweet and very strong. He remembered how this drink had fortified him during his trek through the desert . . . was it only two months ago?

When Wolff had drunk, Ishmael raised his hand to his head and said: "May it agree with thee, sir."

"God grant it may agree with thee."

The formalities were done. Ishmael said: "What of your friends?" He nodded toward the taxi, parked in the middle of the wadi, incongruous among the tents and camels.

"They are not friends," Wolff said.

Ishmael nodded. He was incurious. For all the polite inquiries about one's health, Wolff thought, the nomads were not really interested in what city people did: their lives were so different as to be incomprehensible.

Wolff said: "You still have my box?"

"Yes."

Ishmael would say yes, whether he had it or not, Wolff thought; that was the Arab way. Ishmael made no move to fetch the suitcase. He was incapable of hurrying. "Quickly" meant "within the next few days"; "immediately" meant "tomorrow."

Wolff said: "I must return to the city today."

"But you will sleep in my tent."

"Alas, no."

"Then you will join us in eating."

"Twice alas. Already the sun is low, and I must be back in the city before night falls."

Ishmael shook his head sadly, with the look of one who contemplates a hopeless case. "You have come for your box."

"Yes. Please fetch it, my cousin."

Ishmael spoke to a man standing behind him, who spoke to a younger man, who told a child to fetch the case. Ishmael offered Wolff a cigarette. Wolff took it out of politeness. Ishmael lit the cigarettes with a twig from the fire. Wolff wondered where the cigarettes had come from. The child brought the case and offered it to Ishmael. Ishmael pointed to Wolff.

Wolff took the case and opened it. A great sense of relief flooded over him as he looked at the radio, the book and the key to the code. On the long and tedious train journey his euphoria had vanished, but now it came back, and he felt intoxicated with the sense of power and imminent victory. Once again he knew he was going to win the war. He closed the lid of the case. His hands were unsteady.

Ishmael was looking at him through narrowed eyes. "This is very important to you, this box."

"It's important to the world."

Ishmael said: "The sun rises, and the sun sets. Sometimes it rains. We live, then we die." He shrugged.

He would never understand, Wolff thought; but others would. He stood up. "I thank you, my cousin."

"Go in safety."

"May God protect thee."

Wolff turned around and walked toward the taxi.

∿

Elene saw Wolff walk away from the fire with a suitcase in his hand. "He's coming back," she said. "What now?"

"He'll want to go back to Assyut," Vandam said, not looking at her. "Those radios have no batteries, they have to be plugged in, he has to go somewhere where there's electricity, and that means Assyut."

Billy said: "Can I come in the front?"

"No," Vandam said. "Quiet, now. Not much longer."

"I'm scared of him."

"So am I."

Elene shuddered. Wolff got into the car. "Assyut," he said. Vandam held out his hand, palm upward, and Wolff dropped the key in it. Vandam started the car and turned it around.

They went along the wadi, past the well, and turned onto the road. Elene was thinking about the case Wolff held on his knees. It contained the radio, the book and the key to the *Rebecca* code: how absurd it was that so much should hang on the question of who held that case in his hands, that she should have risked her life for it, that Vandam should have jeopardized his son for it. She felt very tired. The sun was low behind them now, and the smallest objects—boulders, bushes, tufts of grass —cast long shadows. Evening clouds were gathering over the hills ahead.

"Go faster," Wolff said in Arabic. "It's getting dark."

Vandam seemed to understand, for he increased speed. The car bounced and swayed on the unmade road. After a couple of minutes Billy said: "I feel sick."

Elene turned around to look at him. His face was pale and tense, and he was sitting bolt upright. "Go slower," she said to Vandam, then she repeated it in Arabic, as if she had just recalled that he did not speak English.

Vandam slowed down for a moment, but Wolff said: "Go faster." He said to Elene: "Forget about the child."

Vandam went faster.

Elene looked at Billy again. He was as white as a sheet, and seemed to be on the brink of tears. "You bastard," she said to Wolff.

"Stop the car," Billy said.

Wolff ignored him, and Vandam had to pretend not to understand English.

There was a low hump in the road. Breasting it at speed, the car rose a few inches into the air, and came down again with a bump. Billy yelled: "Dad, stop the car! Dad!"

Vandam slammed on the brakes.

Elene braced herself against the dashboard and turned her head to look at Wolff.

For a split second he was stunned with shock. His eyes went to Vandam, then to Billy, then back to Vandam; and she saw in his expression first incomprehension, then astonishment, then fear. She knew he was thinking about the incident on the train, and the Arab boy at the railway station, and the kaffiyeh that covered the taxi driver's face; and then she saw that he knew, he had understood it all in a flash.

The car was screeching to a halt, throwing the passengers forward. Wolff regained his balance. With a rapid movement he threw his left arm around Billy and pulled the boy to him. Elene saw his hand go inside his shirt, and then he pulled out the knife.

The car stopped.

Vandam looked around. At the same moment, Elene saw, his hand went to the side slit of his galabiya—and froze there as he looked into the back seat. Elene turned too.

Wolff held the knife an inch from the soft skin of Billy's throat. Billy was wild-eyed with fear. Vandam looked stricken. At the corners of Wolff's mouth there was the hint of a mad smile.

"Damn it," Wolff said. "You almost had me."

They all stared at him in silence.

"Take off that foolish hat," he said to Vandam.

Vandam removed the kaffiyeh.

"Let me guess," said Wolff. "Major Vandam." He seemed to be enjoying the moment. "What a good thing I took your son for insurance."

"It's finished, Wolff," said Vandam. "Half the British Army is on your trail. You can let me take you alive, or let them kill you."

"I don't believe you're telling the truth," Wolff said. "You wouldn't have brought the Army to look for your son. You'd be afraid those cowboys would shoot the wrong people. I don't think your superiors even know where you are."

Elene felt sure Wolff was right, and she was gripped by despair. She had no idea what Wolff would do now, but she felt sure Vandam had lost the battle. She looked at Vandam, and saw defeat in his eyes.

Wolff said: "Underneath his galabiya, Major Vandam is wearing a pair of khaki trousers. In one of the pockets of the trousers, or possibly in the waistband, you will find a gun. Take it out."

Elene reached through the side slit of Vandam's galabiya and found the gun in his pocket. She thought: How did Wolff know? and then: He guessed. She took the gun out.

She looked at Wolff. He could not take the gun from her without releasing Billy, and if he released Billy, even for a moment, Vandam would do something.

But Wolff had thought of that. "Break the back of the gun, so that the barrel falls forward. Be careful not to pull the trigger by mistake."

She fiddled with the gun.

Wolff said: "You'll probably find a catch alongside the cylinder."

She found the catch and opened the gun.

"Take out the cartridges and drop them outside the car."

She did so.

"Put the gun on the floor of the car."

She put it down.

Wolff seemed relieved. Now, once again, the only weapon in the picture was his knife. He spoke to Vandam. "Get out of the car."

Vandam sat motionless.

"Get out," Wolff repeated. With a sudden precise movement he nicked the lobe of Billy's ear with the knife. A drop of blood welled out.

Vandam got out of the car.

Wolff said to Elene: "Get into the driving seat."

She climbed over the gear stick.

Vandam had left the car door open. Wolff said: "Close the door." Elene closed the door. Vandam stood beside the car, staring in.

"Drive," Wolff said.

The car had stalled. Elene put the gearshift into neutral and turned the key. The engine coughed and died. She hoped it would not go. She turned the key again; again the starter failed.

Wolff said: "Touch the accelerator pedal as you turn the key."

She did what he said. The engine caught and roared.

"Drive," Wolff said.

She pulled away.

"Faster."

She changed up.

Looking in the mirror she saw Wolff put the knife away and release Billy. Behind the car, already fifty yards away, Vandam stood on the desert road, his silhouette black against the sunset. He was quite still.

Elene said: "He's got no water!"

"No," Wolff replied.

Then Billy went berserk.

Elene heard him scream: "You can't leave him behind!" She turned around, forgetting about the road. Billy had leaped on Wolff like an enraged wildcat, punching and scratching and, somehow, kicking; yelling incoherently, his face a mask of childish rage, his body jerking convulsively like one in a fit. Wolff, who had relaxed, thinking the crisis was over, was momentarily powerless to resist. In the confined space, with Billy so close to him, he was unable to strike a proper blow, so he raised his arms to protect himself, and pushed against the boy.

Elene looked back to the road. While she was turning around, the car had gone off course, and now the left-hand front wheel was plowing through the sandy scrub beside the road. She struggled to turn the steering wheel but it seemed to have a will of its own. She stamped on the brake, and the rear of the car began to slide sideways. Too late, she saw a deep rut running across the road immediately in front. The skidding car hit the rut broadside with an impact that jarred her bones. It seemed to bounce upward. Elene came up off the seat momentarily, and when she came down again she unintentionally trod on the accelerator pedal. The car shot forward and began to skid in the other direction. Out of the corner of her eye she saw that Wolff and Billy were being tossed about helplessly, still fighting. The car went off the road into the soft sand. It slowed abruptly, and Elene banged her forehead on the rim of the steering wheel. The whole of the car tilted sideways and seemed to be flying. She saw the desert fall away beside her, and realized the car was in fact rolling. She thought it would go over and over. She fell sideways, grabbing at the wheel and the gear stick. The car did not turn turtle, but perched on its side like a coin dropped edgeways into the sand. The gear shift came off in her hand. She slumped against the door, banging her head again. The car was still.

She got to her hands and knees, still holding the broken-off gear stick, and looked into the rear of the car. Wolff and Billy had fallen in a heap with Wolff on top. As she looked, Wolff moved.

She had hoped he was dead.

She had one knee on the car door and the other on the window. On her right the roof of the car stood up vertically. On her left was the seat. She was looking through the gap between the top of the seat back and the roof.

Wolff got to his feet.

Billy seemed to be unconscious.

Elene felt disoriented and helpless, kneeling on the side window of the car.

Wolff, standing on the inside of the left-hand rear door, threw his weight against the floor of the car. The car rocked. He did it again; the car rocked more. On his third try the car tilted over and fell on all four wheels with a crash. Elene was dizzy. She saw Wolff open the door and get out of the car. He stood outside, crouched and drew his knife. She saw Vandam approaching.

She knelt on the seat, watching. She could not move until her head stopped spinning. She saw Vandam crouch like Wolff, ready to spring, his hands raised protectively. He was red-faced and panting: he had run after the car. They circled. Wolff was limping slightly. The sun was a huge orange globe behind them.

Vandam moved forward, then seemed to hesitate curiously. Wolff lashed out with the knife, but he had been surprised by Vandam's hesitation, and his thrust missed. Vandam's fist lashed out. Wolff jerked back. Elene saw that Wolff's nose was bleeding.

They faced each other again, like boxers in a ring.

Vandam jumped forward again. This time Wolff dodged back. Vandam kicked out, but Wolff was out of range. Wolff jabbed with the knife. Elene saw it rip through Vandam's trousers and draw blood. Wolff stabbed again, but Vandam had stepped away. A dark stain appeared on his trouser leg.

Elene looked at Billy. The boy lay limply on the floor of the car, his eyes closed. Elene clambered over into the back and lifted him onto the seat. She could not tell whether he was dead or alive. She touched his face. He did not stir. "Billy," she said. "Oh, Billy."

She looked outside again. Vandam was down on one knee. His left arm hung limply from a shoulder covered with blood. He held his right arm out in front of him in a defensive gesture. Wolff approached him.

Elene jumped out of the car. She still had the broken-off gear stick in her hand. She saw Wolff bring back his arm, ready to slash at Vandam once more. She rushed up behind Wolff, stumbling in the sand. Wolff struck at Vandam. Vandam jerked sideways, dodging the blow. Elene raised the gear stick high in the air and brought it down with all her might on the back of Wolff's head. He seemed to stand still for a moment.

Elene said: "Oh, God."

Then she hit him again.

She hit him a third time.

He fell down.

She hit him again.

Then she dropped the gear stick and knelt beside Vandam.

"Well done," he said weakly.

"Can you stand up?"

He put a hand on her shoulder and struggled to his feet. "It's not as bad as it looks," he said.

"Let me see."

"In a minute. Help me with this." Using his good arm, he took hold of Wolff's leg and pulled him toward the car. Elene grabbed the unconscious man's arm and heaved. When Wolff was lying beside the car, Vandam lifted Wolff's limp arm and placed the hand on the running board, palm down. Then he lifted his foot and stamped on the elbow. Wolff's arm snapped. Elene turned white. Vandam said: "That's to make sure he's no trouble when he comes round."

He leaned into the back of the car and put a hand on Billy's chest. "Alive," he said. "Thank God."

Billy's eyes opened.

"It's all over," Vandam said.

Billy closed his eyes.

Vandam got into the front seat of the car. "Where's the gear stick?" he said.

"It broke off. That's what I hit him with."

Vandam turned the key. The car jerked. "Good—it's still in gear," he said. He pressed the clutch and turned the key again. The engine fired. He eased out the clutch and the car moved forward. He switched off. "We're mobile," he said. "What a piece of luck."

"What will we do with Wolff?"

"Put him in the boot."

Vandam took another look at Billy. He was conscious now, his eyes wide open. "How are you, son?" said Vandam.

"I'm sorry," Billy said, "but I couldn't help feeling sick."

Vandam looked at Elene. "You'll have to drive," he said. There were tears in his eyes.

29

There was the sudden, terrifying roar of nearby aircraft. Rommel glanced up and saw the British bombers approaching low from behind the nearest line of hills: the troops called them "Party Rally" bombers because they flew in the perfect formation of display aircraft at the prewar Nuremberg parades. "Take cover!" Rommel yelled. He ran to a slit trench and dived in.

The noise was so loud it was like silence. Rommel lay with his eyes closed. He had a pain in his stomach. They had sent him a doctor from Germany, but Rommel knew that the only medicine he needed was victory. He had lost a lot of weight: his uniform hung loosely on him now, and his shirt collars seemed too large. His hair was receding rapidly and turning white in places.

Today was September 1, and everything had gone terribly wrong. What had seemed to be the weak point in the Allied defense line was looking more and more like an ambush. The minefields were heavy where they should have been light, the ground beneath had been quicksand where hard going was expected, and the Alam Halfa ridge, which should have been taken easily, was being mightily defended. Rommel's strategy was wrong; his intelligence had been wrong; his spy had been wrong.

The bombers passed overhead. Rommel got out of the trench. His aides and officers emerged from cover and gathered around him again. He raised his field glasses and looked out over the desert. Scores of vehicles stood still in the sand, many of them blazing furiously. If the enemy would only charge, Rommel thought, we could fight him. But the Allies sat tight, well dug in, picking off the Panzer tanks like fish in a barrel.

It was no good. His forward units were fifteen miles from Alexandria, but they were stuck. Fifteen miles, he thought. Another fifteen miles, and Egypt would have been mine. He looked at the officers around him. As always, their expressions reflected his own: he saw in their faces what they saw in his.

It was defeat.

〜

He knew it was a nightmare, but he could not wake up.

The cell was six feet long by four feet wide, and half of it was taken up by a bed. Beneath the bed was a chamberpot. The walls were of smooth gray stone. A small light bulb hung from the ceiling by a cord. In one end of the cell was a door. In the other end was a small square window, set just above eye level: through it he could see the bright blue sky.

In his dream he thought: I'll wake up soon, then it will be all right. I'll wake up, and there will be a beautiful woman lying beside me on a silk sheet, and I will touch her breasts—and as he thought this he was filled with strong lust—and she will wake up and kiss me, and we will drink champagne . . . But he could not quite dream that, and the dream of the prison cell came back. Somewhere nearby a bass drum was beating steadily. Soldiers were marching to the rhythm outside. The beat was terrifying, terrifying, boom-boom, boom-boom, tramp-tramp, the drum and the soldiers and the close gray walls of the cell and that distant, tantalizing square of blue sky and he was so frightened, so horrified, that he forced his eyes open and he woke up.

He looked around him, not understanding. He was awake, wide awake, no question about it, the dream was over; yet he was still in a prison cell. It was six feet long by four feet wide, and half of it was taken up by a bed. He raised himself from the bed and looked underneath it. There was a chamberpot.

He stood upright. Then, quietly and calmly, he began to bang his head against the wall.

ᗜ

Jerusalem, 24 September 42
My dear Elene,

Today I went to the Western Wall, which is also called the Wailing Wall. I stood before it with many other Jews, and I prayed. I wrote a kvitlach and put it into a crack in the wall. May God grant my petition.

This is the most beautiful place in the world, Jerusalem. Of course I do not live well. I sleep on a mattress on the floor in a little room with five other men. Sometimes I get a little work, sweeping up in a workshop where one of my roommates, a young man, carries wood for the carpenters. I am very poor, like always, but now I am poor in Jerusalem, which is better than rich in Egypt.

I crossed the desert in a British Army truck. They asked me what I would have done if they had not picked me up, and when I said I would have walked, I believe they thought me mad. But this is the sanest thing I ever did.

I must tell you that I am dying. My illness is quite incurable, even if I could afford doctors, and I have only weeks left, perhaps a couple of months. Don't be sad. I have never been happier in my life.

I should tell you what I wrote in my kvitlach. I asked God to grant happiness to my daughter Elene. I believe he will. Farewell,

Your Father.

ᗜ

The smoked ham was sliced as thin as paper and rolled into

dainty cylinders. The bread rolls were home-baked, fresh that morning. There was a glass jar of potato salad made with real mayonnaise and crisp chopped onion. There were a bottle of wine, another bottle of soda and a bag of oranges. And a packet of cigarettes, his brand.

Elene began to pack the food into the picnic basket.

She had just closed the lid when she heard the knock at the door. She took off her apron before going to open it.

Vandam stepped inside, closed the door behind him and kissed her. He put his arms around her and held her painfully tightly. He always did this, and it always hurt, but she never complained, for they had almost lost each other, and now when they were together they were just so grateful.

They went into the kitchen. Vandam hefted the picnic basket and said: "Lord, what have you got in here, the Crown Jewels?"

"What's the news?" Elene asked.

He knew she meant news of the war in the desert. He said: "Axis forces in full retreat, and I quote." She thought how relaxed he was these days. He even talked differently. A little gray was appearing in his hair, and he laughed a lot.

"I think you're one of those men who gets more good-looking as he gets older," she said.

"Wait till my teeth drop out."

They went out. The sky was curiously black, and Elene said "Oh!" in surprise as she stepped into the street.

"End of the world today," Vandam said.

"I've never seen it like this before," Elene said.

They got on the motorcycle and headed for Billy's school. The sky became even darker. The first rain fell as they were passing Shepheard's Hotel. Elene saw an Egyptian drape a handkerchief over his fez. The raindrops were enormous; each one soaked right through her dress to the skin. Vandam turned the bike around and parked in front of the hotel. As they dismounted the clouds burst.

They stood under the hotel canopy and watched the storm. The sheer quantity of water was incredible. Within minutes the gutters overflowed and the pavements were awash. Opposite the hotel the shopkeepers waded through the flood to put up shutters. The cars simply had to stop where they were.

"There's no main drainage in this town," Vandam remarked. "The water has nowhere to go but the Nile. Look at it." The street had turned into a river.

"What about the bike?" Elene said.

"Damn thing will float away," said Vandam. "I'll have to bring it under here." He hesitated, then dashed out on to the pavement, seized the bike by its handlebars and pushed it through the water to the steps of the hotel. When he regained the shelter of the canopy his clothes were thoroughly soaked and his hair was plastered around his head like a mop coming out of a bucket. Elene laughed at him.

The rain went on a long time. Elene said: "What about Billy?"

"They'll have to keep the kids at school until the rain stops."

Eventually they went into the hotel for a drink. Vandam ordered sherry: he had sworn off gin, and claimed he did not miss it.

At last the storm ended, and they went out again; but they had to wait a little longer for the flood to recede. Finally there was only an inch or so of water, and the sun came out. The motorists began to try to start their cars. The bike was not too wet, and it fired first time.

The sun came out and the roads began to steam as they drove to the school. Billy was waiting outside. "What a storm!" he said excitedly. He climbed on to the bike, sitting between Elene and Vandam.

They drove out into the desert. Holding on tightly, her eyes half closed, Elene did not see the miracle until Vandam stopped the bike. The three of them got off and looked around, speechless.

The desert was carpeted with flowers.

"It's the rain, obviously," said Vandam. "But . . ."

Millions of flying insects had also appeared from nowhere, and now butterflies and bees dashed frantically from bloom to bloom, reaping the sudden harvest.

Billy said: "The seeds must have been in the sand, waiting."

"That's it," Vandam said. "The seeds have been there for years, just waiting for this."

The flowers were all tiny, like miniatures, but very brightly colored. Billy walked a few paces from the road and bent down to examine one. Vandam put his arms around Elene and kissed her. It started as a peck on the cheek, but turned into a long, loving embrace.

Eventually she broke away from him, laughing. "You'll embarrass Billy," she said.

"He's going to have to get used to it," Vandam said.

Elene stopped laughing. "Is he?" she said. "Is he, really?"

Vandam smiled, and kissed her again.

THE MAN
FROM
ST. PETERSBURG

ACKNOWLEDGMENTS

In writing this book I was helped by many friends. My grateful thanks to Alan Earney, Pat Golbitz, M. E. Hirsh, Elaine Koster, Diana Levine, Caren Meyer and her moles, Sue Rapp, Pamela Robinson and the staff of Bertram Rota Ltd., Hilary Ross, Christopher Sinclair-Stevenson, Daniel Starer, Colin Tennant, and—alphabetically last but in every other way first—Al Zuckerman.

One can't love humanity.
One can only love people.

—GRAHAM GREENE

ONE

It was a slow Sunday afternoon, the kind Walden loved. He stood at an open window and looked across the park. The broad, level lawn was dotted with mature trees: a Scotch pine, a pair of mighty oaks, several chestnuts and a willow like a head of girlish curls. The sun was high and the trees cast dark, cool shadows. The birds were silent, but a hum of contented bees came from the flowering creeper beside the window. The house was still, too. Most of the servants had the afternoon off. The only weekend guests were Walden's brother George, George's wife, Clarissa, and their children. George had gone for a walk, Clarissa was lying down and the children were out of sight. Walden was comfortable: he had worn a frock coat to church, of course, and in an hour or two he would put on his white tie and tails for dinner, but in the meantime he was at ease in a tweed suit and a soft-collared shirt. Now, he thought, if only Lydia will play the piano tonight, it will have been a perfect day.

He turned to his wife. "Will you play, after dinner?"

Lydia smiled. "If you like."

Walden heard a noise and turned back to the window. At the far end of the drive, a quarter of a mile away, a motor car appeared. Walden felt a twinge of irritation, like the sly stab of pain in his right leg before a rainstorm. Why should a car annoy me? he thought. He was not against motor cars—he owned a Lanchester and used it regularly to travel to and from London —although in the summer they were a terrible nuisance to the village, sending up clouds of dust from the unpaved road as they roared through. He was thinking of putting down a couple of hundred yards of tarmacadam along the street. Ordinarily he would not have hesitated, but the roads had not been his responsibility since 1909 when Lloyd George had set up the Roads Boards—and that, he realized, was the source of his irritation. It had been a characteristic piece of Liberal legislation: they took money from Walden in order to do themselves what he would have done anyway; then they failed to do it. I suppose I'll pave the road myself in the end, he thought; it's just annoying to pay for it twice.

The motor car turned into the gravel forecourt and came to a noisy, shuddering halt opposite the south door. Exhaust fumes drifted in at the window, and Walden held his breath. The driver got out, wearing helmet, goggles and a heavy motoring coat, and opened the door for the passenger. A short man in a black coat and a black felt hat stepped down from the car. Walden recognized the man and his heart sank: the peaceful summer afternoon was over.

"It's Winston Churchill," he said.

Lydia said: "How embarrassing."

The man just refused to be snubbed. On Thursday he had sent a note which Walden had ignored. On Friday he had called on Walden at his London house and had been told that the Earl was not at home. Now he had driven all the way to Norfolk on a Sunday. He would be turned away again. Does he think his stubbornness is impressive? Walden wondered.

He hated to be rude to people, but Churchill deserved it. The Liberal government in which Churchill was a minister was engaged in a vicious attack on the very foundations of English society—taxing landed property, undermining the House of Lords, trying to give Ireland away to the Catholics, emasculating the Royal Navy and yielding to the blackmail of trade unions and damned socialists. Walden and his friends would not shake hands with such people.

The door opened and Pritchard came into the room. He was a tall Cockney with brilliantined black hair and an air of gravity which was transparently fake. He had run away to sea as a boy and had jumped ship in East Africa. Walden, there on safari, had hired him to supervise the native porters, and they had been together ever since. Now Pritchard was Walden's majordomo, traveling with him from one house to another, and as much of a friend as a servant could be.

"The First Lord of the Admiralty is here, my lord," Pritchard said.

"I'm not at home," Walden said.

Pritchard looked uncomfortable. He was not used to throwing out Cabinet ministers. My father's butler would have done it without turning a hair, Walden thought, but old Thomson is graciously retired, growing roses in the garden of that little cottage in the village, and somehow Pritchard has never acquired that unassailable dignity.

Pritchard began to drop his aitches, a sign that he was either very relaxed or very tense. "Mr. Churchill said you'd say not at 'ome, my lord, and 'e said to give you this letter." He proffered an envelope on a tray.

Walden did *not* like to be pushed. He said crossly: "Give it back to him—" Then he stopped and looked again at the handwriting on the envelope. There was something familiar about the large, clear, sloping letters.

"Oh, dear," said Walden.

He took the envelope, opened it and drew out a single sheet of heavy white paper, folded once. At the top was the royal crest, printed in red. Walden read:

> *Buckingham Palace*
> *May 1st, 1914*
>
> *My dear Walden*
> *You will see young Winston.*
> *George R.I*

"It's from the King," Walden said to Lydia.

He was so embarrassed that he flushed. It was *frightfully* bad form to drag the King into something like this. Walden felt like a schoolboy who is told to stop quarreling and get on with his prep. For a moment he was tempted to defy the King. But the consequences . . . Lydia would no longer be received by the Queen, people would be unable to invite the Waldens to parties at which a member of the Royal Family would be present and —worst of all—Walden's daughter, Charlotte, could not be presented at court as a debutante. The family's social life would be wrecked. They might as well go and live in another country. No, there was no question of disobeying the King.

Walden sighed. Churchill had defeated him. In a way it was a relief, for now he could break ranks and no one could blame him. *Letter from the King, old boy,* he would say in explanation; *nothing to be done, you know.*

"Ask Mr. Churchill to come in," he said to Pritchard.

He handed the letter to Lydia. The Liberals really did not understand how the monarchy was supposed to work, he reflected. He murmured: "The King is just not firm enough with these people."

Lydia said: "This is becoming awfully boring."

She was not bored at all, Walden thought; in fact, she probably found it all quite exciting; but she said that because it was the kind of thing an English countess would say, and since she was not English but Russian, she liked to say typically English things, the way a man speaking French would say *alors* and *hein?* a lot.

Walden went to the window. Churchill's motor car was still rattling and smoking in the forecourt. The driver stood beside it, with one hand on the door, as if he had to hold it like a horse to stop it from wandering away. A few servants were gazing at it from a safe distance.

Pritchard came in and said: "Mr. Winston Churchill."

Churchill was forty, exactly ten years younger than Walden. He was a short, slender man who dressed in a way Walden thought was a shade too elegant to be quite gentlemanly. His hair was receding rapidly, leaving a peak at the forehead and two curls at the temples which, together with his short nose and the permanent sardonic twinkle in his eye, gave him a mischievous look. It was easy to see why the cartoonists regularly portrayed him as a malign cherub.

Churchill shook hands and said cheerfully: "Good afternoon, Lord Walden." He bowed to Lydia. "Lady Walden, how do you do." Walden thought: What is it about him that grates so on my nerves?

Lydia offered him tea and Walden told him to sit down. Walden would not make small talk: he was impatient to know what all the fuss was about.

Churchill began: "First of all my apologies, together with the King's, for imposing myself on you."

Walden nodded. He was not going to say it was perfectly all right.

Churchill said: "I might add that I should not have done so, other than for the most compelling reasons."

"You'd better tell me what they are."

"Do you know what has been happening in the money market?"

"Yes. The discount rate has gone up."

"From one and three quarters to just under three percent. It's an enormous rise, and it has come about in a few weeks."

"I presume you know why."

Churchill nodded. "German companies have been factoring debts on a vast scale, collecting cash and buying gold. A few more weeks of this and Germany will have got in everything owing to her from other countries, while leaving her debts to them outstanding—and her gold reserves will be higher than they have ever been before."

"They are preparing for war."

"In this and other ways. They have raised a levy of one billion marks, over and above normal taxation, to improve an army that is already the strongest in Europe. You will remember that in 1909, when Lloyd George increased British taxation by fifteen million pounds sterling, there was almost a revolution. Well, a billion marks is equivalent to *fifty* million pounds. It's the biggest levy in European history—"

"Yes, indeed," Walden interrupted. Churchill was threatening to become histrionic: Walden did not want him making speeches. "We Conservatives have been worried about German militarism for some time. Now, at the eleventh hour, you're telling me that we were right."

Churchill was unperturbed. "Germany will attack France, almost certainly. The question is, will we come to the aid of France?"

"No," Walden said in surprise. "The Foreign Secretary has assured us that we have no obligations to France—"

"Sir Edward is sincere, of course," Churchill said. "But he is mistaken. Our understanding with France is such that we could not possibly stand aside and watch her be defeated by Germany."

Walden was shocked. The Liberals had convinced everyone, him included, that they would not lead England into war; and now one of their leading ministers was saying the opposite. The duplicity of the politicians was infuriating, but Walden forgot that as he began to contemplate the consequences of war. He thought of the young men he knew who would have to fight: the patient gardeners in his park, the cheeky footmen, the brown-faced farm boys, the hell-raising undergraduates, the languid idlers in the clubs of St. James's . . . then that thought was overtaken by another, much more chilling, and he said: "But can we win?"

Churchill looked grave. "I think not."

Walden stared at him. "Dear God, what have you people done?"

Churchill became defensive. "Our policy has been to avoid war, and you can't do that and arm yourself to the teeth at the same time."

"But you have failed to avoid war."

"We're still trying."

"But you think you will fail."

Churchill looked belligerent for a moment, then swallowed his pride. "Yes."

"So what will happen?"

"If England and France together cannot defeat Germany, then we must have another ally, a third country on our side: Russia. If Germany is divided, fighting on two fronts, we can win. The Russian army is incompetent and corrupt, of course —like everything else in that country—but it doesn't matter so long as they draw off part of Germany's strength."

Churchill knew perfectly well that Lydia was Russian, and it was characteristically tactless of him to disparage her country in her presence, but Walden let it pass, for he was highly intrigued by what Churchill was saying. "Russia already has an alliance with France," he said.

"It's not enough," Churchill said. "Russia is obliged to fight if France is the victim of aggression. It is left to Russia to decide whether France is the victim or the aggressor in a particular case. When war breaks out, both sides always claim to be the victim. Therefore the alliance obliges Russia to do no more than fight if she wants to. We need Russia to be freshly and firmly committed to our side."

"I can't imagine you chaps joining hands with the Czar."

"Then you misjudge us. To save England, we'll deal with the devil."

"Your supporters won't like it."

"They won't know."

Walden could see where all this was leading, and the prospect was exciting. "What have you in mind? A secret treaty? Or an unwritten understanding?"

"Both."

Walden looked at Churchill through narrowed eyes. This young demagogue might have a brain, he thought, and that brain might not be working in my interest. So the Liberals want to do a secret deal with the Czar, despite the hatred which the English people have for the brutal Russian regime—but why tell me? They want to rope me in somehow, that much is clear. For what purpose? So that if it all goes wrong they will have a Conservative on whom to put the blame? It will take a plotter more subtle than Churchill to lead me into such a trap.

Walden said: "Go on."

"I have initiated naval talks with the Russians, along the lines of our military talks with the French. They've been going on for a while at a rather low level, and now they are about to get serious. A young Russian admiral is coming to London. His name is Prince Aleksey Andreyevich Orlov."

Lydia said: "Aleks!"

Churchill looked at her. "I believe he is related to you, Lady Walden."

"Yes," Lydia said, and, for some reason Walden could not even guess at, she looked uneasy. "He is the son of my elder sister, which makes him my . . . cousin?"

"Nephew," Walden said.

"I didn't know he had become an admiral," Lydia added. "It must be a recent promotion." She was her usual, perfectly composed self, and Walden decided he had imagined that moment of unease. He was pleased that Aleks would be coming to London: he was very fond of the lad. Lydia said: "He is young to have so much authority."

"He's thirty," Churchill said to Lydia, and Walden recalled that Churchill, at forty, was very young to be in charge of the entire Royal Navy. Churchill's expression seemed to say: The world belongs to brilliant young men like me and Orlov.

But you need me for something, Walden thought.

"In addition," Churchill went on, "Orlov is nephew to the Czar, through his father, the late Prince, and—more importantly—he is one of the few people other than Rasputin whom the Czar likes and trusts. If anyone in the Russian naval establishment can swing the Czar on to our side, Orlov can."

Walden asked the question that was on his mind. "And my part in all this?"

"I want you to represent England in these talks—and I want you to bring me Russia on a plate."

The fellow could never resist the temptation to be melodramatic, Walden thought. "You want Aleks and me to negotiate an Anglo-Russian military alliance?"

"Yes."

Walden saw immediately how difficult, challenging and rewarding the task would be. He concealed his excitement and resisted the temptation to get up and pace about.

Churchill was saying: "You know the Czar personally. You know Russia and speak Russian fluently. You're Orlov's uncle by marriage. Once before you have persuaded the Czar to side with England rather than with Germany—in 1906, when you intervened to prevent the ratification of the Treaty of Bjorko." Churchill paused. "Nevertheless, you were not our first choice to represent Britain at these negotiations. The way things are at Westminster . . ."

"Yes, yes." Walden did not want to start discussing *that*. "However, something changed your mind."

"In a nutshell, you were the Czar's choice. It seems you are the only Englishman in whom he has any faith. Anyway, he sent a telegram to his cousin, His Majesty King George the Fifth, insisting that Orlov deal with you."

Walden could imagine the consternation among the Radicals

when they learned they would have to involve a reactionary old Tory peer in such a clandestine scheme. "I should think you were horrified," he said.

"Not at all. In foreign affairs our policies are not so much at odds with yours. And I have always felt that domestic political disagreements were no reason why your talents should be lost to His Majesty's Government."

Flattery now, Walden thought. They want me badly. Aloud he said: "How would all this be kept secret?"

"It will seem like a social visit. If you agree, Orlov will stay with you for the London season. You will introduce him to society. Am I right in thinking that your daughter is due to come out this year?" He looked at Lydia.

"That's right," she said.

"So you'll be going about a good deal anyway. Orlov is a bachelor, as you know, and obviously very eligible, so we can noise it abroad that he's looking for an English wife. He may even find one."

"Good idea." Suddenly Walden realized that he was enjoying himself. He had used to be a kind of semi-official diplomat under the Conservative governments of Salisbury and Balfour, but for the last eight years he had taken no part in international politics. Now he had a chance to go back on stage, and he began to remember how absorbing and fascinating the whole business was: the secrecy; the gambler's art of negotiation; the conflicts of personalities; the cautious use of persuasion, bullying or the threat of war. The Russians were not easy to deal with, he recalled; they tended to be capricious, obstinate and arrogant. But Aleks would be manageable. When Walden married Lydia, Aleks had been at the wedding, a ten-year-old in a sailor suit: later Aleks had spent a couple of years at Oxford University and had visited Walden Hall in the vacations. The boy's father was dead, so Walden gave him rather more time than he might normally have spent with an adolescent, and was delightfully rewarded by a friendship with a lively young mind.

It was a splendid foundation for a negotiation. I believe I might be able to bring it off, he thought. What a triumph that would be!

Churchill said: "May I take it, then, that you'll do it?"

"Of course," said Walden.

◆§ ┆◆

Lydia stood up. "No, don't get up," she said as the men stood with her. "I'll leave you to talk politics. Will you stay for dinner, Mr. Churchill?"

"I've an engagement in Town, unfortunately."

"Then I shall say good-bye." She shook his hand.

She went out of the Octagon, which was where they always had tea, and walked across the great hall, through the small hall and into the flower room. At the same time one of the under-gardeners—she did not know his name—came in through the garden door with an armful of tulips, pink and yellow, for the dinner table. One of the things Lydia loved about England in general and Walden Hall in particular was the wealth of flowers, and she always had fresh ones cut morning and evening, even in winter when they had to be grown in the hothouses.

The gardener touched his cap—he did not have to take it off unless he was spoken to, for the flower room was notionally part of the garden—and laid the flowers on a marble table, then went out. Lydia sat down and breathed the cool, scented air. This was a good room in which to recover from shocks, and the talk of St. Petersburg had unnerved her. She remembered Aleksey Andreyevich as a shy, pretty little boy at her wedding; and she remembered *that* as the most unhappy day of her life.

It was perverse of her, she thought, to make the flower room her sanctuary. This house had rooms for almost every purpose: different rooms for breakfast, lunch, tea and dinner; a room for billiards and another in which to keep guns; special rooms for washing clothes, ironing, making jam, cleaning silver, hanging game, keeping wine, brushing suits . . . Her own suite had a bedroom, a dressing room and a sitting room. And yet, when she wanted to be at peace, she would come here and sit on a hard chair and look at the crude stone sink and the cast-iron legs of the marble table. Her husband also had an unofficial sanctuary, she had noticed: when Stephen was disturbed about something he would go to the gun room and read the game book.

So Aleks would be her guest in London for the season. They would talk of home, and the snow and the ballet and the bombs; and seeing Aleks would make her think of another young Russian, the man she had not married.

It was nineteen years since she had seen that man, but still the mere mention of St. Petersburg could bring him to mind and make her skin crawl beneath the watered silk of her tea gown. He had been nineteen, the same age as she, a hungry student with long black hair, the face of a wolf and the eyes of a spaniel. He was as thin as a rail. His skin was white, the hair of his body soft, dark and adolescent; and he had clever, clever hands. She blushed now, not at the thought of his body but at the thought of her own, betraying her, maddening her with pleasure, making her cry out shamefully. I was wicked, she thought, and I am wicked still, for I should like to do it again.

She thought guiltily of her husband. She hardly ever thought of him without feeling guilty. She had not loved him when they married, but she loved him now. He was strong-willed and warmhearted, and he adored her. His affection was constant and gentle and entirely lacking in the desperate passion which she had once known. He was happy, she thought, only because he had never known that love could be wild and hungry.

I no longer crave that kind of love, she told herself. I have learned to live without it, and over the years it has become easier. So it should—I'm almost forty!

Some of her friends were still tempted, and they yielded, too. They did not speak to her of their affairs, for they sensed she did not approve; but they gossiped about others, and Lydia knew that at some country-house parties there was a lot of . . . well, adultery. Once Lady Girard had said to Lydia, with the condescending air of an older woman who gives sound advice to a young hostess: "My dear, if you have the Viscountess and Charlie Stott at the same time you simply *must* put them in adjoining bedrooms." Lydia had put them at opposite ends of the house, and the Viscountess had never come to Walden Hall again.

People said all this immorality was the fault of the late King, but Lydia did not believe them. It was true that he had befriended Jews and singers, but that did not make him a rake. Anyway, he had stayed at Walden Hall twice—once as Prince of Wales and once as King Edward VII—and he had behaved impeccably both times.

She wondered whether the new King would ever come. It was a great strain, to have a monarch to stay, but such a thrill to make the house look its very best and have the most lavish meals imaginable and buy twelve new dresses just for one weekend. And if this King were to come, he might grant the Waldens the coveted *entrée*—the right to go into Buckingham Palace by the garden entrance on big occasions, instead of queueing up in The Mall along with two hundred other carriages.

She thought about her guests this weekend. George was Stephen's younger brother: he had Stephen's charm but none of Stephen's seriousness. George's daughter, Belinda, was eighteen, the same age as Charlotte. Both girls would be coming out this season. Belinda's mother had died some years ago and George had married again, rather quickly. His second wife, Clarissa, was much younger than he, and quite vivacious. She had given him twin sons. One of the twins would inherit Walden Hall when Stephen died, unless Lydia gave birth to a boy late in life. I could, she thought; I feel as if I could, but it just doesn't happen.

It was almost time to be getting ready for dinner. She sighed. She felt comfortable and natural in her tea gown, with her fair hair dressed loosely; but now she would have to be laced into a corset and have her hair piled high on her head by a maid. It was said that some of the young women were giving up corsets altogether. That was all right, Lydia supposed, if you were naturally shaped like the figure eight, but she was small in all the wrong places.

She got up and went outside. That under-gardener was standing by a rose tree, talking to one of the maids. Lydia recognized the maid: she was Annie, a pretty, voluptuous, empty-headed girl with a wide, generous smile. She stood with her hands in the pockets of her apron, turning her round face up to the sun and laughing at something the gardener had said. Now *there* is a girl who doesn't need a corset, Lydia thought. Annie was supposed to be supervising Charlotte and Belinda, for the governess had the afternoon off. Lydia said sharply: "Annie! Where are the young ladies?"

Annie's smile disappeared and she dropped a curtsy. "I can't find them, m'lady."

The gardener moved off sheepishly.

"You don't appear to be looking for them," Lydia said. "Off you go."

"Very good, m'lady." Annie ran toward the back of the house. Lydia sighed: the girls would not be there, but she could not be bothered to call Annie back and reprimand her again.

She strolled across the lawn, thinking of familiar and pleasant things, pushing St. Petersburg to the back of her mind. Stephen's father, the seventh Earl of Walden, had planted the west side of the park with rhododendrons and azaleas. Lydia had never met the old man, for he had died before she knew Stephen, but by all accounts he had been one of the great larger-than-life Victorians. His bushes were now in full glorious bloom and made a rather un-Victorian blaze of assorted colors. We must have somebody paint a picture of the house, she thought; the last one was done before the park was mature.

She looked back at Walden Hall. The gray stone of the south front looked beautiful and dignified in the afternoon sunshine. In the center was the south door. The farther, east wing contained the drawing room and various dining rooms, and behind them a straggle of kitchens, pantries and laundries running higgledy-piggledy to the distant stables. Nearer to her, on the west side, were the morning room, the Octagon, and at the corner the library; then, around the corner along the west front, the billiard room, the gun room, her flower room, a smoking room and the estate office. On the second floor, the family bedrooms were mostly on the south side, the main guest rooms on the west side and the servants' rooms over the kitchens to the northeast, out of sight. Above the second floor was an irrational collection of towers, turrets and attics. The whole facade was a riot of ornamental stonework in the best Victorian rococo manner, with flowers and chevrons and sculpted coils of rope, dragons and lions and cherubim, balconies and battlements, flagpoles and sundials and gargoyles. Lydia loved the place, and she was grateful that Stephen—unlike many of the old aristocracy—could afford to keep it up.

She saw Charlotte and Belinda emerge from the shrubbery across the lawn. Annie had not found them, of course. They both wore wide-brimmed hats and summer frocks with schoolgirls' black stockings and low black shoes. Because Charlotte was coming out this season, she was occasionally permitted to put up her hair and dress for dinner, but most of the time Lydia treated her like the child she was, for it was bad for children to grow up too fast. The two cousins were deep in conversation, and Lydia wondered idly what they were talking about. What was on my mind when I was eighteen? she asked herself; and then she remembered a young man with soft hair and clever hands, and she thought: Please, God, let me keep my secrets.

꿎 ꙸ

"Do you think we'll *feel* different after we've come out?" Belinda said.

Charlotte had thought about this before. "I shan't."

"But we'll be grown-up."

"I don't see how a lot of parties and balls and picnics can make a person grown-up."

"We'll have to have corsets."

Charlotte giggled. "Have you ever worn one?"

"No, have you?"

"I tried mine on last week."

"What's it like?"

"Awful. You can't walk upright."

"How did you look?"

Charlotte gestured with her hands to indicate an enormous bust. They both collapsed laughing. Charlotte caught sight of her mother and put on a contrite face in anticipation of a reprimand; but Mama seemed preoccupied and merely smiled vaguely as she turned away.

"It will be fun, though," said Belinda.

"The season? Yes," Charlotte said doubtfully. "But what's the point of it all?"

"To meet the right sort of young man, of course."

"To look for husbands, you mean."

They reached the great oak in the middle of the lawn, and Belinda threw herself down on the seat beneath the tree, looking faintly sulky. "You think coming out is all very silly, don't you?" she said.

Charlotte sat beside her and looked across the carpet of turf to the long south front of Walden Hall. The tall Gothic windows glinted in the afternoon sun. From here the house looked as if it might be rationally and regularly planned, but behind that facade it was really an enchanting muddle. She said: "What's silly is being made to wait so long. I'm not in a hurry to go to balls and leave cards on people in the afternoon and meet young men— I shouldn't mind if I never did those things —but it makes me so angry to be treated like a child still. I hate having supper with Marya; she's quite ignorant, or pretends to be. At least in the dining room you get some conversation. Papa talks about interesting things. When I get bored Marya suggests we play cards. I don't want to *play* anything; I've been playing all my life." She sighed. Talking about it had made her angrier. She looked at Belinda's calm, freckled face with its halo of red curls. Charlotte's own face was oval, with a rather distinctive straight nose and a strong chin, and her hair was thick and dark. Happy-go-lucky Belinda, she thought; these things really don't bother her; *she* never gets intense about anything.

Charlotte touched Belinda's arm. "Sorry. I didn't mean to carry on so."

"It's all right." Belinda smiled indulgently. "You always get cross about things you can't possibly change. Do you remember that time you decided you wanted to go to Eton?"

"Never!"

"You most certainly did. You made a terrible fuss. Papa had gone to school at Eton, you said, so why shouldn't you?"

Charlotte had no memory of that, but she could not deny that it sounded just like her at ten years old. She said: "But do you really think these things can't possibly be different? Coming out, and going to London for the season, and getting engaged, and then marriage . . ."

"You could have a scandal and be forced to emigrate to Rhodesia."

"I'm not quite sure how one goes about having a scandal."

"Nor am I."

They were silent for a while. Sometimes Charlotte wished she were passive like Belinda. Life would be simpler—but then again, it would be awfully dull. She said: "I asked Marya what I'm supposed to *do* after I get married. Do you know what she said?" She imitated her governess's throaty Russian accent. "Do? Why, my child, you will do *nothing.*"

"Oh, that's silly," Belinda said.

"Is it? What do my mother and yours do?"

"They're Good Society. They have parties and stay about at country houses and go to the opera and . . ."

"That's what I mean. Nothing."

"They have babies—"

"Now that's another thing. They make such a *secret* about having babies."

"That's because it's . . . vulgar."

"Why? What's vulgar about it?" Charlotte saw herself becoming *enthusiastic* again. Marya was always telling her not to be *enthusiastic*. She took a deep breath and lowered her voice. "You and I have got to have these babies. Don't you think they might tell us something about how it happens? They're very keen for us to know all about Mozart and Shakespeare and Leonardo da Vinci."

Belinda looked uncomfortable but very interested. She feels the same way about it as I do, Charlotte thought; I wonder how much she knows?

Charlotte said: "Do you realize they grow inside you?"

Belinda nodded, then blurted out: "But how does it start?"

"Oh, it just happens, I think, when you get to about twenty-one. That's really why you have to be a debutante and come out —to make sure you get a husband before you start having babies." Charlotte hesitated. "I think," she added.

Belinda said: "Then how do they get out?"

"I don't know. How big are they?"

Belinda held her hands about two feet apart. "The twins were this big when they were a day old." She thought again, and narrowed the distance. "Well, perhaps this big."

Charlotte said: "When a hen lays an egg, it comes out . . . behind." She avoided Belinda's eyes. She had never had such an intimate conversation with anyone, ever. "The egg seems too big, but it does come out."

Belinda leaned closer and spoke quietly. "I saw Daisy drop a calf once. She's the Jersey cow on the Home Farm. The men didn't know I was watching. That's what they call it, 'dropping' a calf."

Charlotte was fascinated. "What happened?"

"It was horrible. It looked as if her tummy opened up, and there was a lot of blood and things." She shuddered.

"It makes me scared," Charlotte said. "I'm afraid it will happen to me before I find out all about it. Why won't they *tell* us?"

"We shouldn't be talking about such things."

"We've damn well got a right to talk about them!"

Belinda gasped. "Swearing makes it worse!"

"I don't care." It maddened Charlotte that there was no way to find out these things, no one to ask, no book to consult ... She was struck by an idea. "There's a locked cupboard in the library—I bet there are books about all this sort of thing in there. Let's look!"

"But if it's locked . . ."

"Oh, I know where the key is. I've known for years."

"We'll be in terrible trouble if we're caught."

"They're all changing for dinner now. This is our chance." Charlotte stood up.

Belinda hesitated. "There'll be a row."

"I don't care if there is. Anyway, I'm going to look in the cupboard, and you can come if you want." Charlotte turned and walked toward the house. After a moment Belinda ran up beside her, as Charlotte had known she would.

They went through the pillared portico and into the cool, lofty great hall. Turning left, they passed the morning room and the Octagon, then entered the library. Charlotte told herself she was a woman and entitled to know, but all the same she felt like a naughty little girl.

The library was her favorite room. Being on a corner of the house it was very bright, lit by three big windows. The leather-upholstered chairs were old and surprisingly comfortable. In winter there was a fire all day, and there were games and jigsaw puzzles as well as two or three thousand books. Some of the books were ancient, having been here since the house was built, but many were new, for Mama read novels and Papa was interested in lots of different things—chemistry, agriculture, travel, astronomy and history. Charlotte liked particularly to come here on Marya's day off, when the governess was not able to snatch away *Far From the Madding Crowd* and replace it with *The Water Babies*. Sometimes Papa would be here with her, sitting at the Victorian pedestal desk and reading a catalogue of agricultural machinery or the balance sheet of an American railroad, but he never interfered with her choice of books.

The room was empty now. Charlotte went straight to the desk, opened a small, square drawer in one of the pedestals and took out a key.

There were three cupboards against the wall beside the desk. One contained games in boxes and another had cartons of writing paper and envelopes embossed with the Walden crest. The third was locked. Charlotte opened it with the key.

Inside were twenty or thirty books and a pile of old magazines. Charlotte glanced at one of the magazines. It was called *The Pearl.* It did not seem promising. Hastily, she picked out two books at random, without looking at the titles. She closed and locked the cupboard and replaced the key in the desk drawer.

"There!" she said triumphantly.

"Where can we go to look at them?" Belinda hissed.

"Remember the hideaway?"

"Oh! Yes!"

"Why are we whispering?"

They both giggled.

Charlotte went to the door. Suddenly she heard a voice in the hall, calling: "Lady Charlotte . . . Lady Charlotte . . ."

"It's Annie; she's looking for us," Charlotte said. "She's nice, but so dim-witted. We'll go out the other way, quickly." She crossed the library and went through the far door into the billiard room, which led in turn to the gun room; but there was someone in the gun room. She listened for a moment.

"It's my Papa," Belinda whispered, looking scared. "He's been out with the dogs."

Fortunately there was a pair of French doors from the billiard room on to the west terrace. Charlotte and Belinda crept out and closed the doors quietly behind them. The sun was low and red, casting long shadows across the lawns.

"Now how do we get back in?" Belinda said.

"Over the roofs. Follow me!"

Charlotte ran around the back of the house and through the kitchen garden to the stables. She stuffed the two books into the bodice of her dress and tightened her belt so that they should not fall out.

From a corner of the stable yard she could climb, by a series of easy steps, to the roof over the servants' quarters. First she stood on the lid of a low iron bunker which was used to store logs. From there she hauled herself onto the corrugated tin roof of a lean-to shed where tools were kept. The shed leaned against the washhouse. She stood upright on the corrugated tin and lifted herself onto the slate roof of the washhouse. She turned to look behind: Belinda was following.

Lying face down on the sloping slates, Charlotte edged along crabwise, holding on with the palms of her hands and the sides of her shoes, until the roof ended up against a wall. Then she crawled up the roof and straddled the ridge.

Belinda caught up with her and said: "Isn't this dangerous?"

"I've been doing it since I was nine years old."

Above them was the window of an attic bedroom shared by two parlourmaids. The window was high in the gable, its top corners almost reaching the roof, which sloped down on either side. Charlotte stood upright and peeped into the room. No one was there. She pulled herself onto the window ledge and stood up.

She leaned to the left, got an arm and a leg over the edge of the roof and hauled herself onto the slates. She turned back and helped Belinda up.

They lay there for a moment, catching their breath. Charlotte remembered being told that Walden Hall had four acres of roof. It was hard to believe until you came up here and realized you could get lost among the ridges and valleys. From this point it was possible to reach any part of the roofs by using the footways, ladders and tunnels provided for the maintenance men who came every spring to clean gutters, paint drainpipes and replace broken tiles.

Charlotte got up. "Come on, the rest is easy," she said.

There was a ladder to the next roof, then a board footway, then a short flight of wooden steps leading to a small, square door set in a wall. Charlotte unlatched the door and crawled through, and she was in the hideaway.

It was a low, windowless room with a sloping ceiling and a plank floor which would give you splinters if you were not careful. She imagined it had once been used as a storeroom: anyway, it was now quite forgotten. A door at one end led into a closet off the nursery, which had not been used for many years. Charlotte had discovered the hideaway when she was eight or nine and had used it occasionally in the game—which she seemed to have been playing all her life—of escaping from supervision. There were cushions on the floor, candles in jars and a box of matches. On one of the cushions lay a battered and floppy toy dog, which had been hidden here eight years ago after

Marya, the governess, had threatened to throw him away. A tiny occasional table bore a cracked vase full of colored pencils and a red leather writing case. Walden Hall was inventoried every few years, and Charlotte could recall Mrs. Braithwaite, the housekeeper, saying that the oddest things went missing.

Belinda crawled in, and Charlotte lit the candles. She took the two books from her bodice and looked at the titles. One was called *Household Medicine* and the other *The Romance of Lust*. The medical book seemed more promising. She sat on a cushion and opened it. Belinda sat beside her, looking guilty. Charlotte felt as if she were about to discover the secret of life.

She leafed through the pages. The book seemed explicit and detailed on rheumatism, broken bones and measles, but when it arrived at childbirth it suddenly became impenetrably vague. There was some mysterious stuff about cramps, waters breaking, and a cord which had to be tied in two places, then cut with scissors which had been dipped in boiling water. This chapter was evidently written for people who already knew a lot about the subject. There was a drawing of a naked woman. Charlotte noticed, but was too embarrassed to tell Belinda, that the woman in the drawing had no hair in a certain place where Charlotte had a great deal. Then there was a diagram of a baby inside a woman's tummy, but no indication of a passage by which the baby might emerge.

Belinda said: "It must be that the doctor cuts you open."

"Then what did they do in history, before there were doctors?" Charlotte said. "Anyway, this book's no good." She opened the other at random and read aloud the first sentence that came to her eye. "She lowered herself with lascivious slowness until she was completely impaled upon my rigid shaft, whereupon she commenced her delicious rocking movements to and fro." Charlotte frowned, and looked at Belinda.

"I wonder what it means?" said Belinda.

◦§ ʒ◦

Feliks Kschessinsky sat in a railway carriage waiting for the train to pull out of Dover Station. The carriage was cold. He was quite still. It was dark outside, and he could see his own reflection in the window: a tall man with a neat moustache, wearing a black coat and a bowler hat. There was a small suitcase on the rack above his head. He might have been the traveling representative of a Swiss watch manufacturer, except that anyone who looked closely would have seen that the coat was cheap, the suitcase was cardboard and the face was not the face of a man who sold watches.

He was thinking about England. He could remember when, in his youth, he had upheld England's constitutional monarchy as the ideal form of government. The thought amused him, and the flat white face reflected in the window gave him the ghost of a smile. He had since changed his mind about the ideal form of government.

The train moved off, and a few minutes later Feliks was watching the sun rise over the orchards and hop fields of Kent. He never ceased to be astonished at how *pretty* Europe was. When he first saw it he had suffered a profound shock, for like any Russian peasant he had been incapable of imagining that the world could look this way. He had been on a train then, he recalled. He had crossed hundreds of miles of Russia's thinly populated northwestern provinces, with their stunted trees, their miserable villages buried in snow and their winding mud roads; then, one morning, he had woken up to find himself in Germany. Looking at the neat green fields, the paved roads, the dainty houses in the clean villages and the flower beds on the sunny station platform, he had thought he was in Paradise. Later, in Switzerland, he had sat on the veranda of a small hotel, warmed by the sun yet within sight of snow-covered mountains, drinking coffee and eating a fresh, crusty roll, and he had thought: People here must be so happy.

Now, watching the English farms come to life in the early morning, he recalled dawn in his home village—a gray, boiling sky and a bitter wind; a frozen swampy field with puddles of ice and tufts of coarse grass rimed with frost; himself in a worn canvas smock, his feet already numb in felt shoes and clogs; his father striding along beside him, wearing the threadbare robes of an impoverished country priest, arguing that God was good. His father had loved the Russian people because God loved them. It had always been perfectly obvious to Feliks that God hated the people, for He treated them so cruelly.

That discussion had been the start of a long journey, a journey which had taken Feliks from Christianity through socialism to anarchist terror, from Tambov province through St. Petersburg and Siberia to Geneva. And in Geneva he had made the decision which brought him to England. He recalled the meeting. He had almost missed it . . .

⊷ ⊶

He almost missed the meeting. He had been to Cracow, to negotiate with the Polish Jews who smuggled the magazine *Mutiny* across the border into Russia. He arrived in Geneva after dark and went straight to Ulrich's tiny back-street printing shop. The editorial committee was in session—four men and two girls, gathered around a candle, in the rear of the shop behind the gleaming press, breathing the smells of newsprint and oiled machinery, planning the Russian Revolution.

Ulrich brought Feliks up to date on the discussion. He had seen Josef, a spy for the Okhrana, the Russian secret police. Josef secretly sympathized with the revolutionaries and gave the Okhrana false information for their money. Sometimes the anarchists would give him true but harmless tidbits, and in return Josef warned them of Okhrana activities.

This time Josef's news had been sensational. "The Czar wants a military alliance with England," Ulrich told Feliks. "He is sending Prince Orlov to London to negotiate. The Okhrana know about it because they have to guard the Prince on the journey through Europe."

Feliks took off his hat and sat down, wondering whether this was true. One of the girls, a sad, shabby Russian, brought him tea in a glass. Feliks took a half-eaten lump of sugar from his pocket, placed it between his teeth and sipped the tea through the sugar in the peasant manner.

"The point being," Ulrich went on, "that England could then have a war with Germany and make the Russians fight it."

Feliks nodded.

The shabby girl said: "And it won't be the princes and counts who get killed—it will be the ordinary Russian people."

She was right, Feliks thought. The war would be fought by the peasants. He had spent most of his life among those people. They were hard, surly and narrow-minded, but their foolish generosity and their occasional spontaneous outbursts of sheer fun gave a hint of how they might be in a decent society. Their concerns were the weather, animals, disease, childbirth and out-witting the landlord. For a few years, in their late teens, they were sturdy and straight, and could smile and run fast and flirt; but soon they became bowed and gray and slow and sullen. Now Prince Orlov would take those young men in the springtime of their lives and march them in front of cannon to be shot to pieces or maimed forever, no doubt for the very best reasons of international diplomacy.

It was things like this that made Feliks an anarchist.

"What is to be done?" said Ulrich.

"We must blaze the news across the front page of *Mutiny*!" said the shabby girl.

They began to discuss how the story should be handled. Feliks listened. Editorial matters interested him little. He distributed the magazine and wrote articles about how to make bombs, and he was deeply discontented. He had become terribly civilized in Geneva. He drank beer instead of vodka, wore a collar and a tie and went to concerts of orchestral music. He had a job in a bookshop. Meanwhile Russia was in turmoil. The oil workers were at war with the Cossacks, the parliament was impotent and a million workers were on strike. Czar Nicholas II was the most incompetent and asinine ruler a degenerate aristocracy could produce. The country was a powder barrel waiting for a spark, and Feliks wanted to be that spark. But it was fatal to go back. Joe Stalin had gone back, and no sooner had he set foot on Russian soil than he had been sent to Siberia. The secret police knew the exiled revolutionaries better than they knew those still at home. Feliks was chafed by his stiff collar, his leather shoes and his circumstances.

He looked around at the little group of anarchists: Ulrich, the printer, with white hair and an inky apron, an intellectual who loaned Feliks books by Proudhon and Kropotkin but also a man of action who had once helped Feliks rob a bank; Olga, the shabby girl, who had seemed to be falling in love with Feliks until, one day, she saw him break a policeman's arm and became frightened of him; Vera, the promiscuous poetess; Yevno, the philosophy student who talked a lot about a cleansing wave of blood and fire; Hans, the watchmaker, who saw into people's souls as if he had them under his magnifying glass; and Pyotr, the dispossessed Count, writer of brilliant economic tracts and inspirational revolutionary editorials. They were sincere and hardworking people, and all very clever. Feliks knew their importance, for he had been inside Russia among the desperate people who waited impatiently for smuggled newspapers and pamphlets and passed them from hand to hand until they fell to pieces. Yet it was not enough, for economic tracts were no protection against police bullets, and fiery articles would not burn palaces.

Ulrich was saying: "This news deserves wider circulation than it will get in *Mutiny*. I want every peasant in Russia to know that Orlov would lead him into a useless and bloody war over something that concerns him not at all."

Olga said: "The first problem is whether we will be believed."

Feliks said: "The first problem is whether the story is true."

"We can check," Ulrich said. "The London comrades could find out whether Orlov arrives when he is supposed to arrive, and whether he meets the people he needs to meet."

"It's not enough to spread the news," Yevno said excitedly. "We must put a stop to this!"

"How?" said Ulrich, looking at young Yevno over the top of his wire-rimmed spectacles.

"We should call for the assassination of Orlov—he is a traitor, betraying the people, and he should be executed."

"Would that stop the talks?"

"It probably would," said Count Pyotr. "Especially if the assassin were an anarchist. Remember, England gives political asylum to anarchists, and this infuriates the Czar. Now, if one of his princes were killed in England by one of our comrades, the Czar might well be angry enough to call off the whole negotiation."

Yevno said: "What a story we would have then! We could say that Orlov had been assassinated by one of us for treason against the Russian people."

"Every newspaper in the world would carry *that* report," Ulrich mused.

"Think of the effect it would have at home. You know how Russian peasants feel about conscription—it's a death sentence. They hold a funeral when a boy goes into the army. If they learned that the Czar was planning to make them fight a major European war, the rivers would run red with blood . . ."

He was right, Feliks thought. Yevno always talked like that, but this time he was right.

Ulrich said: "I think you're in dreamland, Yevno. Orlov is on a secret mission—he won't ride through London in an open carriage waving to the crowds. Besides, I know the London comrades—they've never assassinated anyone. I don't see how it can be done."

"I do," Feliks said. They all looked at him. The shadows on their faces shifted in the flickering candlelight. "I know how it can be done." His voice sounded strange to him, as if his throat were constricted. "I'll go to London. I'll kill Orlov."

The room was suddenly quiet, as all the talk of death and destruction suddenly became real and concrete in their midst. They stared at him in surprise, all except Ulrich, who smiled knowingly, almost as if he had planned, all along, that it would turn out this way.

◄§ §►

TWO

London was unbelievably rich. Feliks had seen extravagant wealth in Russia and much prosperity in Europe, but not on this scale. Here *nobody* was in rags. In fact, although the weather was warm, everyone was wearing several layers of heavy clothing. Feliks saw carters, street vendors, sweepers, laborers and delivery boys—all sporting fine factory-made coats without holes or patches. All the children wore boots. Every woman had a hat, and such hats! They were mostly enormous things, as broad across as the wheel of a dog cart, and decorated with ribbons, feathers, flowers and fruit. The streets were teeming. He saw more motor cars in the first five minutes than he had in all his life. There seemed to be as many cars as there were horse-drawn vehicles. On wheels or on foot, everyone was rushing.

In Piccadilly Circus all the vehicles were at a standstill, and the cause was one familiar in any city: a horse had fallen and its cart had overturned. A crowd of men struggled to get beast and wagon upright, while from the pavement flower girls and ladies with painted faces shouted encouragement and made jokes.

As he went farther east his initial impression of great wealth

34

was somewhat modified. He passed a domed cathedral which was called St. Paul's, according to the map he had bought at Victoria Station, and thereafter he was in poorer districts. Abruptly, the magnificent facades of banks and office buildings gave place to small row houses in varying states of disrepair. There were fewer cars and more horses, and the horses were thinner. Most of the shops were street stalls. There were no more delivery boys. Now he saw plenty of barefoot children— not that it mattered, for in this climate, it seemed to him, they had no need of boots anyway.

Things got worse as he penetrated deeper into the East End. Here were crumbling tenements, squalid courtyards and stinking alleys, where human wrecks dressed in rags picked over piles of garbage, looking for food. Then Feliks entered Whitechapel High Street, and saw the familiar beards, long hair and traditional robes of assorted Orthodox Jews, and tiny shops selling smoked fish and kosher meat: it was like being in the Russian Pale, except that the Jews did not look frightened.

He made his way to 165 Jubilee Street, the address Ulrich had given him. It was a two-story building that looked like a Lutheran chapel. A notice outside said the Workers Friend Club and Institute was open to all working men regardless of politics, but another notice betrayed the nature of the place by announcing that it had been opened in 1906 by Peter Kropotkin. Feliks wondered whether he would meet the legendary Kropotkin here in London.

He went in. He saw in the lobby a pile of newspapers, also called The Workers Friend but in Yiddish: *Der Arbeiter Fraint.* Notices on the walls advertised lessons in English, a Sunday school, a trip to Epping Forest and a lecture on Hamlet. Feliks stepped into the hall. The architecture confirmed his earlier instinct: this had definitely been the nave of a nonconformist church once upon a time. However, it had been transformed by the addition of a stage at one end and a bar at the other. On the stage a group of men and women appeared to be rehearsing a play. Perhaps this was what anarchists did in England, Feliks thought; that would explain why they were allowed to have clubs. He went over to the bar. There was no sign of alcoholic drink, but on the counter he saw gefilte fish, pickled herring and —joy!—a samovar.

The girl behind the counter looked at him and said, *"Nu?"*
Feliks smiled.

◄§ §►

A week later, on the day that Prince Orlov was due to arrive in
London, Feliks had lunch at a French restaurant in Soho. He
arrived early and picked a table near the door. He ate onion
soup, fillet steak and goat's cheese, and drank half a bottle of red
wine. He ordered in French. The waiters were deferential.
When he finished, it was the height of the lunch-hour rush. At
a moment when three of the waiters were in the kitchen and the
other two had their backs to him he calmly got up, went to the
door, took his coat and hat and left without paying.

He smiled as he walked down the street. He enjoyed stealing.

He had quickly learned how to live in this town on almost no
money. For breakfast he would buy sweet tea and a slab of bread
from a street stall for twopence, but that was the only food he
would pay for. At lunchtime he stole fruit or vegetables from
street stalls. In the evening he would go to a charity soup
kitchen and get a bowl of broth and unlimited bread in return
for listening to an incomprehensible sermon and singing a
hymn. He had five pounds in cash but it was for emergencies.

He was living at Dunstan Houses in Stepney Green, in a
five-story tenement building where lived half the leading
anarchists in London. He had a mattress on the floor in the
apartment of Rudolf Rocker, the charismatic blond German
who edited *Der Arbeiter Fraint*. Rocker's charisma did not work
on Feliks, who was immune to charm, but Feliks respected the
man's total dedication. Rocker and his wife Milly kept open
house for anarchists, and all day—and half the night—there
were visitors, messengers, debates, committee meetings and
endless tea and cigarettes. Feliks paid no rent, but each day he
brought home something—a pound of sausages, a packet of tea,
a pocketful of oranges—for the communal larder. They thought
he bought these things, but of course he stole them.

He told the other anarchists he was here to study at the British
Museum and finish his book about natural anarchism in primitive communities. They believed him. They were friendly, dedicated and harmless: they sincerely believed the revolution could
be brought about by education and trade unionism, by pam-

phlets and lectures and trips to Epping Forest. Feliks knew that most anarchists outside Russia were like this. He did not hate them, but secretly he despised them, for in the end they were just frightened.

Nevertheless, among such groups there were generally a few violent men. When he needed them he would seek them out.

Meanwhile he worried about whether Orlov would come and about how he would kill him. Such worries were useless, and he tried to distract his mind by working on his English. He had learned a little of the language in cosmopolitan Switzerland. During the long train journey across Europe he had studied a school textbook for Russian children and an English translation of his favorite novel, *The Captain's Daughter* by Pushkin, which he knew almost by heart in Russian. Now he read *The Times* every morning in the reading room of the Jubilee Street club, and in the afternoons he walked the streets, striking up conversations with drunks, vagrants and prostitutes—the people he liked best, the people who broke the rules. The printed words in books soon meshed with the sounds all around him, and already he could say anything he needed to. Before long he would be able to talk politics in English.

After leaving the restaurant he walked north, across Oxford Street, and entered the German quarter west of Tottenham Court Road. There were a lot of revolutionists among the Germans, but they tended to be communists rather than anarchists. Feliks admired the discipline of the communists but he was suspicious of their authoritarianism; and besides, he was temperamentally unsuited to party work.

He walked all the way across Regent's Park and entered the middle-class suburb to its north. He wandered around the tree-lined streets, looking into the small gardens of the neat brick villas, searching for a bicycle to steal. He had learned to ride a bicycle in Switzerland, and had discovered that it was the perfect vehicle for shadowing someone, for it was maneuverable and inconspicuous, and in city traffic it was fast enough to keep up with a motor car or a carriage. Sadly, the bourgeois citizens of this part of London seemed to keep their bicycles locked away. He saw one cycle being ridden along the street and was tempted to knock the rider off the machine, but at that moment there were three pedestrians and a baker's van in the road, and

Feliks did not want to create a scene. A little later he saw a boy delivering groceries, but the boy's cycle was too conspicuous, with a large basket on the front and a metal plate hanging from the crossbar, bearing the name of the grocer. Feliks was beginning to toy with alternative strategies when at last he saw what he needed.

A man of about thirty came out of one of the gardens wheeling a bicycle. The man wore a straw boater and a striped blazer which bulged over his paunch. He leaned his cycle against the garden wall and bent down to put on his trouser clips.

Feliks approached him rapidly.

The man saw his shadow, looked up, and muttered: "Good afternoon."

Feliks knocked him down.

The man rolled onto his back and looked up at Feliks with a stupid expression of surprise.

Feliks fell on him, dropping one knee into the middle button of the striped blazer. The man's breath left his body in a whoosh, and he was winded, helpless, gasping for air.

Feliks stood up and glanced toward the house. A young woman stood at a window watching, her hand raised to her open mouth, her eyes wide with fright.

He looked again at the man on the ground: it would be a minute or so before he even thought about getting up.

Feliks climbed on the bicycle and rode away rapidly.

A man who has no fear can do anything he wants, Feliks thought. He had learned that lesson eleven years ago, in a railway siding outside Omsk. It had been snowing . . .

❧ ☙

It was snowing. Feliks sat in an open railway truck, on a pile of coal, freezing to death.

He had been cold for a year, ever since he escaped from the chain gang in the gold mine. In that year he had crossed Siberia, from the frozen north almost to the Urals. Now he was a mere thousand miles from civilization and warm weather. Most of the way he had walked, although sometimes he rode in railcars or on wagons full of pelts. He preferred to ride with cattle, for they kept him warm and he could share their feed. He was vaguely aware that he was little more than an animal himself. He never washed, his coat was a blanket stolen from a horse, his ragged clothes were full of lice and there were fleas in his hair. His favorite food was raw birds' eggs. Once he had stolen a pony, ridden it to death, then eaten its liver. He had lost his sense of time. He knew it was autumn, by the weather, but he did not know what month he was in. Often he found himself unable to remember what he had done the day before. In his saner moments he realized he was half mad. He never spoke to people. When he came to a town or village he skirted it, pausing only to rob the garbage dump. He knew only that he had to keep going west, for it would be warmer there.

But the coal train had been shunted onto a siding, and Feliks thought he might be dying. There was a guard, a burly policeman in a fur coat, who was there to stop peasants from taking coal for their fires . . . As that thought occurred to him, Feliks realized he was having a lucid moment, and that it might be his last. He wondered what had brought it on; then he smelled the policeman's dinner. But the policeman was big and healthy and had a gun.

I don't care, Feliks thought; I'm dying anyway.

So he stood up, and picked up the biggest lump of coal he could carry, and staggered over to the policeman's hut, and went in, and hit the startled policeman over the head with the lump of coal.

There was a pot on the fire and stew in the pot, too hot to eat. Feliks carried the pot outside and emptied it out into the snow; then he fell on his knees and ate the food mixed with cooling snow. There were lumps of potato and turnip, and fat carrots, and chunks of meat. He swallowed them whole. The policeman came out of the hut and hit Feliks with his club, a heavy blow across the back. Feliks was wild with rage that the man should try to stop him from eating. He got up from the ground and flew at the man, kicking and scratching. The policeman fought back with his club, but Feliks could not feel the blows. He got his fingers on the man's throat and squeezed. He would not let go. After a while the man's eyes closed, then his face went blue, then his tongue came out, then Feliks finished the stew.

He ate all the food in the hut, and warmed himself by the fire, and slept in the policeman's bed. When he woke up he was sane. He took the boots and the coat off the corpse and walked to

Omsk. On the way he made a remarkable discovery about himself: he had lost the ability to feel fear. Something had happened in his mind, as if a switch had closed. He could think of nothing that could possibly frighten him. If hungry, he would steal; if chased, he would hide; if threatened, he would kill. There was nothing he wanted. Nothing could hurt him anymore. Love, pride, desire and compassion were forgotten emotions.

They all came back, eventually, except the fear.

When he reached Omsk he sold the policeman's fur coat and bought trousers and a shirt, a waistcoat and a topcoat. He burned his rags and paid one ruble for a hot bath and a shave in a cheap hotel. He ate in a restaurant, using a knife instead of his fingers. He saw the front page of a newspaper, and remembered how to read; and then he knew he had come back from the grave.

᪥

He sat on a bench in Liverpool Street station, his bicycle leaning against the wall beside him. He wondered what Orlov was like. He knew nothing about the man other than his rank and mission. The prince might be a dull, plodding, loyal servant of the Czar, or a sadist and a lecher, or a kindly white-haired old man who liked nothing better than to bounce his grandchildren on his knee. It did not matter: Feliks would kill him anyway.

He was confident he would recognize Orlov, for Russians of that type had not the faintest conception of traveling unobtrusively, secret mission or no.

Would Orlov come? If he did come, and arrived on the very train Josef had specified, and if he subsequently met with the Earl of Walden as Josef had said he would, then there could hardly be any further doubt that Josef's information had been accurate.

A few minutes before the train was due, a closed coach drawn by four magnificent horses clattered by and drove straight onto the platform. There was a coachman in front and a liveried footman hanging on behind. A railwayman in a military-style coat with shiny buttons strode after the coach. The railwayman spoke to the coachman and directed him to the far end of the platform. Then a stationmaster in a frock coat and top hat arrived, looking important, consulting his fob watch and comparing it critically with the station clocks. He opened the carriage door for the passenger to step down.

The railwayman walked past Feliks's bench, and Feliks grabbed his sleeve. "Please, sir," he said, putting on the wide-eyed expression of a naïve foreign tourist. "Is that the King of England?"

The railwayman grinned. "No, mate, it's only the Earl of Walden." He walked on.

So Josef had been right.

Feliks studied Walden with an assassin's eye. He was tall, about Feliks's height, and beefy—easier to shoot than a small man. He was about fifty. Except for a slight limp he seemed fit; he could run away, but not very fast. He wore a highly visible light-gray morning coat and a top hat of the same color. His hair under the hat was short and straight, and he had a spade-shaped beard patterned after that of the late King Edward VII. He stood on the platform, leaning on a cane—potential weapon— and favoring his left leg. The coachman, the footman and the stationmaster bustled about him like bees around the queen. His stance was relaxed. He did not look at his watch. He paid no attention to the flunkies around him. He is used to this, Feliks thought; all his life he has been the important man in the crowd.

The train appeared, smoke billowing from the funnel of the engine. I could kill Orlov now, Feliks thought, and he felt momentarily the thrill of the hunter as he closes with his prey; but he had already decided not to do the deed today. He was here to observe, not to act. Most anarchist assassinations were bungled because of haste or spontaneity, in his view. He believed in planning and organization, which were anathema to many anarchists; but they did not realize that a man could plan his own actions—it was when he began to organize the lives of others that he became a tyrant.

The train halted with a great sigh of steam. Feliks stood up and moved a little closer to the platform. Toward the far end of the train was what appeared to be a private car, differentiated from the rest by the colors of its bright new paintwork. It came to a stop precisely opposite Walden's coach. The stationmaster stepped forward eagerly and opened a door.

Feliks tensed, peering along the platform, watching the shadowed space in which his quarry would appear.

For a moment everyone waited; then Orlov was there. He paused in the doorway for a second, and in that time Feliks's eye photographed him. He was a small man wearing an expensive-looking heavy Russian coat with a fur collar, and a black top hat. His face was pink and youthful, almost boyish, with a small moustache and no beard. He smiled hesitantly. He looked vulnerable. Feliks thought: So much evil is done by people with innocent faces.

Orlov stepped off the train. He and Walden embraced, Russian fashion, but quickly; then they got into the coach.

That was rather hasty, Feliks thought.

The footman and two porters began to load luggage onto the carriage. It rapidly became clear that they could not get everything on, and Feliks smiled to think of his own cardboard suitcase, half empty.

The coach was turned around. It seemed the footman was being left behind to take care of the rest of the luggage. The porters came to the carriage window, and a gray-sleeved arm emerged and dropped coins into their hands. The coach pulled away. Feliks mounted his bicycle and followed.

In the tumult of the London traffic it was not difficult for him to keep pace. He trailed them through the city, along the Strand and across St. James's Park. On the far side of the park the coach followed the boundary road for a few yards, then turned abruptly into a walled forecourt.

Feliks jumped off his bicycle and wheeled it along the grass at the edge of the park until he stood across the road from the gateway. He could see the coach drawn up at the imposing entrance to a large house. Over the roof of the coach he saw two top hats, one black and one gray, disappear into the building. Then the door closed, and he could see no more.

◆§ ﾛ◆

Lydia studied her daughter critically. Charlotte stood in front of a large pier glass, trying on the debutante's gown she would wear to be presented at court. Madame Bourdon, the thin, elegant dressmaker, fussed about her with pins, tucking a flounce here and fastening a ruffle there.

Charlotte looked both beautiful and innocent—just the effect that was called for in a debutante. The dress, of white tulle embroidered with crystals, went down almost to the floor and partly covered the tiny pointed shoes. Its neckline, plunging to waist level, was filled in with a crystal corsage. The train was four yards of cloth-of-silver lined with pale pink chiffon and caught at the end by a huge white-and-silver bow. Charlotte's dark hair was piled high and fastened with a tiara which had belonged to the previous Lady Walden, Stephen's mother. In her hair she wore the regulation two white plumes.

My baby has almost grown up, Lydia thought.

She said: "It's very lovely, Madame Bourdon."

"Thank you, my lady."

Charlotte said: "It's terribly uncomfortable."

Lydia sighed. It was just the kind of thing Charlotte *would* say. Lydia said: "I wish you wouldn't be so frivolous."

Charlotte knelt down to pick up her train. Lydia said: "You don't have to kneel. Look, copy me and I'll show you how it's done. Turn to the left." Charlotte did so, and the train draped down her left side. "Gather it with your left arm, then make another quarter turn to the left." Now the train stretched out along the floor in front of Charlotte. "Walk forward, using your right hand to loop the train over your left arm as you go."

"It works." Charlotte smiled. When she smiled, you could feel the glow. She used to be like this all the time, Lydia thought. When she was little, I always knew what was going on in her mind. Growing up is learning to deceive.

Charlotte said: "Who taught *you* all these things, Mama?"

"Your Uncle George's first wife, Belinda's mother, coached me before I was presented." She wanted to say: These things are easy to teach, but the hard lessons you must learn on your own.

Charlotte's governess Marya came into the room. She was an efficient, unsentimental woman in an iron-gray dress, the only servant Lydia had brought from St. Petersburg. Her appearance had not changed in nineteen years. Lydia had no idea how old she was: Fifty? Sixty?

Marya said: "Prince Orlov has arrived, my lady. Why, Charlotte, you look magnificent!"

It was almost time for Marya to begin calling her "Lady Charlotte," Lydia thought. She said: "Come down as soon as you've changed, Charlotte." Charlotte immediately began to unfasten the shoulder straps which held her train. Lydia went out.

She found Stephen in the drawing room, sipping sherry. He touched her bare arm and said: "I love to see you in summer dresses."

She smiled. "Thank you." He looked rather fine himself, she thought, in his gray coat and silver tie. There was more gray and silver in his beard. *We might have been so happy, you and I . . .* Suddenly she wanted to kiss his cheek. She glanced around the room: there was a footman at the sideboard pouring sherry. She had to restrain the impulse. She sat down and accepted a glass from the footman. "How is Aleks?"

"Much the same as always," Stephen replied. "You'll see, he'll be down in a minute. What about Charlotte's dress?"

"The gown is lovely. It's her attitude that disturbs me. She's unwilling to take anything at face value these days. I should hate her to become *cynical.*"

Stephen refused to worry about that. "You wait until some handsome Guards officer starts paying attention to her—she'll soon change her mind."

The remark irritated Lydia, implying as it did that all girls were the slaves of their romantic natures. It was the kind of thing Stephen said when he did not want to think about a subject. It made him sound like a hearty, empty-headed country squire, which he was not. But he was convinced that Charlotte was no different from any other eighteen-year-old girl, and he would not hear otherwise. Lydia knew that Charlotte had in her makeup a streak of something wild and un-English which had to be suppressed.

Irrationally, Lydia felt hostile toward Aleks on account of Charlotte. It was not his fault, but he represented the St. Petersburg factor, the danger of the past. She shifted restlessly in her chair, and caught Stephen observing her with a shrewd eye. He said: "You can't possibly be nervous about meeting little Aleks."

She shrugged. "Russians are so unpredictable."

"He's not very Russian."

She smiled at her husband, but their moment of intimacy had passed, and now there was just the usual qualified affection in her heart.

The door opened. Be calm, Lydia told herself.

Aleks came in. "Aunt Lydia!" he said, and bowed over her hand.

"How do you do, Aleksey Andreyevich," she said formally. Then she softened her tone and added: "Why, you still look eighteen."

"I wish I were," he said, and his eyes twinkled.

She asked him about his trip. As he replied, she found herself wondering why he was still unmarried. He had a title which on its own was enough to knock many girls—not to mention their mothers—off their feet; and on top of that he was strikingly good-looking and enormously rich. I'm sure he's broken a few hearts, she thought.

"Your brothers and your sister send their love," Aleks was saying, "and ask for your prayers." He frowned. "St. Petersburg is very unsettled now—it's not the town you knew."

Stephen said: "We've heard about this monk."

"Rasputin. The Czarina believes that God speaks through him, and she has great influence over the Czar. But Rasputin is only a symptom. All the time there are strikes, and sometimes riots. The people no longer believe that the Czar is holy."

"What is to be done?" Stephen asked.

Aleks sighed. "Everything. We need efficient farms, more factories, a proper parliament like England's, land reform, trade unions, freedom of speech . . ."

"I shouldn't be in too much of a hurry to have trade unions, if I were you," Stephen said.

"Perhaps. Still, somehow Russia must join the twentieth century. Either we, the nobility, must do it, or the people will destroy us and do it themselves."

Lydia thought he sounded more radical than the Radicals. How things must have changed at home, that a prince could talk like this! Her sister, Tatyana, Aleks's mother, referred in her letters to "the troubles" but gave no hint that the nobility was in real danger. But then, Aleks was more like his father, the old Prince Orlov, a political animal. If he were alive today he would talk like this.

Stephen said: "There is a third possibility, you know; a way in which the aristocracy and the people might yet be united."

Aleks smiled, as if he knew what was coming. "And that is?"

"A war."

Aleks nodded gravely. They think alike, Lydia reflected; Aleks always looked up to Stephen; Stephen was the nearest thing to a father that the boy had, after the old Prince died.

Charlotte came in, and Lydia stared at her in surprise. She was wearing a frock Lydia had never seen, of cream lace lined with chocolate-brown silk. Lydia would never have chosen it— it was rather *striking*—but there was no denying that Charlotte looked ravishing. Where did she buy it? Lydia wondered. When did she start buying clothes without taking me along? Who told her that those colors flatter her dark hair and brown eyes? Does she have a trace of makeup on? And why isn't she wearing a corset?

Stephen was also staring. Lydia noticed that he had stood up, and she almost laughed. It was a dramatic acknowledgment of his daughter's grown-up status, and what was funny was that it was clearly involuntary. In a moment he would feel foolish, and he would realize that standing up every time his daughter walked into a room was a courtesy he could hardly sustain in his own house.

The effect on Aleks was even greater. He sprang to his feet, spilled his sherry and blushed crimson. Lydia thought: Why, he's shy! He transferred his dripping glass from his right hand to his left, so that he was unable to shake with either, and he stood there looking helpless. It was an awkward moment, for he needed to compose himself before he could greet Charlotte, but he was clearly waiting to greet her before he would compose himself. Lydia was about to make some inane remark just to fill the silence when Charlotte took over.

She pulled the silk handkerchief from Aleks's breast pocket and wiped his right hand with it, saying: "How do you do, Aleksey Andreyevich," in Russian. She shook his now-dry right hand, took the glass from his left hand, wiped the glass, wiped the left hand, gave him back the glass, stuffed the handkerchief back into his pocket and made him sit down. She sat beside him and said: "Now that you've finished throwing the sherry around, tell me about Diaghilev. He's supposed to be a strange man. Have you met him?"

Aleks smiled. "Yes, I've met him."

As Aleks talked, Lydia marveled. Charlotte had dealt with the awkward moment without hesitation, and had gone on to ask a question—one which she had presumably prepared in advance —which succeeded in taking Orlov's mind off himself and mak-

ing him feel at ease. And she had done all that as smoothly as
if she had had twenty years' practice. Where had she learned
such poise?

Lydia caught her husband's eye. He too had noted Charlotte's
graciousness, and he was smiling from ear to ear in a glow of
fatherly pride.

◅§ §▻

Feliks paced up and down in St. James's Park, pondering what
he had seen. From time to time he glanced across the road at the
graceful white facade of Walden's house, rising over the high
forecourt wall like a noble head above a starched collar. He
thought: They believe they are safe in there.

He sat on a bench, in a position from which he could still see
the house. Middle-class London swarmed about him, the girls in
their outrageous headgear, the clerks and shopkeepers walking
homeward in their dark suits and bowler hats. There were gossiping nannies with babies in perambulators or overdressed tod-
dlers; there were top-hatted gentlemen on their way to and from
the clubs of St. James's; there were liveried footmen walking
tiny ugly dogs. A fat woman with a big bag of shopping
plumped herself down on the bench beside him and said: "Hot
enough for you?" He was not sure what would be the appropriate reply, so he smiled and looked away.

It seemed that Orlov had realized his life might be in danger
in England. He had shown himself for only a few seconds at the
station, and not at all at the house. Feliks guessed that he had
requested, in advance, that he be met by a closed coach, for the
weather was fine and most people were driving open landaus.

Until today this killing had been planned in the abstract,
Feliks reflected. It had been a matter of international politics,
diplomatic quarrels, alliances and ententes, military possibilities, the hypothetical reactions of faraway Kaisers and Czars.
Now, suddenly, it was flesh and blood; it was a real man, of a
certain size and shape; it was a youthful face with a small moustache, a face which must be smashed by a bullet; it was a short
body in a heavy coat, which must be turned into blood and rags
by a bomb; it was a clean-shaven throat above a spotted tie, a
throat which must be sliced open to gush blood.

Feliks felt completely capable of doing it. More than that, he was eager. There were questions—they would be answered; there were problems—they would be solved; it would take nerve —he had plenty.

He visualized Orlov and Walden inside that beautiful house, in their fine soft clothes, surrounded by quiet servants. Soon they would have dinner at a long table whose polished surface reflected like a mirror the crisp linen and silver cutlery. They would eat with perfectly clean hands, even the fingernails white, and the women wearing gloves. They would consume a tenth of the food provided and send the rest back to the kitchen. They might talk of racehorses or the new ladies' fashions or a king they all knew. Meanwhile the people who were to fight the war shivered in hovels in the cruel Russian climate—yet could still find an extra bowl of potato soup for an itinerant anarchist.

What a joy it will be to kill Orlov, he thought; what sweet revenge. When I have done that I can die satisfied.

He shivered.

"You're catching a cold," said the fat woman.

Feliks shrugged.

"I've got him a nice lamb chop for his dinner, and I've made an apple pie," she said.

"Ah," said Feliks. What on earth was she talking about? He got up from the bench and walked across the grass toward the house. He sat on the ground with his back to a tree. He would have to observe this house for a day or two and find out what kind of life Orlov would lead in London: when he would go out and to where; how he would travel—coach, landau, motor car or cab; how much time he would spend with Walden. Ideally he wanted to be able to predict Orlov's movements and so lie in wait for him. He might achieve that simply by learning his habits. Otherwise he would have to find a way of discovering the Prince's plans in advance—perhaps by bribing a servant in the house.

Then there was the question of what weapon to use and how to get it. The choice of weapon would depend upon the detailed circumstances of the killing. Getting it would depend on the Jubilee Street anarchists. For this purpose the amateur dramatics group could be ignored, as could the Dunstan Houses intellectuals and indeed all those with visible means of support. But there were four or five angry young men who always had money for drinks and, on the rare occasions when they talked politics, spoke of anarchism in terms of expropriating the expropriators, which was jargon for financing the revolution by theft. They would have weapons or know where to get them.

Two young girls who looked like shop assistants strolled by his tree, and he heard one of them say: ". . . told him, if you think just because you take a girl to the Bioscope and buy her a glass of brown ale you can . . ." Then they were past.

A peculiar feeling came over Feliks. He wondered whether the girls had caused it—but no, they meant nothing to him. Am I apprehensive? he thought. No. Fulfilled? No, that comes later. Excited? Hardly.

He finally figured out that he was happy.

It was very odd indeed.

◄§ §►

That night Walden went to Lydia's room. After they had made love she slept, and he lay in the dark with her head on his shoulder, remembering St. Petersburg in 1895.

He was always traveling in those days—America, Africa, Arabia—mainly because England was not big enough for him and his father both. He found St. Petersburg society gay but prim. He liked the Russian landscape and the vodka. Languages came easily to him but Russian was the most difficult he had ever encountered and he enjoyed the challenge.

As the heir to an earldom, Stephen was obliged to pay a courtesy call on the British ambassador, and the ambassador, in his turn, was expected to invite Stephen to parties and introduce him around. Stephen went to the parties because he liked talking politics with diplomats almost as much as he liked gambling with officers and getting drunk with actresses. It was at a reception in the British Embassy that he first met Lydia.

He had heard of her previously. She was spoken of as a paragon of virtue and a great beauty. She *was* beautiful, in a frail, colorless sort of way, with pale skin, pale blond hair and a white gown. She was also modest, respectable and scrupulously polite. There seemed to be nothing to her, and Stephen detached himself from her company quite quickly.

But later he found himself seated next to her at dinner, and he was obliged to converse with her. The Russians all spoke

French, and if they learned a third language it was German, so Lydia had very little English. Fortunately Stephen's French was good. Finding something to talk about was a bigger problem. He said something about the government of Russia, and she replied with the reactionary platitudes that were two-a-penny at the time. He spoke about his enthusiasm, big-game hunting in Africa, and she was interested for a while, until he mentioned the naked black pygmies, at which point she blushed and turned away to talk with the man on her other side. Stephen told himself he was not very interested in her, for she was the kind of girl one married, and he was not planning to marry. Still she left him with the nagging feeling that there was more to her than met the eye.

Lying in bed with her nineteen years later, Walden thought: She still gives me that nagging feeling; and he smiled ruefully in the dark.

He had seen her once more that evening in St. Petersburg. After dinner he had lost his way in the labyrinthine embassy building, and had wandered into the music room. She was there alone, sitting at the piano, filling the room with wild, passionate music. The tune was unfamiliar and almost discordant; but it was Lydia who fascinated Stephen. The pale, untouchable beauty was gone: her eyes flashed, her head tossed, her body trembled with emotion, and she seemed altogether a different woman.

He never forgot that music. Later he discovered that it had been Tchaikovsky's Piano Concerto in B flat minor, and since then he went to hear it played at every opportunity, although he never told Lydia why.

When he left the embassy he went back to his hotel to change his clothes, for he had an appointment to play cards at midnight. He was a keen gambler but not a self-destructive one: he knew how much he could afford to lose, and when he had lost it he stopped playing. Had he run up enormous debts he would have been obliged to ask his father to pay them, and that he could not bear to do. Sometimes he won quite large sums. However that was not the appeal of gambling for him: he liked the masculine companionship, the drinking and the late hours.

He did not keep that midnight rendezvous. Pritchard, his valet, was tying Stephen's tie when the British ambassador knocked on the door of the hotel suite. His Excellency looked as if he had got out of bed and dressed hastily. Stephen's first thought was that some kind of revolution was going on and all the British would have to take refuge in the embassy.

"Bad news, I'm afraid," said the ambassador. "You'd better sit down. Cable from England. It's your father."

The old tyrant was dead of a heart attack at sixty-five.

"Well, I'm damned," Stephen said. "So soon."

"My deepest sympathy," the ambassador said.

"It was very good of you to come personally."

"Not at all. Anything I can do."

"You're very kind."

The ambassador shook his hand and left.

Stephen stared into space, thinking about the old man. He had been immensely tall, with a will of iron and a sour disposition. His sarcasm could bring tears to your eyes. There were three ways to deal with him: you could become like him, you could go under, or you could go away. Stephen's mother, a sweet, helpless Victorian girl, had gone under, and died young. Stephen had gone away.

He pictured his father lying in a coffin and thought: You're helpless at last. Now you can't make housemaids cry, or footmen tremble, or children run and hide. You're powerless to arrange marriages, evict tenants or defeat parliamentary bills. You'll send no more thieves to jail, transport no more agitators to Australia. Ashes to ashes, dust to dust.

In later years he revised his opinion of his father. Now, in 1914, at the age of fifty, Walden could admit to himself that he had inherited some of his father's values: love of knowledge, a belief in rationalism, a commitment to good work as the justification of a man's existence. But back in 1895 there had been only bitterness.

Pritchard brought a bottle of whiskey on a tray and said: "This is a sad day, my lord."

That *my lord* startled Stephen. He and his brother had courtesy titles—Stephen's was Lord Highcombe—but they were always called "sir" by the servants, and "my lord" was reserved for their father. Now, of course, Stephen was the Earl of Walden. Along with the title, he now possessed several thousands of acres in the south of England, a big chunk of Scotland, six racehorses, Walden Hall, a villa in Monte Carlo, a shooting box in Scotland and a seat in the House of Lords.

He would have to live at Walden Hall. It was the family seat, and the Earl always lived there. He would put in electric light, he decided. He would sell some of the farms and invest in London property and North American railroads. He would make his maiden speech in the House of Lords—what would he speak on? Foreign policy, probably. There were tenants to be looked after, several households to be managed. He would have to appear in court in the season, and give shooting parties and hunt balls—

He needed a wife.

The role of Earl of Walden could not be played by a bachelor. Someone must be hostess at all those parties, someone must reply to invitations, discuss menus with cooks, allocate bedrooms to guests and sit at the foot of the long table in the dining room of Walden Hall. There must be a Countess of Walden.

There must be an heir.

"I need a wife, Pritchard."

"Yes, my lord. Our bachelor days are over."

The next day Walden saw Lydia's father and formally asked permission to call on her.

Twenty years later he found it difficult to imagine how he could have been so wickedly irresponsible, even in his youth. He had never asked himself whether she was the right wife for him, only whether she was good countess material. He had never wondered whether he could make her happy. He had assumed that the hidden passion released when she played the piano would be released for him, and he had been wrong.

He called on her every day for two weeks—there was no possibility of getting home in time for his father's funeral—and then he proposed, not to her but to her father. Her father saw the match in the same practical terms as Walden. Walden explained that he wanted to marry immediately, although he was in mourning, because he had to get home and manage the estate. Lydia's father understood perfectly. They were married six weeks later.

What an arrogant young fool I was, he thought. I imagined that England would always rule the world and I would always rule my own heart.

The moon came out from behind a cloud and illuminated the bedroom. He looked down at Lydia's sleeping face. I didn't foresee this, he thought; I didn't know that I would fall helplessly, hopelessly in love with you. I asked only that we should like each other, and in the end that was enough for you but not for me. I never thought that I would *need* your smile, yearn for your kisses, long for you to come to *my* room at night; I never thought that I would be frightened, *terrified* of losing you.

She murmured in her sleep and turned over. He pulled his arm from under her neck, then sat up on the edge of the bed. If he stayed any longer he would nod off, and it would not do to have Lydia's maid catch them in bed together when she came in with the morning cup of tea. He put on his dressing gown and his carpet slippers and walked softly out of the room, through the twin dressing rooms and into his own bedroom. I'm such a lucky man, he thought as he lay down to sleep.

◄§ ŝ►

Walden surveyed the breakfast table. There were pots of coffee, China tea and Indian tea; jugs of cream, milk and cordial; a big bowl of hot porridge; plates of scones and toast; and little pots of marmalade, honey and jam. On the sideboard was a row of silver dishes, each warmed by its own spirit lamp, containing scrambled eggs, sausages, bacon, kidneys and haddock. On the cold table were pressed beef, ham and tongue. The fruit bowl, on a table of its own, was piled with nectarines, oranges, melons and strawberries.

This ought to put Aleks in a good mood, he thought.

He helped himself to eggs and kidneys and sat down. The Russians would have their price, he thought; they would want something in return for their promise of military help. He was worried about what the price might be. If they were to ask for something England could not possibly grant, the whole deal would collapse immediately, and then . . .

It was his job to make sure it did not collapse.

He would have to manipulate Aleks. The thought made him uncomfortable. Having known the boy for so long should have been a help, but in fact it might have been easier to negotiate in a tough way with someone about whom one did not care personally.

I must put my feelings aside, he thought; we must have Russia.

He poured coffee and took some scones and honey. A minute later Aleks came in, looking bright-eyed and well-scrubbed. "Sleep well?" Walden asked him.

"Wonderfully well." Aleks took a nectarine and began to eat it with a knife and fork.

"Is that all you're having?" Walden said. "You used to love English breakfast—I remember you eating porridge, cream, eggs, beef and strawberries and then asking cook for more toast."

"I'm not a growing boy anymore, Uncle Stephen."

I might do well to remember that, Walden thought.

After breakfast they went into the morning room. "Our new five-year plan for the army and navy is about to be announced," Aleks said.

That's what he does, Walden thought; he tells you something before he asks you for something. He remembered Aleks saying: I'm planning to read Clausewitz this summer, Uncle. By the way, may I bring a guest to Scotland for the shooting?

"The budget for the next five years is seven and a half billion rubles," Aleks went on.

At ten rubles to the pound sterling, Walden calculated, that made £750 million. "It's a massive program," he said, "but I wish you had begun it five years ago."

"So do I," said Aleks.

"The chances are that the program will hardly have started before we're at war."

Aleks shrugged.

Walden thought: He won't commit himself to a forecast of how soon Russia might be at war, of course. "The first thing you should do is increase the size of the guns on your dreadnoughts."

Aleks shook his head. "Our third dreadnought is about to be launched. The fourth is being built now. Both will have twelve-inch guns."

"It's not enough, Aleks. Churchill has gone over to fifteen-inch guns for ours."

"And he's right. Our commanders know that, but our politicians don't. You know Russia, Uncle: new ideas are viewed with the utmost distrust. Innovation takes forever."

We're fencing, Walden thought. "What *is* your priority?"

"A hundred million rubles will be spent immediately on the Black Sea fleet."

"I should have thought the North Sea was more important." For England, anyway.

"We have a more Asian viewpoint than you—our bullying neighbor is Turkey, not Germany."

"They might be allies."

"They might indeed." Aleks hesitated. "The great weakness of the Russian Navy," he went on, "is that we have no warm-water port."

It sounded like the beginning of a prepared speech. This is it, Walden thought; we're getting to the heart of the matter now. But he continued to fence. "What about Odessa?"

"On the Black Sea coast. While the Turks hold Constantinople and Gallipoli, they control the passage between the Black Sea and the Mediterranean; so for strategic purposes the Black Sea might as well be an inland lake."

"Which is why the Russian Empire has been trying to push southward for hundreds of years."

"Why not? We're Slavs, and many of the Balkan peoples are Slavs. If they want national freedom, of course we sympathize."

"Indeed. Still, if they get it, they will probably let your navy pass freely into the Mediterranean."

"Slav control of the Balkans would help us. Russian control would help even more."

"No doubt—although it's not on the cards, as far as I can see."

"Would you like to give the matter some thought?"

Walden opened his mouth to speak, then closed it abruptly. This is it, he thought; this is what they want; this is the price. We can't give Russia the Balkans, for God's sake! If the deal depends on that, there will be no deal . . .

Aleks was saying: "If we are to fight alongside you, we must be strong. The area we are talking about is the area in which we need strengthening, so naturally we look to you for help there."

That was putting it as plainly as could be: Give us the Balkans and we'll fight with you.

Pulling himself together, Walden frowned as if puzzled and said: "If Britain had control of the Balkans, we could—at least in theory—give the area to you. But we can't give you what we haven't got, so I'm not sure how we can strengthen you—as you put it—in that area."

Aleks's reply was so quick that it must have been rehearsed. "But you might acknowledge the Balkans as a Russian sphere of influence."

Aah, that's not so bad, Walden thought. That we *might* be able to manage.

He was enormously relieved. He decided to test Aleks's determination before winding up the discussion. He said: "We could certainly agree to favor you over Austria or Turkey in that part of the world."

Aleks shook his head. "We want more than that," he said firmly.

It had been worth a try. Aleks was young and shy, but he could not be pushed around. Worse luck.

Walden needed time to reflect now. For Britain to do as Russia wanted would mean a significant shift in international alignments, and such shifts, like movements of the earth's crust, caused earthquakes in unexpected places.

"You may like to talk with Churchill before we go any farther," Aleks said with a little smile.

You know damn well I will, Walden thought. He realized suddenly how well Aleks had handled the whole thing. First he had scared Walden with a completely outrageous demand; then, when he put forward his real demand, Walden had been so relieved that he welcomed it.

I thought I was going to manipulate Aleks, but in the event he manipulated me.

Walden smiled. "I'm proud of you, my boy," he said.

ᥱᏻ ᏻᥲ

That morning Feliks figured out when, where and how he was going to kill Prince Orlov.

The plan began to take shape in his mind while he read *The Times* in the library of the Jubilee Street club. His imagination was sparked by a paragraph in the Court Circular column:

> *Prince Aleksey Andreyevich Orlov arrived from St. Petersburg yesterday. He is to be the guest of the Earl and Countess of Walden for the London Season. Prince Orlov will be presented to their Majesties the King and Queen at the Court on Thursday, June 4th.*

Now he knew for certain that Orlov would be at a certain place, on a certain date, at a certain time. Information of this kind was essential to a carefully planned assassination. Feliks had anticipated that he would get the information either by speaking to one of Walden's servants or by observing Orlov and identifying some habitual rendezvous. Now he had no need to take the risks involved in interviewing servants or trailing people. He wondered whether Orlov knew that his movements were being advertised by the newspapers, as if for the benefit of assassins. It was typically English, he thought.

The next problem was how to get sufficiently close to Orlov to kill him. Even Feliks would have difficulty getting into a royal palace. But this question also was answered by *The Times*. On the same page as the Court Circular, sandwiched between a report of a dance given by Lady Bailey and the details of the latest wills, he read:

THE KING'S COURT

ARRANGEMENTS FOR CARRIAGES

In order to facilitate the arrangements for calling the carriages of the company at their Majesties' Courts at Buckingham Palace, we are requested to state that in the case of the company having the privilege of the entree at the Pimlico entrance the coachman of each carriage returning to take up is required to leave with the constable stationed on the left of the gateway a card distinctly written with the name of the lady or gentleman to whom the carriage belongs, and in the case of the carriages of the general company returning to take up at the grand entrance a similar card should be handed to the constable stationed on the left of the archway leading to the Quadrangle of the Palace.

To enable the company to receive the advantage of the above arrangements, it is necessary that a footman should accompany each carriage, as no provision can be made for calling the carriages beyond giving the names to the footmen waiting at the door, with whom it rests to bring the carriage. The doors will be open for the reception of the company at 8.30 o'clock.

Feliks read it several times: there was something about the prose style of *The Times* that made it extremely difficult to comprehend. It seemed at least to mean that as people left the palace their footmen were sent running to fetch their carriages, which would be parked somewhere else.

There must be a way, he thought, that I can contrive to be in or on the Walden carriage when it returns to the palace to pick them up.

One major difficulty remained. He had no gun.

He could have got one easily enough in Geneva, but then to have carried it across international frontiers would have been risky: he might have been refused entry into England if his baggage had been searched.

It was surely just as easy to get a gun in London, but he did not know how, and he was most reluctant to make open inquiries. He had observed gun shops in the West End of London and noted that all the customers who went in and out looked thoroughly upper-class: Feliks would not get served in there even if he had the money to buy their beautifully made precision firearms. He had spent time in low-class pubs, where guns were surely bought and sold among criminals, but he had not seen it happen, which was hardly surprising. His only hope was the anarchists. He had got into conversation with those of them whom he thought "serious," but they never talked of weapons, doubtless because of Feliks's presence. The trouble was that he had not been around long enough to be trusted. There were always police spies in anarchist groups, and while this did not prevent the anarchists from welcoming newcomers, it made them wary.

Now the time for surreptitious investigation had run out. He would have to ask directly how guns were to be obtained. It would require careful handling. And immediately afterward he would have to sever his ties with Jubilee Street and move to another part of London, to avoid the risk of being traced.

He considered the young Jewish tearaways of Jubilee Street. They were angry and violent boys. Unlike their parents, they refused to work like slaves in the sweatshops of the East End, sewing the suits that the aristocracy ordered from Savile Row tailors. Unlike their parents, they paid no attention to the conservative sermonizing of the rabbis. But as yet they had not decided whether the solutions to their problems lay in politics or in crime.

His best prospect, he decided, was Nathan Sabelinsky. A man of about twenty, he had rather Slavic good looks, and wore very high stiff collars and a yellow waistcoat. Feliks had seen him around the spielers off the Commercial Road: he must have had money to spend on gambling as well as on clothes.

He looked around the library. The other occupants were an old man asleep, a woman in a heavy coat reading *Das Kapital* in German and making notes, and a Lithuanian Jew bent over a Russian newspaper, reading with the aid of a magnifying glass. Feliks left the room and went downstairs. There was no sign of Nathan or any of his friends. It was a little early for him: if he worked at all, Feliks thought, he worked at night.

Feliks went back to Dunstan Houses. He packed his razor, his clean underwear and his spare shirt in his cardboard suitcase. He told Milly, Rudolf Rocker's wife: "I've found a room. I'll come back this evening to say thank you to Rudolf." He strapped the suitcase to the back seat of the bicycle and rode west to central London, then north to Camden Town. Here he found a street of high, once-grand houses which had been built for pretentious middle-class families who had now moved to the suburbs at the ends of the new railway lines. In one of them Feliks rented a dingy room from an Irishwoman called Bridget. He paid her ten shillings in advance of two weeks' rent.

By midday he was back in Stepney, outside Nathan's home in Sidney Street. It was a small row house of the two-rooms-up-and-two-down type. The front door was wide open. Feliks walked in.

The noise and the smell hit him like a blow. There, in a room about twelve feet square, some fifteen or twenty people were working at tailoring. Men were using machines, women were sewing by hand and children were pressing finished garments. Steam rose from the ironing boards to mingle with the smell of sweat. The machines clattered, the irons hissed and the workers jabbered incessantly in Yiddish. Pieces of cloth cut ready for stitching were piled on every available patch of floor space. Nobody looked up at Feliks: they were all working furiously fast.

He spoke to the nearest person, a girl with a baby at her breast. She was hand-sewing buttons onto the sleeve of a jacket. "Is Nathan here?" he said.

"Upstairs," she said without pausing in her work.

Feliks went out of the room and up the narrow staircase. Each of the two small bedrooms had four beds. Most of them were occupied, presumably by people who worked at night. He found Nathan in the back room, sitting on the edge of a bed, buttoning his shirt.

Nathan saw him and said: "Feliks, *wie gehts*?"

"I need to talk to you," Feliks said in Yiddish.

"So talk."

"Come outside."

Nathan put on his coat and they went out into Sidney Street. They stood in the sunshine, close to the open window of the sweatshop, their conversation masked by the noise from inside.

"My father's trade," said Nathan. "He'll pay a girl fivepence for machining a pair of trousers—an hour's work for her. He'll pay another threepence to the girls who cut, press and sew on buttons. Then he will take the trousers to a West End tailor and get paid ninepence. Profit, one penny—enough to buy one slice of bread. If he asks the West End tailor for tenpence he'll be thrown out of the shop, and the work will be given to one of the dozens of Jewish tailors out in the street with their machines under their arms. I won't live like that."

"Is this why you're an anarchist?"

"Those people make the most beautiful clothes in the world —but did you see how *they* are dressed?"

"And how will things be changed—by violence?"

"I think so."

"I was sure you would feel this way. Nathan, I need a gun."

Nathan laughed nervously. "What for?"

"Why do anarchists usually want guns?"

"You tell me, Feliks."

"To steal from thieves, to oppress tyrants and to kill murderers."

"Which are you going to do?"

"I'll tell you—if you *really* want to know . . ."

Nathan thought for a moment, then said: "Go to the Frying Pan pub on the corner of Brick Lane and Thrawl Street. See Garfield the Dwarf."

"Thank you!" said Feliks, unable to keep the note of triumph out of his voice. "How much will I have to pay?"

"Five shillings for a pinfire."

"I'd rather have something more reliable."

"Good guns are expensive."

"I'll just have to haggle." Feliks shook Nathan's hand. "Thank you."

Nathan watched him climb on his bicycle. "Maybe you'll tell me about it, afterward."

Feliks smiled. "You'll read about it in the papers." He waved a hand and rode off.

He cycled along Whitechapel Road and Whitechapel High Street, then turned right into Osborn Street. Immediately, the character of the streets changed. This was the most run-down part of London he had yet seen. The streets were narrow and very dirty, the air smoky and noisome, the people mostly wretched. The gutters were choked with filth. But despite all that the place was as busy as a beehive. Men ran up and down with handcarts, crowds gathered around street stalls, prostitutes worked every corner and the workshops of carpenters and boot-makers spilled out onto the pavements.

Feliks left his bicycle outside the door of the Frying Pan: if it was taken he would just have to steal another one. To enter the pub he had to step over what looked like a dead cat. Inside was a single room, low and bare, with a bar at the far end. Older men and women sat on benches around the walls, while younger people stood in the middle of the room. Feliks went to the bar and asked for a glass of ale and a cold sausage.

He looked around and spotted Garfield the Dwarf. He had not seen him before because the man was standing on a chair. He was about four feet tall, with a large head and a middle-aged face. A very big black dog sat on the floor beside his chair. He was talking to two large, tough-looking men dressed in leather waistcoats and collarless shirts. Perhaps they were bodyguards. Feliks noted their large bellies and grinned to himself, thinking: I'll eat them up alive. The two men held quart pots of ale, but the dwarf was drinking what looked like gin. The barman handed Feliks his drink and his sausage. "And a glass of the best gin," Feliks said.

A young woman at the bar looked at him and said: "Is that for me?" She smiled coquettishly, showing rotten teeth. Feliks looked away.

When the gin came, he paid and walked over to the group,

who were standing near a small window which looked on to the street. Feliks stood between them and the door. He addressed the dwarf. "Mr. Garfield?"

"Who wants him?" said Garfield in a squeaky voice.

Feliks offered the glass of gin. "May I speak to you about business?"

Garfield took the glass, drained it, and said: "No."

Feliks sipped his ale. It was sweeter and less fizzy than Swiss beer. He said: "I wish to buy a gun."

"I don't know what you've come here for, then."

"I heard about you at the Jubilee Street club."

"Anarchist, are you?"

Feliks said nothing.

Garfield looked him up and down. "What kind of gun would you want, if I had any?"

"A revolver. A good one."

"Something like a Browning seven-shot?"

"That would be perfect."

"I haven't got one. If I had I wouldn't sell it. And if I sold it I'd have to ask five pounds."

"I was told a pound at the most."

"You was told wrong."

Feliks reflected. The dwarf had decided that, as a foreigner and an anarchist, Feliks could be rooked. All right, Feliks thought, we'll play it your way. "I can't afford more than two pounds."

"I couldn't come down below four."

"Would that include a box of ammunition?"

"All right, four pounds including a box of ammunition."

"Agreed," Feliks said. He noticed one of the bodyguards smothering a grin. After paying for the drinks and the sausage, Feliks had three pounds fifteen shillings and a penny.

Garfield nodded at one of his companions. The man went behind the bar and out through the back door. Feliks ate his sausage. A minute or two later the man came back carrying what looked like a bundle of rags. He glanced at Garfield, who nodded. The man handed the bundle to Feliks.

Feliks unfolded the rags and found a revolver and a small box. He took the gun from its wrappings and examined it.

Garfield said: "Keep it down; no need to show it to the whole bleeding world."

The gun was clean and oiled, and the action worked smoothly. Feliks said: "If I do not look at it, how do I know it is good?"

"Where do you think you are, Harrods?"

Feliks opened the box of cartridges and loaded the chambers with swift, practiced movements.

"Put the fucking thing away," the dwarf hissed. "Give me the money quick and fuck off out of it. You're fucking mad."

A bubble of tension rose in Feliks's throat and he swallowed dryly. He took a step back and pointed the gun at the dwarf.

Garfield said: "Jesus, Mary and Joseph."

"Shall I test the gun?" Feliks said.

The two bodyguards stepped sideways in opposite directions so that Feliks could not cover them both with the one gun. Feliks's heart sank: he had not expected them to be that smart. Their next move would be to jump him. The pub was suddenly silent. Feliks realized he could not get to the door before one of the bodyguards reached him. The big dog growled, sensing the tension in the air.

Feliks smiled and shot the dog.

The bang of the gun was deafening in the little room. Nobody moved. The dog slumped to the floor, bleeding. The dwarf's bodyguards were frozen where they stood.

Feliks took another step back, reached behind him and found the door. He opened it, still pointing the gun at Garfield, and stepped out.

He slammed the door, stuffed the gun in his coat pocket and jumped on his bicycle.

He heard the pub door open. He pushed himself off and began to pedal. Somebody grabbed his coat sleeve. He pedaled harder and broke free. He heard a shot, and ducked reflexively. Someone screamed. He dodged around an ice-cream vendor and turned a corner. In the distance he heard a police whistle. He looked behind. Nobody was following him.

Half a minute later he was lost in the warrens of Whitechapel.

He thought: Six bullets left.

◈

THREE

Charlotte was ready. The gown, agonized over for so long, was perfect. To complete it she wore a single blush rose in her corsage and carried a spray of the same flowers, covered in chiffon. Her diamond tiara was fixed firmly to her upswept hair, and the two white plumes were securely fastened. Everything was fine.

She was terrified.

"As I enter the Throne Room," she said to Marya, "my train will drop off, my tiara will fall over my eyes, my hair will come loose, my feathers will lean sideways, and I shall trip over the hem of my gown and go flat on the floor. The assembled company will burst out laughing, and no one will laugh louder than Her Majesty the Queen. I shall run out of the palace and into the park and throw myself into the lake."

"You ought not to talk like that," said Marya. Then, more gently, she added: "You'll be the loveliest of them all."

Charlotte's mother came into the bedroom. She held Charlotte at arm's length and looked at her. "My dear, you're beautiful," she said, and kissed her.

Charlotte put her arms around Mama's neck and pressed her

64

cheek against her mother's, the way she had used to as a child, when she had been fascinated by the velvet smoothness of Mama's complexion. When she drew away, she was surprised to see a hint of tears in her mother's eyes.

"You're beautiful too, Mama," she said.

Lydia's gown was of ivory charmeuse, with a train of old ivory brocade lined in purple chiffon. Being a married lady she wore three feathers in her hair as opposed to Charlotte's two. Her bouquet was sweet peas and petunia roses.

"Are you ready?" she said.

"I've been ready for ages," Charlotte said.

"Pick up your train."

Charlotte picked up her train the way she had been taught. Mama nodded approvingly. "Shall we go?"

Marya opened the door. Charlotte stood aside to let her mother go first, but Mama said: "No, dear—it's your night."

They walked in procession, Marya bringing up the rear, along the corridor and down to the landing. When Charlotte reached the top of the grand staircase she heard a burst of applause.

The whole household was gathered at the foot of the stairs: housekeeper, cook, footmen, maids, skivvies, grooms and boys. A sea of faces looked up at her with pride and delight. Charlotte was touched by their affection: it was a big night for them, too, she realized.

In the center of the throng was Papa, looking magnificent in a black velvet tailcoat, knee breeches and silk stockings, with a sword at his hip and a cocked hat in his hand.

Charlotte walked slowly down the stairs.

Papa kissed her and said: "My little girl."

The cook, who had known her long enough to take liberties, plucked at her sleeve and whispered: "You look wonderful, m'lady."

Charlotte squeezed her hand and said: "Thank you, Mrs. Harding."

Aleks bowed to her. He was resplendent in the uniform of an admiral in the Russian Navy. What a handsome man he is, Charlotte thought; I wonder whether someone will fall in love with him tonight.

Two footmen opened the front door. Papa took Charlotte's elbow and gently steered her out. Mama followed on Aleks's arm. Charlotte thought: If I can just keep my mind blank all evening, and go automatically wherever people lead me, I shall be all right.

The coach was waiting outside. William the coachman and Charles the footman stood at attention on either side of the door, wearing the Walden livery. William, stout and graying, was calm, but Charles looked excited. Papa handed Charlotte into the coach, and she sat down gratefully. I haven't fallen over yet, she thought.

The other three got in. Pritchard brought a hamper and put it on the floor of the coach before closing the door.

The coach pulled away.

Charlotte looked at the hamper. "A picnic?" she said. "But we're only going half a mile!"

"Wait till you see the queue," Papa said. "It will take us almost an hour to get there."

It occurred to Charlotte that she might be more bored than nervous this evening.

Sure enough, the carriage stopped at the Admiralty end of The Mall, half a mile from Buckingham Palace. Papa opened the hamper and took out a bottle of champagne. The basket also contained chicken sandwiches, hothouse peaches and a cake.

Charlotte sipped a glass of champagne but she could not eat anything. She looked out of the window. The pavements were thronged with idlers watching the procession of the mighty. She saw a tall man with a thin, handsome face leaning on a bicycle and staring intently at their coach. Something about his look made Charlotte shiver and turn away.

After such a grand exit from the house, she found that the anticlimax of sitting in the queue was calming. By the time the coach passed through the palace gates and approached the grand entrance she was beginning to feel more her normal self—skeptical, irreverent and impatient.

The coach stopped and the door was opened. Charlotte gathered her train in her left arm, picked up her skirts with her right hand, stepped down from the coach and walked into the palace.

The great red-carpeted hall was a blaze of light and color. Despite her skepticism she felt a thrill of excitement when she saw the crowd of white-gowned women and men in glittering uniforms. The diamonds flashed, the swords clanked and the plumes bobbed. Red-coated Beefeaters stood at attention on either side.

Charlotte and Mama left their wraps in the cloakroom, then, escorted by Papa and Aleks, walked slowly through the hall and up the grand staircase, between the Yeomen of the Guard with their halberds and the massed red and white roses. From there they went through the picture gallery and into the first of three state drawing rooms with enormous chandeliers and mirror-bright parquet floors. Here the procession ended and people stood around in groups, chatting and admiring one another's clothes. Charlotte saw her cousin Belinda with Uncle George and Aunt Clarissa. The two families greeted each other.

Uncle George was wearing the same clothes as Papa, but because he was so fat and red-faced he looked awful in them. Charlotte wondered how Aunt Clarissa, who was young and pretty, felt about being married to such a lump.

Papa was surveying the room as if looking for someone. "Have you seen Churchill?" he said to Uncle George.

"Good Lord, what do you want him for?"

Papa took out his watch. "We must take our places in the Throne Room—we'll leave you to look after Charlotte, if we may, Clarissa." Papa, Mama and Aleks left.

Belinda said to Charlotte: "Your dress is gorgeous."

"It's awfully uncomfortable."

"I *knew* you were going to say that!"

"You're ever so pretty."

"Thank you." Belinda lowered her voice. "I say, Prince Orlov is rather dashing."

"He's very sweet."

"I think he's more than *sweet.*"

"What's that funny look in your eye?"

Belinda lowered her voice even more. "You and I must have a long talk very soon."

"About what?"

"Remember what we discussed in the hideaway? When we took those books from the library at Walden Hall?"

Charlotte looked at her uncle and aunt, but they had turned away to talk to a dark-skinned man in a pink satin turban. "Of course I remember."

"About that."

Silence descended suddenly. The crowd fell back toward the sides of the room to make a gangway in the middle. Charlotte looked around and saw the King and Queen enter the drawing room, followed by their pages, several members of the Royal Family and the Indian bodyguard.

There was a great sigh of rustling silk as every woman in the room sank to the floor in a curtsy.

In the Throne Room, the orchestra concealed in the Minstrels' Gallery struck up "God Save the King." Lydia looked toward the huge doorway guarded by gilt giants. Two attendants walked in backward, one carrying a gold stick and one a silver. The King and Queen entered at a stately pace, smiling faintly. They mounted the dais and stood in front of the twin thrones. The rest of their entourage took their places nearby, remaining standing.

Queen Mary wore a gown of gold brocade and a crown of emeralds. She's no beauty, Lydia thought, but they say he adores her. She had once been engaged to her husband's elder brother, who had died of pneumonia, and the switch to the new heir to the throne had seemed coldly political at the time. However, everyone now agreed that she was a good queen and a good wife. Lydia would have liked to know her personally.

The presentations began. One by one the wives of ambassadors came forward, curtsied to the King, curtsied to the Queen, then backed away. The ambassadors followed, dressed in a great variety of gaudy comic-opera uniforms, all but the United States ambassador who wore ordinary black evening clothes, as if to remind everyone that Americans did not really believe in this sort of nonsense.

As the ritual went on, Lydia looked around the room, at the crimson satin on the walls, the heroic frieze below the ceiling, the enormous candelabra and the thousands of flowers. She loved pomp and ritual, beautiful clothes and elaborate ceremonies; they moved and soothed her at the same time. She caught the eye of the Duchess of Devonshire, who was the Queen's Mistress of the Robes, and they exchanged a discreet smile. She spotted John Burns, the socialist President of the Board of

Trade, and was amused to see the extravagant gilt embroidery on his court dress.

When the diplomatic presentations ended, the King and Queen sat down. The Royal Family, the diplomats and the most senior nobility followed suit. Lydia and Walden, along with the lesser nobility, had to remain standing.

At last the presentation of the debutantes began. Each girl paused just outside the Throne Room while an attendant took her train from her arm and spread it behind her. Then she began the endless walk along the red carpet to the thrones, with all eyes on her. If a girl could look graceful and unselfconscious there, she could do it anywhere.

As the debutante approached the dais she handed her invitation card to the Lord Chamberlain, who read out her name. She curtsied to the King, then to the Queen. Few girls curtsied elegantly, Lydia thought. She had had a great deal of trouble getting Charlotte to practice at all: perhaps other mothers had the same problem. After the curtsies the deb walked on, careful not to turn her back on the thrones until she was safely hidden in the watching crowd.

The girls followed one another so closely that each was in danger of treading on the train of the one in front. The ceremony seemed to Lydia to be less personal, more perfunctory than it had used to be. She herself had been presented to Queen Victoria in the season of 1896, the year after she married Walden. The old Queen had not sat on a throne, but on a high stool which gave the impression that she was standing. Lydia had been surprised at how little Victoria was. She had had to kiss the Queen's hand. That part of the ceremony had now been dispensed with, presumably to save time. It made the court seem like a factory for turning out the maximum number of debs in the shortest possible time. Still, the girls of today did not know the difference and probably would not care if they did.

Suddenly Charlotte was at the entrance, and the attendant was laying down her train, then giving her a gentle push, and she was walking along the red carpet, head held high, looking perfectly serene and confident. Lydia thought: This is the moment I have lived for.

The girl ahead of Charlotte curtsied—and then the unthinkable happened.

Instead of getting up from her curtsy, the debutante looked at the King, stretched out her arms in a gesture of supplication, and cried in a loud voice:

"*Your Majesty, for God's sake stop torturing women!*"

Lydia thought: A suffragette!

Her eyes flashed to her daughter. Charlotte was standing dead still, halfway to the dais, staring at the tableau with an expression of horror on her ashen face.

The shocked silence in the Throne Room lasted for only a second. Two gentlemen-in-waiting were the fastest to react. They sprang forward, took the girl firmly by either arm and marched her unceremoniously away.

The Queen was blushing crimson. The King managed to look as if nothing had happened. Lydia looked again at Charlotte, thinking: Why did my daughter have to be next in line?

Now all eyes were on Charlotte. Lydia wanted to call out to her: Pretend it never happened! Just carry on!

Charlotte stood still. A little color came back into her cheeks. Lydia could see that she was taking a deep breath.

Then she walked forward. Lydia could not breathe. Charlotte handed her card to the Lord Chamberlain, who said: "Presentation of Lady Charlotte Walden." Charlotte stood before the King.

Lydia thought: Careful!

Charlotte curtsied perfectly.

She curtsied again to the Queen.

She half turned, and walked away.

Lydia let out her breath in a long sigh.

The woman standing next to Lydia—a baroness whom she vaguely recognized but did not really know—whispered: "She handled that very well."

"She's my daughter," Lydia said with a smile.

Walden was secretly amused by the suffragette. Spirited girl! he thought. Of course, if *Charlotte* had done such a thing at the court he would have been horrified, but as it was someone else's daughter he regarded the incident as a welcome break in the interminable ceremony. He had noticed how Charlotte had carried on, unruffled: he would have expected no less of her. She was a highly self-assured young lady, and in his opinion Lydia should congratulate herself on the girl's upbringing instead of worrying all the time.

He had used to enjoy these occasions, years ago. As a young man he had quite liked to put on court dress and cut a dash. In those days he had had the legs for it, too. Now he felt foolish in knee breeches and silk stockings, not to mention a damn great steel sword. And he had attended so many courts that the colorful ritual no longer fascinated him.

He wondered how King George felt about it. Walden liked the King. Of course, by comparison with his father Edward VII, George was a rather colorless, mild fellow. The crowds would never shout "Good old Georgie!" the way they had shouted "Good old Teddy!" But in the end they would like George for his quiet charm and his modest way of life. He knew how to be firm, although as yet he did it too rarely; and Walden liked a man who could shoot straight. Walden thought he would turn out very well indeed.

Finally the last debutante curtsied and passed on, and the King and Queen stood up. The orchestra played the national anthem again. The King bowed, and the Queen curtsied, first to the ambassadors, then to the ambassadors' wives, then to the duchesses, and lastly to the ministers. The King took the Queen by the hand. The pages picked up her train. The attendants went out backward. The royal couple left, followed by the rest of the company in order of precedence.

They divided to go into three supper rooms: one for the royal family and their close friends, one for the diplomatic corps and one for the rest. Walden was a friend, but not an intimate friend, of the King: he went with the general assembly. Aleks went with the diplomats.

In the supper room Walden met up with his family again. Lydia was glowing. Walden said: "Congratulations, Charlotte."

Lydia said: "Who was that awful girl?"

"I heard someone say she's the daughter of an architect,' Walden replied.

"That explains it," said Lydia.

Charlotte looked mystified. "Why does that explain it?"

Walden smiled. "Your Mama means that the girl is not quite out of the top drawer."

"But why does she think the King tortures women?"

"She was talking about the suffragettes. But let's not go into all that tonight; this is a grand occasion for us. Let's have supper. It looks marvelous."

There was a long buffet table loaded with flowers and hot and cold food. Servants in the scarlet-and-gold royal livery waited to offer the guests lobster, filleted trout, quail, York ham, plovers' eggs and a host of pastries and desserts. Walden got a loaded plate and sat down to eat. After standing about in the Throne Room for more than two hours he was hungry.

Sooner or later Charlotte would have to learn about the suffragettes, their hunger strikes, and the consequent force-feeding; but the subject was indelicate, to say the least, and the longer she remained in blissful ignorance the better, Walden thought. At her age life should be all parties and picnics, frocks and hats, gossip and flirtation.

But everyone was talking about "the incident" and "that girl." Walden's brother, George, sat beside him and said without preamble: "She's a Miss Mary Blomfield, daughter of the late Sir Arthur Blomfield. Her mother was in the drawing room at the time. When she was told what her daughter had done she fainted right off." He seemed to relish the scandal.

"Only thing she could do, I suppose," Walden replied.

"Damn shame for the family," George said. "You won't see Blomfields at court again for two or three generations."

"We shan't miss them."

"No."

Walden saw Churchill pushing through the crowd toward where they sat. He had written to Churchill about his talk with Aleks, and he was impatient to discuss the next step—but not *here*. He looked away, hoping Churchill would get the hint. He should have known better than to hope that such a subtle message would get through.

Churchill bent over Walden's chair. "Can we have a few words together?"

Walden looked at his brother. George wore an expression of horror. Walden threw him a resigned look and got up.

"Let's walk in the picture gallery," Churchill said.

Walden followed him out.

Churchill said: "I suppose you, too, will tell me that this suffragette protest is all the fault of the Liberal party."

"I expect it is," Walden said. "But that isn't what you want to talk about."

"No indeed."

The two men walked side by side through the long gallery. Churchill said: "We can't acknowledge the Balkans as a Russian sphere of influence."

"I was afraid you'd say that."

"What do they want the Balkans *for*? I mean, forgetting all this nonsense about sympathy with Slav nationalism."

"They want passage through to the Mediterranean."

"That would be to our advantage, if they were our allies."

"Exactly."

They reached the end of the gallery and stopped. Churchill said: "Is there some way we can give them that passage without redrawing the map of the Balkan Peninsula?"

"I've been thinking about that."

Churchill smiled. "And you've got a counterproposal."

"Yes."

"Let's hear it."

Walden said, "What we're talking about here is three stretches of water: the Bosphorus, the Sea of Marmara and the Dardanelles. If we can give them those waterways, they won't need the Balkans. Now, suppose that whole passage between the Black Sea and the Mediterranean could be declared an international waterway, with free passage to ships of all nations guaranteed jointly by Russia and England."

Churchill started walking again, slow and thoughtful. Walden walked beside him, waiting for his answer.

Eventually Churchill said: "That passage *ought* to be an international waterway, in any event. What you're suggesting is that we offer, as if it were a concession, something which we want anyway."

"Yes."

Churchill looked up and grinned suddenly. "When it comes to Machiavellian maneuvering, there's no one to beat the English aristocracy. All right. Go ahead and propose it to Orlov."

"You don't want to put it to the Cabinet?"

"No."

"Not even to the Foreign Secretary?"

"Not at this stage. The Russians are certain to want to modify the proposal—they'll want details of how the guarantee is to be enforced, at least—so I'll go to the Cabinet when the deal is fully elaborated."

"Very well." Walden wondered just how much the Cabinet knew about what Churchill and he were up to. Churchill, too, could be Machiavellian. Were there wheels within wheels?

Churchill said: "Where is Orlov now?"

"In the diplomatic supper room."

"Let's go and put it to him right away."

Walden shook his head, thinking that people were right when they accused Churchill of being impulsive. "This is not the moment."

"We can't wait for the moment, Walden. Every day counts."

It will take a bigger man than you to bully me, Walden thought. He said: "You're going to have to leave that to my judgment, Churchill. I'll put this to Orlov tomorrow morning."

Churchill seemed disposed to argue, but he restrained himself visibly and said: "I don't suppose Germany will declare war tonight. Very well." He looked at his watch. "I'm going to leave. Keep me fully informed."

"Of course. Good-bye."

Churchill went down the staircase and Walden went back into the supper room. The party was breaking up. Now that the King and Queen had disappeared and everyone had been fed there was nothing to stay for. Walden rounded up his family and took them downstairs. They met up with Aleks in the great hall.

While the ladies went into the cloakroom Walden asked one of the attendants to summon his carriage.

All in all, he thought as he waited, it had been a rather successful evening.

◆§ ۶◆

The Mall reminded Feliks of the streets in the Old Equerries Quarter of Moscow. It was a wide, straight avenue that ran from Trafalgar Square to Buckingham Palace. On one side was a series of grand houses including St. James's Palace. On the other side was St. James's Park. The carriages and motor cars of the great were lined up on both sides of The Mall for half its length. Chauffeurs and coachmen leaned against their vehicles, yawning and fidgeting, waiting to be summoned to the palace to collect their masters and mistresses.

The Walden carriage waited on the park side of The Mall. Their coachman, in the blue-and-pink Walden livery, stood beside the horses, reading a newspaper by the light of a carriage lamp. A few yards away, in the darkness of the park, Feliks stood watching him.

Feliks was desperate. His plan was in ruins.

He had not understood the difference between the English words "coachman" and "footman" and consequently he had misunderstood the notice in *The Times* about summoning carriages. He had thought that the driver of the coach would wait at the palace gate until his master emerged, then would come running to fetch the coach. At that point, Feliks had planned, he would have overpowered the coachman, taken his livery and driven the coach to the palace himself.

What happened in fact was that the coachman stayed with the vehicle and the footman waited at the palace gate. When the coach was wanted, the footman would come running, then he and the coachman would go with the carriage to pick up the passengers. That meant Feliks had to overpower two people, not one; and the difficulty was that it had to be done surreptitiously, so that none of the hundreds of other servants in The Mall would know anything was wrong.

Since realizing his mistake a couple of hours ago he had worried at the problem, while he watched the coachman chatting with his colleagues, examining a nearby Rolls-Royce car, playing some kind of game with halfpennies and polishing the carriage windows. It might have been sensible to abandon the plan and kill Orlov another day.

But Feliks hated that idea. For one thing, there was no certainty that another good opportunity would arise. For another, Feliks wanted to kill him now. He had been anticipating the bang of the gun, the way the prince would fall; he had composed the coded cable which would go to Ulrich in Geneva; he had pictured the excitement in the little printing shop, and then the headlines in the world's newspapers, and then the final wave of revolution sweeping through Russia. I can't postpone this any longer, he thought; I want it now.

As he watched, a young man in green livery approached the Walden coachman and said: "What ho, William."

So the coachman's name is William, Feliks thought.

William said: "Mustn't grumble, John."

Feliks did not understand that.

"Anything in the news?" said John.

"Yeah, revolution. The King says that next year all the coachmen can go in the palace for supper and the toffs will wait in The Mall."

"A likely tale."

"You're telling me."

John moved on.

I can get rid of William, Feliks thought, but what about the footman?

In his mind he ran over the probable sequence of events. Walden and Orlov would come to the palace door. The doorman would alert Walden's footman, who would run from the palace to the carriage—a distance of about a quarter of a mile. The footman would see Feliks dressed in the coachman's clothes, and would sound the alarm.

Suppose the footman arrived at the parking place to find that the carriage was no longer there?

That was a thought!

The footman would wonder whether he had misremembered the spot. He would look up and down. In something of a panic he would search for the coach. Finally he would admit defeat and return to the palace to tell his master that he could not find the coach. By which time Feliks would be driving the coach and its owner through the park.

It could still be done!

It was more risky than before, but it could still be done.

There was no more time for reflection. The first two or three footmen were already running down The Mall. The Rolls-Royce car in front of the Walden coach was summoned. William put on his top hat in readiness.

Felix emerged from the bushes and walked a little way toward him, calling: "Hey! Hey, William!"

The coachman looked toward him, frowning.

Feliks beckoned urgently. "Come here, quick!"

William folded his newspaper, hesitated, then walked slowly toward Feliks.

Feliks allowed his own tension to put a note of panic into his voice. "Look at this!" he said, pointing to the bushes. "Do you know anything about this?"

"What?" William said, mystified. He drew level and peered the way Feliks was pointing.

"This." Feliks showed him the gun. "If you make a noise I'll shoot you."

William was terrified. Feliks could see the whites of his eyes in the half dark. He was a heavily built man, but he was older than Feliks. *If he does something foolish and messes this up I'll kill him,* Feliks thought savagely.

"Walk on," Feliks said.

The man hesitated.

I've got to get him out of the light. "Walk, you bastard!"

William walked into the bushes.

Feliks followed him. When they were about fifty yards away from The Mall Feliks said: "Stop."

William stopped and turned around.

Feliks thought: *If he's going to fight, this is where he will do it.* He said: "Take off your clothes."

"What?"

"Undress!"

"You're mad," William whispered.

"You're right—I'm mad! Take off your clothes!"

William hesitated.

If I shoot him, will people come running? Will the bushes muffle the sound? Could I kill him without making a hole in his uniform? Could I take his coat off and run away before anyone arrived?

Feliks cocked the gun.

William began to undress.

Feliks could hear the increasing activity in The Mall: motor cars were started, harnesses jingled, hooves clattered and men shouted to one another and to their horses. Any minute now the footman might come running for the Walden coach. "Faster!" Feliks said.

William got down to his underwear.

"The rest also," Feliks said.

William hesitated. Feliks lifted the gun.

William pulled off his undershirt, dropped his underpants, and stood naked, shivering with fear, covering his genitals with his hands.

"Turn around," said Feliks.

William turned his back.

"Lie on the ground, face down."

He did so.

Feliks put down the gun. Hurriedly, he took off his coat and hat and put on the livery coat and the top hat which William had dropped on the ground. He contemplated the knee breeches and white stockings but decided to leave them: when he was sitting up on the coach no one would notice his trousers and boots, especially in the uncertain light of the street lamps.

He put the gun into the pocket of his own coat and folded the coat over his arm. He picked up William's clothes in a bundle.

William tried to look around.

"Don't move!" Feliks said sharply.

Softly, he walked away.

William would stay there for a while, then, naked as he was, he would try to get back to the Walden house unobserved. It was highly unlikely that he would report that he had been robbed of his clothes before he had a chance to get some more, unless he was an extraordinarily immodest man. Of course if he had known Feliks was going to kill Prince Orlov he might have thrown modesty to the winds—but how could he possibly guess that?

Feliks pushed William's clothes under a bush, then walked out into the lights of The Mall.

This was where things might go wrong. Until now he had been merely a suspicious person lurking in the bushes. From this moment on he was plainly an impostor. If one of William's friends—John, for instance—should look closely at his face, the game would be up.

He climbed rapidly onto the coach, put his own coat on the seat beside him, adjusted his top hat, released the brake and flicked the reins. The coach pulled out into the road.

He sighed with relief. I've got this far, he thought; I'll get Orlov!

As he drove down The Mall he watched the pavements, looking for a running footman in the blue-and-pink livery. The worst possible mischance would be for the Walden footman to see him now, recognize the colors, and jump onto the back of the coach. Feliks cursed as a motor car pulled out in front of him, forcing him to slow the horses to a halt. He looked around anxiously. There was no sign of the footman. After a moment the road was clear and he went on.

At the palace end of the avenue he spotted an empty space on the right, the side of the road farther from the park. The footman would come along the opposite pavement and would not see the coach. He pulled into the space and set the brake.

He climbed down from the seat and stood behind the horses, watching the opposite pavement. He wondered whether he would get out of this alive.

In his original plan there had been a good chance that Walden would get into the carriage without so much as a glance at the coachman, but now he would surely notice that his footman was missing. The palace doorman would have to open the coach door and pull down the steps. Would Walden stop and speak to the coachman, or would he postpone inquiries until he got home? If he were to speak to Feliks, then Feliks would have to reply and his voice would give the game away. What will I do then? Feliks thought.

I'll shoot Orlov at the palace door and take the consequences.

He saw the footman in blue-and-pink running along the far side of The Mall.

Feliks jumped on to the coach, released the brake and drove into the courtyard of Buckingham Palace.

There was a queue. Ahead of him, the beautiful women and the well-fed men climbed into their carriages and cars. Behind him, somewhere in The Mall, the Walden footman was running up and down, hunting for his coach. How long before he returned?

The palace servants had a fast and efficient system for loading guests into vehicles. While the passengers were getting into the carriage at the door, a servant was calling the owners of the second in line, and another servant was inquiring the name of the people for the third.

The line moved, and a servant approached Feliks. "The Earl of Walden," Feliks said. The servant went inside.

They mustn't come out too soon, Feliks thought.

The line moved forward, and now there was only a motor car in front of him. Pray God it doesn't stall, he thought. The chauffeur held the doors for an elderly couple. The car pulled away.

Feliks moved the coach to the porch, halting it a little too far forward, so that he was beyond the wash of light from inside, and his back was to the palace doors.

He waited, not daring to look around.

He heard the voice of a young girl say, in Russian: "And how many ladies proposed marriage to you this evening, Cousin Aleks?"

A drop of sweat ran down into Feliks's eye, and he wiped it away with the back of his hand.

A man said: "Where the devil is my footman?"

Feliks reached into the pocket of the coat beside him and got his hand on the butt of the revolver. Six shots left, he thought.

Out of the corner of his eye he saw a palace servant spring forward, and a moment later he heard the door of the coach being opened. The vehicle rocked slightly as someone got in.

"I say, William, where's Charles?"

Feliks tensed. He imagined he could feel Walden's eyes boring into the back of his head. The girl's voice said: "Come on, Papa," from inside the carriage.

"William's getting deaf in his old age . . ." Walden's words were muffled as he got into the coach. The door slammed.

"Right away, coachman!" said the palace servant.

Feliks breathed out, and drove away.

The release of tension made him feel weak for a moment. Then, as he guided the carriage out of the courtyard, he felt a surge of elation. Orlov was in his power, shut in a box behind him, caught like an animal in a trap. Nothing could stop Feliks now.

He drove into the park.

Holding the reins in his right hand, he struggled to get his left arm into his topcoat. That done, he switched the reins to his left hand and got his right arm in. He stood up and shrugged the coat up over his shoulders. He felt in the pocket and touched the gun.

He sat down again and wound a scarf around his neck.

He was ready.

Now he had to choose his moment.

He had only a few minutes. The Walden house was less than a mile from the palace. He had bicycled along this road the night before, to reconnoiter. He had found two suitable places, where a street lamp would illuminate his victim and there was thick shrubbery nearby into which he could disappear afterward.

The first spot loomed up fifty yards ahead. As he approached it he saw a man in evening dress pause beneath the lamp to light his cigar. He drove past the spot.

The second place was a bend in the road. If there was someone there, Feliks would just have to take a chance, and shoot the intruder if necessary.

Six bullets.

He saw the bend. He made the horses trot a little faster. From inside the coach he heard the young girl laugh.

He came to the bend. His nerves were as taut as piano wire. *Now.*

He dropped the reins and heaved on the brake. The horses staggered and the carriage shuddered and jerked to a halt.

From inside the coach he heard a woman cry and a man shout. Something about the woman's voice bothered him, but there was no time to wonder why. He jumped down to the ground, pulled the scarf up over his mouth and nose, took the gun from his pocket and cocked it.

Full of strength and rage, he flung open the coach door.

<hr />

FOUR

A woman cried out, and time stood still.

Feliks knew the voice. The sound hit him like a mighty blow. The shock paralyzed him.

He was supposed to locate Orlov, point the gun at him, pull the trigger, make sure he was dead with another bullet, then turn and run into the bushes . . .

Instead he looked for the source of the cry, and saw her face. It was startlingly familiar, as if he had last seen it only yesterday, instead of nineteen years ago. Her eyes were wide with panic and her small red mouth was open.

Lydia.

He stood at the door of the coach with his mouth open under the scarf, the gun pointing nowhere, and he thought: My Lydia —here in *this carriage* . . .

As he stared at her he was dimly aware that Walden was moving, with uncanny slowness, close by him on his left; but all Feliks could think was: This is how she used to look, wide-eyed and open-mouthed, when she lay naked beneath me, her legs wrapped around my waist, and she stared at me and began to cry out with delight . . .

Then he saw that Walden had drawn a sword—
For God's sake, a *sword*?
—and the blade was glinting in the lamplight as it swept down, and Feliks moved too slowly and too late, and the sword bit into his right hand, and he dropped the gun and it went off with a bang as it hit the road.

The explosion broke the spell.

Walden drew back the sword and thrust at Feliks's heart. Feliks moved sideways. The point of the sword went through his coat and jacket and stuck into his shoulder. He jumped back reflexively and the sword came out. He felt a rush of warm blood inside his shirt.

He stared down at the road, looking for the gun, but he could not see it. He looked up again, and saw that Walden and Orlov had bumped into one another as they tried simultaneously to get out through the narrow carriage door. Feliks's right arm hung limply at his side. He realized he was unarmed and helpless. He could not even strangle Orlov, for his right arm was useless. He had failed utterly, and all because of the voice of a woman from the past.

After all that, he thought bitterly; after all that.

Full of despair, he turned and ran away.

Walden roared: "Damned villain!"

Feliks's wound hurt at every step. He heard someone running behind him. The footsteps were too light to be Walden's: Orlov was chasing him. He teetered on the edge of hysteria as he thought: Orlov is chasing *me*—and I am running away!

He darted off the road and into the bushes. He heard Walden shout: "Aleks, come back, he's got a gun!" They don't know I dropped it, Feliks thought. If only I still had it I could shoot Orlov now.

He ran a little way farther, then stopped, listening. He could hear nothing. Orlov had given up.

He leaned against a tree. He was exhausted by his short sprint. When he had caught his breath he took off his topcoat and the stolen livery coat and gingerly touched his wounds. They hurt like the devil, which he thought was probably a good sign, for if they had been very grave they would have been numb. His shoulder bled slowly, and throbbed. His hand had been sliced in the fleshy part between thumb and forefinger, and it bled fast.

He had to get out of the park before Walden had a chance to raise the hue and cry.

With difficulty he drew on the topcoat. He left the livery coat on the ground where it lay. He squeezed his right hand under his left armpit, to relieve the pain and slow the flow of blood. Wearily, he headed toward The Mall.

Lydia.

It was the second time in his life that she had caused a catastrophe. The first time, in 1895, in St. Petersburg—

No. He would not allow himself to think about her, not yet. He needed his wits about him now.

He saw with relief that his bicycle was where he had left it, under the overhanging branches of a big tree. He wheeled it across the grass to the edge of the park. Had Walden alerted the police yet? Were they looking for a tall man in a dark coat? He stared at the scene in The Mall. The footmen were still running, the car engines roaring, the carriages maneuvering. How long had it been since Feliks had climbed up onto the Walden coach —twenty minutes? In that time the world had turned over.

He took a deep breath and wheeled the bicycle into the road. Everyone was busy, nobody looked at him. Keeping his right hand in his coat pocket, he mounted the machine. He pushed off and began to pedal, steering with his left hand.

There were bobbies all around the palace. If Walden mobilized them quickly they could cordon off the park and the roads around it. Feliks looked ahead, toward Admiralty Arch. There was no sign of a roadblock.

Once past the arch he would be in the West End and they would have lost him.

He began to get the knack of cycling one-handed, and increased his speed.

As he approached the arch a motor car drew alongside him and, at the same time, a policeman stepped into the road ahead. Feliks stopped the bicycle and prepared to run—but the policeman was merely holding up the traffic to permit another car, belonging presumably to some kind of dignitary, to emerge from a gateway. When the car came out the policeman saluted, then waved the traffic on.

Feliks cycled through the arch and into Trafalgar Square.

Too slow, Walden, he thought with satisfaction.

It was midnight, but the West End was bright with street lights and crowded with people and traffic. There were policemen everywhere and no other cyclists: Feliks was conspicuous. He considered abandoning the bicycle and walking back to Camden Town, but he was not sure he could make the journey on foot: he seemed to be tiring very easily.

From Trafalgar Square he rode up St. Martin's Lane, then left the main streets for the back alleys of Theatreland. A dark lane was suddenly illuminated as a stage door opened and a bunch of actors came out, talking loudly and laughing. Farther on he heard groans and sighs, and passed a couple making love standing up in a doorway.

He crossed into Bloomsbury. Here it was quieter and darker. He cycled north up Gower Street, past the classical facade of the deserted university. Pushing the pedals became an enormous effort, and he ached all over. Just a mile or two more, he thought.

He dismounted to cross the busy Euston Road. The lights of the traffic dazzled him. He seemed to be having difficulty focusing his eyes.

Outside Euston Station he got on the bicycle again and pedaled off. Suddenly he felt dizzy. A street light blinded him. The front wheel wobbled and hit the curb. Feliks fell.

He lay on the ground, dazed and weak. He opened his eyes and saw a policeman approaching. He struggled to his knees.

"Have you been drinkin'?" the policeman said.

"Feel faint," Feliks managed.

The policeman took his right arm and hauled him to his feet. The pain in his wounded shoulder brought Feliks to his senses. He managed to keep his bleeding right hand in his pocket.

The policeman sniffed audibly and said: "Hmm." His attitude became more genial when he discovered that Feliks did not smell of drink. "Will you be all right?"

"In a minute."

"Foreigner, are you?"

The policeman had noticed his accent. "French," Feliks said. "I work at the embassy."

The policeman became more polite. "Would you like a cab?"

"No, thank you. I have only a little way to go."

The policeman picked up the bicycle. "I should wheel it home if I were you."

Feliks took the bicycle from him. "I will do that."

"Very good, sir. Bong noo-wee."

"*Bonne nuit,* officer." With an effort Feliks produced a smile. Pushing the bicycle with his left hand, he walked away. I'll turn into the next alley and sit down for a rest, he resolved. He looked back over his shoulder: the policeman was still watching him. He made himself keep on walking, although he desperately needed to lie down. The next alley, he thought. But when he came to an alley he passed it, thinking: Not this one, but the next.

And in that way he got home.

It seemed hours later that he stood outside the high terraced house in Camden Town. He peered through a fog at the number on the door to make sure this was the right place.

To get to his room he had to go down a flight of stone steps to the basement area. He leaned the bicycle against the wrought-iron railings while he opened the little gate. He then made the mistake of trying to wheel the bicycle down the steps. It slid out of his grasp and fell into the area with a loud clatter. A moment later his landlady, Bridget, appeared at the street door in a shawl.

"What the divil is it?" she called.

Feliks sat on the steps and made no reply. He decided he would not move for a while, until he felt stronger.

Bridget came down and helped him to his feet. "You've had a few too many drinks," she said. She made him walk down the steps to the basement door.

"Give us your key," she said.

Feliks had to use his left hand to take the key from his right trouser pocket. He gave it to her and she opened the door. They went in. Feliks stood in the middle of the little room while she lit the lamp.

"Let's have your coat off," she said.

He let her remove his coat, and she saw the bloodstains. "Have you been fightin'?"

Feliks went and lay on the mattress.

Bridget said: "You look as if you lost!"

"I did," said Feliks, and he passed out.

An agonizing pain brought him around. He opened his eyes to see Bridget bathing his wounds with something that stung like fire. "This hand should be stitched," she said.

"Tomorrow," Feliks breathed.

She made him drink from a cup. It was warm water with gin in it. She said: "I haven't any brandy."

He lay back and let her bandage him.

"I could fetch the doctor but I couldn't be payin' him."

"Tomorrow."

She stood up. "I'll look at you first thing in the morning."

"Thank you."

She went out, and at last Feliks allowed himself to remember.

It has happened in the long run of ages that everything which permits men to increase their production, or even to continue it, has been appropriated by the few. The land belongs to the few, who may prevent the community from cultivating it. The coal-pits, which represent the labour of generations, belong again to the few. The lace-weaving machine, which represents, in its present state of perfection, the work of three generations of Lancashire weavers, belongs also to the few; and if the grandsons of the very same weaver who invented the first lace-weaving machine claim their right to bring one of these machines into motion, they will be told: "Hands off! This machine does not belong to you!" The railroads belong to a few shareholders, who may not even know where is situated the railway which brings them a yearly income larger than that of a medieval king. And if the children of those people who died by the thousands in digging the tunnels should gather and go—a ragged and starving crowd—to ask bread or work from the shareholders, they would be met with bayonets and bullets.

Feliks looked up from Kropotkin's pamphlet. The bookshop was empty. The bookseller was an old revolutionist who made his money selling novels to wealthy women and kept a hoard of subversive literature in the back of the shop. Feliks spent a lot of time in here.

He was nineteen. He was about to be thrown out of the prestigious Spiritual Academy for truancy, indiscipline, long hair and associating with Nihilists. He was hungry and broke, and soon he would be homeless, and life was wonderful. He cared about nothing other than ideas, and he was learning every day new things about poetry, history, psychology and—most of all—politics.

Laws on property are not made to guarantee either to the individual or to society the enjoyment of the produce of their own labour. On the contrary, they are made to rob the producer of a part of what he has created. When, for example, the law establishes Mr. So-and-so's right to a house, it is not establishing his right to a cottage he has built for himself, or to a house he has erected with the help of some of his friends. In that case no one would have disputed his right! On the contrary, the law is establishing his right to a house which is not the product of his labour.

The anarchist slogans had sounded ridiculous when he had first heard them: Property is theft, Government is tyranny, Anarchy is justice. It was astonishing how, when he had really thought about them, they came to seem not only true but crashingly obvious. Kropotkin's point about laws was undeniable. No laws were required to prevent theft in Feliks's home village: if one peasant stole another's horse, or his chair, or the coat his wife had embroidered, then the whole village would see the culprit in possession of the goods and make him give them back. The only stealing that went on was when the landlord demanded rent; and the policeman was there to *enforce* that theft. It was the same with government. The peasants needed no one to tell them how the plow and the oxen were to be shared between their fields: they decided among themselves. It was only the plowing of the landlord's fields that had to be enforced.

We are continually told of the benefits conferred by laws and penalties, but have the speakers ever attempted to balance the benefits attributed to laws and penalties against the degrading effects of these penalties upon humanity? Only calculate all the evil passions awakened in mankind by the atrocious punishments inflicted in our streets! Man is the cruelest animal on earth. And who has pampered and developed the cruel instincts if it is not the king, the judge and the priests, armed with law, who caused flesh to be torn off in strips, boiling pitch to be poured into wounds, limbs to be dislocated, bones to be crushed, men to be sawn asunder to maintain their authority? Only estimate the torrent of depravity let loose in human society by the "informing" which is countenanced by judges, and paid in hard cash by governments, under pretext of assisting in the discovery of "crime." Only go into the jails and study what man becomes when he is steeped in the vice and corruption which oozes from the very walls of our prisons. Finally, consider what corruption, what depravity of mind is kept up among men by the idea of obedience, the very essence of law; of chastisement; of authority having the right to punish; of the necessity for executioners, jailers, and informers—in a word, by all the attributes of law and authority. Consider this, and you will assuredly agree that a law inflicting penalties is an abomination which should cease to exist.

Peoples without political organization, and therefore less depraved than ourselves, have perfectly understood that the man who is called "criminal" is simply unfortunate; and that the remedy is not to flog him, to chain him up, or to kill him, but to help him by the most brotherly care, by treatment based on equality, by the usages of life among honest men.

Feliks was vaguely aware that a customer had come into the shop and was standing close to him, but he was concentrating on Kropotkin.

No more laws! No more judges! Liberty, equality and practical human sympathy are the only effective barriers we can oppose to the anti-social instincts of certain among us.

The customer dropped a book and he lost his train of thought. He glanced away from his pamphlet, saw the book lying on the floor beside the customer's long skirt and automatically bent down to pick it up for her. As he handed it to her he saw her face.

He gasped. "Why, you're an angel!" he said with perfect honesty.

She was blond and petite, and she wore a pale gray fur the color of her eyes, and everything about her was pale and light and fair. He thought he would never see a more beautiful woman, and he was right.

She stared back at him and blushed, but she did not turn away. It seemed, incredibly, that she found something fascinating in him, too.

After a moment he looked at her book. It was *Anna Karenina.* "Sentimental rubbish," he said. He wished he had not spoken, for his words broke the spell. She took the book and turned away. He saw then that there was a maid with her, for she gave the book to the maid and left the shop. The maid paid for the book. Looking through the window, Feliks saw the woman get into a carriage.

He asked the bookseller who she was. Her name was Lydia, he learned, and she was the daughter of Count Shatov.

He found out where the Count lived, and the next day he hung around outside the house in the hope of seeing her. She went in and out twice, in her carriage, before a groom came out and chased Feliks off. He did not mind, for the last time her carriage passed she had looked directly at him.

The next day he went to the bookshop. For hours he read

Bakunin's *Federalism, Socialism and Anti-Theologism* without understanding a single word. Every time a carriage passed he looked out of the window. Whenever a customer came into the shop his heart missed a beat.

She came in at the end of the afternoon.

This time she left the maid outside. She murmured a greeting to the bookseller and came to the back of the shop, where Feliks stood. They stared at one another. Feliks thought: She loves me; why else would she come?

He meant to speak to her, but instead he threw his arms around her and kissed her. She kissed him back, hungrily, opening her mouth, hugging him, digging her fingers into his back.

It was always like that with them: when they met they threw themselves at one another like animals about to fight.

They met twice more in the bookshop and once, after dark, in the garden of the Shatov house. That time in the garden she was in her nightclothes. Feliks put his hands under the woolen nightgown and touched her body all over, as boldly as if she were a street girl, feeling and exploring and rubbing; and all she did was moan.

She gave him money so that he could rent a room of his own, and thereafter she came to see him almost every day for six astonishing weeks.

The last time was in the early evening. He was sitting at the table, wrapped in a blanket against the cold, reading Proudhon's *What Is Property?* by candlelight. When he heard her footstep on the stairs he took his trousers off.

She rushed in, wearing an old brown cloak with a hood. She kissed him, sucked his lips, bit his chin and pinched his sides.

She turned and threw off the cloak. Underneath it she was wearing a white evening gown that must have cost hundreds of rubles. "Unfasten me, quickly," she said.

Feliks began to undo the hooks at the back of the dress.

"I'm on my way to a reception at the British Embassy; I only have an hour," she said breathlessly. "Hurry, please."

In his haste he ripped one of the hooks out of the material. "Damn, I've torn it."

"Never mind!"

She stepped out of the dress, then pulled off her petticoats, her chemise and her drawers, leaving on her corset, hose and shoes.

She flung herself into his arms. As she was kissing him she pulled down his underpants.

She said: "Oh, God, I love the smell of your thing."

When she talked dirty it drove him wild.

She pulled her breasts out of the top of her corset and said: "Bite them. Bite them hard. I want to feel them all evening."

A moment later she pulled away from him. She lay on her back on the bed. Where the corset ended, moisture glistened in the sparse blond hair between her thighs.

She spread her legs and lifted them into the air, opening herself to him. He gazed at her for a moment, then fell on her.

She grabbed his penis with her hands and pushed it inside her greedily.

The heels of her shoes tore the skin of his back and he did not care.

"Look at me," she said. "Look at me!"

He looked at her with adoration in his eyes.

An expression of panic came over her face.

She said: "Look at me, I'm coming!"

Then, still staring into his eyes, she opened her mouth and screamed.

•§ §•

"Do you think other people are like us?" she said.

"In what way?"

"Filthy."

He lifted his head from her lap and grinned. "Only the lucky ones."

She looked at his body, curled up between her legs. "You're so compact and strong, you're perfect," she said. "Look how your belly is flat, and how neat your bottom is, and how lean and hard your thighs are." She ran a finger along the line of his nose. "You have the face of a prince."

"I'm a peasant."

"Not when you're naked." She was in a reflective mood. "Before I met you, I *was* interested in men's bodies, and all that; but I used to pretend I wasn't, even to myself. Then you came along and I just couldn't pretend anymore."

He licked the inside of her thigh.

She shuddered. "Have you ever done this to another girl?"

"No."

"Did you use to pretend, as well?"

"No."

"I think I knew that, somehow. There's a look about you, wild and free like an animal; you never obey anyone, you just do what you want."

"I never before met a girl who would let me."

"They all wanted to, really. Any girl would."

"Why?" he said egotistically.

"Because your face is so cruel and your eyes are so kind."

"Is that why you let me kiss you in the bookshop?"

"I didn't *let* you—I had no choice."

"You could have yelled for help, afterward."

"By then all I wanted was for you to do it again."

"I must have guessed what you were really like."

It was her turn to be egotistical. "What am I really like?"

"Cold as ice on the surface, hot as hell below."

She giggled. "I'm such an actor. Everyone in St. Petersburg thinks I'm so *good*. I'm held up as an example to younger girls, just like Anna Karenina. Now that I know how bad I really am, I have to pretend to be twice as virginal as before."

"You can't be twice as virginal as anything."

"I wonder if they're all pretending," she resumed. "Take my father. If he knew I was here, like this, he'd die of rage. But he must have had the same feelings when he was young—don't you think?"

"I think it's an imponderable," Feliks said. "But what *would* he do, really, if he found out?"

"Horsewhip you."

"He'd have to catch me first." Feliks was struck by a thought. "How old are you?"

"Almost eighteen."

"My God, I could go to jail for seducing you."

"I'd make Father get you out."

He rolled over on to his front and looked at her. "What are we going to do, Lydia?"

"When?"

"In the long term."

"We're going to be lovers until I come of age, and then we'll get married."

He stared at her. "Do you mean that?"

"Of *course.*" She seemed genuinely surprised that he had not made the same assumption. "What else could we do?"

"You want to marry me?"

"Yes! Isn't that what you want?"

"Oh, *yes,*" he breathed. "That's what I want."

She sat up, with her legs spread either side of his face, and stroked his hair. "Then that's what we'll do."

Feliks said: "You never tell me how you manage to get away to come here."

"It's not very interesting," she said. "I tell lies, I bribe servants and I take risks. Tonight, for example. The reception at the embassy starts at half past six. I left home at six o'clock and I'll get there at a quarter past seven. The carriage is in the park— the coachman thinks I'm taking a walk with my maid. The maid is outside this house, dreaming about how she will spend the ten rubles I will give her for keeping her mouth shut."

"It's ten to seven," Feliks said.

"Oh, God. Quick, do it to me with your tongue before I have to go."

❧ ❦

That night Feliks was asleep, dreaming about Lydia's father— whom he had never seen—when they burst into his room carrying lamps. He woke instantly and jumped out of bed. At first he thought students from the university were playing a prank on him. Then one of them punched his face and kicked him in the stomach, and he knew they were the secret police.

He assumed they were arresting him on account of Lydia, and he was terrified for her. Would she be publicly disgraced? Was her father crazy enough to make her give evidence in court against her lover?

He watched the police put all his books and a bundle of letters in a sack. The books were all borrowed, but none of the owners was foolish enough to put his name inside. The letters were from his father and his sister, Natasha—he had never had any letters from Lydia, and now he was thankful for that.

He was marched out of the building and thrown into a four-wheeled cab.

They drove across the Chain Bridge and then followed the

canals, as if avoiding the main streets. Feliks asked: "Am I going to the Litovsky prison?" Nobody replied, but when they went over the Palace Bridge he realized he was being taken to the notorious Fortress of St. Peter and St. Paul, and his heart sank.

On the other side of the bridge the carriage turned left and entered a darkened arched passage. It stopped at a gate. Feliks was taken into a reception hall, where an army officer looked at him and wrote something in a book. He was put in the cab again and driven deeper into the fortress. They stopped at another gate and waited several minutes until it was opened from the inside by a soldier. From there Feliks had to walk through a series of narrow passages to a third iron gate which led to a large damp room.

The prison governor sat at a table. He said: "You are charged with being an anarchist. Do you admit it?"

Feliks was elated. So this was nothing to do with Lydia! "Admit it?" he said. "I boast of it."

One of the policemen produced a book which was signed by the governor. Feliks was stripped naked, then given a green flannel dressing gown, a pair of thick woolen stockings and two yellow felt slippers much too big.

From there an armed soldier took him through more gloomy corridors to a cell. A heavy oak door closed behind him, and he heard a key turn in the lock.

The cell contained a bed, a table, a stool and a washstand. The window was an embrasure in an enormously thick wall. The floor was covered with painted felt, and the walls were cushioned with some kind of yellow upholstery.

Feliks sat on the bed.

This was where Peter I had tortured and killed his own son. This was where Princess Tarakanova had been kept in a cell which flooded so that the rats climbed all over her to save themselves from drowning. This was where Catherine II buried her enemies alive.

Dostoyevsky had been imprisoned here, Feliks thought proudly; so had Bakunin, who had been chained to a wall for two years. Nechayev had died here.

Feliks was at once elated to be in such heroic company and terrified at the thought that he might be here forever.

The key turned in the lock. A little bald man with spectacles came in, carrying a pen, a bottle of ink and some paper. He set them down on the table and said: "Write the names of all the subversives you know."

Feliks sat down and wrote: Karl Marx, Friedrich Engels, Peter Kropotkin, Jesus Christ—

The bald man snatched away the paper. He went to the door of the cell and knocked. Two hefty guards came in. They strapped Feliks to the table and took off his slippers and stockings. They began to lash the soles of his feet with whips.

The torture went on all night.

When they pulled out his fingernails, he began to give them made-up names and addresses, but they told him they knew they were false.

When they burned the skin of his testicles with a candle flame, he named all his student friends, but still they said he was lying.

Each time he passed out they revived him. Sometimes they would stop for a while and allow him to think it was all over at last; then they would begin again, and he would beg them to kill him so that the pain would stop. They carried on long after he had told them everything he knew.

It must have been around dawn that he passed out for the last time.

When he came round he was lying on the bed. There were bandages on his feet and hands. He was in agony. He wanted to kill himself, but he was too weak to move.

The bald man came into the cell in the evening. When he saw him, Feliks began to sob with terror. The man just smiled and went away.

He never came back.

A doctor came to see Feliks each day. Feliks tried without success to pump him for information: Did anyone outside know that Feliks was here? Had there been any messages? Had anyone tried to visit? The doctor just changed the dressings and went away.

Feliks speculated. Lydia would have gone to his room and found the place in disarray. Someone in the house would have told her that the secret police had taken him away. What would she have done then? Would she make frantic inquiries, careless of her reputation? Would she have been discreet, and gone quietly to see the Minister of the Interior with some story about the boyfriend of her maid having been jailed in error?

Every day he hoped for word from her, but it never came.

Eight weeks later he could walk almost normally, and they released him without explanation.

He went to his lodging. He expected to find a message from her there, but there was nothing, and his room had been let to someone else. He wondered why Lydia had not continued to pay the rent.

He went to her house and knocked at the front door. A servant answered. Feliks said: "Feliks Davidovich Kschessinsky presents his compliments to Lydia Shatova—"

The servant slammed the door.

Finally he went to the bookshop. The old bookseller said: "Hello! I've got a message for you. It was brought yesterday by *her* maid."

Feliks tore open the envelope with trembling fingers. It was written, not by Lydia, but by the maid. It read:

> *I have been Let Go and have no job it is all your fault She is wed and gone to England yesterday now you know the wages of Sin.*

He looked up at the bookseller with tears of anguish in his eyes. "Is that all?" he cried.

He learned no more for nineteen years.

◄§ §►

Normal regulations had been temporarily suspended in the Walden house, and Charlotte sat in the kitchen with the servants.

The kitchen was spotless, for of course the family had dined out. The fire had gone out in the great range, and the high windows were wide open, letting in the cool night air. The crockery used for servants' meals was racked neatly in the dresser; the cook's knives and spoons hung from a row of hooks; her innumerable bowls and pans were out of sight in the massive oak cupboards.

Charlotte had had no time to be frightened. At first, when the coach stopped so abruptly in the park, she had been merely puzzled; and after that her concern had been to stop Mama screaming. When they got home she had found herself a little shaky, but now, looking back, she found the whole thing rather exciting.

The servants felt the same way. It was very reassuring to sit around the massive bleached wooden table and talk things over with these people who were so much a part of her life: the cook, who had always been motherly; Pritchard, whom Charlotte respected because Papa respected him; the efficient and capable Mrs. Mitchell, who as housekeeper always had a solution to any problem.

William the coachman was the hero of the hour. He described several times the wild look in his assailant's eyes as the man menaced him with the gun. Basking in the awestruck gaze of the under-house-parlourmaid, he recovered rapidly from the indignity of having walked into the kitchen stark naked.

"Of course," Pritchard explained, "I naturally presumed the thief just wanted William's clothes. I knew Charles was at the palace, so he could drive the coach. I thought I wouldn't inform the police until after speaking to his lordship."

Charles the footman said: "Imagine how I felt when I found the carriage gone! I said to myself, I'm sure it was left here. Oh, well, I thinks, William's moved it. I run up and down The Mall; I look everywhere. In the end I go back to the palace. 'Here's trouble,' I says to the doorman, 'the Earl of Walden's carriage has gone missing.' He says to me: 'Walden?' he says—not very respectful—"

Mrs. Mitchell interrupted: "Palace servants, they think they're better than the nobility—"

"He says to me: 'Walden's gone, mate.' I thought, Gorblimey, I'm for it! I come running through the park, and halfway home I find the carriage, and my lady having hysterics, and my lord with blood on his sword!"

Mrs. Mitchell said: "And after all that, nothing stolen."

"A lewnatic," said Charles. "An ingenious lewnatic."

There was general agreement.

The cook poured the tea and served Charlotte first. "How is my lady now?" she said.

"Oh, she's all right," Charlotte said. "She went to bed and took a dose of laudanum. She must be asleep by now."

"And the gentlemen?"

"Papa and Prince Orlov are in the drawing room, having a brandy."

The cook sighed heavily. "Robbers in the park and suffragettes at the court—I don't know what we're coming to."

"There'll be a socialist revolution," said Charles. "You mark my words."

"We'll all be murdered in our beds," the cook said lugubriously.

Charlotte said: "What did the suffragette mean about the King torturing women?" As she spoke she looked at Pritchard, who was sometimes willing to explain to her things she was not supposed to know about.

"She was talking about force-feeding," Pritchard said. "Apparently it's painful."

"Force-feeding?"

"When they won't eat, they're fed by force."

Charlotte was mystified. "How on earth is that done?"

"Several ways," said Pritchard with a look that indicated he would not go into detail about all of them. "A tube through the nostrils is one."

The under-house-parlourmaid said: "I wonder what they feed them."

Charles said: "Probably 'ot soup."

"I can't believe this," Charlotte said. "Why should they refuse to eat?"

"It's a protest," said Pritchard. "Makes difficulties for the prison authorities."

"Prison?" Charlotte was astonished. "Why are they in prison?"

"For breaking windows, making bombs, disturbing the peace . . ."

"But what do they want?"

There was a silence as the servants realized that Charlotte had no idea what a suffragette was.

Finally Pritchard said: "They want votes for women."

"Oh." Charlotte thought: Did I know that women couldn't vote? She was not sure. She had never thought about that sort of thing.

"I think this discussion has gone quite far enough," said Mrs. Mitchell firmly. "You'll be in trouble, Mr. Pritchard, for putting wrong ideas into my lady's head."

Charlotte knew that Pritchard never got in trouble, because he was practically Papa's friend. She said: "I wonder why they care so much about something like voting?"

There was a ring, and they all looked instinctively at the bell board.

"Front door!" said Pritchard. "At this time of night!" He went out, pulling on his coat.

Charlotte drank her tea. She felt tired. The suffragettes were puzzling and rather frightening, she decided; but all the same she wanted to know more.

Pritchard came back. "Plate of sandwiches, please, Cook," he said. "Charles, take a fresh soda siphon to the drawing room." He began to arrange plates and napkins on a tray.

"Well, come on," Charlotte said. "Who is it?"

"A gentleman from Scotland Yard," said Pritchard.

◆§ ξ◆

Basil Thomson was a bullet-headed man with light-colored receding hair, a heavy moustache and a penetrating gaze. Walden had heard of him. His father had been Archbishop of York. Thomson had been educated at Eton and Oxford and had done service in the Colonies as a Native Commissioner and as Prime Minister of Tonga. He had come home to qualify as a barrister and then had worked in the Prison Service, ending up as Governor of Dartmoor Prison with a reputation as a riot breaker. From prisons he had gravitated toward police work, and had become an expert on the mixed criminal-anarchist milieu of London's East End. This expertise had got him the top job in the Special Branch, the political police force.

Walden sat him down and began to recount the evening's events. As he spoke he kept an eye on Aleks. The boy was superficially calm, but his face was pale, he sipped steadily at a glass of brandy-and-soda and his left hand clutched rhythmically at the arm of his chair.

At one point Thomson interrupted Walden, saying: "Did you notice when the carriage picked you up that the footman was missing?"

"Yes, I did," Walden said. "I asked the coachman where he was, but the coachman seemed not to hear. Then, because there was such a crush at the palace door, and my daughter was telling me to hurry up, I decided not to press the matter until we got home."

"Our villain was relying on that, of course. He must have a cool nerve. Go on."

"The carriage stopped suddenly in the park, and the door was thrown open by the man."

"What did he look like?"

"Tall. He had a scarf or something over his face. Dark hair. Staring eyes."

"All criminals have staring eyes," Thomson said. "Earlier on, had the coachman got a better look at him?"

"Not much. At that time the man wore a hat, and of course it was dark."

"Hm. And then?"

Walden took a deep breath. At the time he had been not so much frightened as angry, but now, when he looked back on it, he was full of fear for what might have happened to Aleks, or Lydia, or Charlotte. He said: "Lady Walden screamed, and that seemed to disconcert the fellow. Perhaps he had not expected to find any women in the coach. Anyway, he hesitated." And thank God he did, he thought. "I poked him with my sword, and he dropped the gun."

"Did you do him much damage?"

"I doubt it. I couldn't get a swing in that confined space, and of course the sword isn't particularly sharp. I blooded him, though. I wish I had chopped off his damned head."

The butler came in, and conversation stopped. Walden realized he had been talking rather loudly. He tried to calm himself. Pritchard served sandwiches and brandy-and-soda to the three men. Walden said: "You'd better stay up, Pritchard, but you can send everyone else to bed."

"Very good, my lord."

When he had gone Walden said: "It is possible that this was just a robbery. I have let the servants think that, and Lady Walden and Charlotte, too. However, a robber would hardly have needed such an elaborate plan, to my mind. I am perfectly certain that it was an attempt on Aleks's life."

Thomson looked at Aleks. "I'm afraid I agree. Have you any idea how he knew where to find you?"

Aleks crossed his legs. "My movements haven't been secret."

"That must change. Tell me, sir, has your life ever been threatened?"

"I live with threats," Aleks said tightly. "There has never been an attempt before."

"Is there any reason why you in particular should be the target of Nihilists or revolutionists?"

"For them, it is enough that I am a p-prince."

Walden realized that the problems of the English establishment, with suffragettes and Liberals and trade unions, were trivial by comparison with what the Russians had to cope with, and he felt a surge of sympathy for Aleks.

Aleks went on in a quiet, controlled voice. "However, I am known to be something of a reformer, by Russian standards. They could pick a more appropriate victim."

"Even in London," Thomson agreed. "There's always a Russian aristocrat or two in London for the season."

Walden said: "What are you getting at?"

Thomson said: "I'm wondering whether the villain knew what Prince Orlov is doing here, and whether his motive for tonight's attack was to sabotage your talks."

Walden was dubious. "How would the revolutionists have found that out?"

"I'm just speculating," Thomson replied. "*Would* this be an effective way to sabotage your talks?"

"Very effective indeed," Walden said. The thought made him go cold. "If the Czar were to be told that his nephew had been assassinated in London by a revolutionist—especially if it were an expatriate Russian revolutionist—he would go through the roof. You know, Thomson, how the Russians feel about our having their subversives here—our open-door policy has caused friction at the diplomatic level for years. Something like this could destroy Anglo-Russian relations for twenty years. There would be no question of an alliance then."

Thomson nodded. "I was afraid of that. Well, there's no more we can do tonight. I'll set my department to work at dawn. We'll search the park for clues, and interview your servants, and I expect we'll round up a few anarchists in the East End."

Aleks said: "Do you think you will catch the man?"

Walden longed for Thomson to give a reassuring answer, but it was not forthcoming. "It won't be easy," Thomson said. "He's obviously a planner, so he'll have a bolt-hole somewhere. We've no proper description of him. Unless his wounds take him to hospital, our chances are slim."

"He may try to kill me again," Aleks said.

"So we must take evasive action. I propose you should move out of this house tomorrow. We'll take the top floor of one of the hotels for you, in a false name, and give you a bodyguard. Lord Walden will have to meet with you secretly, and you'll have to cut out social engagements, of course."

"Of course."

Thomson stood up. "It's very late. I'll set all this in motion."

Walden rang for Pritchard. "You've got a carriage waiting, Thomson?"

"Yes. Let us speak on the telephone tomorrow morning."

Pritchard saw Thomson out, and Aleks went off to bed. Walden told Pritchard to lock up, then went upstairs.

He was not sleepy. As he undressed he let himself relax and feel all the conflicting emotions that he had so far held at bay. He felt proud of himself, at first—after all, he thought, I drew a sword and fought off an assailant: not bad for a man of fifty with a gouty leg! Then he became depressed when he recalled how coolly they had all discussed the diplomatic consequences of the death of Aleks—bright, cheerful, shy, handsome, clever Aleks, whom Walden had seen grow into a man.

He got into bed and lay awake, reliving the moment when the carriage door flew open and the man stood there with the gun; and now he was frightened, not for himself or Aleks, but for Lydia and Charlotte. The thought that they might have been killed made him tremble in his bed. He remembered holding Charlotte in his arms, eighteen years ago, when she had blond hair and no teeth; he remembered her learning to walk and forever falling on her bottom; he remembered giving her a pony of her own, and thinking that her joy when she saw it gave him the biggest thrill of his life; he remembered her just a few hours ago, walking into the royal presence with her head held high, a grown woman and a beautiful one. If she died, he thought, I don't know that I could bear it.

And Lydia: if Lydia were dead I would be alone. The thought made him get up and go through to her room. There was a night-light beside her bed. She was in a deep sleep, lying on her back, her mouth a little open, her hair a blond skein across the pillow. She looked soft and vulnerable. I have never been able to make you understand how much I love you, he thought. Suddenly he needed to touch her, to feel that she was warm and alive. He got into bed with her and kissed her. Her lips responded but she did not wake up. Lydia, he thought, I could not live without you.

․❧ ❨․

Lydia had lain awake for a long time, thinking about the man with the gun. It had been a brutal shock, and she had screamed in sheer terror—but there was more to it than that. There had been something about the man, something about his stance, or his shape, or his clothes, that had seemed dreadfully sinister in an almost supernatural way, as if he were a ghost. She wished she could have seen his eyes.

After a while she had taken another dose of laudanum, and then she slept. She dreamed that the man with the gun came to her room and got into bed with her. It was her own bed, but in the dream she was eighteen years old again. The man put his gun down on the white pillow beside her head. He still had the scarf around his face. She realized that she loved him. She kissed his lips through the scarf.

He made love to her beautifully. She began to think that she might be dreaming. She wanted to see his face. She said *Who are you?* and a voice said *Stephen.* She knew this was not so, but the gun on the pillow had somehow turned into Stephen's sword, with blood on its point; and she began to have doubts. She clung to the man on top of her, afraid that the dream would end before she was satisfied. Then, dimly, she began to suspect that she was doing in reality what she was doing in the dream; yet the dream persisted. Strong physical pleasure possessed her. She began to lose control. Just as her climax began the man in the dream took the scarf from his face, and in that moment Lydia opened her eyes, and saw Stephen's face above her; and then she was overcome by ecstasy, and for the first time in nineteen years she cried for joy.

․❧ ❨․

FIVE

Charlotte looked forward with mixed feelings to Belinda's coming-out ball. She had never been to a town ball, although she had been to lots of country balls, many of them at Walden Hall. She liked to dance and she knew she did it well, but she hated the cattle-market business of sitting out with the wallflowers and waiting for a boy to pick you out and ask you to dance. She wondered whether this might be handled in a more civilized way among the "Smart Set."

They got to Uncle George and Aunt Clarissa's Mayfair house half an hour before midnight, which Mama said was the earliest time one could decently arrive at a London ball. A striped canopy and a red carpet led from the curb to the garden gate, which had somehow been transformed into a Roman triumphal arch.

But even that did not prepare Charlotte for what she saw when she passed through the arch. The whole side garden had been turned into a Roman atrium. She gazed about her in wonderment. The lawns and the flower beds had been covered over with a hardwood dance floor stained in black and white squares to look like marble tiles. A colonnade of white pillars, linked with chains of laurel, bordered the floor. Beyond the pillars, in a kind of cloister, there were raised benches for the sitters-out. In the middle of the floor, a fountain in the form of a boy with a dolphin splashed in a marble basin, the streams of water lit by colored spotlights. On the balcony of an upstairs bedroom a band played ragtime. Garlands of smilax and roses decorated the walls, and baskets of begonias hung from the balcony. A huge canvas roof, painted sky blue, covered the whole area from the eaves of the house to the garden wall.

"It's a miracle!" Charlotte said.

Papa said to his brother: "Quite a crowd, George."

"We invited eight hundred. What the devil happened to you in park?"

"Oh, it wasn't as bad as it sounded," Papa said with a forced smile. He took George by the arm, and they moved to one side to talk.

Charlotte studied the guests. All the men wore full evening dress—white tie, white waistcoat and tails. It particularly suited the young men, or at least the slim men, Charlotte thought: it made them look quite dashing as they danced. Observing the dresses, she decided that hers and her mother's, though rather tasteful, were a trifle old-fashioned, with their wasp waists and ruffles and sweepers: Aunt Clarissa wore a long, straight, slender gown with a skirt almost too tight to dance in, and Belinda had harem pants.

Charlotte realized she knew nobody. Who will dance with me, she wondered, after Papa and Uncle George? However, Aunt Clarissa's younger brother, Jonathan, waltzed with her, then introduced her to three men who were at Oxford with him, each of whom danced with her. She found their conversation monotonous: they said the floor was good, and the band—Gottlieb's—was good, then they ran out of steam. Charlotte tried: "Do you believe that women should have the vote?" The replies she got were: "Certainly not," "No opinion," and "You're not one of *them,* are you?"

The last of her partners, whose name was Freddie, took her into the house for supper. He was a rather sleek young man, with regular features—handsome, I suppose, Charlotte thought—and fair hair. He was at the end of his first year at Oxford. Oxford was rather jolly, he said, but he confessed he was not much of a one for reading books, and he rather thought he would not go back in October.

The inside of the house was festooned with flowers and bright with electric light. For supper there was hot and cold soup, lobster, quail, strawberries, ice cream and hothouse peaches. "Always the same old food for supper," Freddie said. "They all use the same caterer."

"Do you go to a lot of balls?" Charlotte asked.

" 'Fraid so. All the time, really, in the season."

Charlotte drank a glass of champagne-cup in the hope that it would make her feel more gay, then she left Freddie and wandered through a series of reception rooms. In one of them several games of bridge were under way. Two elderly duchesses held court in another. In a third, older men played billiards while younger men smoked. Charlotte found Belinda there with a cigarette in her hand. Charlotte had never seen the point of tobacco, unless one wanted to look sophisticated. Belinda certainly looked sophisticated.

"I adore your dress," Belinda said.

"No, you don't. But *you* look sensational. How did you persuade your stepmother to let you dress like that?"

"She'd like to wear one herself!"

"She seems so much younger than my Mama. Which she is, of course."

"And being a stepmother makes a difference. Whatever happened to you after the court?"

"Oh, it was extraordinary! A madman pointed a gun at us!"

"Your Mama was telling me. Weren't you simply terrified?"

"I was too busy calming Mama. Afterwards I was scared to death. Why did you say, at the palace, that you wanted to have a long talk with me?"

"Ah! Listen." She took Charlotte aside, away from the young men. "I've discovered how they come out."

"What?"

"Babies."

"Oh!" Charlotte was all ears. "Do tell."

Belinda lowered her voice. "They come out between your legs, where you make water."

"It's too small!"

"It stretches."

How awful, Charlotte thought.

"But that's not all," Belinda said. "I've found out how they start."

"How?"

Belinda took Charlotte's elbow and they walked to the far side of the room. They stood in front of a mirror garlanded with roses. Belinda's voice fell almost to a whisper. "When you get married, you know you have to go to bed with your husband."

"Do you?"

"Yes."

"Papa and Mama have separate bedrooms."

"Don't they adjoin?"

"Yes."

"That's so that they can get into the same bed."

"Why?"

"Because, to start a baby, the husband has to put his pego into that place—where the babies come out."

"What's a pego?"

"Hush! It's a thing men have between their legs—haven't you ever seen a picture of Michelangelo's *David*?"

"No."

"Well, it's a thing they make water with. Looks like a finger."

"And you have to do *that* to start babies?"

"Yes."

"And all married people have to do it?"

"Yes."

"How dreadful. Who told you all this?"

"Viola Pontadarvy. She swore it was true."

And somehow Charlotte knew it *was* true. Hearing it was like being reminded of something she had forgotten. It seemed, unaccountably, to make sense. Yet she felt physically shocked. It was the slightly queasy feeling she sometimes got in dreams, when a terrible suspicion turned out to be correct, or when she was afraid of falling and suddenly found she *was* falling.

"I'm jolly glad you found out," she said. "If one got married without knowing . . . how embarrassing it would be!"

"Your mother is supposed to explain it all to you the night before your wedding, but if your mother is too shy you just . . . find out when it happens."

"Thank Heaven for Viola Pontadarvy." Charlotte was struck

by a thought. "Has all this got something to do with . . . bleed-ing, you know, every month?"

"I don't know."

"I expect it has. It's all connected—all the things people don't talk about. Well, now we know why they don't talk about it—it's so disgusting."

"The thing you have to do in bed is called sexual intercourse, but Viola says the common people call it swiving."

"She knows a lot."

"She's got brothers. They told her years ago."

"How did they find out?"

"From older boys at school. Boys are ever so interested in that sort of thing."

"Well," Charlotte said, "it does have a sort of horrid fascina-tion."

Suddenly she saw in the mirror the reflection of Aunt Cla-rissa. "What are you two doing huddled in a corner?" she said. Charlotte flushed, but apparently Aunt Clarissa did not want an answer, for she went on: "Do please move around and talk to people, Belinda—it *is* your party."

She went away, and the two girls moved on through the reception rooms. The rooms were arranged on a circular plan so that you could walk through them all and end up where you had started, at the top of the staircase. Charlotte said: "I don't think I could ever bring myself to do it."

"Couldn't you?" Belinda said with a funny look.

"What do you mean?"

"I don't know. I've been thinking about it. It might be quite nice."

Charlotte stared at her.

Belinda looked embarrassed. "I must go and dance," she said. "See you later on!"

She went down the stairs. Charlotte watched her go, and wondered how many more shocking secrets life had to reveal.

She went back into the supper room and got another glass of champagne-cup. What a peculiar way for the human race to perpetuate itself, she thought. She supposed animals did some-thing similar. What about birds? No, birds had eggs. And such words! *Pego* and *swiving*. All these hundreds of elegant and refined people around her knew those words, but never mentioned them. Because they were never mentioned, they were embarrassing. Because they were embarrassing, they were never mentioned. There was something very *silly* about the whole thing. If the Creator had ordained that people should swive, why pretend that they did not?

She finished her drink and went outside to the dance floor. Papa and Mama were dancing a polka, and doing it rather well. Mama had got over the incident in the park, but it still preyed on Papa's mind. He looked very fine in white tie and tails. When his leg was bad he would not dance, but obviously it was giving him no trouble tonight. He was surprisingly light on his feet for a big man. Mama seemed to be having a wonderful time. She was able to let herself go a bit when she danced. Her usual studied reserve fell away, and she smiled radiantly and let her ankles show.

When the polka was over Papa caught Charlotte's eye and came over. "May I have this dance, Lady Charlotte?"

"Certainly, my lord."

It was a waltz. Papa seemed distracted, but he whirled her around the floor expertly. She wondered whether she looked radiant, like Mama. Probably not. Suddenly she thought of Papa and Mama swiving, and found the idea terribly embarrassing.

Papa said: "Are you enjoying your first big ball?"

"Yes, thank you," she said dutifully.

"You seem thoughtful."

"I'm on my best behavior." The lights and the bright colors blurred slightly, and suddenly she had to concentrate on staying upright. She was afraid she might fall over and look foolish. Papa sensed her unsteadiness and held her a little more firmly. A moment later the dance ended.

Papa took her off the floor. He said: "Are you feeling quite well?"

"Fine, but I was dizzy for a moment."

"Have you been smoking?"

Charlotte laughed. "Certainly not."

"That's the usual reason young ladies feel dizzy at balls. Take my advice: when you want to try tobacco, do it in private."

"I don't think I want to try it."

She sat out the next dance, and then Freddie turned up again. As she danced with him, it occurred to her that all the young men and girls, including Freddie and herself, were supposed to be looking for husbands or wives during the season, especially at balls like this. For the first time she considered Freddie as a possible husband for herself. It was unthinkable.

Then what kind of husband do I want? she wondered. She really had no idea.

Freddie said: "Jonathan just said 'Freddie, meet Charlotte,' but I gather you're called Lady Charlotte Walden."

"Yes. Who are you?"

"Marquis of Chalfont, actually."

So, Charlotte thought, we're socially compatible.

A little later she and Freddie got into conversation with Belinda and Freddie's friends. They talked about a new play, called *Pygmalion*, which was said to be absolutely hilarious but quite vulgar. The boys spoke of going to a boxing match, and Belinda said she wanted to go too, but they all said it was out of the question. They discussed jazz music. One of the boys was something of a connoisseur, having lived for a while in the United States; but Freddie disliked it, and talked rather pompously about "the negrification of society." They all drank coffee and Belinda smoked another cigarette. Charlotte began to enjoy herself.

It was Charlotte's Mama who came along and broke up the party. "Your father and I are leaving," she said. "Shall we send the coach back for you?"

Charlotte realized she was tired. "No, I'll come," she said. 'What time is it?"

"Four o'clock."

They went to get their wraps. Mama said: "Did you have a lovely evening?"

"Yes, thank you, Mama."

"So did I. Who were those young men?"

"They know Jonathan."

"Were they nice?"

"The conversation got quite interesting, in the end."

Papa had called the carriage already. As they drove away from the bright lights of the party, Charlotte remembered what had happened last time they rode in a carriage, and she felt scared.

Papa held Mama's hand. They seemed happy. Charlotte felt excluded. She looked out of the window. In the dawn light she could see four men in silk hats walking up Park Lane, going home from some nightclub perhaps. As the carriage rounded Hyde Park Corner Charlotte saw something odd. "What's that?" she said.

Mama looked out. "What's what, dear?"

"On the pavement. Looks like people."

"That's right."

"What are they doing?"

"Sleeping."

Charlotte was horrified. There were eight or ten of them, up against a wall, bundled in coats, blankets and newspapers. She could not tell whether they were men or women, but some of the bundles were small enough to be children.

She said: "Why do they sleep there?"

"I don't know, dear," Mama said.

Papa said: "Because they've nowhere else to sleep, of course."

"They have no homes?"

"No."

"I didn't know there was anyone that poor," Charlotte said. "How dreadful." She thought of all the rooms in Uncle George's house, the food that had been laid out to be picked at by eight hundred people, all of whom had had dinner, and the elaborate gowns they wore new each season while people slept under newspapers. She said: "We should do something for them."

"We?" Papa said. "What should *we* do?"

"Build houses for them."

"All of them?"

"How many are there?"

Papa shrugged. "Thousands."

"Thousands! I thought it was just those few." Charlotte was devastated. "Couldn't you build small houses?"

"There's no profit in house property, especially at that end of the market."

"Perhaps you should do it anyway."

"Why?"

"Because the strong should take care of the weak. I've heard you say that to Mr. Samson." Samson was the bailiff at Walden Hall, and he was always trying to save money on repairs to tenanted cottages.

"We already take care of rather a lot of people," Papa said. "All the servants whose wages we pay, all the tenants who farm our land and live in our cottages, all the workers in the companies we invest in, all the government employees who are paid out of our taxes—"

"I don't think that's much of an excuse," Charlotte interrupted. "Those poor people are sleeping on the *street*. What will they do in winter?"

Mama said sharply: "Your Papa doesn't need excuses. He was born an aristocrat and he has managed his estate carefully. He is entitled to his wealth. Those people on the pavement are idlers, criminals, drunkards and ne'er-do-wells."

"Even the children?"

"Don't be impertinent. Remember you still have a great deal to learn."

"I'm just beginning to realize how much," Charlotte said.

As the carriage turned into the courtyard of their house, Charlotte glimpsed one of the street sleepers beside the gate. She decided she would take a closer look.

The coach stopped beside the front door. Charles handed Mama down, then Charlotte. Charlotte ran across the courtyard. William was closing the gates. "Just a minute," Charlotte called.

She heard Papa say: "What the devil . . . ?"

She ran out into the street.

The sleeper was a woman. She lay slumped on the pavement with her shoulders against the courtyard wall. She wore a man's boots, woolen stockings, a dirty blue coat and a very large, once-fashionable hat with a bunch of grubby artificial flowers in its brim. Her head was slumped sideways and her face was turned toward Charlotte.

There was something familiar about the round face and the wide mouth. The woman was young . . .

Charlotte cried: "Annie!"

The sleeper opened her eyes.

Charlotte stared at her in horror. Two months ago Annie had been a housemaid at Walden Hall in a crisp clean uniform with a little white hat on her head, a pretty girl with a large bosom and an irrepressible laugh. "Annie, what happened to you?"

Annie scrambled to her feet and bobbed a pathetic curtsy.

"Oh, Lady Charlotte, I was hoping I would see you, you was always good to me, I've nowhere to turn—"

"But how did you get like this?"

"I was let go, m'lady, without a character, when they found out I was expecting the baby; I know I done wrong—"

"But you're not married!"

"But I was courting Jimmy, the under-gardener . . ."

Charlotte recalled Belinda's revelations, and realized that if all that was true it would indeed be possible for girls to have babies without being married. "Where is the baby?"

"I lost it."

"You *lost* it?"

"I mean, it came too early, m'lady, it was born dead."

"How horrible," Charlotte whispered. That was something else she had not known to be possible. "And why isn't Jimmy with you?"

"He run away to sea. He *did* love me, I know, but he was frightened to wed, he was only seventeen . . ." Annie began to cry.

Charlotte heard Papa's voice. "Charlotte, come in this instant."

She turned to him. He stood at the gate in his evening clothes, with his silk hat in his hand, and suddenly she saw him as a big, smug, cruel old man. She said: "This is one of the servants you care for so well."

Papa looked at the girl. "Annie! What is the meaning of this?"

Annie said: "Jimmy run away, m'lord, so I couldn't wed, and I couldn't get another position because you never gave me a character, and I was ashamed to go home, so I come to London . . ."

"You came to London to beg," Papa said harshly.

"Papa!" Charlotte cried.

"You don't understand, Charlotte—"

"I understand perfectly well—"

Mama appeared and said: "Charlotte, get away from that creature!"

"She's not a creature, she's Annie."

"Annie!" Mama shrilled. "She's a fallen woman!"

"That's enough," Papa said. "This family does not hold discussions in the street. Let us go in immediately."

Charlotte put her arm around Annie. "She needs a bath, new clothes and a hot breakfast."

"Don't be ridiculous!" Mama said. The sight of Annie seemed to have made her almost hysterical.

"All right," Papa said. "Take her into the kitchen. The parlourmaids will be up by now. Tell them to take care of her. Then come and see me in the drawing-room."

Mama said: "Stephen, this is insane—"

"Let us go *in*," said Papa.

They went in.

Charlotte took Annie downstairs to the kitchen. A skivvy was cleaning the range and a kitchenmaid was slicing bacon for breakfast. It was just past five o'clock: Charlotte had not realized they started work so early. They both looked at her in astonishment when she walked in, in her ball gown, with Annie at her side.

Charlotte said: "This is Annie. She used to work at Walden Hall. She's had some bad luck but she's a good girl. She must have a bath. Find new clothes for her and burn her old ones. Then give her breakfast."

For a moment they were both dumbstruck; then the kitchenmaid said: "Very good, m'lady."

"I'll see you later, Annie," Charlotte said.

Annie seized Charlotte's arm. "Oh, thank you, m'lady."

Charlotte went out.

Now there will be trouble, she thought as she went upstairs. She did not care as much as she might have. She almost felt that her parents had betrayed her. What had her years of education been for, when in one night she could find out that the most important things had never been taught her? No doubt they talked of protecting young girls, but Charlotte thought deceit might be the appropriate term. When she thought of how ignorant she had been until tonight, she felt so foolish, and that made her angry.

She marched into the drawing room.

Papa stood beside the fireplace holding a glass. Mama sat at the piano, playing double-minor chords with a pained expression on her face. They had drawn back the curtains. The room looked odd in the morning, with yesterday's cigar butts in the ashtrays and the cold early light on the edges of things. It was an evening room, and wanted lamps and warmth, drinks and footmen, and a crowd of people in formal clothes.

Everything looked different today.

"Now, then, Charlotte," Papa began. "You don't understand what kind of woman Annie is. We let her go for a reason, you know. She did something very wrong which I cannot explain to you—"

"I know what she did," Charlotte said, sitting down. "And I know who she did it with. A gardener called Jimmy."

Mama gasped.

Papa said: "I don't believe you have any idea what you're talking about."

"And if I haven't, whose fault is it?" Charlotte burst out. "How did I manage to reach the age of eighteen without learning that some people are so poor they sleep in the street, that maids who are expecting babies get dismissed, and that—that—men are not made the same as women? Don't stand there telling me I don't understand these things and I have a lot to learn! I've spent all my life learning and now I discover most of it was lies! How dare you! How dare you!" She burst into tears, and hated herself for losing control.

She heard Mama say: "Oh, this is too foolish."

Papa sat beside her and took her hand. "I'm sorry you feel that way," he said. "All young girls are kept in ignorance of certain things. It is done for their own good. We have never lied to you. If we did not tell you just how cruel and coarse the world is, that was only because we wanted you to enjoy your childhood for as long as possible. Perhaps we made a mistake."

Mama snapped: "We wanted to keep you out of the trouble that Annie got into!"

"I wouldn't put it quite like that," Papa said mildly.

Charlotte's rage evaporated. She felt like a child again. She wanted to put her head on Papa's shoulder, but her pride would not let her.

"Shall we all forgive each other, and be pals again?" Papa said.

An idea which had been quietly budding in Charlotte's mind now blossomed, and she spoke without thinking. "Would you let me take Annie as my personal maid?"

Papa said: "Well . . ."

"We won't even think of it!" Mama said hysterically. "It is quite out of the question! That an eighteen-year-old girl who is the daughter of an earl should have a scarlet woman as a maid! No, absolutely and finally, no!"

"Then what will she do?" Charlotte asked calmly.

"She should have thought of that when— She should have thought of that before."

Papa said: "Charlotte, we cannot possibly have a woman of bad character to live in this house. Even if I would allow it, the servants would be scandalized. Half of them would give notice. We shall hear mutterings even now, just because the girl has been allowed into the kitchen. You see, it is not just Mama and I who shun such people—it is the whole of society."

"Then I shall buy her a house," Charlotte said, "and give her an allowance and be her friend."

"You've no money," Mama said.

"My Russian grandfather left me something."

Papa said: "But the money is in my care until you reach the age of twenty-one, and I will not allow it to be used for that purpose."

"Then what is to be done with her?" Charlotte said desperately.

"I'll make a bargain with you," Papa said. "I will give her money to get decent lodgings, and I'll see that she gets a job in a factory."

"What would be my part of the bargain?"

"You must promise not to try to make contact with her, ever."

Charlotte felt very tired. Papa had all the answers. She could no longer argue with him, and she did not have the power to insist. She sighed.

"All right," she said.

"Good girl. Now, then, I suggest you go and find her and tell her the arrangement, then say good-bye."

"I'm not sure I can look her in the eye."

Papa patted her hand. "She will be very grateful, you'll see. When you've spoken to her, you go to bed. I'll see to all the details."

Charlotte did not know whether she had won or lost, whether Papa was being cruel or kind, whether Annie should feel saved or spurned. "Very well," she said wearily. She wanted to tell Papa that she loved him, but the words would not come. After a moment she got up and left the room.

❧ ❦

On the day after the fiasco, Feliks was awakened at noon by Bridget. He felt very weak. Bridget stood beside his bed with a large cup in her hand. Feliks sat up and took the cup. The drink was wonderful. It seemed to consist of hot milk, sugar, melted butter and lumps of bread. While he drank it Bridget moved around his room, tidying up, singing a sentimental song about boys who gave their lives for Ireland.

She went away and came back again with another Irish-woman of her own age who was a nurse. The woman stitched his hand and put a dressing on the puncture wound in his shoulder. Feliks gathered from the conversation that she was the local abortionist. Bridget told her that Feliks had been in a fight in a pub. The nurse charged a shilling for the visit and said: "You won't die. If you'd had yourself seen to straightaway you wouldn't have bled so much. As it is you'll feel weak for days."

When she had gone, Bridget talked to him. She was a heavy, good-natured woman in her late fifties. Her husband had got into some kind of trouble in Ireland and they had fled to the anonymity of London, where he died of the booze, she said. She had two sons who were policemen in New York and a daughter who was in service in Belfast. There was a vein of bitterness in her which showed in an occasional sarcastically humorous re-mark, usually at the expense of the English.

While she was explaining why Ireland should have Home Rule, Feliks went to sleep. She woke him again in the evening to give him hot soup.

On the following day his physical wounds began visibly to heal, and he started to feel the pain of his emotional wounds. All the despair and self-reproach which he had felt in the park as he ran away now came back to him. Running away! How could it happen?

Lydia.

She was now Lady Walden.

He felt nauseated.

He made himself think clearly and coolly. He had known that she married and went to England. Obviously the Englishman she married was likely to be both an aristocrat and a man with a strong interest in Russia. Equally obviously, the person who negotiated with Orlov had to be a member of the Establishment and an expert on Russian affairs. I couldn't have guessed it would turn out to be the same man, Feliks thought, but I should have realized the possibility.

The coincidence was not as remarkable as it had seemed, but it was no less shattering. Twice in his life Feliks had been utterly, blindly, deliriously happy. The first time was when, at the age of four—before his mother died—he had been given a red ball. The second was when Lydia fell in love with him. But the red ball had never been taken from him.

He could not imagine a greater happiness than that which he had had with Lydia—nor a disappointment more appalling than the one that followed. There had certainly been no such highs and lows in Feliks's emotional life since then. After she left he began to tramp the Russian countryside, dressed as a monk, preaching the anarchist gospel. He told the peasants that the land was theirs because they tilled it; that the wood in the forest belonged to anyone who felled a tree; that nobody had a right to govern them except themselves, and because self-government was no government it was called anarchy. He was a wonderful preacher and he made many friends, but he never fell in love again, and he hoped he never would.

His preaching phase had ended in 1899, during the national student strike, when he was arrested as an agitator and sent to Siberia. The years of wandering had already inured him to cold, hunger and pain; but now, working in a chain gang, using wooden tools to dig out gold in a mine, laboring on when the man chained to his side had fallen dead, seeing boys and women flogged, he came to know darkness, bitterness, despair and finally hatred. In Siberia he had learned the facts of life: steal or starve, hide or be beaten, fight or die. There he had acquired cunning and ruthlessness. There he had learned the ultimate truth about oppression: that it works by turning its victims against each other instead of against their oppressors.

He escaped, and began the long journey into madness, which ended when he killed the policeman outside Omsk and realized that he had no fear.

He returned to civilization as a full-blooded revolutionist. It seemed incredible to him that he had once scrupled to throw bombs at the noblemen who maintained those Siberian convict mines. He was enraged by the government-inspired pogroms against the Jews in the west and south of Russia. He was sickened by the wrangling between Bolsheviks and Mensheviks at the second congress of the Social Democratic Party. He was inspired by the magazine that came from Geneva, called *Bread and Liberty*, with the quote from Bakunin on its masthead: "The urge to destroy is also a creative urge." Finally, hating the government, disenchanted with the socialists and convinced by the anarchists, he went to a mill town called Bialystock and founded a group called Struggle.

Those had been the glory years. He would never forget young Nisan Farber, who had knifed the millowner outside the synagogue on the Day of Atonement. Feliks himself had shot the chief of police. Then he took the fight to St. Petersburg, where he founded another anarchist group, The Unauthorized, and planned the successful assassination of the Grand Duke Sergey. That year—1905—in St. Petersburg there were killings, bank robberies, strikes and riots: the revolution seemed only days away. Then came the repression—more fierce, more efficient and a great deal more bloodthirsty than anything the revolutionists had ever done. The secret police came in the middle of the night to the homes of The Unauthorized, and they were all arrested except Feliks, who killed one policeman and maimed another and escaped to Switzerland, for by then nobody could stop him, he was so determined and powerful and angry and ruthless.

In all those years, and even in the quiet years in Switzerland that followed, he had never loved anyone. There had been people of whom he had grown mildly fond—a pig-keeper in Georgia, an old Jewish bomb-maker in Bialystock, Ulrich in Geneva—but they tended to pass into and then out of his life. There had been women, too. Many women sensed his violent nature and shied away from him, but those of them who found him attractive found him extremely so. Occasionally he had yielded to the temptation, and he had always been more or less disappointed. His parents were both dead and he had not seen his sister for twenty years. Looking back, he could see his life since Lydia as a slow slide into anesthesia. He had survived by becoming less and less sensitive, through the experiences of imprisonment, torture, the chain gang and the long, brutal escape from Siberia. He no longer cared even for himself: this, he had decided, was the meaning of his lack of fear, for one could only be afraid on account of something for which one cared.

He liked it this way.

His love was not for people, it was for *the* people. His compassion was for starving peasants in general, and sick children and frightened soldiers and crippled miners in general. He hated nobody in particular: just all princes, all landlords, all capitalists and all generals.

In giving his personality over to a higher cause he knew he was like a priest, and indeed like one priest in particular: his father. He no longer felt diminished by this comparison. He respected his father's high-mindedness and despised the cause it served. He, Feliks, had chosen the right cause. His life would not be wasted.

This was the Feliks that had formed over the years, as his mature personality emerged from the fluidity of youth. What had been so devastating about Lydia's scream, he thought, was that it had reminded him that there might have been a different Feliks, a warm and loving man, a sexual man, a man capable of jealousy, greed, vanity and fear. Would I rather be that man? he asked himself. That man would long to stare into her wide gray eyes and stroke her fine blond hair, to see her collapse into helpless giggles as she tried to learn how to whistle, to argue with her about Tolstoy, to eat black bread and smoked herrings with her and to watch her screw up her pretty face at her first taste of vodka. That man would be *playful*.

He would also be *concerned*. He would wonder whether Lydia was happy. He would hesitate to pull the trigger for fear she might be hit by a ricochet. He might be reluctant to kill her nephew in case she were fond of the boy. That man would make a poor revolutionist.

No, he thought as he went to sleep that night; I would not want to be that man. He is not even dangerous.

In the night he dreamed that he shot Lydia, but when he woke up he could not remember whether it had made him sad.

On the third day he went out. Bridget gave him a shirt and a coat which had belonged to her husband. They fitted badly, for he had been shorter and wider than Feliks. Feliks's own trousers and boots were still wearable, and Bridget had washed the blood off.

He mended the bicycle, which had been damaged when he dropped it down the steps. He straightened a buckled wheel, patched a punctured tire, and taped the split leather of the saddle. He climbed on and rode a short distance, but he realized immediately that he was not yet strong enough to go far on it. He walked instead.

It was a glorious sunny day. At a secondhand clothes stall in Mornington Crescent he gave a halfpenny and Bridget's husband's coat for a lighter coat that fitted him. He felt peculiarly happy, walking through the streets of London in the summer weather. I've nothing to be happy about, he thought; my clever, well-organized, daring assassination plan fell to pieces because a woman cried out and a middle-aged man drew a sword. What a fiasco!

It was Bridget who had cheered him up, he decided. She had seen that he was in trouble and she had given help without thinking twice. It reminded him of the great-heartedness of the people in whose cause he fired guns and threw bombs and got himself sliced up with a sword. It gave him strength.

He made his way to St. James's Park and took up his familiar station opposite the Walden house. He looked across at the pristine white stonework and the high, elegant windows. You can knock me down, he thought, but you can't knock me out; if you knew I was back here again, you'd tremble in your patent-leather shoes.

He settled down to watch. The trouble with a fiasco was that it put the intended victim on his guard. It would now be very difficult indeed to kill Orlov because he would be taking precautions. But Feliks would find out what those precautions were, and he would evade them.

At eleven A.M. the carriage went out, and Feliks thought he saw behind the glass a spade-shaped beard and a top hat: Walden. It came back at one. It went out again at three, this time with a feminine hat inside, belonging presumably to Lydia, or perhaps to the daughter of the family; whoever it was returned at five. In the evening several guests came and the family apparently dined at home. There was no sign of Orlov. It rather looked as if he had moved out.

I'll find him, then, he thought.

On his way back to Camden Town he bought a newspaper. When he arrived home Bridget offered him tea, so he read the paper in her parlor. There was nothing about Orlov either in the Court Circular or the Social Notes.

Bridget saw what he was reading. "Interesting material, for a fellow such as yourself," she said sarcastically. "You'll be making up your mind which of the balls to attend tonight, no doubt."

Feliks smiled and said nothing.

Bridget said: "I know what you are, you know. You're an anarchist."

Feliks was very still.

"Who are you going to kill?" she said. "I hope it's the bloody King." She drank tea noisily. "Well, don't stare at me like that. You look as if you're about to slit me throat. You needn't worry, I won't tell on you. My husband did for a few of the English in his time."

Feliks was nonplussed. She had guessed—and she approved! He did not know what to say. He stood up and folded his newspaper. "You're a good woman," he said.

"If I was twenty years younger I'd kiss you. Get away before I forget myself."

"Thank you for the tea," Feliks said. He went out.

He spent the rest of the evening sitting in the drab basement room, staring at the wall, thinking. Of course Orlov was lying low, but where? If he was not at the Walden house, he might be at the Russian Embassy, or at the home of one of the embassy staff, or at a hotel, or at the home of one of Walden's friends. He might even be out of London, at a house in the country. There was no way to check all the possibilities.

It was not going to be so easy. He began to worry.

He considered following Walden around. It might be the best he could do, but it was unsatisfactory. Although it was possible for a bicycle to keep pace with a carriage in London, it could be exhausting for the cyclist, and Feliks knew that he could not contemplate it for several days. Suppose then that, over a period of three days, Walden visited several private houses, two or three offices, a hotel or two and an embassy—how would Feliks find out which of those buildings Orlov was in? It was possible, but it would take time.

Meanwhile the negotiations would be progressing and war drawing nearer.

And suppose that, after all that, Orlov was still living in Walden's house and had decided simply not to go out?

Feliks went to sleep gnawing at the problem and woke up in the morning with the solution.

He would ask Lydia.

He polished his boots, washed his hair and shaved. He borrowed from Bridget a white cotton scarf which, worn around his throat, concealed the fact that he had neither collar nor tie. At the secondhand clothes stall in Mornington Crescent he found a bowler hat which fitted him. He looked at himself in the stallholder's cracked, frosted mirror. He looked dangerously respectable. He walked on.

He had no idea how Lydia would react to him. He was quite sure that she had not recognized him on the night of the fiasco: his face had been covered and her scream had been a reaction to the sight of an anonymous man with a gun. Assuming he could get in to see her, what would she do? Would she throw him out? Would she immediately begin to tear off her clothes, the way she had used to? Would she be merely indifferent, thinking of him as someone she knew in her youth and no longer cared for?

He wanted her to be shocked and dazed and still in love with him, so that he would be able to make her tell him a secret.

Suddenly he could not remember what she looked like. It was very odd. He knew she was a certain height, neither fat nor thin, with pale hair and gray eyes; but he could not bring to mind a picture of her. If he concentrated on her nose he could see that, or he could visualize her vaguely, without definite form, in the bleak light of a St. Petersburg evening; but when he tried to focus on her she faded away.

He arrived at the park and hesitated outside the house. It was ten o'clock. Would they have got up yet? In any event, he thought he should probably wait until Walden left the house. It occurred to him that he might even see Orlov in the hall—at a time when he had no weapon.

If I do, I'll strangle him with my hands, he thought savagely.

He wondered what Lydia was doing right now. She might be dressing. Ah, yes, he thought, I can picture her in a corset, brushing her hair before a mirror. Or she might be eating breakfast. There would be eggs and meat and fish, but she would eat a small piece of a soft roll and a slice of apple.

The carriage appeared at the entrance. A minute or two later someone got in and it drove to the gate. Feliks stood on the opposite side of the road as it emerged. Suddenly he was looking straight at Walden, behind the window of the coach, and Walden was looking at him. Feliks had an urge to shout: "Hey, Walden, I fucked her first!" Instead he grinned and doffed his hat. Walden inclined his head in acknowledgment, and the carriage passed on.

Feliks wondered why he felt so elated.

He walked through the gateway and across the courtyard. He saw that there were flowers in every window of the house, and he thought: Ah, yes, she always loved flowers. He climbed the steps to the porch and pulled the bell at the front door.

Perhaps she will call the police, he thought.

A moment later a servant opened the door. Feliks stepped inside. "Good morning," he said.

"Good morning, sir," the servant said.

So I *do* look respectable. "I should like to see the Countess of Walden. It is a matter of great urgency. My name is Konstantin Dmitrich Levin. I am sure she will remember me from St. Petersburg."

"Yes, sir. Konstantin . . . ?"

"Konstantin Dmitrich Levin. Let me give you my card." Feliks fumbled inside his coat. "Ach! I brought none."

"That's all right, sir. Konstantin Dmitrich Levin."

"Yes."

"If you will be so good as to wait here, I'll see if the Countess is in."

Feliks nodded, and the servant went away.

◆§ §◆

SIX

The Queen Anne bureau-bookcase was one of Lydia's favorite pieces of furniture in the London house. Two hundred years old, it was of black lacquer decorated in gold with vaguely Chinese scenes of pagodas, willow trees, islands and flowers. The flap front folded down to form a writing table and to reveal red-velvet-lined pigeonholes for letters and tiny drawers for paper and pens. There were large drawers in the bombé base, and the top, above her eye level as she sat at the table, was a bookcase with a mirrored door. The ancient mirror showed a cloudy, distorted reflection of the morning room behind her.

On the writing table was an unfinished letter to her sister, Aleks's mother, in St. Petersburg. Lydia's handwriting was small and untidy. She had written, in Russian: *I don't know what to think about Charlotte* and then she had stopped. She sat, looking into the cloudy mirror, musing.

It was turning out to be a very eventful season in the worst possible way. After the suffragette protest at the court and the madman in the park, she had thought there could be no more catastrophes. And for a few days life had been calm. Charlotte was successfully launched. Aleks was no longer around to disturb Lydia's equanimity, for he had fled to the Savoy Hotel and did not appear at society functions. Belinda's ball had been a huge success. That night Lydia had forgotten her troubles and had a wonderful time. She had danced the waltz, the polka, the two-step, the tango and even the Turkey Trot. She had partnered half the House of Lords, several dashing young men, and —most of all—her husband. It was not really chic to dance with one's own husband quite as much as she had. But Stephen looked so fine in his white tie and tails, and he danced so well, that she had given herself up to pleasure. Her marriage was definitely in one of its happier phases. Looking back over the years, she had the feeling that it was often like this in the season. And then Annie had turned up to spoil it all.

Lydia had only the vaguest recollection of Annie as a housemaid at Walden Hall. One could not possibly know all the servants at an establishment as large as that: there were some fifty indoor staff, and then the gardeners and grooms. Nor was one known to all the servants: on one famous occasion, Lydia had stopped a passing maid in the hall and asked her whether Lord Walden was in his room, and had received the reply: "I'll go and see, Madam—what name shall I say?"

However, Lydia remembered the day Mrs. Braithwaite, the housekeeper at Walden Hall, had come to her with the news that Annie would have to go because she was pregnant. Mrs. Braithwaite did not say "pregnant," she said "overtaken in moral transgression." Both Lydia and Mrs. Braithwaite were embarrassed, but neither was shocked: it had happened to housemaids before and it would happen again. They had to be let go—it was the only way to run a respectable house—and naturally they could not be given references in those circumstances. Without a "character" a maid could not get another job in service, of course; but normally she did not need a job, for she either married the father of the child or went home to mother. Indeed, years later, when she had brought up her children, such a girl might even find her way back into the house, as a laundry-maid or kitchen-maid, or in some other capacity which would not bring her into contact with her employers.

Lydia had assumed that Annie's life would follow that course. She remembered that a young under-gardener had left without giving notice and run away to sea—that piece of news had come to her attention because of the difficulty of finding boys to work as gardeners for a sensible wage these days—but of course no one ever told her the connection between Annie and the boy.

We're not harsh, Lydia thought; as employers we're relatively generous. Yet Charlotte reacted as if Annie's plight were my fault. I don't know where she gets her ideas. What was it she said? "I know what Annie did and I know who she did it with." In Heaven's name, where did the child learn to speak like that? I dedicated my whole life to bringing her up to be pure and clean and decent, not like me *don't even think that*—

She dipped her pen in the inkwell. She would have liked to share her worries with her sister, but it was so hard in a letter. It was hard enough in person, she thought. Charlotte was the one with whom she really wanted to share her thoughts. Why is it that when I try I become shrill and tyrannical?

Pritchard came in. "A Mr. Konstantin Dmitrich Levin to see you, my lady."

Lydia frowned. "I don't think I know him."

"The gentleman said it was a matter of urgency, m'lady, and seemed to think you would remember him from St. Petersburg." Pritchard looked dubious.

Lydia hesitated. The name was distinctly familiar. From time to time Russians whom she hardly knew would call on her in London. They usually began by offering to take back messages, and ended by asking to borrow the passage money. Lydia did not mind helping them. "All right," she said. "Show him in."

Pritchard went out. Lydia inked her pen again, and wrote: *What can one do when the child is eighteen years old and has a will of her own? Stephen says I worry too much. I wish—*

I can't even talk to Stephen properly, she thought. He just makes soothing noises.

The door opened, and Pritchard said: "Mr. Konstantin Dmitrich Levin."

Lydia spoke over her shoulder in English. "I'll be with you in a moment, Mr. Levin." She heard the butler close the door as she wrote: *—that I could believe him.* She put down her pen and turned around.

He spoke to her in Russian. "How are you, Lydia?"

Lydia whispered: "Oh, my *God.*"

It was as if something cold and heavy descended over her

heart, and she could not breathe. Feliks stood in front of her: tall, and thin as ever, in a shabby coat with a scarf, holding a foolish English hat in his left hand. He was as familiar as if she had seen him yesterday. His hair was still long and black, without a hint of gray. There was that white skin, the nose like a curved blade, the wide, mobile mouth and the sad soft eyes.

He said: "I'm sorry to shock you."

Lydia could not speak. She struggled with a storm of mixed emotions: shock, fear, delight, horror, affection and dread. She stared at him. He was *older.* His face was lined: there were two sharp creases in his cheeks, and downturning wrinkles at the corners of his lovely mouth. They seemed like lines of pain and hardship. In his expression there was a hint of something which had not been there before—perhaps ruthlessness, or cruelty, or just inflexibility. He looked tired.

He was studying her, too. "You look like a girl," he said wonderingly.

She tore her eyes away from him. Her heart pounded like a drum. Dread became her dominant feeling. If Stephen should come back early, she thought, and walk in here now, and give me that look that says Who is this man? and I were to blush, and mumble, and—

"I wish you'd say something," Feliks said.

Her eyes returned to him. With an effort, she said: "Go away."

"No."

Suddenly she knew she did not have the strength of will to make him leave. She looked over to the bell which would summon Pritchard. Feliks smiled as if he knew what was in her mind.

"It's been nineteen years," he said.

"You've aged," she said abruptly.

"You've changed."

"What did you expect?"

"I expected this," he said. "That you would be afraid to admit to yourself that you are happy to see me."

He had always been able to see into her soul with those soft eyes. What was the use of pretending? He knew all about pretending, she recalled. He had understood her from the moment he first set eyes on her.

"Well?" he said. "Aren't you happy?"

"I'm frightened, too," she said, and then she realized she had admitted to being happy. "And you?" she added hastily. "How do you feel?"

"I don't feel much at all, anymore," he said. His face twisted into an odd, pained smile. It was a look she had never seen on him in the old days. She felt intuitively that he was telling the truth at that moment.

He drew up a chair and sat close to her. She jerked back convulsively. He said: "I won't hurt you—"

"Hurt me?" Lydia gave a laugh that sounded unexpectedly brittle. "You'll ruin my life!"

"You ruined mine," he replied; then he frowned as if he had surprised himself.

"Oh, Feliks, I didn't mean to."

He was suddenly tense. There was a heavy silence. He gave that hurt smile again, and said: "What happened?"

She hesitated. She realized that all these years she had been longing to explain it to him. She began: "That night you tore my gown . . ."

◦§ ৪◦

"What are you going to do about this tear in your gown?" Feliks asked.

"The maid will put a stitch in it before I arrive at the embassy," Lydia replied.

"Your maid carries needles and thread around with her?"

"Why else would one take one's maid when one goes out to dinner?"

"Why indeed?" He was lying on the bed watching her dress. She knew that he loved to see her put her clothes on. He had once done an imitation of her pulling up her drawers which had made her laugh until it hurt.

She took the gown from him and put it on. "Everybody takes an hour to dress for the evening," she said. "Until I met you I had no idea it could be done in five minutes. Button me up."

She looked in the mirror and tidied her hair while he fastened the hooks at the back of her gown. When he had finished he kissed her shoulder. She arched her neck. "Don't start again," she said. She picked up the old brown cloak and handed it to him.

He helped her on with it. He said: "The lights go out when you leave."

She was touched. He was not often sentimental. She said: "I know how you feel."

"Will you come tomorrow?"

"Yes."

At the door she kissed him and said: "Thank you."

"I love you dearly," he said.

She left him. As she went down the stairs she heard a noise behind her and looked back. Feliks's neighbor was watching her from the door of the next apartment. He looked embarrassed when he caught her eye. She nodded politely to him, and he withdrew. It occurred to her that he could probably hear them making love through the wall. She did not care. She knew that what she was doing was wicked and shameful but she refused to think about it.

She went out into the street. Her maid was waiting on the corner. Together they walked to the park where the carriage was waiting. It was a cold evening, but Lydia felt as if she were glowing with her own warmth. She often wondered whether people could tell, just by looking at her, that she had been making love.

The coachman put down the step of the carriage for her and avoided her eyes. He knows, she thought with surprise; then she decided that that was fanciful.

In the coach the maid hastily repaired the back of Lydia's gown. Lydia changed the brown cloak for a fur wrap. The maid fussed with Lydia's hair. Lydia gave her ten rubles for her silence. Then they were at the British Embassy.

Lydia composed herself and went in.

It was not difficult, she found, to assume her other personality and become the modest, virginal Lydia whom polite society knew. As soon as she entered the real world she was terrified by the brute power of her passion for Feliks and she became quite genuinely a trembling lily. It was no act. Indeed, for most of the hours in the day she felt that this well-behaved maiden was her real self, and she thought she must be somehow possessed while she was with Feliks. But when he was there, and also when she was alone in bed in the middle of the night, she knew that it was her official persona that was evil, for it would have denied her the greatest joy she had ever known.

So she entered the hall, dressed in becoming white, looking young and a little nervous.

She met her cousin Kiril, who was nominally her escort. He was a widower of thirty-something years, an irritable man who worked for the Foreign Minister. He and Lydia did not much like each other, but because his wife was dead, and because Lydia's parents did not enjoy going out, Kiril and Lydia had let it be known that they should be invited together. Lydia always told him not to trouble to call for her. This was how she managed to meet Feliks clandestinely.

"You're late," Kiril said.

"I'm sorry," she replied insincerely.

Kiril took her into the salon. They were greeted by the ambassador and his wife, and then introduced to Lord Highcombe, elder son of the Earl of Walden. He was a tall, handsome man of about thirty, in well-cut but rather sober clothes. He looked very English, with his short, light-brown hair and blue eyes. He had a smiling, open face which Lydia found mildly attractive. He spoke good French. They made polite conversation for a few moments, then he was introduced to someone else.

"He seems rather pleasant," Lydia said to Kiril.

"Don't be fooled," Kiril told her. "Rumor has it that he's a tearaway."

"You surprise me."

"He plays cards with some officers I know, and they were telling me that he drinks them under the table some nights."

"You know so much about people, and it's always bad."

Kiril's thin lips twisted in a smile. "Is that my fault or theirs?"

Lydia said: "Why is he here?"

"In St. Petersburg? Well, the story is that he has a very rich and domineering father, with whom he doesn't see eye to eye; so he's drinking and gambling his way around the world while he waits for the old man to die."

Lydia did not expect to speak to Lord Highcombe again, but the ambassador's wife, seeing them both as eligible, seated them side by side at dinner. During the second course he tried to make conversation. "I wonder whether you know the Minister of Finance?" he said.

"I'm afraid not," Lydia said coldly. She knew all about the man, of course, and he was a great favorite of the Czar; but he had married a woman who was not only divorced but also Jewish, which made it rather awkward for people to invite him. She suddenly thought how scathing Feliks would be about such prejudices; then the Englishman was speaking again.

"I should be most interested to meet him. I understand he's terribly energetic and forward-looking. His Trans-Siberian Railway project is marvelous. But people say he's not very refined."

"I'm sure Sergey Yulevich Witte is a loyal servant of our adored sovereign," Lydia said politely.

"No doubt," Highcombe said, and turned back to the lady on his other side.

He thinks I'm boring, Lydia thought.

A little later she asked him: "Do you travel a great deal?"

"Most of the time," he replied. "I go to Africa almost every year, for the big game."

"How fascinating! What do you shoot?"

"Lion, elephant . . . a rhinoceros, once."

"In the jungle?"

"The hunting is in the grasslands to the east, but I did once go as far south as the rain forest, just to see it."

"And is it how it is pictured in books?"

"Yes, even to the naked black pygmies."

Lydia felt herself flush, and she turned away. Now why did he have to say that? she thought. She did not speak to him again. They had conversed enough to satisfy the dictates of etiquette, and clearly neither of them was keen to go further.

After dinner she played the ambassador's wonderful grand piano for a while; then Kiril took her home. She went straight to bed to dream of Feliks.

The next morning after breakfast a servant summoned her to her father's study.

The count was a small, thin, exasperated man of fifty-five. Lydia was the youngest of his four children—the others were a sister and two brothers, all married. Their mother was alive but in continual bad health. The count saw little of his family. He seemed to spend most of his time reading. He had one old friend who came to play chess. Lydia had vague memories of a time when things were different and they were a jolly family around a big dinner table; but it was a long time ago. Nowadays a summons to the study meant only one thing: trouble.

When Lydia went in he was standing in front of the writing table, his hands behind his back, his face twisted with fury. Lydia's maid stood near the door with tears on her cheeks. Lydia knew then what the trouble was, and she felt herself tremble.

There was no preamble. Her father began by shouting: "You have been seeing a boy secretly!"

Lydia folded her arms to stop herself shaking. "How did you find out?" she said with an accusing look at the maid.

Her father made a disgusted noise. "Don't look at *her*," he said. "The coachman told me of your extraordinarily long walks in the park. Yesterday I had you followed." His voice rose again. "How could you act like that—like a peasant girl?"

How much did he know? Not everything, surely! "I'm in love," Lydia said.

"In love?" he roared. "You mean you're in heat!"

Lydia thought he was about to strike her. She took several paces backward and prepared to run. He knew everything. It was total catastrophe. What would he do?

He said: "The worst of it is, you can't possibly marry him."

Lydia was aghast. She was prepared to be thrown out of the house, cut off without a penny and humiliated; but he had in mind worse punishment than that. "Why can't I marry him?" she cried.

"Because he's practically a serf and an anarchist to boot. Don't you understand—you're ruined!"

"Then let me marry him and live in ruin!"

"No!" he yelled.

There was a heavy silence. The maid, still in tears, sniffed monotonously. Lydia heard a ringing in her ears.

"This will kill your mother," the count said.

Lydia whispered: "What are you going to do?"

"You'll be confined to your room for now. As soon as I can arrange it, you'll enter a convent."

Lydia stared at him in horror. It was a sentence of death.

She ran from the room.

Never to see Feliks again—the thought was utterly unbearable. Tears rolled down her face. She ran to her bedroom. She could not possibly suffer this punishment. I shall die, she thought; I shall die.

Rather than leave Feliks forever she would leave her family forever. As soon as this idea occurred to her she knew it was the only thing to do—and the time to do it was now, before her father sent someone to lock her into her room.

She looked in her purse: she had only a few rubles. She opened her jewelry case. She took out a diamond bracelet, a gold chain and some rings, and stuffed them into her purse. She put on her coat and ran down the back stairs. She left the house by the servants' door.

She hurried through the streets. People stared at her, running in her fine clothes, with tears on her face. She did not care. She had left society for good. She was going to elope with Feliks.

She quickly became exhausted and slowed to a walk. Suddenly the whole affair did not seem so disastrous. She and Feliks could go to Moscow, or to a country town, or even abroad, perhaps Germany. Feliks would have to find work. He was educated, so he could at least be a clerk, possibly better. She might take in sewing. They would rent a small house and furnish it cheaply. They would have children, strong boys and pretty girls. The things she would lose seemed worthless: silk dresses, society gossip, ubiquitous servants, huge houses and delicate foods.

What would it be like, living with him? They would get into bed and actually go to sleep together—how romantic! They would take walks, holding hands, not caring who saw that they were in love. They would sit by the fireside in the evenings, playing cards or reading or just talking. Any time she wanted, she could touch him, or kiss him, or take off her clothes for him.

She reached his house and climbed the stairs. What would his reaction be? He would be shocked, then elated; then he would become practical. They would have to leave immediately, he would say, for her father could send people after them to bring her back. He would be decisive. "We'll go to X," he would say, and he would talk about tickets and a suitcase and disguises.

She took out her key, but the door to his apartment hung

open and askew on its hinges. She went in, calling: "Feliks, it's me—oh!"

She stopped in the doorway. The whole place was in a mess, as if it had been robbed, or there had been a fight. Feliks was not there.

Suddenly she was terribly afraid.

She walked around the small apartment, feeling dazed, stupidly looking behind the curtains and under the bed. All his books were gone. The mattress had been slashed. The mirror was broken, the one in which they had watched themselves making love one afternoon when it had been snowing outside.

Lydia wandered aimlessly into the hallway. The occupant of the next apartment stood in his doorway. Lydia looked at him. "What happened?" she said.

"He was arrested last night," the man replied.

And the sky fell in.

She felt faint. She leaned against the wall for support. Arrested! Why? Where was he? Who had arrested him? How could she elope with him if he was in jail?

"It seems he was an anarchist." The neighbor grinned suggestively and added: "Whatever else he might have been."

It was too much to bear, that this should have happened on the very day that Father had—

"Father," Lydia whispered. "Father did this."

"You look ill," the neighbor said. "Would you like to come in and sit down for a moment?"

Lydia did not like the look on his face. She could not cope with this leering man on top of everything else. She pulled herself together and, without answering him, made her way slowly down the stairs and went out into the street.

She walked slowly, going nowhere, wondering what to do. Somehow she had to get Feliks out of jail. She had no idea how to go about it. She should appeal to the Minister of the Interior? To the Czar? She did not know how to reach them except by going to the right receptions. She could write—but she needed Feliks *today*. Could she visit him in jail? At least then she would know how he was, and he would know she was fighting for him. Maybe, if she arrived in a coach, dressed in fine clothes, she could overawe the jailer . . . But she did not know where the jail was—there might be more than one—and she did not have her carriage; and if she went home her father would lock her up and she would never see Feliks—

She fought back the tears. She was so ignorant of the world of police and jails and criminals. Whom could she ask? Feliks's anarchist friends would know all about that sort of thing, but she had never met them and did not know where to find them.

She thought of her brothers. Maks was managing the family estate in the country, and he would see Feliks from Father's point of view and would completely approve of what Father had done. Dmitri—empty-headed, effeminate Dmitri—would sympathize with Lydia but be helpless.

There was only one thing to do. She must go and plead with her father for Feliks's release.

Wearily, she turned around and headed for home.

Her anger toward her father grew with every step she took. He was supposed to love her, care for her and ensure her happiness—and what did he do? Tried to ruin her life. She knew what she wanted; she knew what would make her happy. Whose life was it? Who had the right to decide?

She arrived home in a rage.

She went straight to the study and walked in without knocking. "You've had him arrested," she accused.

"Yes," her father said. His mood had altered. His mask of fury had gone, to be replaced by a thoughtful, calculating look.

Lydia said: "You must have him released immediately."

"They are torturing him, at this moment."

"No," Lydia whispered. "Oh, no."

"They are flogging the soles of his feet—"

Lydia screamed.

Father raised his voice. "—with thin, flexible canes—"

There was a paper knife on the writing table.

"—which quickly cut the soft skin—"

I will kill him—

"—until there is so much blood—"

Lydia went berserk.

She picked up the paper knife and rushed at her father. She lifted the knife high in the air and brought it down with all her might, aiming at his skinny neck, screaming all the while: "I hate you, I hate you, I hate you—"

He moved aside, caught her wrist, forced her to drop the knife and pushed her into a chair.

She burst into hysterical tears.

After a few minutes her father began to speak again, calmly, as if nothing had happened. "I could have it stopped immediately," he said. "I can have the boy released whenever I choose."

"Oh, please," Lydia sobbed. "I'll do anything you say."

"Will you?" he said.

She looked up at him through her tears. An access of hope calmed her. Did he mean it? Would he release Feliks? "Anything," she said, "anything."

"I had a visitor while you were out," he said conversationally. "The Earl of Walden. He asked permission to call on you."

"Who?"

"The Earl of Walden. He was Lord Highcombe when you met him last evening, but his father died in the night so now he's the Earl. 'Earl' is the English for 'Count.' "

Lydia stared at her father uncomprehendingly. She remembered meeting the Englishman, but she could not understand why her father was suddenly rambling on about him. She said: "Don't torture me. Tell me what I must do to make you release Feliks."

"Marry the Earl of Walden," her father said abruptly.

Lydia stopped crying. She stared at him, dumbstruck. Was he really saying this? It sounded insane.

He continued: "Walden will want to marry quickly. You would leave Russia and go to England with him. This appalling affair could be forgotten and nobody need know. It's the ideal solution."

"And Feliks?" Lydia breathed.

"The torture would stop today. The boy would be released the moment you leave for England. You would never see him again as long as you live."

"No," Lydia whispered. "In God's name, no."

They were married eight weeks later.

❧ ☙

"You really tried to stab your father?" Feliks said with a mixture of awe and amusement.

Lydia nodded. She thought: Thank God, he has not guessed the rest of it.

Feliks said: "I'm proud of you."

"It was a terrible thing to do."

"He was a terrible man."

"I don't think so anymore."

There was a pause. Feliks said softly: "So, you never betrayed me, after all."

The urge to take him into her arms was almost irresistible. She made herself sit frozen still. The moment passed.

"Your father kept his word," he mused. "The torture stopped that day. They let me out the day after you left for England."

"How did you know where I had gone?"

"I got a message from the maid. She left it at the bookshop. Of course she didn't know of the bargain you had made."

The things they had to say were so many and so weighty that they sat in silence. Lydia was still afraid to move. She noticed that he kept his right hand in his coat pocket all the time. She did not remember his having that habit before.

"Can you whistle yet?" he said suddenly.

She could not help laughing. "I never got the knack."

They lapsed into quiet again. Lydia wanted him to leave, and with equal desperation she wanted him to stay. Eventually she said: "What have you been doing since then?"

Feliks shrugged. "A good deal of traveling. You?"

"Bringing up my daughter."

The years in between seemed to be an uncomfortable topic for both of them.

Lydia said: "What made you come here?"

"Oh . . . " Feliks seemed momentarily confused by the question. "I need to see Orlov."

"Aleks? Why?"

"There's an anarchist sailor in jail—I have to persuade Orlov to release him . . . You know how things are in Russia; there's no justice, only influence."

"Aleks isn't here anymore. Someone tried to rob us in our carriage, and he got frightened."

"Where can I find him?" Feliks said. He seemed suddenly tense.

"The Savoy Hotel—but I doubt if he'll see you."

"I can try."

"This is important to you, isn't it?"

"Yes."

"You're still . . . political?"

"It's my life."

"Most young men lose interest as they grow older."

He smiled ruefully. "Most young men get married and have a family."

Lydia was full of pity. "Feliks, I'm so sorry."

He reached out and took her hand.

She snatched it back and stood up. "Don't touch me," she said.

He looked at her in surprise.

"I've learned my lesson, even if you haven't," she said. "I was brought up to believe that lust is evil, and destroys. For a while, when we were . . . together . . . I stopped believing that, or at least I pretended to stop. And look what happened—I ruined myself and I ruined you. My father was right—lust does destroy. I've never forgotten that, and I never will."

He looked at her sadly. "Is that what you tell yourself?"

"It's true."

"The morality of Tolstoy. Doing good may not make you happy, but doing wrong will certainly make you unhappy."

She took a deep breath. "I want you to go away now, and never come back."

He looked at her in silence for a long moment; then he stood up. "Very well," he said.

Lydia thought her heart would break.

He took a step toward her. She stood still, knowing she should move away from him, unable to do so. He put his hands on her shoulders and looked into her eyes, and then it was too late. She remembered how it used to be when they looked into each other's eyes, and she was lost. He drew her to him and kissed her, folding her into his arms. It was just like always, his restless mouth on her soft lips, busy, loving, gentle; she was melting. She pushed her body against his. There was a fire in her loins. She shuddered with pleasure. She searched for his hands and held them in her own, just to have something to hold, a part of his body to grip, to squeeze with all her might—

He gave a shout of pain.

They broke apart. She stared at him, nonplussed.

He held his right hand to his mouth. She saw that he had a nasty wound, and in squeezing his hand she had made it bleed. She moved to take his hand, to say sorry, but he stepped back. A change had come over him, the spell was broken. He turned and strode to the door. Horrified, she watched him go out. The door slammed. Lydia gave a cry of loss.

She stood for a moment gazing at the place where he had been. She felt as if she had been ravaged. She fell into a chair. She began to shake uncontrollably.

Her emotions whirled and boiled for minutes, and she could not think straight. Eventually they settled, leaving one predominant feeling: relief that she had not yielded to the temptation to tell him the last chapter of the story. That was a secret lodged deep within her, like a piece of shrapnel in a healed-over wound; and there it would stay until the day she died, when it would be buried with her.

•◦§ §◦•

Feliks stopped in the hall to put on his hat. He looked at himself in the mirror, and his face twisted into a grin of savage triumph. He composed his features and went out into the midday sunshine.

She was so gullible. She had believed his half-baked story about an anarchist sailor, and she had told him, without a second's hesitation, where to find Orlov. He was exultant that she was still so much in his power. She married Walden for my sake, he thought, and now I have made her betray her husband.

Nevertheless, the interview had had its dangerous moments for him. As she was telling her story he had watched her face, and a dreadful grief had welled up within him, a peculiar sadness that made him want to cry; but it had been so long since he had shed tears that his body seemed to have forgotten how, and those dangerous moments had passed. I'm not really vulnerable to sentiment, he told himself: I lied to her, betrayed her trust in me, kissed her and ran away; I *used* her.

Fate is on my side today. It's a good day for a dangerous task.

He had dropped his gun in the park, so he needed a new

weapon. For an assassination in a hotel room a bomb would be best. It did not have to be aimed accurately, for wherever it landed, it would kill everyone in the room. If Walden should happen to be there with Orlov at the time, so much the better, Feliks thought. It occurred to him that then Lydia would have helped him kill her husband.

So?

He put her out of his mind and began to think about chemistry.

He went to a chemist's shop in Camden Town and bought four pints of a common acid in concentrated form. The acid came in two two-pint bottles, and cost four shillings and fivepence including the price of the bottles, which was refundable.

He took the bottles home and put them on the floor of the basement room.

He went out again, and bought another four pints of the same acid in a different shop. The chemist asked him what he was going to use it for. "Cleaning," he said, and the man seemed satisfied.

In a third chemist's he bought four pints of a different acid. Finally he bought a pint of pure glycerine and a glass rod a foot long.

He had spent sixteen shillings and eightpence, but he would get four shillings and threepence back for the bottles when they were empty. That would leave him with just under three pounds.

Because he had bought the ingredients in different shops, none of the chemists had any reason to suspect that he was going to make explosives.

He went up to Bridget's kitchen and borrowed her largest mixing bowl.

"Would you be baking a cake?" she asked him.

He said: "Yes."

"Don't blow us all up, then."

"I won't."

Nevertheless she took the precaution of spending the afternoon with a neighbor.

Feliks went back downstairs, took off his jacket, rolled up his sleeves and washed his hands.

He put the mixing bowl in the washbasin.

He looked at the row of large brown bottles, with their ground-glass stoppers, lined up on the floor.

The first part of the job was not very dangerous.

He mixed the two kinds of acid together in Bridget's kitchen bowl, waited for the bowl to cool, then rebottled the two-to-one mixture.

He washed the bowl, dried it, put it back into the sink and poured the glycerine into it.

The sink was fitted with a rubber plug on a chain. He wedged the plug into the drain hole sideways, so that it was partly blocked. He turned on the tap. When the water level reached almost to the rim of the kitchen bowl, he turned the tap partly but not completely off, so that the water was flowing out as fast as it was flowing in and the level in the sink stayed constant without overflowing into the kitchen bowl.

The next part had killed more anarchists than the Okhrana.

Gingerly, he began to add the mixed acids to the glycerine, stirring gently but constantly with the glass rod.

The basement room was very warm.

Occasionally a wisp of reddish-brown smoke came off the bowl, a sign that the chemical reaction was beginning to get out of control; then Feliks would stop adding acid, but carry on stirring, until the flow of water through the washbasin cooled the bowl and moderated the reaction. When the fumes were gone he waited a minute or two, then carried on mixing.

This is how Ilya died, he recalled; standing over a sink in a basement room, mixing acids and glycerine: perhaps he was impatient. When they finally cleared the rubble, there was nothing left of Ilya to bury.

Afternoon turned into evening. The air became cooler but Feliks perspired all the same. His hand was as steady as a rock. He could hear children in the street outside, playing a game and chanting a rhyme: "Salt, mustard, vinegar, *pepper*, salt, mustard, vinegar, *pepper.*" He wished he had ice. He wished he had electric light. The room filled with acid fumes. His throat was raw. The mixture in the bowl stayed clear.

He found himself daydreaming about Lydia. In the daydream she came into the basement room, stark naked, smiling, and he told her to go away because he was busy.

"Salt, mustard, vinegar, *pepper.*"

He poured the last bottle of acid as slowly and gently as the first.

Still stirring, he increased the stream of water from the tap so that it overflowed into the bowl; then he meticulously washed away the surplus acids.

When he had finished he had a bowl of nitroglycerine.

It was an explosive liquid twenty times as powerful as gunpowder. It could be detonated by a blasting cap, but such a detonator was not essential, for it could also be set off by a lighted match or even the warmth from a nearby fire. Feliks had known a foolish man who carried a bottle of nitroglycerine in the breast pocket of his coat until the heat of his body detonated it and killed him and three other people and a horse on a St. Petersburg street. A bottle of nitroglycerine would explode if smashed, or just dropped on the floor, or shaken, or even jerked hard.

With the utmost care, Feliks dipped a clean bottle into the bowl and let it fill slowly with the explosive. When it was full he closed the bottle, making sure that there was no nitroglycerine caught between the neck of the bottle and the ground-glass stopper.

There was some liquid left in the bowl. Of course it could not be poured down the sink.

Feliks went over to his bed and picked up the pillow. The stuffing seemed to be cotton waste. He tore a small hole in the pillow and pulled out some of the stuff. It was chopped rag mixed with a few feathers. He poured some of it into the nitroglycerine remaining in the bowl. The stuffing absorbed the liquid quite well. Feliks added more stuffing until all the liquid was soaked up; then he rolled it into a ball and wrapped it in newspaper. It was now much more stable, like dynamite—in fact dynamite was what it was. It would detonate much less readily than the pure liquid. Lighting the newspaper might do it, and it might not: what was really required was a paper drinking straw packed with gunpowder. But Feliks did not plan to use the dynamite, for he needed something reliable and immediate.

He washed and dried the mixing bowl again. He plugged the sink, filled it with water, then gently placed the bottle of nitroglycerine in the water, to keep cool.

He went upstairs and returned Bridget's kitchen bowl.

He came back down and looked at the bomb in the sink. He thought: I wasn't afraid. All afternoon, I was never frightened of dying. I still have no fear.

That made him glad.

He went off to reconnoiter the Savoy Hotel.

❦

SEVEN

Walden observed that both Lydia and Charlotte were subdued at tea. He, too, was thoughtful. The conversation was desultory.

After he had changed for dinner, Walden sat in the drawing room sipping sherry, waiting for his wife and his daughter to come down. They were to dine out, at the Pontadarvys'. It was another warm evening. So far it had been a fine summer for weather, if for nothing else.

Shutting Aleks up in the Savoy Hotel had not done anything to hasten the slow pace of negotiating with the Russians. Aleks inspired affection like a kitten, and had the kitten's surprisingly sharp teeth. Walden had put to him the counterproposal, an international waterway from the Black Sea to the Mediterranean. Aleks had said flatly that this was not good enough, for in wartime—when the strait would become vital—neither Britain nor Russia, with the best will in the world, could prevent the Turks from closing the channel. Russia wanted not only the right of passage but also the power to enforce that right.

While Walden and Aleks argued about how Russia might be given that power, the Germans had completed the widening of the Kiel Canal, a strategically crucial project which would en-

able their dreadnoughts to pass from the North Sea battle-
ground to the safety of the Baltic. In addition, Germany's gold
reserves were at a record high, as a result of the financial ma-
neuvers that had prompted Churchill's visit to Walden Hall in
May. Germany would never be better prepared for war: every
day that passed made an Anglo-Russian alliance more indispens-
able. But Aleks had true nerve—he would make no concessions
in haste.

And, as Walden learned more about Germany—its industry,
its government, its army, its natural resources—he realized that
it had every chance of replacing Britain as the most powerful
nation in the world. Personally he did not much mind whether
Britain was first, second or ninth, so long as she was free. He
loved England. He was proud of his country. Her industry
provided work for millions, and her democracy was a model for
the rest of the world. Her population was becoming more educated, and following that process, more of her people had the
vote. Even the women would get it sooner or later, especially if
they stopped breaking windows. He loved the fields and the
hills, the opera and the music hall, the frenetic glitter of the
metropolis and the slow, reassuring rhythms of country life. He
was proud of her inventors, her playwrights, her businessmen
and her craftsmen. England was a damn good place, and it was
not going to be spoiled by squareheaded Prussian invaders, not
if Walden could help it.

He was worried because he was not sure he *could* help it. He
wondered just how far he really understood modern England,
with its anarchists and suffragettes, ruled by young firebrands
like Churchill and Lloyd George, swayed by even more disrup-
tive forces such as the burgeoning Labor Party and the ever-
more-powerful trade unions. Walden's kind of people still ruled
—the wives were Good Society and the husbands were the Establishment—but the country was not as governable as it had
used to be. Sometimes he had a terribly depressing feeling that
it was all slipping out of control.

Charlotte came in, reminding him that politics was not the
only area of life in which he seemed to be losing his grip. She
was still wearing her tea gown. Walden said: "We must go
soon."

"I'll stay at home, if I may," she said. "I've a slight headache."

"There'll be no hot dinner, unless you warn Cook quickly."

"I shan't want it. I'll have a tray in my room."

"You look a little pale. Have a small glass of sherry; it'll give you an appetite."

"All right."

She sat down and he poured the drink for her. As he gave it to her he said: "Annie has a job and a home, now."

"I'm glad," she replied coldly.

He took a deep breath. "It must be said that I was at fault in that affair."

"Oh!" Charlotte said, astonished.

Is it so rare for me to admit that I'm in the wrong? he wondered. He went on: "Of course, I didn't know that her . . . young man . . . had run off and she was ashamed to go to her mother. But I should have inquired. As you quite rightly said, the girl was my responsibility."

Charlotte said nothing, but sat beside him on the sofa and took his hand. He was touched.

He said: "You have a kind heart, and I hope you'll always stay that way. Might I also be permitted to hope that you will learn to express your generous feelings with a little more . . . equanimity?"

She looked up at him. "I'll do my best, Papa."

"I often wonder whether we've protected you too much. Of course, it was your Mama who decided how you should be brought up, but I must say I agreed with her nearly all the time. There are people who say that children ought not to be protected from, well, what might be called the facts of life; but those people are very few, and they tend to be an awfully coarse type."

They were quiet for a while. As usual, Lydia was taking forever to dress for dinner. There was more that Walden wanted to say to Charlotte, but he was not sure he had the courage. In his mind he rehearsed various openings, none of which was less than acutely embarrassing. She sat with him in contented silence, and he wondered whether she had some idea of what was going on in his mind.

Lydia would be ready in a moment. It was now or never. He cleared his throat. "You'll marry a good man, and together with him you'll learn about all sorts of things that are mysterious and perhaps a little worrying to you now." That might be enough, he thought; this was the moment to back down, to duck the issue. Courage! "But there is one thing you need to know in advance. Your mother should tell you, really, but somehow I think she may not, so I shall."

He lit a cigar, just to have something to do with his hands. He was past the point of no return. He rather hoped Lydia would come in now to put a stop to the conversation; but she did not.

"You said you know what Annie and the gardener did. Well, they aren't married, so it was wrong. But when you are married, it's a very fine thing to do indeed." He felt his face redden and hoped she would not look up just now. "It's very good just physically, you know," he plunged on. "Impossible to describe, perhaps a bit like feeling the heat from a coal fire . . . However, the main thing is, the thing I'm sure you don't realize, is how wonderful the whole thing is spiritually. Somehow it seems to express all the affection and tenderness and respect and . . . well, just the love there is between a man and his wife. You don't necessarily understand that when you're young. Girls especially tend to see only the, well, coarse aspect; and some unfortunate people never discover the good side of it at all. But if you're expecting it, and you choose a good, kind, sensible man for your husband, it's sure to happen. So that's why I've told you. Have I embarrassed you terribly?"

To his surprise she turned her head and kissed his cheek. "Yes, but not as much as you've embarrassed yourself," she said.

That made him laugh.

Pritchard came in. "The carriage is ready, my lord, and my lady is waiting in the hall."

Walden stood up. "Not a word to Mama, now," he murmured to Charlotte.

"I'm beginning to see why everybody says you're such a good man," Charlotte said. "Enjoy your evening."

"Good-bye," he said. As he went out to join his wife he thought: Sometimes I get it right, anyway.

⌇

After that, Charlotte almost changed her mind about going to the suffragette meeting.

She had been in a rebellious mood, following the Annie incident, when she saw the poster stuck to the window of a jeweler's shop in Bond Street. The headline VOTES FOR WOMEN had caught her eye; then she had noticed that the hall in which the meeting was to be held was not far from her house. The notice did not name the speakers, but Charlotte had read in the newspapers that the notorious Mrs. Pankhurst often appeared at such meetings without prior warning. Charlotte had stopped to read the poster, pretending (for the benefit of Marya, who was chaperoning her) to be looking at a tray of bracelets. As she was reading, a boy came out of the shop and began to scrape the poster off the window. There and then Charlotte decided to go to the meeting.

Now Papa had shaken her resolution. It was a shock to see that he could be fallible, vulnerable, even humble; and even more of a revelation to hear him talk of sexual intercourse as if it were something beautiful. She realized that she was no longer raging inwardly at him for allowing her to grow up in ignorance. Suddenly she saw his point of view.

But none of that altered the fact that she was still horribly ignorant, and she could not trust Mama and Papa to tell her the whole truth about things, especially about things like suffragism. I *will* go, she decided.

She rang the bell for Pritchard and asked for a salad to be brought up to her room; then she went upstairs. One of the advantages of being a woman was that no one ever cross-questioned you if you said you had a headache: women were *supposed* to have headaches every now and then.

When the tray came, she picked at the food for a while, until the time came when the servants would be having their supper; then she put on a hat and coat and went out.

It was a warm evening. She walked quickly toward Knightsbridge. She felt a peculiar sense of freedom, and realized that she had never before walked the streets of a city unaccompanied. I could do anything, she thought. I have no appointments and no chaperone. Nobody knows where I am. I could have dinner in a restaurant. I could catch a train to Scotland. I could take a room in a hotel. I could ride on an omnibus. I could eat an apple in the street, and drop the core in the gutter.

She felt conspicuous, but nobody looked at her. She had always had the vague impression that if she went out alone strange men would embarrass her in unspecified ways. In reality they did not seem to see her. The men were not lurking; they were all going somewhere, wearing their evening clothes or their worsted suits or their frock coats. How could there be any danger? she thought. Then she remembered the madman in the park, and she began to hurry.

As she approached the hall she noticed more and more women heading the same way. Some were in pairs or in groups, but many were alone like Charlotte. She felt safer.

Outside the hall was a crowd of hundreds of women. Many wore the suffragette colors of purple, green and white. Some were handing out leaflets or selling a newspaper called *Votes for Women*. There were several policemen about, wearing rather strained expressions of amused contempt. Charlotte joined the queue to get in.

When she reached the door, a woman wearing a steward's armband asked her for sixpence. Charlotte turned, automatically, then realized she did not have Marya, or a footman, or a maid, to pay for things. She was alone, and she had no money. She had not anticipated that she would have to pay to get into the hall. She was not quite sure where she would have got sixpence even if she had foreseen the need.

"I'm sorry," she said. "I haven't any money . . . I didn't know . . ." She turned to leave.

The steward reached out to stop her. "It's all right," the woman said. "If you've no money, you get in free." She had a middle-class accent, and although she spoke kindly, Charlotte imagined that she was thinking: Such fine clothes, and no money!

Charlotte said: "Thank you . . . I'll send you a check . . ." Then she went in, blushing furiously. Thank Heaven I didn't try to have dinner in a restaurant or catch a train, she thought. She had never needed to worry about carrying money around with her. Her chaperone always had petty cash, Papa kept accounts with all the shops in Bond Street, and if she wanted to have lunch at Claridge's or morning coffee in the Café Royal she would simply leave her card on the table and the bill would be sent to Papa. But this was one bill he would not pay.

She took her seat in the hall quite close to the front: she did not want to miss anything, after all this trouble. If I'm going to do this kind of thing often, she thought, I'll have to think of a

way to get my hands on proper money—grubby pennies and
gold sovereigns and crumpled banknotes.

She looked around her. The place was almost full of women,
with just a scattering of men. The women were mostly middle-
class, wearing serge and cotton rather than cashmere and silk.
There were a few who looked distinctly more well-bred than the
average—they talked more quietly and wore less jewelry—and
those women seemed—like Charlotte—to be wearing last year's
coats and rather undistinguished hats, as if to disguise themselves. As far as Charlotte could see, there were no working-class
women in the audience.

Up on the platform was a table draped with a purple, green
and white "Votes for Women" banner. A small lectern stood on
the table. Behind it was a row of six chairs.

Charlotte thought: All these women—rebelling against men!
She did not know whether to be thrilled or ashamed.

The audience applauded as five women walked onto the stage.
They were all impeccably dressed in rather less-than-fashiona-
ble clothes—not a hobble skirt or a cloche hat among them.
Were these really the people who broke windows, slashed paintings and threw bombs? They looked too respectable.

The speeches began. They meant little to Charlotte. They
were about organization, finance, petitions, amendments, divisions and by-elections. She was disappointed: she was learning
nothing. Ought she to read books about this before going to a
meeting, in order to understand the proceedings? After almost
an hour she was ready to leave. Then the current speaker was
interrupted.

Two women appeared at the side of the stage. One was an
athletic-looking girl in a motoring coat. Walking with her, and
leaning on her for support, was a small, slight woman in a
pale-green spring coat and a large hat. The audience began to
applaud. The women on the platform stood up. The applause
grew louder, with shouts and cheers. Someone near Charlotte
stood up, and in seconds a thousand women were on their feet.

Mrs. Pankhurst walked slowly to the lectern.

Charlotte could see her quite clearly. She was what people
called a handsome woman. She had dark, deep-set eyes, a wide,
straight mouth and a strong chin. She would have been beautiful
but for a rather fat, flat nose. The effects of her repeated impris-

onments and hunger strikes showed in the fleshlessness of her face and hands and the yellow color of her skin. She seemed weak, thin and feeble.

She raised her hands, and the cheering and applause died down almost instantly.

She began to speak. Her voice was strong and clear, although she did not seem to shout. Charlotte was surprised to notice that she had a Lancashire accent.

She said: "In 1894 I was elected to the Manchester Board of Guardians, in charge of the workhouse. The first time I went into that place I was horrified to see little girls seven and eight years old on their knees scrubbing the cold stones of the long corridors. These little girls were clad, summer and winter, in thin cotton frocks, low in the neck and short-sleeved. At night they wore nothing at all, nightdresses being considered too good for paupers. The fact that bronchitis was epidemic among them most of the time had not suggested to the Guardians any change in the fashion of the clothes. I need hardly add that, until I arrived, all the Guardians were men.

"I found that there were pregnant women in that workhouse, scrubbing floors, doing the hardest kind of work, almost until their babies came into the world. Many of them were unmarried women; very, very young, mere girls. These poor mothers were allowed to stay in the hospital after confinement for a short two weeks. Then they had to make a choice of staying in the workhouse and earning their living by scrubbing and other work—in which case they were separated from their babies—or of taking their discharges. They could stay and be paupers, or they could leave—leave with a two-week-old baby in their arms, without hope, without home, without money, without anywhere to go. What became of those girls, and what became of their hapless infants?"

Charlotte was stunned by the public discussion of such delicate matters. Unmarried mothers . . . mere girls . . . without home, without money . . . And why should they be separated from their babies in the workhouse? Could this be true?

There was worse to come.

Mrs. Pankhurst's voice rose a fraction. "Under the law, if a man who ruins a girl pays down a lump sum of twenty pounds, the boarding home is immune from inspection. As long as a baby farmer takes only one child at a time, the twenty pounds being paid, the inspectors cannot inspect the house."

Baby farmers . . . a man who ruins a girl . . . the terms were unfamiliar to Charlotte, but they were dreadfully self-explanatory.

"Of course the babies die with hideous promptness, and then the baby farmers are free to solicit another victim. For years women have tried to get the Poor Law changed, to protect all illegitimate children, and to make it impossible for any rich scoundrel to escape liability for his child. Over and over again it has been tried, but it has always failed—" here her voice became a passionate cry "—because the ones who really care about the thing are mere women!"

The audience burst into applause, and a woman next to Charlotte cried: "Hear, hear!"

Charlotte turned to the woman and grabbed her arm. "Is this true?" she said. "Is this *true*?"

But Mrs. Pankhurst was speaking again.

"I wish I had time, and strength, to tell you of all the tragedies I witnessed while I was on that board. In our out-relief department, I was brought into contact with widows who were struggling desperately to keep their homes and families together. The law allowed these women relief of a certain very inadequate kind, but for herself and one child it offered no relief except the workhouse. Even if the woman had a baby at her breast she was regarded, under the law, as an able-bodied man. Women, we are told, should stay at home and take care of their children. I used to astound my men colleagues by saying to them: 'When women have the vote they will see that mothers *can* stay at home and care for their children!'

"In 1899 I was appointed to the office of Registrar of Births and Deaths in Manchester. Even after my experience on the Board of Guardians I was shocked to be reminded over and over again of what little respect there was in the world for women and children. I have had little girls of thirteen come to my office to register the births of their babies—illegitimate, of course. There was nothing that could be done in most cases. The age of consent is sixteen years, but a man can usually claim that he thought the girl was over sixteen. During my term of office, a very young mother of an illegitimate child exposed her baby and it died. The girl was tried for murder and sentenced to death.

The man who was, from the point of view of justice, the real murderer of the baby, received no punishment at all.

"Many times in those days I asked myself what was to be done. I had joined the Labour Party, thinking that through its councils something vital might come, some demand for women's enfranchisement that the politicians could not possibly ignore. Nothing came.

"All these years my daughters had been growing up. One day Christabel startled me with the remark: 'How long you women have been trying for the vote. For my part, I mean to get it.' Since that day I have had two mottoes. One has been: 'Votes for women.' The other: 'For my part, I mean to get it!' "

Someone shouted: "So do I!" and there was another outburst of cheering and clapping. Charlotte was feeling dazed. It was as if she, like Alice in the story, had walked through the looking glass and found herself in a world where nothing was what it seemed. When she had read in the newspapers about suffragettes, no mention had been made of the Poor Law, of thirteen-year-old mothers (was it *possible*?) or of little girls catching bronchitis in the workhouse. Charlotte would have believed none of it had she not seen with her own eyes Annie, a decent, ordinary maid from Norfolk, sleeping on a London pavement after being "ruined" by a man. What did a few broken windows matter while this sort of thing was going on?

"It was many years before we lighted the torch of militancy. We had tried every other measure, and our years of work and suffering and sacrifice had taught us that the Government would not yield to right and justice, but it would yield to expediency. We had to make every department of English life insecure and unsafe. We had to make English law a failure and the courts theatres of farce; we had to discredit the Government in the eyes of the world; we had to spoil English sports, hurt business, destroy valuable property, demoralize the world of Society, shame the churches, upset the whole orderly conduct of life! We had to do as much of this guerrilla warfare as the people of England would tolerate. When they came to the point of saying to the Government: 'Stop this, in the only way it can be stopped, by giving the women of England representation,' then we should extinguish our torch.

"The great American statesman Patrick Henry summed up

the causes that led to the American revolution like this: 'We have petitioned, we have remonstrated, we have supplicated, we have prostrated ourselves at the foot of the throne, and it has all been in vain. We must fight—I repeat it, sir, we must fight.' Patrick Henry was advocating killing people as the proper means of securing the political freedom of *men*. The suffragettes have not done that and never will. In fact, the moving spirit of militancy is a deep and abiding reverence for human life.

"It was in this spirit that our women went forth to war last year. On January thirty-first a number of putting greens were burned with acids. On February seventh and eighth telegraph and telephone wires were cut in several places and for some hours all communication between London and Glasgow was suspended. A few days later windows in various of London's smartest clubs were broken, and the orchid houses at Kew were wrecked and many valuable blooms destroyed by cold. The jewel room at the Tower of London was invaded and a showcase broken. On February eighteenth a country house which was being built at Walton-on-the-Hill for Mr. Lloyd George was partially destroyed, a bomb having been exploded in the early morning before the arrival of the workmen.

"Over one thousand women have gone to prison in the course of this agitation, have suffered their imprisonment, have come out of prison injured in health, weakened in body but not in spirit. Not one of those women would, if women were free, be lawbreakers. They are women who seriously believe that the welfare of humanity demands this sacrifice; they believe that the horrible evils which are ravaging our civilization will never be removed until women get the vote. There is only one way to put a stop to this agitation; there is only one way to break down this agitation. It is not by deporting us!"

"No!" someone shouted.

"It is not by locking us up in jail!"

The whole crowd shouted: "No!"

"It is by doing us justice!"

"Yes!"

Charlotte found herself shouting with the rest. The little woman on the platform seemed to radiate righteous indignation. Her eyes blazed, she clenched her fists, she tilted up her chin, and her voice rose and fell with emotion.

"The fire of suffering whose flame is upon our sisters in prison is burning us also. For we suffer with them, we partake of their affliction, and we shall share their victory by-and-by. This fire will breathe into the ear of many a sleeper the one word 'Awake,' and she will arise to slumber no more. It will descend with the gift of tongues upon many who have hitherto been dumb, and they will go forth to preach the news of deliverance. Its light will be seen afar off by many who suffer and are sorrowful and oppressed, and will irradiate their lives with a new hope. For the spirit which is in women today cannot be quenched; it is stronger than all tyranny, cruelty and oppression; it is stronger—even—than—death—itself!"

◆§ ﴾◆

During the day a dreadful suspicion had dawned on Lydia.

After lunch she had gone to her room to lie down. She had been unable to think about anything but Feliks. She was still vulnerable to his magnetism: it was foolish to pretend otherwise. But she was no longer a helpless girl. She had resources of her own. And she was determined that she would not lose control, would not let Feliks wreck the placid life she had so carefully made for herself.

She thought of all the questions she had not asked him. What was he doing in London? How did he earn his living? How had he known where to find her?

He had given Pritchard a false name. Clearly he had been afraid that she would not let him in. She realized why "Konstantin Dmitrich Levin" had seemed familiar: it was the name of a character in *Anna Karenina,* the book she had been buying when she first met Feliks. It was an alias with a double meaning, a sly mnemonic which lit up a host of dim memories, like a taste recalled from childhood. They had argued about the novel. It was brilliantly real, Lydia had said, for she knew what it was like when passion was released in the soul of a respectable woman; Anna *was* Lydia. But the book was not about Anna, said Feliks; it was about Levin and his search for the answer to the question: "How should I live?" Tolstoy's answer was: "In your heart you know what is right." Feliks argued that it was this kind of empty-headed morality—deliberately ignorant of history, economics and psychology—which had led to the utter incompetence and degeneracy of the Russian ruling class. That was the night they ate pickled mushrooms and she tasted vodka for the first time. She had been wearing a turquoise dress which turned her gray eyes blue. Feliks had kissed her toes, and then—

Yes, he was sly, to remind her of all that.

Had he been in London a long time, she wondered, or had he come just to see Aleks? There was presumably a reason for approaching an admiral in London about the release of a sailor imprisoned in Russia. For the first time it occurred to Lydia that Feliks might not have told her the truth about that. After all, he was still an anarchist. In 1895 he had been determinedly nonviolent, but he might have changed.

If Stephen knew that I had told an anarchist where to find Aleks . . .

She had worried about it through tea. She had worried about it while the maid was putting up her hair, with the result that the job was not properly done and she looked a fright. She had worried about it through dinner, with the result that she had been less than vivacious with the Marchioness of Quort, Mr. Chamberlain and a young man called Freddie who kept hoping aloud that there was nothing seriously wrong with Charlotte.

She recalled Feliks's cut hand, which had caused him to give such a shout when she squeezed it. She had only glimpsed the wound but it looked as if it had been bad enough to need stitches.

Nevertheless, it was not until the end of the evening, when she sat in her bedroom at home brushing her hair, that it occurred to her to connect Feliks with the madman in the park.

The thought was so frightening that she dropped a gold-backed hairbrush onto the dressing table and broke a glass vial of perfume.

What if Feliks had come to London to kill Aleks?

Suppose it was Feliks who had attacked the coach in the park, not to rob them but to get at Aleks? Had the man with the gun been Feliks's height and build? Yes, roughly. And Stephen had wounded him with his sword . . .

Then Aleks had left the house because he was frightened (or perhaps, she now realized, because he *knew* the "robbery" had been an assassination attempt) and Feliks had not known where to find him, so he had asked Lydia . . .

She stared at herself in the mirror. The woman she saw there had gray eyes, fair eyebrows, blond hair, a pretty face and the brain of a sparrow.

Could it be true? Could Feliks have deceived her so? Yes—because he had spent nineteen years imagining that she had betrayed him.

She picked up the pieces of broken glass from the vial and put them in a handkerchief; then she mopped up the spilled perfume. She did not know what to do now. She had to warn Stephen, but how? "By the way, an anarchist called this morning and asked me where Aleks had gone; and because he used to be my lover I told him . . ." She would have to make up a story. She thought for a while. Once upon a time she had been an expert barefaced liar, but she was out of practice. Eventually she decided she could get away with a combination of the lies Feliks had told to her and to Pritchard.

She put on a cashmere robe over the silk nightgown and went through to Stephen's bedroom.

He was sitting at the window, in pajamas and a dressing gown, with a small glass of brandy in one hand and a cigar in the other, looking out over the moonlit park. He was surprised to see her come in, for it was always he who went to her room in the night. He stood up with a welcoming smile and embraced her. She realized that he misunderstood her visit: he thought she had come to make love.

She said: "I want to talk to you."

He released her. He looked disappointed. "At this time of night?"

"I think I may have done something awfully silly."

"You'd better tell me about it."

They sat down on opposite sides of the cold fireplace. Suddenly Lydia wished she *had* come to make love. She said: "A man called this morning. He said he had known me in St. Petersburg. Well, the name was familiar and I thought I vaguely recalled him . . . You know how it is, sometimes—"

"What was his name?"

"Levin

"Go on

"He said he wanted to see Prince Orlov."

Stephen was suddenly very attentive. "Why?"

"Something to do with a sailor who had been unjustly imprisoned. This . . . Levin . . . wanted to make a personal plea for the man's release."

"What did you say?"

"I told him the Savoy Hotel."

"Damn," Stephen cursed, then apologized: "Pardon me."

"Afterward it occurred to me that Levin might have been up to no good. He had a cut hand—and I remembered that you had cut the madman in the park . . . so, you see, it dawned on me gradually . . . I've done something dreadful, haven't I?"

"It's not your fault. In fact it's mine. I should have told you the truth about the man in the park, but I thought it better not to frighten you. I was wrong."

"Poor Aleks," Lydia said. "To think that someone would want to kill him. He's so sweet."

"What was Levin like?"

The question unsettled Lydia. For a moment she had been thinking of "Levin" as an unknown assassin; now she was forced to describe Feliks. "Oh . . . tall, thin, with dark hair, about my age, obviously Russian; a nice face, rather lined . . ." She tailed off. *And I yearn for him.*

Stephen stood up. "I'll go and rouse Pritchard. He can drive me to the hotel."

Lydia wanted to say: No, don't, take me to bed instead; I need your warmth and tenderness. She said: "I'm so sorry."

"It may be for the best," Stephen said.

She looked at him in surprise. "Why?"

"Because, when he comes to the Savoy Hotel to assassinate Aleks, I shall catch him."

And then Lydia knew that before this was over one of the two men she loved would surely kill the other.

◆§ §◆

Feliks gently lifted the bottle of nitroglycerine out of the sink. He crossed the room as if he were walking on eggshells. His pillow was on the mattress. He had enlarged the rip until it was about six inches long, and now he put the bottle through the hole and into the pillow. He arranged the stuffing all around the bottle so that the bomb lay cocooned in shock-absorbing material. He picked up the pillow and, cradling it like a baby, placed it in his open suitcase. He closed the case and breathed more easily.

He put on his coat, his scarf and his respectable hat. Carefully, he turned the cardboard suitcase on to its edge, then picked it up.

He went out.

The journey into the West End was a nightmare.

Of course he could not use the bicycle, but even walking was nerve-wracking. Every second he visualized that brown glass bottle in its pillow; every time his foot hit the pavement he imagined the little shock wave which must travel up his body and down his arm to the case; in his mind he saw the molecules of nitroglycerine vibrating faster and faster under his hand.

He passed a woman washing the pavement in front of her house. He went by on the road, in case he should slip on the wet flagstones, and she jeered: "A-scared of getting yer feet wet, toff?"

Outside a factory in Euston a crowd of apprentices poured through the gates chasing a football. Feliks stood stock still as they rushed all around him, jostling and fighting for the ball. Then someone kicked it clear and they were gone as quickly as they had arrived.

Crossing the Euston Road was a dance with death. He stood at the curb for five minutes, waiting for a good-sized gap in the stream of traffic; and then he had to walk across so fast he was almost running.

In Tottenham Court Road he went into a high-class stationer's. It was calm and hushed in the shop. He set the suitcase down gently on the counter. An assistant in a morning coat said: "Can I help you, sir?"

"I need an envelope, please."

The assistant raised his eyebrows. "Just the one, sir?"

"Yes."

"Any particular kind, sir?"

"Just plain, but good quality."

"We have blue, ivory, eau-de-nil, cream, beige—"

"White."

"Very good, sir."

"And a sheet of paper."

"One sheet of paper, sir."

They charged him threepence. On principle he would have preferred to run off without paying, but he could not run with the bomb in his case.

Charing Cross Road teemed with people on their way to work in shops and offices. It was impossible to walk at all without getting buffeted. Feliks stood in a doorway for a while, wondering what to do. Finally he decided to carry the case in his arms to protect it from the scurrying hordes.

In Leicester Square he took refuge in a bank. He sat at one of the writing tables where the customers made out their checks. There was a tray of pens and an inkwell. He put the case on the floor between his feet. He relaxed for a moment. Frock-coated bank clerks padded softly by with papers in their hands. Feliks took a pen and wrote on the front of his envelope:

> *Prince A. A. Orlov*
> *The Savoy Hotel*
> *Strand, London W.*

He folded the blank sheet of paper and slipped it inside the envelope, just for the sake of its weight: he did not want the envelope to seem empty. He licked the gummed flap and sealed it shut. Then he reluctantly picked up the suitcase and left the bank.

In Trafalgar Square he dipped his handkerchief in the fountain and cooled his face with it.

He passed Charing Cross Station and walked east along the embankment. Near Waterloo Bridge a small group of urchins lounged against the parapet, throwing stones at the seagulls on the river. Feliks spoke to the most intelligent-looking boy.

"Do you want a penny?"

"Yes, guv!"

"Are your hands clean?"

"Yes, guv!" The boy showed a pair of filthy hands.

They would have to do, Feliks thought. "Do you know where the Savoy Hotel is?"

"Too right!"

Feliks assumed this meant the same as "Yes, guv." He handed the boy the envelope and a penny. "Count to a hundred slowly, then take this letter to the hotel. Do you understand?"

"Yes, guv!"

Feliks mounted the steps to the bridge. It was thronged with men in bowler hats coming across the river from the Waterloo side. Feliks joined the procession.

He went into a newsagent's and bought *The Times*. As he was leaving a young man rushed in through the door. Feliks stuck out his arm and stopped the man, shouting: "Look where you're going!"

The man stared at him in surprise. As Feliks went out he heard the man say to the shopkeeper: "Nervous type, is he?"

"Foreigner," said the shopkeeper, and then Feliks was outside.

He turned off the Strand and went into the hotel. In the lobby he sat down and placed the suitcase on the floor between his feet. Not much farther now, he thought.

From his seat he could see both doors and the hall porter's desk. He put his hand inside his coat and consulted an imaginary fob watch, then opened his newspaper and settled down to wait, as if he were early for an appointment.

He pulled the suitcase closer to his seat and stretched out his legs either side of it, to protect it against an accidental kick from a careless passerby. The lobby was crowded: it was just before ten o'clock. This is when the ruling class has breakfast, Feliks thought. He had not eaten: he had no appetite today.

He examined the other people in the lobby over the top of *The Times*. There were two men who might be detectives. Feliks wondered whether they might impede his escape. But even if they hear the explosion, he thought, how will they know which of the dozens of people walking through this lobby was responsible for it? Nobody knows what I look like. Only if I were being chased would they know. I'll have to make sure I'm not chased.

He wondered whether the urchin would come. After all, the boy had his penny already. Perhaps by now he had thrown the envelope into the river and gone off to the sweet shop. If so, Feliks would simply have to go through the whole rigmarole again until he found an honest urchin.

He read an article in the newspaper, looking up every few seconds. The government wanted to make those who gave money to the Women's Social and Political Union liable to pay for damage done by suffragettes. They planned to bring in special legislation to make this possible. How foolish governments are when they become intransigent, Feliks thought; everyone will just give money anonymously.

Where was that urchin?

He wondered what Orlov was doing right now. In all probability he was in one of the rooms of the hotel, a matter of yards above Feliks's head, eating breakfast, or shaving, or writing a letter, or having a discussion with Walden. I'd like to kill Walden too, Feliks thought.

It was not impossible that the two of them should walk through the lobby at any minute. That was too much to hope for. What would I do if it happened? thought Feliks.

I would throw the bomb, and die happy.

Through the glass door he saw the urchin.

The boy came along the narrow road which led to the hotel entrance. Feliks could see the envelope in his hand: he held it by one corner, almost distastefully, as if it were dirty and he were clean instead of the reverse. He approached the door but was stopped by a commissionaire in a top hat. There was some discussion, inaudible from inside, then the boy went away. The commissionaire came into the lobby with the envelope in his hand.

Feliks tensed. Would it work?

The commissionaire handed in the envelope at the bell captain's desk.

The captain looked at it, picked up a pencil, scribbled something in the top right-hand corner—a room number?—and summoned a bellboy.

It was working!

Feliks stood up, gently lifted his case and headed for the stairs.

The bellboy passed him on the first floor and went on up.

Feliks followed.

It was almost too easy.

He allowed the bellboy to get one flight of stairs ahead, then he quickened his step to keep him in view.

On the fifth floor the boy walked along the corridor.

Feliks stopped and watched.

The boy knocked on a door. It was opened. A hand came out and took the envelope.

Got you, Orlov.

The bellboy made a pantomime of going away and was called

back. Feliks could not hear the words. The boy received a tip. He said: "Thank you very much indeed, sir, very kind of you." The door closed.

Feliks started to walk along the corridor.

The boy saw his case and reached for it, saying: "Can I help you with that, sir?"

"No!" Feliks said sharply.

"Very good, sir," said the boy, and he passed on.

Feliks walked to the door of Orlov's room. Were there no more security precautions? Walden might imagine that a killer could not get into a London hotel room, but Orlov would know better. For a moment Feliks was tempted to go away and do some more thinking, or perhaps more reconnaissance; but he was too close to Orlov now.

He put the suitcase down on the carpet outside the door.

He opened the case, reached inside the pillow and carefully withdrew the brown bottle.

He straightened up slowly.

He knocked on the door.

⋙ ⋘

EIGHT

Walden looked at the envelope. It was addressed in a neat, characterless hand. It had been written by a foreigner, for an Englishman would have put *Prince Orlov* or *Prince Aleksey* but not *Prince A. A. Orlov*. Walden would have liked to know what was inside, but Aleks had moved out of the hotel in the middle of the night, and Walden could not open it in his absence—it was, after all, another gentleman's mail.

He handed it back to Basil Thomson, who had no such scruples.

Thomson ripped it open and took out a single sheet of paper. "Blank!" he said.

There was a knock at the door.

They all moved quickly. Walden went over to the windows, away from the door and out of the line of fire, and stood behind a sofa, ready to duck. The two detectives moved to either side of the room and drew their guns. Thomson stood in the middle of the room behind a large overstuffed easy chair.

The knock came again.

Thomson called: "Come in—it's open."

The door opened, and there he stood.

Walden clutched at the back of the sofa. He *looked* frightening.

He was a tall man in a bowler hat and a black coat buttoned to the neck. He had a long, gaunt, white face. In his left hand he held a large brown bottle. His eyes swept the room, and he understood in a flash that this was a trap.

He lifted the bottle and said: "Nitro!"

"Don't shoot!" Thomson barked at the detectives.

Walden was sick with fear. He knew what nitroglycerine was: if the bottle fell they would all die. He wanted to live; he did not want to die in an instant of burning agony.

There was a long moment of silence. Nobody moved. Walden stared at the face of the killer. It was a shrewd, hard, determined face. Every detail was imprinted on Walden's mind in that short, terrible pause: the curved nose, the wide mouth, the sad eyes, the thick black hair showing beneath the brim of the hat. Is he mad? Walden wondered. Bitter? Heartless? Sadistic? The face showed only that he was fearless.

Thomson broke the silence. "Give yourself up," he said. "Put the bottle on the floor. Stop being a fool."

Walden was thinking: If the detectives shoot, and the man falls, could I get to him in time to catch the bottle before it crashes onto the floor—

No.

The killer stood motionless, bottle raised high. He's looking at me, not Thomson, Walden realized; he's studying me, as if he finds me fascinating; taking in the details, wondering what makes me tick. It's a personal look. He's as interested in me as I am in him.

He has realized Aleks isn't here—what will he do now?

The killer spoke to Walden in Russian: "You're not as stupid as you look."

Walden thought: Is he suicidal? Will he kill us all and himself too? Better keep him talking—

Then the man was gone.

Walden heard his footsteps running down the corridor.

Walden made for the door. The other three were ahead of him.

Out in the corridor, the detectives knelt on the floor, aiming their guns. Walden saw the killer running away with a queer fluid step, his left arm hanging straight down by his side, holding the bottle as steady as possible while he ran.

If it goes off now, Walden thought, will it kill us at this distance? Probably not.

Thomson was thinking the same. He said: "Shoot!"

Two guns crashed.

The killer stopped and turned.

Was he hit?

He swung back his arm and hurled the bottle at them.

Thomson and the two detectives threw themselves flat. Walden realized in a flash that if the nitroglycerine exploded anywhere near them it would be no use to be lying flat.

The bottle turned over and over in the air as it flew at them. It was going to hit the floor five feet away from Walden. If it landed it would surely explode.

Walden ran *toward* the flying bottle.

It descended in a flat arc. He reached for it with both hands. He caught it. His fingers seemed to slip on the glass. He fumbled it, panicking; he almost lost it; then he grasped it again—

Don't slip Christ Jesus don't slip—

—and like a goalkeeper catching a football he drew it to his body, cushioning it against his chest, and spun around in the direction of travel of the bottle; then he lost his balance, and fell to his knees, and steadied himself, still holding the bottle, and thinking: I'm going to die.

Nothing happened.

The others stared at him, on his knees, cradling the bottle in his arms like a newborn baby.

One of the detectives fainted.

⋘ ⋙

Feliks stared in amazement at Walden for a split second longer; then he turned and raced down the stairs.

Walden was amazing. What a nerve, to catch that bottle!

He heard a distant shout: "Go after him!"

It's happening again, he thought; I'm running away again. What is the matter with me?

The stairs were endless. He heard running footsteps behind him. A shot rang out.

On the next landing he crashed into a waiter with a tray. The waiter fell, and crockery and food flew everywhere.

The pursuer was one or two flights behind him. He reached

the foot of the staircase. He composed himself and walked into the lobby.

It was still crowded.

He felt as if he were walking a tightrope.

Out of the corner of his eye he spotted the two men he had identified as possibly detectives. They were deep in conversation, looking worried: they must have heard distant gunfire.

He walked slowly across the lobby, fiercely resisting the urge to break into a run. He had the illusion that everyone was staring at him. He looked ahead fixedly.

He reached the door and went out.

"Cab, sir?" said the doorman.

Feliks jumped into a waiting cab and it pulled away.

As it turned into the Strand he looked back at the hotel. One of the detectives from upstairs burst out of the door, followed by the two from the lobby. They spoke to the doorman. He pointed at Feliks's cab. The detectives drew their guns and ran after the cab.

The traffic was heavy. The cab stopped in the Strand.

Feliks jumped out.

The cabbie shouted: "Oi! What's on, John?"

Feliks dodged through the traffic to the far side of the road and ran north.

He looked back over his shoulder. They were still after him.

He had to stay ahead until he could lose himself somewhere, in a maze of back alleys, or a railway station.

A uniformed policeman saw him running and watched suspiciously from the other side of the street. A minute later the detectives saw the policeman and yelled at him. He joined the chase.

Feliks ran faster. His heart pounded and his breath came in ragged gasps.

He turned a corner and found himself in the fruit and vegetable market of Covent Garden.

The cobbled streets were jammed with motor lorries and horse-drawn wagons. Everywhere there were market porters carrying wooden trays on their heads or pushing handcarts. Barrels of apples were being manhandled off wagons by heavily muscled men in undershirts. Boxes of lettuce and tomatoes and strawberries were bought and sold by men in bowler hats, and fetched and carried by men in caps. The noise was terrific.

Feliks plunged into the heart of the market.

He hid behind a stack of empty crates and peered through the slats. After a moment he saw his pursuers. They stood still, looking around. There was some conversation; then the four of them split up to search.

So Lydia betrayed me, Feliks thought as he caught his breath. Did she know in advance that I was after Orlov to kill him? No, she can't have. She wasn't acting a part that morning; she wasn't dissembling when she kissed me. But if she believed the story about getting a sailor out of jail, surely she would never have said anything to Walden. Well, perhaps later she realized that I had lied to her, so then she warned her husband, because she didn't want to have any part in the killing of Orlov. She didn't exactly betray me.

She won't kiss me next time.

There won't be a next time.

The uniformed policeman was coming his way.

He moved around the stack of crates and found himself alone in a little backwater, concealed by the boxes all around him.

Anyway, he thought, I escaped their trap. Thank God for nitroglycerine.

But *they* are supposed to be afraid of *me.*

I am the hunter; I am the one who sets traps.

It's Walden, he's the danger. Twice now he has got in the way. Who would have thought an aristocrat with gray hair would have had so much spunk?

He wondered where the policeman was. He peeped out.

He came face to face with the man.

The policeman's face was forming into an expression of astonishment when Feliks grabbed him by the coat and jerked him into the little enclosure.

The policeman stumbled.

Feliks tripped him. He fell on the floor. Feliks dropped on top of him and got him by the throat. He began to squeeze.

Feliks hated policemen.

He remembered Bialystock, when the strikebreakers—thugs with iron bars—had beaten up the workers outside the mill, while the police looked on unmoving. He remembered the pogrom, when the hooligans ran wild in the Jewish quarter, setting fire to houses and kicking old men and raping the young girls, while the police watched, laughing. He recalled Bloody Sunday, when the troops fired round after round into the peaceful crowd in front of the Winter Palace, and the police watched, cheering. He saw in his mind the police who had taken him to the Fortress of St. Peter and St. Paul to be tortured, and those who had escorted him to Siberia and stolen his coat, and those who had burst into the strike meeting in St. Petersburg with their truncheons waving, hitting the women's heads—they always hit the women.

A policeman was a worker who had sold his soul.

Feliks tightened his grip.

The man's eyes closed, and he stopped struggling.

Feliks squeezed harder.

He heard a sound.

His head whipped around.

A small child of two or three years stood there, eating an apple, watching him strangle the policeman.

Feliks thought: What am I waiting for?

He let the policeman go.

The child walked over and looked down at the unconscious man.

Feliks looked out. He could not see any of the detectives.

The child said: "Is he sleepy?"

Feliks walked away.

He got out of the market without seeing any of his pursuers.

He made his way to the Strand.

He began to feel safe.

In Trafalgar Square he caught an omnibus.

◄§ ß►

I almost died, Walden kept thinking; I almost died.

He sat in the hotel suite while Thomson gathered his team of detectives. Somebody gave him a glass of brandy-and-soda, and that was when he noticed that his hands were shaking. He could not put from his mind the image of that bottle of nitroglycerine in his hands.

He tried to concentrate on Thomson. The policeman changed

visibly as he spoke to his men: he took his hands out of his pockets, he sat on the edge of his chair, and his voice altered from a drawl to a crisp snap.

Walden began to calm down as Thomson was talking. "This man has slipped through our fingers," Thomson said. "It is not going to happen a second time. We know something about him now, and we're going to find out a great deal more. We know he was in St. Petersburg during or before 1895, because Lady Walden remembers him. We know he's been to Switzerland, because the suitcase in which he carried the bomb was Swiss. And we know what he looks like."

That face, Walden thought; and he clenched his fists.

Thomson went on: "Watts, I want you and your lads to spend a little money in the East End. The man is almost certainly Russian, so he's probably an anarchist and Jewish, but don't count on it. Let's see if we can put a name to him. If we can, cable Zurich and St. Petersburg and ask for information.

"Richards, you start with the envelope. It was probably bought singly, so a shop assistant might remember the sale.

"Woods, you work on the bottle. It's a Winchester bottle with a ground-glass stopper. The name of the manufacturer is stamped on the bottom. Find out who in London they supply it to. Send your team around all the shops and see whether any chemists remember a customer answering to the description of our man. He will have bought the ingredients for nitroglycerine in several different shops, of course; and if we can find those shops we will know where in London to look for him."

Walden was impressed. He had not realized that the killer had left behind so many clues. He began to feel better.

Thomson addressed a young man in a felt hat and a soft collar. "Taylor, yours is the most important job. Lord Walden and I have seen the killer briefly, but Lady Walden has had a good long look at him. You'll come with us to see her ladyship, and with her help and ours you'll draw a picture of the fellow. I want the picture printed tonight and distributed to every police station in London by midday tomorrow."

Surely, Walden thought, the man cannot escape us now. Then he remembered that he had thought the same when they set the trap here in the hotel room; and he began to tremble again.

Feliks looked in the mirror. He had had his hair cut very short, like a Prussian, and he had plucked his eyebrows until they were thin lines. He would stop shaving immediately, so that in a day he would look scruffy and in a week his beard and moustache would cover his distinctive mouth and chin. Unfortunately there was nothing he could do about his nose. He had bought a pair of secondhand spectacles with wire rims. The lenses were small so he could look over the top of them. He had changed his bowler hat and black coat for a blue sailor's pea jacket and a tweed cap with a peak.

A close look would still reveal him as the same man, but to a casual glance he was completely different.

He knew he had to leave Bridget's house. He had bought all his chemicals within a mile or two of here, and when the police learned that, they would begin a house-to-house search. Sooner or later they would end up in this street, and one of the neighbors would say: "I know him; he stops in Bridget's basement."

He was on the run. It was humiliating and depressing. He had been on the run at other times, but always after killing someone, never before.

He gathered up his razor, his spare underwear, his homemade dynamite and his book of Pushkin stories, and tied them all up in his clean shirt. Then he went to Bridget's parlor.

"Jesus, Mary and Joseph, what have you done to your eyebrows?" she said. "You used to be a handsome man."

"I must leave," he said.

She looked at his bundle. "I can see your luggage."

"If the police come, you don't have to lie to them."

"I'll say I threw you out because I suspected you were an anarchist."

"Good-bye, Bridget."

"Take off those daft glasses and kiss me."

Feliks kissed her cheek and went out.

"Good luck, boy," she called after him.

He took the bicycle and, for the third time since he had arrived in London, he went looking for lodgings.

He rode slowly. He was no longer weak from the sword wounds, but his spirit was sapped by his sense of failure. He went through North London and the City, then crossed the river at London Bridge. On the far side he headed southeast, passing a pub called The Elephant and Castle.

In the region of the Old Kent Road he found the kind of slum where he could get cheap accommodation and no questions asked. He took a room on the fifth floor of a tenement building owned, the caretaker told him lugubriously, by the Church of England. He would not be able to make nitroglycerine here: there was no water in the room, nor indeed in the building—just a standpipe and a privy in the courtyard.

The room was grim. There was a telltale mousetrap in the corner, and the one window was covered with a sheet of newspaper. The paint was peeling and the mattress stank. The caretaker, a stooped, fat man shuffling in carpet slippers and coughing, said: "If you want to mend the window, I can get glass cheap."

Feliks said: "Where can I keep my bicycle?"

"I should bring it up here if I were you; it'll get nicked anywhere else."

With the bicycle in the room there would be just enough space to get from the door to the bed.

"I'll take the room," Feliks said.

"That'll be twelve shillings, then."

"You said three shillings a week."

"Four weeks in advance."

Feliks paid him. After buying the spectacles and trading in the clothes, he now had one pound and nineteen shillings.

The caretaker said: "If you want to decorate, I can get you half-price paint."

"I'll let you know," said Feliks. The room was filthy, but that was the least of his problems.

Tomorrow he had to start looking for Orlov again.

⋘ ⋙

"Stephen! Thank Heaven you're all right!" said Lydia.

He put his arm around her. "Of course I'm all right."

"What happened?"

"I'm afraid we didn't catch our man."

Lydia almost fainted with relief. Ever since Stephen had said "I shall catch the man," she had been terrified twice over: terrified that Feliks would kill Stephen, and terrified that if not, she would be responsible for putting Feliks in jail for the second time in her life. She knew what he had gone through the first time, and the thought nauseated her.

"You know Basil Thomson, I think," Stephen said, "and this is Mr. Taylor, the police artist. We're all going to help him draw the face of the killer."

Lydia's heart sank. She would have to spend hours visualizing her lover in the presence of her husband. When will this end? she thought.

Stephen said: "By the way, where is Charlotte?"

"Shopping," Lydia told him.

"Good. I don't want her to know anything about this. In particular I don't want her to know where Aleks has gone."

"Don't tell me, either," Lydia said. "I'd rather not know. That way I shan't be able to make the same mistake again."

They sat down, and the artist got out his sketchbook.

Over and over again he drew that face. Lydia could have drawn it herself in five minutes. At first she tried to make the artist get it wrong, by saying "Not quite" when something was exactly right and "That's it" when something was crucially awry; but Stephen and Thomson had both seen Feliks clearly, if briefly, and they corrected her. In the end, fearful of being found out, she cooperated properly, knowing all the time that she might still be helping them to put Feliks in prison again. They ended up with a very good likeness of the face Lydia loved.

After that her nerves were so bad that she took a dose of laudanum and went to sleep. She dreamed that she was going to St. Petersburg to meet Feliks. With the devastating logic of dreams, it seemed that she drove to catch the ship in a carriage with two duchesses who, in real life, would have expelled her from polite society had they known of her past. However, they made a mistake and went to Bournemouth instead of Southampton. There they stopped for a rest, although it was five o'clock and the ship sailed at seven. The duchesses told Lydia that they slept together at night and caressed each other in a perverted way. Somehow this came as no surprise at all, although they were both extremely old. Lydia kept saying "We must go, now," but they took no notice. A man came with a message for Lydia.

It was signed "Your anarchist lover." Lydia said to the messenger: "Tell my anarchist lover that I'm *trying* to get the seven o'clock boat." There: the cat was out of the bag. The duchesses exchanged knowing winks. At twenty minutes to seven, still in Bournemouth, Lydia realized that she had not yet packed her luggage. She raced around throwing things into cases but she could never find anything and the seconds ticked by and she was already too late and somehow her case *would not* fill up, and she panicked and went without her luggage and climbed on the carriage and drove herself, and lost her way on the seafront at Bournemouth and could not get out of town and woke up without getting anywhere near Southampton.

Then she lay in bed with her heart beating fast, her eyes wide open and staring at the ceiling, and she thought: It was only a dream. Thank God. Thank God!

Feliks went to bed miserable and woke up angry.

He was angry with himself. The killing of Orlov was not a superhuman task. The man might be guarded, but he could not be locked away in an underground vault like money in a bank; besides, even bank vaults could be robbed. Feliks was intelligent and determined. With patience and persistence he would find a way around all the obstacles they would put in his path.

He was being hunted. Well, he would not be caught. He would travel by the back streets, avoid his neighbors and keep a constant lookout for blue police uniforms. Since he had begun his career of violence he had been hunted many times, but he had never been caught.

So he got up, washed at the standpipe in the courtyard, remembered not to shave, put on his tweed cap, his pea jacket and his spectacles, had breakfast at a tea stall and cycled, avoiding the main roads, to St. James's Park.

The first thing he saw was a uniformed policeman pacing up and down outside the Walden house.

That meant he could not take up his usual position for observing the house. He had to retreat much farther into the park and watch from a distance. He could not stay in the same place for too long, either, in case the policeman was alert and keen-eyed enough to notice.

At about midday a motor car emerged from the house. Feliks ran for his bicycle.

He had not seen the car go in, so presumably it was Walden's. Previously the family had always traveled in a coach, but there was no reason why they should not have both horse-drawn and motor vehicles. Feliks was too far away to be able to guess who was inside the car. He hoped it was Walden.

The car headed for Trafalgar Square. Feliks cut across the grass to intercept it.

The car was a few yards ahead of him when he reached the road. He kept up with it easily around Trafalgar Square, then it drew ahead of him as it headed north on Charing Cross Road.

He pedaled fast, but not desperately so. For one thing he did not want to draw attention to himself, and for another he wanted to conserve his strength. But he was too cautious, for when he reached Oxford Street the car was out of sight. He cursed himself for a fool. Which direction had it taken? There were four possibilities: left, straight on, right or sharp right.

He guessed, and went straight on.

In the traffic jam at the north end of Tottenham Court Road he saw the car again, and breathed a sigh of relief. He caught up with it as it turned east. He risked going close enough to see inside. In the front was a man in a chauffeur's cap. In the back was someone with gray hair and a beard: Walden!

I'll kill him too, Feliks thought; by Christ I'll kill him.

In the traffic jam outside Euston Station he passed the car and got ahead, taking the chance that Walden might look at him when the car caught up again. He stayed ahead all down Euston Road, looking back over his shoulder continually to check that the car was still following him. He waited at the junction by King's Cross, breathing hard, until the car passed him. It turned north. He averted his face as it went by, then followed.

The traffic was fairly heavy, and he was able to keep pace, although he was tiring. He began to hope that Walden was going to see Orlov. A house in North London, discreet and suburban, might be a good hiding place. His excitement mounted. He might be able to kill them both.

After half a mile or so the traffic began to thin out. The car was large and powerful. Feliks had to pedal faster and faster. He was sweating heavily. He thought: How much farther?

Heavy traffic at Holloway Road gave him a brief rest; then the car picked up speed along Seven Sisters Road. He went as fast as he could. Any minute now the car might turn off the main road; it might be only minutes from its destination. All I want is some luck! he thought. He summoned up his last reserves of strength. His legs hurt now, and his breath came in ragged gasps. The car pulled remorselessly away from him. When it was a hundred yards ahead and still accelerating, he gave up.

He coasted to a halt and sat on the bicycle at the side of the road, bent over the handlebars, waiting to recover. He felt faint.

It was always the way, he thought bitterly: the ruling class fought in comfort. There was Walden, sitting comfortably in a big smooth car, smoking a cigar, not even having to drive.

Walden was plainly going out of town. Orlov could be anywhere north of London within half a day's journey by fast motor car. Feliks was utterly defeated—again.

For want of a better idea, he turned around and headed back toward St. James's Park.

❧ ☙

Charlotte was still tingling from Mrs. Pankhurst's speech.

Of course there would be misery and suffering while all power was in the hands of one half of the world, and that half had no understanding of the problems of the other half. Men accepted a brutish and unjust world because it was brutish and unjust not to them but to women. If women had power, there would be nobody left to oppress.

The day after the suffragette meeting her mind teemed with speculations of this kind. She saw all the women around her—servants, shop assistants, nurses in the park, even Mama—in a new light. She felt she was beginning to understand how the world worked. She no longer resented Mama and Papa for lying to her. They had not really lied to her, except by omission; besides, insofar as deceit was involved, they deceived themselves almost as much as they had deceived her. And Papa had spoken frankly to her, against his evident inclinations. Still she wanted to find out things for herself, so that she could be sure of the truth.

In the morning she got hold of some money by the simple expedient of going shopping with a footman and saying to him: "Give me a shilling." Later, while he waited with the carriage at the main entrance to Liberty's in Regent Street, she slipped out of a side entrance and walked to Oxford Street where she found a woman selling the suffragette newspaper *Votes For Women.* The paper cost a penny. Charlotte went back to Liberty's and, in the ladies' cloakroom, hid the newspaper under her dress. Then she returned to the carriage.

She read the paper in her room after lunch. She learned that the incident at the palace during her debut had not been the first time that the plight of women had been brought to the attention of the King and Queen. Last December three suffragettes in beautiful evening gowns had barricaded themselves inside a box at Covent Garden. The occasion was a gala performance of *Jeanne d'Arc* by Raymond Roze, attended by the King and Queen with a large entourage. At the end of the first act one of the suffragettes stood up and began to harangue the King through a megaphone. It took them half an hour to break down the door and get the women out of the box. Then forty more suffragettes in the front rows of the gallery stood up, threw showers of pamphlets down into the stalls and walked out en masse.

Before and after this incident the King had refused to give an audience to Mrs. Pankhurst. Arguing that all subjects had an ancient right to petition the King about their grievances, the suffragettes announced that a deputation would march to the palace, accompanied by thousands of women.

Charlotte realized that the march was to take place today—this afternoon—now.

She wanted to be there.

It was no good understanding what was wrong, she told herself, if one did nothing about it. And Mrs. Pankhurst's speech was still ringing in her ears: "The spirit which is in women today cannot be quenched . . ."

Papa had gone off with Pritchard in the motor car. Mama was lying down after lunch, as usual. There was nobody to stop her.

She put on a dowdy dress and her most unprepossessing hat and coat; then she went quietly down the stairs and out of the house.

❦

Feliks walked about the park, keeping the house always in view, racking his brains.

Somehow he had to find out where Walden was going in the motor car. How might that be achieved? Could he try Lydia again? He might, at some risk, get past the policeman and into the house, but would he get out again? Would Lydia not raise the alarm? Even if she let him go, she would hardly tell him the secret of Orlov's hiding place, now that she knew why he wanted to know. Perhaps he could seduce her—but where and when?

He could not follow Walden's car on a bike. Could he follow in another car? He could steal one, but he did not know how to drive them. Could he learn? Even then, would Walden's chauffeur not notice that he was being followed?

If he could hide in Walden's motor car . . . That meant getting inside the garage, opening the trunk, spending several hours inside—all in the hope that nothing would be put inside the trunk before the journey. The odds against success were too high for him to risk everything on that gamble.

The chauffeur must know, of course. Could he be bribed? Made drunk? Kidnapped? Feliks's mind was elaborating these possibilities when he saw the girl come out of the house.

He wondered who she was. She might be a servant, for the family always came and went in coaches; but she had come out of the main entrance, and Feliks had never seen servants do that. She might be Lydia's daughter. She might know where Orlov was.

Feliks decided to follow her.

She walked toward Trafalgar Square. Leaving his bicycle in the bushes, Feliks went after her and got a closer look. Her clothes did not look like those of a servant. He recalled that there had been a girl in the coach on the night he had first tried to kill Orlov. He had not taken a good look at her, because all his attention had been—disastrously—riveted to Lydia. During his many days observing the house he had glimpsed a girl in the carriage from time to time. This was probably the girl, Feliks decided. She was sneaking out on a clandestine errand while her father was away and her mother was busy.

There was something vaguely familiar about her, he thought as he tailed her across Trafalgar Square. He was quite sure he had never looked closely at her, yet he had a strong sense of *déjà vu* as he watched her trim figure walk, straight-backed and with a determined quick pace, through the streets. Occasionally he saw her face in profile when she turned to cross a road, and the tilt of her chin, or perhaps something about the eyes, seemed to strike a chord deep in his memory. Did she remind him of the young Lydia? Not at all, he realized: Lydia had always looked small and frail, and her features were all delicate. This girl had a strong-looking, angular face. It reminded Feliks of a painting by an Italian artist which he had seen in a gallery in Geneva. After a moment the name of the painter came back to him: Modigliani.

He got still closer to her, and a minute or two later he saw her full face. His heart skipped a beat and he thought: she's just beautiful.

Where was she going? To meet a boyfriend, perhaps? To buy something forbidden? To do something of which her parents would disapprove, such as go to a moving-picture show or a music hall?

The boyfriend theory was the likeliest. It was also the most promising possibility from Feliks's point of view. He could find out who the boyfriend was and threaten to give away the girl's secret unless she would tell him where Orlov was. She would not do it readily, of course, especially if she had been told that an assassin was after Orlov; but given the choice between the love of a young man and the safety of a Russian cousin, Feliks reckoned that a young girl would choose romance.

He heard a distant noise. He followed the girl around a corner. Suddenly he was in a street full of marching women. Many of them wore the suffragette colors of green, white and purple. Many carried banners. There were *thousands* of them. Somewhere a band played marching tunes.

The girl joined the demonstration and began to march.

Feliks thought: Wonderful!

The route was lined with policemen, but they mostly faced inward, toward the women, so Feliks could dodge along the pavement behind their backs. He went with the march, keeping the girl in sight. He had been in need of a piece of luck, and he had been given one. She was a secret suffragette! She was vulnerable to blackmail, but there might be more subtle ways of manipulating her.

One way or another, Feliks thought, I'll get what I want from her.

❦ ❧

Charlotte was thrilled. The march was orderly, with female stewards keeping the women in line. Most of the marchers were well-dressed, respectable-looking types. The band played a jaunty two-step. There were even a few men, carrying a banner which read: "Fight the Government That Refuses to Give Women the Parliamentary Vote." Charlotte no longer felt like a misfit with heretical views. Why, she thought, all these thousands of women think and feel as I do! At times in the last twenty-four hours she had wondered whether men were right in saying that women were weak, stupid and ignorant, for she sometimes *felt* weak and stupid and she really was ignorant. Now she thought: If we educate ourselves we won't be ignorant; if we think for ourselves we won't be stupid; and if we struggle together we won't be weak.

The band began to play the hymn "Jerusalem," and the women sang the words. Charlotte joined in lustily:

> *I will not cease from mental fight*
> *Nor shall my sword sleep in my hand*

I don't care if anybody sees me, she thought defiantly—not even the duchesses!

> *Till we have built Jerusalem*
> *In England's green and pleasant land.*

The march crossed Trafalgar Square and entered The Mall. Suddenly there were many more policemen, watching the women intently. There were also many spectators, mostly male, along either side of the road. They shouted and whistled derisively. Charlotte heard one of them say: "All you need is a good swiving!" and she blushed crimson.

She noticed that many women carried a staff with a silver arrow fixed to its top. She asked the woman nearest her what that symbolized.

"The arrows on prison clothing," the woman replied. "All the women who carry that have been to jail."

"To jail!" Charlotte was taken aback. She had known that a few suffragettes had been imprisoned, but as she looked around she saw hundreds of silver arrows. For the first time it occurred to her that she might end the day in prison. The thought made her feel weak. I won't go on, she thought. My house is just there, across the park; I can be there in five minutes. Prison! I would die! She looked back. Then she thought: I've done nothing wrong! Why am I afraid that I shall go to prison? Why should I not petition the King? Unless we do this, women will always be weak, ignorant and stupid. Then the band began again, and she squared her shoulders and marched in time.

The facade of Buckingham Palace loomed up at the end of The Mall. A line of policemen, many on horseback, stretched across the front of the building. Charlotte was near the head of the procession: she wondered what the leaders intended to happen when they reached the gates.

She remembered once coming out of Derry & Toms and seeing an afternoon drunk lurching at her across the pavement. A gentleman in a top hat had pushed the drunk aside with his walking cane, and the footman had quickly helped Charlotte up into the carriage which was waiting at the curb.

Nobody would rush to protect her from a jostling today.

They were at the palace gates.

Last time I was here, Charlotte thought, I had an invitation.

The head of the procession came up against the line of policemen. For a moment there was deadlock. The people behind pressed forward. Suddenly Charlotte saw Mrs. Pankhurst. She wore a jacket and skirt of purple velvet, a high-necked white blouse and a green waistcoat. Her hat was purple with a huge white ostrich feather and a veil. She had detached herself from the body of the march and somehow had managed, unnoticed, to reach the far gate of the palace courtyard. She was such a brave little figure, marching with her head held high to the King's gate!

She was stopped by a police inspector in a flat hat. He was a huge, burly man, and looked at least a foot taller than she. There was a brief exchange of words. Mrs. Pankhurst stepped forward. The inspector barred her way. She tried to push past him. Then, to Charlotte's horror, the policeman grabbed Mrs. Pankhurst in a bear hug, lifted her off her feet and carried her away.

Charlotte was enraged—and so was every other woman in sight. The marchers pressed fiercely against the police line. Charlotte saw one or two break through and run toward the palace, chased by constables. The horses shifted, their iron hooves clattering threateningly on the pavement. The line began to break up. Several women struggled with policemen and were thrown to the ground. Charlotte was terrified of being manhandled. Some of the male bystanders rushed to the aid of the police, and then jostling turned into fighting. A middle-aged woman close to Charlotte was grabbed by the thighs. "Unhand me, sir!" she said indignantly. The policeman said: "My old dear, I can grip you where I like today!" A group of men in straw boaters waded into the crowd, pushing and punching the women, and Charlotte screamed. Suddenly a team of suffragettes wielding Indian clubs counterattacked, and straw boaters flew everywhere. There were no longer any spectators: everyone was in the melee. Charlotte wanted to run away but every way she turned she saw violence. A fellow in a bowler picked up a young woman by getting one arm across her breasts and one hand in the fork of her thighs, and Charlotte heard him say: "You've been wanting this for a long time, haven't you?" The bestiality of it all horrified Charlotte: it was like one of those medieval paintings of Purgatory in which everyone is suffering unspeakable tortures; but it was real and she was in the middle of it. She was pushed from behind and fell down, grazing her hands and bruising her knees. Someone trod on her hand. She tried to get up and was knocked down again. She realized she might be trampled by a horse and die. Desperately, she grabbed the skirts of a woman's coat and hauled herself to her feet. Some of the women were throwing pepper into the eyes of the men, but it was impossible to throw accurately, and they succeeded in incapacitating as many women as men. The fighting became vicious. Charlotte saw a woman lying on the ground with blood streaming from her nose. She wanted to help the woman but she could not move—it was as much as she could do to stay upright. She began to feel angry as well as scared. The men, police and civilians alike, punched and kicked women with relish. Charlotte thought hysterically: Why do they *grin* so? To her horror she felt a large hand grasp her breast. The hand squeezed and twisted. She turned, clumsily shoving the arm away from her.

She was confronted by a man in his middle twenties, well-dressed in a tweed suit. He put out his hands and grabbed both her breasts, digging his fingers in hard. Nobody had *ever* touched her there. She struggled with the man, seeing on his face a wild look of mingled hatred and desire. He yelled: "This is what you need, ain't it?" Then he punched her in the stomach with his fist. The blow seemed to sink into her belly. The shock was bad and the pain was worse, but what made her panic was that she could not breathe. She stood, bending forward, with her mouth open. She wanted to gasp, she wanted to scream, but she could do neither. She felt sure she was going to die. She was vaguely aware of a very tall man pushing past her, dividing the crowd as if it were a field of wheat. The tall man grabbed the lapel of the man in the tweed suit and hit him on the chin. The blow seemed to knock the young man off his feet and lift him into the air. The look of surprise on his face was almost comical. At last Charlotte was able to breathe, and she sucked in air with a great heave. The tall man put his arm firmly around her shoulders and said in her ear: "This way." She realized she was being rescued, and the sense of being in the hands of someone strong and protective was such a relief that she almost fainted.

The tall man propelled her toward the edge of the crowd. A police sergeant struck at her with a truncheon. Charlotte's protector raised his arm to ward off the blow, then gave a shout of pain as the wooden club landed on his forearm. He let go of Charlotte. There was a brief flurry of blows; then the sergeant was lying on the ground, bleeding, and the tall man was once again leading Charlotte through the crush.

Suddenly they were out of it. When Charlotte realized she was safe she began to cry, sobbing softly as tears ran down her cheeks. The man made her keep walking. "Let's get right away," he said. He spoke with a foreign accent. Charlotte had no will of her own: she went where he led her.

After a while she began to recover her composure. She realized they were in the Victoria area. The man stopped outside a Lyons Corner House and said: "Would you like a cup of tea?"

She nodded, and they went in.

He led her to a chair, then sat opposite her. She looked at him for the first time. For an instant she was frightened again. He had a long face with a curved nose. His hair was very short but his cheeks were unshaven. He looked somehow rapacious. But then she saw that there was nothing but compassion in his eyes.

She took a deep breath and said: "How can I ever thank you?"

He ignored the question. "Would you like something to eat?"

"Just tea." She had recognized his accent, and she began to speak Russian. "Where are you from?"

He looked pleased that she could speak his language. "I was born in Tambov province. You speak Russian very well."

"My mother is Russian, and my governess."

A waitress came, and he said: "Two teas, please, love."

Charlotte thought: He is learning English from Cockneys. She said in Russian: "I don't even know your name. I'm Charlotte Walden."

"Feliks Kschessinsky. You were brave, to join that march."

She shook her head. "Bravery had nothing to do with it. I simply didn't know it would be like that." She was thinking: Who and what is this man? Where did he come from? He *looks* fascinating. But he's guarded. I'd like to know more about him.

He said: "What did you expect?"

"On the march? I don't know . . . Why do those men *enjoy* attacking women?"

"This is an interesting question." He was suddenly animated, and Charlotte saw that he had an attractive, expressive face. "You see, we put women on a pedestal and pretend they are pure in mind and helpless in body. So, in polite society at least, men must tell themselves that they feel no hostility toward women, ever; nor do they feel lust for women's bodies. Now, here come some women—the suffragettes—who plainly are not helpless and need not be worshiped. What is more, they break the law. They deny the myths that men have made themselves believe, and they can be assaulted with impunity. The men feel cheated, and they give expression to all the lust and anger which they have been pretending not to feel. This is a great release of tension, and they enjoy it."

Charlotte looked at him in amazement. It was fantastic—a complete explanation, just like that, off the top of his head! I like this man, she thought. She said: "What do you do for a living?"

He became guarded again. "Unemployed philosopher."

The tea came. It was strong and very sweet, and it restored Charlotte somewhat. She was intrigued by this weird Russian, and she wanted to draw him out. She said: "You seem to think that all this—the position of women in society and so on—is just as bad for men as it is for women."

"I'm sure of it."

"Why?"

He hesitated. "Men and women are happy when they love." A shadow passed briefly across his face and was gone. "The relation of love is not the same as the relation of worship. One worships a god. Only human beings can be loved. When we worship a woman we cannot love her. Then, when we discover she is not a god, we hate her. This is sad."

"I never thought of that," Charlotte said wonderingly.

"Also, every religion has good gods and bad gods. The Lord and the Devil. So, we have good women and bad women; and you can do anything you like to the bad women, for example, suffragettes and prostitutes."

"What are prostitutes?"

He looked surprised. "Women who sell themselves for—" He used a Russian word that Charlotte did not know.

"Can you translate that?"

"Swiving," he said in English.

Charlotte flushed and looked away.

He said: "Is this an impolite word? I'm sorry, I know no other."

Charlotte screwed up her courage and said in a low voice: "Sexual intercourse."

He reverted to Russian. "I think *you* have been put on a pedestal."

"You can't imagine how awful it is," she said fiercely. "To be so ignorant! Do women really sell themselves that way?"

"Oh, yes. Respectable married women must pretend not to like sexual intercourse. This sometimes spoils it for the men, so they go to the prostitutes. The prostitutes pretend to like it very much, although since they do it so often with so many different people, they don't really enjoy it. Everyone ends up pretending."

These things are *just* what I need to know! thought Charlotte. She wanted to take him home and chain him up in her room, so that he could explain things to her day and night. She said: "How did we get like this—all this pretending?"

"The answer is a lifetime study. At least. However, I'm sure it has to do with power. Men have power over women, and rich men have power over poor men. A great many fantasies are required to legitimize this system—fantasies about monarchy, capitalism, breeding and sex. These fantasies make us unhappy, but without them someone would lose his power. And men will not give up power, even if it makes them miserable."

"But what is to be done?"

"A famous question. Men who will not give up power must have it taken from them. A transfer of power from one faction to another faction *within the same class* is called a coup, and this changes nothing. A transfer of power from one *class* to another is called a revolution, and this does change things." He hesitated. "Although the changes are not necessarily the ones the revolutionaries sought." He went on: "Revolutions occur only when the people rise up en masse against their oppressors—as the suffragettes seem to be doing. Revolutions are always violent, for people will always kill to retain power. Nevertheless they happen, for people will always give their lives in the cause of freedom."

"Are you a revolutionary?"

He said in English: "I'll give you three guesses."

Charlotte laughed.

&

It was the laugh that did it.

While he spoke, a part of Feliks's mind had been watching her face, gauging her reactions. He warmed to her, and the affection he felt was somehow familiar. He thought: I am supposed to bewitch her, but she is bewitching me.

And then she laughed.

She smiled widely; crinkles appeared in the corners of her brown eyes; she tipped back her head so that her chin pointed forward; she held up her hands, palms forward, in a gesture that was almost defensive; and she chuckled richly, deep in her throat.

Feliks was transported back in time twenty-five years. He saw a three-roomed hut leaning against the side of a wooden church. Inside the hut a boy and a girl sat opposite one another at a crude table made of planks. On the fire was a cast-iron pot containing a cabbage, a small piece of bacon fat and a great deal of water. It was almost dark outside and soon the father would be home for his supper. Fifteen-year-old Feliks had just told his eighteen-year-old sister, Natasha, the joke about the traveler and the farmer's daughter. She threw back her head and laughed.

Feliks stared at Charlotte. She looked exactly like Natasha. He said: "How old are you?"

"Eighteen."

There occurred to Feliks a thought so astonishing, so incredible and so devastating that his heart stood still.

He swallowed, and said: "When is your birthday?"

"The second of January."

He gasped. She had been born exactly seven months after the wedding of Lydia and Walden; nine months after the last occasion on which Feliks had made love to Lydia.

And Charlotte looked exactly like Feliks's sister, Natasha.

And now Feliks knew the truth.

Charlotte was his daughter.

❧ ❦

NINE

"What is it?" Charlotte said.

"What?"

"You look as if you'd seen a ghost."

"You reminded me of someone. Tell me all about yourself."

She frowned at him. He seemed to have a lump in his throat, she thought. She said: "You've got a cold coming."

"I never catch colds. What's your earliest memory?'

She thought for a moment. "I was brought up in a country house called Walden Hall, in Norfolk. It's a beautiful gray stone building with a very lovely garden. In summer we had tea outdoors, under the chestnut tree. I must have been about four years old when I was first allowed to have tea with Mama and Papa. It was very dull. There was nothing to investigate on the lawn. I always wanted to go around to the back of the house, to the stables. One day they saddled a donkey and let me ride it. I had seen people ride, of course, and I thought I knew how to do it. They told me to sit still or I would fall off, but I didn't believe them. First somebody took the bridle and walked me up and down. Then I was allowed to take the reins myself. It all seemed so easy that I gave him a kick, as I had seen people do

189

to horses, and made him trot. Next thing I knew, I was on the ground in tears. I just couldn't *believe* I had really fallen!" She laughed at the memory.

"It sounds like a happy childhood," Feliks said.

"You wouldn't say that if you knew my governess. Her name is Marya and she's a Russian dragon. 'Little ladies *always* have clean hands.' She's still around—she's my chaperone now."

"Still—you had good food, and clothes, and you were never cold, and there was a doctor when you were sick."

"Is that supposed to make you happy?"

"I would have settled for it. What's your *best* memory?"

"When Papa gave me my own pony," she said immediately. "I had wanted one so badly, it was like a dream come true. I shall never forget that day."

"What's he like?"

"Who?"

Feliks hesitated. "Lord Walden."

"Papa? Well . . ." It was a good question, Charlotte thought. For a complete stranger, Feliks was remarkably interested in her. But she was even more interested in him. There seemed to be some deep melancholy beneath his questions: it had not been there a few minutes ago. Perhaps that was because he had had an unhappy childhood and hers seemed so much better. "I think Papa is probably a terribly *good* man . . ."

"But?"

"He will treat me as a child. I know I'm probably frightfully naïve, but I'll never be anything else unless I learn. He won't explain things to me the way—well, the way you do. He gets very embarrassed if he talks about . . . men and women, you know . . . and when he speaks of politics his views seem a bit, I don't know, smug."

"That's completely natural. All his life he's got everything he wanted, and got it easily. Of course he thinks the world is wonderful just as it is, except for a few small problems which will get ironed out in time. Do you love him?"

"Yes, except for the moments when I hate him." The intensity of Feliks's gaze was beginning to make her uncomfortable. He seemed to be drinking in her words and memorizing her facial expressions. "Papa is a very lovable man. Why are you so interested?"

He gave a peculiar, twisted smile. "I've been fighting the ruling class all my life, but I rarely get the chance to talk to one of them."

Charlotte could tell that this was not the real reason, and she wondered vaguely why he should lie to her. Perhaps he was embarrassed about something—that was usually the reason why people were less than honest with her. She said: "I'm not a member of the ruling class, any more than one of my father's dogs is."

He smiled. "Tell me about your mother."

"She has bad nerves. Sometimes she has to take laudanum."

"What's laudanum?"

"Medicine with opium in it."

He raised his eyebrows. "That sounds ominous."

"Why?"

"I thought the taking of opium was considered degenerate."

"Not if it's for medical reasons."

"Ah."

"You're skeptical."

"Always."

"Come, now, tell me what you mean."

"If your mother needs opium, I suspect it is because she is unhappy, rather than because she is ill."

"Why should she be unhappy?"

"You tell me, she's *your* mother."

Charlotte considered. Was Mama unhappy? She certainly was not *content* in the way Papa seemed to be. She worried too much, and she would fly off the handle without much provocation. "She's not relaxed," she said. "But I can't think of any reason why she should be unhappy. I wonder if it has to do with leaving your native country?"

"That's possible," Feliks said, but he did not sound convinced. "Have you any brothers and sisters?"

"No. My best friend is my cousin Belinda; she's the same age as me."

"What other friends have you got?"

"No other friends, just acquaintances."

"Other cousins?"

"Twin boys, six years old. Of course I've loads of cousins in Russia, but I've never seen any of them, except Aleks, who's much older than me."

"And what are you going to do with your life?"

"What a question!"

"Don't you know?"

"I haven't made up my mind."

"What are the alternatives?"

"That's the big question, really. I mean, I'm expected to marry a young man of my own class and raise children. I suppose I shall have to marry."

"Why?"

"Well, Walden Hall won't come to me when Papa dies, you know."

"Why not?"

"It goes with the title—and I can't be the Earl of Walden. So the house will be left to Peter, the elder of the twins."

"I see."

"And I couldn't make my own living."

"Of course you could."

"I've been trained for nothing."

"Train yourself."

"What would I do?"

Feliks shrugged. "Raise horses. Be a shopkeeper. Join the civil service. Become a professor of mathematics. Write a play."

"You talk as if I might do anything I put my mind to."

"I believe you could. But I have one quite serious idea. Your Russian is perfect—you could translate novels into English."

"Do you really think I could?"

"I've no doubt whatsoever."

Charlotte bit her lip. "Why is it that you have such faith in me and my parents don't?"

He thought for a minute, then smiled. "If I had brought you up, you would complain that you were forced to do serious work all the time and never allowed to go dancing."

"You've no children?"

He looked away. "I never married."

Charlotte was fascinated. "Did you want to?"

"Yes."

She knew she ought not to go on, but she could not resist it: she wanted to know what this strange man had been like when he was in love. "What happened?"

"The girl married someone else."

"What was her name?"

"Lydia."

"That's my mother's name."

"Is it?"

"Lydia Shatova, she was. You must have heard of Count Shatov, if you ever spent any time in St. Petersburg."

"Yes, I did. Do you carry a watch?"

"What? No."

"Nor do I." He looked around and saw a clock on the wall. Charlotte followed his glance. "Heavens, it's five o'clock! I intended to get home before mother came down for tea." She stood up.

"Will you be in trouble?" he said, getting up.

"I expect so." She turned to leave the café.

He said: "Oh, Charlotte . . ."

"What is it?"

"I don't suppose you could pay for the tea? I'm a very poor man."

"Oh! I wonder whether I've any money. Yes! Look, elevenpence. Is that enough?"

"Of course." He took sixpence from the palm of her hand and went to the counter to pay. It's funny, Charlotte thought, the things you have to remember when you're not in Society. What would Marya think of me, buying a cup of tea for a strange man? She would have apoplexy.

He gave her the change and held the door for her. "I'll walk part of the way with you."

"Thank you."

Feliks took her arm as they walked along the street. The sun was still strong. A policeman walked toward them, and Feliks made her stop and look in a shop window while he passed. She said: "Why don't you want him to see us?"

"They may be looking for people who were seen on the march."

Charlotte frowned. That seemed a bit unlikely, but he would know better than she.

They walked on. Charlotte said: "I love June."

"The weather in England is wonderful."

"Do you think so? You've never been to the South of France, then."

"You have, obviously."

"We go every winter. We've a villa in Monte Carlo." She was struck by a thought. "I hope you don't think I'm boasting."

"Certainly not." He smiled. "You must have realized by now that I think great wealth is something to be ashamed of, not proud of."

"I suppose I should have realized, but I hadn't. Do you despise me, then?"

"No, but the wealth isn't yours."

"You're the most interesting person I've ever met," Charlotte said. "May I see you again?"

"Yes," he said. "Have you got a handkerchief?"

She took one from her coat pocket and gave it to him. He blew his nose. "You *are* catching a cold," she said. "Your eyes are streaming."

"You must be right." He wiped his eyes. "Shall we meet at that café?'

"It's not a frightfully attractive place, is it?" she said. "Let's think of somewhere else. I know! We'll go to the National Gallery. Then, if I see somebody I know, we can pretend we aren't together.'

"All right."

"Do you like paintings?"

"I'd like you to educate me."

"Then it's settled. How about the day after tomorrow, at two o'clock?"

"Fine."

It occurred to her that she might not be able to get away. "If something goes wrong, and I have to cancel, can I send you a note?"

"Well .   er . . . I move about a lot . . ." He was struck by a thought. "But you can always leave a message with Mrs. Bridget Callahan at number nineteen, Cork Street, in Camden Town."

She repeated the address. "I'll write that down as soon as I get home. My house is just a few hundred yards away." She hesitated. "You must leave me here. I hope you won't be offended, but it really would be best if no one saw me with you."

"Offended?" he said with his funny, twisted smile. "No, not at all."

She held out her hand. "Good-bye."

"Good-bye." He shook her hand firmly.

She turned around and walked away. There will be trouble when I get home, she thought. They will have found out that I'm not in my room, and there will be an inquisition. I'll say I went for a walk in the park. They won't like it.

Somehow she did not care what they thought. She had found a true friend. She was very happy.

When she reached the gate she turned and looked back. He stood where she had left him, watching her. She gave a discreet wave. He waved back. For some reason he looked vulnerable and sad, standing there alone. That was silly, she realized, as she remembered how he had rescued her from the riot: he was very tough indeed.

She went into the courtyard and up the steps to the front door.

⌘ ☙

Walden arrived at Walden Hall suffering from nervous indigestion. He had rushed away from London before lunch as soon as the police artist had finished drawing the face of the assassin, and he had eaten a picnic and drunk a bottle of Chablis on the way down, without stopping the car. As well as that, he was nervous.

Today he was due for another session with Aleks. He guessed that Aleks had a counterproposal and expected the Czar's approval of it by cable today. He hoped the Russian Embassy had had the sense to forward cables to Aleks at Walden Hall. He hoped the counterproposal was something reasonable, something he could present to Churchill as a triumph.

He was fiercely impatient to get down to business with Aleks, but he knew that in reality a few minutes made no difference, and it was always a mistake to appear eager during a negotiation; so he paused in the hall and composed himself before walking into the Octagon.

Aleks sat at the window, brooding, with a great tray of tea and cakes untouched beside him. He looked up eagerly and said: "What happened?"

"The man came, but I'm afraid we failed to catch him," Walden said.

Aleks looked away. "He came to kill me . . ."

Walden felt a surge of pity for him. He was young, he had a huge responsibility, he was in a foreign country and a killer was stalking him. But there was no point in letting him brood. Walden put on a breezy tone of voice. "We have the man's description now—in fact the police artist has made a drawing of him. Thomson will catch him in a day or so. And you're safe here—he can't possibly find out where you are."

"We thought I was safe at the hotel—but he found out I was there."

"That can't happen again." This was a bad start to a negotiating session, Walden reflected. He had to find a way to turn Aleks's mind to more cheerful subjects. "Have you had tea?"

"I'm not hungry."

"Let's go for a walk—it will give you an appetite for dinner."

"All right." Aleks stood up.

Walden got a gun—for rabbits, he told Aleks—and they walked down to the Home Farm. One of the two bodyguards provided by Basil Thomson followed ten yards behind them.

Walden showed Aleks his champion sow, the Princess of Walden. "She's won first prize in the East Anglian Agricultural Show for the last two years." Aleks admired the sturdy brick cottages of the tenants, the tall white-painted barns, and the magnificent shire horses.

"I don't make any money out of it, of course," Walden said. "All the profit is spent on new stock, or drainage, or buildings, or fencing . . . but it sets a standard for the tenanted farms; and the Home Farm will be worth a lot more when I die than it was when I inherited it."

"We can't farm like this in Russia," Aleks said. Good, thought Walden; he's thinking of something else. Aleks went on: "Our peasants won't use new methods, won't touch machinery, won't take care of new buildings or good tools. They are still serfs, psychologically if not legally. When there is a bad harvest and they are starving, do you know what they do? They burn the empty barns."

The men were mowing hay in the South Acre. Twelve laborers made a ragged line across the field, stooped over their scythes, and there was a steady swish, swish as the tall stalks fell like dominoes.

Samuel Jones, the oldest of the laborers, finished his row first.

He came over, scythe in hand, and touched his cap to Walden. Walden shook his calloused hand. It was like grasping a rock.

"Did your lordship find time to go to that there exhibition in Lunnun?" Samuel said.

"Yes, I did," Walden replied.

"Did you see that mowing machine you was talking about?"

Walden put on a dubious face. "It's a beautiful piece of engineering, Sam—but I don't know . . ."

Sam nodded. "Machinery never does the job as well as a laborer."

"On the other hand, we could cut the hay in three days instead of a fortnight—and by getting it in that much faster we run less risk of rain. Then we could rent the machine to the tenanted farms."

"You'd need fewer laborers, too," Sam said.

Walden pretended to be disappointed. "No," he said, "I couldn't let anyone go. It would just mean we need not take on gypsies to help around harvest time."

"It wouldn't make that much difference, then."

"Not really. And I'm a bit concerned about how the men would take to it—you know young Peter Dawkins will find any excuse to make trouble."

Sam made a noncommittal sound.

"Anyway," Walden continued, "Mr. Samson is going to take a look at the machine next week." Samson was the bailiff. "I say!" Walden said as if he had been struck by an idea. "I don't suppose you'd want to go with him, Sam?"

Sam pretended not to care much for the idea. "To Lunnun?" he said. "I went there in 1888. Didn't like it."

"You could go up on the train with Mr. Samson—perhaps take young Dawkins with you—see the machine, have your dinner in London, and come back in the afternoon."

"I dunno what my missus would say."

"I'd be glad to have your opinion of the machine, though."

"Well, I should be interested."

"That's settled, then. I'll tell Samson to make the arrangements." Walden smiled conspiratorially. "You can give Mrs. Jones to understand I practically forced you to go."

Sam grinned. "I'll do that, m'lord."

The mowing was almost done. The men stopped work. Any

rabbits would be hidden within the last few yards of hay. Walden called Dawkins over and gave him the gun. "You're a good shot, Peter. See if you can get one for yourself and one for the Hall."

They all stood on the edge of the field, out of the line of fire, then cut the last of the hay from the side, to drive the rabbits into the open field. Four came out, and Dawkins got two with his first round and one with his second. The gunfire made Aleks wince.

Walden took the gun and one of the rabbits; then he and Aleks walked back toward the Hall. Aleks shook his head in admiration. "You have a wonderful way with the men," he said. "I never seem to be able to strike the right balance between discipline and generosity."

"It takes practice," Walden said. He held up the rabbit. "We don't really need this at the Hall—but I took it to remind them that the rabbits are mine, and that any they have are a gift from me, not theirs by right." If I had a son, Walden thought, this is how I would explain things to him.

"One proceeds by discussion and consent," Aleks said.

"It's the best method—even if you have to give something away."

Aleks smiled. "Which brings us back to the Balkans."

Thank Heaven—at last, Walden thought.

"Shall I sum up?" Aleks went on. "We are willing to fight on your side against Germany, and you are willing to recognize our right to pass through the Bosphorus and the Dardanelles. However, we want not just the right but the power. Our suggestion, that you should recognize the whole of the Balkan Peninsula from Rumania to Crete as a Russian sphere of influence did not meet with your approval: no doubt you felt it was giving us too much. My task, then, was to formulate a lesser demand: one which would secure our sea passage without committing Britain to an unreservedly pro-Russian Balkan policy."

"Yes." Walden thought: He has a mind like a surgeon's knife. A few minutes ago I was giving him fatherly advice, and now, suddenly, he seems my equal—at the least. I suppose this is how it is when your son becomes a man.

"I'm sorry it has taken so long," Aleks said. "I have to send coded cables via the Russian Embassy to St. Petersburg, and discussion at this distance just can't be as quick as I should like."

"I understand," said Walden, thinking: Come on—out with it!

"There is an area of about ten thousand square miles, from Constantinople to Adrianople—it amounts to half of Thrace—which is at present part of Turkey. Its coastline begins in the Black Sea, borders the Bosphorus, the Sea of Marmara and the Dardanelles, and finishes in the Aegean Sea. In other words, it guards the whole of the passage between the Black Sea and the Mediterranean." He paused. "Give us that, and we're on your side."

Walden concealed his excitement. Here was a real basis for bargaining. He said: "The problem remains, that it isn't ours to give away."

"Consider the possibilities if war breaks out," Aleks said. "One: If Turkey is on our side we will have the right of passage anyway. However, this is unlikely. Two: If Turkey is neutral, we would expect Britain to insist on our right of passage as a sign that Turkey's neutrality was genuine; and failing that, to support our invasion of Thrace. Three: If Turkey is on the German side—which is the likeliest of the three possibilities—then Britain would concede that Thrace is ours as soon as we can conquer it."

Walden said dubiously: "I wonder how the Thracians would feel about all this."

"They would rather belong to Russia than to Turkey."

"I expect they'd like to be independent."

Aleks gave a boyish smile. "Neither you nor I—nor, indeed, either of our governments—is in the least concerned about what the inhabitants of Thrace might prefer."

"Quite," Walden said. He was forced to agree. It was Aleks's combination of boyish charm and thoroughly grown-up brains which kept putting Walden off balance. He always thought he had the discussion firmly under control, until Aleks came out with a punch line which showed that *he* had been controlling it all along.

They walked up the hill that led to the back of Walden Hall. Walden noticed the bodyguard scanning the woods on either side. Dust puffed around his heavy brown brogues. The ground was dry: it had hardly rained for three months. Walden was excited about Aleks's counterproposal. What would Churchill say? Surely the Russians could be given part of Thrace—who cared about Thrace?

They crossed the kitchen garden. An under-gardener was watering lettuces. He touched his cap to them. Walden searched for the man's name, but Aleks beat him to it. "A fine evening, Stanley," said Aleks.

"We could do with a shower, your highness."

"But not too much, eh?"

"Quite so, your highness."

Aleks is learning, Walden thought.

They went into the house. Walden rang for a footman. "I'll send a telegram to Churchill making an appointment for tomorrow morning. I'll motor to London first thing."

"Good," Aleks said. "Time is running short."

◦§ ‍§◦

Charlotte got a big reaction from the footman who opened the door to her.

"Oh! Thank goodness you're home, Lady Charlotte!" he said.

Charlotte gave him her coat. "I don't know why you should thank goodness, William."

"Lady Walden has been worried about you," he said. "She asked that you should be sent to her as soon as you arrived."

"I'll just go and tidy myself up," Charlotte said.

"Lady Walden did say 'immediately'—"

"And I said I'll go and tidy up." Charlotte went up to her room.

She washed her face and unpinned her hair. There was a dull, muscular ache in her tummy, from the punch she had received, and her hands were grazed, but not badly. Her knees were sure to be bruised, but no one ever saw them. She went behind the screen and took off her dress. It seemed undamaged. I don't *look* as if I've been in a riot, she thought. She heard her bedroom door open.

"Charlotte!" It was Mama's voice.

Charlotte slipped into a robe, thinking: Oh, dear, she's going to be hysterical. She came from behind the screen.

"We've been frantic with worry!" Mama said.

Marya came into the room behind her, looking self-righteous and steely-eyed.

Charlotte said: "Well, here I am, safe and sound, so you can stop worrying now."

Mama reddened. "You impudent child!" she shrilled. She stepped forward and slapped Charlotte's face.

Charlotte fell back and sat down heavily on the bed. She was stunned, not by the blow but by the idea of it. Mama had never struck her before. Somehow it seemed to hurt more than all the blows she had received during the riot. She caught Marya's eye and saw a peculiar look of satisfaction on her face.

Charlotte recovered her composure and said: "I shall never forgive you for that."

"That you should speak of forgiving me!" In her rage Mama was speaking Russian. "And how soon should I forgive you for joining a mob outside Buckingham Palace?"

Charlotte gasped. "How did you know?"

"Marya saw you marching along The Mall with those . . . those suffragettes. I feel so *ashamed*. God knows who else saw you. If the King ever finds out we shall be banished from the court."

"I see." Charlotte was still smarting from the slap. She said nastily: "So you weren't worried about my safety, just the family reputation."

Mama looked hurt. Marya butted in: "We were worried about both."

"Keep quiet, Marya," said Charlotte. "You've done enough damage with your tongue."

"Marya did the right thing!" Mama said. "How could she *not* tell me?"

Charlotte said: "Don't you think women should have the vote?"

"Certainly not—and you shouldn't think so, either."

"But I do," Charlotte said. "There it is."

"You know nothing—you're still a child."

"We always come back to that, don't we? I'm a child, and I know nothing. Who is responsible for my ignorance? Marya has been in charge of my education for fifteen years. As for being a child, you know perfectly well that I'm nothing of the kind. You would be quite happy to see me married by Christmas. And some girls are mothers by the age of thirteen, married or not."

Mama was shocked. "Who tells you such things?"

"Certainly not Marya. She never told me anything important. Nor did you."

Mama's voice became almost pleading. "You have no need of such knowledge—you're a lady."

"You see what I mean? You want me to be ignorant. Well, I don't intend to be."

Mama said plaintively: "I only want you to be happy!"

"No, you don't," Charlotte said stubbornly. "You want me to be like you."

"No, no, no!" Mama cried. "I don't want you to be like me! I don't!" She burst into tears, and ran from the room.

Charlotte stared after her, mystified and ashamed.

Marya said: "You see what you've done."

Charlotte looked her up and down: gray dress, gray hair, ugly face, smug expression. "Go away, Marya."

"You've no conception of the trouble and heartache you've caused this afternoon."

Charlotte was tempted to say: If you had kept your mouth shut there would have been no heartache. Instead she said: "Get out."

"You listen to me, little Charlotte—"

"I'm *Lady* Charlotte to you."

"You're little Charlotte, and—"

Charlotte picked up a hand mirror and hurled it at Marya. Marya squealed. The missile was badly aimed and smashed against the wall. Marya scuttled out of the room.

Now I know how to deal with *her*, Charlotte thought.

It occurred to her that she had won something of a victory. She had reduced Mama to tears and chased Marya out of her room. That's something, she thought; I may be stronger than they after all. They deserved rough treatment: Marya went to Mama behind my back, and Mama slapped me. But I didn't grovel and apologize and promise to be good in future. I gave as good as I got. I should be proud.

So why do I feel so ashamed?

•§ ¿•

I hate myself, Lydia thought.

I know how Charlotte feels, but I can't *tell* her that I understand. I always lose control. I never used to be like this. I was always calm and dignified. When she was a little girl I could laugh at her peccadilloes. Now she's a woman. Dear God, what have I done? She's tainted with the blood of her father, of Feliks, I'm sure of it. What am I going to do? I thought if I pretended she was Stephen's daughter she might actually become like a daughter of Stephen—innocent, ladylike, English. It was no good. All those years the bad blood was in her, dormant, and now it's coming out; now the amoral Russian peasant in her ancestry is taking her over. When I see those signs I panic, I can't help it. I'm cursed, we're all cursed, the sins of the fathers are visited upon the children, even unto the third and fourth generation, when will I be forgiven? Feliks is an anarchist and Charlotte is a suffragette; Feliks is a fornicator and Charlotte talks about thirteen-year-old mothers; she has no idea how awful it is to be possessed by passion; my life was ruined, hers will be too, that's what I'm afraid of, that's what makes me shout and cry and get hysterical and smack her, but, sweet Jesus, don't let her ruin herself, she's all I've lived for. I shall lock her away. If only she would marry a nice boy, soon, before she has time to go right off the rails, before everybody realizes there is something wrong with her breeding. I wonder if Freddie will propose to her before the end of the season—that would be the answer—I must make sure he does, I *must* have her married, quickly! Then it will be too late for her to ruin herself; besides, with a baby or two she won't have time. I must make sure she meets Freddie more often. She's quite pretty, she'll be a good enough wife to a strong man who can keep her under control, a decent man who will love her without unleashing her dark desires, a man who will sleep in an adjoining room and share her bed once a week with the light out, Freddie is just right for her, then she'll never have to go through what I've been through, she'll never have to learn the hard way that lust is wicked and destroys, the sin won't be passed down yet another generation, she won't be wicked like me. She thinks I want her to be like me. If only she knew. If only she knew!

&ᵉᵍ ᵉᵃ&

Feliks could not stop crying.

People stared at him as he walked through the park to retrieve his bicycle. He shook with uncontrollable sobs and the tears poured down his face. This had never happened to him before and he could not understand it. He was helpless with grief.

He found the bicycle where he had left it, beneath a bush, and the familiar sight calmed him a little. What is happening to me? he thought. Lots of people have children. Now I know that I have, too. So what? And he burst into tears again.

He sat down on the dry grass beside the bicycle. She's so beautiful, he thought. But he was not weeping for what he had found; he was weeping for what he had lost. For eighteen years he had been a father without knowing it. While he was wandering from one grim village to another, while he was in jail, and in the gold mine, and walking across Siberia, and making bombs in Bialystock, she had been growing up. She had learned to walk, and to talk, and to feed herself and tie her bootlaces. She had played on a green lawn under a chestnut tree in summer, and had fallen off a donkey and cried. Her "father" had given her a pony while Feliks had been working on the chain gang. She had worn white frocks in summer and woolen stockings in winter. She had always been bilingual in Russian and English. Someone else had read storybooks to her; someone else had said "I'll catch you!" and chased her, screaming with delight, up the stairs; someone else had taught her to shake hands and say "How do you do?"; someone else had bathed her and brushed her hair and made her finish up her cabbage. Many times Feliks had watched Russian peasants with their children and had wondered how, in their lives of misery and grinding poverty, they managed to summon up affection and tenderness for the infants who took the bread from their mouths. Now he knew: the love just came, whether you wanted it or not. From his recollections of other people's children he could visualize Charlotte at different stages of development: as a toddler with a protruding belly and no hips to hold up her skirt; as a boisterous seven-year-old, tearing her frock and grazing her knees; as a lanky, awkward girl of ten with ink on her fingers and clothes always a little too small; as a shy adolescent, giggling at boys, secretly trying her mother's perfume, crazy about horses, and then—

And then this beautiful, brave, alert, inquisitive, admirable young woman.

And I'm her father, he thought.

Her *father.*

What was it she had said? *You're the most interesting person I've ever met—may I see you again?* He had been preparing to say good-bye to her forever. When he knew that he would not have to, his self-control had begun to disintegrate. She thought he had a cold. Ah, she was young still, to make such bright, cheerful remarks to a man whose heart was breaking.

I'm becoming maudlin, he thought; I must pull myself together.

He stood up and picked up the bicycle. He mopped his face with the handkerchief she had given him. It had a bluebell embroidered in one corner, and he wondered whether she had done that herself. He mounted the bicycle and headed for the Old Kent Road.

It was supper time but he knew he would not be able to eat. That was just as well, for his money was running low and tonight he did not have the spirit to steal. He looked forward now to the darkness of his tenement room, where he could spend the night alone with his thoughts. He would go over every minute of this encounter, from the moment she emerged from the house to that last good-bye wave.

He would have liked a bottle of vodka for company, but he could not afford it.

He wondered whether anyone had ever given Charlotte a red ball.

The evening was mild but the city air was stale. The pubs of the Old Kent Road were already filling up with brightly dressed working-class women and their husbands, boyfriends or fathers. On impulse, Feliks stopped outside one. The sound of an elderly piano wafted through the open door. Feliks thought: I'd like someone to smile at me, even if it's only a barmaid. I could afford half a pint of ale. He tied his bicycle to a railing and went in.

The place was stifling, full of smoke and the unique beery smell of an English pub. It was early, but already there was a good deal of loud laughter and feminine squeals. Everyone seemed enormously cheerful. Feliks thought: Nobody knows how to spend money better than the poor. He joined the crush at the bar. The piano began a new tune, and everyone sang.

> *Once a young maiden climbed an old man's knee*
> *Begged for a story, "Do, uncle, please,*
> *Why are you single, why live alone?*
> *Have you no babies, have you no home?"*
> *"I had a sweetheart, years, years ago;*
> *Where is she now, pet, you will soon know*
> *List to my story, I'll tell it all;*
> *I believed her faithless, after the ball."*

The stupid, sentimental, empty-headed damn song brought tears to Feliks's eyes, and he left the pub without ordering his beer.

He cycled away, leaving the laughter and music behind. That kind of jollity was not for him; it never had been and never would be. He made his way back to the tenement and carried the bicycle up the stairs to his room on the top floor. He took off his hat and coat and lay on the bed. He would see her again in two days. They would look at paintings together. He would go to the municipal bathhouse before meeting her, he decided. He rubbed his chin: there was nothing he could do to make the beard grow decently in two days. He cast his mind back to the moment when she came out of the house. He had seen her from a distance, never dreaming . . .

What was I thinking of at that moment? he wondered.

And then he remembered.

I was asking myself whether she might know where Orlov is.

I haven't thought about Orlov all afternoon.

In all probability she *does* know where he is; if not, she could find out.

I might use her to help me kill him.

Am I capable of that?

No, I am not. I will not do it. No, no, no!

What is happening to me?

❧ ❧

Walden saw Churchill at the Admiralty at twelve noon. The First Lord was impressed. "Thrace," he said. "Surely we can give them half of Thrace. Who the devil cares if they have the whole of it!'"

"That's what I thought," Walden said. He was pleased with Churchill's reaction. "Now, will your colleagues agree?"

"I believe they will," Churchill said thoughtfully. "I'll see Grey after lunch and Asquith this evening."

"And the Cabinet?" Walden did not want to do a deal with Aleks only to have it vetoed by the Cabinet.

"Tomorrow morning."

Walden stood up. "So I can plan to go back to Norfolk late tomorrow."

"Splendid. Have they caught that damned anarchist yet?"

"I'm having lunch with Basil Thomson of the Special Branch —I'll find out then."

"Keep me informed."

"Naturally."

"And thank you. For this proposal, I mean." Churchill looked out of the window dreamily. "Thrace!" he murmured to himself. "Who has ever even heard of it?"

Walden left him to his reverie.

He was in a buoyant mood as he walked from the Admiralty to his club in Pall Mall. He usually ate lunch at home, but he did not want to trouble Lydia with policemen, especially as she was in a rather strange mood at the moment. No doubt she was worried about Aleks, as Walden was. The boy was the nearest thing to a son that they had: if anything should happen to him—

He went up the steps of his club and, just inside the door, handed his hat and gloves to a flunky. "What a lovely summer we're having, my lord," the man said.

The weather had been remarkably fine for months, Walden reflected as he went up to the dining room. When it broke there would probably be storms. We shall have thunder in August, he thought.

Thomson was waiting. He looked rather pleased with himself. What a relief it will be if he's caught the assassin, Walden thought. They shook hands, and Walden sat down. A waiter brought the menu.

"Well?" said Walden. "Have you caught him?"

"All but," Thomson said.

That meant no, Walden thought. His heart sank. "Oh, *damn,*" he said.

The wine waiter came. Walden asked Thomson: "Do you want a cocktail?"

"No, thank you."

Walden approved. Cocktails were a nasty American habit. "Perhaps a glass of sherry?"

"Yes, please."

"Two," Walden said to the waiter.

They ordered Brown Windsor soup and poached salmon, and Walden chose a bottle of hock to wash it down.

Walden said: "I wonder if you realize quite how important this is? My negotiations with Prince Orlov are almost complete. If he were to be assassinated now the whole thing would fall through—with serious consequences for the security of this country."

"I do realize, my lord," Thomson said. "Let me tell you what progress we've made. Our man is Feliks Kschessinsky. That's so hard to say that I propose we call him Feliks. He is forty, the son of a country priest, and he comes from Tambov province. My opposite number in St. Petersburg has a very thick file on him. He has been arrested three times and is wanted in connection with half a dozen murders."

"Dear God," Walden muttered.

"My friend in St. Petersburg adds that he is an expert bomb maker and an extremely vicious fighter." Thomson paused. "You were terribly brave, to catch that bottle." Walden gave a thin smile: he preferred not to be reminded.

The soup came and the two men ate in silence for a while. Thomson sipped his hock frugally. Walden liked this club. The food was not as good as he got at home, but there was a relaxed atmosphere. The chairs in the smoking room were old and comfortable, the waiters were old and slow, the wallpaper was faded and the paintwork was dull. They still had gas lighting. Men such as Walden came here because their homes were spick and span and feminine.

"I thought you said you had all but caught him," Walden said as the poached salmon arrived.

"I haven't told you the half of it yet."

"Ah."

"At the end of May he arrived at the Jubilee Street anarchist club in Stepney. They didn't know who he was, and he told them lies. He's a cautious man—quite rightly so, from his point of view, for one or two of those anarchists are working for me.

My spies reported his presence, but the information didn't come to my notice at that stage because he appeared to be harmless. Said he was writing a book. Then he stole a gun and moved on."

"Without telling anyone where he was going, of course."

"That's right."

"Slippery fellow."

A waiter collected their plates and said: "Will you have a slice off the joint, gentlemen? It's mutton today."

They both had mutton with red-currant jelly, roast potatoes and asparagus.

Thomson said: "He bought the ingredients for his nitroglycerine in four different shops in Camden Town. We made house-to-house inquiries there." Thomson took a mouthful of mutton.

"And?" Walden asked impatiently.

"He's been living at nineteen Cork Street, Camden, in a house owned by a widow called Bridget Callahan."

"But he's moved on."

"Yes."

"Damn it, Thomson, can't you see the fellow's cleverer than you?"

Thomson looked at him coolly and made no comment.

Walden said: "I beg your pardon, that was discourteous of me, the fellow's got me rattled."

Thomson went on: "Mrs. Callahan says she threw Feliks out because she thought he was a suspicious character."

"Why didn't she report him to the police?"

Thomson finished his mutton and put down his knife and fork. "She says she had no real reason to. I found that suspicious, so I checked up on her. Her husband was an Irish rebel. If she knew what our friend Feliks was up to, she might well have been sympathetic."

Walden wished Thomson would not call Feliks "our friend." He said: "Do you think she knows where the man went?"

"If she does, she won't say. But I can't think why he should tell her. The point is, he may come back."

"Are you having the place watched?"

"Surreptitiously. One of my men has already moved into the basement room as a tenant. Incidentally, he found a glass rod of the kind used in chemistry laboratories. Evidently Feliks made up his nitroglycerine right there in the sink."

It was chilling to Walden to think that in the heart of London anyone could buy a few chemicals, mix them together in a wash-hand-basin, and make a bottle of dreadfully explosive liquid—then walk with it into a suite in a West End hotel.

The mutton was followed by a savory of *foie gras*. Walden said: "What's your next move?"

"The picture of Feliks is hanging up in every police station in the County of London. Unless he locks himself indoors all day, he's bound to be spotted by an observant bobby sooner or later. But just in case that should be later rather than sooner, my men are visiting cheap hotels and lodging houses, showing the picture."

"Suppose he changes his appearance?"

"It's a bit difficult in his case."

Thomson was interrupted by the waiter. Both men refused the Black Forest gateau and chose ices instead. Walden ordered half a bottle of champagne.

Thomson went on: "He can't hide his height, nor his Russian accent. And he has distinctive features. He hasn't had time to grow a beard. He may wear different clothes, shave himself bald or wear a wig. If I were he I should go about in a uniform of some kind—as a sailor, or a footman, or a priest. But policemen are alert to that sort of thing."

After their ices they had Stilton cheese and sweet biscuits with some of the club's vintage port.

It was all too vague, Walden felt. Feliks was *loose*, and Walden would not feel safe until the fellow was locked up and chained to the wall.

Thomson said: "Feliks is clearly one of the top killers of the international revolutionist conspiracy. He is very well informed: for example, he knew that Prince Orlov was going to be here in England. He is also clever, and formidably determined. However, we have hidden Orlov away."

Walden wondered what Thomson was getting at.

"By contrast," Thomson went on, "you are still walking about the streets of London as large as life."

"Why should I not?"

"If I were Feliks, I would now concentrate on you. I would follow you in the hope that you might lead me to Orlov; or I would kidnap you and torture you until you told me where he was."

Walden lowered his eyes to hide his fear. "How could he do that alone?"

"He may have help. I want you to have a bodyguard."

Walden shook his head. "I've got my man Pritchard. He would risk his life for me—he has done, in the past."

"Is he armed?"

"No."

"Can he shoot?"

"Very well. He used to come with me to Africa in my big-game hunting days. That's when he risked his life for me."

"Then let him carry a pistol."

"All right," Walden assented. "I'll be going to the country tomorrow. I've got a revolver there which he can have."

To finish the meal Walden had a peach and Thomson took a melba pear. Afterward they went into the smoking room for coffee and biscuits. Walden lit a cigar. "I think I shall walk home, for my digestion's sake." He tried to say it calmly, but his voice sounded oddly high-pitched.

"I'd rather you didn't," Thomson said. "Haven't you brought your carriage?"

"No—"

"I should be happier about your safety if you were to go everywhere in your own vehicles from now on."

"Very well," Walden sighed. "I shall have to eat less."

"For today, take a cab. Perhaps I'll accompany you."

"Do you really think that's necessary?"

"He might be waiting for you outside this club."

"How would he find out which club I belong to?"

"By looking you up in *Who's Who.*"

"Yes, of course." Walden shook his head. "One just doesn't think of these things."

Thomson looked at his watch. "I should get back to the Yard . . . if you're ready."

"Certainly."

They left the club. Feliks was not lying in wait outside. They took a cab to Walden's house; then Thomson took the cab on to Scotland Yard. Walden went into the house. It felt empty. He decided to go to his room. He sat at the window and finished his cigar.

He felt the need to talk to someone. He looked at his watch: Lydia would have had her siesta, and would now be putting on a gown ready to have tea and receive callers. He went through to her room.

She was sitting at her mirror in a robe. She looks strained, he thought; it's all this trouble. He put his hands on her shoulders, looking at her reflection in the mirror, then bent to kiss the top of her head. "Feliks Kschessinsky."

"*What?*" She seemed frightened.

"That's the name of our assassin. Does it mean something to you?"

"No."

"I thought you seemed to recognize it."

"It . . . it rings a bell."

"Basil Thomson has found out all about the fellow. He's a killer, a thoroughly evil type. It's not impossible that you might have come across him in St. Petersburg—that would explain why he seemed vaguely familiar when he called here, and why his name rings a bell."

"Yes—that must be it."

Walden went to the window and looked out over the park. It was the time of day when nannies took their charges for a walk. The paths were crowded with perambulators, and every bench was occupied by gossiping women in unfashionable clothes. It occurred to Walden that Lydia might have had some connection with Feliks, back in St. Petersburg—some connection which she did not want to admit. The thought was shaming, and he pushed it out of his mind. He said: "Thomson believes that when Feliks realizes Aleks is hidden away, he will try to kidnap me."

Lydia got up from her chair and came to him. She put her arms around his waist and laid her head on his chest. She did not speak.

Walden stroked her hair. "I must go everywhere in my own coach, and Pritchard must carry a pistol."

She looked up at him, and to his surprise he saw that her gray eyes were full of tears. She said: "Why is this happening to us? First Charlotte gets involved in a riot, then you're threatened—it seems we're all in jeopardy."

"Nonsense. You're in no danger, and Charlotte is only being a silly girl. And I'll be well protected." He stroked her sides. He could feel the warmth of her body through the thin robe—she was not wearing her corset. He wanted to make love to her, right now. They had never done it in daylight.

He kissed her mouth. She pressed her body against his, and he realized that she, too, wanted to make love. He could not remember her being like this ever before. He glanced toward the door, thinking to lock it. He looked at her, and she gave a barely perceptible nod. A tear rolled down her nose. Walden went to the door.

Someone knocked.

"Damn!" Walden said quietly.

Lydia turned her face away from the door and dabbed at her eyes with a handkerchief.

Pritchard came in. "Excuse me, my lord. An urgent telephone communication from Mr. Basil Thomson. They have tracked the man Feliks to his lodging. If you want to be in at the kill, Mr. Thomson will pick you up here in three minutes"

"Get my hat and coat," Walden told him.

◆§ ᶳ◈

TEN

When Feliks went out to get the morning paper he seemed to see children every way he turned. In the courtyard a group of girls played a game involving dancing and chanting. The boys were playing cricket with a wicket chalked on the wall and a piece of rotten planking for a bat. In the street, older boys were pushing handcarts. He bought his newspaper from an adolescent girl. Coming back to his room, his way was blocked by a naked baby crawling up the stairs. As he looked at the child—it was a girl—she stood up unsteadily and slowly toppled backward. Feliks caught her and put her down on the landing. Her mother came out of an open door. She was a pale young woman with greasy hair, already very pregnant with another child. She scooped the baby girl up off the floor and disappeared back into her room with a suspicious look at Feliks.

Every time he considered exactly how he would bamboozle Charlotte into telling him the whereabouts of Orlov, he seemed to run up against a brick wall in his mind. He visualized getting the information out of her sneakily, without her knowing she was telling him; or by giving her a cock-and-bull story like the one he had given Lydia; or by telling her straight out that he wanted to kill Orlov; and his imagination recoiled at each scene.

When he thought about what was at stake he found his feelings ridiculous. He had a chance to save millions of lives and possibly spark the Russian Revolution—and he was worried about lying to an upper-class girl! It was not as if he intended to do her any harm—just use her, deceive her and betray her trust, his own daughter, whom he had only just met . . .

To occupy his hands he began to fashion his homemade dynamite into a primitive bomb. He packed the nitroglycerine-soaked cotton waste into a cracked china vase. He considered the problem of detonation. Burning paper alone might not be sufficient. He stuffed half a dozen matches into the cotton so that only their bright red heads showed. It was difficult to get the matches to stand upright because his hands were unsteady.

My hands never shake.

What is happening to me?

He twisted a piece of newspaper into a taper and stuck one end into the middle of the match heads, then tied the heads together with a length of cotton. He found it very difficult to tie the knot.

He read all the international news in *The Times*, plowing doggedly through the turgid English sentences. He was more or less sure that there would be a war, but more or less sure no longer seemed enough. He would have been happy to kill a useless idler like Orlov, then find out that it had been to no purpose. But to destroy his relationship with Charlotte to no purpose . . .

Relationship? What relationship?

You know what relationship.

Reading *The Times* made his head ache. The print was too small and his room was dark. It was a wretchedly conservative newspaper. It ought to be blown up.

He longed to see Charlotte again.

He heard shuffling footsteps on the landing outside, then there was a knock at the door.

"Come in," he called carelessly.

The caretaker came in, coughing. "Morning."

"Good morning, Mr. Price." What did the old fool want now?

"What's that?" said Price, nodding at the bomb on the table.

"Homemade candle," Feliks said. "Lasts months. What do you want?"

"I wondered if you needed a spare pair of sheets. I can get them at a very low price—"

"No, thank you," Feliks said. "Good-bye."

"Good-bye, then." Price went out.

I should have hidden that bomb, Feliks thought.

What is happening to me?

⌘

"Yes, he's in there," Price said to Basil Thomson.

Tension knotted in Walden's stomach.

They sat in the back of a police car parked around the corner from Canada Buildings, where Feliks was. With them was an inspector from the Special Branch and a uniformed superintendent from Southwark police station.

If they could catch Feliks now, then Aleks would be safe: what a relief that will be, Walden thought.

Thomson said: "Mr. Price went to the police station to report that he had rented a room to a suspicious character with a foreign accent who had very little money and was growing a beard as if to change his appearance. He identified Feliks from our artist's drawing. Well done, Price."

"Thank you, sir."

The uniformed superintendent unfolded a large-scale map. He was maddeningly slow and deliberate. "Canada Buildings consists of three five-story tenements around a courtyard. Each building has three stairwells. As you stand at the entrance to the courtyard, Toronto House is on your right. Feliks is on the middle staircase and the top floor. Behind Toronto House is the yard of a builder's merchant."

Walden contained his impatience.

"On your left is Vancouver House, and behind Vancouver House is another street. The third building, straight ahead of you as you stand at the courtyard entrance, is Montreal House, which backs on to the railway line."

Thomson pointed to the map. "What's that, in the middle of the courtyard?"

"The privy," replied the superintendent. "And a real stinker, too, with all those people using it."

Walden thought: Get on with it!

Thomson said: "It seems to me that Feliks has three ways out of the courtyard. First, the entrance: obviously we'll block that. Second, at the opposite end of the courtyard on the left, the alley between Vancouver House and Montreal House. It leads to the next street. Put three men in the alley, superintendent."

"Very good, sir."

"Third, the alley between Montreal House and Toronto House. This alley leads to the builder's yard. Another three men in there."

The superintendent nodded.

"Now, do these tenements have back windows?"

"Yes, sir."

"So Feliks has a fourth escape route from Toronto House: out of the back window and across the builder's yard. Better put six men in the builder's yard. Finally, let's have a nice show of strength right here in the middle of the courtyard, to encourage him to come along quietly. Does all that meet with your approval, superintendent?"

"More than adequate, I'd say, sir."

He doesn't know what kind of man we're dealing with, Walden thought.

Thomson said: "You and Inspector Sutton here can make the arrest. Got your gun, Sutton?"

Sutton pulled aside his coat to show a small revolver strapped under his arm. Walden was surprised: he had thought that no British policeman ever carried a firearm. Obviously the Special Branch was different. He was glad.

Thomson said to Sutton: "Take my advice—have it in your hand when you knock on his door." He turned to the uniformed superintendent. "You'd better take my gun."

The superintendent was mildly offended. "I've been twenty-five years in the force and never felt the lack of a firearm, sir, so if it's all the same to you I shan't begin now."

"Policemen have died trying to arrest this man."

"I'm afraid I've never been taught to shoot, sir."

Good God, Walden thought despairingly, how can people like us deal with people like Feliks?

Thomson said: "Lord Walden and I will be at the courtyard entrance."

"You'll stay in the car, sir?"

"We'll stay in the car."

Let's *go,* thought Walden.

"Let's go," said Thomson.

◦§ ﻬ◦

Feliks realized he was hungry. He had not eaten for more than twenty-four hours. He wondered what to do. Now that he had stubble on his chin and working-class clothes, he would be watched by shopkeepers so it would be more difficult for him to steal.

He pulled himself up at that thought. It's *never* difficult to steal, he told himself. Let's see: I could go to a suburban house —the kind where they are likely to have only one or two servants—and walk in at the tradesmen's entrance. There would be a maid in the kitchen, or perhaps a cook. "I am a madman," I would say with a smile, "but if you make me a sandwich I won't rape you." I would move toward the door to block her escape. She might scream, in which case I should go away and try another house. But, most likely, she would give me the food. "Thank you," I would say. "You are kind." Then I would walk away. It is never difficult to steal.

Money was a problem. Feliks thought: As if I could afford a pair of sheets! The caretaker was an optimist. Surely he knew that Feliks had no money . . .

Surely he knows I've no money.

On reflection, Price's reason for coming to Feliks's room was suspicious. Was he just optimistic? Or was he *checking?* I seem to be slowing down, Feliks thought. He stood up and went to the window.

Jesus *Christ.*

The courtyard was alive with blue-uniformed policemen.

Feliks stared down at them in horror.

The sight made him think of a nest of worms, wriggling and crawling over one another in a hole in the ground.

His instincts screamed: Run! Run! Run!

Where?

They had blocked all exits from the courtyard.

Feliks remembered the back windows.

He ran from his room and along the landing to the back of the tenement. There a window looked out on to the builder's yard behind. He peered down into the yard and saw five or six policemen taking up positions among the piles of bricks and stacks of planking. There was no escape that way.

That left only the roof.

He ran back to his room and looked out. The policemen were still, all but two men—one in uniform and one in plain clothes —who were walking purposefully across the courtyard toward Feliks's stair.

He picked up his bomb and the box of matches and ran down to the landing below. A small door with a latch gave access to a cupboard beneath the stairs. Feliks opened the door and placed the bomb inside. He lit the paper fuse and closed the cupboard door. He turned around. He had time to run up the stairs before the fuse burned down—

The baby girl was crawling up the stairs.

Shit.

He picked her up and dashed through the door into her room. Her mother sat on the dirty bed, staring vacantly at the wall. Feliks thrust the baby into her arms and yelled: "Stay here! Don't move!" The woman looked scared.

He ran out. The two men were one floor down. Feliks raced up the stairs—

Don't blow now don't blow now don't

—to his landing. They heard him, and one shouted: "Hey, you!" They broke into a run.

Feliks dashed into his room, picked up the cheap straight-backed chair, carried it out to the landing and positioned it directly under the trapdoor leading to the loft.

The bomb had not exploded.

Perhaps it would not work.

Feliks stood on the chair.

The two men hit the stairs.

Feliks pushed open the trapdoor.

The uniformed policeman shouted: "You're under arrest!"

The plainclothes man raised a gun and pointed it at Feliks.

The bomb went off.

There was a big dull thud like something very heavy falling

and the staircase broke up into matchwood which flew everywhere and the two men were flung backward and the debris
burst into flames and Feliks hauled himself up into the loft.

&

"Damn, he's exploded a damn bomb!" Thomson shouted.

Walden thought: It's going wrong—again.

There was a crash as shards of glass from a fourth-floor window hit the ground.

Walden and Thomson jumped out of the car and ran across
the courtyard.

Thomson picked two uniformed policemen at random. "You
and you—come inside with me." He turned to Walden. "You
stay here." They ran inside.

Walden backed across the courtyard, looking up at the windows of Toronto House.

Where is Feliks?

He heard a policeman say: "He've gorn out the back, you
mark my words."

Four or five slates fell off the roof and shattered in the courtyard—loosened, Walden assumed, by the explosion.

Walden kept feeling the urge to look back over his shoulder,
as if Feliks might suddenly appear behind him, from nowhere.

The residents of the tenements were coming to their doors
and windows to see what was going on, and the courtyard began
to fill with people. Some of the policemen made halfhearted
attempts to send them back inside. A woman ran out of Toronto
House screaming: "Fire!"

Where is Feliks?

Thomson and a policeman came out carrying Sutton. He was
unconscious, or dead. Walden looked more closely. No, he was
not dead: his pistol was gripped in his hand.

More slates fell off the roof.

The policeman with Thomson said: "It's a bloody mess in
there."

Walden said: "Did you see where Feliks is?"

"Couldn't see anything."

Thomson and the policeman went back inside.

More slates fell—

Walden was struck by a thought. He looked up.

There was a hole in the roof, and Feliks was climbing up through it.

"There he is!" Walden yelled.

They all watched, helpless, as Feliks crawled out of the loft and scrambled up the roof to the ridge.

If I had a gun—

Walden knelt over the unconscious body of Sutton and prized the pistol from his fingers.

He looked up. Feliks was kneeling on the peak of the roof. I wish it were a rifle, Walden thought as he lifted the gun. He sighted along the barrel. Feliks looked at him. Their eyes met.

ఆ ఈ

Feliks moved.

A shot rang out.

He felt nothing.

He began to run.

It was like running along a tightrope. He had to hold out his arms for balance, he had to place his feet squarely on the narrow ridge, and he had to avoid thinking about the fifty-foot drop to the courtyard.

There was another shot.

Feliks panicked.

He ran at top speed. The end of the roof loomed up. He could see the downsloping roof of Montreal House ahead. He had no idea how wide was the gap between the two buildings. He slowed down, hesitating; then Walden fired again.

Feliks ran full tilt at the end of the ridge.

He jumped.

He flew through the air. He heard his own voice, as if distantly, screaming.

He caught a momentary glimpse of three policemen, in the alley fifty feet below him, staring up at him openmouthed.

Then he hit the roof of Montreal House, landing hard on his hands and knees.

The impact winded him. He slid backward down the roof. His feet hit the gutter. It seemed to give under the strain, and he thought he was going to slide right off the edge of the roof and fall, fall, endlessly—but the gutter held and he stopped sliding.

He was frightened.

A distant corner of his mind protested: But I'm never frightened!

He scrambled up the roof to the peak and then down the other side.

Montreal House backed on to the railway. There were no policemen on the lines or the embankment. They didn't anticipate this, Feliks thought exultantly; they thought I was trapped in the courtyard; it never occurred to them that I might escape over the rooftops.

Now all I have to do is get down.

He peered over the gutter at the wall of the building beneath him. There were no drainpipes—the gutters emptied through spouts which jutted out from the edge of the roof, like gargoyles. But the top-floor windows were close to the eaves and had wide ledges.

With his right hand Feliks grasped the gutter and pulled it, testing its strength.

Since when have I cared whether I live or die?

(You know since when.)

He positioned himself over a window, gripped the gutter with both hands, and slowly eased himself over the edge.

For a moment he hung free.

His feet found the window ledge. He took his right hand from the gutter and felt the brickwork around the window for a handhold. He got his fingers into a shallow groove, then let go of the gutter with his other hand.

He looked through the window. Inside, a man saw him and shouted in fright.

Feliks kicked the window in and dropped into the room. He pushed the frightened occupant aside and rushed out through the doorway.

He ran down the stairs four at a time. If he could reach the ground floor he could get out through the back windows and onto the railway line.

He reached the last landing and stopped at the top of the last flight of stairs, breathing hard. A blue uniform appeared at the front entrance. Feliks spun around and raced to the back of the landing. He lifted the window. It stuck. He gave a mighty heave and threw it open. He heard boots running up the stairs. He clambered over the windowsill, eased himself out, hung by his hands for a moment, pushed himself away from the wall and dropped.

He landed in the long grass of the railway embankment. To his right, two men were jumping over the fence of the builder's yard. A shot came from his far left. A policeman came to the window from which Feliks had jumped.

He ran up the embankment to the railway.

There were four or five pairs of lines. In the distance a train was approaching fast. It seemed to be on the farthermost track. He suffered a moment of cowardice, frightened to cross in front of the train; then he broke into a run.

The two policemen from the builder's yard and the one from Montreal House chased him across the tracks. From the far left a voice shouted: "Clear the field of fire!" The three pursuers were making it difficult for Walden to get a shot.

Feliks glanced over his shoulder. They had fallen back. A shot rang out. He began to duck and zigzag. The train sounded very loud. He heard its whistle. There was another shot. He turned aside suddenly, then stumbled and fell onto the last pair of railway lines. There was a terrific thunder in his ears. He saw the locomotive bearing down on him. He jerked convulsively, catapulting himself off the track and onto the gravel on the far side. The train roared past his head. He caught a split-second glimpse of the engineman's face, white and scared.

He stood up and ran down the embankment.

◈

Walden stood at the fence watching the train. Basil Thomson came up beside him.

Those policemen who had got onto the railway line ran across to the last track, then stood there, helpless, waiting for the train to pass. It seemed to take forever.

When it had gone, there was no sign of Feliks.

"The bugger's got away," a policeman said.

Basil Thomson said: "God damn it all to hell."

Walden turned away and walked back to the car.

◈

Feliks dropped down on the far side of a wall and found himself in a poor street of small row houses. He was also in the goalmouth of an improvised soccer pitch. A group of small boys in large caps stopped playing and stared at him in surprise. He ran on.

It would take them a few minutes to redeploy the police on the far side of the railway line. They would come looking for him, but they would be too late: by the time they got a search under way he would be half a mile from the railway and still moving.

He kept running until he reached a busy shopping street. There, on impulse, he jumped on an omnibus.

He had escaped, but he was terribly worried. This kind of thing had happened to him before, but previously he had never been scared, he had never panicked. He remembered the thought that had gone through his mind as he slid down the roof: I don't want to die.

In Siberia he had lost the ability to feel fear. Now it had come back. For the first time in years, he wanted to stay alive. I have become human again, he thought.

He looked out of the window at the mean streets of southeast London, wondering whether the dirty children and the white-faced women could look at him and see a reborn man.

It was a disaster. It would slow him down, cramp his style, interfere with his work.

I'm afraid, he thought.

I want to live.

I want to see Charlotte again.

◄§ §►

ELEVEN

The first tram of the day woke Feliks with its noise. He opened his eyes and watched it go by, striking bright blue sparks from the overhead cable. Dull-eyed men in working clothes sat at its windows, smoking and yawning, on their way to jobs as street cleaners and market porters and road menders.

The sun was low and bright, but Feliks was in the shade of Waterloo Bridge. He lay on the pavement with his head to the wall, wrapped in a blanket of newspapers. On one side of him was a stinking old woman with the red face of a drunkard. She looked fat, but now Feliks could see, between the hem of her dress and the tops of her man's boots, a few inches of dirty white legs like sticks; and he concluded that her apparent obesity must be due to several layers of clothing. Feliks liked her: last night she had amused all the vagrants by teaching him the vulgar English words for various parts of the body. Feliks had repeated them after her and everyone had laughed.

On his other side was a red-haired boy from Scotland. For him, sleeping in the open was an adventure. He was tough and wiry and cheerful. Looking now at his sleeping face, Feliks saw that he had no morning beard: he was terribly young. What would happen to him when winter came?

There were about thirty of them in a line along the pavement, all lying with their heads to the wall and their feet toward the road, covered with coats or sacks or newspapers. Feliks was the first to stir. He wondered whether any of them had died in the night.

He got up. He ached after a night on the cold street. He walked out from under the bridge into the sunshine. Today he was to meet Charlotte. No doubt he looked and smelled like a tramp. He contemplated washing himself in the Thames, but the river appeared to be dirtier than he was. He went looking for a municipal bathhouse.

He found one on the south side of the river. A notice on the door announced that it would open at nine o'clock. Feliks thought that characteristic of social-democratic government: they would build a bathhouse so that working men could keep clean, then open it only when everyone was at work. No doubt they complained that the masses failed to take advantage of the facilities so generously provided.

He found a tea stall near Waterloo station and had breakfast. He was severely tempted by the fried-egg sandwiches but he could not afford one. He had his usual bread and tea and saved the money for a newspaper.

He felt contaminated by his night with the deadbeats. That was ironic, he thought, for in Siberia he had been glad to sleep with pigs for warmth. It was not difficult to understand why he felt differently now: he was to meet his daughter, and she would be fresh and clean, smelling of perfume and dressed in silk, with gloves and a hat and perhaps a parasol to shade her from the sun.

He went into the railway station and bought *The Times*, then sat on a stone bench outside the bathhouse and read the paper while he waited for the place to open.

The news shocked him to the core.

AUSTRIAN HEIR AND HIS WIFE MURDERED

SHOT IN BOSNIAN TOWN

A STUDENT'S POLITICAL CRIME

BOMB THROWN EARLIER IN THE DAY

THE EMPEROR'S GRIEF

*The Austro-Hungarian Heir-Presumptive, the Archduke Francis Fer-
dinand, and his wife, the Duchess of Hohenberg, were assassinated yesterday morning at Serajevo, the capital of Bosnia. The actual assassin is
described as a high school student, who fired bullets at his victims with
fatal effect from an automatic pistol as they were returning from a
reception at the Town Hall.*

*The outrage was evidently the fruit of a carefully-laid plot. On their
way to the Town Hall the Archduke and his Consort had narrowly
escaped death. An individual, described as a compositor from Trebinje,
a garrison town in the extreme south of Herzegovina, had thrown a bomb
at their motor-car. Few details of this first outrage have been received. It
is stated that the Archduke warded off the bomb with his arm, and that
it exploded behind the car, injuring the occupants of the second carriage.*

*The author of the second outrage is stated to be a native of Grahovo,
in Bosnia. No information as to his race or creed is yet forthcoming. It
is presumed that he belongs to the Serb or Orthodox section of the Bosnian
population.*

*Both criminals were immediately arrested, and were with difficulty
saved from being lynched.*

*While this tragedy was being enacted in the Bosnian capital, the aged
Emperor Francis Joseph was on his way from Vienna to his summer
residence at Ischl. He had an enthusiastic send-off from his subjects in
Vienna and an even more enthusiastic reception on reaching Ischl.*

Feliks was stunned. He was delighted that another useless
aristocratic parasite had been destroyed, another blow struck
against tyranny; and he felt ashamed that a schoolboy had been
able to kill the heir to the Austrian throne while he, Feliks, had
failed repeatedly to kill a Russian prince. But what occupied his
mind most was the change in the world political picture that
must surely follow. The Austrians, with the Germans backing
them, would take their revenge on Serbia. The Russians would
protest. Would the Russians mobilize their army? If they were
confident of British support, they probably would. Russian mobilization would mean German mobilization; and once the Germans had mobilized no one could stop their generals from going
to war.

Feliks painstakingly deciphered the tortured English of the
other reports, on the same page, to do with the assassination.

There were stories headlined OFFICIAL REPORT OF THE CRIME, AUSTRIAN EMPEROR AND THE NEWS, TRAGEDY OF A ROYAL HOUSE, and SCENE OF THE MURDER (From Our Special Correspondent). There was a good deal of nonsense about how shocked and horrified and grieved everyone was; plus repeated assertions that there was no cause for undue alarm, and that tragic though it was, the murder would make no real difference to Europe—sentiments which Feliks had already come to recognize as being characteristic of *The Times,* which would have described the Four Horsemen of the Apocalypse as strong rulers who could do nothing but good for the stability of the international situation.

So far there was no talk of Austrian reprisals, but it would come, Feliks was sure. And then—

Then there would be war.

There was no real reason for Russia to go to war, Feliks thought angrily. The same applied to England. It was France and Germany that were belligerent: the French had been wanting since 1871 to win back their lost territories of Alsace and Lorraine, and the German generals felt that Germany would be a second-class power until she began to throw her weight about.

What might stop Russia from going to war? A quarrel with her allies. What would cause a quarrel between Russia and England? The killing of Orlov.

If the assassination in Sarajevo could start a war, another assassination in London could stop a war.

And Charlotte could find Orlov.

Wearily, Feliks contemplated afresh the dilemma that had haunted him for the last forty-eight hours. Was anything changed by the murder of the Archduke? Did that give him the right to take advantage of a young girl?

It was almost time for the bathhouse to open. A small crowd of women carrying bundles of washing gathered around the door. Feliks folded his newspaper and stood up.

He knew that he *would* use her. He had not resolved the dilemma—he had simply decided what to do. His whole life seemed to lead up to the murder of Orlov. There was a momentum in his progress toward that goal, and he could not be deflected, even by the knowledge that his life had been founded on a mistake.

Poor Charlotte.

The doors opened, and Feliks went into the bathhouse to wash.

◦§ ȝ◦

Charlotte had it all planned. Lunch was at one o'clock when the Waldens had no guests. By two-thirty Mama would be in her room, lying down. Charlotte would be able to sneak out of the house in time to meet Feliks at three. She would spend an hour with him. By four-thirty she would be at home in the morning room, washed and changed and demurely ready to pour tea and receive callers with Mama.

It was not to be. At midday Mama ruined the whole plan by saying: "Oh, I forgot to tell you—we're lunching with the Duchess of Middlesex at her house in Grosvenor Square."

"Oh, dear," Charlotte said. "I really don't feel like a luncheon party."

"Don't be silly, you'll have a lovely time."

I said the wrong thing, Charlotte thought immediately. I should have said I've got a splitting headache and I can't possibly go. I was too halfhearted. I could have lied if I'd known in advance but I can't do it on the spur of the moment. She tried again. "I'm sorry, Mama, I don't want to go."

"You're coming, and no nonsense," Mama said. "I want the Duchess to get to know you—she really is most useful. And the Marquis of Chalfont will be there."

Luncheon parties generally started at one-thirty and went on past three. I might be home by three-thirty, so I could get to the National Gallery by four, Charlotte thought; but by then he will have given up and gone away, and besides, even if he is still waiting, I would have to leave him almost immediately in order to be home for tea. She wanted to talk to him about the assassination: she was eager to hear his views. She did not want to have lunch with the old Duchess and—

"Who is the Marquis of Chalfont?"

"You know, Freddie. He's charming, don't you think?"

"Oh, him. Charming? I haven't noticed." I could write a note, address it to that place in Camden Town, and leave it on the hall table on my way out for the footman to post; but Feliks doesn't actually live at that address, and anyway he wouldn't get the note before three o'clock.

Mama said: "Well, notice him today. I fancy you may have bewitched him."

"Who?"

"*Freddie.* Charlotte, you really must pay a little attention to a young man when he pays attention to you."

So that was why she was so keen on this lunch party. "Oh, Mama, don't be silly—"

"What's silly about it?" Mama said in an exasperated voice.

"I've hardly spoken three sentences to him."

"Then it's not your conversation that has bewitched him."

"Please!"

"All right, I won't tease. Go and change. Put on that cream dress with the brown lace—it suits your coloring."

Charlotte gave in, and went up to her room. I suppose I should be flattered about Freddie, she thought as she took off her dress. Why can't I get interested in any of these young men? Maybe I'm just not ready for all that yet. At the moment there's too much else to occupy my mind. At breakfast Papa said there would be a war, because of the shooting of the Archduke. But girls aren't supposed to be too interested in that sort of thing. The summit of my ambition should be to get engaged before the end of my first season—that's what Belinda is thinking about. But not all girls are like Belinda—remember the suffragettes.

She got dressed and went downstairs. She sat and made idle conversation while Mama drank a glass of sherry; then they went to Grosvenor Square.

The Duchess was an overweight woman in her sixties: she made Charlotte think of an old wooden ship rotting beneath a new coat of paint. The lunch was a real hen party. If this were a play, Charlotte thought, there would be a wild-eyed poet, a discreet Cabinet Minister, a cultured Jewish banker, a Crown Prince, and at least one remarkably beautiful woman. In fact, the only men present, apart from Freddie, were a nephew of the Duchess and a Conservative M.P. Each of the women was introduced as the wife of so-and-so. If I ever get married, Charlotte thought, I shall insist on being introduced as myself, not as somebody's wife.

Of course it was difficult for the Duchess to have interesting parties because so many people were banned from her table: all Liberals, all Jews, anybody in trade, anybody who was on the stage, all divorcées, and all of the many people who had at one time or another offended against the Duchess's idea of what was the done thing. It made for a dull circle of friends.

The Duchess's favorite topic of conversation was the question of what was ruining the country. The main candidates were subversion (by Lloyd George and Churchill), vulgarity (Diaghilev and the post-Impressionists), and supertax (one shilling and threepence in the pound).

Today, however, the ruin of England took second place to the death of the Archduke. The Conservative M.P. explained at somewhat tedious length why there would be no war. The wife of a South American ambassador said in a little-girlish tone which infuriated Charlotte: "What I don't understand is why these Nihilists want to throw bombs and shoot people."

The Duchess had the answer to that. Her doctor had explained to her that all suffragettes had a nervous ailment known to medical science as hysteria; and in her view the revolutionists suffered from the male equivalent of this disease.

Charlotte, who had read *The Times* from cover to cover that morning, said: "On the other hand, perhaps the Serbs simply don't want to be ruled by Austria." Mama gave her a black look, and everyone else glanced at her for a moment as if she were quite mad and then ignored what she had said.

Freddie was sitting next to her. His round face always seemed to gleam slightly. He spoke to her in a low voice. "I say, you do say the most outrageous things."

"What was outrageous about it?" Charlotte demanded.

"Well, I mean to say, anyone would think you approved of people shooting Archdukes."

"I think if the Austrians tried to take over England, you would shoot Archdukes, wouldn't you?"

"You're priceless," Freddie said.

Charlotte turned away from him. She was beginning to feel as if she had lost her voice: nobody seemed to hear anything she said. It made her very cross.

Meanwhile the Duchess was getting into her stride. The lower classes were idle, she said; and Charlotte thought: You who have never done a day's work in your life! Why, the Duchess said, she understood that nowadays each workman had a lad to carry his tools around: surely a man could carry his own tools, she said as a footman held out for her a silver salver of boiled potatoes. Beginning her third glass of sweet wine, she said that they drank so much beer in the middle of the day that they were incapable of working in the afternoon. People today wanted to be mollycoddled, she said as three footmen and two maids cleared away the third course and served the fourth; it was no business of the government's to provide Poor Relief and medical insurance and pensions. Poverty would encourage the lower orders to be thrifty, and that was a virtue, she said at the end of a meal which would have fed a working-class family of ten for a fortnight. People must be self-reliant, she said as the butler helped her rise from the table and walk into the drawing room.

By this time Charlotte was boiling with suppressed rage. Who could blame revolutionists for shooting people like the Duchess?

Freddie handed her a cup of coffee and said: "She's a marvelous old warhorse, isn't she?"

Charlotte said: "I think she's the nastiest old woman I've ever met."

Freddie's round face became furtive and he said: "Hush!"

At least, Charlotte thought, no one could say I'm encouraging him.

A carriage clock on the mantel struck three with a tinkling chime. Charlotte felt as if she were in jail. Feliks was now waiting for her on the steps of the National Gallery. She had to get out of the Duchess's house. She thought: What am I doing here when I could be with someone who talks sense?

The Conservative M.P. said: "I must get back to the House." His wife stood up to go with him. Charlotte saw her way out.

She approached the wife and spoke quietly. "I have a slight headache," she said. "May I come with you? You must pass my house on the way to Westminster."

"Certainly, Lady Charlotte," said the wife.

Mama was talking to the Duchess. Charlotte interrupted them and repeated the headache story. "I know Mama would like to stay a little longer, so I'm going with Mrs. Shakespeare. Thank you for a lovely lunch, your grace."

The Duchess nodded regally.

I managed that rather well, Charlotte thought as she walked out into the hall and down the stairs.

She gave her address to the Shakespeares' coachman and

added: "There's no need to drive into the courtyard—just stop outside."

On the way, Mrs. Shakespeare advised her to take a spoonful of laudanum for the headache.

The coachman did as he had been told, and at three-twenty Charlotte was standing on the pavement outside her home, watching the coach drive off. Instead of going into the house she headed for Trafalgar Square.

She arrived just after three-thirty and ran up the steps of the National Gallery. She could not see Feliks. He's gone, she thought; after all that. Then he emerged from behind one of the massive pillars, as if he had been lying in wait, and she was so pleased to see him she could have kissed him.

"I'm sorry to have made you wait about," she said as she shook his hand. "I got involved in a dreadful luncheon party."

"It docsn't matter, now that you're here." He was smiling, but uneasily, like—Charlotte thought—someone saying hello to a dentist before having a tooth pulled.

They went inside. Charlotte loved the cool, hushed museum, with its glass domes and marble pillars, gray floors and beige walls, and the paintings shouting out color and beauty and passion. "At least my parents taught me to look at pictures," she said.

He turned his sad dark eyes on her. "There's going to be a war."

Of all the people who had spoken of that possibility today, only Feliks and Papa had seemed to be *moved* by it. "Papa said the same thing. But I don't understand why."

"France and Germany both think they stand to gain a lot by war. Austria, Russia and England may get sucked in."

They walked on. Feliks did not seem to be interested in the paintings. Charlotte said: "Why are you so concerned? Shall you have to fight?"

"I'm too old. But I think of all the millions of innocent Russian boys, straight off the farm, who will be crippled or blinded or killed in a cause they don't understand and wouldn't care about if they did."

Charlotte had always thought of war as a matter of men killing one another, but Feliks saw it as men being killed by war. As usual, he showed her things in a new light. She said: "I never looked at it that way."

"The Earl of Walden never looked at it that way either. That's why he will let it happen."

"I'm sure Papa wouldn't let it happen if he could help—"

"You're wrong," Feliks interrupted. "He is making it happen."

Charlotte frowned, puzzled. "What do you mean?"

"That's why Prince Orlov is here."

Her puzzlement deepened. "How do you know about Aleks?"

"I know more about it than you do. The police have spies among the anarchists, but the anarchists have spies among the police spies. We find things out. Walden and Orlov are negotiating a treaty, the effect of which will be to drag Russia into the war on the British side."

Charlotte was about to protest that Papa would not do such a thing; then she realized that Feliks was right. It explained some of the remarks passed between Papa and Aleks while Aleks was staying at the house, and it explained why Papa was shocking his friends by consorting with Liberals like Churchill.

She said: "Why would he do that?"

"I'm afraid he doesn't care how many Russian peasants die so long as England dominates Europe."

Yes, of course, Papa would see it in those terms, she thought. "It's awful," she said. "Why don't you *tell* people? Expose the whole thing—shout it from the rooftops!"

"Who would listen?"

"Wouldn't they listen in Russia?"

"They will if we can find a dramatic way of bringing the thing to their notice."

"Such as?"

Feliks looked at her. "Such as kidnapping Prince Orlov."

It was so outrageous that she laughed, then stopped abruptly. It crossed her mind that he might be playing a game, pretending in order to make a point; then she looked at his face and knew that he was deadly serious. For the first time she wondered whether he was perfectly sane. "You don't mean that," she said incredulously.

He smiled awkwardly. "Do you think I'm crazy?"

She knew he was not. She shook her head. "You're the sanest man I ever met."

"Then sit down, and I'll explain it to you."

She allowed herself to be led to a seat.

"The Czar already distrusts the English, because they let political refugees like me come to England. If one of us were to kidnap his favorite nephew there would be a real quarrel—and then they could not be sure of each other's help in a war. And when the Russian people learn what Orlov was trying to do to them, they will be so angry that the Czar will not be able to make them go to war anyway. Do you see?"

Charlotte watched his face as he talked. He was quiet, reasonable and only a little tense. There was no mad light of fanaticism in his eye. Everything he said made sense, but it was like the logic of a fairy tale—one thing followed from another, but it seemed to be a story about a different world, not the world she lived in.

"I do see," she said, "but you can't kidnap Aleks; he's such a nice man."

"That *nice man* will lead a million other nice men to their deaths if he's allowed to. This is *real*, Charlotte; not like the battles in these paintings of gods and horses. Walden and Orlov are discussing *war*—men cutting each other open with swords, boys getting their legs blown off by cannonballs, people bleeding and dying in muddy fields, screaming in pain with no one to help them. This is what Walden and Orlov are trying to arrange. Half the misery in the world is caused by nice young men like Orlov who think they have the right to organize wars between nations."

She was struck by a frightening thought. "You've already tried once to kidnap him."

He nodded. "In the park. You were in the carriage. It went wrong."

"Oh, my word." She felt sickened and depressed.

He took her hand. "You know I'm right, don't you?"

It seemed to her that he *was* right. His world was the real world: she was the one who lived in a fairy tale. In fairyland the debutantes in white were presented to the King and Queen, and the Prince went to war, and the Earl was kind to his servants who all loved him, and the Duchess was a dignified old lady, and there was no such thing as sexual intercourse. In the real world Annie's baby was born dead because Mama let Annie go without a reference, and a thirteen-year-old mother was condemned

to death because she had let her baby die, and people slept on
the streets because they had no homes, and there were baby
farms, and the Duchess was a vicious old harridan, and a grinning man in a tweed suit punched Charlotte in the stomach
outside Buckingham Palace.

"I know you're right," she said to Feliks.

"That's very important," he said. "You hold the key to the
whole thing."

"Me? Oh, no!"

"I need your help."

"No, please don't say that!"

"You see, I can't find Orlov."

It's not fair, she thought; it has all happened too quickly. She
felt miserable and trapped. She wanted to help Feliks, and she
could see how important it was, but Aleks was her cousin, and
he had been a guest in her house—how could she betray him?

"Will you help me?" Feliks said.

"I don't know where Aleks is," she said evasively.

"But you could find out."

"Yes."

"Will you?"

She sighed. "I don't know."

"Charlotte, you must."

"There's no *must* about it!" she flared. "Everyone tells me
what I *must* do—I thought you had more respect for me!"

He looked crestfallen. "I wish I didn't have to ask you."

She squeezed his hand. "I'll think about it."

He opened his mouth to protest, and she put a finger to his lips
to silence him. "You'll have to be satisfied with that," she said.

◈

At seven-thirty Walden went out in the Lanchester, wearing
evening dress and a silk hat. He was using the motor car all the
time, now: in an emergency it would be faster and more maneuverable than a carriage. Pritchard sat in the driving seat with
a revolver holstered beneath his jacket. Civilized life seemed to
have come to an end. They drove to the back entrance of Number Ten Downing Street. The Cabinet had met that afternoon to discuss the deal Walden had worked out with Aleks.

Now Walden was to hear whether or not they had approved it.

He was shown into the small dining room. Churchill was already there with Asquith, the Prime Minister. They were leaning on the sideboard drinking sherry. Walden shook hands with Asquith.

"How do you do, Prime Minister."

"Good of you to come, Lord Walden."

Asquith had silver hair and a clean-shaven face. There were traces of humor in the wrinkles around his eyes, but his mouth was small, thin-lipped and stubborn-looking, and he had a broad, square chin. Walden thought there was in his voice a trace of Yorkshire accent which had survived the City of London School and Balliol College, Oxford. He had an unusually large head which was said to contain a brain of machine-like precision; but then, Walden thought, people always credit prime ministers with more brains than they've got.

Asquith said: "I'm afraid the Cabinet would not approve your proposal."

Walden's heart sank. To conceal his disappointment he adopted a brisk manner. "Why not?"

"The opposition came mainly from Lloyd George."

Walden looked at Churchill and raised his eyebrows.

Churchill nodded. "You probably thought, like everyone else, that L.G. and I vote alike on every issue. Now you know otherwise."

"What's his objection?"

"Matter of principle," Churchill answered. "He says we're passing the Balkans around like a box of chocolates: help yourself, choose your favorite flavor, Thrace, Bosnia, Bulgaria, Serbia. Small countries have their rights, he says. That's what comes of having a Welshman in the Cabinet. A Welshman and a solicitor, too; I don't know which is worse."

His levity irritated Walden. This is his project as much as mine, he thought: why isn't the man as dismayed as I am?

They sat down to dinner. The meal was served by one butler. Asquith ate sparingly. Churchill drank too much, Walden thought. Walden was gloomy, mentally damning Lloyd George with every mouthful.

At the end of the first course Asquith said: "We must have this treaty, you know. There will be a war between France and Germany sooner or later; and if the Russians stay out of it, Germany will conquer Europe. We can't have that."

Walden asked: "What must be done to change Lloyd George's mind?"

Asquith smiled thinly. "If I had a pound note for every time that question has been asked I'd be a rich man."

The butler served a quail to each man and poured claret. Churchill said: "We must come up with a modified proposal which will meet L.G.'s objection."

Churchill's casual tone infuriated Walden. "You know perfectly well it's not that simple," he snapped.

"No indeed," Asquith said mildly. "Still, we must try. Thrace to be an independent country under Russian protection, something like that."

"I've spent the past month beating them down," Walden said wearily.

"Still, the murder of poor old Francis Ferdinand changes the complexion of things," Asquith said. "Now that Austria is getting aggressive in the Balkans again, the Russians need more than ever that toehold in the area which, in principle, we're trying to give them."

Walden set aside his disappointment and began to think constructively. After a moment he said: "What about Constantinople?"

"What do you mean?"

"Suppose we offered Constantinople to the Russians—would Lloyd George object to that?"

"He might say it was like giving Cardiff to the Irish Republicans," Churchill said.

Walden ignored him and looked at Asquith.

Asquith put down his knife and fork. "Well. Now that he has made his principled stand, he may be keen to show how reasonable he can be when offered a compromise. I think he may buy it. Will it be enough for the Russians?"

Walden was not sure, but he was buoyed by his new idea. Impulsively he said: "If you can sell it to Lloyd George, I can sell it to Orlov."

"Splendid!" said Asquith. "Now, then, what about this anarchist?"

Walden's optimism was punctured. "They're doing everything possible to protect Aleks, but still it's damned worrying."

"I thought Basil Thomson was a good man."

"Excellent," Walden said. "But I'm afraid Feliks might be even better."

Churchill said: "I don't think we should let the fellow *frighten* us—"

"I *am* frightened, gentlemen," Walden interrupted. "Three times Feliks has slipped through our grasp: the last time we had thirty policemen to arrest him. I don't see how he can get at Aleks now, but the fact that I can't see a way doesn't mean that he can't see a way. And we know what will happen if Aleks is killed: our alliance with Russia will fall through. Feliks is the most dangerous man in England."

Asquith nodded, his expression somber. "If you're less than perfectly satisfied with the protection Orlov is getting, please contact me directly."

"Thank you."

The butler offered Walden a cigar, but he sensed that he was finished here. "Life must go on," he said, "and I must go to a crush at Mrs. Glenville's. I'll smoke my cigar there."

"Don't tell them where you had dinner," Churchill said with a smile.

"I wouldn't dare—they'd never speak to me again." Walden finished his port and stood up

"When will you put the new proposal to Orlov?" Asquith asked.

"I'll motor to Norfolk first thing in the morning."

"Splendid."

The butler brought Walden's hat and gloves, and he took his leave.

Pritchard was standing at the garden gate, chatting to the policeman on duty. "Back to the house," Walden told him.

He had been rather rash, he reflected as they drove. He had promised to secure Aleks's consent to the Constantinople plan, but he was not sure how. It was worrying. He began to rehearse the words he would use tomorrow.

He was home before he had made any progress. "We'll need the car again in a few minutes, Pritchard."

"Very good, my lord."

Walden entered the house and went upstairs to wash his hands. On the landing he met Charlotte. "Is Mama getting ready?" he said.

"Yes, she'll be a few minutes. How goes your politicking?"

"Slowly."

"Why have you suddenly got involved in all that sort of thing again?"

He smiled. "In a nutshell: to stop Germany conquering Europe. But don't you worry your pretty little head—"

"I shan't worry. But where on earth have you hidden Cousin Aleks?"

He hesitated. There was no harm in her knowing; yet, once she knew, she would be capable of accidentally letting the secret out. Better for her to be left in the dark. He said: "If anyone asks you, say you don't know." He smiled and went on up to his room.

◆§ ﻉ◆

There were times when the charm of English life wore thin for Lydia.

Usually she liked crushes. Several hundred people would gather at someone's home to do nothing whatsoever. There was no dancing, no formal meal, no cards. You shook hands with the hostess, took a glass of champagne, and wandered around some great house chatting to your friends and admiring people's clothes. Today she was struck by the pointlessness of the whole thing. Her discontent took the form of nostalgia for Russia. There, she felt, the beauties would surely be more ravishing, the intellectuals less polite, the conversations deeper, the evening air not so balmy and soporific. In truth she was too worried—about Stephen, about Feliks and about Charlotte—to enjoy socializing.

She ascended the broad staircase with Stephen on one side of her and Charlotte on the other. Her diamond necklace was admired by Mrs. Glenville. They moved on. Stephen peeled off to talk to one of his cronies in the Lords: Lydia heard the words "Amendment Bill" and listened no more. They moved through the crowd, smiling and saying hello. Lydia kept thinking: What am I doing here?

Charlotte said: "By the way, Mama, where has Aleks gone?"

"I don't know, dear," Lydia said absently. "Ask your father. Good evening, Freddie."

Freddie was interested in Charlotte, not Lydia. "I've been thinking about what you said at lunch," he said. "I've decided that the difference is, we're English."

Lydia left them to it. *In my day,* she thought, *political discussions were decidedly* not *the way to win a man; but perhaps things have changed. It begins to look as if Freddie will be interested in whatever Charlotte wants to talk about. I wonder if he will propose to her. Oh, Lord, what a relief that would be.*

In the first of the reception rooms, where a string quartet played inaudibly, she met her sister-in-law, Clarissa. They talked about their daughters, and Lydia was secretly comforted to learn that Clarissa was terribly worried about Belinda.

"I don't mind her buying those ultra-fashionable clothes and showing her ankles, and I shouldn't mind her smoking cigarettes if only she were a little more discreet about it," Clarissa said. "But she goes to the most dreadful places to listen to nigger bands playing jazz music, and last week she went to a boxing match!"

"What about her chaperone?"

Clarissa sighed. "I've said she can go out without a chaperone if she's with girls we know. Now I realize that was a mistake. I suppose Charlotte is always chaperoned."

"In theory, yes," Lydia said. "But she's frightfully disobedient. Once she sneaked out and went to a suffragette meeting." Lydia was not prepared to tell Clarissa the whole disgraceful truth: "a suffragette meeting" did not sound quite as bad as "a demonstration." She added: "Charlotte is interested in the most unladylike things, such as politics. I don't know where she gets her ideas."

"Oh, I feel the same," Clarissa said. "Belinda was always brought up with the very best of music, and good society, and wholesome books and a strict governess . . . so naturally one wonders where on earth she got her taste for vulgarity. The worst of it is, I can't make her realize that I am worried for her happiness, not my own."

"Oh, I'm so glad to hear you say that!" Lydia said. "It's *just* how I feel. Charlotte seems to think there's something false or silly about our protecting her." She sighed. "We must marry them off quickly, before they come to any harm."

"Absolutely! Is anyone interested in Charlotte?"

"Freddie Chalfont."

"Ah, yes, I'd heard that."

"He even seems to be prepared to talk politics to her. But I'm afraid she's not awfully interested in him. What about Belinda?"

"The opposite problem. She likes them all."

"Oh, dear!" Lydia laughed, and moved on, feeling better. In some ways Clarissa, as a stepmother, had a more difficult task than Lydia I suppose I have much to be thankful for, she thought.

The Duchess of Middlesex was in the next room. Most people stayed on their feet at a crush, but the Duchess, characteristically, sat down and let people come to her. Lydia approached her just as Lady Gay-Stephens was moving away.

"I gather Charlotte is quite recovered from her headache," the Duchess said.

"Yes, indeed; it's kind of you to inquire."

"Oh, I wasn't inquiring," the Duchess said. "My nephew saw her in the National Gallery at four o'clock."

The National Gallery! What in Heaven's name was she doing there? She had sneaked out again! But Lydia was not going to let the Duchess know that Charlotte had been misbehaving. "She has always been fond of art," she improvised.

"She was with a man," the Duchess said. "Freddie Chalfont must have a rival."

The little minx! Lydia concealed her fury. "Indeed," she said, forcing a smile.

"Who is he?"

"Just one of their set," Lydia said desperately.

"Oh, no," said the Duchess with a malicious smile. "He was about forty, and wearing a tweed cap."

"A tweed cap!" Lydia was being humiliated and she knew it, but she hardly cared. Who could the man be? What was Charlotte thinking of? Her reputation—

"They were holding hands," the Duchess added, and she smiled broadly, showing rotten teeth.

Lydia could no longer pretend that everything was all right.

"Oh, my God," she said. "What has the child got into now?"

The Duchess said: "In my day the chaperone system was found effective in preventing this sort of thing."

Lydia was suddenly very angry at the pleasure the Duchess was taking in this catastrophe. "That was a hundred years ago," she snapped. She walked away. A tweed cap! Holding hands! Forty years old! It was too appalling to be contemplated. The cap meant he was working-class, the age meant he was a lecher, and the hand-holding implied that matters had already gone far, perhaps too far. What can I do, she thought helplessly, if the child goes out of the house without my knowledge? Oh, Charlotte, Charlotte, you don't know what you're doing to yourself!

***

"What was the boxing match like?" Charlotte asked Belinda.

"In a horrid sort of way it was terribly exciting," Belinda said. "These two enormous men wearing nothing but their shorts, standing there trying to beat each other to death."

Charlotte did not see how that could be exciting. "It sounds dreadful."

"I got so worked up"— Belinda lowered her voice —"that I almost let Peter Go Too Far."

"What do you mean?"

"You know. Afterwards, in the cab on the way home. I let him . . . kiss me, and so on."

"What's *and so on?*"

Belinda whispered: "He kissed my bosom."

"Oh!" Charlotte frowned. "Was it nice?"

"Heavenly!"

"Well, well." Charlotte tried to picture Freddie kissing her bosom, and somehow she knew it would not be heavenly.

Mama walked past and said: "We're leaving, Charlotte."

Belinda said: "She looks cross."

Charlotte shrugged. "Nothing unusual in that."

"We're going to a coon show afterward—why don't you come with us?"

"What's a coon show?"

"Jazz. It's wonderful music."

"Mama wouldn't let me."

"Your Mama is so old-fashioned."

"You're telling me! I'd better go."

"Bye."

Charlotte went down the stairs and got her wrap from the cloakroom. She felt as if two people were inhabiting her skin, like Dr. Jekyll and Mr. Hyde. One of them smiled and made polite conversation and talked to Belinda about girlish matters; the other thought about kidnapping and treachery, and asked sly questions in an innocent tone of voice.

Without waiting for her parents she went outside and said to the footman: "The Earl of Walden's car."

A couple of minutes later the Lanchester pulled up at the curb. It was a warm evening, and Pritchard had the hood down. He got out of the car and held the door for Charlotte.

She said: "Pritchard, where is Prince Orlov?"

"It's supposed to be a secret, my lady."

"You can tell me."

"I'd rather you asked your Papa, m'lady."

It was no good. She could not bully these servants who had known her as a baby. She gave up, and said: "You'd better go into the hall and tell them I'm waiting in the car."

"Very good, m'lady."

Charlotte sat back on the leather seat. She had asked the three people who might have known where Aleks was, and none of them would tell her. They did not trust her to keep the secret, and the maddening thing was that they were of course quite right. She still had not decided whether to help Feliks, however. Now, if she could not get the information he wanted, perhaps she would not have to make the agonizing decision. What a relief that would be.

She had arranged to meet Feliks the day after tomorrow, same place, same time. What would he say when she turned up empty-handed? Would he despise her for failing? No, he was not like that. He would be terribly disappointed. Perhaps he would be able to think of another way to find out where Aleks was. She could not wait to see him again. He was so interesting, and she learned so much from him, that the rest of her life seemed unbearably dull without him. Even the anxiety of this great dilemma into which he had thrown her was better than the boredom of choosing dresses for yet another day of empty social routine.

Papa and Mama got into the car and Pritchard drove off. Papa said: "What's the matter, Lydia? You look rather upset."

Mama looked at Charlotte. "What were you doing in the National Gallery this afternoon?"

Charlotte's heart missed a beat. She had been found out. Someone had spied on her. Now there would be trouble. Her hands started to shake and she held them together in her lap. "I was looking at pictures."

"You were with a man."

Papa said: "Oh, *no*. Charlotte, what *is* all this?"

"He's just somebody I met," Charlotte said. "You wouldn't approve of him."

"Of course we wouldn't approve!" Mama said. "He was wearing a tweed cap!"

Papa said: "A tweed cap! Who the devil is he?"

"He's a terribly *interesting* man, and he understands things—"

"And he holds your hand!" Mama interrupted.

Papa said sadly: "Charlotte, how vulgar! In the National Gallery!"

"There's no romance," Charlotte said. "You've nothing to fear."

"Nothing to fear?" Mama said with a brittle laugh. "That evil old Duchess knows all about it, and she'll tell everyone."

Papa said: "How could you do this to your Mama?"

Charlotte could not speak. She was close to tears. She thought: I did nothing wrong, just held a conversation with someone who talks sense! How can they be so—so brutish? I hate them!

Papa said: "You'd better tell me who he is. I expect he can be paid off."

Charlotte shouted: "I should think he's one of the few people in the world who can't!"

"I suppose he's some Radical," Mama said. "No doubt it is he who has been filling your head with foolishness about suffragism. He probably wears sandals and eats potatoes with the skins on." She lost her temper. "He probably believes in Free Love! If you have—"

"No, I haven't," Charlotte said. "I told you, there's no romance." A tear rolled down her nose. "I'm not the romantic type."

"I don't believe you for a minute," Papa said disgustedly. "Nor will anyone else. Whether you realize it or not, this episode is a social catastrophe for all of us."

"We'd better put her in a convent!" Mama said hysterically, and she began to cry.

"I'm sure that won't be necessary," Papa said.

Mama shook her head. "I didn't mean it. I'm sorry to be so shrill, but I just get so *worried* . . ."

"However, she can't stay in London, after this."

"Certainly not."

The car pulled into the courtyard of their house. Mama dried her eyes so that the servants would not see her upset. Charlotte thought: And so they will stop me from seeing Feliks, and send me away, and lock me up. I wish now I had promised to help him, instead of hesitating and saying I would think about it. At least then he would know I'm on his side. Well, they won't win. I shan't live the life they have mapped out for me. I shan't marry Freddie and become Lady Chalfont and raise fat, complacent children. They can't keep me locked away forever. As soon as I'm twenty-one I'll go and work for Mrs. Pankhurst, and read books about anarchism, and start a rest home for unmarried mothers, and if I ever have children I will never, never tell them lies.

They went into the house. Papa said: "Come into the drawing room."

Pritchard followed them in. "Would you like some sandwiches, my lord?"

"Not just now. Leave us alone for a while, would you, Pritchard?"

Pritchard went out.

Papa made a brandy-and-soda and sipped it. "Think again, Charlotte," he said. "Will you tell us who this man is?"

She wanted to say: He's an anarchist who is trying to prevent your starting a war! But she merely shook her head.

"Then you must see," he said almost gently, "that we can't possibly trust you."

You could have, once, she thought bitterly; but not anymore.

Papa spoke to Mama. "She'll just have to go to the country for a month; it's the only way to keep her out of trouble. Then, after the Cowes Regatta, she can come to Scotland for the shooting."

He sighed. "Perhaps she'll be more manageable by next season."

Mama said: "We'll send her to Walden Hall, then."

Charlotte thought: They're talking about me as if I weren't here.

Papa said: "I'm driving down to Norfolk in the morning, to see Aleks again. I'll take her with me."

Charlotte was stunned.

Aleks was at Walden Hall.

I never even thought of that!

Now I know!

"She'd better go up and pack," Mama said.

Charlotte stood up and went out, keeping her face down so that they should not see the light of triumph in her eyes.

※

TWELVE

At a quarter to three Feliks was in the lobby of the National Gallery. Charlotte would probably be late, like last time, but anyway he had nothing better to do.

He was nervy and restless, sick of waiting and sick of hiding. He had slept rough again the last two nights, once in Hyde Park and once under the arches at Charing Cross. During the day he had hidden in alleys and railway sidings and patches of waste ground, coming out only to get food. It reminded him of being on the run in Siberia, and the memory was unpleasant. Even now he kept moving, going from the lobby into the domed rooms, glancing at the pictures, and returning to the lobby to look for her. He watched the clock on the wall. At half past three she still had not come. She had got involved in another dreadful luncheon party.

She would surely be able to find out where Orlov was. She was an ingenious girl, he was certain. Even if her father would not tell her straightforwardly, she would think of a way to discover the secret. Whether she would pass the information on was another matter. She was strong-willed, too.

He wished . . .

He wished a lot of things. He wished he had not deceived her. He wished he could find Orlov without her help. He wished human beings did not make themselves into princes and earls and kaisers and czars. He wished he had married Lydia and known Charlotte as a baby. He wished she would come: it was four o'clock.

Most of the paintings meant nothing to him: the sentimental religious scenes, the portraits of smug Dutch merchants in their lifeless homes. He liked Bronzino's *Allegory,* but only because it was so sensual. Art was an area of human experience which he had passed by. Perhaps one day Charlotte would lead him into the forest and show him the flowers. But it was unlikely. First, he would have to live through the next few days, and escape after killing Orlov. Even that much was not certain. Then he would have to retain Charlotte's affection despite having used her, lied to her and killed her cousin. That was close to impossible, but even if it happened he would have to find ways of seeing her while avoiding the police . . . No, there was not much chance he would know her after the assassination. He thought: Make the most of her now.

It was four-thirty.

She's not just late, he thought with a sinking heart: she is unable to come. I hope she's not in trouble with Walden. I hope she didn't take risks and get found out. I wish she would come running up the steps, out of breath and a little flushed, with her hat slightly awry and an anxious look on her pretty face, and say: "I'm terribly sorry to have made you wait about, I got involved in . . ."

The building seemed to be emptying out. Feliks wondered what to do next. He went outside and down the steps to the pavement. There was no sign of her. He went back up the steps and was stopped at the door by a commissionaire. "Too late, mate," the man said. "We're closing." Feliks turned away.

He could not wait about on the steps in the hope that she would come later, for he would be too conspicuous right here in Trafalgar Square. Anyway, she was now two hours late: she was not going to come.

She was not going to come.

Face it, he thought: she has decided to have nothing more to do with me, and quite sensibly. But would she not have come, if only to tell me that? She might have sent a note—

She might have sent a note.

She had Bridget's address. She *would* have sent a note.

Feliks headed north.

He walked through the alleys of Theatreland and the quiet squares of Bloomsbury. The weather was changing. All the time he had been in England it had been sunny and warm, and he had yet to see rain. But for the last day or so the atmosphere had seemed oppressive, as if a storm were slowly gathering.

He thought: I wonder what it is like to live in Bloomsbury, in this prosperous middle-class atmosphere, where there is always enough to eat and money left over for books. But after the revolution we will take down the railings around the parks.

He had a headache. He had not suffered headaches since childhood. He wondered whether it was caused by the stormy air. More likely it was worry. After the revolution, he thought, headaches will be prohibited.

Would there be a note from her waiting at Bridget's house? He imagined it. "Dear Mr. Kschessinsky, I regret I am unable to keep our appointment today. Yours truly, Lady Charlotte Walden." No, it would surely not be like that. "Dear Feliks, Prince Orlov is staying at the home of the Russian Naval Attaché, 25A Wilton Place, third floor, left front bedroom. Your affectionate friend, Charlotte." That was more like it. "Dear Father, Yes—I have learned the truth. But my 'Papa' has locked me in my room. Please come and rescue me. Your loving daughter, Charlotte Kschessinsky." Don't be a damned fool.

He reached Cork Street and looked along the road. There were no policemen guarding the house, no hefty characters in plain clothes reading newspapers outside the pub. It looked safe. His heart lifted. There's something marvelous about a warm welcome from a woman, he thought, whether she's a slip of a girl like Charlotte or a fat old witch like Bridget. I've spent too much of my life with men—or alone.

He knocked on Bridget's door. As he waited, he looked down at the window of his old basement room, and saw that there were new curtains. The door opened.

Bridget looked at him and smiled widely. "It's my favorite

international terrorist, begod," she said. "Come in, you darling man."

He went into her parlor.

"Do you want some tea? It's hot."

"Yes, please." He sat down. "Did the police trouble you?"

"I was interrogated by a superintendent. You must be a big cheese."

"What did you tell him?"

She looked contemptuous. "He'd left his truncheon at home —he got nothing out of me."

Feliks smiled. "Have you got a letter—"

But she was still talking. "Did you want your room back? I've let it to another fellow, but I'll chuck him out—he's got side-whiskers, and I never could abide side-whiskers."

"No, I don't want my room—"

"You've been sleeping rough, I can tell by the look on you."

"That's right."

"Whatever it was you came to London to do, you haven't done it yet."

"No."

"Something's happened—you've changed."

"Yes."

"What, then?"

He was suddenly grateful for someone to whom he could talk about it. "Years ago I had a love affair. I didn't know it, but the woman had a baby. A few days ago . . . I met my daughter."

"Ah." She looked at him with pity in her eyes. "You poor bugger. As if you didn't have enough on your mind already. Is she the one that wrote the letter?"

Feliks gave a grunt of satisfaction. "There's a letter."

"I supposed that's what you came for." She went to the mantelpiece and reached behind the clock. "And is the poor girl mixed up with oppressors and tyrants?"

"Yes."

"I thought so from the crest. You don't get much luck, do you?" She handed him the letter.

Feliks saw the crest on the back of the envelope. He ripped it open. Inside were two pages covered with neat, stylish handwriting.

Walden Hall
July 1st, 1914

Dear Feliks,
       By the time you get this you will have waited in vain for me at
our rendezvous. I am most awfully sorry to let you down. Unfortunately
I was seen with you on Monday and it is assumed I have a clandestine
lover!!!

If she's in trouble she seems cheerful enough about it, Feliks
thought.

       I have been banished to the country for the rest of the season. However,
it is a blessing in disguise. Nobody would tell me where Aleks was, but
now I know because he is here!!!

Feliks was filled with savage triumph. "So that's where the
rats have their nest."
Bridget said: "Is this child helping you?"
"She was my only hope."
"Then you deserve to look troubled."
"I know."

       Take a train from Liverpool Street station to Waldenhall Halt. This
is our village. The house is three miles out of the village on the north road.
However, don't come to the house of course!!! On the left-hand side of the
road you will see a wood. I always ride through the wood, along the bridle
path, before breakfast between 7 and 8 o'clock. I will look out for you each
day until you come.

Once she decided whose side she was on, Feliks thought, there
were no half measures.

       I'm not sure when this will get sent. I will put it on the hall table as
soon as I see some other letters for posting there: that way, nobody will
see my handwriting on an envelope, and the footman will just pick it up
along with all the rest when he goes to the post office.

"She's a brave girl," Feliks said aloud.

       I am doing this because you are the only person I ever met who talks
sense to me.   .

                              Yours most affectionately,
                              Charlotte.

Feliks sat back in his seat and closed his eyes. He was so proud of her, and so ashamed of himself, that he felt close to tears.

Bridget took the letter from his unresisting fingers and began to read.

"So she doesn't know you're her father," she said.

"No."

"Why is she helping you, then?"

"She believes in what I'm doing."

Bridget made a disgusted noise. "Men like yourself always find women to help them. I should know, bechrist." She read on. "She writes like a schoolgirl."

"Yes."

"How old is she?"

"Eighteen."

"Old enough to know her own mind. Aleks is the one you're after?"

Feliks nodded.

"What is he?"

"A Russian prince."

"Then he deserves to die."

"He's dragging Russia into war."

Bridget nodded. "And you're dragging Charlotte into it."

"Do you think I'm doing wrong?"

She handed the letter back to him. She seemed angry. "We'll never be sure, will we?"

"Politics is like that."

"Life is like that."

Feliks tore the envelope in half and dropped it in the wastepaper bin. He intended to rip up the letter but he could not bring himself to do it. When it's all over, he thought, this may be all I have to remember her by. He folded the two sheets of paper and put them in his coat pocket.

He stood up. "I've got a train to catch."

"Do you want me to make you a sandwich to take with you?"

He shook his head. "Thank you, I'm not hungry."

"Have you money for your fare?"

"I never pay train fares."

She put her hand into the pocket of her apron and took out a sovereign. "Here. You can buy a cup of tea as well."

"It's a lot of money."

"I can afford it this week. Away with you before I change my mind."

Feliks took the coin and kissed her good-bye. "You have been kind to me."

"It's not for you, it's for my Sean, God rest his merry soul."

"Good-bye."

"Good luck to you, boy."

Feliks went out.

⊷§ §⊷

Walden was in an optimistic mood as he entered the Admiralty building. He had done what he had promised: he had sold Constantinople to Aleks. The previous afternoon Aleks had sent a message to the Czar recommending acceptance of the British offer. Walden was confident that the Czar would follow the advice of his favorite nephew, especially after the assassination in Sarajevo. He was not so sure that Lloyd George would bend to the will of Asquith.

He was shown into the office of the First Lord of the Admiralty. Churchill bounced up out of his chair and came around his desk to shake hands. "We sold it to Lloyd George," he said triumphantly.

"That's marvelous!" Walden said. "And I sold it to Orlov!"

"I knew you would. Sit down."

I might have known better than to expect a thank you, Walden thought. But even Churchill could not damp his spirits today. He sat on a leather chair and glanced around the room, at the charts on the walls and the naval memorabilia on the desk. "We should hear from St. Petersburg at any time," he said. "The Russian Embassy will send a note directly to you."

"The sooner the better," Churchill said. "Count Hayes has been to Berlin. According to our intelligence, he took with him a letter asking the Kaiser whether Germany would support Austria in a war against Serbia. Our intelligence also says the answer was yes."

"The Germans don't want to fight Serbia—"

"No," Churchill interrupted, "they want an excuse to fight France. Once Germany mobilizes, France will mobilize, and that will be Germany's pretext for invading France. There's no stopping it now."

"Do the Russians know all this?"

"We've told 'em. I hope they believe us."

"Can nothing be done to make peace?"

"Everything is being done," Churchill said. "Sir Edward Grey is working night and day, as are our ambassadors in Berlin, Paris, Vienna and St. Petersburg. Even the King is firing off telegrams to his cousins, Kaiser 'Willy' and Czar 'Nicky.' It'll do no good."

There was a knock at the door, and a young male secretary came in with a piece of paper. "A message from the Russian ambassador, sir," he said.

Walden tensed.

Churchill glanced at the paper and looked up with triumph in his eyes. "They've accepted."

Walden beamed. "Bloody good show!"

The secretary went out. Churchill stood up. "This calls for a whiskey-and-soda. Will you join me?"

"Certainly."

Churchill opened a cupboard. "I'll have the treaty drafted overnight and bring it down to Walden Hall tomorrow afternoon. We can have a little signing ceremony tomorrow night. It will have to be ratified by the Czar and Asquith, of course, but that's a formality—so long as Orlov and I sign as soon as possible."

The secretary knocked and came in again. "Mr. Basil Thomson is here, sir."

"Show him in."

Thomson came in and spoke without preamble. "We've picked up the trail of our anarchist again."

"Good!" said Walden.

Thomson sat down. "You'll remember that I put a man in his old basement room in Cork Street, just in case he should go back there."

"I remember," Walden said.

"He did go back there. When he left, my man followed him."

"Where did he go?"

"To Liverpool Street station." Thomson paused. "And he bought a ticket to Waldenhall Halt."

THIRTEEN

Walden went cold.

His first thought was for Charlotte. She was vulnerable there: the bodyguards were concentrating on Aleks, and she had nobody to protect her but the servants. How could I have been so stupid? he thought.

He was nearly as worried for Aleks. The boy was almost like a son to Walden. He thought he was safe in Walden's home—and now Feliks was on his way there, with a gun or a bomb, to kill him, and perhaps Charlotte too, and sabotage the treaty—

Walden burst out: "Why the devil haven't you stopped him?"

Thomson said mildly: "I don't think it's a good idea for one man alone to go up against our friend Feliks, do you? We've seen what he can do against several men. He seems not to care about his own life. My chappie has instructions to follow him and report."

"It's not enough—"

"I *know*, my lord," Thomson interrupted.

Churchill said: "Let us be calm, gentlemen. At least we know where the fellow is. With all the resources of His Majesty's

Government at our disposal we shall catch him. What do you propose, Thomson?"

"As a matter of fact I've already done it, sir. I spoke by telephone with the chief constable of the county. He will have a large detachment of men waiting at Waldenhall Halt to arrest Feliks as he gets off the train. Meanwhile, in case anything should go wrong, my chappie will stick to him like glue."

"That won't do," Walden said. "Stop the train and arrest him before he gets anywhere near my home."

"I did consider that," Thomson said. "The dangers outweigh the advantages. Much better to let him go on thinking he's safe, then catch him unawares."

Churchill said: "I agree."

"It's not your home!" Walden said.

"You're going to have to leave this to the professionals," Churchill said.

Walden realized he could not overrule them. He stood up. "I shall motor to Walden Hall immediately. Will you come, Thomson?"

"Not tonight. I'm going to arrest the Callahan woman. Once we've caught Feliks, we have to mount a prosecution, and she may be our chief witness. I'll come down tomorrow to interrogate Feliks."

"I don't know how you can be so confident," Walden said angrily.

"We'll catch him this time," Thomson said.

"I hope to God you're right."

◄§ ξ►

The train steamed into the falling evening. Feliks watched the sun setting over the English wheatfields. He was not young enough to take mechanical transport for granted: he still found traveling by train almost magical. The boy who had walked in clogs across the muddy Russian meadows could not have dreamed this.

He was alone in the carriage but for a young man who seemed intent on reading every line of this evening's *Pall Mall Gazette*. Feliks's mood was almost gay. Tomorrow morning he would see Charlotte. How fine she would look on a horse, with the wind streaming her hair. They would be working together. She would tell him where Orlov's room was, where he was to be found at different times of day. She would help him get hold of a weapon.

It was her letter that had made him so cheerful, he realized. She was on *his* side now, come what may. Except—

Except that he had told her he was going to kidnap Orlov. Each time he recalled this he wanted to squirm in his seat. He tried to put it out of his mind, but the thought was like an itch that could not be ignored and had to be scratched. Well, he thought, what is to be done? I must begin to prepare her for the news, at least. Perhaps I should tell her that I am her father. What a shock it will be.

For a moment he was tempted by the idea of going away, vanishing and never seeing her again; leaving her in peace. No, he thought; that is not her destiny, nor is it mine.

I wonder what *is* my destiny, after the killing of Orlov? Shall I die? He shook his head, as if he could get rid of the thought like shaking off a fly. This was no time for gloom. He had plans to make.

How will I kill Orlov? There will be guns to steal in an earl's country house: Charlotte can tell me where they are, or bring me one. Failing that there will be knives in the kitchen. And I have my bare hands.

He flexed his fingers.

Will I have to go into the house, or will Orlov come out? Shall I do it by day or by night? Shall I kill Walden, too? Politically the death of Walden would make no difference, but I should like to kill him anyway. So it's personal—so what?

He thought again of Walden catching the bottle. Don't underestimate that man, he told himself.

I must be careful that Charlotte has an alibi—no one must ever know she helped me.

The train slowed down and entered a little country station. Feliks tried to recall the map he had looked at in Liverpool Street station. He seemed to remember that Waldenhall Halt was the fourth station after this one.

His traveling companion at last finished the *Pall Mall Gazette* and put it down on the seat beside him. Feliks decided that he could not plan the assassination until he had seen the lay of the land, so he said: "May I read your newspaper?"

The man seemed startled. Englishmen did not speak to strangers on trains, Feliks recalled. "By all means," the man said.

Feliks had learned that this phrase meant yes. He picked up the paper. "Thank you."

He glanced at the headlines. His companion stared out of the window, as if embarrassed. He had the kind of facial hair that had been fashionable when Feliks was a boy. Feliks tried to remember the English word . . . "side-whiskers," that was it.

Side-whiskers.

Did you want your room back? I've let it to another fellow, but I'll chuck him out—he's got side-whiskers, and I never could abide side-whiskers.

And now Feliks recalled that this man had been behind him in the queue at the ticket office.

He felt a stab of fear.

He held the newspaper in front of his face in case his thoughts should show in his expression. He made himself think calmly and clearly. Something Bridget had said had made the police suspicious enough to place a watch on her house. They had done that by the simple means of having a detective live in the room Feliks had vacated. The detective had seen Feliks call, had recognized him and had followed him to the station. Standing behind Feliks in the queue, he had heard him ask for Waldenhall Halt and bought himself a ticket to the same destination. Then he had boarded the train along with Feliks.

No, not quite. Feliks had sat in the train for ten minutes or so before it pulled out. The man with the side-whiskers had jumped aboard at the last minute. What had he been doing in those few missing minutes?

He had probably made a phone call.

Feliks imagined the conversation as the detective sat in the stationmaster's office speaking into a telephone:

"The anarchist returned to the house in Cork Street, sir. I'm following him now."

"Where are you?"

"At Liverpool Street station. He bought a ticket to Waldenhall Halt. He's on the train now."

"Has it left?"

"Not for another . . . seven minutes."

"Are there any police in the station?"

"Just a couple of bobbies."

"It's not enough . . . this man is dangerous."

"I can have the train delayed while you get a team down here."

"Our anarchist might get suspicious and bolt for it. No. You stay with him . . ."

And what, Feliks wondered, would they do then? They could either take him off the train somewhere along the route or wait to catch him at Waldenhall Halt.

Either way he had to get off the train, fast.

What to do about the detective? He must be left behind, on the train, unable to give the alarm, so that Feliks would have time to get clear.

I could tie him up, if I had anything to tie him with, Feliks thought. I could knock him out if I had something heavy and hard to hit him with. I could strangle him, but that would take time, and someone might see. I could throw him off the train, but I want to leave him on the train . . .

The train began to slow down. They might be waiting for me at the next station, he thought. I wish I had a weapon. Does the detective have a gun? I doubt it. I could break the window and use a shard of glass to cut his throat—but that would surely draw a crowd.

I must get off the train.

A few houses could be seen alongside the railway track. They were coming into a village or a small town. The brakes of the train squealed, and a station slid into view. Feliks watched intently for signs of a police trap. The platform appeared empty. The locomotive shuddered to a halt with a hiss of steam.

People began to get off. A handful of passengers walked past Feliks's window, heading for the exit: a family with two small children, a woman with a hatbox, a tall man in tweeds.

I could hit the detective, he thought, but it's so hard to knock somebody unconscious with just your fists.

The police trap could be at the next station. I must get off now.

A whistle blew.

Feliks stood up.

The detective looked startled.

Feliks said: "Is there a toilet on the train?"

The detective was thrown by this. "Er . . . sure to be," he said.

"Thank you." He doesn't know whether to believe me, Feliks thought.

He stepped out of the compartment and into the corridor.

He ran to the end of the carriage. The train chuffed and jerked forward. Feliks looked back. The detective poked his head out of the compartment. Feliks went into the toilet and came back out again. The detective was still watching. The train moved a little faster. Feliks went to the carriage door. The detective came running.

Feliks turned back and punched him full in the face. The blow stopped the detective in his tracks. Feliks hit him again, in the stomach. A woman screamed. Feliks got him by the coat and dragged him into the toilet. The detective struggled and threw a wild punch which caught Feliks in the ribs and made him gasp. He got the detective's head in his hands and banged it against the edge of the washbasin. The train picked up speed. Feliks banged the detective's head again, and then again. The man went limp. Feliks dropped him and stepped out of the toilet. He went to the door and opened it. The train was moving at running speed. A woman at the other end of the corridor watched him, white-faced. Feliks jumped. The door banged shut behind him. He landed running. He stumbled and regained his balance. The train moved on, faster and faster.

Feliks walked to the exit.

"You left it a bit late," said the ticket man.

Feliks nodded and handed over his ticket.

"This ticket takes you three more stations," the ticket man said.

"I changed my mind at the last minute."

There was a squeal of brakes. They both looked along the track. The train was stopping: someone had pulled the emergency brake. The ticket man said: "Here, what's going on?"

Feliks forced himself to shrug unconcernedly. "Search me," he said. He wanted to run, but that would be the worst thing he could do.

The ticket man hovered, torn between his suspicion of Feliks and his concern for the train. Finally he said: "You wait here," and ran along the platform. The train stopped a couple of hundred yards out of the station. Feliks watched the ticket man run to the end of the platform and down on to the embankment.

He looked around. He was alone. He walked briskly out of the station and into the town.

A few minutes later a car with three policemen in it went past him at top speed, heading for the station.

On the outskirts of the town Feliks climbed over a gate and went into a wheatfield, where he lay down to wait for nightfall.

❦

The big Lanchester roared up the drive to Walden Hall. All the lights were on in the house. A uniformed policeman stood at the door, and another was patrolling, sentry-fashion, along the terrace. Pritchard brought the car to a halt. The policeman at the entrance stood to attention and saluted. Pritchard opened the car door and Walden got out.

Mrs. Braithwaite, the housekeeper, came out of the house to greet him. "Good evening, my lord."

"Hello, Mrs. Braithwaite. Who's here?"

"Sir Arthur is in the drawing room with Prince Orlov."

Walden nodded and they entered the house together. Sir Arthur Langley was the Chief Constable and an old school friend of Walden's.

"Have you dined, my lord?" said Mrs. Braithwaite.

"No."

"Perhaps a piece of game pie, and a bottle of burgundy?"

"I leave it to you."

"Very good, my lord."

Mrs. Braithwaite went away and Walden entered the drawing room. Aleks and Sir Arthur were leaning on the mantelpiece with brandy glasses in their hands. Both wore evening dress.

Sir Arthur said: "Hello, Stephen. How are you?"

Walden shook his hand. "Did you catch the anarchist?"

"I'm afraid he slipped through our fingers—"

"Damnation!" Walden exclaimed "I was afraid of that! No one would listen to me." He remembered his manners, and shook hands with Aleks. "I don't know what to say to you, dear boy—you must think we're a lot of fools." He turned back to Sir Arthur. "What the devil happened, anyway?"

"Feliks hopped off the train at Tingley."

"Where was Thomson's precious detective?"

"In the toilet with a broken head."

"Marvelous," Walden said bitterly. He slumped into a chair.

"By the time the town constabulary had been roused, Feliks had melted away."

"He's on his way here, do you realize that?"

"Yes, of course," said Sir Arthur in a soothing tone.

"Your men should be instructed that next time he is sighted he's to be shot."

"Ideally, yes—but of course they don't have guns."

"They damn well should have!"

"I think you're right, but public opinion—"

"Before we discuss that, tell me what is being done."

"Very well. I've got five patrols covering the roads between here and Tingley."

"They won't see him in the dark."

"Perhaps not, but at least their presence will slow him down, if not stop him altogether."

"I doubt it. What else?"

"I've brought a constable and a sergeant to guard the house."

"I saw them outside."

"They'll be relieved every eight hours, day and night. The Prince already has two bodyguards from the Special Branch, and Thomson is sending four more down here by car tonight. They'll take twelve-hour shifts, so he'll always have three men with him. My men aren't armed but Thomson's are—they have revolvers. My recommendation is that until Feliks is caught, Prince Orlov should remain in his room and be served his food and so on by the bodyguards."

Aleks said: "I will do that."

Walden looked at him. He was pale but calm. He's very brave, Walden thought. If I were he, I should be raging about the incompetence of the British police. Walden said: "I don't think a few bodyguards is enough. We need an army."

"We'll have one by tomorrow morning," Sir Arthur replied. "We're mounting a search, beginning at nine o'clock."

"Why not at dawn?"

"Because the army has to be mustered. A hundred and fifty men will be coming here from all over the county. Most of them are now in bed—they have to be visited and given their instructions, and they have to make their ways here."

Mrs. Braithwaite came in with a tray. There was cold game pie, half a chicken, a bowl of potato salad, bread rolls, cold sausages, sliced tomatoes, a wedge of Cheddar cheese, several kinds of chutney and some fruit. A footman followed with a bottle of wine, a jug of milk, a pot of coffee, a dish of ice cream, an apple tart and half of a large chocolate cake. The footman said: "I'm afraid the burgundy hasn't had time to breathe, my lord—shall I decant it?"

"Yes, please."

The footman fussed with a small table and a place setting. Walden was hungry but he felt too tense to eat. I don't suppose I shall be able to sleep, either, he thought.

Aleks helped himself to more brandy. He is drinking steadily, Walden realized. His movements were deliberate and machine-like, as if he had himself rigidly under control.

"Where is Charlotte?" Walden said suddenly.

Aleks answered: "She went to bed."

"She mustn't leave the house while all this is going on."

Mrs. Braithwaite said: "Shall I tell her, my lord?"

"No, don't wake her. I'll see her at breakfast." Walden took a sip of wine, hoping it would relax him a little. "We could move you again, Aleks, if it would make you feel better."

Aleks gave a tight little smile. "I don't think there's much point, do you? Feliks always manages to find me. The best plan is for me to hide in my room, sign the treaty as soon as possible, and then go home."

Walden nodded. The servants went out. Sir Arthur said: "Um, there is something else, Stephen." He seemed embarrassed. "I mean, the question of just what made Feliks suddenly catch a train to Waldenhall Halt."

In all the panic Walden had not even considered that. "Yes—how in Heaven's name did he find out?"

"As I understand it, only two groups of people knew where Prince Orlov had gone. One is the embassy staff, who of course have been passing telegrams and so on to and fro. The other group is your people here."

"A traitor among my servants?" Walden said. The thought was chilling.

"Yes," said Sir Arthur hesitantly. "Or, of course, among the family."

◆§ ۆ◆

Lydia's dinner party was a disaster. With Stephen away, his brother, George, had to sit in as host, which made the numbers uneven. More seriously, Lydia was so distracted that her conversation was barely polite, let alone sparkling. All but the most kindhearted guests asked after Charlotte, knowing full well that she was in disgrace. Lydia just said that she had gone to the country for a few days' rest. She spoke mechanically, hardly knowing what she was saying. Her mind was full of nightmares: Feliks being arrested, Stephen being shot, Feliks being beaten, Stephen bleeding, Feliks running, Stephen dying. She longed to tell someone how she felt, but with her guests she could talk only of last night's ball, the prospects for the Cowes Regatta, the Balkan situation and Lloyd George's budget.

Fortunately they did not linger after dinner: they were all going to a ball, or a crush, or a concert. As soon as the last one had left Lydia went into the hall and picked up the telephone. She could not speak to Stephen, for Walden Hall was not yet on the phone, so she called Winston Churchill's home in Eccleston Square. He was out. She tried the Admiralty, Number Ten and the National Liberal Club without success. She *had* to know what had happened. Finally she thought of Basil Thomson, and she telephoned Scotland Yard. Thomson was still at his desk, working late.

"Lady Walden, how are you," he said.

Lydia thought: People *will* be polite! She said: "What is the news?"

"Bad, I'm afraid. Our friend Feliks has slipped through our fingers again."

Relief washed over Lydia in a tidal wave. "Thank . . . thank you," she said.

"I don't think you need to worry too much," Thomson went on. "Prince Orlov is well guarded, now."

Lydia blushed with shame: she had been so pleased that Feliks was all right that she had momentarily forgotten to worry about

Aleks and Stephen. "I . . . I'll try not to worry," she said. "Good night."

"Good night, Lady Walden."

She put down the phone.

She went upstairs and rang for her maid to come and unlace her. She felt distraught. Nothing was resolved, everyone she loved was still in danger. How long could it go on? Feliks would not give up, she was sure, unless he got caught.

The maid came and unbuttoned her gown and unlaced her corset. Some ladies confided in their maids, Lydia knew. She did not. She had once, in St. Petersburg . . .

She decided to write to her sister, for it was too early to go to bed. She told the maid to bring writing paper from the morning room. She put on a wrap and sat by the open window, staring into the darkness of the park. The evening was close. It had not rained for three months, but during the last few days the weather had become thundery, and soon there would surely be storms.

The maid brought paper, pens, ink and envelopes. Lydia took a sheet of paper and wrote: *Dear Tatyana—*

She did not know where to begin. How can I explain about Charlotte, she thought, when I don't understand her myself? And I daren't say anything about Feliks, for Tatyana might tell the Czar, and if the Czar knew how close Aleks had come to being killed . . .

Feliks is so *clever*. How on earth did he find out where Aleks is hiding? We wouldn't even tell Charlotte!

Charlotte.

Lydia went cold.

Charlotte

She stood upright and cried: "Oh, no!"

He was about forty, and wearing a tweed cap.

A sense of inevitable horror possessed her. It was like one of those crucifying dreams in which you think of the worst thing that could possibly happen and that thing immediately begins to happen: the ladder falls, the child is run over, the loved one dies.

She buried her face in her hands. She felt dizzy.

I must think, I must try to *think*.

Please, God, help me think.

Charlotte met a man in the National Gallery. That evening, she asked me where Aleks was. I didn't tell her. Perhaps she asked Stephen, too: he wouldn't have told her. Then she was sent home, to Walden Hall, and of course she discovered that Aleks was there. Two days later Feliks went to Waldenhall Halt.

Make this be a dream, she prayed; make me wake up, now, please, and find myself in my own bed, make it be morning.

It was not a dream. Feliks was the man in the tweed cap. Charlotte had met her father. They had been holding hands.

It was horrible, horrible.

Had Feliks told Charlotte the truth, had he said: "I am your real father," had he revealed the secret of nineteen years? Did he even know? Surely he must have. Why else would she be . . . collaborating with him?

My daughter, conspiring with an anarchist to commit murder. She must be helping him still.

What can I do? I must warn Stephen—but how can I do that without telling him he's not Charlotte's father? I wish I could *think*.

She rang for her maid again. I must find a way to put an end to this, she thought. I don't know what I'm going to do but I must do something. When the maid came she said: "Start packing. I shall leave first thing in the morning. I have to go to Walden Hall."

◦◦◦

After dark Feliks headed across the fields. It was a warm, humid night, and very dark: heavy cloud hid the stars and the moon. He had to walk slowly for he was almost blind. He found his way to the railway line and turned north.

Walking along the tracks he could go a little faster, for there was a faint shine on the steel lines, and he knew there would be no obstacles. He passed through dark stations, creeping along the deserted platforms. He heard rats in the empty waiting rooms. He had no fear of rats: once upon a time he had killed them with his hands and eaten them. The names of the stations were stamped on sheet-metal signs, and he could read them by touch.

When he reached Waldenhall Halt he recalled Charlotte's directions: *The house is three miles out of the village on the north road.*

The railway line was running roughly north-northeast. He followed it another mile or so, measuring the distance by counting his paces. He had reached one thousand six hundred when he bumped into someone.

The man gave a shout of surprise and then Feliks had him by the throat.

An overpowering smell of beer came from the man. Feliks realized he was just a drunk going home, and relaxed his grip.

"Don't be frightened," the man said in a slurred voice.

"All right," Feliks said. He let go.

"It's the only way I can get home, see, without getting lost."

"On your way, then."

The man moved on. A moment later he said: "Don't go to sleep on the line—the milk train comes at four o'clock."

Feliks made no reply and the drunk shuffled off.

Feliks shook his head, disgusted with himself for being so jumpy: he might have killed the man. He was weak with relief. This would not do.

He decided to find the road. He moved off the railway line, stumbled across a short stretch of rough ground, then came up against a flimsy three-wire fence. He waited for a moment. What was in front of him? A field? Someone's back garden? The village green? There was no darkness like a dark night in the country, with the nearest street light a hundred miles away. He heard a sudden movement close to him, and out of the corner of his eye he saw something white. He bent down and fumbled on the ground until he found a small stone, then threw it in the direction of the white thing. There was a whinny, and a horse cantered away.

Feliks listened. If there were dogs nearby the whinny ought to make them bark. He heard nothing.

He stooped and clambered through the fence. He walked slowly across the paddock. Once he stumbled into a bush. He heard another horse but did not see it.

He came up against another wire fence, climbed through it and bumped into a wooden building. Immediately there was a tremendous noise of chickens clucking. A dog started to bark. A light came on in the window of a house. Feliks threw himself flat and lay still. The light showed him that he was in a small farmyard. He had bumped into the henhouse. Beyond the farmhouse he could see the road he was looking for. The chickens quieted, the dog gave a last disappointed howl and the light went out. Feliks walked to the road.

It was a dirt road bordered by a dry ditch. Beyond the ditch there seemed to be woodland. Feliks remembered: *On the left hand side of the road you will see a wood.* He was almost there.

He walked north along the uneven road, his hearing strained for the sound of someone approaching. After more than a mile he sensed that there was a wall on his left. A little farther on, the wall was broken by a gate, and he saw a light.

He leaned on the iron bars of the gate and peered through. There seemed to be a long drive. At its far end he could see, dimly illuminated by a pair of flickering lamps, the pillared portico of a vast house. As he watched, a tall figure walked across the front of the house: a sentry.

In that house, he thought, is Prince Orlov. I wonder which is his bedroom window?

Suddenly he heard the sound of a car approaching very fast. He ran back ten paces and threw himself into the ditch. A moment later the car's headlights swept along the wall and it pulled up in front of the gate. Someone got out.

Feliks heard knocking. There must be a gatehouse, he realized: he had not seen it in the darkness. A window was opened and a voice shouted: "Who's there?"

Another voice replied: "Police, from the Special Branch of Scotland Yard."

"Just a minute."

Feliks lay perfectly still. He heard footsteps as the man who had got out of the car moved around restlessly. A door was opened. A dog barked, and a voice said: "Quiet, Rex!"

Feliks stopped breathing. Was the dog on a lead? Would it smell Feliks? Would it come snuffling along the ditch and find him and start to bark?

The iron gates creaked open. The dog barked again. The voice said: "Shut *up*, Rex!"

A car door slammed and the car moved off up the drive. The ditch was dark again. Now, Feliks thought, if the dog finds me I can kill it and the gatekeeper and run away . . .

He tensed, ready to jump up as soon as he heard a snuffling sound near to his ear.

The gates creaked shut.

A moment later the gatehouse door slammed.

Feliks breathed again.

᪣ ᪣

FOURTEEN

Charlotte woke at six o'clock. She had drawn back the curtains of her bedroom windows so that the first rays of the sun would shine on her face and rouse her from sleep: it was a trick she had used years ago, when Belinda was staying over, and the two of them had liked to roam around the house while the grown-ups were still in bed and there was no one to tell them to behave like little ladies.

Her first thought was for Feliks. They had failed to catch him —he was so clever! Today he would surely be waiting for her in the wood. She jumped out of bed and looked outside. The weather had not yet broken: he would have been dry in the night, anyway.

She washed in cold water and dressed quickly in a long skirt, riding boots and a jacket. She never wore a hat for these morning rides.

She went downstairs. She saw nobody. There would be a maid or two in the kitchen, lighting fires and heating water, but otherwise the servants were still in bed. She went out of the south front door and almost bumped into a large uniformed policeman.

"Heavens!" she exclaimed. "Who are you?"

"Constable Stevenson, Miss."

He called her *Miss* because he did not know who she was. "I'm Charlotte Walden," she said.

"Pardon me, m'lady."

"That's all right. What are you doing here?"

"Guarding the house, m'lady."

"Oh, I see: guarding the Prince, you mean. How reassuring. How many of you are there?"

"Two outside and four inside. The inside men are armed. But there'll be a lot more later."

"How so?"

"Big search party, m'lady. I hear there'll be a hundred and fifty men here by nine. We'll get this anarchist chappie—never you fear."

"How splendid."

"Was you thinking of going riding, m'lady? I shouldn't, if I was you. Not today."

"No, I shan't," Charlotte lied.

She walked away, around the east wing of the house to the back. The stables were deserted. She went inside and found her mare, Spats, so called because of the white patches on her forelegs. She talked to her for a minute, stroking her nose, and gave her an apple. Then she saddled her, led her out of the stable and mounted her.

She rode away from the back of the house and around the park in a wide circle, staying out of sight and out of earshot of the policeman. She galloped across the west paddock and jumped the low fence into the wood. She walked Spats through the trees until she came to the bridle path, then let her trot.

It was cool in the wood. The oak and beech trees were heavy with leaf, shading the path. In the patches where the sun came through, dew rose from the ground like wisps of steam. Charlotte felt the heat of those stray sunbeams as she rode through them. The birds were very loud.

She thought: What can he do against a hundred and fifty men? His plan was impossible now: Aleks was too well guarded and the hunt for Feliks was too well organized. At least Charlotte could warn him off.

She reached the far end of the wood without seeing him. She

was disappointed: she had been sure he would be here today. She began to worry, for if she did not see him she could not warn him, and then he would surely be caught. But it was not yet seven o'clock: perhaps he had not begun to watch out for her. She dismounted and walked back, leading Spats. Perhaps Feliks had seen her and was waiting to check whether she had been followed. She stopped in a glade to watch a squirrel. They did not mind people, although they would run away from dogs. Suddenly she felt she was being watched. She turned around, and there he was, looking at her with a peculiarly sad expression.

He said: "Hello, Charlotte."

She went to him and held both his hands. His beard was quite full, now. His clothes were covered with bits of greenery. "You look dreadfully tired," she said in Russian.

"I'm hungry. Did you bring food?"

"Oh, dear, no!" She had brought an apple for her horse and nothing for Feliks. "I didn't think of it."

"Never mind. I've been hungrier."

"Listen," she said. "You must go away, immediately. If you leave now you can escape."

"Why should I escape? I want to kidnap Orlov."

She shook her head. "It's impossible now. He has armed bodyguards, the house is patrolled by policemen and by nine o'clock there will be a hundred and fifty men searching for you."

He smiled. "And if I escape, what will I do with the rest of my life?"

"But I won't help you commit suicide!"

"Let's sit on the grass," he said. "I have something to explain to you."

She sat with her back against a broad oak tree. Feliks sat in front of her and crossed his legs, like a Cossack. Dappled sunlight played across his weary face. He spoke rather formally, in complete sentences which sounded as if they might have been rehearsed. "I told you I was in love, once, with a woman called Lydia; and you said: 'That's my mother's name.' Do you remember?"

"I remember everything you've ever said to me." She wondered what this was all about.

"It *was* your mother."

She stared at him. "You were in love with Mama?"

"More than that. We were lovers. She used to come to my apartment, alone—do you understand what I mean?"

Charlotte blushed with confusion and embarrassment. "Yes, I do."

"Her father, your grandfather, found out. The old Count had me arrested; then he forced your mother to marry Walden."

"Oh, how terrible," Charlotte said softly. For some reason she was frightened of what he might say next.

"You were born seven months after the wedding."

He seemed to think that was very significant. Charlotte frowned.

Feliks said: "Do you know how long it takes for a baby to grow and be born?"

"No."

"It takes nine months, normally, although it can take less."

Charlotte's heart was pounding. "What are you getting at?"

"You might have been conceived before the wedding."

"Does that mean you might be my father?" she said incredulously.

"There's more. You look *exactly* like my sister Natasha."

Charlotte's heart seemed to rise into her throat and she could hardly speak. "You think you *are* my father?"

"I'm sure of it."

"Oh, God." Charlotte put her face in her hands and stared into space, seeing nothing. She felt as if she were waking from a dream and could not yet figure out which aspects of the dream had been real. She thought of Papa, but he was not her Papa; she thought of Mama, having a lover; she thought of Feliks, her friend and suddenly her father . . .

She said: "Did they lie to me even about this?"

She was so disoriented that she felt she would not be able to stand upright. It was as if someone had told her that all the maps she had ever seen were forgeries and she really lived in Brazil; or that the real owner of Walden Hall was Pritchard; or that horses could talk but merely kept silent by choice; but it was much worse than all those things. She said: "If you were to tell me that I am a boy, but my mother always dressed me in girl's clothing . . . it would be like this."

She thought: Mama . . . and Feliks? That made her blush again

Feliks took her hand and stroked it. He said: "I suppose all the love and concern that a man normally gives to his wife and children went, in my case, into politics. I have to try to get Orlov, even if it's impossible; the way a man would have to try to save his child from drowning, even if the man could not swim."

Charlotte suddenly realized how confused Feliks must feel about *her,* the daughter he had never really had. She understood, now, the odd, painful way he had looked at her sometimes.

"You poor man," she said.

He bit his lip. "You have such a generous heart."

She did not know why he should say that. "What are we going to do?"

He took a deep breath. "Could you get me inside the house and hide me?"

She thought for a moment. "Yes," she said.

◄§ §►

He mounted the horse behind her. The beast shook its head and snorted, as if offended that it should be expected to carry a double weight. Charlotte urged it into a trot. She followed the bridle path for a while, then turned off it at an angle and headed through the wood. They went through a gate, across a paddock, and into a little lane. Feliks did not yet see the house: he realized she was circling around it to approach from the north side.

She was an astonishing child. She had such strength of character. Had she inherited it from him? He wanted to think so. He was very happy to have told her the truth about her birth. He had the feeling she had not quite accepted it, but she would. She had listened to him turn her world upside down, and she had reacted with emotion but without hysteria—she did not get *that* kind of equanimity from her mother.

From the lane they turned into an orchard. Now, looking between the tops of the trees, Feliks could see the roofs of Walden Hall. The orchard ended in a wall. Charlotte stopped the horse and said: "You'd better walk beside me from here. That way, if anyone should glance out of a window, they won't be able to see you very easily."

Feliks jumped off. They walked alongside the wall and followed it around a corner. "What's behind the wall?" Feliks asked.

"Kitchen garden. Better not talk, now."

"You're marvelous," Feliks whispered, but she did not hear.

They stopped at the next corner. Feliks could see some low buildings and a yard. "The stables," Charlotte murmured. "Stay here for a moment. When I give you the signal, follow me as fast as you can."

"Where are we going?"

"Over the roofs."

She rode into the yard, dismounted, and looped the reins over a rail. Feliks watched her cross to the far side of the little yard, look both ways, then come back and look inside the stables.

He heard her say: "Oh, hello, Peter."

A boy of about twelve years came out, taking off his cap. "Good morning, m'lady."

Feliks thought: How will she get rid of him?

Charlotte said: "Where's Daniel?"

"Having his breakfast, m'lady."

"Go and fetch him, will you, and tell him to come and unsaddle Spats."

"I can do it, m'lady."

"No, I want Daniel," Charlotte said imperiously. "Off you go."

Marvelous, Feliks thought.

The boy ran off. Charlotte turned toward Feliks and beckoned. He ran to her.

She jumped onto a low iron bunker, then climbed onto the corrugated tin roof of a lean-to shed, and from there got onto the slate roof of a one-story stone building.

Feliks followed.

They edged along the slate roof, moving sideways on all fours, until it ended up against a brick wall; then they crawled up the slope to the ridge of the roof.

Feliks felt dreadfully conspicuous and vulnerable.

Charlotte stood upright and peeped through a window in the brick wall.

Feliks whispered: "What's in there?"

"Parlormaids' bedroom. But they're downstairs by now, laying the breakfast table."

She clambered onto the window ledge and stood upright. The bedroom was an attic room and the window was in the gable end, so that the roof peaked just above the window and sloped down either side. Charlotte moved along the sill, then cocked her leg over the edge of the roof.

It looked dangerous. Feliks frowned, frightened that she would fall. But she hauled herself onto the roof with ease.

Feliks did the same.

"Now we're out of sight," Charlotte said.

Feliks looked around. She was right: they could not be seen from the ground. He relaxed a fraction.

"There are four acres of roof," Charlotte told him.

"Four acres! Most Russian peasants haven't got that much land."

It was quite a sight. On all sides were roofs of every material, size and pitch. Ladders and strips of decking were provided so that people could move around without treading on the slates and tiles. The guttering was as complex as the piping in the oil refinery Feliks had seen at Batum. "I've never seen such a big house," he said.

Charlotte stood up. "Come on, follow me."

She led him up a ladder to the next roof, along a board footway, then up a short flight of wooden steps leading to a small, square door set in a wall. She said: "At one time this must have been the way they got out onto the roofs for maintenance—but now everybody has forgotten about it." She opened the door and crawled through.

Gratefully, Feliks followed her into the welcoming darkness.

Lydia borrowed a motor car and driver from her brother-in-law, George, and, having lain awake all night, left London very early. The car entered the drive at Walden Hall at nine o'clock, and she was astonished to see, in front of the house and spreading over the park, hundreds of policemen, dozens of vehicles and scores of dogs. George's driver threaded the car through the crowd to the south front of the house. There was an enormous tea urn on the lawn, and the policemen were queueing up with cups in their hands. Pritchard walked by carrying a mountain of sandwiches on a huge tray and looking harassed. He did not even notice that his mistress had arrived. A trestle table had been set up on the terrace, and behind it sat Stephen with Sir

Arthur Langley, giving instructions to half a dozen police officers who stood in front of them in a semicircle. Lydia went over to them. Sir Arthur had a map in front of him. She heard him say: "Each team will have a local man, to keep you on the correct route, and a motorcyclist to dash back here and report progress every hour." Stephen looked up, saw Lydia, and left the group to speak to her.

"Good morning, my dear, this is a pleasant surprise, how did you get here?"

"I borrowed George's car. What is going on?"

"Search parties."

"Oh." With all these men looking for him, how could Feliks possibly escape?

Stephen said: "Still, I wish you had stayed in Town. I should have been happier for your safety."

"And I should have spent every minute wondering whether bad news was on its way." And what would count as good news? she wondered. Perhaps if Feliks were simply to give up and go away. But he would not do that, she was sure. She studied her husband's face. Beneath his customary poise there were signs of tiredness and tension. Poor Stephen: first his wife, and now his daughter, deceiving him. A guilty impulse made her reach up and touch his cheek. "Don't wear yourself out," she said.

A whistle blew. The policemen hastily drained their teacups, stuffed the remains of sandwiches into their mouths, put on their helmets and formed themselves into six groups, each around a leader. Lydia stood with Stephen, watching. There were a lot of shouted orders and a good deal more whistling. Finally they began to move out. The first group went south, fanning out across the park, and entered the wood. Two more headed west, into the paddock. The other three groups went down the drive toward the road.

Lydia regarded her lawn. It looked like the site of a Sunday-school outing when all the children have gone home. Mrs. Braithwaite began to organize the clearing-up with a pained expression on her face. Lydia went into the house.

She met Charlotte in the hall. Charlotte was surprised to see her. "Hello, Mama," she said. "I didn't know you were coming down."

"One gets so bored in Town," Lydia said automatically, then she thought: What rubbish we talk.

"How did you get here?"

"I borrowed Uncle George's car." Lydia saw that Charlotte was making small talk, and thinking of something else.

"You must have started very early," Charlotte said.

"Yes." Lydia wanted to say: Stop it! Let's not pretend! Why don't we speak the truth? But she could not bring herself to do it.

"Have all those policemen gone yet?" Charlotte asked. She was looking at Lydia in a strange way, as if seeing her for the first time. It made Lydia uncomfortable. I wish I could read my daughter's mind, she thought.

She replied: "Yes, they've all gone."

"Splendid."

That was one of Stephen's words—splendid. There was, after all, something of Stephen in Charlotte: the curiosity, the determination, the poise—since she had not inherited those things, she must have acquired them simply by imitating him . . .

Lydia said: "I hope they catch this anarchist," and watched Charlotte's reaction.

"I'm sure they will," Charlotte said gaily.

She's very bright-eyed, Lydia thought. Why should she look that way, when hundreds of policemen are combing the county for Feliks? Why is she not depressed and anxious, as I am? It must be that she does *not* expect them to catch him. For some reason she thinks he is safe.

Charlotte said: "Tell me something, Mama. How long does it take for a baby to grow and be born?"

Lydia's mouth fell open and the blood drained from her face. She stared at Charlotte, thinking: She knows! She knows!

Charlotte smiled and nodded, looking faintly sad. "Never mind," she said. "You've answered my question." She went on down the stairs.

Lydia held on to the banister, feeling faint. Feliks had told Charlotte. It was just too cruel, after all these years. She felt angry at Feliks: why had he ruined Charlotte's life this way? The hall spun around her head, and she heard a maid's voice say: "Are you all right, my lady?"

Her head cleared. "A little tired, after the journey," she said. "Take my arm."

The maid took her arm and together they walked upstairs to Lydia's room. Another maid was already unpacking Lydia's cases. There was hot water ready for her in the dressing room. Lydia sat down. "Leave me now, you two," she said. "Unpack later."

The maids went out. Lydia unbuttoned her coat but did not have the energy to take it off. She thought about Charlotte's mood. It had been almost vivacious, even though there was obviously a lot on her mind. Lydia understood that; she recognized it; she had sometimes felt that way. It was the mood you were in when you had spent time with Feliks. You felt that life was endlessly fascinating and surprising, that there were important things to be done, that the world was full of color and passion and change. Charlotte had seen Feliks, and she believed him to be safe.

Lydia thought: What am I going to do?

Wearily, she took off her clothes. She spent time washing and dressing again, taking the opportunity to calm herself. She wondered how Charlotte felt about Feliks's being her father. She obviously liked him very much. People do, Lydia thought; people love him. Where had Charlotte got the strength to hear such news without collapsing?

Lydia decided she had better take care of the housekeeping. She looked in the mirror and composed her face; then she went out. On the way downstairs she met a maid with a tray laden with sliced ham, scrambled eggs, fresh bread, milk, coffee and grapes. "Who is that for?" she asked.

"For Lady Charlotte, m'lady," said the maid.

Lydia passed on. Had Charlotte not even lost her appetite? She went into the morning room and sent for Cook. Mrs. Rowse was a thin, nervous woman who never ate the kind of rich food she prepared for her employers. She said: "I understand Mr. Thomson will be arriving for lunch, m'lady, and Mr. Churchill also for dinner." Lydia discussed the menus with her, then sent her away. Why on earth was Charlotte having such a massive breakfast in her room? she wondered. And so late! In the country Charlotte was normally up early and had finished breakfast before Lydia surfaced.

She sent for Pritchard and made the table plan with him. Pritchard told her that Aleks was having all his meals in his room until further notice. It made little difference to the table plan: they still had too many men, and in the present situation Lydia could hardly invite people to make up the right numbers. She did the best she could, then sent Pritchard away.

Where had Charlotte seen Feliks? And why was she confident that he would not be caught? Had she found him a hiding place? Was he in some impenetrable disguise?

She moved around the room, looking at the pictures, the little bronzes, the glass ornaments, the writing desk. She had a headache. She began to rearrange the flowers in a big vase by the window, and knocked over the vase. She rang for someone to clear up the mess, then left the room.

Her nerves were very bad. She contemplated taking some laudanum. These days it did not help her as much as it had used to.

What will Charlotte do now? Will she keep the secret? Why don't children talk to one?

She went along to the library with the vague idea of getting a book to take her mind off everything. When she walked in she gave a guilty start on seeing that Stephen was there, at his desk. He looked up at her as she entered, smiled in a welcoming way, and went on writing.

Lydia wandered along the bookshelves. She wondered whether to read the Bible. There had been a great deal of Bible-reading in her childhood, and family prayers and much church-going. She had had stern nurses who were keen on the horrors of hell and the penalties of uncleanliness, and a Lutheran German governess who talked a great deal about sin. But since Lydia had committed fornication and brought retribution upon herself and her daughter, she had never been able to take any consolation from religion. I should have gone into that convent, she thought, and put myself right with God; my father's instinct was correct.

She took a book at random and sat down with it open on her lap. Stephen said: "That's an unusual choice for you." He could not read the title from where he was sitting, but he knew where all the authors were placed on the shelves. He read so many books, Lydia did not know how he found the time. She looked at the spine of the book she was holding. It was Thomas Hardy's *Wessex Poems*. She did not like Hardy: did not like those deter mined, passionate women nor the strong men whom they made helpless.

They had often sat like this, she and Stephen, especially when they first came to Walden Hall. She recalled nostalgically how she would sit and read while he worked. He had been less tranquil in those days, she remembered: he used to say that nobody could make money out of agriculture anymore, and that if this family were to continue to be rich and powerful it would have to get ready for the twentieth century. He had sold off some farms at that time, many thousands of acres at very low prices; then he had put the money into railroads and banks and London property. The plan must have worked, for he soon stopped looking worried.

It was after the birth of Charlotte that everything seemed to settle down. The servants adored the baby and loved Lydia for producing her. Lydia got used to English ways and was well liked by London society. There had been eighteen years of tranquillity.

Lydia sighed. Those years were coming to an end. For a while she had buried the secrets so successfully that they tormented nobody but her, and even she had been able to forget them at times; but now they were coming out. She had thought that London was at a safe distance from St. Petersburg, but perhaps California would have been a better choice; or it might be that nowhere was far enough. The time of peace was over. It was all falling apart. What would happen now?

She looked down at the open page, and read:

> *She would have given a world to breathe "yes" truly,*
> *So much his life seemed hanging on her mind,*
> *And hence she lied, her heart persuaded throughly*
> *'Twas worth her soul to be a moment kind.*

Is that me? she wondered. Did I give my soul when I married Stephen in order to save Feliks from incarceration in the For tress of St. Peter and St. Paul? Ever since then I've been playing a part, pretending I'm not a wanton, sinful, brazen whore. But I am! And I'm not the only one. Other women feel the same Why else would the Viscountess and Charlie Stott want adjoining bedrooms? And why would Lady Girara tell me about them with a wink, if she did not understand how they felt? If I had been just a little wanton, perhaps Stephen would have come to my bed more often, and we might have had a son. She sighed again.

"Penny for 'em," Stephen said.

"What?"

"A penny for your thoughts."

Lydia smiled. "Will I never stop learning English expressions? I've never heard that one."

"Nobody ever stops learning. It means tell me what you're thinking."

"I was thinking about Walden Hall going to George's son when you die."

"Unless we have a son."

She looked at his face: the bright blue eyes, the neat gray beard. He was wearing a blue tie with white spots.

He said: "Is it too late?"

"I don't know," she said, thinking: That depends on what Charlotte does next.

"Do let's keep trying," he said.

This was an unusually frank conversation: Stephen had sensed that she was in a mood to be candid. She got up from her chair and went over to stand beside him. He had a bald spot on the back of his head, she noticed. How long had that been there? "Yes," she said, "let's keep trying." She bent down and kissed his forehead; then, on impulse, she kissed his lips. He closed his eyes.

After a moment she broke away. He looked a little embarrassed: they rarely did this sort of thing during the day, for there were always so many servants about. She thought: Why do we live the way we do, if it doesn't make us happy? She said: "I *do* love you."

He smiled. "I know you do."

Suddenly she could stand it no longer. She said: "I must go and change for lunch before Basil Thomson arrives."

He nodded.

She felt his eyes following her as she left the room. She went upstairs, wondering whether there might still be a chance that she and Stephen could be happy.

She went into her bedroom. She was still carrying the book of poems. She put it down. Charlotte held the key to all this. Lydia had to talk to her. One *could* say difficult things, after all, if one had the courage; and what now was left to lose? Without having a clear idea of what she would say, she headed for Charlotte's room on the next floor.

Her footsteps made no noise on the carpet. She reached the top of the staircase and looked along the corridor. She saw Charlotte disappearing into the old nursery. She was about to call out, then stopped herself. What had Charlotte been carrying? It had looked very like a plate of sandwiches and a glass of milk.

Puzzled, Lydia went along to Charlotte's bedroom. There on the table was the tray Lydia had seen the maid carrying. All the ham and all the bread had gone. Why would Charlotte order a tray of food, then make sandwiches of it and eat it in the nursery? There was nothing in the nursery, as far as Lydia knew, except furniture covered with dust sheets. Was Charlotte so anxious that she needed to retreat into the cosy world of childhood?

Lydia decided to find out. She felt uneasy about interrupting Charlotte's private ritual, whatever it was; but then she thought: It's my house, she's my daughter, and perhaps I ought to know. And it might create a moment of intimacy, and help me say what I need to say. So she left Charlotte's bedroom and went along the corridor and into the nursery.

Charlotte was not there.

Lydia looked around. There was the old rocking horse, his ears making twin peaks in the dust sheet. Through an open door she could see the schoolroom, with maps and childish drawings on the wall. Another door led to the bedroom: that, too, was empty but for shrouds. Will all this ever be used again? Lydia wondered. Will we have nurses, and diapers, and tiny, tiny clothes; and a nanny, and toy soldiers, and exercise books filled with clumsy handwriting and ink blots?

But where was Charlotte?

The closet door was open. Suddenly Lydia remembered: of course! Charlotte's hideaway! The little room she thought no one else knew of, where she used to go when she had been naughty. She had furnished it herself, with bits and pieces from around the house, and everyone had pretended not to know how certain things had disappeared. One of the few indulgent decisions Lydia had made was to allow Charlotte her hideaway, and to forbid Marya to "discover" it; for Lydia herself hid away sometimes, in the flower room, and she knew how important it was to have a place of your own.

So Charlotte still used that little room! Lydia moved closer, more reluctant now to disturb Charlotte's privacy, but tempted all the same. No, she thought; I'll leave her be.

Then she heard voices.

Was Charlotte talking to herself?

Lydia listened carefully.

Talking to herself in Russian?

Then there was another voice, a man's voice, replying in Russian, in low tones; a voice like a caress, a voice which sent a sexual shudder through Lydia's body.

Feliks was in there.

Lydia thought she would faint. Feliks! Within touching distance! Hidden, in Walden Hall, while the police searched the county for him! Hidden by Charlotte.

I mustn't scream!

She put her fist to her mouth and bit herself. She was shaking.

I must get away. I can't think straight. I don't know what to do.

Her head ached horribly. I need a dose of laudanum, she thought. That prospect gave her strength. She controlled her trembling. After a moment she tiptoed out of the nursery.

She almost ran along the corridor and down the stairs to her room. The laudanum was in the dresser. She opened the bottle. She could not hold the spoon steady, so she took a gulp directly from the bottle. After a few moments she began to feel calmer. She put the bottle and the spoon away and closed the drawer. A feeling of mild contentment began to come over her as her nerves settled down. Her head ached less. Nothing would really matter now for a while. She went to her wardrobe and opened the door. She stood staring at the rows of dresses, totally unable to make up her mind what to wear for lunch.

Feliks paced the tiny room like a caged tiger, three steps each way, bending his head to avoid the ceiling, listening to Charlotte.

"Aleks's door is always locked," she said. "There are two armed guards inside and one outside. The inside ones won't unlock the door unless their colleague outside tells them to."

"One outside, and two inside." Feliks scratched his head and cursed in Russian. Difficulties, there are always difficulties, he thought. Here I am, right in the house, with an accomplice in the household, and still it isn't easy. Why shouldn't I have the luck of those boys in Sarajevo? Why did it have to turn out that I'm a part of this family? He looked at Charlotte and thought: Not that I regret it.

She caught his look, and said: "What?"

"Nothing. Whatever happens, I'm glad I found you."

"Me too. But what are you going to do about Aleks?"

"Could you draw a plan of the house?"

Charlotte made a face. "I can try."

"You must know it, you've lived here all your life."

"Well, I know this part, of course—but there are bits of the house I've never been in. The butler's bedroom, the housekeeper's rooms, the cellars, the place over the kitchens where they store flour and things . . ."

"Do your best. One plan for each floor."

She found a piece of paper and a pencil among her childish treasures and knelt at the little table.

Feliks ate another sandwich and drank the rest of the milk. She had taken a long time to bring him the food because the maids had been working in her corridor. As he ate he watched her draw, frowning and biting the end of her pencil. At one point she said: "One doesn't realize how difficult this is until one tries it." She found an eraser among her old crayons and used it frequently. Feliks noticed that she was able to draw perfectly straight lines without using a rule. He found the sight of her like this very touching. So she must have sat, he thought, for years in the schoolroom, drawing houses, then Mama and "Papa," and later the map of Europe, the leaves of the English trees, the park in winter . . . Walden must have seen her like this many times.

"Why have you changed your clothes?" Feliks asked.

"Oh, everybody has to change all the time here. Every hour

of the day has its appropriate clothes, you see. You must show your shoulders at dinner time but not at lunch. You must wear a corset for dinner but not for tea. You can't wear an indoor gown outside. You can wear woolen stockings in the library but not in the morning room. You can't imagine the rules I have to remember."

He nodded. He was no longer capable of being surprised by the degeneracy of the ruling class.

She handed him her sketches, and he became businesslike again. He studied them. "Where are the guns kept?" he said.

She touched his arm. "Don't be so abrupt," she said. "I'm on your side—remember?"

Suddenly she was grown-up again. Feliks smiled ruefully. "I had forgotten," he said.

"The guns are kept in the gun room." She pointed it out on the plan. "You really did have an affair with Mama."

"Yes."

"I find it so hard to believe that she would do such a thing."

"She was very wild, then. She still is, but she pretends otherwise."

"You really think she's still like that?"

"I know it."

"Everything, *everything* turns out to be different from how I thought it was."

"That's called growing up."

She was pensive. "What should I call you, I wonder?"

"What do you mean?"

"I should feel very strange, calling you Father."

"Feliks will do for now. You need time to get used to the idea of me as your father."

"Shall I have time?"

Her young face was so grave that he held her hand. "Why not?"

"What will you do when you have Aleks?"

He looked away so that she should not see the guilt in his eyes. "That depends just how and when I kidnap him, but most likely I'll keep him tied up right here. You'll have to bring us food, and you'll have to send a telegram to my friends in Geneva, in code, telling them what has happened. Then, when the news has achieved what we want it to achieve, we'll let Orlov go."

"And then?"

"They will look for me in London, so I'll go north. There seem to be some big towns—Birmingham, Manchester, Hull—where I could lose myself. After a few weeks I'll make my way back to Switzerland, then eventually to St. Petersburg—that's the place to be, that's where the revolution will start."

"So I'll never see you again."

You won't want to, he thought. He said: "Why not? I may come back to London. You may go to St. Petersburg. We might meet in Paris. Who can tell? If there is such a thing as Fate, it seems determined to bring us together." I wish I could believe this, I wish I could.

"That's true," she said with a brittle smile, and he saw that she did not believe it either. She got to her feet. "Now I must get you some water to wash in."

"Don't bother. I've been a good deal dirtier than this. I don't mind."

"But I do. You smell awful. I'll be back in a minute."

With that she went out.

ᴥᵎ ᵇᴥ

It was the dreariest luncheon Walden could remember in years. Lydia was in some kind of daze. Charlotte was silent but uncharacteristically nervy, dropping her cutlery and knocking over a glass. Thomson was taciturn. Sir Arthur Langley attempted to be convivial but nobody responded. Walden himself was withdrawn, obsessed by the puzzle of how Feliks had found out that Aleks was at Walden Hall. He was tortured by the ugly suspicion that it had something to do with Lydia. After all, Lydia had told Feliks that Aleks was at the Savoy Hotel; and she had admitted that Feliks was "vaguely familiar" from St. Petersburg days. Could it be that Feliks had some kind of hold on her? She had been behaving oddly, as if distracted, all summer. And now, as he thought about Lydia in a detached way for the first time in nineteen years, he admitted to himself that she was sexually lukewarm. Of course, well-bred women were supposed to be like that; but he knew perfectly well that this was a polite fiction, and that women generally suffered the same longings as men. Was it that Lydia longed for someone else, someone from her past? That would explain all sorts of things which until now had not seemed to need explanation. It was perfectly horrible, he found, to look at his lifetime companion and see a stranger.

After lunch Sir Arthur went back to the Octagon, where he had set up his headquarters. Walden and Thomson put on their hats and took their cigars out onto the terrace. The park looked lovely in the sunshine, as always. From the distant drawing room came the crashing opening chords of the Tchaikovsky piano concerto: Lydia was playing. Walden felt sad. Then the music was drowned by the roar of a motorcycle as another messenger came to report the progress of the search to Sir Arthur. So far there had been no news.

A footman served coffee, then left them alone. Thomson said: "I didn't want to say this in front of Lady Walden, but I think we may have a clue to the identity of the traitor."

Walden went cold.

Thomson said: "Last night I interviewed Bridget Callahan, the Cork Street landlady. I'm afraid I got nothing out of her. However, I left my men to search her house. This morning they showed me what they had found." He took from his pocket an envelope which had been torn in half, and handed the two pieces to Walden.

Walden saw with a shock that the envelope bore the Walden Hall crest.

Thomson said: "Do you recognize the handwriting?"

Walden turned the pieces over. The envelope was addressed:

Mr. F. Kschessinsky
c/o 19 Cork Street
London, N.

Walden said: "Oh, dear God, not Charlotte." He wanted to cry.

Thomson was silent.

"She led him here," Walden said. "My own daughter." He stared at the envelope, willing it to disappear. The handwriting was quite unmistakable, like a juvenile version of his own script.

"Look at the postmark," Thomson said. "She wrote it as soon as she arrived here. It was mailed from the village."

"How could this happen?" Walden said.

Thomson made no reply.

"Feliks was the man in the tweed cap," Walden said. "It all

fits." He felt hopelessly sad, almost bereaved, as if someone dear to him had died. He looked out over his park, at trees planted fifty years ago by his father, at a lawn that had been cared for by his family for a hundred years, and it all seemed worthless, worthless. He said quietly: "You fight for your country, and you are betrayed from within by socialists and revolutionists; you fight for your class, and you're betrayed by Liberals; you fight for your family, and even they betray you. Charlotte! Why, Charlotte, why?" He felt a choking sensation. "What a damnable life this is, Thomson. What a damnable life."

"I'll have to interview her," Thomson said.

"So will I." Walden stood up. He looked at his cigar. It had gone out. He threw it away. "Let's go in."

They went in.

In the hall Walden stopped a maid. "Do you know where Lady Charlotte is?"

"I believe she's in her room, my lord. Shall I go and see?"

"Yes. Tell her I wish to speak to her in her room immediately."

"Very good, m'lord."

Thomson and Walden waited in the hall. Walden looked around. The marble floor, the carved staircase, the stucco ceiling, the perfect proportions—worthless. A footman drifted by silently, eyes lowered. A motorcycle messenger came in and headed for the Octagon. Pritchard crossed the hall and picked up the letters for posting from the hall table, just as he must have the day Charlotte's treacherous letter to Feliks was written. The maid came down the stairs.

"Lady Charlotte is ready to see you, my lord."

Walden and Thomson went up.

Charlotte's room was on the second floor at the front of the house, looking over the park. It was sunny and light, with pretty fabrics and modern furniture. It's a long time since I've been in here, Walden thought vaguely.

"You look rather fierce, Papa," Charlotte said.

"I've reason to be," Walden replied. "Mr. Thomson has just given me the most dreadful piece of news of my whole life."

Charlotte frowned.

Thomson said: "Lady Charlotte, where is Feliks?"

Charlotte turned white. "I've no idea, of course."

Walden said: "Don't be so damned cool!"

"How dare you swear at me!"

"I beg your pardon."

Thomson said: "Perhaps if you'd leave it to me, my lord   "

"Very well." Walden sat down in the window seat, thinking: How did I find myself apologizing?

Thomson addressed Charlotte. "Lady Charlotte, I'm a policeman, and I can prove that you have committed conspiracy to murder. Now my concern, and your father's, is to let this go no further; and, in particular, to ensure that you will not have to go to jail for a period of many years."

Walden stared at Thomson. Jail! Surely he's merely frightening her. But no, he realized with a sense of overwhelming dread; he's right, she's a criminal . . .

Thomson went on: "As long as we can prevent the murder, we feel we can cover up your participation. But if the assassin succeeds, I will have no option but to bring you to trial—and then the charge will not be conspiracy to murder but accessory to murder. In theory you could be hanged "

"No!" Walden shouted involuntarily

"Yes," Thomson said quietly.

Walden buried his face in his hands.

Thomson said: "You must save yourself that agony—and not only yourself, but your Mama and Papa. You must do everything in your power to help us find Feliks and save Prince Orlov."

It could not be, Walden thought desperately. He felt as if he were going insane. My daughter could not be hanged. But if Aleks is killed, Charlotte will have been one of the murderers. But it would never come to trial. Who was Home Secretary? McKenna. Walden did not know him. But Asquith would intervene to prevent a prosecution . . . wouldn't he?

Thomson said: "Tell me when you last saw Feliks."

Walden watched Charlotte, waiting for her response. She stood behind a chair, gripping its back with both hands. Her knuckles showed white, but her face appeared calm. Finally she spoke. "I have nothing to tell you."

Walden groaned aloud. How could she continue to be like this now that she was found out? What was going on in her mind? She seemed a stranger. He thought: When did I lose her?

"Do you know where Feliks is now?" Thomson asked her.
She said nothing.

"Have you warned him of our security precautions here?"
She looked blank.

"How is he armed?"
Nothing.

"Each time you refuse to answer a question, you become a little more guilty, do you realize that?"

Walden noticed a change of tone in Thomson's voice, and looked at him. He seemed genuinely angry now.

"Let me explain something to you," Thomson said. "You may think that your Papa can save you from justice. He is perhaps thinking the same thing. But if Orlov dies, I swear to you that I will bring you to trial for murder. Now think about that!"

Thomson left the room.

◄§ §►

Charlotte was dismayed to see him go. With a stranger in the room she had just about managed to keep her composure. Alone with Papa she was afraid she would break down.

"I'll save you if I can," Papa said sadly.

Charlotte swallowed thickly and looked away. I wish he'd be angry, she thought; I could cope with that.

He looked out of the window. "I'm responsible, you see," he said painfully. "I chose your mother, I fathered you, and I brought you up. You're nothing but what I've made you. I can't understand how this has happened, I really can't." He looked back at her. "Can you explain it to me, please?"

"Yes, I can," she said. She was eager to make him understand, and she was sure he would, if she could tell it right. "I don't want you to succeed in making Russia go to war, because if you do, millions of innocent Russians will be killed or wounded to no purpose."

He looked surprised. "Is that it?" he said. "Is *that* why you've done these awful things? Is that what Feliks is trying to achieve?"

Perhaps he *will* understand, she thought joyfully. "Yes," she said. She went on enthusiastically: "Feliks also wants a revolution in Russia—even you might think that could be a good thing

—and he believes it will begin when the people there find out that Aleks has been trying to drag them into war."

"Do you think I want a war?" he said incredulously. "Do you think I would like it? Do you think it would do me any good?"

"Of course not—but you'd let it happen, under certain circumstances."

"Everyone would—even Feliks, who wants a revolution, you tell me. And if there's to be a war, we must win it. Is that an evil thing to say?" His tone was almost pleading.

She was desperate for him to understand. "I don't know whether it's evil, but I do know it's wrong. The Russian peasants know nothing of European politics, and they care less. But they will be shot to pieces, and have their legs blown off, and all awful things like that because you made an agreement with Aleks!" She fought back tears. "Papa, can't you see that's wrong?"

"But think of it from the British point of view—from your own personal point of view. Imagine that Freddie Chalfont and Peter and Jonathan go to war as officers, and their men are Daniel the groom, and Peter the stable lad, and Jimmy the bootboy, and Charles the footman, and Peter Dawkins from the Home Farm—wouldn't you want them to get some help? Wouldn't you be *glad* that the whole of the Russian nation was on their side?"

"Of course—especially if the Russian nation had chosen to help them. But they won't choose, will they, Papa? You and Aleks will choose. You should be working to prevent war, not to win it."

"If Germany attacks France, we have to help our friends. And it would be a disaster for Britain if Germany conquered Europe."

"How could there be a bigger disaster than a war?"

"Should we never fight, then?"

"Only if we're invaded."

"If we don't fight the Germans in France, we'll have to fight them here."

"Are you sure?"

"It's likely."

"When it happens, then we should fight."

"Listen. This country hasn't been invaded for eight hundred and fifty years. Why? Because we've fought other people on their territory, not ours. That is why you, Lady Charlotte Walden, grew up in a peaceful and prosperous country."

"How many wars were fought to prevent war? If we had not fought on other people's territory, would they have fought at all?"

"Who knows?" he said wearily. "I wish you had studied more history. I wish you and I had talked more about this sort of thing. With a son, I would have—but Lord! I never dreamed my daughter would be interested in foreign policy! And now I'm paying the price for that mistake. What a price. Charlotte, I promise you that the arithmetic of human suffering is not as straightforward as this Feliks has led you to believe. Could you not believe me when I tell you that? Could you not trust me?"

"No," she said stubbornly.

"Feliks wants to *kill* your cousin. Does that make no difference?"

"He's going to kidnap Aleks, not kill him."

Papa shook his head. "Charlotte, he's tried twice to kill Aleks and once to kill me. He has killed many people in Russia. He's not a kidnapper, Charlotte, he's a murderer."

"I don't believe you."

"But why?" he said plaintively.

"Did you tell me the truth about suffragism? Did you tell me the truth about Annie? Did you tell me that in democratic Britain most people still can't vote? Did you tell me the truth about sexual intercourse?"

"No, I didn't." To her horror, Charlotte saw that his cheeks were wet with tears. "It may be that everything I ever did, as a father, was mistaken. I didn't know the world would change the way it has. I had no idea of what a woman's role would be in the world of 1914. It begins to look as if I have been a terrible failure. But I did what I thought best for you, because I loved you, and I still do. It's not your politics that are making me cry. It's the betrayal, you see. I mean, I shall fight tooth and nail to keep you out of the courts, even if you do succeed in killing poor Aleks, because you're my daughter, the most important person in the world to me. For you I will let justice and reputation and England go to hell. I would do wrong for you, without a moment's hesitation. For me, you come above all principles, all politics, everything. That's how it is in families. What hurts me so much is that you will not do the same for me. Will you?"

She wanted desperately to say yes.

"Will you be loyal to me, for all that I may be in the wrong, just because I am your father?"

But you're not, she thought. She bowed her head; she could not look at him.

They sat in silence for a minute. Then Papa blew his nose. He got up and went to the door He took the key out of the lock, and went outside. He closed the door behind him. Charlotte heard him turn the key, locking her in.

She burst into tears.

⌒

It was the second appalling dinner party Lydia had given in two days. She was the only woman at the table. Sir Arthur was glum because his vast search operation had utterly failed to turn up Feliks. Charlotte and Aleks were locked in their rooms. Basil Thomson and Stephen were being icily polite to each other, for Thomson had found out about Charlotte and Feliks, and had threatened to send Charlotte to jail. Winston Churchill was there. He had brought the treaty with him and he and Aleks had signed it, but there was no rejoicing on that account, for everyone knew that if Aleks were to be assassinated, then the Czar would refuse to ratify the deal. Churchill said that the sooner Aleks was off English soil the better. Thomson said he would devise a secure route and arrange a formidable bodyguard, and Aleks could leave tomorrow. Everyone went to bed early, for there was nothing else to do.

Lydia knew she would not sleep. Everything was unresolved. She had spent the afternoon in an indecisive haze, drugged with laudanum, trying to forget that Feliks was there in her house. Aleks would leave tomorrow: if only he could be kept safe for a few more hours . . . She wondered whether there might be some way she could make Feliks lie low for another day. Could she go to him and tell him a lie, say that he would have his opportunity of killing Aleks tomorrow night? He would never believe her. The scheme was hopeless. But once she had conceived the idea of going to see Feliks she could not get it out of her mind. She thought: Out of this door, along the passage, up the stairs, along another passage, through the nursery, through the closet, and there . . .

She closed her eyes tightly and pulled the sheet up over her head. Everything was dangerous. It was best to do nothing at all, to be motionless, paralyzed. Leave Charlotte alone, leave Feliks alone, forget Aleks, forget Churchill.

But she did not know what was going to *happen*. Charlotte might go to Stephen and say: "You're not my father." Stephen might kill Feliks. Feliks might kill Aleks. Charlotte might be accused of murder. Feliks might come here, to my room, and kiss me.

Her nerves were bad again and she felt another headache coming on. It was a very warm night. The laudanum had worn off, but she had drunk a lot of wine at dinner and she still felt woozy. For some reason her skin was tender tonight, and every time she moved, the silk of her nightdress seemed to scrape her breasts. She was irritable, both mentally and physically. She half-wished Stephen would come to her, then she thought: No, I couldn't bear it.

Feliks's presence in the nursery was like a bright light shining in her eyes, keeping her awake. She threw off the sheet, got up and went to the window. She opened it wider. The breeze was hardly cooler than the air in the room. Leaning out and looking down, she could see the twin lamps burning at the portico, and the policeman walking along the front of the house, his boots crunching distantly on the gravel drive.

What was Feliks doing up there? Was he making a bomb? Loading a gun? Sharpening a knife? Or was he sleeping, content to wait for the right moment? Or wandering around the house, trying to find a way to get past Aleks's bodyguards?

There's nothing I can do, she thought; nothing.

She picked up her book. It was Hardy's *Wessex Poems*. Why did I choose this? she thought. It opened at the page she had looked at that morning. She turned up the night-light, sat down and read the whole poem. It was called "Her Dilemma."

The two were silent in a sunless church,
Whose mildewed walls, uneven paving-stones,
And wasted carvings passed antique research;
And nothing broke the clock's dull monotones.

Leaning against a wormy poppy-head,
So wan and worn that he could scarcely stand,
—For he was soon to die,—he softly said,
"Tell me you love me!"—holding hard her hand.

She would have given a world to breathe "yes" truly,
So much his life seemed hanging on her mind,
And hence she lied, her heart persuaded throughly
'Twas worth her soul to be a moment kind.

But the sad need thereof, his nearing death,
So mocked humanity that she shamed to prize
A world conditioned thus, or care for breath
Where Nature such dilemmas could devise.

That's right, she thought; when life is like this, who can do right?

Her headache was so bad she thought her skull would split. She went to the drawer and took a gulp from the bottle of laudanum. Then she took another gulp.

Then she went to the nursery.

⇛ ⇝

FIFTEEN

Something had gone wrong. Feliks had not seen Charlotte since midday, when she had brought him a basin, a jug of water, a towel and a cake of soap. There must have been some kind of trouble to keep her away—perhaps she had been forced to leave the house, or perhaps she felt she might be under observation. But she had not given him away, evidently, for here he was.

Anyway, he did not need her anymore

He knew where Orlov was and he knew where the guns were. He was not able to get into Orlov's room, for the security seemed too good; so he would have to make Orlov come out. He knew how to do that

He had not used the soap and water, because the little hideaway was too cramped to allow him to stand up straight and wash himself, and anyway he did not care much about cleanliness; but now he was very hot and sticky, and he wanted to feel fresh before going about his work, so he took the water out into the nursery.

It felt very strange, to be standing in the place where Charlotte had spent so many hours of her childhood. He put the thought out of his mind: this was no time for sentiment. He took off all his clothes and washed himself by the light of a single candle. A familiar, pleasant feeling of anticipation and excitement filled him, and he felt as if his skin were glowing. I shall win tonight, he thought savagely, no matter how many I have to kill. He rubbed himself all over roughly with the towel. His movements were jerky, and there was a tight sensation in the back of his throat which made him want to shout. This must be why warriors yell war cries, he thought. He looked down at his body and saw that he had the beginnings of an erection.

Then he heard Lydia say: "Why, you've grown a beard."

He spun around and stared into the darkness, stupefied.

She came forward into the circle of candlelight. Her blond hair was unpinned and hung around her shoulders. She wore a long, pale nightdress with a fitted bodice and a high waist. Her arms were bare and white. She was smiling.

They stood still, looking at one another. Several times she opened her mouth to speak, but no words came out. Feliks felt the blood rush to his loins. How long, he thought wildly, how long since I stood naked before a woman?

She moved, but it did not break the spell. She stepped forward and knelt at his feet. She closed her eyes and nuzzled his body. As Feliks looked down on her unseeing face, candlelight glinted off the tears on her cheeks.

◄§ §►

Lydia was nineteen again, and her body was young and strong and tireless The simple wedding was over, and she and her new husband were in the little cottage they had taken in the country. Outside, snow fell quietly in the garden. They made love by candlelight. She kissed him all over, and he said: "I have always loved you, all these years," although it was only weeks since they had met. His beard brushed her breasts, although she could not remember his growing a beard. She watched his hands, busy all over her body, in all the secret places, and she said: "It's you, you're doing this to me, it's you, Feliks, Feliks," as if there had ever been anyone else who did these things to her, who gave her this rolling, swelling pleasure. With her long fingernail she scratched his shoulder. She watched as the blood welled up, then leaned forward and licked it greedily. "You're an animal," he said. They touched one another busily, all the time; they were like children let loose in a sweet shop, moving restlessly from one thing to another, touching and looking and tasting, unable to believe in their astonishing good fortune. She said: "I'm so glad we ran away together," and for some reason that made him look sad, so she said: "Stick your finger up me," and the sad look went and desire masked his face, but she realized that she was crying, and she could not understand why. Suddenly she realized that this was a dream, and she was terrified of waking up, so she said: "Let's do it now, quickly," and they came together, and she smiled through her tears and said: "We fit." They seemed to move like dancers, or courting butterflies, and she said: "This is ever so nice, dear Jesus this is ever so nice," and then she said: "I thought this would never happen to me again," and her breath came in sobs. He buried his face in her neck, but she took his head in her hands and pushed it away so that she could see him. Now she knew that this was not a dream. She was awake. There was a taut string stretched between the back of her throat and the base of her spine, and every time it vibrated, her whole body sang a single note of pleasure which got louder and louder. "Look at me!" she said as she lost control, and he said gently: "I'm looking," and the note got louder. "I'm wicked!" she cried as the climax hit her. "Look at me, I'm wicked!" and her body convulsed, and the string got tighter and tighter and the pleasure more piercing until she felt she was losing her mind, and then the last high note of joy broke the string and she slumped and fainted.

❧ ☙

Feliks laid her gently on the floor. Her face in the candlelight was peaceful, all the tension gone; she looked like one who had died happy. She was pale, but breathing normally. She had been half asleep, probably drugged, Feliks knew, but he did not care. He felt drained and weak and helpless and grateful, and very much in love. We could start again, he thought: she's a free woman, she could leave her husband, we could live in Switzerland, Charlotte could join us—

This is not an opium dream, he told himself. He and Lydia had made such plans before, in St. Petersburg, nineteen years ago; and they had been utterly impotent against the wishes of respectable people. It doesn't happen, not in real life, he thought; they would frustrate us all over again.

They will never let me have her.

But I shall have my revenge.

He got to his feet and quickly put on his clothes. He picked up the candle. He looked at her once more. Her eyes were still closed. He wanted to touch her once more, to kiss her soft mouth. He hardened his heart. Never again, he thought. He turned and went through the door.

He walked softly along the carpeted corridor and down the stairs. His candle made weird moving shadows in the doorways. I may die tonight, but not before I have killed Orlov and Walden, he thought. I have seen my daughter, I have lain with my wife; now I will kill my enemies, and then I can die.

On the second-floor landing he stepped on a hard floor and his boot made a loud noise. He froze and listened. He saw that there was no carpet here, but a marble floor. He waited. There was no noise from the rest of the house. He took off his boots and went on in his bare feet—he had no socks.

The lights were out all over the house. Would anyone be roaming around? Might someone come down to raid the larder, feeling hungry in the middle of the night? Might a butler dream he heard noises and make a tour of the house to check? Might Orlov's bodyguards need to go to the bathroom? Feliks strained his hearing, ready to snuff out the candle and hide at the slightest noise.

He stopped in the hall and took from his coat pocket the plans of the house Charlotte had drawn for him. He consulted the ground-floor plan briefly, holding the candle close to the paper, then turned to his right and padded along the corridor.

He went through the library into the gun room.

He closed the door softly behind him and looked around. A great hideous head seemed to leap at him from the wall, and he jumped, and grunted with fear. The candle went out. In the darkness he realized he had seen a tiger's head, stuffed and mounted on the wall. He lit the candle again. There were trophies all around the walls: a lion, a deer, and even a rhinoceros. Walden had done some big-game hunting in his time. There was also a big fish in a glass case.

Feliks put the candle down on the table. The guns were racked along one wall. There were three pairs of double-barreled shotguns, a Winchester rifle and something that Feliks thought must be an elephant gun. He had never seen an elephant gun. He had never seen an elephant. The guns were secured by a chain through their trigger guards. Feliks looked along the chain. It was fastened by a large padlock to a bracket screwed into the wooden end of the rack.

Feliks considered what to do. He had to have a gun. He thought he might be able to snap the padlock, given a tough piece of iron such as a screwdriver to use as a lever; but it seemed to him that it might be easier to unscrew the bracket from the wood of the rack and then pass chain, padlock and bracket through the trigger guards to free the guns.

He looked again at Charlotte's plan. Next to the gun room was the flower room. He picked up his candle and went through the communicating door. He found himself in a small, cold room with a marble table and a stone sink. He heard a footstep. He doused his candle and crouched down. The sound had come from outside, from the gravel path: it had to be one of the sentries. The light of a torch flickered outside. Feliks flattened himself against the door, beside the window. The light grew stronger and the footsteps became louder. They stopped right outside and the torch shone in through the window. By its light Feliks could see a rack over the sink and a few tools hanging by hooks: shears, secateurs, a small hoe and a knife. The sentry tried the door against which Feliks stood. It was locked. The footsteps moved away and the light went. Feliks waited a moment. What would the sentry do? Presumably he had seen the glimmer of Feliks's candle. But he might think it had been the reflection of his own torch. Or someone in the house might have had a perfectly legitimate reason to go into the flower room. Or the sentry might be the ultracautious type, and come and check.

Leaving the doors open, Feliks went from the flower room, through the gun room, and into the library, feeling his way in the dark, holding his unlit candle in his hand. He sat on the floor in the library behind a big leather sofa and counted slowly to one thousand. Nobody came. The sentry was not the cautious type.

He went back into the gun room and lit the candle. The

windows were heavily curtained here—there had been no curtains in the flower room. He went cautiously into the flower room, took the knife he had seen over the rack, came back into the gun room and bent over the gun rack. He used the blade of the knife to undo the screws that held the bracket to the wood of the rack. The wood was old and hard, but eventually the screws came loose and he was able to unchain the guns.

There were three cupboards in the room. One held bottles of brandy and whiskey, together with glasses. Another held bound copies of a magazine called *Horse and Hound* and a huge leather-bound ledger marked "Game Book." The third was locked: that must be where the ammunition was kept.

Feliks broke the lock with the garden knife.

Of the three types of gun available—Winchester, shotgun or elephant gun—he preferred the Winchester. However, as he searched through the boxes of ammunition he realized there were no cartridges here either for the Winchester or for the elephant gun: those weapons must have been kept as souvenirs. He had to be content with a shotgun. All three pairs were twelve-bore, and all the ammunition consisted of cartridges of number-six shot. To be sure of killing his man he would have to fire at close range—no more than twenty yards, to be absolutely certain. And he would have only two shots before reloading.

Still, he thought, I only want to kill two people.

The image of Lydia lying on the nursery floor kept coming back to him. When he thought of how they had made love, he felt exultant. He no longer felt the fatalism which had gripped him immediately afterward. Why should I die? he thought. And when I have killed Walden, who knows what might happen then?

He loaded the gun

❧ ❧

And now, Lydia thought, I shall have to kill myself.

She saw no other possibility. She had descended to the depths of depravity for the second time in her life. All her years of self-discipline had come to nothing, just because Feliks had returned. She could not live with the knowledge of what she was She wanted to die, now

She considered how it might be done. What could she take that was poisonous? There must be rat poison somewhere on the premises, but of course she did not know where. An overdose of laudanum? She was not sure she had enough. You could kill yourself with gas, she recalled, but Stephen had converted the house to electric light. She wondered whether the top stories were high enough for her to die by jumping from a window. She was afraid she might merely break her back and be paralyzed for years. She did not think she had the courage to slash her wrists; and besides, it would take so long to bleed to death. The quickest way would be to shoot herself. She thought she could probably load a gun and fire it: she had seen it done innumerable times. But, she remembered, the guns were locked up.

Then she thought of the lake. Yes, that was the answer. She would go to her room and put on a robe; then she would leave the house by a side door, so that the policemen should not see her; and she would walk across the west side of the park, beside the rhododendrons, and through the woods until she came to the water's edge; then she would just keep walking, until the cool water closed over her head; then she would open her mouth, and a minute or so later it would be all over.

She left the nursery and walked along the corridor in the dark. She saw a light under Charlotte's door, and hesitated. She wanted to see her little girl one last time. The key was in the lock on the outside. She unlocked the door and went in.

Charlotte sat in a chair by the window, fully dressed but asleep. Her face was pale but for the redness around her eyes. She had unpinned her hair. Lydia closed the door and went over to her. Charlotte opened her eyes.

"What's happened?" she said.

"Nothing," Lydia said. She sat down.

Charlotte said: "Do you remember when Nannie went away?"

"Yes. You were old enough for a governess, and I didn't have another baby."

"I had forgotten all about it for years. I've just remembered. You never knew, did you, that I thought Nannie was my mother?"

"I don't know . . . did you think so? You always called me Mama, and her Nannie . . ."

"Yes." Charlotte spoke slowly, almost desultorily, as if she were lost in the fog of distant memory. "You were Mama, and Nannie was Nannie, but everybody had a mother, you see, and when Nannie said you were my mother, I said don't be silly, Nannie, *you* are my mother. And Nannie just laughed. Then you sent her away. I was brokenhearted."

"I never realized . . ."

"Marya never told you, of course—what governess would?" Charlotte was just repeating the memory, not accusing her mother, just explaining something. She went on: "So you see, I have the wrong mother, and now I have the wrong father, too. The new thing made me remember the old, I suppose."

Lydia said: "You must hate me. I understand. I hate myself."

"I don't hate you, Mama. I've been dreadfully angry toward you, but I've never hated you."

"But you think I'm a hypocrite."

"Not even that."

A feeling of peace came over Lydia.

Charlotte said: "I'm beginning to understand why you're so fiercely respectable, why you were so determined that I should never know anything of sex . . . you just wanted to save me from what happened to you. And I've found out that there are hard decisions, and that sometimes one can't tell what's good and right to do; and I think I've judged you harshly, when I had no right to judge you at all . . . and I'm not very proud of myself."

"Do you know that I love you?"

"Yes . . . and I love you, Mama, and that's why I feel so wretched."

Lydia was dazed. This was the last thing she had expected. After all that had happened—the lies, the treachery, the anger, the bitterness—Charlotte still loved her. She was suffused with a kind of tranquil joy. Kill myself? she thought. Why should I kill myself?

"We should have talked like this before," Lydia said.

"Oh, you've no idea how much I wanted to," Charlotte said. "You were always so good at telling me how to curtsy, and carry my train, and sit down gracefully, and put up my hair . . . and I longed for you to explain important things to me in the same way—about falling in love and having babies—but you never did."

"I never could," Lydia said. "I don't know why."

Charlotte yawned. "I think I'll sleep now." She stood up.

Lydia kissed her cheek, then embraced her.

Charlotte said: "I love Feliks, too, you know; that hasn't changed."

"I understand," said Lydia. "I do, too."

"Goodnight, Mama."

"Goodnight."

Lydia went out quickly and closed the door behind her. She hesitated outside. What would Charlotte do if the door were left unlocked? Lydia decided to save her the anxiety of the decision. She turned the key in the lock.

She went down the stairs, heading for her own room. She was so glad she had talked to Charlotte. Perhaps, she thought, this family could be mended, after all; I've no idea how, but surely it might be done. She went into her room.

"Where have you been?" said Stephen.

◆§ ἔ◆

Now that Feliks had a weapon, all he had to do was get Orlov out of his room. He knew how to do that. He was going to burn the house down.

Carrying the gun in one hand and the candle in the other, he walked—still barefoot—through the west wing and across the hall into the drawing room. Just a few more minutes, he thought; give me just a few more minutes and I will be done. He passed through two dining rooms and a serving room and entered the kitchens. Here Charlotte's plans became vague, and he had to search for the way out. He found a large rough-hewn door closed with a bar. He lifted the bar and quietly opened the door.

He put out his candle and waited in the doorway. After a minute or so he found he could just about make out the outlines of the buildings. That was a relief: he was afraid to use the candle outside because of the sentries.

In front of him was a small cobbled courtyard. On its far side, if the plan was right, there was a garage, a workshop, and—a petroleum tank.

He crossed the yard. The building in front of him had once been a barn he guessed. Part of it was enclosed—the workshop, perhaps—and the rest was open. He could vaguely make out the great round headlamps of two large cars. Where was the fuel tank? He looked up. The building was quite high. He stepped forward, and something hit his forehead. It was a length of flexible pipe with a nozzle at the end. It hung down from the upper part of the building.

It made sense: they put the cars in the barn and the petroleum tank in the hayloft. They simply drove the cars into the courtyard and filled them with fuel from the pipe.

Good! he thought.

Now he needed a container: a two-gallon can would be ideal. He entered the garage and walked around the cars, feeling with his feet, careful not to stumble over anything noisy.

There were no cans

He recalled the plans again. He was close to the kitchen garden. There might be a watering can in that region. He was about to go and look when he heard a sniff.

He froze.

The policeman went by.

Feliks could hear the beat of his own heart.

The light from the policeman's oil lamp meandered around the courtyard. Did I shut the kitchen door? Feliks thought in a panic. The lamp shone on the door: it looked shut.

The policeman went on.

Feliks realized he had been holding his breath, and he let it out in a long sigh.

He gave the policeman a minute to get some distance away; then he went in the same direction, looking for the kitchen garden.

He found no cans there, but he stumbled over a coil of hose. He estimated its length at about a hundred feet. It gave him a wicked idea

First he needed to know how frequently the policeman patrolled. He began to count. Still counting, he carried the garden hose back to the courtyard and concealed it and himself behind the motor cars.

He had reached nine hundred and two when the policeman came around again.

He had about fifteen minutes.

He attached one end of the hose to the nozzle of the petroleum pipe, then walked across the courtyard, paying out the hose as he went. He paused in the kitchen to find a sharp meat skewer and to relight his candle. Then he retraced his steps through the house, laying the hose through the kitchen, the serving room, the dining rooms, the drawing room, the hall and the passage, and into the library. The hose was heavy, and it was difficult to do the job silently. He listened all the while for footsteps, but all he heard was the noise of an old house settling down for the night. Everyone was in bed, he was sure; but would someone come down to get a book from the library, or a glass of brandy from the drawing room, or a sandwich from the kitchen?

If that were to happen now, he thought, the game would be up.

Just a few more minutes—just a few more minutes!

He had been worried about whether the hose would be long enough, but it just reached through the library door. He walked back, following the hose, making holes in it every few yards with the sharp point of the meat skewer.

He went out through the kitchen door and stood in the garage. He held his shotgun two-handed, like a club.

He seemed to wait an age.

At last he heard footsteps. The policeman passed him and stopped, shining his torch on the hose, and gave a grunt of surprise.

Feliks hit him with the gun.

The policeman staggered.

Feliks hissed: "Fall down, damn you!" and hit him again with all his might.

The policeman fell down, and Feliks hit him again with savage satisfaction.

The man was still.

Feliks turned to the petroleum pipe and found the place where the hose was connected. There was a tap to stop and start the flow of petroleum.

Feliks turned on the tap.

◄§ §►

"Before we were married," Lydia said impulsively, "I had a lover."

"Good lord!" said Stephen

Why did I say that? she thought. Because lying about it has made everyone unhappy, and I'm finished with all that.

She said: "My father found out about it. He had my lover jailed and tortured. He said that if I would agree to marry you, the torture would stop immediately; and that as soon as you and I had left for England, my lover would be released from jail."

She watched his face. He was not as hurt as she had expected, but he was horrified. He said: "Your father was wicked."

"I was wicked to marry without love."

"Oh . . ." Now Stephen looked pained. "For that matter, I wasn't in love with you. I proposed to you because my father had died and I needed a wife to be Countess of Walden. It was later that I fell so desperately in love with you. I'd say I forgive you, but there's nothing to forgive."

Could it be this easy? she thought. Might he forgive me everything and go on loving me? It seemed that, because death was in the air, anything was possible. She found herself plunging on. "There's more to be told," she said, "and it's worse."

His expression was painfully anxious. "You'd better tell me."

"I was . . . I was already with child when I married you."

Stephen paled. "Charlotte!"

Lydia nodded silently.

"She . . . she's not mine?"

"No."

"Oh, God."

Now I have hurt you, she thought; this you never dreamed. She said: "Oh, Stephen, I am so dreadfully sorry."

He stared at her. "Not mine," he said stupidly. "Not mine."

She thought of how much it meant to him: more than anyone else the English nobility talked about breeding and bloodlines. She remembered him looking at Charlotte and murmuring: "Bone of my bones, and flesh of my flesh"; it was the only verse of the Bible she had ever heard him quote. She thought of her own feelings, of the mystery of the child starting life as part of oneself and then becoming a separate individual, but never completely separate: it must be the same for men, she thought; sometimes one thinks it isn't, but it must be.

His face was gray and drawn. He looked suddenly older. He said: "Why are you telling me this now?"

I can't, she thought; I can't reveal any more, I've hurt him so much already. But it was as if she was on a downhill slope and could not stop. She blurted: "Because Charlotte has met her real father, and she knows everything."

"Oh, the poor child." Stephen buried his face in his hands.

Lydia realized that his next question would be: Who is the father? She was overcome by panic. She could not tell him that. It would kill him. But she *needed* to tell him; she wanted the weight of these guilty secrets to be lifted forever. Don't ask, she thought; not yet, it's too much.

He looked up at her. His face was frighteningly expressionless. He looked like a judge, she thought, impassively pronouncing sentence; and she was the guilty prisoner in the dock.

Don't ask.

He said: "And the father is Feliks, of course."

She gasped.

He nodded, as if her reaction was all the confirmation he needed.

What will he do? she thought fearfully. She watched his face, but she could not read his expression: he was like a stranger to her.

He said: "Oh, dear God in Heaven, what have we done."

Lydia was suddenly garrulous. "He came along just when she was beginning to see her parents as frail human beings, of course; and there he was, full of life and ideas and iconoclasm . . . just the kind of thing to enchant an independent-minded young girl . . . I know, something like that happened to me . . . and so she got to know him, and became fond of him, and helped him . . . but she loves you, Stephen, she's yours in that way. People can't help loving you . . . can't help it . . ."

His face was wooden. She wished he would curse, or cry, or abuse her, or even beat her, but he sat there looking at her with that judge's face, and said: "And you? Did you help him?"

"Not intentionally, no . . . but I haven't helped you, either. I am such a hateful, evil woman."

He stood up and held her shoulders. His hands were cold as the grave. He said: "But are you mine?"

"I wanted to be, Stephen—I really did."

He touched her cheek, but no love showed in his face. She shuddered. She said: "I told you it was too much to forgive."

He said: "Do you know where Feliks is?"

She made no reply. If I tell, she thought, it will be like killing Feliks. If I don't tell, it will be like killing Stephen.

"You do know," he said.

She nodded dumbly.

"Will you tell me?"

She looked into his eyes. If I tell him, she thought, will he forgive me?

Stephen said: "Choose."

She felt as if she were falling headlong into a pit.

Stephen raised his eyebrows expectantly.

Lydia said: "He's in the house."

"Good God! Where?"

Lydia's shoulders slumped. It was done. She had betrayed Feliks for the last time. "He's been hiding in the nursery," she said dejectedly.

His expression was no longer wooden. His cheeks colored and his eyes blazed with fury.

Lydia said: "Say you forgive me . . . please?"

He turned around and ran from the room.

◄§ §►

Feliks ran through the kitchen and through the serving room, carrying his candle, the shotgun and his matches. He could smell the sweet, slightly nauseating vapor of petrol. In the dining room a thin, steady jet was spouting through a hole in the hosepipe. Feliks shifted the hose across the room, so that the fire would not destroy it too quickly, then struck a match and threw it on to a petrol-soaked patch of rug. The rug burst into flames.

Feliks grinned and ran on.

In the drawing room he picked up a velvet cushion and held it to another hole in the hosepipe for a minute. He put the cushion down on a sofa, set fire to it and threw some more cushions onto it. They blazed merrily.

He ran across the hall and along the passage to the library. Here the petrol was gushing out of the end of the pipe and running over the floor. Feliks pulled handfuls of books off the shelves and threw them on the floor into the spreading puddle. Then he crossed the room and opened the communicating door to the gun room. He stood in the doorway for a moment, then threw his candle into the puddle.

There was a noise like a huge gust of wind and the library caught fire. Books and petrol burned fiercely. In a moment the curtains were ablaze, then the seats and the paneling caught. The petrol continued to pour out of the hosepipe, feeding the fire. Feliks laughed aloud.

He turned into the gun room. He stuffed a handful of extra cartridges into the pocket of his coat. He went from the gun room into the flower room. He unbolted the door to the garden, opened it quietly and stepped out.

He walked directly west, away from the house, for two hundred paces, containing his impatience. Then he turned south for the same distance, and finally he walked east until he was directly opposite the main entrance to the house, looking at it across the darkened lawn.

He could see the second police sentry standing in front of the portico, illuminated by the twin lamps, smoking a pipe. His colleague lay unconscious, perhaps dead, in the kitchen courtyard. Feliks could see the flames in the windows of the library, but the policeman was some distance away from there and he had not noticed them yet. He would see them at any moment.

Between Feliks and the house, about fifty yards from the portico, was a big old chestnut tree. Feliks walked toward it across the lawn. The policeman seemed to be looking more or less in Feliks's direction, but he did not see him. Feliks did not care: if he sees me, he thought, I'll shoot him dead. It doesn't matter now. No one could stop the fire. Everyone will have to leave the house. Any minute now, any minute now, I'll kill them both.

He came up behind the tree and leaned against it, with the shotgun in his hands.

Now he could see flames at the opposite end of the house, in the dining-room windows.

He thought: What are they doing in there?

◄§ §►

Walden ran along the corridor to the bachelor wing and knocked on the door of the Blue Room, where Thomson was sleeping. He went in.

"What is it?" Thomson's voice said from the bed.

Walden turned on the light. "Feliks is in the house."

"Good God!" Thomson got out of bed. "How?"

"Charlotte let him in," Walden said bitterly.

Thomson was hastily putting on trousers and a jacket. "Do we know where?"

"In the nursery. Have you got your revolver?"

"No, but I've got three men with Orlov, remember? I'll peel two of them off and then take Feliks."

"I'm coming with you."

"I'd rather—"

"Don't argue!" Walden shouted. "I want to see him die."

Thomson gave a queer, sympathetic look, then ran out of the room. Walden followed.

They went along the corridor to Aleks's room. The bodyguard outside the door stood up and saluted Thomson. Thomson said: "It's Barrett, isn't it?"

"Yes, sir."

"Who's inside?"

"Bishop and Anderson, sir."

"Get them to open up."

Barrett tapped on the door.

Immediately a voice said: "Password?"

"Mississippi," said Barrett.

The door opened. "What's on, Charlie? Oh, it's you, sir."

Thomson said: "How is Orlov?"

"Sleeping like a baby, sir."

Walden thought: Let's get on with it!

Thomson said: "Feliks is in the house. Barrett and Anderson, come with me and his lordship. Bishop, stay inside the room. Check that your pistols are loaded, please, all of you."

Walden led the way along the bachelor wing and up the back stairs to the nursery suite. His heart was pounding, and he felt the curious mixture of fear and eagerness which had always come over him when he got a big lion in the sights of his rifle.

He pointed at the nursery door.

Thomson whispered: "Is there electric light in that room?"

"Yes," Walden replied.

"Where's the switch?"

"Left-hand side of the door, at shoulder height."

Barrett and Anderson drew their pistols.

Walden and Thomson stood either side of the door, out of the line of fire.

Barrett threw open the door, Anderson dashed in and stepped to one side, and Barrett threw the light switch.

Nothing happened.

Walden looked into the room.

Anderson and Barrett were checking the schoolroom and the bedroom. A moment later Barrett said: "No one here, sir."

The nursery was bare and bright with light. There was a bowl of dirty water on the floor, and next to it a crumpled towel.

Walden pointed to the closet door. "Through there is a little attic."

Barrett opened the closet door. They all tensed. Barrett went through with his gun in his hand.

He came back a moment later. "He *was* there."

Thomson scratched his head.

Walden said: "We must search the house."

Thomson said: "I wish we had more men."

"We'll start with the west wing," Walden said. "Come *on.*"

They followed him out of the nursery and along the corridor to the staircase. As they went down the stairs Walden smelled smoke. "What's that?" he said.

Thomson sniffed.

Walden looked at Barrett and Anderson: neither of them was smoking.

The smell became more powerful, and now Walden could hear a noise like wind in the trees.

Suddenly he was filled with fear. "My house is on fire!" he shouted. He raced down the stairs.

The hall was full of smoke.

Walden ran across the hall and pushed open the door of the drawing room. Heat hit him like a blow and he staggered back. The room was an inferno. He despaired: it could never be put out. He looked along to the west wing, and saw that the library was afire too. He turned. Thomson was right behind him Walden shouted: "My house is burning down!"

Thomson took his arm and pulled him back to the staircase Anderson and Barrett stood there. Walden found he could breathe and hear more easily in the center of the hall. Thomson was very cool and collected. He began to give orders.

"Anderson, go and wake up those two bobbies outside. Send one to find a garden hose and a tap. Send the other running to the village to telephone for a fire engine. Then run up the back stairs and through the servants' quarters, waking everyone. Tell them to get out the quickest way they can, then gather on the front lawn to be counted. Barrett, go wake up Mr. Churchill and make sure he gets out. I'll fetch Orlov. Walden, you get Lydia and Charlotte. Move!"

Walden ran up the stairs and into Lydia's room. She was sitting on the chaise longue in her nightdress, and her eyes were red with weeping. "The house is on fire," Walden said breathlessly. "Go out quickly on to the front lawn. I'll get Charlotte." Then he thought of something: the dinner bell. "No," he said. "You get Charlotte. I'll ring the bell."

He raced down the stairs again, thinking: Why didn't I think of this before? In the hall was a long silk rope which would ring bells all over the house to warn guests and servants that a meal was about to be served. Walden pulled on the rope, and heard faintly the response of the bells from various parts of the house. He noticed a garden hose trailing through the hall. Was somebody fighting the fire already? He could not think who. He kept on pulling the rope.

◦§ §◦

Feliks watched anxiously. The blaze was spreading too quickly. Already large areas of the second floor were burning—he could see the glow in the windows. He thought: Come out, you fools. What were they doing? He did not want to burn everyone in the house—he wanted them to come out. The policeman in the portico seemed to be asleep. I'll give the alarm myself, Feliks thought desperately; I don't want the wrong people to die—

Suddenly the policeman looked around. His pipe fell out of his mouth. He dashed into the porch and began to hammer on the door. At last! thought Feliks. Now raise the alarm, you fool! The policeman ran around to a window and broke it.

Just then the door opened and someone rushed out in a cloud of smoke. It's happening, Feliks thought. He hefted the shotgun and peered through the darkness. He could not see the face of the newcomer. The man shouted something, and the policeman ran off. I've got to be able to see their faces, Feliks thought; but if I go too close I'll be seen too soon. The newcomer rushed back into the house before Feliks could recognize him. I'll have to get nearer, Feliks thought, and take the chance. He moved across the lawn. Within the house, bells began to ring.

Now they will come, thought Feliks.

❧ ☙

Lydia ran along the smoke-filled corridor. How could this happen so *quickly*? In her room she had smelled nothing, but now there were flames flickering underneath the doors of the bedrooms she passed. The whole house must be blazing. The air was too hot to breathe. She reached Charlotte's room and turned the handle of the door. Of course, it was locked. She turned the key. She tried again to open the door. It would not move. She turned the handle and threw her weight against the door. Something was wrong, the door was jammed, Lydia began to scream and scream—

"Mama!" Charlotte's voice came from within the room.

Lydia bit her lip hard and stopped screaming. "Charlotte!"

"Open the door!"

"I can't I can't I can't—"

"It's locked!"

"I've unlocked it and it won't open and the house is on fire oh dear Jesus help me help—"

The door shook and the handle rattled as Charlotte tried to open it from the inside.

"Mama!"

"Yes!"

"Mama, stop screaming and listen carefully to me—the floor has shifted and the door is wedged in its frame—it will have to be broken down—go and fetch help!"

"I can't leave you—"

"MAMA! GO AND GET HELP OR I'LL BURN TO DEATH!"

"Oh, God—all right!" Lydia turned and ran, choking, toward the staircase.

❧ ☙

Walden was still ringing the bell. Through the smoke he saw Aleks, flanked by Thomson and the third detective, Bishop coming down the stairs. Lydia and Churchill and Charlotte should be here, too, he thought; then he realized that they might come down any one of several staircases: the only place to check was out on the front lawn where everyone had been told to gather.

"Bishop!" shouted Walden. "Come here!"

The detective ran across.

"Ring this. Keep going as long as you can."

Bishop took the rope and Walden followed Aleks out of the house.

⤙ ⤚

It was a very sweet moment for Feliks.

He lifted the gun and walked toward the house.

Orlov and another man walked toward him. They had not yet seen him. As they came closer, Walden appeared behind them.

Like rats in a trap, Feliks thought triumphantly.

The man Feliks did not know looked back over his shoulder and spoke to Walden.

Orlov was twenty yards away.

This is it, Feliks thought.

He put the stock of the gun to his shoulder, aimed carefully at Orlov's chest and—just as Orlov opened his mouth to speak —pulled the trigger.

A large black hole appeared in Orlov's nightshirt as an ounce of number-six shot, about four hundred pellets, tore into his body. The other two men heard the bang and stared at Feliks in astonishment. Blood gushed from Orlov's chest, and he fell backward.

I did it, Feliks thought exultantly; I killed him.

Now for the other tyrant.

He pointed the gun at Walden. "Don't move!" he yelled.

Walden and the other man stood motionless.

They all heard a scream.

Feliks looked in the direction from which the sound came.

Lydia was running out of the house with her hair on fire.

Feliks hesitated for a split second, then he dashed toward her.

Walden did the same.

As he ran, Feliks dropped the gun and tore off his coat. He

reached Lydia a moment before Walden. He wrapped the coat around her head, smothering the flames.

She pulled the coat off her head and yelled at them: "Charlotte is trapped in her room!"

Walden turned and ran toward the house.

Feliks ran with him.

❧ ☙

Lydia, sobbing with fright, saw Thomson dart forward and pick up the shotgun Feliks had dropped.

She watched in horror as Thomson raised it and took aim at Feliks's back.

"No!" she screamed. She threw herself at Thomson, knocking him off balance.

The gun discharged into the ground.

Thomson stared at her in bewilderment.

"Don't you know?" she shouted hysterically. "He's suffered enough!"

❧ ☙

Charlotte's carpet was smoldering.

She put her fist to her mouth and bit her knuckles to stop herself from screaming.

She ran to her washstand, picked up the jug of water and threw it into the middle of the room. It made more smoke, not less.

She went to the window, opened it and looked out. Smoke and flames poured out of the windows below her. The wall of the house was faced with smooth stone: there was no way to climb down. If I have to I'll jump; it will be better than burning, she thought. The idea terrified her and she bit her knuckles again.

She ran to the door and shook the handle impotently.

"Somebody, help, quickly!" she screamed.

Flames rose from the carpet, and a hole appeared in the center of the floor.

She ran around the edge of the room to be near the window, ready to jump.

She heard someone sobbing and realized it was she.

❧ ☙

The hall was full of smoke. Feliks could hardly see. He stayed close behind Walden, thinking: Not Charlotte, I won't let Charlotte die, not Charlotte.

They ran up the staircase. The whole second floor was ablaze. The heat was terrific. Walden dashed through a wall of flame and Feliks followed him.

Walden stopped outside a door and was seized by a fit of coughing. Helpless, he pointed at the door. Feliks rattled the handle and pushed the door with his shoulder. It would not move. He shook Walden and shouted: "Run at the door!" He and Walden—still coughing—stood on the other side of the corridor, facing the door.

Feliks said: "Now!"

They threw themselves at the door together.

The wood split but the door stayed shut.

Walden stopped coughing. His face showed sheer terror. 'Again!" he shouted at Feliks.

They stood against the opposite wall.

"Now!"

They threw themselves at the door.

It cracked a little more.

From the other side of the door, they heard Charlotte scream.

Walden gave a roar of anger. He looked about him desperately. He picked up a heavy oak chair. Feliks thought it was too heavy for Walden to lift, but Walden raised it above his head and smashed it against the door. The wood began to splinter.

In a frenzy of impatience Feliks put his hands into the crack and began to tear at the splintered wood. His fingers became slippery with blood.

He stood back and Walden swung with the chair again. Again Feliks pulled out the shards. His hands were full of splinters. He heard Walden muttering something and realized it was a prayer. Walden swung the chair a third time. The chair broke, its seat and legs coming away from its back; but there was a hole in the door big enough for Feliks—but not for Walden—to crawl through.

Feliks dragged himself through the hole and fell into the bedroom.

The floor was on fire, and he could not see Charlotte.

"Charlotte!" he shouted at the top of his voice.

"Here!" Her voice came from the far side of the room.

Feliks ran around the outside of the room where the fire was less. She was sitting on the sill of the open window, breathing in ragged gulps. He picked her up by the waist and threw her over his shoulder. He ran back around the edge of the room to the door.

Walden reached through the door to take her.

◦§ ﹩◦

Walden put his head and one shoulder through the hole to take Charlotte from Feliks. He could see that Feliks's face and hands were burned black and his trousers were on fire. Charlotte's eyes were open and wide with terror. Behind Feliks, the floor began to collapse. Walden got one arm beneath Charlotte's body. Feliks seemed to stagger. Walden withdrew his head, put his other arm through the hole and got his hand under Charlotte's armpit. Flames licked around her nightdress and she screamed. Walden said: "All right, Papa's got you." Suddenly he was taking her entire weight. He drew her through the hole. She fainted and went limp. As he pulled her out the bedroom floor fell in, and Walden saw Feliks's face as Feliks dropped into the inferno.

Walden whispered: "May God have mercy on your soul."

Then he ran downstairs.

◦§ ﹩◦

Lydia was held in an iron grip by Thomson, who would not let her go into the blazing house. She stood, staring at the door, willing the two men to appear with Charlotte.

A figure appeared. Who was it?

It came closer. It was Stephen. He was carrying Charlotte.

Thomson let Lydia go. She ran to them. Stephen laid Charlotte gently on the grass. Lydia stared at him in a panic. She said: "What—what—"

"She's not dead," Stephen said. "Just fainted."

Lydia got down on the grass, cradled Charlotte's head in her lap and felt her chest beneath her left breast. There was a strong heartbeat.

"Oh, my baby," Lydia said.

Stephen sat beside her. She looked at him. His trousers had

burned and his skin was black and blistered. But he was alive.

She looked toward the door.

Stephen saw her glance.

Lydia became aware that Churchill and Thomson were standing near, listening.

Stephen took Lydia's hand. "He saved her," he said. "Then he passed her to me. Then the floor fell in. He's dead."

Lydia's eyes filled with tears. Stephen saw, and squeezed her hand. He said: "I saw his face as he fell. I don't think I'll ever forget it, as long as I live. You see, his eyes were open, and he was conscious, but—he wasn't frightened. In fact he looked . . . satisfied."

The tears streamed down Lydia's face.

Churchill spoke to Thomson. "Get rid of the body of Orlov."

Poor Aleks, Lydia thought, and she cried for him too.

Thomson said incredulously: "What?"

Churchill said: "Hide it, bury it, throw it into the fire, I don't care how you do it, I just want you to get rid of that body."

Lydia stared at him aghast, and through a film of tears she saw him take a sheaf of papers from the pocket of his dressing-gown.

"The agreement is signed," Churchill said. "The Czar will be told that Orlov died by accident, in the fire that burned down Walden Hall. Orlov was not murdered, do you understand? There was no assassin." He looked around at each of them with his aggressive, pudgy face set in a fierce scowl. "There was never anybody called Feliks."

Stephen stood up and went over to where Aleks's body lay. Someone had covered his face. Lydia heard Stephen say: "Aleks, my boy . . . what am I going to say to your mother?" He bent down and folded the hands over the hole in the chest.

Lydia looked at the fire, burning down all those years of history, consuming the past.

Stephen came over and stood beside her. He whispered: "There was never anybody called Feliks."

She looked up at him. Behind him, the sky in the east was pearly gray. Soon the sun would rise, and it would be a new day.

⋘ ⋙

EPILOGUE

On August 2, 1914, Germany invaded Belgium. Within days the German army was sweeping through France. Toward the end of August, when it seemed that Paris might fall, vital German troops were withdrawn from France to defend Germany against a Russian invasion from the east; and Paris did not fall.

In 1915 the Russians were officially given control of Constantinople and the Bosphorus.

Many of the young men Charlotte had danced with at Belinda's ball were killed in France. Freddie Chalfont died at Ypres. Peter came home shell-shocked. Charlotte trained as a nurse and went to the front.

In 1916 Lydia gave birth to a boy. The delivery was expected to be difficult because of her age, but in the event there were no problems. They called the boy Aleks.

Charlotte caught pneumonia in 1917 and was sent home. During her convalescence she translated *The Captain's Daughter* by Pushkin into English.

After the war the women got the vote. Lloyd George became Prime Minister. Basil Thomson got a knighthood.

Charlotte married a young officer she had nursed in France.

The war had made him a pacifist and a socialist, and he was one of the first Labour Members of Parliament. Charlotte became the leading English translator of nineteenth-century Russian fiction. In 1931 the two of them went to Moscow and came home declaring that the USSR was a workers' paradise. They changed their minds at the time of the Nazi-Soviet pact. Charlotte's husband was a junior minister in the Labour government of 1945.

Charlotte is still alive. She lives in a cottage on what used to be the Home Farm. The cottage was built by her father for his bailiff, and it is a spacious, sturdy house full of comfortable furniture and bright fabrics. The Home Farm is now a housing estate, but Charlotte likes to be surrounded by people. Walden Hall was rebuilt by Lutyens and is now owned by the son of Aleks Walden.

Charlotte is sometimes a little confused about the recent past but she remembers the summer of 1914 as if it were yesterday. A rather distant look comes into those sad brown eyes, and she's off on one of her hair-raising stories.

She's not all memories, though. She denounces the Communist Party of the Soviet Union for giving socialism a bad name and Margaret Thatcher for giving feminism a bad name. If you tell her that Mrs. Thatcher is no feminist, she will say that Brezhnev is no socialist.

She doesn't translate anymore, of course, but she is reading *The Gulag Archipelago* in the original Russian. She says Solzhenitsyn is self-righteous but she's determined to finish the book. As she can read only for half an hour in the morning and half an hour in the afternoon, she calculates that she will be ninety-nine by the time she gets to the end.

Somehow I think she'll make it.